P.S. —
See Maps!!
I worked out how to do maps.
So you're not original ANY LONGER ;-)

THE HEART OF LICHIEN

To Sharon,
Guess what?
All those wonderful days and nights we spent reading and writing — you plotting 'Worthy to Fall' — all paid off!!
I did it!
Book two will be out Jan 2006
Love you heaps &
Miss you ever more
Tammy
xxxxx

Sasheer sighed, lifting a hand to rub his eyes in annoyance and irritation. "Why are you so stubborn?"

"Just tell me if I have any family left alive in the Southland," Kellen persisted peevishly.

"You have none." Sasheer stated, visibly restraining his temper.

"Why?" Kellen snarled, no longer feeling cold as he glared at the infuriating man.

"Because they did not survive."

"The war?" Kellen asked, when Sasheer did not elaborate.

"Yes! The cursed war!" Sasheer snapped. "Your entire family is dead. Uncles, aunts and cousins! Is that what you wanted to hear?"

A brief flaring of pain hit him as Kellen imagined the deaths of relatives he had never even known. What else had he never been told? What else did this man know of his life that he wasn't aware of? "Who are you?"

The Heart of Lichien

T. S. Clayton

Copyright © 2004 by T. S. Clayton.

Library of Congress Number: 2004094999
ISBN : Hardcover 1-4134-6300-2
       Softcover 1-4134-6299-5

All rights reserved. No part of this book may be reproduced or transmitted in any form or by any means, electronic or mechanical, including photocopying, recording, or by any information storage and retrieval system, without permission in writing from the copyright owner.

This is a work of fiction. Names, characters, places and incidents either are the product of the author's imagination or are used fictitiously, and any resemblance to any actual persons, living or dead, events, or locales is entirely coincidental.

This book was printed in the United States of America.

To order additional copies of this book, contact:
Xlibris Corporation
1-888-795-4274
www.Xlibris.com
Orders@Xlibris.com
25405

CHAPTER ONE

It was raining. A continuous, depressing type of rain that enshrouded the entire land and turned everything gray. It made the ground soggy, the grass overlush, and gave each tree the appearance of weeping. An annoying type of drizzle, which could saturate any man or beast within minutes.

Kellen hated the rain and he sighed, disgruntled, and contemplated his pale, wet fingers. He was thoroughly drenched, and he wondered why he was standing there, in the rain, before he dismissed the thought as unworthy. He shook his head and took stock of his situation. He was pressed up against the side of an old barn, trying to find the courage to complete the task Bains had given him. *Bains!* He squinted up at the dark rain clouds and cursed.

When his friend had first suggested they raid the old abandoned farmhouse, it had not been raining, and he had been bored, so the adventure had sounded like fun. Only now he was no longer smiling. He took another deep, steadying breath then slowly counted to ten before chancing a sneak look around the corner of the decaying barn. Nothing moved in the fine drizzle. The huge farmhouse sat a hundred paces away, a drab outline in the rain, and at the side rail, three dark horses were tethered exactly where Bains had predicted they would be. Like ghosts, unmoving and obscure. He exhaled and leaned back against the barn wall. *So far, so good.* Now all he had to do was reach the horses, steal the gold, and get away before the Black Guard returned. Simple. So why had an insidious doubt crept into his mind?

He hesitated then moved closer to the edge of the barn, his fingers digging into the soft, damp wood while he swept his gaze over the vacant courtyard before him. The cobblestones were dark with puddles, and he knew they would be slippery. The house was ominously silent; even the horses were motionless, like stone statues of mystical beauty. He could feel his heart starting to pound in his chest and briefly closed his eyes, reciting the litany of safety that all travelers used. Only he wasn't a traveler.

Bains was standing watch by the main gates and would alert him if more of the Black Guard approached. But, somehow, that knowledge did not ease his worry. In all honesty, he was a little scared of the Black Guard, scared of their size, reputation, strange appearance, and—it was whispered—they had forbidden powers. They were the enemy, the frightening invaders from across the White Sea. From North Ridge.

He sank back against the wet wood a second time and berated himself for his hesitation. If his brother could go off and join the Ihovian army to fight the Black Guard in the border war, then surely he could face three harmless horses and steal a bag of gold. All he had to do was move.

He hardened his resolve, straightened, and looked at the tranquil courtyard. The rain was like a mist, and he readying himself for the dash across wet stones. It would only take moments, precious moments, and then he would be safe.

With that thought in mind, he stepped out of hiding. Rain hit him anew, washing over him, and he wiped his eyes, crouching low and hurriedly navigated the slippery ground. He approached the horses then stopped, abruptly sensing *something*, and he glanced around. Nothing moved in the stillness, and he crouched low, his fingers settling against the cold cobbles while he studied his surroundings. The butterflies in his stomach somersaulted, and he cursed his overactive paranoia. His brother had always accused him of seeing faces in the dark, or of hearing voices at the night, and he forcibly pushed his panic aside.

Then *something* featherlike brushed his cheek, and he whipped his head around, seeing nothing, staring wide-eyed at the horses and the silent house beyond. The irritating rain was now forgotten as he used every sense he possessed to focus on his surroundings. Nothing.

Yet he was positive something had touched him, a heat, a burning warmth, an awareness—something not tangible—and he almost bolted. Only that was the action of a scared child, and he snarled at his fear, unclenching his fingers. He looked again at the patiently waiting horses and reminded himself that he only had to retrieve one bag of gold. Just one for his holdings, for his adopted family, so they could survive the harsh winter months ahead.

Shaking off his uncertainty, he stood from his protective crouch and straightened his shoulders. He felt exposed, like he was being watched, studied or observed, and he shook off the sensations, covering his unease by walking with determination toward the horses. He wiped wet hair from his eyes and listening for sounds from inside the darkened house. There was no noise, and his brows drew down in speculation.

Like all within this isolated district, he had heard the rumors that suggested that the Black Guard were systematically stripping Ihova of wealth. He knew that in a few days, the Black Guard would move on to plunder the next defenseless community, and he knew that the Black Guard went mostly unchallenged due to the fact that all the able-bodied men were away, conscripted into King Arikaines' army.

Up until that moment, the war had seemed surreal and so far away from what he recognized as reality. Incomprehensible, except for the news that wearied travelers brought. Only now he was looking at the dreaded mounts belonging to the fabled Black Guard, and according to Bains' older brother, all the Black Guard were supposed to carry the wealth and gold from raids in their packs. Why, he did not know and had never thought to question the information—a decision he was now regretting.

"Great," he muttered, wishing he had volunteered to stand watch, so Bains could do the actual heroics and steal the gold. Besides, *Bains got on so much better with horses,* he reminded himself. Bains was also more suited to be the dashing, adventurous hero. He smiled at that thought.

Calming his nerves, he remembered the last words Bains had

spoken to him before they had separated. "Be careful, Kell, and whatever happens, just remember to keep your pretty head down."

His smile widened in memory, for he knew his appearance was in direct contrast to the normal Ihovian characteristics. Where he was pale and dark like the moon's reflection on a winter's night, Bains was tanned, and as light as the sun on a summer's day. In his mind he could picture Bains' tousled blond head, Bains' unrepentant, cocky grin and dancing blue eyes. Grinning as that image replaced the dismay in his mind, he closed his eyes and concentrated on his objective. He just had to remember the plan.

Feeling more confident, he touched the small dagger at his belt and cautiously approached the three inky black horses, noting how they each pulled against their restraints to look at him. He could sympathize, for he disliked the rain also. Settling a calming hand on the flank of the first horse, he gently caressed the wet hair, studying the tethered animals and noting their nervousness. He frowned, remembering that the Black Guard were reputed to always travel in groups of four. *So why only three horses?*

Dismissing the oddity, he glanced at the packs hanging across the top of each saddle and bit his lower lip in a mixture of excitement and fear. This was what he had come for. He darted another quick look toward the old house then moved closer to the second animal.

Leaving one hand on the horse's rump, he eyed the bulging packs and gently stroked the horse's damp flank. He ran his fingers up the coarse hair, trailing his fingertips over the beautifully crafted saddle before lifting his eyes to meet the unblinking stare of the tethered horse. The horse flicked its tail, and he frowned before attempting to give the animal a reassuring smile. Despite the cool, damp weather, he found he was hot and sweaty, and he tried to imagine what the animal was thinking. *Did a horse think?* He had no idea. *Were they even ordinary horses, or spellbound like the legendary Deathwalkers?* Evil, terrifying monsters encased in mystical beauty and powerful magics.

He shuddered and tried to dismiss the childhood tales from his mind which spoke of dark, nightmarish horror, and he glanced around to reassure himself that he was alone. He was safe and very much alive. He had too vivid an imagination at the best of times, and he swallowed before looking at the horse again. It was just a horse. An ordinary horse, like any other horse, and he moved closer to the animal, reaching up to stroke the silky, wet nose.

He released a tense breath and gentled the animal's agitation. "Shhh, shhh, it's all right. Just stay quiet," he whispered, feeling those large unblinking eyes settle unerringly on him. Again a sliver of unease touched him, winding its way into his mind, and he stilled in apprehension, suddenly feeling *something* icy and sharp brush against his shoulder. The coldness of it sucked all life from his bones.

He froze, transfixed, and stared wide-eyed into the misty rain, just catching a glimpse of patterned darkness—a blackness so bleak and so complete that nothing else existed for a frightening moment. Then a deadly swirl of movement disturbed the rain, so fleeting that he wasn't sure he saw anything at all. His heart hammered in his chest, and his breathing was coming in hot, unrestrained gusts, as he stared at the empty space not two paces away. But the ripples of darkness were gone, the sensations of dread vanishing into nothing.

"Cursed stars," he mouthed the words, his fingers gripping the saddle pommel hard. He felt ill and strangely exhausted. What he had seen—was it real or imagined? Slowly, he released his death grip on the wet leather, flexing his fingers, refusing to believe in the impossible—in childhood fairytales.

He turned and stared again at the saddle, at the wet horses, at the muddy ground, at the silent house, then at his fingers. Nothing. Absolutely nothing and he hardened his resolve to finish his task and get away from the Black Guard and their taint as swiftly as possible. Muttering under his breath, he attacked the buckle on the saddle pack, working the swollen leather loose—when abruptly he was engulfed a second time. Imprisoned in a web of suffocation and despair, of hatred and pain. The sensations stole all breath from his lungs, silenced his sharp cry, crippled his instinctive reactions, and held him immobile. *Witchcraft?*

The unknown terrified him, and he struggled to break free of the constricting embrace, hearing softly hissed words in a language he did not understand and could not comprehend. Old words, cruel words, echoed in his mind. Words accompanied by pictures that ghosted across his vision—pictures of darkness, of death, of sacrifice and blood, of betrayal and murder. Then just as abruptly, he was released, the images fracturing in the mist, and he staggered backward, swinging around in the rain to glare in every direction.

He was panting hard, trembling, his own heartbeat a deafening thunder in his ears—yet nothing was there. The house was silent, and the only movement came from the horses as they shied away from him.

He released an explosive breath, rattled, battling to get his fear under control. He had never felt anything so chilling, so sinister or so deathly before, and he eyed the innocent-looking animals in mistrust. *Horses,* he had his doubts that they were ordinary horses. He should leave . . . but . . .

Determinedly, he went back to the second horse and swiftly worked the wet leather loose, unbuckling the pack. In no time, he had the pouch open, and he reached inside, his fingers encountering the welcome feel of a coin sack. No doubt it was white Ihovian gold stolen from his neighbors, and he scowled, shoving the gold into his tunic before removing a second sack. Perfect.

He had defied the Black Guard, and he turned to make a hasty retreat. Only the sound of a slamming door alerted him to trouble, and he stopped dead in his tracks. Instinctively, he dropped into a crouch and peered up under the horse's legs, seeing two of the Black Guard walk down the front steps of the farmhouse. Both guards were extremely tall and covered in gleaming black armor, making them look like giants—giants that reflected darkness and doom.

He hissed a curse and cast a worried glance over toward the old barn, then back again at the house. That was his safest escape route, if he was quick. Behind the house was a low sidewall and, beyond that, a meadow until the woodland. Open country.

Gazing one final time under the horse's muscular black legs to check the position of the Black Guard, and froze when he heard a piercing scream. His eyes went wide as he saw Bains being dragged into the front courtyard by a fourth guard who was mounted on a huge stallion.

The fourth guard! He pressed against the wall of the old house and exhaled, his thoughts in disarray as he berated himself for not listening to the rumors, not listening to his own instincts. He slid down the rough stone and hid behind the horses, thinking hard while watching his friend's plight. He could hear Bains yelling abuse at the guard, his friend's words marred by pain and anger, his cries ending in a plea.

Scared for them both, he watched as Bains' hands were tied behind his back, as the fourth guard brutally dragged his captive closer to the house by Bains' longish hair. Then the guard dismounted his massive warhorse with a grunt and shoved his protesting captive onto the wet cobblestones.

Horrified, he found he could not look away, mesmerized by the impossible, watching how the guard so callously unsheathed his sword and rested the tip under Bains' chin. That silenced Bains' cursing, and an eerie silence fell.

Then the guard spoke in the guttural northern dialect, the words harsh, incomprehensible, yet the hissed words made the other guards snicker. The sound broke the unnatural spell in Kellen's mind, and he sagged back against the cold stone and then mentally searched for a way to help Bains escape. He had one blunt knife, but he knew that would be useless against the guards' armor and long blades. He explored his other pockets, his fingers lingering on the two bags of gold, and he briefly wondered if he could use them to trade. *Probably not.* He glanced again under the legs of the horses and saw Bains was now gasping for breath, saw how the guard tormented him in sport.

Feeling his anger resurface, he forced himself to think, to work out an alternative. He could not leave, not without Bains, and he slowly pushed himself upright, pressing into the coldness at his back. At the front of the manor, the largest guard kicked the prisoner, repeating the action until Bains screamed for mercy.

Kellen glared at the guard and found that most of his fear had vanished, and he instinctively pulled his small dagger free with the intention of rushing forward to rescue his friend. Impulsiveness took over, and he was sure that all he had to do was distract the guard long enough, so Bains could find his feet and run.

He pushed away from the security of the wall and moved past the horses, faltering abruptly when he was swiftly and silently wrapped within an invisible embrace. An intense coldness, a cord of ice wrapped around his throat, stealing his voice, paralyzing all his responses—and he gasped, but no sound came out, his skin burning from the brief contact. He shuddered and dropped his dagger.

Then the pain was gone, leaving him shaken and vulnerable while a wicked little voice laughed in his ear. Fear coiled in his stomach, and he turned, his eyes falling on a shimmering image within the rain that was as beautiful as it was disturbing. The image solidified into darkness that evolved further into a figure of a tall cloak-wrapped man. A dreamlike apparition of perfection, power and beauty, enshrouded in death, and he felt his jaw drop. *It had to be an illusion*, and he rubbed his eyes, squinting at the fading apparition but only saw the rain-soaked courtyard. Shocked, he inhaled, feeling dazed and disorientated.

What was that thing? Backing away, he bumped into the horses and was thrust forward by their agitation, slipping on the wet cobblestones. He went down hard, landing in a puddle and spitting out water. "Damn horse—"

"Seize him!"

Hearing the barked order, Kellen lifted his lashes and saw two of the Black Guard approach, and he scrambled to his feet. He cursed again then snatched up his fallen dagger and wiped his wet, nervous hands down his leather leggings. This was not how he had wanted to face the enemy.

He backed away and searched the faces of his enemy, refusing to give up victory. Wicked glee contorted the snarling faces of the guards, and he took another step backward. The inky black armor mirrored the bleakness of the rain, and he fleetingly wondered how they kept sane encased in all that metal. He watched them circle him expertly, and he realized the futility of his position, but stubbornness bolstered his determination. And with luck, it would give Bains a chance to escape.

"Little rabbit, do you think that toy frightens me?"

The words were growled in his own language, the speech stilted, but the meaning unmistakable, and Kellen held his ground; he gritted his teeth and moved to his left when one guard made the predictable lunge. He struck out with his dagger, feeling it sink into something soft, and he staggered away, even more startled that his aim had been true. He stared at the guard he had injured, kicking out in fright when a second guard seized him from behind. His wrist was locked in a painful grip, and he was forced to release his dagger. It fell to the wet ground unnoticed.

"Pretty child, your life is now mine," the first guard spat. He lifted his hand away from the injury and snarled. Dark blood covered his gloved hand.

Kellen opened his mouth to voice his defiance but was silenced effectively when leather-clad fingers locked around his throat. He gasped, choking, and was unable to put up much resistance as he was manhandled over toward Bains' prone form. Then he was released and shoved to the ground next to his friend.

"Great plan," Kellen said hoarsely.

"You should have run," Bains wheezed, his wide blue eyes showing nothing but a disheartening hopelessness.

"I couldn't leave you," he whispered back. He fingered his throat, shocked by Bains' expression.

"Enough!"

The roared command made Kellen jump, and he glanced up at their captors. He wondered if he could talk his way out of trouble. He had to try, and he slowly pushed himself up, keeping his eyes locked on the largest guard. He figured this man was the commander. "What do you want with us?"

"It speaks!" the commander leered in amusement, folding his arms.

Not enthused by the reaction, Kellen balled his fists and glared at the foreigners. That show of insolence earned him a club from behind, and his knees buckled, dropping him awkwardly to the slippery cobblestones a second time. The jolt caused him to bite his inside lip, and he spat out blood before raising his eyes to glare up at the commander. Dark, contemptuous eyes stared back, and he shuddered.

"So, my little rabbit, tell me—has your gutless pretender prince got children now running his raids?"

Confused by the question, Kellen didn't answer and was slapped hard for his hesitation. More blood flooded his mouth, and he blinked, seeing bright spots of light swim before his vision, disorientating him. "What do you want with us?" he repeated, lifting his lashes and daring to look at the commander again.

"Answer the question. Or I will kill your friend," the commander said, his voice overloud in the sudden silence.

Swallowing, Kellen looked down at his friend, hoping Bains would have an answer, but Bains looked truly afraid.

"Where is your cowardly prince? Tell me!" the commander repeated, placing his boot on Bains' chest and shoving the youth down to lie sprawled on the wet ground.

Jolted by the shout, Kellen could only shake his head, not understanding. "What prince?" he croaked. "Ihova is ruled by King Arikaines."

A sharp, cracking sound captured Kellen's complete attention, and he felt ill as he watched the commander shatter Bains' ribs with his boot. Then the blond Ihovian's strangled scream died, and the youth sagged, collapsing on the wet stones like a limp sack. "No," Kellen gasped, instinctively reaching for his friend and seeing how the blue eyes blinked at him in astonishment. Bains' fingers stretched out toward him in petition, and Kellen hiccoughed on a scared breath, seeing the same guard exert more pressure on Bains' chest with his boot. The dazed blond struggled to breathe, blood bubbling up in his mouth to stain graying lips a bright red.

Fists clenching in horror and rage, Kellen watched helplessly as Bains' blue eyes slowly clouded over. There was no accusation in their depth, just trust and loyalty.

"I will not ask you again!" the guard growled, removing his heavy boot and passing his sword to one of his men. Then the commander strode over to Kellen and gripped him by the collar and lifted him effortlessly off the ground. "Give me the rebel camp, and I'll spare your friend's life."

Kellen licked very dry lips, his eyes darting back to Bains' semiconscious body. *Rebel camp?* He knew nothing about a rebel camp.

"Kell, don't—"

A second guard immediately kicked Bains to stop his protest, and the injured youth whimpered in agony.

"No!" Kellen tried to struggle free, to fight back and prevent the inevitable. Nothing was worth his best friend's life. Not gold and not this rebel camp. "You demonspawn!" he spat in impotent fury.

The commander laughed, strengthening his hold on the struggling young man, turning him to hiss his next words warningly. "Your cowardly little excuse of a kingdom is no match for my Lord Kalern, the Lord of All Shadows. So just tell me where that half-witted imbecile calling himself a prince is hiding, and I might let *you* live."

The names meant nothing to him, he knew nothing about a prince, his only concern was Bains, and he tried to loosen the fingers locked in his tunic. He felt himself shaken, experienced the strength behind this giant man's grip and tried to shove his own fear aside. "I know nothing!"

The commander's eyes narrowed further. "By your coloring, you are not even Ihovian. So what do you owe this dying land, boy? What are you doing here? What is the Ihovian throne paying your people?"

"You will not win," Kellen said, tears of rage misting his eyes as he challenged the guard. The words were innate, coming out of him easily, like he had known them all his life, and he was stunned by his own boldness and sudden clarity of thought. From where the knowledge came, he did not know, but he flung his anger at the sneering guard. "One will come of the bloodline and challenge for control! That one will shatter Lichien's heart, and you will all be destroyed!"

"What was that squeak?" the commander half-laughed, hauling the resisting young man closer. He enclosed the slender throat and squeezed, watching his captive fight for every breath. "I think that was a direct refusal to cooperate."

Abruptly released and dropped unceremoniously to the wet ground, Kellen coughed, his eyes watering, his head spinning as he stared up at the commander. But the big man only took his sword back from the other guard and went to stand over Bains' motionless body. Fear prickled along every nerve, and Kellen instinctively flicked his eyes down to Bains, seeing how weak and pale his friend was, how hard Bains struggled to remain conscious, and he knew what was coming next.

"Lord Kalern does not tolerate rebellion," the commander snarled then drove his sword into the prone man's chest.

"No!" Kellen gasped hoarsely. His heart pounded, his insides churning in pain and loss. Bains only cried out once, his body arching slightly before falling lifeless on the rain-soaked stones to lie so still. Shocked by the grotesque act, he could only stare in disbelief at Bains' dead, broken body.

"Now, answer my question!"

Snapping back to the present with that growled demand, Kellen tore his eyes away from Bains and tried to deny his tears. His grief. But it was impossible, and he lashed out at the commander, his attack uncoordinated and weak. The big man grunted in laughter, turning to look at his associates in amusement. The other three guards showed little interest, and the commander swung back to push Kellen roughly away.

The thrust sent him falling to sit on the wet ground a second time, and Kellen snarled—incensed—hastily standing and rushing his enemy again. Four against one, but he didn't care. Anguish governed his thinking, guided his hands, a desperate need to lash out and kill—and something loosened inside him. Then a rush of burning heat swept up his legs to engulf the pain blossoming in his chest.

It was a shock, jolting him enough to focus his mind, causing him to hiccough on a breath before he stared down at his tingling feet. The heat was strange—dancing around his feet, hot, yet not consuming—filling him with an incredible surge of energy, driving away his grief. Then the heat was moving, creeping up past his thighs into his abdomen and chest, and Kellen slowly lifted his eyes to pin the commander with grim determination. This man would pay for Bains' death.

He let that thought germinate in his mind then raised one arm, willing the heat into his fingers and feeling the wash of energy obey his desire. Vaguely, he noticed how his skin appeared unchanged, yet a liquid fire seemed to engulf his hand. A tangible, yet unseen force, which filled his head with visions of darkness and light. It gave him hope, and for the first time in his life, he felt truly powerful.

"Insolent child," the commander said, reaching for the entranced young man. "Congratulations on killing your friend. Now you will taste the hospitality of a northern prison camp, and I will be interested to see how long a tasty specimen like you lasts within the caverns of Gerthwin."

Foul breath assaulted his face, bringing his focus back to the commander, and Kellen blinked. He stared at the commander, his mind so full of new images, seeing a darkness that changed into a sea of tranquility and light. Then the commander was touching him, shaking him in fury, and Kellen was given a glimpse into the man's mind. He watched fascinated, picturing the guard's fragile life force hanging by a thread, malleable to his will. Vulnerable—so vulnerable—and he raised his hand, splaying his fingers against the commander's metal breastplate. Under the black armor drummed the commander's heart, and he flexed his fingers, willing the organ to burst. Just like Bains' heart had burst.

Abruptly, the commander faltered, and Kellen snatched his hand away from the black armor, leaving his palm imprinted in the cold metal. That stunned him, and he stepped back, his eyes going up to the commander's paling face. The big guard was opening his mouth, trying to inhale, shock dilating the dark pupils, and for one spellbinding, terrifying moment, Kellen could even *hear* the commander's innermost thoughts, could *taste* all the lives this one had taken. The vast rushing sound of voices assaulted him, and he twisted away, growing fearful at what he had done. At what he had willed with a simple thought.

Before him, the commander toppled forward, those sightless eyes accusing and fixed in death. Astounded, he felt the energy bleed out of his limbs, the heat washing away through his feet into the wet earth, deserting him.

"Witchcraft! Seize him! Lord Jorean has ordered the death of all such cursed souls!"

The shout snapped him alert, and Kellen ran with as much speed as he could muster, darting past the tethered horses toward the back of the old farmhouse. Then he was scrambling over the low stonewall and running into the long grass of the meadow. Behind him, he heard the guards shouting in their harsh native language, and he glanced around, slipping over in the wet grass. An arrow whistled past him, and he ducked, looking back to see the dark shadow of a guard turn back toward the house. He knew they would come after him on horseback, and he hastily climbed to his feet. In the distance, he could see the dense woodlands, and he knew that was his only hope.

He ran for another fifty paces and then paused, searching around. A small wooden bridge was to his right, and he vaguely remembered there was a gully and creek near the forest. He felt so disorientated by what had happened that he almost fell a second time when he heard the distinctive echo of horses' hooves on cobblestones. Cursing with feeling, he shook hair out of his eyes and scrambling urgently forward, only to tumble down a deceptively hidden, steep gully.

Gasping in surprise, he slid down the muddy embankment, landing face first in the small stream. He lifted his head and coughed out water and dirt, blinking to clear his vision while his limbs trembled in fatigue. Cold rain mingled with his tears, and he pushed his dark, unruly hair away before attempting to lever himself up. He never made it. Without warning, he was seized from behind and restrained before a large gloved hand clamped over his mouth, cutting off his shocked cry. "Wha—"

"Hush, child."

Forced to submit, Kellen closed his eyes, giving up the fight when his arms were immobilized with practiced speed behind his back. He grunted in pain, feeling himself half-dragged and half-carried toward the low wooden bridge, which spanned the narrow gully.

"Hush!"

It was an urgent whisper, hot in his ear, and Kellen tried to suck in a breath when the hand covering his mouth tightened. Moments later, the loud clattering of horses' hooves hitting the wooden bridge overhead made him jump, and he glanced up. He saw black shadows pass overhead, then he blinked rapidly as mud and water dripped down from the cracks in the old wood. Again, he was held tighter, and he wanted to protest, knowing he would be bruised. It wasn't until the horses had gone, and the silence had stretched for long moments, before he was turned and allowed a glimpse of his captor. The man was huge, encased in armor, and extremely hairy. But he was not a Black Guard.

"Now I'm going to let Ryland release you, but . . ." The speaker appeared next to the giant, his face lighting up into an appealing smile, almost friendly. "But you must first promise not to call out."

Squinting at the speaker, Kellen considered the words for a second then nodded, glad when the big man who was holding him so securely released his grip. He reached out a hand to steady himself then sat down hard on the embankment, not really caring who or what his new captors were. Rather, he had lost control; everything that had happened and that was now unfolding was a direct result to what he had done. What he and Bains had tried to do. *God! Bains . . .* He shuddered, feeling the cold rain eat into his flesh and bones. Squeezing his eyes tightly shut did not stop the images of death and horror replaying in his mind, and he shuddered again. Reality dissolved, and he raised his hands to stare at his bloodstained fingers. Only the blood was long gone, washed away in the rain, but still he felt tainted. Cursed. His best friend was now dead, and nothing would ever be the same again.

"Lad?"

Kellen forced himself to glance up when a massive hand squeezed his shoulder.

"You may like to explain why the Black Guard are so interested in you, and what you are doing with a bag of stolen Ihovian coin?"

The question was from the same blond with the friendly smile, and Kellen noted with some surprise that this man had managed to liberate a coin bag from out of his possession.

He pulled away from the large hand restraining him and flexed his cramped fingers. *The blond was good*, he acknowledged silently, feeling inside his tunic and finding the second bag also gone. He must have dropped it during his flight. Licking his dry lips, he glanced up wide-eyed at the three men who were watching him so intently. They were Ihovian, or at least two of the men were, Kellen decided, and he bit his lip in speculation. The speaker was tall, lean and rain soaked; dressed in forest greens; and possessed clear, direct eyes. Clipped to his belt were two long knives, and Kellen felt a prickle of uneasiness sweep him again. *Could these be the rebels the Black Guard asked about?*

"I think our little thief has lost his voice."

"Or nerve—"

"No," a deep voice behind Kellen rumbled. "Shock. Look, he is covered in blood."

He glanced back toward the man who had spoken, and Kellen suppressed a shiver. It was the hairy giant. The man was intimidatingly big, dressed in heavy armor much like that of the Black Guard, only larger. He also sported a thick, dark beard and black hair that stuck out from under his helmet in unruly tufts. "Don't you rust?" It was the first thing that came to mind, and Kellen bit the words off, not believing he had actually verbalized that thought.

The big man gave a deep snort of laugher, which was cut short when the third member of the party slid down the embankment beside the bridge with an elegance that impressed Kellen. This third man said nothing, just made a gesture with his hand, and before Kellen knew it, he was roughly pulled back and pressed into the unforgiving, cold dirt bank a second time. Thankfully, his mouth was not covered, and he held his breath, listening for the approach of horses.

Loud hooves abruptly pounded above them as horses crossed the small bridge, heading back toward the farmhouse. Only after they were gone and the silence was broken again by the sound of frogs croaking in the rain was Kellen allowed to move his cramped limbs.

"I think we should go." It was the third member of the little group who spoke. He made a cutting gesture with his hand and then turned away, slinging a small bag over his shoulder.

Disconcerted at how quickly he had been entangled in new events, Kellen found himself unceremoniously dragged to his feet and ushered out from under the low bridge. In mute displeasure, he realized he felt no safer now than he had in the hands of the Black Guard.

"It will not take those black vultures long to work out that the lad is no longer in the immediate area. Then they will make a more thorough search of the woodlands."

"Don't worry; we'll be long gone," the tall blond who had first spoken said in an offhanded way. "Just bring the boy."

Disgruntled, and wanting to protest that he was not a *boy*, Kellen almost fell when he was shoved forward, noting that his hard-earned thievery had achieved nothing. His single bag of white-gold coins disappeared into the speaker's pack. *He must be their leader*, Kellen decided, and the huge monster behind guarding his escape—*his jailer.*

CHAPTER TWO

The stream in the gully was cold. Muttering under his breath, Kellen glanced around, getting sick of being referred to as *the boy*. His boots were soaked, his clothes dripping wet, and he was given no answers to his questions, just silenced with a look from the big steel-encased warrior. Apart from that, they ignored him, until he was hauled out of the gully near the eastern edge of the valley about two leagues from the bridge. He was only mildly relieved when they entered the forest, as the massive trees gave them partial shelter from the rain.

The atmosphere in the forest was chilling, cold, and damp, with not even the crickets disturbing the eerie silence. No one spoke, and Kellen took the opportunity to study the men around him, anything to take his mind off what had just happened to him and Bains.

The leader was tall, with his hair neatly pulled back and tied with leather thongs. His expression was serious, his clothing a mix of cloth and leather, well worn with a partial insignia on his belt strap. The design was hard to make out in the gloom, but Kellen had the strangest feeling he had seen that insignia before. *But where?* The second man scouting ahead was of a similar build and coloring, and his clothing identified him clearly as Ihovian. Like the leader, the scout was carrying a crossbow slung over his shoulder and a long sword and knife strapped to his left boot. His hawklike features were fierce, giving Kellen the firm impression that this man missed nothing. Fidgeting, Kellen tried to avoid the perceptive blue-eyed gaze that returned his curious appraisal.

Then behind him, following up the rear of the group, was the giant—Ryland—and Kellen half-turned, immediately feeling a large hand grip his shoulder to keep him facing forward and moving. In fact, he had never seen such an enormous man before, and he shuddered, intimidated by his own musings. This giant was not Ihovian, nor was he a Black Guard, and Kellen frowned over that, wondering why two Ihovian hunters would team up with such an unusual warrior. Where had the silent threesome come from, and where were they now taking him? What had they been doing in that gully? His overactive imagination supplied him with numerous possibilities, and he wished Bains were with him. But Bains was dead.

Stumbling a little, Kellen struggled to keep up with the fast pace his captors enforced, getting disconcerted by the many changes in direction as they weaved through the lush forest, until he had soon lost his bearings. He became disorientated, and as the sun set, he could just make out the mountain range ahead, and he started to wonder if he would ever see his holdings again.

Demoralized, cold, and hungry, he shivered, finding it harder and harder to keep the pace as the evening gloom turned into a cheerless darkness. And still it rained. Slowly, his body turned as numb as his bruised mind, until he lost all track of time.

* * *

Hours later and in the deep blackness of night, they reached an old stone cottage hidden within the forest, and Kellen was too relieved to even protest when he was pushed inside and told to sit. A fire was lit in the old grate, flooding the room in warm light, and he sighed before gratefully sinking to sit on a bench. All his limbs ached from the vigorous march and the biting cold. The other three men secured the shutters on the windows then unloaded their bags and checked the shelves and cupboards.

A loud noise made him jump, and Kellen glanced up in time to see the sturdy door being closed and bolted shut. He risked a look at his captors and watched the giant ease off his helmet, dropping it on the long wooden table with a loud thump. Then all eyes turned to him.

"Well, that was a waste of effort." This was from the blond Ihovian, the bowman, who now stood by the bolted door.

"Maybe and maybe not," the leader said softly, walking over to stand near Kellen and hand him a dry blanket. "Let me take a look at your injuries, boy."

"I'll be fine," Kellen muttered, accepting the thick woolen blanket and seeing the blood that stained his leather tunic.

"Good," the leader said. "But dry yourself before your muscles cool down, or you will get cramp."

Fingering the coarse blanket, Kellen wiped his face, avoiding eye contact with his captors as a renewed feeling of apprehension engulfed him. Would they kill him, or let him go? Risking a glance up, he saw that the tall leader returned his look calmly before dragging a chair over to straddle it. Those vivid blue eyes then pinned him expertly.

"So, let us start again," the leader said, giving a small yet firm smile. "What is your name?"

"Kellen," he said after careful thought. There was really no benefit in lying.

The leader nodded. "Tell me, what were you doing robbing the Black Guard? Surely you must know to be caught means death?"

"Yes," Kellen said very slowly. *Bains' death.* "We had not intended to be caught."

"It did not look like that to me." The giant scowled at him. "Soon as those guards hit the meadows, they would have seen you, and your sorry little carcass would be locked in a dungeon by now. If not dead."

"That wouldn't have happened if we—" Kellen stopped abruptly and frowned, studying his hands.

"We?" the leader questioned shrewdly. "You've said that twice now. Is your friend captured?"

A disturbing bubble of memory threatened to escape, and Kellen bit down on his sudden panic, clamping his mouth shut. He just shook his head in reply.

"I . . . see." The leader released a slow breath, his eyes taking on a sympathetic shadow. "I am sorry."

"It shouldn't have happened. I should have stopped it, but I froze. I—" The words were rash and out before Kellen could stop them.

"There was probably nothing you could have done. The Black Guard do not take prisoners." Now the leader had moved and was crouching down by his side, close yet not touching.

"But I could have..."

"What? What could you have tried?"

"I don't know. Something," Kellen whispered, his eyes haunted as he remembered the commander's horror-filled gaze and shocking death.

The leader regarded at him for a long moment. "Do you have family around here, Kellen?"

"I don't even know where here is."

The man rephrased the question with a half smile. "Family near the old farmhouse then?"

"No," Kellen shook his head, "they're all dead."

The leader stood up with a sigh and walked over to the silent bowman who was leaning against the far wall. The bowman's eyes were direct, sliding from Kellen to the leader before he hissed something softly. The two exchanged heated words, with the bowman speaking passionately in a fast whisper as if trying to convince his companion of something important. Watching the exchange, Kellen saw the familial affection, the small indications that linked them as closer than friends, and he blinked, feeling as if he was given a strange glimpse, or insight, into a very complex relationship.

Images flashed into his mind, places, faces etched from another's mind flickered before his eyes. Pictures of *beauty, of marbled terraces, adorned maidens, regal banquets, two young boys playing behind a massive throne,* and Kellen blinked, startled. Then just as abruptly, the strange fragments were gone, and he refocused on the two Ihovian hunters by the bolted door. What had he seen, where had the knowledge come from, or how had he suddenly picked up on the undercurrents between these two men, he did not know, but he felt as if the bowman was the younger, yet the stronger. *More than friends.* Curious, Kellen tried to strain his ears to hear more of the whispered conversation and found that the giant was studying him in amusement.

"So tell me, lad, how many others knew of your attempt to rob the guard?"

"None." That was not strictly true, but Kellen was not going to admit to anything else. He had more than likely already said too much. Eyeing the big warrior, he was confused by the strange accent and formal speech patterns, wondering from where the giant had originated. "It would have worked, except for . . ."

"Except for what?"

The question surprised him by its unexpectedness and deceptive mildness, and Kellen swung his eyes back on the leader. The man was examining him again, and he inhaled nervously. *Who to trust?* Yet he got the impression that none of his three captors meant him any real harm. Glancing around, he considered his next words with care. "I think they were expecting a raid. Bains had . . . had everything worked out too well." He tried to shrug off the memories. "Now that I think about it—it had to be a trap."

"Why do you say that?" The question was sharp and direct, and Kellen apprehensively looked at the man by the door. The searching, pale blue eyes spoke of intelligence and wry humor, and Kellen turned away, deciding he preferred the more approachable façade of the leader.

"Well . . ." Kellen took a deep breath and then sighed, deciding he had to trust someone. It would be easier to tell the truth now than later. "There were three of the Black Guard inside the house. The gold was outside. A fourth guard had to be hiding in the surrounding shed with his horse, otherwise there would've been four horses tethered. Also, Bains would have seen any approaching rider from the front gate, as that farmhouse is visible for a league in every direction."

The tall blond leader nodded approvingly. "I think you are right, young Kellen. It probably *was* a trap. But not for you. It is unfortunate that you and your friend stumbled into it." He cast a sideways glance at the man by the door, hearing the other snort in disgust. "Tell me, what was this gold you stole for?"

"The holdings where I live. Without it, we cannot buy supplies and the livestock will die, and the farm will be abandoned." Somehow it all seemed so far away now. So unimportant.

The fire crackled as the silence lengthened, and Kellen dragged his mind back to the present and noted the leader's wordless sympathy.

"Entertaining tale, but it still leaves us in a quandary," the giant said, stripping off his mail shirt. Underneath the armor, his cotton tunic was marked with rust spots.

Kellen looked over at the big warrior and blinked, his gaze falling on all the stored armor, weapons, and supplies in the back of the small cottage. Suddenly, it all clicked into place, and he found himself voicing his suspicions before the thought was complete. "You were going to steal that gold . . ." he trailed off, getting a very direct blue-eyed glare. "They were waiting for you; that was why they kept asking me—"

"Asking you what?"

Kellen stared up at the tall man and felt his jaw sag. "You!" he breathed. "They called you the pretender prince of Ihova!"

"Really?"

"But I thought . . . ?"

The tall leader waved his questions away and paced the length of the small room.

"What does worry me is that they were waiting. Setting up a trap," the bowman interjected as his concerned gaze followed the leader's pacing. "Dale—"

"Rather, do you not mean 'who betrayed us'?" the giant corrected while he took out a stone and started to hone his sword.

"That can't be possible!"

"Dale." The bowman moved, stopping the leader's agitated movements with a hand as he offered softly spoken words. "But the trap almost worked. If we hadn't been delayed, then the Black Guard would have you now. And you know how much that twisted schemer Jorean would like nothing more than to see your head swing from the battlements in Ihova. Especially since he is offering a very tempting reward for information."

Kellen stared unashamedly at the tall Ihovian warriors. He had known that insignia looked familiar, but he had never imagined he would ever see—let alone meet—"You're Prince Lesendal of Hanlin?"

Sweeping his eyes down, the leader just nodded then placed a reassuring hand on the bowman's shoulder. "A title and throne which I hope one day to win back, my young friend."

"I . . . does that mean your father the king is . . . ?"

"Dead," the prince finished very softly. "They took Ihova City in the space of a day, before we even knew what was happening. My father had sent peace envoy after peace envoy, but—" he stopped, pain washing over his face. "We were betrayed from within. My sister and I are the only two surviving members of the house of Hanlin, and I will not rest until my father and brothers are avenged."

Kellen just stared at him, trying to remember all he could of the royal family and the beautiful city. Was this what he had glimpsed only moments before? But his memories were different to the surreal images. In reality, Ihova City was a three-day ride to the west and he had only been there once, as a child. Yet, he still recalled the high white stone buildings, the trees, and the river, which ran down the center of the city. The tranquil gardens and clean roads, the carriages and the beautifully dressed people. It had been a place of splendor, culture, and learning.

Regaining his composure, the prince gave a wry smile. "So, young Kellen, it seems I am in your debt. I just wish this day had not been so costly to you and your friend." He gestured to the other two men in the room. "Introductions are in order, I think. This is Salimen," he gestured to the bowman first, "and Ryland. And yes, we were after the gold. Anything to irritate the Hoindrite army that is marching across our soil. Anything to stop Lord Jorean from claiming victory. Anything to cause chaos and buy much needed support for our cause." He slowly unclenched his fist. "But that is not your concern."

"But, my lord, if you are going to fight the Black Guard then you will need an army," Kellen reasoned. "If the city is taken then—"

"Ryland is from Haonia, and it seems that the Black Guard under Jorean's control have already desolated his kingdom as well as our western neighbors, the Cardonen. After they finish with Ihova, the guard intend to march into Dalisen. Then it will be into Vernonz or Kalhorn." The prince took a steadying breath. "Soon there will be no army remaining within the entire Southland to fight the Hoindrites unless I can raise enough gold to buy support."

Mercenaries? The prince was talking about mercenaries, and Kellen shuddered, having heard more than one horror tale about their eastern cousins. "But what of the Ihovian army, my lord?"

"All but destroyed by the Deathwalkers."

Kellen gasped. "Deathwalkers?" he mouthed, never wanting to believe those creatures from legend were real. An old childhood litany rose in his mind, his brother's voice whispering the taunt: *"If you don't behave the Raveners, Deathwalkers, Drow, and Mindwipes will eat you."* Shaking his head to dislodge the memory, Kellen risked a glance up at the frowning prince. "My lord?"

"I am sorry, Kellen. This is not your burden." The prince turned away from him, looking defeated and exhausted.

"But, my lord, if you need an army, then I would be willing to fight for Ihova."

"No."

"I am old enough," Kellen declared, willing the other to listen. "I want to help. I can fight."

"Kellen, how old are you?"

"Seventeen." He willed the other to believe him.

"Really?"

"Yes."

"And are you old enough to die?" Again it was quietly asked, the prince's perceptive blue eyes locking on him. "Like your young friend died today?"

The reminder was harsh, and Kellen paled. "What is my alternative?" he asked a little brokenly. "Am I to now wait to be hunted down by the Black Guard and then dragged off for their amusement? Do you think I want to be sent to their caverns in Gerthwin?"

"Caverns?" the prince repeated and raised a questioning brow. "The northern caverns of Gerthwin are only whispered rumors, nothing substantial. Where did you hear about the caverns?"

"One of the guards said he would send me there," Kellen explained, remembering the frightening encounter and the foul breath of the commander. Yet had the commander spoken of Gerthwin aloud, or had that name just mysteriously popped into his head? Maybe he was losing his mind. "He said that I would not last long in the caverns."

"I see." The prince eyed him with concern as Salimen whistled through his teeth. "Then you had better come with us until we can at least ensure your safety. We have a safe haven in the mountains."

"But—" Kellen started to protest.

The Ihovian prince lifted a finger, and Kellen closed his mouth obediently.

"In the morning, we will be leaving for the high country to the west. You will come with us, and if the war continues to go badly, then at least you will be safe from the Black Guard." He gave a soft laugh, trying to lighten the mood. "I would hate to see you killed after we went to so much trouble rescuing you."

"Thanks," Kellen muttered, far from happy.

The prince walked away and pulled wrapped food items from his pack. He handed out the rations, stopping last in front of Kellen. "Just one final thing bothers me, Kellen," the prince said, "how did you manage to escape the guard?"

Feeling uncomfortable with that particular question, Kellen just shrugged. "Luck," he mumbled even as he saw in his mind the commander's face as the man's heart burst apart. How he had accomplished such a feat, he did not know, and he definitely was not willing to share his secret. Not now and maybe never. He was too scared of rejection, too scared of the curse, witchcraft.

Ryland laughed, recapturing Kellen's attention as the big man sat next to him. "You just used your wits, lad. For I can tell you, intelligence is not one of the guards' stronger points." He scratched his bearded chin, glancing over at the prince. "You know, Lesendal, he might prove useful up in the stronghold. He is of legal age."

"We'll see . . ." Prince Lesendal said then tore a piece of bread from the round loaf and handed it to Kellen. "You can be our lucky charm until then. Which means Sasheer should be waiting where he is supposed to be waiting."

"That would be a miracle. Sasheer is outside the realm of luck and all that is associated with the term," Ryland growled. "You have a misguided faith in that disreputable man."

"No, my friend," Lesendal grinned. "I believe he is the only one that can aid us in this war."

"Aid or destroy?" Ryland questioned, letting his dark eyes sweep up to Salimen, looking for support. But the bowman ignored him. "Have you considered that Sasheer might be the reason behind this war?"

"Never," Lesendal dismissed. "I have known him all my life, and I trust him implicitly."

"Maybe so, but Lesendal, a man who does not appear to age—can you truly know and trust such a man? Is he even a man?" Ryland questioned.

"You are overly suspicious." Lesendal waved the questions away.

"One of us has to be," Ryland cautioned, his voice a deep rumble.

Kellen watched wide-eyed as the big warrior glared at the prince for a moment and then looked away, obviously dissatisfied. "Ryland," he started, taken back when Ryland's darkening gaze pinned him so swiftly. "Who, or what, is this Sasheer?"

"A historian, or so he tells everyone," Ryland explained. "He is a charlatan, a manipulator of the weak. He wanders the Twelve Kingdoms of the south meddling in politics and trade. He is a fraud, if you ask me. All he ever did when visiting my kingdom was drink the ale, seduce maidens, and spend the money given him by the throne to buy books!"

"Ryland!" Lesendal laughed.

"What sane man buys books?" Ryland growled, ignoring Lesendal's laughter. "I am sorry, but I have seen what I have seen. If you insist on trusting him, then I must protect your back. And if the young lad is to be a traveling companion, then he needs to know the dangers also."

Lesendal just shook his head and appealed to Salimen, who smiled back, amused. "I think, my Haonian friend, you are just sore because Sasheer has beaten you at every dice game you've challenged him to."

CHAPTER THREE

Early the following morning, Kellen found himself back in the forest, walking behind Prince Lesendal's tall figure. Thinking about the previous chaotic day, he could not believe how one event could change his life so drastically. He was excited, yet awed, by the three men with him, his mind racing with what he had learned and seen. But the memory of Bains' death weighed on him, and he glanced down at his fingers, seeing that they were clean of blood. Yet he still wiped them on his leggings, wishing the guilt would disappear as easily. He wished he had acted sooner to save Bains' life, wished he could remember how he had killed the commander, but even thinking about that incredible moment was frightening. Fear and dread shadowed his elation. So was it witchcraft?

A confusing panic loomed in the back of his mind, and Kellen forced it away, thinking about other problems. Like where was Prince Lesendal taking him? Would the three remaining enemy guards hunt him? Who was this Lord Kalern, and why had the commander whispered his name in reverence? Was Lord Kalern related to Lord Jorean? How big was Lesendal's rebel army? And who was Sasheer?

He was so consumed by these churning thoughts that Kellen did not realize the others had stopped until he smacked into the back of Lesendal's stationary frame. Blinking, he mumbled a hasty apology, hearing Ryland's deep rumbling laugh behind.

"So wearied already, young Kellen?"

"No," Kellen said, in defense. He most definitely did not want to be thought of as a helpless child. But the prince was not listening. Instead, Lesendal was cautiously turning to scan the quiet woodlands with an expert eye.

Becoming aware of their surroundings for the first time in over an hour, Kellen also looked around, pushing his long hair behind one ear, noting that Salimen was drifting silently through the woods off to his right—ghostlike in appearance. Even the giant Ryland was motionless. "What—"

The prince just raised a hand, and Kellen swallowed the rest of his question, paying more attention to the silence permeating the area. Nothing moved; no fresh breeze of air disturbed the foliage, and Kellen held his breath, becoming very conscious of the strange stillness. He frowned, noticing that even the rain had stopped, and that the birds were unusually quiet. A hazy brightness cast a gloom over the area, and he was very glad when Lesendal relaxed. Then Salimen walked back to them, shaking his head.

"I told you we would lose those trackers," Ryland said dryly.

Blinking at that, Kellen wondered when they had been sighted and tracked. It was disturbing to think he had missed something so vital.

"I prefer to be careful," Lesendal said.

"It was the pass at White Falls which lost them," Salimen decided smugly.

"So now what?" Ryland asked. "Do you want to continue on under these conditions or go back to the foothills?"

Considering that, the prince turned to look at Kellen as if weighing up the alternatives. "No, I think we have time to see if Sasheer has reached the meeting point."

"It is a waste of effort," Ryland said.

"He will have information we need," Lesendal said pointedly.

Raising a hand in compliance, Ryland only nodded, falling into place behind Kellen again as they set off west. "I do not know why you trust him. There are safer—easier—ways of getting information. More inexpensive ways as well."

"Ryland, I know you don't want to believe this, but he is extremely talented and perceptive," Lesendal answered. "Plus he is not asking for any payment."

"Talented?" Ryland snorted in disgust. "Lesendal, he is nothing more than a Trickster!"

"Ryland!" Lesendal turned, whispering urgently. "Cursed bones, man! Keep your voice down! And don't ever say that again! Especially not in Sasheer's hearing, or you will learn a very hard lesson."

Shocked by the hissed tone more than the words, Kellen held his breath, watching Lesendal turn and walk away. A dozen paces ahead, Salimen could be seen scouting the narrow track for traps, and Kellen shifted his gaze between the two Ihovian warriors, seeing how Salimen made some obscure gesture toward the prince. If anything, the silent communication calmed the prince, and Lesendal chuckled before returning the hand signal.

Curious about what had upset the prince in the first place, Kellen cast Ryland an appraising glance and was not surprised to see how the Haonian was still scowling. Considering all that he had witnessed, Kellen let the silence stretch before he carefully broached the topic.

"Ryland?" Kellen began, receiving only a grunt of acknowledgment. He slowed his pace and waited until Ryland was walking at his side before continuing. "Can I ask you a question?" He got another grunt and risked an assessing glance up at the massive warrior. "Ryland, what precisely is a Trickster?"

"A Trickster?"

"Yes, well . . . you know, what you were just talking about," he added helpfully. "I mean, I've heard of them in stories and such. In legends, but I have always thought they were supposed to be all-powerful mythical beings who inspired courage . . ." Kellen trailed off, worried by the way Ryland had turned to glare at him in annoyance. "That is just what I've heard," he defended hastily. "I just thought you might know, since you mentioned it to Prince Hanlin."

"It seems your education is terribly lacking," Ryland said. "In my kingdom, you would be reprimanded for such a remark and then sent back to basic schooling."

Kellen blushed at the thought. "I've never been to a proper school."

"It should be mandatory in all young. A good, learned education is just as important as a strong physical education," Ryland said.

"Well, I probably missed out because my family seemed to travel around. My mother disliked discussing history. She said the Twelve Kingdoms were misguided."

"Hmm . . ." Ryland eyed him a little disapprovingly. "Misguided?" he repeated before shaking his head. "And what did your father say?"

"I can't remember," Kellen answered. "He died when I was very young."

"I imagine he was a farmer," Ryland said. "A man of the land. He must have instructed you in the family beliefs."

"I have no memory of it," Kellen shrugged. "My mother moved us from holding to holding when I was young," he said, remembering how lost and disorientated he had been. "She had family in Ihova, and she wanted to find sponsors for my brother and me. She died not long after from a strange illness."

"I'm sorry, lad," Ryland said in sincerity, placing a large gloved hand on Kellen's shoulder in sympathy. "What of your brother?"

"We stayed on the holding, moving into the workers' cottage. Then when Wyran was old enough, he left to join the Ihovian army. That was two years ago," Kellen ended, only a little pain coloring his voice as he thought about his older brother.

"An honorable goal," Ryland nodded in approval.

Shaking off the uncomfortable memory, Kellen looked back at Ryland. "You were going to tell me what a Trickster is," he prompted.

Ryland considered him then looked ahead toward the prince before slowing his pace. When Lesendal was completely out of earshot, he turned back to Kellen. "There are many different types of men who walk the combined lands, lad. Just remember that each land has its own legends and beliefs of such things, but I will tell you what I know and have read. What is taught in Haonia." He took a deep breath, clearly considering his words carefully. "Some men, warriors, or leaders are portrayed as good or as misguided. Some are naive, greedy, twisted, or just plain evil. Then there is another group of men—creatures—who are separate again. They have cast themselves in a higher role to us mere mortals and believe they are better than we are. Or so they like to bemoan. Of this group, you have those who are called Tricksters, Spellcasters, and Mageborns."

Enthralled by the mystery, Kellen drank in Ryland's words. "Are they all the same?"

"Hardly," Ryland said. "A Trickster is no more than a glorified—and overpaid, if you ask me—entertainer. They can perform spectacular illusions and dazzle the weak-minded, but really they are nothing more than frauds. Their power, for it is a type of power, is in their speech as they twist and manipulate the unwary. They stand out among men, dress in long flowing robes, and have a snobbish disposition." Ryland shook his head in disgust. "Vile parasites."

Trying to imagine such a robed man, Kellen frowned. "And this Sasheer, whom the prince talks about, is like this?"

Ryland paused briefly and cleared his throat. "In all honesty, no," he admitted. "But he does act like a glorified Court Trickster, and that infuriates me."

"Maybe that is why he does it," Kellen offered.

Ryland spiked him with a look of concern. "You cannot be serious?" Then held up a hand. "Nay, lad, say nothing more. You are better at rebuking me gently than my elders, it seems. Lesendal might be right for once. Perhaps you are a lucky charm."

"I . . . umm, doubt it," Kellen hesitated. "So what are the others?" he asked, seeing how the prince was walking beside Salimen. The two men were talking and paying him no heed. "Are they magic users?"

"Spellcasters use old magics," Ryland clarified. "I was taught, when I was very young, that the four lands used to contain vast magics until the war against the Mages bled all the magic from the land. Then the races separated, and true magic was lost forever."

Reeling from this information, Kellen wanted to ask so much more, wanted to know it all. No one had ever told him this history. "The war?"

"The Coastal Mage War," Ryland corrected. "That was over four thousand years ago according to the scrolls I have heard read.

Magic faded as the old races diminished. And now men have no dealings with the remnants of the other lands—with the mystical races. It is said, that even now, the earth on the mainland is infected with the old ones' taint, with wild pockets of fire. That is another reason why we have no dealings with those outside the Southland."

Wide-eyed, Kellen absorbed it all. He knew many within his isolated holdings had shunned the mainland, but he had never been told why. "So all the magic is gone?"

"From what I have heard, real magic—yes. If ever it existed in the first place. That sort of magic has never touched the Southland. And what the other races possess, like the Dwarves and Elves, has never been clear and is of no concern to us—to man."

"Until now?"

"I doubt this war we are having with Lord Jorean will interest the other nations across the White Sea on the mainland," Ryland said, gesturing toward the horizon. "Unless, of course, the trade lines with the Lancooti are disrupted."

"Lancooti?" Kellen repeated, becoming diverted from the subject by this new term. He had so many questions. He wanted to ask Ryland if he had ever seen an Elf or sailed over the ocean that separated them from the other lands. He wanted to know what the land looked like over the sea.

"The Lancooti are the sand people who live beyond the Divide. They trade openly with the mainland of Sennovia. We trade with the mainland through them."

Storing that information away, Kellen went back to their original topic. "So these Spellcasters—this magic," he prompted, "what sort of magic was it if it wasn't real? How can magic not be real?"

Eyeing him in curiosity, Ryland shrugged. "I do not know. Earthen power from plants is considered a type of magic. Sleight of hand and smoke images. Though who can say? I have never met anyone who has seen real magic."

"And over the sea?" Kellen pushed. He had to find something that would explain what had happened to the commander. Maybe it was the commander's own dark magic which had killed the man?

"Who knows?" Ryland said then leaned down to wrap an arm around Kellen's shoulder before giving him a wide grin. "Kellen, it is not our business to concern ourselves with foreign nations. We live in the south. Remember that."

"I'll try," he said, thinking that remark seemed a little narrow-minded. What was over the White Sea that none in the south was allowed to see? "So what of the others?"

"Others?"

"You mentioned three groups of men. Tricksters, Spellcasters, and . . ."

"Oh yes, the Mageborn," the big man nodded, seeing Lesendal stop ahead and look back. The prince was frowning and scanning the undergrowth. "They are myth only," he answered dismissively. "Come, we had best hurry."

Myth? Quickening his pace, Kellen could not help but think on all that Ryland had told him, and he glanced around, speculating on the idea that if the Deathwalkers of childhood legends were real, then what about the other evil creatures strong men only whispered about in the dead of night? Could they be real also?

* * *

They reached the old bridge, which broached a fast-running stream, and Kellen studied the area, feeling edgy as the stillness of the place ate into his nerves. He sensed tension, a building anticipation of danger, an awareness growing in the atmosphere around him. A sensation of coldness—and his eyes widened as he realized it was the same coldness he had experienced at the farmhouse. He scanned the misty forest, the brilliant green of plants and moss giving the place a mystical glow, and he shivered, half-expecting to see the figure of a man cloaked in darkness loom up in the shadows. Who or what had the cloaked figure been? He shivered a second time as icy fingers of dread skimmed his body and brushed his cheek. More supernatural madness? Or just his overworked paranoia? He shuddered, and he tried to push the unsettling thoughts away.

The forest was unnaturally quiet, dormant, and lifeless, with not even the sound of insects disturbing the peace. A cool breeze lightly stirred the foliage, played in his hair, whispered over his senses, but it too failed to dispel the fear which seeped into his bones and traveled down his spine in a flood of goosebumps. He swiveled, his hand going to the dagger at his waist, and he scrutinized the area. But there was nothing to be seen. Only an eerie tranquility, and then a hand settled heavily on his shoulder, and he jumped, gasping in fright.

"You sense it too, lad?"

It was Ryland, and Kellen released an explosive breath. "It is like . . ." he searched for a word to describe the ill feeling.

"Death," Ryland finished for him. "Come on, lad, we cannot wait here much longer. It is not safe."

Swallowing the lump in his throat, Kellen did not move for a long moment, watching the others move away from the bridge before he got his legs working. *Death?* He glanced around one last time at the lifelessness of the forest and wondered what had happened to this place to kill the brightness. And what had happened to the man named Sasheer. If Sasheer was some enchanted Trickster like Ryland stated, then what could have happened to him? Dismissing the troubling idea, he hurried after the other men.

* * *

They walked in silence, the shadows lengthening to indicate late afternoon. Falling in behind the prince, Kellen rolled his shoulder back and glanced around at the hushed forest. The sun-dappled undergrowth and massive trees looked ordinary, yet there was something about the old forest that bothered him. Like the air was charged with expectancy, like something unspeakable was on the verge of happening. A foreboding that frightened and excited him.

The bridge was now far behind them, and the sky darkening, the thick canopy overhead locking in an oppressive dampness. Beneath his feet, twigs cracked, and Kellen tried to tread lightly, imitating the prince's surefootedness. His fingers strayed to touch his small dagger again, and he glanced sideways, just catching a glimpse of wraithlike, inky blackness. A shadowlike image of night; and he froze, the warning dying on his lips even as Salimen gave a clipped call before his crossbow twanged.

Abruptly, the forest came alive with activity, and Kellen instinctively crouched low in the damp undergrowth. He felt Ryland reach for him and shove him toward a thick tree stump. Then the big warrior raised his massive sword and slashed at one of the four guards who circled in menacingly. Lesendal had pulled a second guard from the saddle, fending off a black sword with his knife as he tangled their legs to fall and roll into the dense undergrowth. Salimen threw his crossbow at the third guard in defense, pulling out his sword as he sprang out of the way of the charging horse's hooves.

Everything happened so fast, Kellen barely had time to blink, and then he felt those same fingers of foreboding wrap around his throat and cut off his air. He gasped, feeling smothered, falling back against the tree and staring up into blackness. A hooded cowl and the most intensely dark eyes he had ever seen focused on him. Eyes brimming with pain and sadness. Glistening with hatred, or was it anger?

He struggled for breath, reaching for the invisible fingers in an attempt to loosen the ghost's hold and sucked in a breath when he was released. The image of darkness before him fractured, then vanished into nothing, and he coughed, staring around wildly but seeing only the trees and foliage.

Dazed, he turned and scanned the undergrowth, the sounds of fighting reaching his ears. It was frightening and strange, and he heard Ryland shout some sort of battle cry in his native tongue. Then the large man rammed his opponent up against a tree and sliced the guard open from abdomen to shoulder. Blood gushed out, covering the ground, and Kellen turned away, seeing that Lesendal had killed his guard also. Salimen held his captive on the ground in a neck lock while the doomed man thrashed uselessly in the throws of death.

Soon, too soon, there was only silence surrounding them again. Salimen stood, a self-satisfied grin on his handsome face, before he dropped his victim, then bent down to retrieve his sword.

"Well, that certainly warmed the blood," Ryland said as he wiped his blade on the damp clothing of his dead opponent.

"Good shooting, Sal," Lesendal acknowledged, gripping his countryman's shoulder. "But it is a pity you had to kill this one. It would be interesting to know why they were this far inside the forest."

"The 'why' is because you are here. I keep telling you, Dale, we have an informer in the group," Salimen said, tired of having to repeat the obvious.

"But I trust everyone at the settlement with my life."

"I know you do; that's why I believe you should let me handle this when we get back to base camp."

Considering that, Lesendal glanced around again, his eyes falling on Kellen's white face. "Fine," he sighed then turned when Ryland walked back toward them, holding the reins of the four black horses.

"Thank the cursed stars that the Black Guard always travel in groups of four. I think it must be a failing in their training or something. But who am I to argue?" Ryland grinned. "Now we have the advantage. Our mounts await."

Lesendal just nodded and cleaned his sword before resheathing it. "Let's search them before we go."

Feeling disconnected with his surroundings and his companions, Kellen could only stare at Lesendal in bewildered shock as the prince searched the dead. Instead he lifted his own hand and massaged his bruised throat. A ghost had tried to kill him.

* * *

As evening descended, Kellen found his shock was fading. Rather he was consumed with frustration, and he glared at the spot between his horse's ears. He was extremely uncomfortable, bouncing up and down in the hard saddle, fighting the reins and this stubborn mount. He had never ridden a horse before and could honestly say he hoped never to ride again. His backside was numb, his thighs were cramped in protested, and it felt like every tooth in his head was on the verge of falling out, while the horse fought every little command he tried to give it. *Perverse horse.* Then to make matters worse, he was positive the others knew of his plight and were silently laughing at him.

They stopped on dusk, and Kellen was amazed to see they had entered a small makeshift camp. He had been so engrossed with just staying upright that he had hardly noticed anything since leaving the forest. But now, looking around, he saw canvas-type tents dotting the dirt-swept clearing, horse pens, chickens, goats, and large fire pits. People were walking around all dressed in the similar forest greens, children played by one pool, while women tended the cooking meat over each pit. Behind him, tall blond Ihovians stood guard, watching the winding trail he had just endured.

"Come on, lad. They tell me dinner is almost ready, so there is just time to wash up."

It was Ryland by his side, and Kellen looked at the Haonian then focused on the ground. He was suddenly unsure if his legs would hold his weight.

"Here, let me help you down."

Before he knew it, Ryland had him by the back of his belt and out of the saddle in a swift twist. He staggered and glared up at the big man. "That has to be probably one of the worst things I have ever experienced."

Laughing good-naturedly, Ryland wrapped an arm around his shoulders and dragged him away to the water troughs. "Come on, or we will miss all the food and verbal sparks."

"The what?" Kellen asked, sore all over and feeling sorry for himself.

"Lesendal's a little upset, and when he gets like that, heads usually roll," Ryland laughed again, "it is usually best to leave him to Sal."

"Oh," Kellen frowned, intrigued as he dried his hands. Next to him, Ryland continued to grin in knowing anticipation. "So what happens now?"

Ryland sobered a little as he went to stand near one of the fires. The tasty smell of cooking meat was overpowering, and Kellen found his mouth watering while his stomach growled. "One of the watchmen by the gate said a scouting group was due back this night, so we will probably wait here until Lesendal gets their report."

"Then what?" Kellen pushed.

The big warrior shrugged, eyeing off the roasting meat. "It depends."

"I mean, what will happen to me?"

Ryland's direct gaze pinned him in speculation. "One of two things, I should imagine."

"Such as?" Kellen asked, feeling his hunger vanishing under the uncertainty.

"Either you will stay here for a while, or one of the supply envoys will take you up into the mountains. There is a secret stronghold there."

Blinking at Ryland, Kellen turned and went to sit on one of the low logs at the fire's edge. So he was to be cast off, handed on to others. But what of his old life? What of the holdings and Bains' family? He glanced up as Ryland handed him a strip of hot, moist meat, its smell enticing.

"What eats at your soul, lad?"

The words were haunting, and Kellen straightened with a jolt, eyeing the other man in apprehension as he met the shrewd brown eyes. "I just . . ."

"You are thinking about those you leave behind."

"I told you I have no family," Kellen rushed in excuse.

"I heard what you said, but I also saw how you said it," Ryland reprimanded. "Know this, if it will make you feel better, I will make sure some of the gold you stole makes it to the holdings in the area of the old farmhouse."

"You would do that for me?" Kellen asked, surprised.

"It is the least I can do for someone who averted a disaster."

Hearing those soft words, Kellen's gaze caught the image of Lesendal and Salimen over Ryland's broad shoulder. The two seemed to be arguing while Lesendal held another man back. "Ryland?"

"Yes, lad?" Ryland answered, concentrating on his meal.

"Who is Salimen?"

Lifting a brow, Ryland looked around to where the two men were standing. "Ah," his grin started again, "Salimen and Lesendal are very . . . close. Cousins. Or so everyone says," he said, reaching for more hot food. "Now eat up, lad, before the meat gets cold."

Tasting the spicy food, Kellen nevertheless watched the two men curiously as Lesendal lead Salimen away from the group, grabbing his shirt to pull him back a few more times. *Cousins?* "They look more like brothers."

Ryland sighed. "Lad, it is best not to delve into other people's business; trust me on this. Lesendal is the rightful heir to the Ihovian throne, and Salimen is his closest friend and adviser. I think Salimen is officially Lesendal's uncle's youngest son or something like that. Therefore—cousins."

Kellen waited, expecting more, but Ryland seemed very reluctant to finish. "Ryland, how long have you been here?" He asked, deciding to change the angle of his questions.

"About six months. I, and some of my clan, came across the ice range after sealing the gem mines. We got there just before the Black Guard destroyed the clans." He frowned, his expression darkening in remembrance. "Then we ventured into Vernonz looking for aid, but Nizzizanan had already signed a peace treaty with Lord Jorean, so we fled into Dalisen."

"Nizz who?" Kellen asked, not even trying to pronounce that name.

"You do not know the names of the kings of the Twelve Kingdoms?" Ryland asked, shocked.

"I think that might be another one of those areas in my schooling that I missed out on," Kellen offered.

"Can you read?"

"Yes." Kellen was quite proud of that fact, for that was one skill his older brother had not fully mastered.

"Good. Then when you get to the stronghold, read your history."

"Fine. But until then can you at least finish telling me your story?"

Ryland seemed to consider him for a long moment, and it seemed to Kellen that the other man might just take it upon himself to educate him personally. "Nizzizanan is the old hierarch king of Vernonz. He has ruled in peace for over half a century, but I should have suspected that his sons would sell him out. The Black Guard took his city in less than a day."

"Ryland, who actually is this Jorean?"

"Lord Jorean," Ryland corrected as he frowned. "He is from the north, from across the White Sea—the lands of Hoindrea. I have heard it said that he is the brother of King Falron from the Ice Ranges to the north of the Ridges. And that his people trade in black gold taken, I imagine, from the vast mines under Dusk Mountain."

"So why is he here?" Kellen asked.

Considering that, Ryland studied his toes which were warming in front of the fire before he answered. "Four seasons ago, Lord Jorean was visiting King Falimar of Wericonon on some diplomatic errand. What exactly, I do not know, but very soon after his arrival, it was rumored that he had been appointed royal adviser to the throne of Wericonon when the king's two sons died in a tragic accident. Then when the king passed away in his sleep a few months later, this corrupt upstart must have either bribed or murdered much of the royal court because suddenly he was crowned king of Wericonon. Then from there, he started bringing in the Black Guard and disrupting the trade lines between the Lancooti and the Twelve Kingdoms, isolating some of our major supply routes out of Herston, until war broke out between Wericonon and Cardonen." Ryland shrugged. "His movements were insidious at first, but after he hit my home of Haonia, it became almost too late to stop his advancement across the south."

"He went from your kingdom into Dalisen?" Kellen asked, wide-eyed. He could vaguely recall stories he had heard circulating before the Hoindrite army had invaded Ihova.

Ryland waved the question away. "In Dalisen, they believed their peace envoys had worked because the Hoindrite army bypassed them and invaded Ranhoy and Ihova. So I and my surviving clansmen came here and offered our aid to the throne of Ihova only to find Lesendal's father had been betrayed also by his oldest son."

Kellen's jaw dropped. "And Lesendal?"

"He was not in the city at the time of the attack, or he would have been killed. Only a few escaped."

"So he and Salimen were . . ." he trailed off.

Ryland raised an amused brow. "You are back to that question, I see."

"I heard them talking earlier this afternoon about a traitor."

"Aye," Ryland nodded. "That is true. It is just hard for Lesendal to accept. Everything in his life was ordered. Preordained. Ihova is a strange kingdom, lad. Trust, loyalty, and honor are the backbone of this society and what his older brother did shook him hard. If it had not been for Salimen, we would have lost him months ago," Ryland said. "Lesendal and his younger sister, Kessendra, are the only surviving heirs to the throne. And as long as they live, Lord Jorean's victory over the Ihovian throne will never be complete."

Looking away from Ryland, Kellen let his eyes drift over the Ihovian campsite, absorbing the unsettling news. "So this Lord Jorean has taken five of the Twelve Kingdoms already," he mused.

"Six. Maybe more. It is hard to get accurate reports," Ryland said.

"But what does he want?"

"That is the question," Ryland said, as his frown returned. "He has made no demands. Has taken few prisoners. He has even bypassed the gem mines without even attempting to enter them. If you ask me, I would say he is simply trying to wipe out every living soul within the Twelve Kingdoms."

Trying to come to terms with all that, Kellen put his food aside. "That makes no sense."

"I agree."

"And Kalern?"

"Who?" Ryland asked, reaching for more hot meat.

"I heard one of the Black Guard talk of a Lord Kalern."

"Never heard of him," Ryland shrugged, reaching for his ale.

Kellen wondered if he had heard the name correctly. "So Prince Lesendal has a sister. Where is his sister now? Is she in this stronghold?"

"Aye," Ryland nodded. "You may even get to see her if you watch your manners."

"What's she like?" he asked.

This time Ryland grinned. "She is the fairest maiden I have ever seen. Sheer beauty with a radiance that blocks out everything but the sun. Pure innocence. She is the heart of Ihova."

Imagining her, Kellen smiled. "I hope I see her."

Ryland cuffed him gently. "She is not for you, lad, so do not even think about it. I believe she is already betrothed."

"To who?" Kellen could not help but ask.

"To whom," Ryland corrected automatically. "It was to Salimen, but with the war, that may change," Ryland said. "Lesendal will need new alliances. Now come, let us find you a bed for this night. For the air gets very cold up here."

CHAPTER FOUR

One moment he was drifting in the pleasant void of nothingness, and the next, he was sitting up, wide awake. Rubbing his eyes, Kellen wondered what had woken him. Over by the gates, he saw people running, saw a dozen Ihovian rebel hunters hastily dress beside one of the large fire pits, while others loaded pack horses. He watched them curiously and then caught a glimpse of Lesendal as the prince struggled into his leather jerkin, striding toward the gates.

It was early, the sun only a pale glimmer of dawn light that touched the tops of the trees in the forest valley below. The early-morning chill was refreshing, the crispness of the air pleasant, and Kellen pushed his bedding aside. He stood, straightening his own clothing, then ran fingers through his long tangled hair, tying it back before he approached the front gate. He could hear anguished voices, and the closer he got, the clearer the words.

"It's gone, all gone."

"There must be some sort of mistake."

"No mistake."

Stopping a few paces away, Kellen studied the tall, lean man facing the prince. The Ihovian scout looked half-dead, his clothing ripped and bloodied as he gripped one of the watchmen for support.

"But there has to be . . ."

"None, my lord. The stronghold is gone. Destroyed by fire," the scout said, his voice tight.

"And my sister, Kessendra?" Lesendal's voice was empty, hollow, as he stared at the bedraggled messenger.

"I fear captured by Hoindrite warriors of the Black Guard, my lord."

Turning away, Kellen felt the shock eat into him as his mind sluggishly registered the information. The secret stronghold, gone? Princess Kessendra captured? What were they to do now? He looked for Ryland, stopping a heartbeat later as the morning breeze swirled around him, his long hair obscuring his vision for an instant. Around him the atmosphere changed, the temperature dropping to a frigid coldness, and he glanced down at his hands, his breath frosting the air. Puzzled, he lifted his gaze and caught the beginnings of an image in the air by his side. A dark vision, which for a moment reflected the morning light before it shifted and vanished.

Shivering anew, he stared at the spot, his eyes overlarge. Then a cold brush of fingers caressed his cheek, burning his skin, freezing his jaw in an icy pain. He stepped back, away from the coldness, only to feel a tantalizing puff of air twist around his ankles and wind up his legs. It immobilized him, pushed him off balance, and he staggered back, tripping to land in an ungraceful heap in the dirt.

Then just as swiftly he was released, the returning sounds of the waking camp hit his ears. He shook his head, feeling disorientated, feeling warmer air touch him, returning all his senses to normal. He fingered his jaw, feeling his chilled skin, knowing he had not imagined the pain, and exhaled hard, before shifting his gaze to study the camp in suspicion. Nothing seemed out of place, yet *something* had touched him. He was sure of it. He climbed to his feet slowly and dusted off his britches.

He straightened his tunic and narrowed his eyes. Was this some remnant of northern magic that had infected him when he'd touched the commander of the Black Guard? He tried to think clearly, rationally, tried to banish his innate panic.

He closed his eyes and ordered his thinking, managing to calm his confusion with a few slow breaths. Maybe if he ignored the oddity, it would go away? Deciding to do just that, he opened his eyes and was immediately engulfed a second time in a shifting world of silence, strange images, and freezing blackness. Ice-cold, invisible fingers gripped his chin, forcing his head up, and he blinked, gasped in surprise, seeing nothing recognizable yet he could hear a deep, cruel laugh feather over his senses. This was more than his simple, overworked paranoia, and he definitely was not imagining it. Shocked, he swatted at the invisible fingers.

Then as before, the strange sensations were gone, leaving him standing in the middle of the encampment swiping at nothing. He cursed, feeling embarrassed when he noticed that a number of people were watching him warily and muttering amongst themselves. Backing away, he left the gate area and went to his makeshift bed, his thoughts in confusion.

He brooded, while he observed the activity of the camp around him. Orange dawn light bathed the mountain region, warm sunshine spreading down into the camp. The disturbing news from the gate was traveling fast among the Ihovians, and he heard a few anguished cries as grief permeated the atmosphere, subduing the rebels as optimism was replaced by anger. Watching all this, he sat alone on a log, contemplating his choices and his own bleak future.

* * *

It was well past dawn when Kellen became aware of the scouting party that was preparing to leave the camp and investigate the remains of the stronghold. The idea of them going worried him, and not because he feared that the Black Guard would attack while the camp was defenseless, rather it was because of the heaviness in the atmosphere, of the emotions building behind the tall gates. An unnatural depression, like something tainted which was about to descend on them all.

Getting up, he moved away from the dead embers of last night's fire and walked toward the gates, trying to loosen stiff muscles and sore joints, and shake off the ill feelings. The ride yesterday had left him aching, and he stretched, his eyes going back to the scouts as they filed out of the camp in silence. Then the large gates closed behind the rebel hunters with an eerie finality.

Again a sliver of unease knifed him, and he stared at the gates, finding that he was wordlessly willing the scouts back. He had the strangest feeling something sinister was about to happen, but he was powerless to voice his knowledge. Instead, he stood motionless, frozen in place. With sightless eyes, he stared—at the solid wood of the massive gates, at the reinforced timbers, at the steel girders and the pickets, at the remaining hunters, at the grim determination of the Ihovians. Everything seemed in order, yet he hugged his chest hard, trembling in trepidation as an unsettling tingling of cold energy started in his toes and swiftly traveled up his tense thighs to flood his upper body. It was the second time such a rush of power had engulfed him, and he forced himself to blink and to look down at his legs. They were unchanged. He no longer knew what was happening to him, what he was experiencing or how to make it stop.

The camp around him was still, abnormally so, and he wanted to voice a warning. But of what? A faint breeze stirred the air, and he tasted the aroma of smoke, of death, in the back of his throat, and his first instinct was to flee. But he was caught, trapped in place, held prisoner by an invisible force—that entity—a voiceless, powerful, and extremely dangerous thing which had shadowed his steps from the manor house. In that instant, he understood. He comprehended the vastness of his enemy's arsenal and knew he was hopelessly outclassed. So had this unseen power used him, tracked him only, so it could find the rebels and destroy them?

That realization scared him, and Kellen opened his mouth to shout for help—but nothing came out. Around him the camp abruptly blurred; the sunlight fractured into many colors, and he saw the Ihovian people through a haze as they moved in slow motion. Light became dark, and darkness became a brightness that stung the eyes and captured the soul. Fear and frustration welled in his chest, and he wanted to scream, but he couldn't. He tried to catch the attention of an Ihovian guard, but they were oblivious to him, looking right through him. Then the light intensified, and he lifted his eyes to see the tops of the massive gates.

Hanging there like deathly apparitions were dazzling shadows of whiteness—wraithlike forms that loomed up behind the closed gates to hang poised in the still dawn light. The eeriest thing was, he knew with certainty that all the scouts beyond the gates were dead even though not a single cry had been uttered. He wanted to react, to fight, but could not break the bonds holding him, instead he shuddered in desperation as the gates to the camp were abruptly and violently blown open.

Only then when he was released did his perception shift, and he could see the wraiths for what they were. He yelled a warning, but his cry was lost as the watchman by the gates managed to sound the alarm before he was cut down. Around him the Ihovians scrambled for their weapons, those who could fight and those who were too young to fight, women and children and all so unprepared. None of them stood a chance as mounted warriors of the Black Guard swept into the camp with grotesque, deathlike shadows at their sides, shades of death that stalked the living and killed without mercy, creatures of flesh, once alive but now forever cursed. Kellen gasped, staggering backward. Now that he could see again, he stared in disbelief at the deathly shadows that killed all in their path. A childhood horror. Deathwalkers. Only these were far from being a myth.

Understanding struck Kellen as the dark shapes advanced, reaching for their victims lovingly, their touch meaning pain and death wrapped in the arms of decaying flesh. No swords, arrows, or fire could stop the Deathwalkers. Cutting off a limb only meant a new one grew back, more horrid than the first. To cut one in half produced two identical versions of the first. These creatures felt no pain, no fear, no restraint, as their original souls were bound under a potent enchantment, making them perfect weapons against their own race. Nightmares come to life. Nothing tangible could break the spell, and he wrenched himself free from the icy embrace of his invisible enemy to back away from a Deathwalker's hypnotic approach.

Someone behind him swore, and he turned to see Ryland's reckless charge into the arms of death. "Ryland—no!" Kellen shouted as he braced hands against the Haonian's chest. The jarring contact opened a window in his mind, and he was bathed instantly in the warrior's turbulent emotions. Ryland was beyond fear, beyond anger, because these dark wraiths had been responsible for the death of his clan. Ryland's family, home—even the babes. They had broken the warrior's spirit when his son had fallen prey and been turned into a walking wraith.

Startled by the power of his vision, Kellen reeled backward when Ryland shoved him aside and then charged the Deathwalker stalking them. "NO!" Kellen shouted a second time, grabbing Ryland's sword arm, preventing the warrior from carrying the strike through. "No," Kellen petitioned, more softly, watching how the insane rage marring Ryland's face subsided. "You can't kill it like this."

"Out of my way!"

Licking his lips, Kellen shook his head. He did not have time to explain; he just knew that to rush into a Deathwalker's embrace meant death. How he knew was even more startling, and Kellen dismissed his apprehension when he saw Ryland raise his sword anew. Then the Haonian was moving toward the seductive, beckoning creature.

Muttering under his breath, Kellen intercepted the big man by simply bowling him over.

"Kellen, you idiot!" Ryland spat, disentangling himself as he climbed back to his feet.

"Ryland, no!" Kellen pleaded. "Listen to me. This is not the way. You have to—" He stopped and blinked, bewildered, realizing he knew exactly how to stop them. *But how? Why?* It was like a forgotten memory, a personal knowledge.

Refusing to think anymore about the instinctive knowledge, Kellen climbed to his feet and stepped in front of his friend, willing that strange, tingling sensation to return to his limbs. In an instant, the heat seeped up from the ground and washed into him, filling him with unimaginable vibrancy. He thrust out his hands, deliberately stepping into the Deathwalker and physically halting the creature's approach with his outstretched arm.

The Deathwalker stared at him from lidless eyes, once human, but now horribly disfigured; its mouth opened as foul fumes swam from out of its chest. Like wasps, the fumes engulfed his face and shoulders, and Kellen closed his eyes tightly. Appalled, he almost relented, choking, fighting his inner fear, imagining his own flesh withering and dying as the Deathwalker's curse swept over him.

Then he remembered the image of Ryland's son in his mind, and he pushed the vivid images away to concentrate, bringing into play that deep, inborn knowledge he sensed at the periphery of his mind. Energy gathered at his fingertips, and he grunted in exertion, releasing the heat all at once and scorching the creature from inside out. Fire poured from his outstretched fingers, piercing the creature's black heart. Then just as swiftly, the foul stench was gone, and in his hands, Kellen held only dust as a woman's scream of hopeless despair echoed in his head before it was gone. Freed from eternal torment.

"Ke . . . Kell . . . Kellen . . ." Ryland was staring at him like he was some kind of monster. "Kellen?"

"I—" Kellen stopped and swallowed, shaking uncontrollably. He turned his hand and let the dust spill to the ground, feeling suddenly exhausted and sick.

"Ryland!"

Before Kellen could speak, Salimen was there, grabbing them both and pulling them toward the compound's far wall. "We have to retreat. Quickly."

Diverted, Ryland cast Kellen an apprehensive glance then followed the Ihovian to the wall at the back of the camp.

"Sal!" It was Lesendal. The prince hurried forward and cast an expert eye over them all. Blood was on his face, in his hair, under his nails, and liberally covering his sword. "I don't like it, but we have to retreat. Go into the trees as we have done before and then start again. How they found us or the location of the stronghold, I have no idea, but I will find out."

"We both will," Salimen promised as he pushed Kellen toward the hole in the rear wall. "I will watch our backs. Now go, and go swiftly."

Unable to think as a numbing exhaustion sank into him, Kellen went where he was pushed, finding himself standing outside the camp facing a dense forest to his left and a sheer drop to his right.

Around him, people were fleeing, running for the trees, and he leaned heavily against the outer wall of the camp, too tired to think or move. *No*, he corrected silently; he didn't want to think, didn't want to recall what he had just done as it was too disconcerting. First, the guard, and now this. *It had to be more than coincidence, didn't it?* And what of the dark visions?

More people came through the small opening, and Kellen slid slowly down to sit on the damp ground. *Let them find me*, he thought, *I no longer have the energy to care or to fight.* He was a danger to himself and to others; all he ever did was cause death.

Closing his eyes, Kellen tried not to listen to the sounds of anguish around him. He could hear screams and raised voices off in the woods, while behind him he heard fighting. Steel hitting steel. The crackling of fire as the Black Guard burned the huts and canvas dwellings. *Why did they always use fire?* Shaking his head, Kellen wanted to sob, but his eyes were dry. *And Ryland calls me his good luck charm!* More like a curse.

"Cursed bones! Kellen, what are you doing?"

It was hissed in exasperation, and Kellen found himself roughly hauled to his feet. He opened his eyes and saw Ryland holding him by his shirt front while Lesendal and Salimen fought the Black Guard who came through the hole in the outer wall.

"Now move, lad, or you will die," Ryland growled.

"We are dead no matter where we go," Kellen said, watching the Black Guard start to fan out from the main gate.

Ryland ignored him as he turned back to see the two Ihovians walk away from the compound, both looking fierce as they held their swords ready. "We cannot escape through the forest. Kellen is right; it is a death trap."

"Then we go over the cliff," Salimen said with anger.

Lesendal regarded him then gave a crooked smile. "Why not? We have nothing left to lose."

They went to the edge and gazed out across the valley and lands far below. It would be more than three leagues down, Kellen estimated, and he stepped back as vertigo hit him. He had never liked heights.

"If I remember rightly, Johan once told me there was a ledge down here somewhere. He found it when he first scouted this area looking for a camp site," Salimen said.

"I don't see anything," Lesendal offered, leaning dangerously far out over the edge.

"I'll go take a look, shall I?" Salimen decided as he glanced around. "I don't think we have the luxury of time on our side."

"Sal, just be careful," Lesendal admonished.

"Watch my back," Salimen whispered as he lowered himself over the edge, searching for footholds. Slowly, he disappeared while Lesendal and Ryland hid themselves in the trees, waiting for patrolling members of the Black Guard.

Crouching behind a rock, Kellen waited, nervous, refusing to look over the edge, afraid of what he might see, so he kept his eyes locked on the ground. Time seemed to crawl, and he fully expected them to be caught, but the guard never came any closer than the hole in the camp's outer wall. Then just when everything settled, Kellen jumped when Salimen's grinning face reappeared over the ledge, startling him. He glared at the bowman, noting the vicious-looking cut on his forehead as fair hair covered his face in a messy display, making him appear terribly young. "Don't do that," Kellen hissed and received an unrepentant grin in return.

"Kell, go and get Lesendal, but do it quietly," Salimen instructed.

Nodding, Kellen peered around his rock and searched out the prince. Lesendal was motionless, making Kellen wonder if he were still alive or if he had been killed without any of them knowing or seeing. Running his eyes over the surrounding area, he debated his choices before carefully inching forward. The woods around them were ominously quiet, and he did not trust his senses as he caught Ryland's attention and mouthed Lesendal's name.

Ryland nodded and alerted the prince, and Kellen breathed a sigh of relief when the others cautiously made their way back to his position.

"Sal?" Lesendal whispered urgently as the bowman raised his head again.

"There is a large ledge just under this face. It is a little difficult to get to, but I have found this vine, and if you tie it around that rock and conceal it, you should be able to use it to get down here."

Lesendal cast a dubious glance at Ryland, and the other man nodded his consent. "Okay, Sal, give me the vine."

After they had tied the vine securely and hidden it as best they could with leaves, branches, and rocks, each of them slowly climbed down with Salimen's help.

The ledge was not very big. In fact, Kellen believed Salimen had exaggerated in his assessment as he sat huddled against the back wall with his face turned away from the distressing view of the land below. Despite what the perverse bowman said, *no*, he did not find the view fascinating, exhilarating, or inspiring. In fact, he wondered if it might not have been better to have taken their chances with the Black Guard in the forest.

All in all, it was a very long, cold, and disturbing night.

* * *

At dawn, Salimen volunteered to go up and scout out the land, and Lesendal reluctantly agreed. Surprisingly, the Ihovian was back within a very short time, and Salimen had a smirk on his face that could only mean trouble, but of a different sort.

"Sal?"

"You can all come up. It is safe now."

"How do you know that? You have barely been away?" Ryland asked.

"Trust me; it's safe." And then Salimen was gone again.

Lesendal raised a brow and looked at Ryland. "I'll go first just to make sure, you follow with the boy."

"Fine," Ryland nodded as he loosened his sword.

The climb back up was ghastly, and Kellen was very glad to be back on solid ground as he collapsed to his knees and sucked in a deep breath. He was hungry, tired, cold, and thirsty, and he did not believe things could get any worse. So far he had managed to avoid Ryland's eye, not wanting to discuss the previous day at all.

"And who's this, then?"

It was a new voice, light in timbre, and it held a wealth of amusement behind the tone. Lifting his head with effort, Kellen blinked then stared at the man standing before him. A sudden wash of familiarity engulfed his senses, and he saw an image in his mind. *Two young men, identical in looks, with long dark hair and magical spheres in their hands.* Then just as mysteriously, the image vanished.

Frowning, Kellen studied the new arrival, noting the man was of average height with long dark hair, haphazardly tied back off his face. His clothing was dark and dusty, and he had a feel about him that spoke of recklessness, yet also of beauty beyond compare. Meeting the dark gaze watching him, Kellen still had the strangest impression that something calculating and undeniably dangerous lurked behind those assessing eyes—and then gasped as he was jolted by a mental slap. It was like a door was slammed deep in his mind to block out necessary truths, to block out this bedraggled young man's real identity. Stunned, Kellen stared at this dark enigma.

"This is Kellen," Lesendal answered tiredly as he looked around. "We rescued him from some of the Hoindrite Black Guard, and so far, he has been like a lucky charm. Amazingly, we are all still alive."

"I see," the stranger said, a little annoyance creeping into his tone. He turned to the prince. "I am sorry to hear what happened at the stronghold."

"If you had been here, it might not have happened," Salimen shot back.

The stranger ignored him. "Kessendra is alive; I have discerned that much, and I would guess she has either been taken to Jorean's camp, or more likely back to Wericonon."

"I will not rest until she is safe!" Lesendal vowed.

"And your kingdom?" the stranger asked.

Lesendal suddenly looked very defeated. "I do not know. My people are scattered, probably captured. That raid was too precisely planned, which means my supply lines are probably also gone."

The new arrival nodded and paced away as if thinking. Watching all this, Kellen felt the tension in Ryland, yet the ease in Salimen and Lesendal, and he assumed this was the much-talked-about Sasheer. He eyed the stranger up and down, taking in the travel-stained shirt and leathers, and tried to picture this man in one of those long theatrical robes Ryland described that all Tricksters wore. But somehow, it did not seem appropriate.

"And you, Sasheer?" Salimen asked. "We needed you here! Where have you been?" It was a thinly veiled accusation.

Lifting his head, the stranger sighed and walked over to the tall Ihovian. "There are greater concerns in the world than just the problems of Ihova, Salimen. To save your home, I think you must let it go, or you will lose the entire Southland. There is more at stake here than just what Jorean is doing, and I think it is about time I found out what precisely that might be."

They all stared at Sasheer, bemused. "I don't understand," Lesendal said. "What else could be more important? If we stop Jorean, we will win."

"Lesendal, Jorean is just an instrument of this war. He is talented but expendable. While you waste all your time fighting him, the real force behind this war takes another land. No, I think it is time we had a good look at what is happening outside the south."

"But—"

Sasheer shrugged, the action remarkably elegant and regal despite his dusty appearance. His half smile was disturbingly superior, and his mannerisms like those from an age-long dead, full of grace, yet so dismissive. "Besides, Kessendra will not be kept in Wericonon for long."

"Why not?" Lesendal demanded. "You don't think he would trade her to the Westlands for more weapons. Do you?"

"That is what you must find out," Sasheer said very quietly. "Now, I think we had best leave this area before the Black Guard return." He gave a crooked smile. "It would seem you are compelled to trust me. Yes?"

"Do not count on it," Ryland muttered.

"Oh come, come, Ryland, please use that brain I know you

have hidden in that woolly head of yours," Sasheer chastised mockingly. "To reclaim your clan's insignia rights and find Kessendra, you will have to go west. Think about it, all of you." With that, he turned and started to walk away.

"I swear I am going to kill that arrogant, smug bastard one day and—"

"Ryland," Lesendal soothed as he looked after the retreating figure. "For the moment, I think we have no choice. Sasheer is our only hope at this stage."

"I hate to admit it, but he's also right," Salimen added. "It is to Wericonon we should be directing our effort, not Jorean. No matter how tempting a target he makes."

Lesendal looked up at that as if a point had just clarified. "Okay, so we will follow Sasheer, at least for the time being?"

"Aye," Ryland nodded solemnly, as Salimen also agreed.

Lesendal then turned to Kellen. "I'm sorry, boy, but I think you had best come with us. Maybe we can find a safe place for you along the way."

Not enjoying being made to feel like a burden or a child, Kellen nodded, given little choice. Turning his eyes on Sasheer's impatiently waiting figure, he was intrigued by the image this man produced in his mind. Strength emanated from the slender frame, and Kellen narrowed his eyes, watching how Sasheer returned his appraisal with wicked delight.

Taken aback by the frank assessment he saw in those changeable blue-black eyes, Kellen lifted his chin in silent challenge. This man was treacherous. Sasheer's grin widened in acknowledgment before the man turned away and gestured for the others to follow him. Stunned by the brief yet silent exchange, Kellen promised himself to find out who and what Sasheer was. He also vowed that he would find a way to return to his home and exact a vengeance of his own.

Regardless of what the others thought of him.

CHAPTER FIVE

Pausing for a breath, Kell kept his eyes focused on the narrow track ahead and tried to ignore the sheer drop on his left. The much discussed and admired "strategic northern valley" and vast forest below, which Salimen seemed particularly proud of, was a daunting sight. To him it was just a very long way down, and seeing the abundant treetops far below only made him light-headed and nauseated.

Ever since they had entered the steep range, Lesendal and Salimen had argued constantly about what might have gone wrong within their security arrangements and careful planning at the campsite and stronghold. All Kellen could pick up from their fast and often-heated words were the terms "must have," "couldn't have," "I can't accept that," and "I warned you about this." The hushed discussion had been interesting to a point, but now, as far as Kellen was concerned, he did not really care about what had gone wrong, rather the fact that it had gone wrong. Turning back, he saw that Salimen was still talking passionately to Lesendal, and Kellen rolled his eyes, stopping to rest against a large bolder and rub his fatigued thighs. His legs felt dead, and he was exhausted.

Glancing up from his resting position, he gave a weak smile as the two Ihovians went past him, Salimen not even drawing breath as he continued to argue some obscure point. Lesendal only spared him a curious look before countering Salimen's arguments.

Amused, Kellen's eyes followed the two hunters, being drawn past both Ihovians to the stationary figure further up the steep track. Sasheer. The man had said very little since that first meeting earlier in the morning, only leading them out of the forest area and up toward Dargor's Peak. It was a natural boundary between

Ihova and Selston, that much he did know, and Kellen wondered what the mysterious man's plans were. Is Sasheer trustworthy?

It was a disquieting thought, and Kellen squinted up, studying the puzzling man. Maybe this Sasheer was leading them into another trap? He let his eyes sweep over to the prince, but Lesendal seemed unconcerned, and Kellen remembered how Lesendal had suggested earlier that they should stop at one of the rebels' hidden supply bases before continuing. But Sasheer had counseled against it, warning that with the Hoindrite Black Guard knowing their campsite location, it was, therefore, probable that the Black Guard would also know all the supply stations. Frowning over that, Kellen had to admit the explanation had sounded logical. But was it?

"Are you all right, lad?"

Kellen jumped and glanced up, seeing Ryland watching him in concern. Shaking off his lingering doubts, he sent the warrior a hesitant smile. He had forgotten that Ryland had appointed himself rear guard for the company. "By the stars, Ryland, can't you make some noise instead of creeping up on a person like that?"

The big man stroked his beard as he laughed softly. "You were sitting so still; I was afraid you might have fallen asleep."

"No, just resting my legs." Kellen turned and looked back up at the other members of the small company and saw that the dark-haired Sasheer was staring down at him. Only the expression on Sasheer's face was far from reassuring. "How much further is it, Ryland?"

"Lesendal says a couple more hours. It seems that the only place to set up a camp in these passes is on the other side of the peak." Ryland shrugged, repositioning his heavy armor. "That of course will depend on what we find at the peak."

"Like what?" Kell asked suspiciously.

"Not far from the top is a checkpoint, I believe. More a formality rather than a proper Customs post, allowing passage between the two kingdoms. But now, with the war, I do not know."

"You think some of the Black Guard might be waiting?" Kellen asked. "Shouldn't we warn the others?"

"What, and miss out on a good fight?" Ryland gave him a wide grin. "Nay. I welcome the chance to warm the blood."

"But you could be killed," Kellen said, appalled.

"There is that slim possibility, I suppose," Ryland agreed before his eyes became speculative, and he grinned. "But I doubt it. Not with you in the company. My lucky charm."

"I . . ." Kellen felt a flush creep over his cheeks, and he looked away, uneasy. *How can I explain why I feel far from lucky?* He felt cursed.

"Without you, I would be dead," Ryland continued seriously. "I do not know how you did it, lad, how you stopped a Deathwalker with your bare hands, but I am grateful. I am also now in your debt. My life is yours. So long as I live, you will never need to fear the Black Guard. My strength is your strength." He settled a steel-clad hand on Kellen's shoulder and squeezed gently. "Now we had best move before Sasheer's glares turn into something more."

Without thinking, Kellen twisted a little and cast a glance back up the rugged track to the man in question and found Ryland's assessment very accurate. Sasheer was indeed glaring down at them, those dark eyes judging him, weighing him, and obviously finding him wanting. He stood abruptly and got his sore legs working. Dragging in a deep breath, he forced himself to climb the steep track until he was level with Lesendal. He ignored Sasheer's eyes, and to his amazement, he found Salimen was still muttering about the injustices of Lord Jorean's raid.

"Salimen, would you please desist? At least until I am out of hearing," Sasheer said, his eyes briefly touching the bowman before he turned back to look at the rest of the company. Sweeping a hand sideways, he gestured to the sheer rock walls ahead of them. "Be careful of your footing during this next stretch. When I came through here a few days ago, there had already been one or two small rockslides."

"Traps?" Salimen asked, ignoring Sasheer's glare.

"There are more deadly forces in the universe than the Hoindrite Black Guard," Sasheer quipped, his eyes narrowing in annoyance. Then he was looking past Salimen to capture Ryland's gaze. "Ryland, watch the boy and try not to fall behind this time."

Kellen clamped his jaw and scowled after Sasheer's arrogant figure. *Boy?* He hated that term, hated the implications and tone of the word with a passion, because that had been how his older brother, Wyran, had teased him. Whenever they had argued, Wyran always ended the argument by mocking his opinions by degrading him as *the boy* in front of others.

"Sounds like fun," Salimen muttered as he followed after the agile Sasheer. "You're a real comedian, Sasheer," he added sarcastically.

Falling in behind the prince, Kellen brooded over the remark, taking very little note of his surroundings until he realized they were completely encased in towering rock walls and narrowing ledges. The views were gone, as was some of the light, and he started to concentrate on where he was putting his feet. In one way, he was glad the deadly drop was gone, but in another way, the oppressiveness of the narrow track was worse than the view across the valley.

Shaking off his growing discomfort, Kellen watched Lesendal, noting how the other man moved. The prince was surefooted and an experienced tracker, and he started to mimic the Ihovian's methods.

They climbed in silence for a long time, stopping briefly to have a drink or to catch their breath, and then Sasheer would lead the way again.

Touching the cold rock walls on either side of the pass, Kellen let his fingers trail the uneven stone, his brows drawing down into a frown. An odd prickling of apprehension permeated the atmosphere in the confined pass, and Kellen felt the tensions rise around him. He searched around cautiously, glanced behind at Ryland, and saw how the bigger man appeared crowded in the narrow passage. How Ryland's face was marred by fierce concentration and determination.

Looking ahead, Kellen noted how Lesendal was checking his knives while Salimen had drawn his sword. *So maybe it isn't just me?* Maybe it was just the oppressive dimness and humidity of the passage that made all of them uneasy?

He looked past the Ihovians to the track ahead and saw how steep the incline had become. This was not a pass he would ever want to attempt in the dark. That was probably the reason for his uneasiness, he decided. So much had happened to him over the last three days that now he found he was jumping at shadows, expecting the worst, expecting more of those Deathwalkers to pounce on him. He swallowed, quickening his pace to catch up with Lesendal.

Lesendal was struggling over a partially blocked section of track while Salimen and Sasheer waited at the top of the incline. The bowman gave his usual cocky grin as he reached down to help pull the prince up.

Sucking in a deep breath, Kellen reached for a handhold in order to climb over the fallen stones and, in that instant, froze as everything around him changed. It was as if time had stilled, and his eyes went wide with a vision—and he saw.

Salimen battled to pull Lesendal up the last few feet of stone. Sasheer turned ever so slowly toward him and frowned. The layers of dirt and dust magically vanished from around Sasheer to expose a very young wide-eyed man who reached down to offer help. But Kellen turned away as Ryland came charging up from behind, a shout on the big warrior's lips.

The vision abruptly cleared, and Kellen blinked. He was again standing in the middle of the pass, locked in place with his hand outstretched while Salimen pulled Lesendal up the final few feet of incline. Stunned, Kellen gasped, feeling shocked and fearful and not at all sure about what he had glimpsed. Real or imagined? It was like a premonition, yet, and he slowly reached out a second time to touch the cold rock at his side.

Cold dampness greeted his fingers, the stone's texture imprinting on his senses. It was icy like death, and he snatched his hand away when an insidious tingle of power filtered through the rock and up his arm. He stared at his hand then stared at the drab rock wall. It was like the rock was alive, like the mountain was alive, and he cautiously reached over to touch the stone a second time.

Again, a surge of energy rushed up his hand, only this time it was stronger, more insistent, and it definitely had a sinister feel. He shuddered, feeling a faint vibration travel up through his feet, and he removed his hand from the cold stone to stare at the passage surrounding him in growing horror. The implications of what he had sensed were staggering, because he knew with a chilling certainty that they were about to experience an earthquake. He could feel it in the stone, feel it under his feet, and almost taste it in the air.

About to turn and warn Ryland of the imminent danger, Kellen hesitated as he felt a brush of chilly fingers against his face. So intimate a caress, capturing his attention like a ghost breeze kissing his skin. Then the seductive spell was broken when numerous tiny pebbles showered him from overhead. He lifted his eyes, recognizing that familiar, real presence and seeing the ripple in the air before him—inky blackness that blotted out all light, the image of a cowled and bowed head—before the darkness fractured. So fleeting, so frightening, that Kellen gazed up toward the two Ihovians and met Sasheer's dark, hypnotic eyes.

He sucked in a startled gasp, seeing how regal Sasheer was in that instant, how powerful, as the mysterious man's appearance became crystalline in his mind. Like a door had been flung wide open, and Kellen reeled mentally from what he glimpsed.

Towering marble castles awash in sunlight. A magnificence of splendor—supreme confidence, unsurpassable power, orderly submission. Under the archway stood a man, a bewitchingly handsome man, immaculate, dressed in a long, flowing robe with darkly braided hair. At his side was a similar man, a beloved and cherished brother, whose image dissolved into the unsubstantial haziness of stormy blue eyes. Then destruction. Pain. Betrayal. Loss and despair followed by a soul-shattering cry of anguish.

Taken aback, Kellen watched as Sasheer raised a dark brow in silent inquiry, almost in challenge. Then just as quickly, the dark blue fathomless eyes changed. The vision he had of Sasheer returned to normal, as Kellen watched how Sasheer started to frown as if he sensed the approach of danger. Then Kellen was shocked at how swiftly Sasheer reacted, at how skillfully Sasheer maneuvered around

Lesendal and Salimen to reach down to him with a hand outstretched. "Kellen, here. Now, MOVE!"

It was a sharp order, snapping him alert, and Kellen found himself obeying without question, just stopping at the last instant from reaching out to Sasheer as he remembered Ryland. The warrior believed he was a lucky charm, and if he abandoned Ryland now, the other would die. He knew it, could see the truth reflected in Sasheer's changeable eyes, and he yanked his arm back. Disobeying the command was hard, and Kellen closed his eyes, shutting out Sasheer's presence before he blindly turned back to find Ryland.

He got no further than two steps when he heard Sasheer hiss something uncomplimentary, but it was too late because he could feel the first strong vibrations of the approaching earthquake. The low rumble in the rock around increased, and he threw himself at Ryland, crashing into the Haonian and pushing the other man backward, so that they both fell against the shuddering rock face.

Under them the ground started to shake violently as rocks fell from overhead, pelting them with painful projectiles. Dust rose up in a choking cloud, obscuring the dimness even more, and Kellen felt Ryland wrench on his arm, dragging him under a small overhang. The sound of rocks falling, of the mountain shaking, was deafening, and Kellen huddled against Ryland's chest, waiting for the deadly vibrations to subside.

The terror seemed to go on and on endlessly, and Kellen coughed, only moving after Ryland assured him the worst was over. He then peered out from under the narrow alcove and waited for the dust to settle, worried about the others.

"Cursed stones, lad, are you all right?"

Kellen only nodded as he looked at his filthy friend. Both of them were bleeding from small wounds.

"I wonder what set that off?" Ryland continued to mutter as he checked his sword and other weapons.

"I don't know," Kellen said vaguely, remembering all too clearly the dark presence that seemed intent on killing him. He reached out and touched the stonewall but sensed nothing, no malignant presence, and he saw no glimpses of seductive darkness. *Am I going* mad? And what of Sasheer's reaction? What of the images he had perceived which clung to Sasheer like a living cloak? *Was the man good or evil?* He didn't know.

"Come. We had best see if the others are all right and try to get out of these passes before nightfall."

Nodding his agreement, Kellen cautiously glanced behind them before following as Ryland stepped over the fallen stone fragments.

Reaching the area where the rockslide had occurred, it took them a long while to clear some of the debris and climb over what could not be moved. Eventually, they were reunited with Lesendal and Sasheer. The prince informed them that Salimen had gone to scout ahead just in case the small rockslide was more than coincidence.

Grateful, Kellen sat on a large boulder and was surprised when Sasheer walked over to him and peered at him in curiosity. It was far from reassuring and made him even more wary.

"Do you want to talk about it?"

Thrown by the directness of the question, Kellen just blinked, startled. "Umm . . ." Again those dark blue black eyes pinned him, and Kellen shivered. There was an ageless knowledge behind their gaze. An ageless beauty mingled with pain, loss, regret that was all overshadowed by a will of iron. This man was definitely not a person he wanted to provoke. "What would there be to talk about?" he asked instead, praying Sasheer would leave him alone.

Sasheer gave a secretive smile and nodded slowly as he looked away, his expression speculative. "Maybe nothing. Then again, maybe everything."

Kellen tried to pretend that he misunderstood Sasheer's meaning and looked at Ryland for help. But the warrior was talking with Lesendal and oblivious to his discomfort. "I don't understand," he said, knowing it was a lame answer. Worse, he knew that Sasheer knew he was lying, and he cringed.

"Oh, I think you do understand." Sasheer gave him that smug, knowing smile before the other man leaned down very close to whisper the next few words. "It is not a sin to be different or to ask for help. Try and remember that if you can."

Watching Sasheer walk away, Kellen's thoughts whirled. *Different?* He most definitely did not want to be different. Nor did he want this mysterious Sasheer's help, and he certainly did not want to trust the peculiar man. Relaxing when Salimen returned, he edged closer to the Ihovians and hid behind Ryland. Anything to get away from Sasheer's perceptive gaze.

CHAPTER SIX

By nightfall, they had crossed the border and entered into the kingdom of Selston. There was no trace of the Customs post or the patrolling sentry, and Kellen wondered if the kingdom of Selston was not already conquered. Sasheer did not appear to be surprised by their lack of reception, and he speculated on this, his imagination coming up with nasty alternatives.

Everyone in the group was as equally quiet, and Kellen entertained the idea that they may have had similar thoughts, until Lesendal accepted Sasheer's comments with no arguments. Brooding over that, he trailed the trusting prince as they started down the trail that would take them west into Selston's mountainous region.

A short while later, Sasheer turned off the main track onto a narrow partially hidden trail that wound around a large boulder, coming to a sparse clearing which was surrounded on three sides by a rock face, with the fourth side facing out toward the land below. Thankfully it was darkening, so Kellen was spared the discomfort of knowing exactly how high up they were this time. Instead he glanced around the bare clearing.

It was an old campsite, and he watched the other members of the company fall into some sort of unvoiced routine. Salimen disappeared back the way they had just traveled while Lesendal set about preparing a fire. Ryland collected wood while scouting the area. Only Sasheer seemed motionless as he stood facing the ledge, staring out into the darkness, deep in thought.

"Can I do anything?" Kellen asked, approaching the prince.

"Help, Ryland."

Nodding, Kellen went and helped Ryland, and by the time he had collected all the wood Ryland had instructed him to find, he felt they had enough to build a house, let alone a fire. He was about to voice his complaint when Salimen returned with a couple of rabbits.

"Well, at least we don't have to sleep hungry tonight. I, for one, feel like something hot," Salimen declared as he laid the dead animals down and started to prepare them.

"You've lost half the meat with the arrow," Lesendal observed, peering over his cousin's shoulder.

Turning and giving the other a sour glare, Salimen sighed. "It is all I had, so stop complaining. You should be pleased I caught anything at all."

"I am sure we can buy food once we find a village inn," Ryland added, rubbing his well-rounded middle. "These scrawny specimens could hardly feed a child. It would be nice to taste the ale from a warm taproom and savor a hearty stew."

Salimen scowled at him.

"That is if you have money," Ryland ended, avoiding the bowman's eyes.

"We'll trade something," Salimen muttered before glancing over at Sasheer. "We are going down into Selston, I take it."

"That depends," Sasheer's smile was cynical, his voice a distant sound before he sighed and turned back to look at the men by the fire. He walked over to warm himself, drawing his long cloak tightly around his lean frame. To Kellen, it seemed that Sasheer was wrapping himself in the darkness, his eyes almost all black, making him look like a creature of the night. Then the strange guide blinked, and his eyes lightened in color, the darkness lifting from around him.

"Depends on what?" Lesendal asked, walking over to crouch next to Sasheer.

"On a number of things," Sasheer returned evasively, his eyes touching Kellen again.

Refusing to show how unsettled he was by this man's strangeness, Kellen steeled his nerves and glared back impassively. He hated being manipulated. Wyran had always tried to manipulate him, and he had become very adept at blocking his brother's advantage.

Salimen cast a pointed look at Lesendal then looked at Sasheer.

"Well, enlighten me—us," Lesendal pushed. Kellen saw him glance around the group and then fix his gaze on Sasheer. Sasheer ducked his head down to hide a self-mocking smile, before he sighed, coming to a decision.

"It will depend greatly on what Dalzere finds," Sasheer said.

"Oh great!" Salimen was on his feet, the rabbits forgotten, as he glared at Sasheer. "You didn't tell us *he* was involved in this venture."

"You didn't ask—"

"I shouldn't have to!" Salimen cut back. "He isn't allowed anywhere within the borders of the Twelve Kingdoms!"

"What utter nonsense," Sasheer dismissed.

"Sasheer!" Lesendal stared at him, shocked.

"You risk all our lives if any of us are caught in his presence. Doesn't that mean anything to you?" Salimen reminded him.

Sasheer rubbed a hand over his face before looking up at the angry bowman. "Salimen—Dalzere has done more for your misguided cause and misty kingdom than any other person I know. Besides, he is my partner, and we rarely travel apart."

"I don't care if he is a holy relic; he is still not allowed access into the Twelve Kingdoms! It is the law!" Salimen said stubbornly. "We've had this discussion before! By the gods, Sasheer, if you are as learned as you say, then you know why it is the law, and why his kind are killed on sight." The bowman gestured around in agitation, his face flushed with anger. "And I have seen you in court without Dalzere, so don't tell me he always travels with you!"

"Sal," Lesendal placed a hand on the other's chest to calm him and waited until his cousin took a few deep breaths. Then he turned to confront Sasheer.

"Your laws were written as a safeguard and are perhaps more narrow-minded than I would like. In Dalzere's case, they are wrong," Sasheer stated, crossing his arms, his expression unrelenting.

"That is beside the point," Lesendal said.

"Excuse me, but who is Dalzere?" Ryland asked, bemused. He glanced between the three men. "A criminal from across the White Sea?"

"No. Try death incarnate," Salimen supplied in a growl, his gaze hard as Sasheer rolled his eyes in mock dramatics.

"He is—" Lesendal took a deep breath and hesitated. "If I was being diplomatic, I would say he is... he is a... Ranger. Like Sasheer." He lifted a questioning brow. "Is that correct?"

"Essentially," Sasheer nodded, clearly amused at the prince's discomfort.

"Feel free to elaborate," Ryland said. "Especially since it seems our life may depend on it."

"Sasheer?" Lesendal gestured toward the Ranger for an answer.

"All you need know is that Dalzere is here to help you, just as I am."

"He's a Drow, Sasheer!" Salimen cursed impatiently.

"Drow?" Ryland repeated, shocked. His eyes widened, his disbelief clear as his gaze went from Lesendal to Sasheer for confirmation. "Are you insane? How can you let a creature like that live? Let alone allow him access into the Twelve Kingdoms! It is forbidden."

Sasheer sighed again, wearily looking around at the angry faces of the company. "Yes, Dalzere is a Drow—in appearance. But not in spirit."

"You can't control the demonspawn of Sethesthovaln!" Salimen snapped.

"Lesendal, I warned you about Sasheer and his kind; now it looks like we will be paying with more than just our mortal lives." Ryland turned and walked away in disgust.

"Now, that's enough!" Sasheer broke in, a touch of anger coloring his normally level tone. "I am tired of this petty bickering which seems to plague the mentality of your small-minded kingdoms! You are all so self-absorbed in your own immediate survival that I think you have forgotten that the Twelve Kingdoms only make up *part* of the Southland. And that beyond your borders and across the Divide lies a land larger than any of you can imagine. A land that will swallow you like the night swallows the sun, only in your case, you will not survive the darkness unless you wake up to yourselves and start to comprehend the bigger issues."

They all stared at him; even Ryland looked doubtful as he turned back toward the crackling fire. Nothing further was said for a prolonged moment, and Kellen jumped as a piece of burning wood popped loudly.

Intrigued and slightly startled by the intense emotions surrounding him, Kellen first eyed the two Ihovians, seeing their discomfort and confusion. He then looked at Ryland and saw the Haonian's face was a mix of disbelief and stubborn dislike, while Sasheer just raised a hand and petitioned for calm. It was a strange, uneasy peace, and Kellen blinked as the silence stretched. Instinctively, his eyes were drawn back to Sasheer, and he studied the man's outstretched hand before looking up into those dangerous eyes. Then he remembered what Sasheer had said—*Dalzere is my partner*—which meant instant death in Ihova, and that cast suspicion on all Sasheer's motives. On his true loyalties. So who was this man who trusted a Drow to guard his sleep?

Lesendal's soft voice broke the strained silence. "You accuse us of being small-minded. Yet why should we be interested in what is happening outside the Twelve Kingdoms?"

"Lesendal, who do you think is really behind the wars sweeping across the kingdoms?" Sasheer asked.

"Lord Jorean of Wericonon," Lesendal answered, the name coming out like a sneer. "Everyone knows of his lust for power and how he has been trading with the Westlands for men and weapons. It is a good example of *why* the law should be obeyed and contact with the other lands beyond the Divide avoided."

"Jorean is only a puppet king for Kalern; I thought you understood that," Sasheer snapped, ignoring Lesendal's frown and Salimen's uncomplimentary mutterings. "I explained that to you months ago. I told you Jorean was not your real enemy."

"Our minds were on other things," Salimen said. "The king had just been betrayed, our families murdered, so I don't think anyone was thinking beyond survival and revenge when you showed up."

"Salimen, I rarely expect you to think," Sasheer said, his sarcasm clear, "but, Lesendal, I, at least, hoped you would have understood the dangers facing your people and your neighbors. Now I am starting to doubt your fledgling grasp of knowledge."

"I did understand," Lesendal defended. "I put together a fighting force, but we were continually undermined."

"Betrayed," Salimen supplied.

"All right, betrayed," Lesendal corrected. He exhaled hard, rubbing his face before looking again at Sasheer. "I sent envoys for help into Kalhorn and Olvaronia, but neither returned or replied."

"Your messages probably never got through," Sasheer said.

"We might have had a better chance if you had carried the messages or at least stayed with us," Lesendal accused. "Why did you abandon us?"

"I never abandoned you. But as I said, there is more happening in the lands than you know. An urgent matter arose, with which I had to deal immediately."

"Such as?" Salimen asked as Ryland came and stood poised behind the bowman. "Tell us, Sasheer, what could be more important than the death of a kingdom?"

"The death of all four lands." Sasheer captured their gaze and held it. Again there was a silence, which Sasheer broke this time. "As it turned out, I was far too late, and an entire bloodline died before I could intervene." He glanced down at his hands and shuddered, closing his eyes tightly for a second before lifting his lashes to encompass Kellen in his gaze. Kellen felt the weight of Sasheer's stare and was glad when the Ranger turned back to Lesendal. "I did send Dalzere to Wericonon to gather information which I hoped would aid your kingdom as well as your neighbors."

"You sent the Drow into Wericonon territory?" Lesendal asked, shocked.

"Yes, about seven months ago," Sasheer nodded, his gaze becoming troubled. "I have not heard from him since."

"Then he is dead," Lesendal predicted as both Salimen and Ryland nodded in agreement.

"No . . ." Sasheer shook his head. "He will be here; I trust in his skill and talent for survival. Now I ask that you trust mine. Trust me."

"You ask the near impossible," Salimen said quietly, his expression uncompromising.

"I ask what I have always asked for from you, Salimen, which is an open mind, nothing more," Sasheer said, and Kellen observed how the Ranger's eyes narrowed as he deliberately captured Salimen's gaze. After a prolonged moment, the Ihovian turned away, a slow flush touching his cheeks.

Lesendal stepped between the two men and broke the exchange. "To trust you, you must trust us and tell us what is really going on," he countered.

With a thoughtful expression on his face, Sasheer sat down and indicated the others should sit as well. Kellen caught the curious gaze Sasheer sent his way and hesitated. "All right. I'll try to explain it to *all* of you." Sasheer's words softened to a whisper as he again turned toward Kellen, gesturing for him to sit.

With slight apprehension, Kellen accepted the invitation and sat across from the mysterious man, still not trusting Sasheer's outward appearance. It was obvious he was not telling them everything.

"A brief history lesson, since your knowledge of the lands across the White Sea is severely limited. Try, if you can, to suspend your disbelief and hear what I say," Sasheer admonished, his gaze briefly flicking toward Salimen. "As I have told you before, Jorean is only the figurehead of Kalern's army."

"Kalern? Who is this Kalern?" Ryland questioned. "Kell mentioned the name to me a few days ago."

Sasheer shot the bigger man an irritated look as he interrupted then just raised a hand, stalling other questions and speculation. His gaze slipped to Kellen across from him, who glared back. "Is this true, Kellen?"

"Yes," Kellen said, feeling awkward. "One of the Black Guard mentioned a Lord Kalern."

"I see. It seems I have a lot to educate you all about." Sasheer sighed, sweeping his eyes around the group. "First, let me tell you who Kalern is."

Kellen watched as Sasheer cleared his throat, the dark gaze

homing in on the fire between them before Sasheer's voice became gentle and almost hypnotic. The story unfolded, and despite his dislike of the man, Kellen found he was enthralled.

"Many years ago, there were two brothers—twins—who were identical in every aspect of looks, deeds, and personality. They were the youngest sons of a very prominent family in a magnificent city far to the east on the mainland of Sennovia. A city which is now long gone, destroyed by war to sink back into the earth which spawned it." Sasheer paused. "But in that magical time, within the old laws, the twins—because of their rank as second born within the family—were given to the temple as gifts of service to the gods. They were sold at a tender age into the priesthood. Now, this arrangement had worked for centuries within this finely controlled and prosperous society, until war erupted against the city and its people." Sasheer stopped, hesitating, as if to consider his next words carefully. "This war had a catastrophic effect on all living within the city. The whole idea of rebellion against the city's rulers was unimaginable, and many councilmen and advisers to the throne reacted rashly and harshly toward the surrounding nations that came to challenge their laws. Needless to say, sanity was set aside, and powers were abused as vile creatures were created to defend the city. And the effects of that overreaction backlashed throughout the four lands. The Southland included."

"The Great War," Lesendal whispered.

Glancing at the prince, Sasheer nodded. "Yes. That is the name some give to it. Many races were reduced to near extinction by that war, yet the killing still continued. It was senseless, like a stone rolling down a hill, gaining momentum on both sides, until something had to be done to preserve life." Sasheer took a deep breath, sadness creeping into his tone. "So something was done. A horrible and irreversible decision was made to end the war." He paused again, his eyes darkening. "A number of the city's talented Mageborn lords combined their power and skill to bring about the downfall of their once-majestic society. To stop the slaughter."

"You're talking about the end of the Great War, when the Coastal Mage Society was destroyed. That was over four thousand years ago," Lesendal said. "I have never heard it told so explicated before, but as I recall, the history states that there were twelve Mageborn lords that defied their king and betrayed their own people in order to save the four lands. They were traitors, yet heroes. Responsible for the death of all magical talent—or something similar. I don't know for certain, but the history books all state that the configuration of the four lands was changed that fateful day."

Lesendal smiled and went on with confidence. "And that was when a great warrior named Byront took his clan and crossed what today is called the White Sea and settled the Southland. He vowed that his people would never again mix with the other nations, for fear of a second great war erupting and the land being totally consumed," Lesendal finished with a grin. Salimen nodded in agreement.

Kellen looked at the prince, feeling dismayed that he had never been told this story as a child. But then, his family had traveled around so much in his early years that he found it hard to remember which kingdom was his birthplace.

"You do your teachers proud," Sasheer said. "It was precisely 3,897 years ago. And indeed, Byront was a competent warrior. But that is not strictly why he traveled with his people to the south."

Lesendal and Salimen blinked at him. "What?" they said in unison. "Are you saying our history is wrong?" Lesendal added, his tone slightly outraged.

Sasheer brushed the question aside. "What version of the truth you were taught is not the question here. Rather the point is—what happened to those twins."

"You still have not told us who Kalern is," Ryland said.

"I am getting to that." Sasheer stopped just short of snapping, exhaling slowly through his nose before continuing. "Before this ancient city—"

"Mitthsombaine," Salimen interjected, his blond brows drawn down into a frown of displeasure. "That city was called Mitthsombaine."

"Thank you, Salimen," Sasheer remarked sarcastically then waved the bowman's protest aside. "Before the twelve Mageborns dismantled Mitthsombaine's inner defenses, and the surrounding nations destroyed both her beauty and all those who lived within the marble walls, a number of families escaped. The twins belonged to one of these prominent, ruling families," Sasheer said with heavy emphasis. His eyes swept the scowling faces. Kellen stared back, watching how the Ranger's mouth twitched up into an amused smile.

"So these twins escaped death and started a new society of Mages?" Salimen asked, bewildered. "What has that got to do with the war today?"

"Let me finish," Sasheer moderated his glare. "The problem lay not in the fact that the twins escaped, but rather in the fact that they were sworn to protect the twelve Mageborns who had defied their society. They became guardians if you will."

"Sasheer, will you get to the point!" Lesendal demanded. "At this rate, Jorean will catch us in the pass, and we will still be no closer to working out your cryptic clues."

Sighing, Sasheer sat back and rubbed a hand over his face. "I don't have the patience for this," he muttered then shook his head and pinned each man with a harassed look. "For the twelve Mageborns to destroy Mitthsombaine's defenses, they needed power. Raw power. So in a desperate move, each Mage donated his focus stone to form one large stone of immense power. One large, acutely sensitive focus stone that could absorb the user's will. In this case, the will of the twelve Mageborns who dared to challenge their colleagues and destroyed the ruling lords of Mitthsombaine." He exhaled hard and regained his composure. "The stone was directed at Mitthsombaine's heart, and its power utterly breached the city's magical defenses."

"We have heard this before, Sasheer," Lesendal said. "The city was made defenseless, and the other nations came in and destroyed everything. Those twelve became heroes."

Sasheer looked at Lesendal and said nothing for a long moment. "Heroes? You think so?" He swept a hand across the fire, and the flames died down, turning an incredible blue that poured heat into the atmosphere. "They were forever cursed. And the taint of Mitthsombaine was not destroyed—just buried to lie dormant. Like a festering wound," he hissed.

"The city is buried?" Salimen repeated, a little shocked. "I thought the city . . . it had to be obliterated."

"Only on the surface," Sasheer said.

"So Mitthsombaine is still there," Salimen continued in growing horror, "in theory."

"Haunted and sealed with blood. Ancient blood," Sasheer said. "The evil survived."

"So the twelve failed?" Ryland clarified.

"Not in the way you imagine," Sasheer said. "You see, the power that was used to bring down so corrupt a society did work. It worked very well. It was the rebound of that power that changed history. The rebound hit the twelve stones, fusing them into an angry ball of energy, creating a new awareness, and that awareness turned on the twelve."

"A stone that can think?" Kellen asked, watching as Sasheer's mouth curled up in a ghost smile.

"An ordinary Mage focus stone is the mirror of its master's heart. Twelve focus stones held together by a fragile spell reflected twelve hearts. Twelve individual intentions. The minds of twelve Mageborns." Sasheer cast his eyes around the group to make sure they understood the implications of what he was saying. "Very dangerous. And although the original purpose of the twelve was of pure intent, the rebound backlash from Mitthsombaine was of blackened discontent. Of a deep, malignant hatred of all who opposed Mitthsombaine."

"Please tell me, this stone was destroyed?" Salimen asked.

"If only." Sasheer rubbed his temple as if an old hurt plagued him. "Rather, it killed the guards and entrapped two of the guardians in a magical enchantment."

"The twins," Lesendal guessed.

"The twins," Sasheer confirmed. "One twin was thrown from the link, and the second was ensnared. That twin died a good, honest-hearted man, and what was born in his place by the stone's influence was a tragedy. A madness, if you will. An evil specter of everything that the twelve Mageborns had tried to destroy. A mockery." He looked up, his eyes still shadowed, reflecting the light of the subdued fire. "At a loss to know what to do, a few of the Mageborns tried to reverse the original spell that held the focus stones together. But the stone, now with a growing consciousness of its own, sensed their plan and took action."

"How?" Kellen found himself asking. He was absorbed in the tale of magic and loss. Captured by the images and words produced in his mind by Sasheer's persuasive voice. He tensed when Sasheer met his gaze directly, a small pleased smile playing over Sasheer's lips.

"It used, reanimated, the body of the ensnarled—dead—guardian and forced him to kill two of the Mageborns. If he felt anguish, the stone squashed those emotions." Sasheer's voice became a distant murmur. "The stone then forced him to kill his kin. Forced him to watch as his twin brother died an agonizing death. That act ripped him apart—" Sasheer shook his head, "and he went insane. The stone delighted in that reaction."

Anger permeated Sasheer's tone, and he paused to take a deep breath. "Once driven past the point of madness, this once guardian escaped with the stone, leaving the remaining ten Mageborns in a state of confusion and despair. He left behind older kin," he paused again. "So his older brothers went after him."

"And they killed him, put this walking dead man out of his misery, and destroyed the stone. Right? There is a happy ending. Yes?" Salimen asked. "Because I have never heard this tale before, and if there were some evil stone still around, we would all be in serious trouble. Please tell me, Sasheer, that this is one of your fairytales."

Sasheer's grin turned dark and dangerous. "I wish it were."

"So what happened?" Lesendal asked, frowning. "As a child, I remember hearing this chilling tale once when my grandmother had read from some old scrolls."

"The stone secured its continued existence by hiding deep

within the Colbart Mountains region. A once lush and fertile land that was later named Death Peaks after it subverted the shy Drow inhabitants."

"Shy?" Salimen scoffed in disbelief. Beside him, Ryland muttered a similar comment of mistrust.

"You should study your history better, Salimen," Sasheer reprimanded. "Many things have changed—or been forced to change over the centuries. As it was, it took the Mageborns a century to track the stone and find the captive guardian. By then he was unrecognizable." He took a breath. "The stone had gathered an impressive army of protectors. It sent out Drow assassins to kill the remaining Mageborns, to kill the Sun Elves who had affiliated themselves with the Mageborns, and to subvert some of the creatures hidden deep within the black pits of Death Peaks."

"Are you saying the Drow became evil because of this stone?" Lesendal asked. "And I take it the stone is still within Death Peaks."

"The Sun Elves gave the stone a name. They called it 'Lichien,' meaning *mind darkness* in the Elvish tongue, because its evil taint had affected the cold, nonliving stone of deep caverns and caves. It created an army of mindless warriors among the Drow—turning some into evil drones known as Mindwipes."

"And the Mageborns?" Salimen asked. "What did they do?"

"Within time, they tracked the original guardian and found Lichien, and they tried to destroy them both." Sasheer swallowed. "They failed."

"I do not understand," Ryland said, as the silence stretched.

"You don't understand what?" Sasheer lifted a questioning brow, looking very tired.

"So who is Kalern?" the big man asked, still bemused.

"I thought that would be obvious. Kalern is the insane young guardian who is in possession of the stone. He is Lichien's slave," Sasheer whispered. "He is a direct descendant of the original Coastal Mage Society. A man once denied a position within the Great Hall of Mages, a man sent to the priesthood because he was second born. A man bent on revenge. And believe me when I say he has inherited all of Mitthsombaine's bad traits and improved upon them."

"But it's just impossible," Salimen said in disbelief.

"Why?" Sasheer asked reasonably.

"It would mean he's . . . he's—"

"He died 3,897 years ago, Salimen. He is just the shell of the man he used to be. A walking vessel totally consumed by Lichien's will."

"But, it's still impossible!"

"Why?" Sasheer cocked a brow. "Don't marry that concept of improbability, because you will find there is very little in the world which is actually impossible. It all comes down to your point of view."

* * *

After a very strained supper, Kellen sat beside the subdued fire and just watched the other four men. He was numb, awed, after having heard Sasheer's haunting story, stunned after watching how Sasheer had changed the fire with so little effort and how none of his companions had commented. But then Sasheer had said nothing was impossible.

Although he knew that the basic idea and realization should worry him, somehow it did not. Maybe it was because everything still seemed weird, so that the very idea of a four-thousand-year-old walking corpse and an evil, living stone seemed almost normal. Normal, that was, in comparison to the idea that a Drow was coming here. A Drow, he was actually going to see a real Drow—*to see a Drow is to see death*—or so he had been taught. Yet so much of what he had been taught was vague, and he had never heard anything like what Sasheer had shared.

Dragging in a slow breath, Kellen relaxed his tense muscles, flexed his fingers, and held them out over the fire. Had Sasheer worked magic or trickery? What was he? And how had he survived traveling with a Drow? A Drow he called partner and friend. It was obvious Lesendal and Salimen knew of this creature—this man—so maybe the litany was wrong. Just like everything else.

Casting a curious glance over at the two Ihovians, Kellen noticed Salimen was already asleep while Lesendal stood watch. Ryland was sitting on the other side of the fire, sharpening his sword. The sound of stone on steel a solid reality in the dimness, and he cautiously moved, so he could glimpse the last member of their group. Sasheer. The man was a contradiction, and Kellen stared unashamedly at the dark figure. Sasheer stood on the edge of the firelight, staring outward like a chiseled statue. How old was the man? He seemed to know so much, to feel so old, yet to look at him, Kellen was reminded of a young farmhand. A Trickster? *Maybe*, but did a Trickster possess the ability to mask true age? To mask clear perception? Studying Sasheer now, he noted how the silent man seemed contained, with arms folded across his chest. His cloak was pulled tight, his long braided hair appearing to have a life of its own as a few wayward strands fluttered in the faint, chilly breeze. Yet there was also something so familiar about him that troubled Kellen. Scared him to the bone.

"Try and get some sleep, lad, for tomorrow will be a big day."

Jumping when Ryland's deep voice shattered his thoughts, Kellen turned back and nodded. On his peripheral vision, he saw Sasheer turn and walk back to his own makeshift bedroll, and Kellen held his breath until the other man turned away.

Giving up on his confusion, he settled in his blanket and courted sleep. But try as he might to dismiss his concerns, there was one question that hovered persistently in the back of his mind. Why would a powerful creature like Kalern, who controlled a living stone of power, attack the Southland? What could this Kalern possibly hope to gain from such a war? As sleep claimed him, that last thought wound its way into his dreams.

* * *

"The war has ended, and you, my confused little warrior, have failed, just like all the rest of your family who failed miserably before you."

Edging backward, Kellen glanced around the dark cavern in disbelief and fright. How he had ended up sitting on this cold, wet floor, he could not understand. His last memory was of the campsite and of Ryland sitting next to him, sharpening his sword.

"Reality is only what your mind perceives as real. And here, with me, you are very real, my lovely, young captive."

Licking his lips, Kellen found they were torn and bleeding. As were his hands and knees, and he risked another glance up at the magnificent being standing before him.

Kalern.

He knew this man, recognized those features and that voice as well as he knew his own. Knew this man intimately. Only he did not know how he knew, but the information was burned deep inside his mind, screaming to get out.

Lifting his gaze, Kellen stared at the shadowed lord before him, a mixture of fear and anger curling in his gut. Kalern was tall with unblemished, pale skin and hair as dark as a ravens, which hung down his back. He was adorned in silk and velvet, rubies and diamonds, but that was not this lord's most striking feature. It was his eyes. Their hypnotic, seductive quality and changeable color which could disarm, and at the moment, those dark eyes were watching him in amusement. So like Sasheer in appearance and stance, and Kellen frowned, remembering how Sasheer had looked, how his eyes reflected such dangerous beauty. That memory troubled him, and he backed away from Kalern, hearing words form in his mind. Words that insistently refused to be ignored.

"One will come," Kalern whispered in a half chant then grinned in malicious delight. "So are you the one who will challenge for control? Or are you, my naive child, the one who will sacrifice his soul?"

The words echoed in his mind over and over, burning into his brain, making his eyes water—and Kellen sucked in a painful breath, only to jump a moment later when Kalern reached down and caressed his cheek with ice-cold fingers.

"Do you know the prophecy, Kellen? Are the words imprinted on your soul?"

Shying away from the touch, Kellen tried to deny the whispered provocation.

"Do you dream about the prophecy?"

Closing his eyes, Kellen tried to deny the suggestion laced into Kalern's voice but found himself helplessly obeying. Unable to deny the pull of Kalern's sexual appeal and will.

"Tell me the prophecy," Kalern whispered persuasively. "Tell me . . ."

"One—" Kellen tried to resist, but it was impossible, especially when Kalern's dark eyes locked on him. Panic infused him, but still the words bubbled forth. "One will come of the bloodline and challenge for control," Kellen recited. "That one will touch a lost soul and shatter a divided heart. If the lost soul is restored, then innocence will be sacrificed."

"Yes," Kalern purred. "A curse, a blessing, a promise."

Willing his hands to stop trembling, Kellen blinked, stunned by what he had just said. Stunned by the effect the words had on his mind and body.

"So young and fragile, with that same unique beauty Aserties and Serine had. You could be them."

"What are you going to do with me?" Kellen found his voice was only a squeak, barely audible as he battled both his panic and anger, hating the power Kalern exerted over him. He did not want to believe this reality.

Kalern gave a seductive smile as he leaned in closer, his eyes now shining in the subdued firelight of the damp cavern. "I am going to kill you, Kellen. Just like I killed my beloved brother, Aserties. Just like I forced Sasheer to . . . kill—" Kalern stopped abruptly and laughed wickedly. "Poor Serine. I loved him, you know. But he had to die, just like you have to die."

"No!" Kellen screamed hoarsely as he felt Kalern's icy breath feather over his face. Saw his death in the dark, hypnotic eyes. "No . . ."

"Kellen!"

Shaken hard, Kellen snapped awake to meet an identical set of dark eyes, only these were frowning at him in worry. Panicking, he tried to break free from the hands that held him securely.

"Kellen!"

He was shaken again, and he blinked as fingers bit into his arms, causing pain. "One will come," he whispered in remembrance, looking back up into the same changeable, dark gaze of his captor, seeing only concern now. "One will come..."

"Yes," the other whispered back, his grip slackening as those amazing eyes softened in affection, mirroring mild surprise. "So, I was wrong. It was not Wyran; it was you all along."

Swallowing, Kellen blinked again, feeling the remains of his nightmare fall away, and he refocused on Sasheer's hauntingly familiar face. "I . . . you . . ."

"You were dreaming."

Coming more awake, Kellen relaxed further, glad when Sasheer released him completely. "I have never had a dream like that before," he said, and he glanced around the campsite, regaining his composure with effort. Ryland and the prince were asleep. Of Salimen, there was no evidence.

"So it begins," Sasheer predicted in a soft tone as he turned his face up to stare at the night stars. "I should not keep doubting the power of prophecy." He looked back at Kellen and gave a half smile. "Rest now, for tomorrow will be a long day."

"But," wanting to protest and ask what the nightmare had meant, what Sasheer had meant by the words "not Wyran," Kellen found his eyes treacherously closing a second time as Sasheer reached over and brushed his temple with cool, familiar fingers.

:Sleep:

The word was deep within his mind, a seductive, warm sound that filled him with comfort. Then, before he could argue, Kellen found himself tumbling down into a restful slumber where no dark shadows could find him.

CHAPTER SEVEN

The next day dawned clear with the promise of mild autumn warmth. Shaking off the remains of some bad dream, Kellen found it was a pleasure to look down on the valley and forest below without the veil of rain or mist. How different the land looked just on the other side of Dargor's Peak. Brighter and sunnier, and in the peacefulness of the morning light, he found it hard to believe that war threatened all this beauty and tranquility. But it did, and he now knew that the enemy was an ancient evil.

Frowning over that, he considered all that Sasheer had said, and he found it hard to fathom how a stone could live and think and subvert both Drow and men alike. It did not seem possible. Maybe something strange had happened many thousands of years ago, but he found it much easier to believe in the idea that a dark, evil and very *old* lord was behind the wars in the Southland rather than blaming a fabled stone.

During a meager breakfast, Kellen discovered that his friends were also reluctant to discuss Sasheer's story of the previous night. Some things were best left in the darkness, he decided, so he hastily finished his food and gathered his blanket. Lesendal and Salimen busied themselves with scouting the area, returning to the peak, and checking the Customs post before bringing news back.

"Nothing," Salimen said in frustration, shrugging off his bow and rubbing a sore shoulder. "It's as if there has never been a Customs post in this pass."

"We found no trace of anything," Lesendal added. "Living or dead."

"That is strange," Ryland frowned.

"Very," Lesendal confirmed. "I know for a fact that Ihova and Selston shared the responsibility of maintaining this post."

"Things are speeding up faster than I anticipated," Sasheer said, going over and resting against a sun-warmed boulder. He stood staring out across the valley far below, his gaze dark, distant, and unfocused.

"What does that mean?" Salimen watched him in suspicion.

Sasheer blinked, turned, and raised a brow. "I would guess that Selston has fallen to Kalern's forces. Probably Olaronia as well."

"So quickly? But how?" Lesendal asked.

"If that were the case, surely we would have heard," Salimen said. "Fairytales will not help us now, Sasheer. And I am still not certain you were not just spinning us an entertaining story last night, because I have never read anything like what you said in the history books—and I do read."

"Then I will refrain from stating the obvious about Ihova's inadequate library," Sasheer said with mild sarcasm.

"How dare you?"

"Sal," Lesendal warned, shaking his head and blocking Salimen's instinctive reaction. "Let's just agree to disagree at present. Concentrate on the facts," he advised.

Kellen held his breath, feeling a tingling start in his lower limbs, and he shifted his gaze from Salimen's tense frame to Sasheer's seemingly relaxed sprawl. He blinked, almost hearing his own heartbeat pound in building tension and seeing a web of light dance around Sasheer's frame. So intricate, so beautiful, and then Salimen was breathing out hard and nodding his acceptance of Lesendal's warning. Only then did Kellen release his anxious breath and looked again at Sasheer, catching the Ranger's amused grin, which played across that mischievous mouth.

"Stop playing with us, Sasheer," Lesendal continued. "I need the truth from you."

"I told you the truth. What you choose to believe is not my problem."

"Sasheer!" Lesendal growled.

Sasheer gave a long-suffering sigh and then moved in a fluid motion, gesturing around the clearing in a negligent way. "Believe what fantasy stories you like, but trust me when I say Kalern is very real. So is Lichien."

Like a glimmer of precious truth, Kellen felt those words hit his mind hard, and he knew they were a fact. He knew that Sasheer was not lying, and he shuddered. Kalern was real, which meant his nightmare last night *was* . . . *was* . . . he didn't want to think about that.

"Kalern controls Jorean," Lesendal said, seeing Sasheer give him a rewarding smile. He glared at the infuriating man. "Kalern is behind the war then."

"Lichien and Kalern are well practiced in war," Sasheer corrected, sweeping his eyes around the group and stopping to watch Kellen for a moment before looking back to the prince. "The army here in the Southland will only be the tip of their true forces."

"But what do they want with the Southland?" Ryland asked, serious.

"Lichien wants the total destruction of the Twelve Kingdoms," Sasheer told them, all traces of his mocking smile gone.

"But why?" Ryland persisted.

"And the only way to stop Lichien is to strike directly at its heart," Sasheer said, not answering Ryland's question. He glanced at Kellen a second time, his eyes appraising.

"So we head toward Wericonon," Lesendal decided. "If this Kalern is anywhere in the south, then he will be in Wericonon."

"Dale," Salimen started with a sigh.

"No. It is obvious we have miscalculated. If Kessendra is alive, then that is where she will be." Lesendal lifted his gaze and looked directly at the Ranger. "That's also where your Drow will be—if he lives."

Sasheer studied the prince curiously before nodding. "All right. But I suggest we wait until dusk before leaving the safety of this clearing. For there are many other creatures roaming your lands now. Creatures more dangerous than the Black Guard."

* * *

Trudging along, behind Lesendal, Kellen glanced at the rocky trail and sparse foliage. Gone were the sunshine, warm breeze, and picturesque beauty of the valleys. Now they were in old woodlands that smelled of rotting trees, mould, and stagnant water. A heavy gloom was slowly settling across the land, and he, for one, did not think the countryside looked any better in the dark than it did in daylight. They had been traveling since early evening, and ahead, he could see dark objects looming up which, he presumed, were more decaying trees. At the bottom of the mountain trail, they had crossed a small winding stream that stank, and he was glad that Sasheer had continued on without stopping. The Ranger was leading them steadily northwest.

The Drow had not shown, and Kellen was not sure if he was disappointed, thankful, or relieved. He was finding it hard enough to understand Sasheer without adding a Drow into the mix. The tension between the Ihovians and Sasheer was already strained, and as he glanced around, as an uncomfortable feeling of awareness hit his senses. An eeriness of being watched slithered across his nerves, and he scanned the darkened woods.

Ahead, he could just make out Lesendal's blond hair and face when the other looked back in the moonlight. The prince's clothing of dark greens and browns blended in perfectly with the night. In front of Lesendal, both Salimen and Sasheer were now swallowed by the darkness, and he glanced behind at Ryland. The Haonian warrior was a short distance away, his battleaxe held loosely in his hands while he, too, scanned the murky woodland.

Nothing seemed out of place, and he berated himself for overreacting, releasing his tension in a slow exhale. Looking ahead, he concentrated on where he was walking so as to not trip over some protruding root or fallen branch. Yet, in the back of his mind that feeling of being watched, of being studied, remained. He shook off the unease, trying to relax, and then a moment later, a swift brush of energy swept past his ear, and he spun around trying to focus on the oddity. It felt similar, yet also different to his other unpleasant encounters with the invisible entity. This touch—presence, wasn't cold, or malignant in feel, and he frowned, puzzled, as it brushed him a second time. He saw Ryland approach, and he turned back to the track, pretending nothing was wrong, silently focusing on this entity and willing it to appear.

A warm breeze rushed past his face, teasingly, and Kellen almost stumbled from the startling fact that this time he didn't feel threatened. Rather there was a playful quality about this invisible creature's aura—an elusive awareness with a definite sense of intelligence.

Elated by his progress in reading this creature, Kellen tentatively pushed his thoughts out, wondering if he could make contact. He was excited and scared, wanting to know so badly what it was he had encountered that tragic, rainy day yet also terrified of learning that this persuasive spirit was real. He reached out with his mind and hand at the same time and felt a rush of heat wash along his fingertips then down his body. A burning spark of seductive desire.

He pulled back, stunned. His brow drew down in astonishment, and he did nothing more for a long moment, just concentrating on walking and keeping up with Lesendal. Only his mind was spinning in a hundred different directions. *What was that thing?* It was so unlike his original encounter that he was sure it had to be a different creature. Was that possible?

Bewildered, he called the creature mentally, stunned when it responded and probed the warm presence that swirled at his side. He could see tiny reflections of light twinkle in the darkness, and he wondered if any of his friends could see this amazing display of warmth. He glanced back at Ryland, but the warrior showed no evidence of witnessing the shimmering phenomenon.

Picking up the pace, he kept a careful eye on the floating beads of light, seeing how they changed color, finding that his nervousness decreased with each step. The undercurrents of playfulness permeated the encounter, and he smiled, wondering if he could make the creature solidify even more.

He lifted a hand and trailed his fingers through the air, his palm tingling, heat charging up his arm, firing into his chest and loins. Despite the chilly evening and cold breeze, he started to sweat under his leathers, and he removed his hand from the fractured figments of light to wipe his palm against his chest. Only the seductive memory of the entity's heat remained to fuel his vivid imagination and make him believe in new delightful possibilities.

"Stop that!" he mouthed, feeling his lips spread into a grin at his own foolishness. *Now I'm talking to thin air!* How his life had changed in only a few days. From ignorance, to watching a friend die, to killing a man, seeing spirits and visions, and destroying a fabled Deathwalker. *So is this thing as real as a Deathwalker?* If so, then he wanted to see it.

Pushing embarrassment and hot desire away, he glared at the patterned flows of light and willed the creature to appear. Nothing happened, and he sighed in frustration, swiping at the light currents, feeling the euphoric effects of laughter wash over him anew. Dismissing those feelings, he threw his annoyance back at the creature and froze when the warmth turned into a burning heat.

What he saw then startled and shocked him, and he closed his eyes to block the image, only the vision increased tenfold. Before him stood a very petite and beautiful woman with large luminescent eyes, long flaming hair, flawless white skin—and he noted with uneasy desire that she was wearing very little. His jaw dropped, and he forced his eyes open, but she remained before him, hovering above the damp leaves. Tiny filaments of light surrounded her, and she looked unearthly, like a fantasy sent to fulfill each and every dream he'd ever had. Then without realizing it, he found his eyes were trailing down her body, noting her blatant invitation as the soft, transparent material covering her tiny frame slipped from bare shoulders. He groaned, so tempted by her exotic beauty, by her sheer perfection.

Frozen in time, Kellen stared unashamedly, watching her lips move, seeing her lashes flutter as more of her wrap fell away, her skin like velvet, her lips a red desire.

"Kell?"

He gasped when Ryland gripped his shoulder, shuddering, and feeling perspiration run down his spine. Before him, the image vanished, and he peered up at Ryland, startled. It was obvious Ryland had not seen anything.

"Come on, lad, pick up the pace, or we will never get out of this depressing forest."

Nodding, he got his stiff legs working, suddenly very glad for the darkness and the fact Ryland could not see his face, or the state his body was in. Taking a deep, steadying breath, he wiped his sweaty palms against his leather pants. *Who is she? And where does she come from?* Nervously, he searched the woodlands, but she was gone and all traces of the lingering feel of her invisible presence had vanished also. He extended his senses, probing the atmosphere but encountered nothing.

Disappointed despite his initial fear, he considered all he had seen. Real or imagined? Yet she had been in direct contrast to the first entity he had encountered. So maybe they were creatures brought into the Southland by the Black Guard? Maybe these spirits were enemy spies? Maybe one of the Black Guard had sent them to track Lesendal? That was a terrifying thought, and Kellen panicked for a moment, remembering the ambush in the forest, the raid on the stronghold, and the earthquake. Was it possible? Yet Sasheer said nothing was impossible. Worrying at his lower lip, he hurried to catch up with the prince. At least now he knew the invisible touches were real and, in all probability, an enemy. So all he had to do now was work out a way to kill it, before it killed them.

* * *

They stopped hours later, and Kellen paid scant attention to the conversation as Lesendal and Sasheer discussed the best way through the mountainous track ahead. They were avoiding all inhabited areas of Selston, using the hilly range on Selston's eastern border to cut across, unnoticed, into the kingdom of Olvaronia. It would take about two weeks of constant walking—or so Salimen predicted as he drew a rough map in the dirt, pinpointing their approximate position.

"I do not like it," Ryland said as he studied the map.

"Neither do I," Sasheer agreed. "But for once, Salimen is right."

"Why, thank you," the bowman muttered sarcastically.

"We should avoid Selston and cut across into Olvaronia then detour up into her marshlands. If we do that, we should come out near the river township of Herston, nestled in the foothills of the Divide," Sasheer said.

"You are assuming an awful lot," Salimen returned, glaring at the Ranger. Sasheer ignored him. "Those marshes are deadly, especially this time of year."

"I have been through them before, and I can get us through them again. It is the quickest way to Herston," Sasheer said, his tone inviting no arguments.

"No doubt," Salimen replied, tart. "But what if Olvaronia has fallen to Jorean, or this Kalern you insist on talking about? If that is the case, then Herston will be closed to all travelers. It is too valuable a position to just leave unguarded."

"Herston will appear normal despite its capture. I'd say it fell months ago to Kalern," Sasheer said, rubbing out the hastily drawn map with his boot.

"So why are we going there then?" Salimen asked, irritated.

"Sal," Lesendal sighed, and shook his head, "let's get out of Selston first and into Olvaronia before we decide what is and isn't safe. I am willing to trust in Sasheer's judgments, and I ask you to do the same. All right?"

Clamping his jaw shut, the bowman just gave a tight nod then turned away to gather his gear.

Lesendal frowned and then looked at Sasheer in appeal, but the Ranger just shook his head before he turned and started down the grassy trail.

CHAPTER EIGHT

It took them over five long weeks to cross the swamplands in Olvaronia and then reach the Divide on its northern border. The weather turned colder with the approach of winter, and the smell of snow was thick in the air before the first few small flakes fluttered down, much to Kellen's disgust, especially since he was finding that his list of dislikes far outweighed his current likes. Between Lesendal's moodiness, Salimen's complaints, and Sasheer's sarcastic baiting of both Ihovians, he wondered how any of them had managed to survive the stressful trek through the swamplands. Only Ryland's steadfast presence was a welcomed comfort in this time of confusion, and Kellen found he spent a lot of time reviewing his life.

The short interlude of soft, dry snow falling was rapidly followed by cold, sweeping rain and an icy wind that chilled him to the bone. The land turned bleak; the trees resembled dark smudges on the countryside, and the ground became muddy, murky pools of water. Then the desolation increased as they started to find first one, then another burnt out and abandoned village on the edge of the swamplands. Thatched roofs had been destroyed by fire and partially pulled down by looters. Thick, black soot mingled with the rain, turning the ground a dirty slate gray and emphasizing the lifelessness of the place. It was a chilling reminder of the war, of death, and of the unseen enemy they were fighting.

Sasheer and Salimen finally seemed to agree on abandoning their attempt to reach Herston and to head directly for the Divide. Once through the mountainous pass, Sasheer said that he believed they could gain information from the Lancooti and then accurately decide on a new route. And according to Sasheer, there would be only one pass free of Lord Jorean's patrols, and that was because of its treacherous route in winter.

Glancing up at the impressive mountains before him, Kellen pulled his cape closer, shivering from the cold and eyeing the snowdrifts, not looking forward to the dangerous climb.

Frostbite was a real danger, and to stop himself from thinking about the burning pain, he started to fantasize about the warmth in the kitchens back at the holdings. He imagined those old noisy kitchens, the heat, the food, the roaring fires, and how he had slept near the furnace in winter. He remembered the delicious smells, the comforting heat that had lulled him to sleep, and Kellen found he was stumbling, half asleep, until a solid hand steadied him, and he glimpsed up at Ryland's concerned face. Icicles hung from the big man's beard; snow rested in the curls escaping the warrior's helmet, and Kellen nodded, understanding and accepting his friend's silent help.

He forced himself to keep walking, picturing the images in his mind of hot stew and steaming, fresh bread. It helped to ease his numbness, and it helped him to forget the disturbing nightmares that invaded his sleep almost nightly. Nightmares of a dark cavern, of the sensual, immaculately dressed, shadowed lord.

Pushing that memory away, Kellen focused on his surroundings, lifting his head and seeing Sasheer watch him in concern and speculation. For some reason, ever since that first night when Sasheer had woken him, the dreams had not been as intrusive. Now they were just snatched images that intruded on his subconscious, that twisted his thinking and then vanished to leave him unsure and bewildered.

Avoiding Sasheer's piercing gaze, Kellen fixed his attention on Lesendal's tall frame, hoping that Salimen's predictions would be correct, and that the temperature would increase when they reached the other side of this range. Anything to forget about the biting winds which tore at his clothing.

"Why such dark thoughts?"

Groaning, Kellen sneaked a second look up and was surprised to find Sasheer now walking beside him. Cursing silently for not paying more attention, he cast a cautious look around and found that the other members of the company were taking no notice of his plight.

"Kellen?"

Risking another glance up, he tried to school his expression. "I was just thinking about home."

"Of course. This must be hard for you. I imagine you are concerned about your brother," Sasheer said.

Frowning, Kellen looked properly at Sasheer. *My brother? How does Sasheer know about Wyran?* "No," he said carefully, "my brother is dead." Remarkably, Sasheer's blue eyes darkened, and he blinked, wondering if the change was a trick of the light or something else—something more sinister.

"Wyran?"

Startled when Sasheer whispered his brother's name, Kellen stopped and stared at the man next to him. "How did . . . do you know his name?"

Grabbing the young man's arm, Sasheer got them walking again as Kellen's stare searched his face. "I met him briefly awhile ago," he answered evasively. "Tell me when and how he died."

Swallowing, Kellen hunted for something to say, something that would describe his inner anger at Wyran and also his hurt at being abandoned—his love-hate relationship with his stubborn brother. Only nothing came to mind. He pulled free of Sasheer's grip.

"Well?"

"I don't know when he died exactly, only that he did when he joined the Ihovian army last spring."

"That idiot!" Sasheer swore with real feeling, seeming to forget about Kellen's presence for a second. "I had told him specifically not to involve himself in the events unfolding around him. What was he thinking?"

"I . . . I really don't know." Rubbing his arm where Sasheer's fingers had bitten into his muscles, Kellen studied Sasheer's eyes. He saw fear, anger, and compassion mirrored in the changeable gaze.

"So you truly are alone, the last of your line. Almost a man, yet still a child, with a powerful potential for destruction welling inside your mind. How did I miss seeing you before this?"

It was more a statement than a question, and it was spoken with such eeriness that Kellen shuddered. Then just as quickly, Sasheer attempted to smile at him. That was even more frightening.

"So tell me, how did you meet Lesendal and his band of part-time rebels?"

"They found me," Kellen said, unsure if he should say more. "They took me to their camp because I don't think they knew exactly what else to do with me."

"I see. And now?"

"And now, what?" Kellen repeated, feeling very isolated and annoyed that Lesendal and especially Ryland would leave him to Sasheer's mercies for this long. But the others were ignoring him, and he really did not want to have this conversation with Sasheer.

"Are you following Lesendal because you believe in his cause? Or are you only here because you have nowhere else to go?"

The words were harsh, yet so typical of Sasheer, and Kellen clamped his jaw. He wanted to shout at Sasheer, and he stared ahead, seeing Salimen cast him a swift, apologetic look. So was this how Salimen felt most of the time while dealing with Sasheer? Did the bowman want to strangle the cynical Ranger like he did? "What else am I supposed to do?" he said, letting his anger show. Only Sasheer laughed. "Where else am I supposed to go now that my home is gone?"

"There are always choices," Sasheer said, his tone amused. "You just have to know what to choose."

"And how am I to do that?" Kellen demanded louder, not caring if his voice carried. Sasheer annoyed him more than anyone he had ever met. "I don't even know what's going on half the time, and what I have heard I don't understand. Or believe!"

"Then find out the truth."

The calmness and simplicity of Sasheer's tone just proved to irritate Kellen further. He glared at Sasheer. "And how am I to do that when we're stuck up here on some cold and desolate mountain?"

"This region is called the Divide."

Thrown again by the quietness of the comment, by the reasonable tone, Kellen battled to hang onto his temper, directing a scowl at the man beside him. That didn't work, so he scowled at the drab gray rock and snow-covered track. *Why couldn't Sasheer just shout back?* It would make him feel so much better. "So?" he asked in the most irritating way possible.

Sasheer chuckled. "Nice try, child," he said then sobered. "Tell me, Kellen, do you know what the Divide is?"

He hated being patronized, and he ground his teeth together and admitted that Salimen was right—*Sasheer is an arrogant bastard.* "Should I know what it is? Should I care?" he asked in deliberate provocation. "All I know is that I am freezing my legs off, and your company is the last thing I want or need."

Sasheer laughed in delight then placed a hand on Kellen's shoulder. "This massive range we're crossing stretches for over a thousand leagues from coastline to coastline, with only a few places that are accessible to cross. It completely cuts off the Southland from the rest of the known world, sheltering the kingdoms with its protective barrier. On the other side of the Divide are the Lancooti, mostly nomadic tribes scattered across the Sandlands. They are traders, smugglers, and thieves who barter their goods with silver at Engleton seaport. With pirates, Kellen," Sasheer added in an aside, his smile infectious.

Despite himself, Kellen was curious about the Lancooti, and he felt his resentment melt away. He just hated the way Sasheer could manipulate his responses.

"The Lancooti as a people are flamboyant, passionate, excitable, and hospitable, but beware of anything they offer you. And, Kellen, I'll warn you now; you cannot trust them," Sasheer stated, pausing, and Kellen felt the warning sink into his mind. "Remember that when we meet the Lancooti scouts on the other side of this range."

Nodding, Kellen did not know whether he should be angry or thankful for the information. He dared a look up at Sasheer's face. Those eyes were a deep azure color at present, an ageless knowledge invading their depths.

"See how a little knowledge can change your perspective?"

The amusement behind Sasheer's words still stung, but Kellen begrudgingly nodded. He still felt it was unjust that Sasheer could exasperate him so easily, but then he also had to admit that Sasheer was the best person to educate him about the land outside of Ihova. But did he want to be educated?

"If your mother had spent the money given her on educating her sons, rather than on buying shares in a worthless holding, then maybe you would not feel so ill prepared now."

Those uncalled-for words fired his indignation anew, and Kellen shut down all the charitable thoughts he was having about Sasheer. Instead, he shot the Ranger another sideways glance of pure dislike. *Cursed stars!* But how did Sasheer know so much about his family? Was Sasheer reading his mind? Was mind reading even possible? "How do you know about my mother?"

"I know your family, Kellen. I knew your brother, and I had known your father and uncle before that."

Kellen blinked at Sasheer, dissecting the comment and finding no judgment or sarcasm in the Ranger's words this time, only sincere regret. So how had Sasheer known his father? He was not old enough to have known his father. "If you knew . . . then . . . then you would know how my father died?"

"In a hunting accident," Sasheer said. "In the woodlands of Rye in Olvaronia."

Kellen's mind whirled. His father had died a long time ago; in fact, he had little memory of him, yet he remembered his mother telling him that his father had died while in the woodlands of Rye. Nothing else—just the name had stuck in his memory. He had never known how his father had died. Until now. So how did Sasheer know? And then Sasheer had admitted to knowing Wyran, and his uncle?

"Don't dwell on it, Kellen."

"But you just said . . ." he trailed off. "I might have other family in Ihova if my father had a brother," his face broke into a hopeful smile. "I could go back. I have family."

"No."

It was very soft and very final, and Kellen jolted to a stop, turning to stare at Sasheer. He saw Sasheer reach out and grab his shoulder before those long fingers squeezed gently. "What do you mean, no?" he had to ask, had to know. "I am not a pawn in some power struggle. I will not be manipulated."

"I'm not trying to manipulate you," Sasheer said with an edge of exasperation. "Rather, I am trying to help you. If you'll let me."

Kellen only stared at him in distrust.

"You have a great potential, a powerful Gift that is maturing, and from what I have seen over the last few weeks, you are in grave danger of losing control of that Gift. I can feel your panic when you wake, can sense your confusion."

"I want none of this!" Kellen snapped.

"Kellen—"

"No!" His anger returned, unheeded, and he turned on Sasheer and snarled at him. "Stay out of my mind!"

"I am not in your mind," Sasheer clarified. "What you see in your dreams is not me."

"No!" Raising a hand to his head, Kellen hissed the denial, not wanting to mention his dreams. Nightmares, visions he had believed he'd successfully hidden from Sasheer. He would not talk about them—ever. "You talk of my family, so what do you know of them?"

Sasheer sighed, lifting a hand to rub his eyes in annoyance and irritation. "Why are you so stubborn?"

"Just tell me if I have any family left alive in the Southland," Kellen persisted peevishly.

"You have none," Sasheer stated, visibly restraining his temper.

"Why?" Kellen snarled, no longer feeling cold as he glared at the infuriating man.

"Because they did not survive."

"The war?" Kellen asked, when Sasheer did not volunteer more.

"Yes! The cursed war!" Sasheer snapped. "Your entire family is dead. Uncles, aunts, and cousins! Is that what you wanted to hear?"

A brief flaring of pain hit him as Kellen imagined the deaths of relatives he had never even known. What else had he never been told? What else did this man know of his life that he wasn't aware of? "Who are you?" He found he was whispering the question urgently, needing to know as he unconsciously stepped closer to Sasheer. He no longer saw the snow around them, or felt the icy wind, for now he was totally focused on Sasheer, his entire body awaiting this important answer.

Sasheer pursed his lips as if considering the request seriously, before he turned and gave Kellen a disgruntled look. "I have already told you."

"No." Kellen shook his head, reaching out to grab Sasheer and pull the other man back. He had to know now, had to learn the truth in that instant before he lost the nerve or courage. "I want the truth. I can sense your age, regardless of what your appearance says. You are not what you appear. So if I am to believe you, then you have to tell me the truth," he petitioned, allowing himself for once to sink into Sasheer's powerful eyes, to challenge the man silently to deny him an answer.

"Truth?" Sasheer breathed, the wind around them catching the word and ripping it away. He gave a twisted, cynical smile. "What is truth except another excuse for weak men to clutch at?"

Shaking his head, Kellen felt Ryland walk past them. The Haonian eyed them both in curiosity, not saying a word. In the back of his mind, Kellen wondered what the others must be thinking, what they must be perceiving of this exchange. "Who are you?" He repeated, pushing his senses out to see past the facade that Sasheer wore, to see past those barriers, and abruptly he glimpsed a deluge of intense images, which stole his breath away.

Brilliant colors skipped over gray stone, and in the corner was a man. A man sitting isolated on a barren floor. In this man's arms was the body of another man. Silken robes of deep, vibrant richness and long shining hair contrasted the damming pool of blood that sat around the two men.

The man sobbed. Sobbed so hard that the vibrations of his pain and anguish filled the room. He started to rock, clutching the body in his arms. Long fingers smoothed back soft hair, those same fingers caressed gray lips and moved up to close partially open eyes. Dead eyes. Then the man lifted his face and cried out in grief.

So much agony, so much helplessness and vulnerability. When there was no more sound, the man raised a bloody, bejeweled dagger and threw it aside.

Jolted back to the present, Kellen stepped away from Sasheer, shaken by what he had just witnessed. He stared at the Ranger, locking his gaze with Sasheer's and noting how those defiant eyes were now a vivid, shining blue. Then a tear rolled down Sasheer's pale face as he wrenched his gaze away with a small cry of dismay.

Drawn to Sasheer, yet also repulsed, Kellen tentatively reached over and touched Sasheer's shoulder, not surprised when he felt muscles tremble under his fingers. "Sasheer?" He moved closer. "I am sorry—"

"Don't say it." The other shook his head, the muscles under Kellen's fingers relaxing a little before Sasheer turned around. "It is just a . . ." he hesitated, his voice strained, "a memory of long ago. Best forgotten."

Dropping his hand, Kellen did not know what to say. He did not want to intrude, but neither did he want to forget what he had just been shown.

"You want to know if you can trust me," Sasheer said, his voice still unsteady. He was looking away, not meeting Kellen's searching eyes. "I can't give you the reassurances you ask for. All I can tell you is that I am a friend to your family. And yes, I knew your father, Hargon—and yes, I knew Wyran. I was not there to help them when they needed me. For that, I am sorry. I hope you will allow me to help you."

Not completely satisfied by the answer, Kellen hesitated. He turned away and glanced ahead, noting that the others had stopped also and now waited, careful not to intrude. Lesendal was rubbing his hands together, warming them. Salimen, his blond hair a mass of whiteness in the wind, turned to say something to the prince. Only Ryland looked concerned as he stood guard further up the track. It was almost surreal, and Kellen found that his senses were numb, isolated. So could he trust Sasheer? Did he have any choice?

Shaking his head, Kellen let his eyes touch the man beside him, noting the worried frown marring Sasheer's handsome face. "So what happens now?"

Sasheer shrugged. "First, we have to get higher into the Divide. Then we cross into the narrow pass and escape the worst of the winter effect. From there, we can cut through the range and go down into the Sandlands." He looked away, his eyes clearing. "It should take a week, but on the other side of the Divide, the weather will be warmer."

CHAPTER NINE

Sitting on a large boulder, Kellen moodily studied the land around him. They had exited the high peaks of the Divide days earlier, leaving behind the chilling blasts of snowdrifts and biting cold. Upon reaching the lower northern tracks of the Divide, they had been hit with warmer weather, and then two days later, they had been faced with the glare of a hot sun reflecting off vast grasslands. He had been amazed at the rapid change in conditions from one side of the Divide to the other. It was like entering a different world. Even the sun was different—hotter, brighter, and the air was drier. The tang of salt was strong in the breeze, crusting his lips and burning his eyes. Then at dusk, when the evening winds picked up, the grass seemed to sing.

Strange but wonderful, and Kellen spent the first few days in this new and unusual world just staring around in wonderment, listening to the music the long grass made. He found that even Lesendal and Ryland viewed this grassland with awed eyes. Only Salimen looked unaffected, a response that seemed to amuse Sasheer, much to the bowman's annoyance.

That had been two days ago. Now he was used to the strange grasslands, the eerie music of the evening, and the salty taste on everything. In fact, he was starting to feel sick in this great expanse of nothing—a feeling that was shared by Ryland. The warrior had sat with him complaining about the sun and the heat, the lack of trees, of water—but determined to remain in his armor.

"I would feel even more exposed under this unrelenting sun if I were to succumb and remove my armor," Ryland had pronounced, his deep voice almost challenging the elements of this strange grassland to respond.

Remembering that, Kellen frowned. He wanted to escape the endless plains of grass that swayed in the breeze. He wanted to see the hard, wet earth again, to feel the wetness of rain on his face, instead of the burn of salt in his eyes. But Sasheer counseled that they had to wait for the Lancooti scouts to bring them into the Sandlands, because to venture into the land without invitation resulted in death to all unwary travelers.

It was a chilling thought; the Lancooti were such a different culture to what he had been brought up to accept. But waiting was arduous, so he had appointed himself as watch, sitting on one of the largest sandstone rocks in the area and studying the grass as it swayed and danced to the breeze. A hypnotic sight.

The camp behind him was almost a domestic haven as Ryland polished the buckles on his armor and sharpened his blades. Salimen was cutting himself new arrows, while Lesendal patched holes in his leathers. Sasheer seemed asleep by the cold fire pit, oblivious to everything around, a state Kellen suspected was false. He had been unable to relax, so he had gathered twigs, explored the immediate area and now watched for riders. It was better than just sitting around doing nothing.

Squinting, he noticed a curious cloud of dust, and he watched in fascination as the dust spiraled upward, until he realized with a jolt that horses were approaching. Standing, he called back, "Riders!"

"Yes, I've seen them," Salimen acknowledged. "You'd better wake Sasheer."

Wondering why that task had fallen to him, Kellen approached the still form and crouched down, lightly placing a hand on the Ranger's arm. "We have company."

Sasheer came awake instantly. "Good," he said, giving Kellen an absent glance. Then Sasheer was squinting in the direction of the riders, his smile satisfied.

"Sasheer, is it safe to be taken by these people? You said yourself they can't be trusted. So, won't they be working with Kalern and his army?" Kellen asked.

"I doubt it."

"But why?" Kellen persisted.

"Because there is nothing here in these sand dunes for Kalern to capture."

"I don't understand."

Sasheer gave him a steady look, an impatient look, before the Ranger sighed and placed an arm around Kellen's shoulder, leading him toward the others. "These grasslands run the entire length of the Divide and then stretch out toward the coast of the White Sea. Apart from the semipermanent tent cities, which change location depending on the weather, there is nothing to be captured here except the seaport of Engleton. And that is run by disreputable pirate traders, so I doubt Kalern would waste his energy on them."

Digesting this, Kellen frowned. "So why is he wasting his energy on fighting the south if he is not interested in the gem mines or the rich cities? Why does he want to destroy the Twelve Kingdoms?"

"Because they represent everything he hates."

Far from satisfied with that muttered response, Kellen wished Sasheer would just tell him the plain truth, not these annoying half-truths. But the closest he had come to getting an honest answer from the irritating man had been up in the pass when the Ranger had been shaken and strangely vulnerable. For a moment, he had glimpsed Sasheer's true soul, and Kellen had wanted to press Sasheer further for information but had felt strangely hesitant. Thinking about that encounter, Kellen frowned, lifting his eyes to watch the Lancooti riders' approach. The group stopped a dozen paces away, all unsmiling and all armed with wicked-looking crossbows.

One rider dismounted and advanced, while the others all held their crossbows aimed at them. Their faces were very tanned, and their hair was a mixture of bright, dyed colors, some long, some short, and all tied off with beads. Their clothing also appeared mismatched at first, but as the dust settled, Kellen could see it was a combination of flowing garments and decorative jewelry. Exotic, yet practical.

"I hope you are right about this," Lesendal said to Sasheer, giving the man approaching them a strained smile.

"Trust me."

"Gods, I hate it when he says that," Salimen sighed.

Stepping forward, Sasheer bowed and then made a curious gesture with his hand before drawing a symbol in the dirty sand. The Lancooti scout stilled, his eyes going wide before he peered closer at the intruder. No one moved for a very long second, and then the scout gave a hesitant smile and reached out to embrace the hand Sasheer offered. The Lancooti spoke then in a language which none of them understood, musical, fluid and as soft as the summer wind. Mesmerizing, and Kellen blinked when Sasheer answered in the same unusual style. The scout grinned and then rubbed out the symbol drawn in the dirt with his foot before he gestured back to the waiting riders.

"Well?" Ryland half-growled, edging closer to Sasheer.

"His name is Koti, and he is from the Sessti tribe," Sasheer said softly, not taking his eyes off the Lancooti in question. When he got no reply, he glanced back at the others and saw their blank looks.

"And that's all he said?" Lesendal asked pointedly.

"No. He is under orders to take all trespassers to the elders of GarFamita for questioning," Sasheer informed him dryly.

"Gara, what?" Ryland repeated, tightening his armor's straps. "Maybe we should fight our way out. After all there are only six of them."

Sasheer glared at the big warrior, placing a hand warningly on Ryland's sword arm. "GarFamita is the city of the Famita nomads, who currently are the leading tribe of all Lancooti. They have been in control of the Sandlands for the last twenty years, and their chief is Lasdajar. She is a reasonable woman and will not harm us unless you force her hand."

"A woman?" Ryland uttered in disbelief and contempt.

"You know her?" Lesendal asked incredulously.

"You are forgetting that I know almost everyone. I have had dealings with her tribe in the past. If you don't provoke the Lancooti, we will have no trouble," Sasheer said, looking at Ryland, and then Salimen. "Is that understood?"

"I hear you, Ranger," Ryland growled, taking his hand off his sword.

"Good." Sasheer turned, striding toward the waiting Lancooti. "Now come. Koti says we will ride with them."

"Is that understood?" Salimen mimicked, rolling his eyes skyward. Ryland grinned as Lesendal shook his head. The prince then gestured to Salimen using a hand signal before following Ryland.

Seeing the action, Kellen debated asking the bowman what the hand signals meant. But he dismissed the thought when he realized that they would have to ride more horses. He hated riding.

* * *

The grasslands seemed endless, and Kellen despaired of ever reaching the end of the rolling dunes and seeing something beside murky green stalks of grass. Even the blistering change of thinning grass tuffs and darker sand dunes would be welcome, he decided. And with the wind, there was no distinguishable trail, just more sand, more grass, and more heat.

The scout he was perched behind was a competent rider, a fact Kellen was especially grateful for. And the horse was mild mannered, so he was able to study their new associates, marveling at the exotic dress sense, the intermix of colors and fabric that extended to the horse's reigns, and detailed beading of the horse's mane and tail. It certainly wasn't for camouflage purposes as the grass was a dull color in contrast, and at present, it reached his thighs, pulling against his clothing, cutting into his skin. Kellen was glad when they reached the top of one steep, grassy incline to stare down on the vast leagues of shimmering sand dunes below.

The horse never hesitated, nor did the scout, plunging down the slope, and Kellen hung on tightly, glancing back to watch the others. He was relieved when Lesendal, Salimen, and even Ryland looked uncomfortable facing this new grassless expanse. But the Lancooti scout he was perched behind never said a word, never indicated he was even aware of Kellen's presence, so Kellen just gripped the saddle harder and gritted his teeth, finding that the sun's glare was blinding, and the heat was suffocating.

Now he wished for the sticky long grass to return.

* * *

They seemed to travel for leagues. Never a fast pace, with each new mound of sand merging in with the next distant mound. The sun beat down on him, making him dizzy, and Kellen's head ached; his mouth was parched, and he was finding that the air was dusty, although the tang of salt had diminished.

They traveled on and on. It felt like endless hours before they stopped atop one rippling sand dune and looked down on the valley below. There, a huge multicolored structure stood. The colors gleaming in the sunlight, dazzling to the eye, a spectacle of magnificence and beauty amid such desolate bleakness.

Relieved, Kellen peered at the city they approached, realizing a long while later just how massive the structure was. The walls were not solid as he first perceived; they were moving, constantly moving, and the colors of the outer walls blended perfectly with the yellow rock and sand mounds. He also noted that the valley floor was made up more of slated rock than sand, giving a feeling of stability.

The gates before them swung open, and they were met with numerous Lancooti guards lining the entrance, holding spears, and eyeing them in distrust. Swallowing nervously, Kellen swiveled in the saddle to see the gates shut behind them with finality. It was eerie, and he glanced up, noting intricate carving in the hard sandstone that was both beautiful and puzzling. All the abodes around them appeared solid, but he realized that was only illusion, for when the stiff breeze touched the walls near him, the seemingly solid walls rippled sluggishly.

Awed, he stared at the magnificence of the place, seeing people crowd the marketplace as color dazzled the eye at every turn. Color and music, a noise that was lively, oddly inviting and vibrant, just like the unusual people. The labyrinth of homes and markets made

Kellen lose his sense of direction, and he looked around anxiously, only catching fleeting glimpses of the sun amidst the tall canvaslike walls and flags that fluttered from every rooftop. This was nothing like he could have ever imagined.

"It's amazing," Salimen said, for once his tone lack any sarcasm.

Every road circled inward, and eventually, they stopped inside a sheltered courtyard, where the vibrancy was toned down, and a respectful silence seemed to permeate the air. He dismounted and followed the others into a large canvassed pavilion. Sasheer drew them all aside and told them that this was the home of the ruling house, and that they should be polite and mind their manners.

"But I thought you said these people were not our enemies?" Salimen hissed, glaring at the Ranger.

Sasheer turned back to him and gave a humorless smile. "After spending weeks in your company, Salimen, I can start to understand why the Lancooti avoid contact with the Twelve Kingdoms."

Salimen's gaze darkened. "Why you—"

"Save it, Sal," Lesendal advised.

"Don't aggravate our hosts," Sasheer added then turned on his toes and followed the beckoning Lancooti scout.

Digesting that, Kellen stared around wide-eyed, ducking under silken drapes to enter a larger area that was regally decorated with fountains, with birds of all colors, and with a wide carved staircase that led up into an even more spacious and inviting atmosphere. Patterned pavilion sheets divided and sectioned off numerous areas. He had never seen anything so big or so extravagantly stunning, and he turned, seeing that Ryland and the Ihovians were looking similarly amazed.

Their guide, Koti, stopped them and went to talk with another of these multicolored Lancooti guards before he came forward and spoke briefly to Sasheer again.

After he had gone, Lesendal asked, "Well?"

"He has handed us over to the sentinel of the Famita tribe. Someone will be informed of our arrival shortly, and then I imagine, we will be escorted to the baths before being presented to Lasdajar."

He looked at each of them. "Don't worry, we are not prisoners. Their customs are just different to your own."

"A bath," Ryland said with distaste.

"You won't rust, my friend, so long as you take your armor off," Salimen quipped.

Then a number of women arrived and bowed before them, gesturing for them to follow. Ryland was the first to move.

* * *

Feeling acutely self-conscious when he was led into a huge room, Kellen glanced around, seeing that the others were nowhere in sight. Turning back, his worst nightmares were realized when he was faced with a large tub of water, surrounded by furs and wool cloths. One of the Lancooti had just left him, indicating with a sharp gesture that he should use the bath, before the screen partition was tied closed. Speculating if he would be allowed to leave, he dismissed the idea almost at once as he slowly unlaced his tunic and leather pants. Pulling off his boots, he dropped them on the smooth floor, wiggling his toes, noticing the dirt and stones that showered the floor in his boots' wake.

He had to admit that he did need a wash; apart from the infrequent rainstorms, he had not seriously considered his physical state. And now, looking down at himself, he had to grant he was filthy.

He stripped then gingerly stepped into the tepid tub. He winced as he sank below the surface, deciding that he had better wash his hair, not a task he ever liked doing.

Enjoying the brief privacy, he realized that this was the first time he had been alone in weeks, the first time he had been allowed the luxury of being warm and being able to sit and think in complete solitude. He missed Ihova, missed his holding, and missed Bains. Tears unbidden clouded his eyes, and he scrubbed viciously at his face, not wanting to cry. But he felt so disassociated with his life at present. He had no idea where they were going, except Lesendal was driven to find his sister, Kessendra—a princess—and that

Ryland had vowed to help him if it meant killing the enemy that had destroyed his kingdom. They were not hard to understand; even Salimen and all his contrary moods was easy to comprehend. It was Sasheer that baffled him. What motivated the Ranger? The need to find his Drow traveling companion?

Thinking about that, Kellen let his fingers trail through the tepid water. So what would happen to him when Lesendal found his sister, and Ryland had his revenge, and Sasheer was reunited with the Drow? What would he do?

Such gloomy thoughts were depressing, and he looked over the edge of his huge tub and picked up his filthy clothing, dragging them into the water. If he was clean, he may as well have clean clothing. Washing the few items, he stood up, wringing out his clothing and placing them over the bench beside the tub. With that done, he started to consider what he could wear while his clothing dried and jumped when he was touched—brushed—by something that wasn't visible.

He stood still, his mind rapidly going over a number of alternative plans when the same warmth circled him a second time. Only this time, he *felt* a definite, seductive touch. That worried him even more, and he sank back into the cooling water.

He scanned the room for the invisible presence, trying to locate its position. From the feel of this entity's touch, he guessed it was the feminine creature he had glimpsed in the woodlands. She was warm and approachable, whereas the other entity he had sensed in Ihova was cold, malicious, and deadly. He moved to the edge of the tub and gripped the old wood, peering over the timber to eye the room warily. The atmosphere almost vibrated with her presence, a strong sexual overtone of playful delight and gentle teasing. Groaning, Kellen clamped his teeth tightly shut and concentrated on willing the creature away. :*Leave me alone*: He sent the thought out, trying to make it a command and knew he had failed when he heard laughter.

Bright stars! He frowned in the direction of the laughter and reached out to pick up a drying cloth. He anxiously grabbed the first one he could find and exited the tub, spilling water over the floor as he wrapped the towel around his waist. It covered modesty, and he glared in the direction of his tormentor. "All right," he grumbled. "I know what you look like, so you might as well show yourself."

Again he was treated to bubbling laughter, and then something touched the back of his legs, making his hair stand on end.

"Stop playing games." He tried to make it sound like an order, but it came out more like a plea. Controlling his emotions, he forced his mind to concentrate and was rewarded when the space before him shimmered, the light intensifying before a being slowly solidified. It was the same woman he had seen in the woodlands, and he sighed in relief, recognizing her mischievous emerald eyes that danced in mirth and unspoken promise.

Swallowing hard, he ignored the blatant stare. "What are you?"

"What would you like me to be?"

"Informative," he shot back, knowing that he was blushing again and almost positive the entity could read his thoughts. Then as if to confirm his suspicions, she giggled, reaching out with a finger to trail a pattern down his chest. He slapped her hand away but connected with nothing. Instead, he saw the colors surrounding her shift and distort before she solidified a second time. "You're not flesh and blood. So what are you?" he asked.

"You are the one called Kellen?"

"Yes," he answered, hesitating as she drifted closer. He noticed she had ignored his question. "You're female?" It was almost a squeak, and he closed his mouth quickly when her fingers danced across his face.

"Why, of course," she purred, another invisible thread of warmth caressing down his cheek and neck. "You are a very lovely specimen for your kind, Kellen."

"Umm, thanks."

"It is a pity I am not allowed to have you."

Not sure if he was relieved or disappointed, he frowned. "What are you?" he asked again.

"I am Terrica."

He waited, watching as she swayed, moving sensually closer.

She looked human, moved like a human, and he was so tempted by her feminine charms, yet he knew she wasn't real. Lifting a hand, he tried to push her back, finding his hands disappeared into nothing, that the colors making her shifted. He stepped back. "Terrica," he repeated. "And what is that precisely?"

She laughed again, a hot, breathy sound, before she reached between them and tangled fingers in his long damp hair. This felt very real, and Kellen noticed that parts of her had become substantial. Tentatively he reached up and touched her hand, his fingers encountering warm, soft skin. Awed, he raised his eyes to stare into her magnificent green gaze. "Who are you?" he whispered.

"I cannot tell you that. What I can tell you is of greater importance."

"What could be more important than learning who you are? What you are? Who the other of your kind is?"

"The other?" Her brow drew down, her eyes troubled.

"A colder entity, just like you. Only this colder one seems determined to get me killed." Kellen stopped, not missing how her gaze became unfocused and how anxious her expression became.

"Then this is even more important. You must be very careful here in GarFamita. Everything is not as it seems."

Blinking at her, Kellen was about to ask what she meant, when one of the flaps opened behind him, and he felt her vanish abruptly as one of the Lancooti entered, carrying a bundle of clean clothing for him.

The servant placed the clothing on a low chair then left. Waiting for the flap to close completely, Kellen scanned the area urgently, but Terrica was gone.

* * *

Oddly disturbed by the visit, Kellen slowly followed behind his Lancooti sentinel walking down the spacious stairs, deciding not to mention anything about her visit to the others. Not that he could explain it properly anyway. He had tried to think of a way to explain her to Ryland, Lesendal, or even Sasheer, but then he would have to talk about what happened with the Deathwalker, and he didn't want to go there. They would think he was mad. Sasheer already believed he was a stubborn fool, and this would only confirm the Ranger's words.

Lost in thought, he tripped over a thick floor rug and glanced up when he heard the Lancooti sentinel mutter something unflattering about his clumsiness. Ahead, the others were already seated, while a large woman in multicolored silk robes talked with them. Numerous ferns plants and flowers dotted the room, all lit by sunlight spilling into the area from overhead vents. It looked appealing to the senses, a delightful display of hospitality, designed to relax visitors.

Standing where the sentinel left him, Kellen wondered if he was supposed to just walk forward and interrupt the discussions or wait until they had finished. He was about to back out of the room when cool fingers touched his arm. He spun around, expecting to see Terrica—but instead saw a pretty young woman. She was flesh and blood, real, and her eyes were the color of night.

Not moving for a long moment, Kellen watched as she beckoned for him to follow her out of the chamber and into an even warmer, sun-dappled room. He obliged. Here, the canvas walls were pulled back; ferns lined one wall, and flowers decorated the tables. The intoxicating perfume of the flowers was addictive and pleasing, helping him to relax, and he sank down to sit on soft cushions.

"You are one of the visitors from across the Divide?"

The female's voice was light and appealing, and Kellen found himself responding to her genuine smile. She had dark orange hair that was tied back in intricate designs. Tiny beads and slender crystals hung from her ears and clothing. Bells tinkled as she moved, as she knelt on the cushions opposite him. A very pleasant, teasing sound that lulled him. "Yes. You speak our language?" he asked, accepting the drink she pressed into his hands.

"We who work in GarFamita palace must learn."

He nodded and returned her smile.

"My name is Tontie."

"I'm Kellen."

"Kel-len," her smile grew wider as she looked him over. "Which kingdom are you from?"

Her question surprised him. "You know the Southland?"

"Oh yes. We know all the Twelve Kingdoms. We trade with you, so we must understand you. To make a good trade, you have to know the people." She tilted her head to one side, and Kellen watched with fascination as sparkling beads jingled from her ears almost hypnotically. "I cannot place your origins. You seem to fit no standard characteristics of the Twelve Kingdoms." Her smile was sweet.

Thrown by her question, Kellen raised a brow, his eyes straying to her slender neck and the strings of jewelry adorning her bodice before he coughed politely and cast a cautionary glance over at the door. Maybe it would be safer if he went and waited for the others. "My friends and I are from a few different kingdoms," he began.

"Yes, I recognized the Ihovians," Tontie said, leaning closer to him, her fingers straying against his wrist. "They all look the same. They are all tall and blond, blue green eyes, with limited imagination."

Slightly offended, Kellen was about to object when she touched his wrist again, her fingers electric. "Which is your kingdom?"

"I am Ihovian," he said.

She shook her head. "You cannot be. You are tall, and your complexion is fair enough to be Ihovian, but your hair and eyes are too dark to be remotely related to their race," she whispered. "You must be trying to trick me because I cannot place you."

"No," he assured her, "I am Ihovian."

She shook her head negatively, her smile faltering. "You are not Ihovian. Do not tease me like this."

"But I'm not teasing you. It is true. I am Ihovian," Kellen defended, feeling offended that she would persist in this line of questioning. He had to be Ihovian, because that was all he knew. All he had ever been, could ever remember.

"You lie," she insisted, her smile disappearing. "I am trained to read races; it is my specialty. Your big companion is Haonian, while the other two, as I said, are probably upper-class Ihovian nobles—"

"And Sasheer?" Kellen interjected, curious that she had left the Ranger out of her summary.

"Pardon?" She stopped and blinked at him.

"The other member of our group," Kellen clarified. "Sasheer. Which kingdom is he from?"

"He is not from the Southland. He is a Watcher," she said simply, as if he should have known that fact.

"A Watcher?" he asked, bemused. "What is a Watcher?"

She hesitated, as if weighing him up. "Are you testing me still?" She glanced over at the Lancooti sentinels near the archway. "For I know he is from the old time."

Hairs on the back of his neck rose in warning as the two of the sentinels turned toward them. Uncertain, Kellen reached for his small blade, realizing too late that it had been taken from him after his bath. *What is going on here?* Was this a trap of some sort, and if so, why had the Lancooti singled him out?

Her dark eyes narrowed further, becoming speculative. "From what land are you, Kel-len?"

He ignored her question, latching on to her last comments instead. "Are there other Watchers? Other Watchers, here in GarFamita?" he asked, looking down at her loveliness a second time but no longer tempted. She was dangerous, and suddenly he no longer felt safe within this tent city. Seeing how she reacted, he very carefully reached out with his senses and tried to read her intentions, just like he had reached out to read the rock wall in the pass and the Deathwalkers in the camp.

"Your asking that makes no sense."

A prickling of fear brushed him, and he wondered if it was his own feelings or hers. Concentrating harder on the emotion he was experiencing, he was unexpectedly engulfed in a well of confused thoughts, sensing her panic, her jumbled thoughts, even as her breathing increased. Then her thoughts became a sound in his mind.

What is he? What is his old knowledge, his strange strengths? What is his land, his kingdom? Is he part of the conspiracy? Does he know the Watchers' plans for us? Will they help us?

"Tontie, how many other Watchers are there?" he asked, shaking his head to break the connection between them. "Are there any here in GarFamita?" His voice was a hushed whisper as he grabbed her hands, holding them tightly, willing her to answer.

She gasped at the contact, her pupils dilating swiftly, her thoughts perplexed as she sagged against his side. All her vibrant energy seemed to vanish as she tried to focus her eyes on him. "What . . . ar . . . re . . . y—you?"

Touching cool fingers to her paling cheek, Kellen watched in horror as she fell against his chest, her head landing on his shoulder. Had he done this? Was she injured? He glanced up nervously at the two sentinels, but they had dismissed his presence, chatting with another flamboyantly dressed male. Exhaling in relief, he moved so he could look down into her relaxed face. She appeared to be in some sort of a daze, a trance, and he bit his lip in worry. "Tontie?"

"You smell so powerful, so addictive . . ."

Frowning harder, he touched her chin, tilting her face upward. "Tontie, this is very important. What is a Watcher?"

"The preservers of life."

Filing that away, he questioned her further. "Are there any other Watchers here, besides Sasheer?"

"Only one."

"And who is that?"

"Dalzere."

Realizing she had passed out, Kellen carefully lowered her down onto the soft seat and got up, straightening his borrowed clothing, and glanced around. She appeared to be asleep but would not stay that way for long; he was sure, and he was worried what would happen when she awoke. Obviously she had wanted something specific from him and had not succeeded in getting it. What unnerved him was what would happen when she reported her failure to her superiors.

There was also the unsettling fact of *what* he had done to her and *how* he had done it. He was starting to dread this ability, scared now to mention it to any of the others, but it seemed to be getting worse. Stronger. Yet Sasheer had offered him help. But help to do what?

Refusing to think about it, Kellen concentrated on the only two points that were clear in his mind: first, that he had been warned by Terrica, and second, that this Dalzere—Sasheer's friend—was here. Maybe he was a prisoner? Maybe it was a trap set by Kalern, and they were all doomed?

Looking at the landing below, he saw Salimen standing off to one side, and he hurried down to the bowman's side, avoiding the two sentinels.

"Kellen! I was beginning to think we had lost you," Salimen said.

"No." He shook his head, still shocked by what had happened. "And don't even to think about leaving me here when you leave. This place gives me the creeps."

With one brow going up, Salimen considered him seriously. "We wouldn't leave you."

"Salimen," Kellen licked his lips and lowered his voice, "Dalzere's here somewhere."

"Are you sure?" The blond's eyes widened. "Where did you hear that from?"

"One of the women upstairs," Kellen said evasively. "Do you think he is a prisoner?"

The other gave a short laugh. "Kell, he is a Drow." Salimen laid an arm across Kellen's shoulder and leaned in closer. "Nothing can harm a Drow except a beheading," he paused, doubt coming into his voice. "Even then I've heard stories which say that not even a beheading can kill a Drow." His smile became reassuring. "Besides, if Dalzere is here, then Sasheer probably knows, so don't worry."

"Salimen, what am I?" Kellen found himself asking all of a sudden. The bowman gave him a puzzled look, and he cast his eyes down apprehensively. "It's just that one of these Lancooti told me that with my coloring I can't be Ihovian."

"What would they know?" Salimen asked then stopped, seeing Kellen's fearful gaze.

Risking another look up, Kellen met Salimen's clear light blue eyes. There was no deceit or mockery in their depths as Salimen cupped his cheek.

"You are Ihovian, Kellen, in every way that counts. In honor and loyalty. And I am proud to have you as a kinsman. Never forget that," Salimen ended with a smile, his lips curving up mischievously. "Now come," he urged. "I hate official meetings, and I hear there is a thriving market down by the west wall. I think we should investigate."

CHAPTER TEN

Following Salimen through the labyrinth-like markets, Kellen found that the stalls and various racks wound all around the inside wall of the city. Pockets of business being transacted, and lively haggling could be heard echoing between the thick, canvassed walls. And to his surprise, Kellen discovered that this was indeed a temporary city, despite its seemingly solid foundations. Everything was movable, and he gasped more than once at how often different stallholders quarreled, only to pack all their belongings and move to another section in the noisy tract of markets.

He was told that GarFamita was the largest Lancooti city, and that the Famita tribe was the most respected, feared, and wealthy tribe in the area. Only the Solanndite tribe who inhabited the western edge of the Sandlands was considered a worthy adversary by the many who lived and affiliated themselves with the Famita. Talkative stall owners told them that if war were to descend on the Sandlands, it would be the untrustworthy Solanndites who would disgrace the tribes by inviting Kalern's forces in.

This had surprised Kellen, particularly since the Lancooti talked of Kalern so openly. The name had not even been whispered in Ihova.

"Is Kalern in the Sandlands at present?" Salimen asked softly. He kept his eyes purposely down while he pretended to examine a yard of beautifully crafted fabric. The stallholder seemed to falter then shrug.

"That was woven by the maidens from Javousa, a talented tribe renowned for such intricate designs. Five gold coins for you," the Lancooti said.

Salimen looked up at that and glared at the stallholder, and Kellen felt sure he was about to argue. Holding his breath, Kellen let his eyes go from the bland face of the Lancooti to Salimen's disgruntled expression, then to his amazement, the Ihovian took out his coin bag and carefully counted out the five pieces named. "Five. White gold," Salimen stressed, just baring his teeth in false friendliness. "For the maidens of Javousa."

"You have exquisite taste for a southerner," the Lancooti assured him, rolling the fabric swiftly and presenting it with a flourish. Then he stepped closer, his words hushed, and Kellen had to strain to hear.

"The salt pits have been closed to all, and I hear that the Bluff has fallen to the Black Guard. All is not as it seems, my southern friend." Then the Lancooti was moving away, calling out to other buyers, bartering his goods, and ignoring them as if they were invisible.

Stunned, Kellen blinked around at the magnificent colors, hearing the rhythmic sound of bells and music and a sea of chaotic voices that drowned out clear thinking. He jumped as Salimen touched his shoulder and indicating they should leave. He didn't argue, casting one last glance at the markets before following Salimen back to the palace.

*   *   *

Salimen said nothing to him during the long walk back to the massive royal house, and Kellen didn't offer any question, just glad when they entered the tranquil courtyard. Here the silence was absolute, like being in a different world to the madness outside in the market area. Here even the Lancooti sentinels looked drab compared to their numerous tribesmen outside the palace walls.

Climbing the immaculate staircase that led up to the audience halls, Kellen was relieved to see his friends were still there. He trailed Salimen as they went to the long table, and Kellen took the seat offered next to the Ryland. Scanning the heavy-laden table, Kellen's nose picked out the tasty aromas of the food being served, and his stomach growled.

"What's happening, Ryland?" he asked as he accepted a plate of food gratefully.

"Where have you been?" Ryland returned, genuinely pleased to see him. "I was starting to worry, lad."

"Oh, Sal took me around the markets," he shrugged.

"Spying, was he?"

Kellen hid his grin, shrugging again and sampling the food before him. He was starving. "So what's happening? I hope we are not staying here too long."

"No," Ryland rubbed his beard as he gazed over at the bowman, noting how Salimen was talking quietly with Lesendal. "According to Lasdajar, it seems the Lancooti as a nation are neutral in the war, trading with both sides, but would still prefer it if we left quietly and quickly. They have even offered us a tracker to take us safely through the dunes and across the grasslands into Engleton."

"Are we going?"

"I would assume so."

Digesting that, Kellen stopped eating as another worry occurred to him. "Do you think this tracker can be trusted?" he asked, remembering the young girl called Tontie and how she had tried to get information out of him.

"Sasheer knows of him, but whether that means we can trust him, I do not know, lad."

Being reminded of the Ranger, Kellen glanced around for the man in question. Sasheer was sitting further down the table with an older woman, the pair deep in conversation. "Ryland, how long have you known Sasheer?"

The bigger man let out a loud breath, his eyes darkening as he considered the question. "Probably for about ten years. Why do you ask?"

"It's just that I heard one of the Lancooti call him a Watcher, and I thought you might know what that is."

Stroking his beard in thought, Ryland scowled, his eyes getting that faraway look. "A Watcher... now where have I heard that before?"

"You know what that is?" Kellen interrupted excitedly.

"No, but it sounds vaguely familiar for some reason."

Sitting back in disappointment, Kellen again chanced a look up at the mysterious man. "I also heard that Dalzere was here in GarFamita."

"Huh!" Ryland snorted. "Salimen has been spying," he leant down closer. "The Drow apparently was here, lad, but now he is gone."

"Gone where?"

"To Engleton. Or so Lasdajar told us."

"But why? What's in Engleton?"

"I do not know, but I feel we are going to find out."

* * *

Waking the next morning before the sun had even graced the dunes with its golden glow, Kellen pulled on his clean clothing. Searching around for his woven tunic, he discovered it was missing, so he had to make do with one of the paler leather tunics left out for him by the invisible Lancooti servants. Stretching sore limbs, he noticed how honed his muscles had become from all the traveling, and he grinned. He had to admit that he was starting to look more like his older brother everyday, and he stopped that thought, remembering Wyran was dead. Killed by the war. By Kalern's forces. Closing his eyes, he tried not to think about Wyran, and turned as Ryland called him a second time.

Struggling into his boots, he gathered his few belongings, shoving them into a bag before leaving the canvassed alcove to find his friends. He found a sentinel waiting for him outside his small sleeping alcove, and he silently followed the guard to the stables at the rear of the massive palace area. The others greeted him with somber smiles.

"Good, we are all here now," Sasheer said as he looked around the group. "This is Peleyia, and he has kindly consented to guide us safely through the dunes which lead to Engleton seaport. Lasdajar has loaned us these horses, so saddle up. I would like to get to the coast as quickly as possible."

Kellen eyed off their new guide and rolled his eyes. The Lancooti was slender, exotically decorated in layers of delicate fabric and strips of leather all sewn together into a multicolored traveling outfit. The most sedate thing about this guide was his hair. It was long and one color, a pale lavender, with only a few beads dangling down his back. *He's another Tontie,* Kellen thought despairingly. This guide also looked young, very young as he gave a cocky grin before smoothly swinging up into his saddle. *And overconfident,* Kellen added silently to his list of complaints, not wanting to like or trust the Lancooti.

Shaking his head, he then looked at his horse, noting that the animal was staring back at him, and not with much confidence or liking either. *Terrific.* He could tell that this was going to be a very unpleasant trip.

* * *

By early evening, Kellen was hoping they would have either reached the seaport or found another canvassed city, as his muscles protested the abuse of the long ride. Instead they were surrounded by a barren wilderness of sand dunes and sporadic patches of tough salt grass. Resigned to a cold night, he had helped Ryland set up camp in a sheltered gully, assisting Salimen to raise the tents given them by Lasdajar.

After dinner, he lifted his eyes to the darkening sky and noted the few faint stars, which had already appeared. He cast a glance over at the silent Lancooti guide, deciding to break the ice and speak with him. *I shouldn't be so distrustful,* he decided. *Maybe not all Lancooti are like Tontie.* Standing, he stretched and then hobbled with care over to the guide, ignoring Sasheer as the other watched him in curiosity and amusement.

He sat slowly opposite the Lancooti and kept silent, just observing as the young tracker skillfully wove and braided six narrow lengths of toughened leather strands.

"What is that for?" he asked after a while, impressed as the other nimbly knotted the ends off.

"Precaution. I hate going anywhere without a strong rope. You never know when a quick escape might be needed."

The Lancooti's voice was accented and light. Accepting the explanation, Kellen saw Salimen glance over at him in silent warning, before he moved away to take his turn at watch.

"You're Kellen, aren't you?"

Looking up, Kellen nodded. He regarded the brief, friendly smile that graced the Lancooti's mouth and decided to ignore Salimen's cautious warning and talk to this guide, and see if there was any information he could learn. "I don't know much about your kingdom in the Sandlands, but how far is it to Engleton?"

The Lancooti gave him a perceptive smile, his face lighting up in the firelight as he pushed hair behind one ear. "You are not used to riding, are you?" The Lancooti reached into one of his packs and pulled out a pouch. "Here, rub this into your sore muscles. It will ease some of the ache."

"Umm, thanks," Kellen said, surprised by the offer as he accepted the small pouch. Had the man read his feelings, like Tontie had tried to do? Or had the man simply seen he was a poor rider?

"If the weather holds, it will take maybe three more days of steady riding to cross the plains," the Lancooti said. "Also, on this side of the Divide, we do not think of ourselves as a kingdom. There is too much bickering between the tribes for that to become reality."

"I thought you were at peace with each other, that Lasdajar has ruled the Sandlands for a long time."

"She has, but that does not stop the fighting. Many do not always agree with the Famita's decisions."

"And you are of the Famita tribe?"

"No," the Lancooti's fringe fell into his eyes as he shook his head, his smile suddenly blinding. "I am of the Welconin tribe. We are further east of here."

"So how come you work for the Famita?" Kellen asked, starting to like this man's openness despite himself.

"I was bonded to her tribe as payment for a service."

"They can do that?" Kellen asked, shocked.

"When they have the silver and gold, they can do anything."

"So . . . so when will you go home?"

"When I have either collected enough silver to pay off the debt, or when the Famita tribe is defeated in war." The Lancooti looked sideways at Kellen. "With either plan, I am not holding my breath."

Realizing that he still knew so little about this strange culture, Kellen ventured another question: "So how much will you earn for taking us safely to Engleton?"

"Nothing."

"Nothing! Then how can you even start to save to buy back your freedom?" Horrified, Kellen wondered how anyone could live like this.

The guide only chuckled as he sat cross-legged. Slowly, he wound up the leather rope he had just made, tying it to his pack. "There are other alternatives."

"Like what?"

"Thievery for instance."

"You steal?" The idea was incredulous.

"I am very good at it."

"You would have to be," Kellen cut back. "Where I come from, to steal and be caught means death."

The Lancooti shrugged unconcerned. "It is the same here. The penalty adds a sort of excitement and challenge to the risk."

Not believing this, Kellen stared openmouthed at the young guide, seeing the amused smile that graced the Lancooti's thin lips. Despite his initial feeling, he found he was starting to grin also. "So why are you taking us to Engleton if you are not going to get paid?"

"I owe Sasheer a favor," the Lancooti turned a little more toward Kellen as he settled backward to lean against his pack, "and even if I didn't, I would jump at the chance of getting out of GarFamita for even a few days."

"Everything is just so different over here to what I am used to," Kellen said, amazed that so vibrant a culture could also be so restrictive. "Do you know that in my home of Ihova, it has rained nonstop for six months, and that when we entered the Divide, it was snowing?"

"If it rained that much here then GarFamita would be washed out to sea." The Lancooti's face brightened. "Now that would be a pleasant sight!"

Unable to stop his smile, Kellen laughed softly as the other laughed also. Suddenly, he realized how much he had missed just talking with someone his own age. Someone who was not of royalty, who treated him equally and not like an inexperienced child. Regardless of their obvious cultural differences, he needed a friend, and so he grinned at the Lancooti, glad when the guide returned the grin. "Can I call you Peleyia?"

"Please. Though my friends call me Pel."

"And mine used to call me Kell," he offered, extending a hand and waiting until the Lancooti took it and shook it. "Now, what can you tell me about Engleton seaport?"

* * *

Holding down the hat, which Peleyia had given him the morning before, Kellen scanned the grasslands ahead of them. The wind had picked up strongly, doubling the long salt grass over, as the clouds overhead raced, promising a vicious storm. He tightened his hold on the reigns, feeling the horse under him tremble, and he glanced around at the other members of the company. Peleyia had predicted earlier that they would be hit with a storm before sunset, only Kellen had not expected anything like this—from scorching, hot days to thunder and stormy afternoons. At present, Peleyia was out with Salimen, searching for a sand cave in which they could shelter for the night, and he hoped they were successful before the storm rolled down on top of them all.

Feeling a movement beside him, he turned, recognizing Sasheer's familiar aura before the other pulled his protective cape aside and nudged his agitated mount closer.

"I have noticed that you and Peleyia are getting on very well."

"So?" His defenses rose swiftly, and Kellen looked warily at the Ranger. Sasheer had hardly spoken two words to him since they had met the Lancooti.

"Just be careful; and don't get too involved in one of his impractical side adventures."

"Like what?" Kellen knew he sounded sullen but could not help himself. Sasheer just brought out the worst in him.

"Kellen, don't make me spell this out."

"He's my friend!" he protested, gripping his cloak tighter as a gust of wind hit them in savage gusts.

"I am not saying he can't be. Only that you keep some common sense when we enter Engleton. It is a dangerous place, and I would prefer it if you came out of the seaport alive and in one piece." Sasheer pinned the younger man with a very serious look. "Peleyia is wild, and I just want you to stop and think before you do anything rash. Understood?"

Giving a curt nod, Kellen looked away.

"And while we are discussing the subject of common sense and courtesy—next time you feel the urge to flex your mental muscles, please show a bit more decorum. I had a hard time explaining that young girl's condition to Lasdajar," Sasheer reprimanded.

Feeling his cheeks darken in color, Kellen squirmed in his saddle before meeting the dark blue gaze still pinned on him. "I didn't do anything. Well, not intentionally . . ."

"Your wide-eyed innocence might devastate the farm girls, Kellen, but it has no effect on me," Sasheer said then turned away.

"But I didn't do anything!" Kellen repeated louder. The injustice of Sasheer's statement resurrected all his smoldering anger and confusion over the last few months' chaotic events.

"You have a Gift, and until you acknowledge the fact and seek out guidance, I am unable to help you."

"And who says I want your help?" he cut back, gripping his reins fiercely as he glared at the Ranger. It seemed to have no effect as Sasheer only gave him a reproving look. "How can I trust you when I don't even know who or what you are?"

"Kellen!"

Ignoring the sting of the wind, Kellen challenged Sasheer to answer, even as a small voice inside his mind shrieked a warning about this type of suicidal behavior. After all, Sasheer was dangerous; that much he had worked out. Was he mad for deliberately wanting to provoke this man? "I must be crazy to listen to you, when you have done nothing for me, or Lesendal and Ihova! You're just playing with us, making us follow a trail to this imaginary creature you've invented for your own amusement!"

"Ah, progress at last." Sasheer raised a knowing brow, his eyes hardening. "You are now at least angry, and not hiding behind your normal gloomy face of self-pity."

Locking his jaw, Kellen felt the familiar build of heat flash up into his chest, suffocating him as he battled to control it, scared suddenly by its intensity. His fear increased the build of power and heat, and he knew that he had little chance stopping the dangerous curl of energy from escaping as he stared at Sasheer. Just as he'd had no chance of stopping the flare of energy that had killed the Hoindrite commander or the Deathwalker—and he shuddered. Sasheer was right; he was unstable, and in that instant, he wanted to lash out, to strike at the man who was sitting so calmly next to him and who so easily denounced his life and feelings. But deep down he knew Sasheer was not to blame; deep down he knew it was his own insecurities and his own fear of the unknown that were the problem.

Sucking in a ragged breath, he tried to push the heat away, but it refused to go, curling tighter in his chest and gut. Just one touch, one wrong word . . . his world narrowed to a blade of pure heat and rage, and he barely noticed the storm around him as reality faded. Insecurity plagued him; he had lost control of everything and was running toward an enemy he didn't understand, trapped in the company of men who terrified him.

He fought to breath, feeling the burning tingle of energy spread from his chest to rush down his arms and legs. He was consumed by the sensual heat, by the heady power, and he glanced fearfully down at his fingers, feeling them swell with liquid fire. His skin wanted to burst open, yet his hands looked exactly the same, unchanged by the volatile force gathering inside him. Then he caught sight of Sasheer reaching over to touch him, and he wanted to scream a warning. *No!* He did not want to be responsible for this man's death, *no,* but he could not move, could not speak, and he could only stared wide-eyed at Sasheer. The Ranger was pulling off a leather glove, then those long pale fingers were gripping his shaking hands hard, almost bruising them, and Kellen closed his eyes in panic and *waited, waited,* only nothing happened. Nothing at all for a long moment, and then abruptly, the painful buildup of power was bleeding away, vanishing out of his body, leaving only a bone-deep exhaustion. Stunned, he lifted heavy lids and stared at Sasheer, meeting the other man's very bright and very angry glare.

"You are out of control." The words were hissed in a controlled rage. "You either accept my help, or I will be forced to take steps to bind you. I don't really want to do that, but you are giving me little choice."

Unable to protest, he sucked in a ragged breath, battling a mind-numbing lethargy that left him vulnerable to Sasheer's anger. Then he started to tremble from reaction, even his teeth chattering. "Wwwhat are yyyou?"

"I have already told you; I am your friend," Sasheer said, his expression far from friendly.

Tears stung his eyes, and he looked down at Sasheer's hand, feeling those long fingers embrace his icy skin so warmly. Despite the cold words, Sasheer's touch offered a strange comfort. Then Sasheer squeezed his hand, and Kellen sighed, feeling as if all his defiance was suddenly crushed out of him. "I don't understand any of this," he said honestly. "I never asked for it, and I don't want it."

Sasheer edged his horse a little closer, and the big roan neighed unhappily. "Kellen, sometimes it is not possible to choose your own destiny, no matter how unfair things seem to be."

"But why me?" he almost sobbed. "Have I done something so terrible that I now need to be punished?"

If anything, Sasheer's expression softened, becoming sympathetic as a small smile played across his mouth, and his eyes reflected his understanding of Kellen's innate horror and fear. "This ability of yours is as much a part of you as your stubbornness. It permeates your entire being."

Not knowing how to cope with this almost-human-appearing Sasheer, Kellen swept his gaze away, turning his face up into the wind, feeling the first heavy drops of rain caress his cheeks. He was in a void now, caught between acceptance of what Sasheer offered so silently, and regret over what he used to be. But in that instant, he felt no fear; then Sasheer was removing his hand, his warmth, leaving him bereaved, and he was jolted back to reality. He blinked and saw Lesendal turn his horse and ride back to them.

"We have to get out of this wind," Lesendal shouted as he steadied his horse and gestured to the storm front approaching.

Agreeing, Sasheer checked Ryland's position behind before briefly glancing one final time at Kellen. Then he was leading them down the dunes, flowing the path Salimen and Peleyia had taken earlier.

Numbly, Kellen got his horse moving, his mind so full of conflicting thoughts. What had just happened? Was it possible that Sasheer could tap into his emotions and absorb this wild energy?

The rain started to fall harder, and then it was pelting down on them as small pieces of hail swept in with the destructive wind. Just managing to control his agitated horse, Kellen was grateful when Salimen abruptly loomed before them, waving them over. Battling with the reins, he got the animal moving, ducking for cover when the hailstones increased in size. So this was what Peleyia had meant by desert storms. Loud thunder cracked overhead, and lightning arced down, hitting the dunes behind them while the wind whipped up sharp sand gusts.

The others around him halted and dismounted, and Kellen reluctantly did the same. He caught a glimpse of Peleyia's pale features in a lightning flash as the Lancooti beckoned them into a narrow cave mouth.

Breathing a sigh of relief when he escaped the savage storm, Kellen pulled his obstinate horse further inside the cave before he leaned heavily against a sandy wall. Ryland was the last inside the narrow entranceway, his voice angry as he swore choice phrases, slapping his stubborn horse on the rump to move it impatiently toward the back of the dark cavern.

"Just lovely!" Ryland cursed again. "Sasheer, I think I would rather face Kalern himself, and all his vile Deathwalkers, than a storm I cannot fight!"

CHAPTER ELEVEN

Two days later, they entered Engleton. The seaport was alive with activity as people from all different lands busily moved down the numerous streets and alleyways. Kellen had never seen anything like it, had never imagined that a city could be so packed with people of all different cultures. Carts, horses, dogs, and people moved either side of the street.

Some of the ladies were dressed in the most fashionable designs, hitching their skirts up over dusty steps outside the numerous shops that lined the right side of the street. Then the clientele further on changed, and gone were the bright colors, to be replaced by casually dressed farmers and boisterous sailors.

The stout dwellings were made out of a combination of wood and stone, and they all faced the sea, with peculiar wooden decks hanging out over the streets and laneways. On all these decks hung lanterns and signs, welcoming customers, their cramped overhangs teeming with noisy activity.

Rowdy shouting and music drew his attention, and Kellen watched, astounded, as a brawl spilled out of one establishment into the street, halting traffic, before the local law enforcement, who looked no better than the sparring men, arrived and separated the drunken party.

Ryland was watching with a grin plastered across his face as Salimen pointed out something else. Across the main street, a group of skinny boys were eyeing them off with interest, until one spotted the Lancooti and gasped before scrambling away.

"Not a good sign," Salimen commented, giving the lavender-haired Lancooti a questioning glance.

"Are you in any particular trouble at the moment, here in

Engleton?" Sasheer asked idly, cursing when he saw Ryland loosen his sword.

"Not . . . really," Peleyia said.

"Oh, that sounds encouraging," Salimen muttered. Kellen watched him glancing around for an escape route, seeing Lesendal do the same.

"I could do with a good fight," Ryland ventured, drawing his sword and resting it across his pommel, so it was in clear sight of all the ruffians.

"Put that thing away. They are not going to challenge us," Sasheer said in exasperation. "This place is a breeding ground for criminals, not warriors."

"Pity."

"So what do we do now?" Lesendal asked.

"Find a place to stay then look around."

"For what?" Salimen asked, giving the Ranger a curious look.

"Information."

"Information?" Lesendal repeated curiously.

"Everything that happens in the Southland and across the White Sea ends up here, eventually, and is sorted," Sasheer said. "All types of gossip, truth, and rumors can be purchased, for a price. For instance, if you ask the right questions, I bet we could find out what King Nizzizanon of Vernonz had for breakfast last week."

"You're not serious," Lesendal said in a shocked voice.

"Very. It is this sort of merchandise which makes Engleton so valuable. Probably why Kalern has left the city alone." A cynical smile crossed Sasheer's face.

Realization dawned on the prince's face, and he swept his eyes around the area a second time. "You think he has spies here?"

"Undoubtedly," Sasheer nodded, slowing his mount to a sedate walk as they approached the hectic seafront marketplace. "I imagine this is how he learns the secrets of the Twelve Kingdoms."

"If that is the case, do you think it is wise to be seen so openly? Lesendal might be recognized," Ryland added, drawing his horse level with the prince's.

"We were probably identified before we entered the gates," Sasheer said, unconcerned.

"So what do we do now?" the prince asked.

"Find accommodation," Sasheer repeated. "Then see what information we can glean for ourselves." He grinned then. "Two can play this game."

"How about that inn over there?" Peleyia pointed to a dark red building that had stables around the back. "It has a respectable name."

"No," Sasheer shook his head. "I know a better place. Follow me."

* * *

Handing over the reins of his horse to the scruffy-looking boy who manned the stables, Kellen trailed behind Lesendal as they entered the rundown inn. Once through the old wooden doors, the aroma of old cooking, stale smoke, and beer assaulted his senses, and Kellen watched Sasheer give Salimen silver coins and direct him to purchase rooms for the night. The interior of the inn was dark, and Kellen decided not to look too closely at the furnishings or walls as he silently followed the others up the creaking stairs.

"This is the best you can do?" Lesendal accused, eyeing the room Salimen had secured for them and then glaring at Sasheer in distrust. He glanced around the large room, not missing the holes in the threadbare carpet, or the paint peeling on the walls. Nor the thin mattresses on the wooden bunks, or sparse pillows. "I think Pel had a better suggestion earlier."

"This is more secluded. The residents of this section ask fewer questions." Sasheer sat down on the side of one bunk and tested the straw mattress. "Trust me; we will be better off here."

Begrudgingly accepting that, Lesendal paced across the thin carpet to the single window. He pushed the curtain aside and scanned the road outside.

"So what now?" Ryland asked.

"I suggest that Lesendal, Salimen, and I go for a look around.

If there is any news available concerning royal prisoners from the kingdoms, then we will find it. Also, I would like to find out what Kalern is up to. And what the Dwarves are doing in Engleton."

"Yes," Salimen nodded. "I've never heard of them ever leaving the Northlands before."

"Occasionally they will, but it is rare to find them so openly in the south," Sasheer said.

"And what of me and the lads?" Ryland asked.

"I would like you to keep watch downstairs and let me know if anything suspicious happens," Sasheer said, eyeing Ryland as the big man checked his blade.

"Like what?"

"Any unwarranted interest in our arrival," Sasheer elaborated before turning to face Kellen and Peleyia. "You both stay here and keep out of sight."

"What of your friend Dalzere," Kellen ventured. "Maybe we could look for him?"

"No, he will find us," Sasheer said, his eyes darkening in thought. Then he shook his head to dismiss further questions and went to join Lesendal at the window, scanning the area outside. "It will be dark soon. We had best wait until then."

* * *

Left alone when the others silently filed out, Kellen felt abandoned even as Ryland ruffled his hair in affection before closing the door. Sighing, he collapsed down onto one of the hard beds.

"So what was all that about?" Peleyia asked, raising a curious brow and glancing over at Kellen's sprawled frame.

"Lesendal's trying to find his sister," Kellen said indifferently. "She was supposedly taken by Jorean's forces in Ihova a few months ago."

"Then she's probably dead."

"Maybe. Sasheer thinks she might be alive because she is a princess."

Peleyia whistled through his teeth. "A princess? That would mean Lesendal's—"

"Heir to the Ihovian throne," Kellen confirmed.

"I didn't recognize him or his name," Peleyia said, frowning.

"He's the youngest son. I think." Kellen shrugged, trying to remember what Ryland had told him about Ihova's royal family. It seemed too long ago. In another world.

"So who is Salimen?"

"His cousin, or so they say. From what I've heard, he was engaged to Lesendal's sister."

A slow smile graced the Lancooti's mouth. "Do you know how much we could get for this type of information?" His eyes lit up dangerously. "We'd make a killing!"

"Pel . . ." Kellen admonished, even as his smile grew.

"And what about the Haonian? Ryland? Is he royalty as well?"

"I don't really know." Leaning up on his elbows, Kellen eyed his friend. "How long have you known Sasheer?"

"Most of my life. Why?"

"He must have been young when you meet him."

Peleyia shrugged and came to sit beside Kellen on the lumpy mattress. "Yes and no," he said then shrugged again. "I have never seen him change; he always looks the same."

"But that's not possible."

"Who is to say what is and isn't possible in this world?" the Lancooti asked. "I have seen many things and have come to learn that anything is conceivable."

Digesting that, Kellen licked his lips in speculation. He remembered Sasheer had said the same to Salimen. "Do you know of this Dalzere that Sasheer speaks of?"

"The Drow?" The Lancooti asked, raising a brow. "Yes, I have seen him and know who he is. But—" he hesitated, his eyes losing focus, "but I have never gotten close enough to speak with him."

"What's he like?" Kellen asked as he pushed himself further up the bed, his mind supplying him with ghoulish images. Every story he had heard always described the Drow as deathlike creatures. Dark and ugly, filthy, with deformed limbs, grotesque features and foul breath. He found it strange to think that a man like Sasheer would travel with such a vile creature. The idea fascinated and appalled him, yet he wanted to learn as much as he could about this Drow, and about Sasheer. "I bet he's ugly."

"Who? Dalzere?" Peleyia questioned, seeing Kellen nod. Licking his lips, Peleyia considered his answer. "He's just like any other Elf, except for his skin color, which is a deep, opalescent ebony. He's tall, with long jet-black hair to his waist, and I think his reputation is enhanced by the fact that he refuses to wear anything but black." Peleyia shrugged again, an impish smile showing through. "I guess his appearance is a statement or challenge." He paused, his eyebrows drawing down. "From what I can remember, his most striking feature is his eyes. They are amber. Like one of those dune cats you see at the edge of the Divide."

Enthralled, Kellen wondered if they would ever catch up with this illusive creature. "He must be deadly—"

"Fast with his hands, or so I've heard," Peleyia assured, his smile easy. "You think Dalzere is in Engleton?"

"That's what Sasheer believes," Kellen replied.

"Really?"

"Ah-huh," Kell nodded. "I heard it mentioned when we were in GarFamita."

"Why don't *we* go find him?" Peleyia suggested. He gave a mischievous grin. "We could look around and see if there is any news of him in the taverns."

"But Sasheer said—"

"Sasheer won't be back for hours, and I, for one, will die of boredom if I don't get out of this stuffy room. Besides, I know a few tricks which will keep us out of trouble." Peleyia leaned forward and peered at Kellen in challenge, his tone becoming persuasive. "That's if you're game?"

Feeling his pulse start to quicken in excitement, Kellen found himself returning the smile as Peleyia levered himself off the bed. "But what about Ryland?"

"He'll never know we are gone. I promise." Peleyia's grin widened even more. "We'll go out the window." Saying that, the

Lancooti extinguished the candles and moved to the long window, carefully drawing back the old curtain to look out into the evening darkness. "Come on. This will be fun."

* * *

Hiding in the shadows as the five drunken pirates swaggered past them; Kellen was acutely reminded of his last foolhardy adventure with Bains. Only that adventure had ended in—*no*, he wasn't going to think about that. Not now.

"Come on," Peleyia stopped and scowled, looking closely at Kellen. "You all right?"

"Fine," Kellen said, refusing to think about the disastrous past. Peleyia was not Bains, and as far as he knew, there were no Black Guard in Engleton.

"Then follow me."

The words were a whisper of sound in his ear only, as Peleyia's cool fingers touched his shoulder. Crouching low, Kellen imitated his friend's movements as they skirted the outside of the crowded, noisy, and rowdy tavern. Peleyia paused at the swing doors then stood upright and boldly entered.

Following the Lancooti's example, Kellen squinted through the haze of smoke, eyeing the crowd, mesmerized by the vibrancy inside the tavern, reveling in the sight. He had never seen such crudeness and appeal, and he blinked in awe as a bottle was smashed over a man's head. The drunkard staggered toward them before two other men joined in the fight. A lady squealed, her blouse being torn to expose an ample breast, and Kellen felt his eyes widen even more. But far from being upset, the lady then proceeded to join the fight.

"Kell?"

Turning, he saw Peleyia motion him over as the fight escalated, and he ducked behind old stairs, feeling the Lancooti squeeze in next to him.

"I have an acquaintance over there who has agreed, reluctantly, to meet with us. So stay low and follow me," Peleyia instructed, tugging on his tunic and dragging him against the wall past an overturned table.

Before Kellen could protest, the lean Lancooti was agilely sidestepping brawlers as he weaved across the chaotic room. Taking a deep breath, Kellen followed. He got three steps before slipping on the wet floor and landing on his behind. He had to scramble out of the way of two fighters, crawling between the agitated men and managing to reach the safety of the counter near the bar. He climbed to his feet and searched out Peleyia, determined to keep up with his surefooted friend.

Untangling himself from yet another overinebriated reveler, Kellen eventually reached the back of the room beside the open fire pit and found Peleyia already deep in conversation with a plump, filthy-looking woman. She stopped midsentence and eyed him up and down.

"It's all right; he's with me," Peleyia assured her.

"I don't know if I can trust you anymore, Pel. There have been some very nasty characters putting out money for information about your activities."

"It's nothing," he dismissed.

"I don't like you hunting me down either, especially with that dog, Haron, in town. Do you know what he will do to me if you're caught here?"

"Carley, Carley, have I ever been caught? No—so just relax," Peleyia soothed. "I just need some information urgently, then I'll be gone."

"And how will you pay?" Despite her protests, Carley's expression hardened.

"The usual way, only I'll need a little time."

"Pel, as good as you are, I'll need more than just your persuasive words this time." Her gaze switched to Kellen. "What of the pretty one? Is he for sale?"

Covering his smile, Peleyia placed a hand on Kellen's arm to stop his protest. He shook his head negatively. "No. He's with me."

"Ah," she breathed, her eyes lighting up in understanding.

"Carley, I need to know if a certain distinctive westerner has been seen in town recently."

"Dark and deadly?"

"Sounds like him," he smiled appealingly, his light eyes darting up to survey the room.

"I don't know," she started, her gaze centering on him before it encompassed Kellen again. "Where are you from, lad?"

"Carley . . ." Peleyia warned. "We don't have time for games."

"I have to get something out of this, you little sand rat, and you never know what an easterner like him might know."

Startled by her assessment, Kellen blinked. *Easterner?* Yet she sounded so confident.

"He knows nothing," Peleyia cut in, distracting her by stepping closer and whispering in her ear. "I have heard that the Solanndites might have signed with Kalern."

"Old news," she quipped then sighed. She reached out and stroked Peleyia's smooth cheek with the back of her fingers. "What I wouldn't give to be young again."

The general noise of fighting around them was broken when the Engleton security force invaded the place to arrest the fighters. People scattered everywhere; windows thrown open, and bodies trampled.

Getting crushed in the mad rush, Kellen just managed to grab Peleyia before they could be separated, finding himself plastered against the other's back as they fell through a broken door into a side alley. The woman Carley was issuing orders to three other men before turning back to them.

"I'd hide that shapely rear of yours if I were you, Pel, and take lover boy with you." Bending down swiftly, she gave him a kiss full on the lips. "Go buy a drink in the Scholes bar," she breathed and then was gone.

Getting up, Kellen scowled and knew he was blushing as he glared after her. "What did she mean by that comment?" he demanded.

"People always think the worst of me," Peleyia grinned impishly, looking far from upset. "Don't let it worry you. Now come on," he dismissed as he hooked a finger in the other's belt and hastily got them out of there.

Half an hour later, they were outside another noisy tavern. Peering at the sign that was hanging only by one hook and swinging in the night breeze, Kellen shook his head, not wanting to get any closer to the unsavory place.

"Carley said the Drow was here," Peleyia explained.

"I didn't hear her say that."

"That's because you weren't listening."

"Pel . . ."

"What?"

"I have a bad feeling about this," Kellen said, shivering. He glanced around, hearing a hissed moan in the darkness behind him, and prayed it was just the wind.

"There is nothing to worry about."

"How do you know?" Kellen asked, starting to wish that they had stayed in the room.

"I just do. Trust me."

"But, Pel, I think—"

"Shh," Peleyia raised a finger to his lips, his smile persuasive. "We are not going in the tavern. Just to the back to see Dedrea. She works in the kitchens and will be able to tell us who is in the tavern." He grinned again. "So don't think, just move."

Rounding a corner, they entered a back alley that ran parallel with the tavern. Rubbish littered the ground, and the smell of rotting food even overpowered the scent of fish from the markets and docks. Kellen raised a hand to cover his nose, gagging on the smell, and almost ran into Peleyia when the Lancooti stopped dead in his tracks. "Pel?" he asked, peering over his friend's shoulder to see six men abruptly materialize out of the shadows.

Kellen instinctively took a step backward and froze, becoming aware of a new danger—an invisible danger. Icy fingers caressed him as cold hatred washed down his spine with loving familiarity— and he sucked in a sharp breath. He closed his eyes, knowing what it was and not surprised when the creature's mocking laughter filled his ears. *Oh bright stars!* He should have known, should have heeded his instincts.

He battled to calm his breathing and opened his eyes, feeling layers of emotions feather down to smother him. The entity deliberately dulled his responses, slowed time, and he wanted to scream, needing to warn Peleyia. He had a bad feeling in the pit of his stomach that heralded danger and death, and he stared at the Lancooti, so sure that this evil creature was about to take Peleyia from him just as it had taken Bains.

No! He tried to get the word out but failed. He felt the creature's gloating anger curl around him, and he wished with all his heart that Terrica would appear and balance out the darkness so he could fight back. But he remained alone and isolated within the evil entity's world of blackness and silence.

He tried to order his thinking, pitting his will against the entity's, willing it to materialize—and suddenly, shards of polished blackness shimmered in the air in front of him, coldly reflecting the moon's pale light. The image of a man wrapped in a dark cowl solidified, and he watched as this deadly foe lifted its head to reveal white skin. Skin the color of new snow, with eyes as dark as pitch. Expressionless—then just as abruptly, the image fractured into a thousand splinters of darkness.

He gasped as he was released, then blinked, seeing Peleyia raise a hand and try to reason with the six men who were rapidly encircling them. He dragged in a breath and glanced around, half-expecting the entity to reappear, but he could sense nothing. And he trusted that lack of sensation even less.

"Umm, fellers, I'm sure we can work this out and trade something useful," Peleyia was saying as he backed way from the thugs, his hands spread out in appeal.

"Haron wants you for that last little prank you pulled. It cost him a fortune," one thug growled.

"I'm mortified, but hey, that's business. It's nothing personal," Peleyia admonished.

"Pel," Kellen hissed, gripping the Lancooti's arm, wanting to warn him of the unseen dangers gathering around them. He knew with a sinking realization that disaster was about to strike.

"Everything is personal, you stinking, dirty Welconin! And I can honestly say I've been looking forward to wiping that smug grin off your arrogant face," the thug snarled as he took out a wicked-looking knife.

"Now, Derome, there is no need to get insulting," Peleyia said, eyeing off the approaching men before turning and shoving Kellen back toward the main street. "Run, Kell, and whatever you do, don't look back!"

"But—" Feeling himself propelled forward, Kellen didn't have time to argue. He could hear harsh swearing behind and the ring of steel hitting stone.

"Run!"

He fumbled for his own dagger, really wishing he had invested in a bigger knife while in GarFamita. Then he was jerked to a halt by a hand in his hair. Tears sprang to his eyes before he was spun around and slammed against the side of the tavern. He lifted his dagger in defense but gasped as he was roughly disarmed. *I really need to spend more time learning the sword,* he decided as he gritted his teeth.

A thick-set man with an angry-looking rash under his stubble lifted the hilt of his sword in readiness to strike, and Kellen moved. He kicked the man in the shins, then aimed a punch at the man's midriff, encountering solid muscle. He gasped, his knuckles cracking, but he still refused to give up, reeling from a glancing blow to his temple. Then just as abruptly, his attacker fell backward, the large sword falling loudly to the stones at his feet before the thick-set hit the ground.

Stunned by his dramatic rescue, he was about to thank Peleyia, when he saw that the Lancooti was pinned under two larger men. His friend stood no chance of winning the encounter as the first man flicked out a cruel-looking blade, preparing to plunge it into Peleyia's chest.

No . . . in desperation, Kellen searched for his dagger. He stepped over the fallen pirate at his feet and picked up the man's wicked-looking sword. Raising it above his head, he prepared to charge, but was struck from behind. He stumbled, half-falling to the wet ground. He dropped the sword and half-turned only to see his new attacker fall dead to the cobbled ground by his side.

He gasped in shock. Then the sound of bones cracking made Kellen glance around, and he just caught sight of another assailant smashing into the stonewall beside him. The man slid to the ground, unconscious. Stunned, he searched for his rescuer. A tall dark shape stepped elegantly over the prone ruffian before leaping forward to yank the two men off Peleyia. Seeing how their odds had drastically diminished, those who could still stand made a dash for the alley's entrance.

Standing, Kellen dubiously approached the shadowed figure as his rescuer reached down and helped Peleyia to his feet. He noticed with relief that the cruel, dark entity had also vanished, and he released a tense sigh.

"Are you both all right?" It was a soft, musical sound, elemental in nature.

"Dalzere," Peleyia said, breathless. "I am indebted to you."

"What where you doing out here?"

"Looking for you, actually," Peleyia offered as he wiped blood from his split lip. He grimaced.

Their rescuer said nothing; instead he turned, and Kellen got his first glimpse of this creature in the muted light. Death incarnate. A picture of delicate perfection and unearthly, dark beauty mixed—nothing like he had expected. In the back of his mind, the childhood litany played in his head—*Cursed is the one who is bespelled by the gaze of a Drow.* A Drow Elf. Fear and fascination warred within him. Then the Drow turned away, breaking the spell, and Kellen found he could breathe again.

"Does Sasheer know you are both out here?" Dalzere asked.

Pel hesitated. "Well . . ."

"Just as I imagined," the newcomer said irritably before indicating for them to move. "I will escort you children back to the inn."

"Great," Peleyia complained. He grabbed Kellen's arm and swung him around, making him walk. "This is going to do wonders for my reputation!"

Glancing back over his shoulder, Kellen just remembered to close his mouth as he felt those golden eyes of the Drow sweep over him. He shuddered, allowing Peleyia to steer him back to their room. Somehow he could not imagine Sasheer understanding.

CHAPTER TWELVE

"I don't understand! What were you both thinking?" Sasheer demanded as he eyed the youths in annoyance.

"I doubt *thinking* played any part in the excursion," Dalzere remarked, leaning back against a wall in the dim room. The Ihovians attempted to ignore him, while Ryland stared at him with a look of dislike and grudging respect.

"We can't stay here," Lesendal said into the sudden silence, dragging his eyes away from the Drow to scowl at Sasheer.

Sasheer looked up, his gaze narrowing. Exhaling, he turned to his friend and partner and lifted a brow, asking wordlessly for Dalzere to answer the prince's unvoiced question.

"It is as safe a place as any," Dalzere confirmed solemnly. "We were not observed in returning here."

Sasheer swept his shrewd gaze from Dalzere to the other occupants in the room, then he walked over to one of the bunks and collapsed inelegantly on it. He muttered something in a language that sounded ethereal, his expression annoyed.

Kellen followed Sasheer's irritated gaze and was surprised by what he noticed. On his left was the Drow, and on his right stood Lesendal, Salimen, and Ryland, with the Ihovians making no effort to hide their hostility. He swallowed nervously, darting his eyes back to Dalzere's dark figure. He attempted not to stare at the magnificent creature before him, thrilled and frightened by the idea of actually seeing a Drow—talking with a Drow. Especially a Drow who knew Sasheer so well, and who would be able to tell him about the secretive Ranger.

Returning his attention to the others, Kellen saw how Lesendal shifted his gaze to Sasheer, the prince valiantly trying to pretend the Drow did not exist. While Salimen brooded, intermittently glaring at Dalzere and then shifting his glare to the back of Lesendal's head. Even Ryland was unsettled as he kept a firm hold on the hilt of his sword. Only Peleyia seemed disinterested as he slouched by the window, muttering about his reputation being in ruins.

"All right," Sasheer said, his manner more conciliatory. "Ryland, did you see anything tonight downstairs in the tavern taproom?"

"Nothing out of the ordinary," Ryland said. He flexed his fingers around the massive hilt of his sword. "The customers who entered appeared to be regulars."

Sasheer nodded. "We discovered very little also, except that the Dwarves have split into five different factions. Why, I'm not sure. Yet."

"There was also no word on Kess, or anyone else from home," Lesendal said to Ryland in a quiet voice.

"Dalzere?" Sasheer threw the question at his friend, and Kellen did not miss how both Ihovians tensed, animosity clear in their eyes. "I was expecting you at Dargor's Peak weeks ago. What happened?"

"I got trapped in the mountains by early snow outside Herston," Dalzere said, his voice carrying that musical quality. "As you suspected, the river town was well under Kalern's control, and I had a difficult time getting past the patrols without alerting any Mindwipes. By the time I crossed the Divide, I figured you would either be heading toward GarFamita or Engleton." He shrugged, an easy, fluid gesture that looked effortless. "I arrived here two days ago, scouted the coast, and was about to head back toward the Divide when I heard Peleyia was in town." He turned, giving the Lancooti a thin smile. "I put two and two together and went looking for him."

Lesendal turned and faced the tall Drow, his posture stiff. "And my sister? Did you learn anything of her while in Wericonon?" His tone was neutral, but the prejudice showed in his eyes.

"Yes," Dalzere inclined his head. One corner of his mouth twitched up in wicked amusement.

"And?" Salimen growled, stepping around Lesendal to confront the Drow. His hand strayed to his bow.

Dalzere's eyes narrowed, his stance not altering, but Kellen got the impression he was ready for anything.

"Salimen," Sasheer broke in, "he is not your enemy."

"You want to kill me?" It was quietly spoken, a murmur of seductive sound that caressed the ears. Dalzere lifted his hands, spreading his arms wide, seeming to offer the Ihovian bowman a clear and open shot at him.

"Give me strength," Sasheer muttered, rolling his eyes and stifling an exasperated groan. "Dalzere, is this really necessary?"

Dalzere ignored the Ranger, looking solely at the blond Ihovian. "Go ahead; I will give you one free shot. But miss, Ihovian, and you are mine." It was a deadly promise, his vulnerability tempting as he stood there, black leather gleaming in the candlelight, highlighting his tall frame, flowing black hair, and golden eyes. A picture of deadliness and beauty mixed.

Salimen snarled, dropped his crossbow on the bed and drew his fine blade. His face was twisted in fury as he lunged forward, getting stopped by Lesendal, as the prince stepped across his path and imprisoned his sword arm.

"Sal! That's enough!" Lesendal shook his cousin hard. "Look at yourself; look at us! We should not be fighting amongst ourselves. In that, at least, Sasheer is correct."

"But he's a Drow!"

"I know," Lesendal soothed as he dragged Salimen over to the other side of the room. He forcefully turned him away from the Drow, cupping his cousin's face. "But we are no longer in Ihova, and if you remember, earlier tonight, we saw Dwarves and Sun Elves down in the marketplace. Our world is changing, Sal, and I think we must learn to change with it."

Kellen held his breath, stunned, yet fascinated by the volatile emotions. He had never seen Salimen so out of control, and he risked a brief glance in Sasheer's direction. The Ranger looked resigned, amused even, and Kellen found his fingers were curling into a fist, anticipating trouble—then Salimen released an explosive breath, and a measure of sanity returned to his eyes as he nodded, accepting Lesendal's lead.

"Maybe we should give him the benefit of a doubt, let him prove to us that he is not like the rest of his race," Lesendal said, releasing Salimen's sword arm and turning to face the Drow. "Tell me, Drow, what of my sister, Kessendra? Have you news?"

Dalzere raised one finely pointed brow and seemed to consider the prince's request before casting a look at Sasheer. The Ranger said nothing, and he returned his gaze to the Ihovians. "All southerners captured were shipped by sea to the mainland of Sennovia within days of arriving in Wericonon. So if she survived the march, then I would say she is on her way to the caverns in Gerthwin, beneath North Ridge."

Lesendal said nothing, his face paling with the news, and Kellen felt his own heart contract in shared sympathy for the prince. He knew how much Lesendal loved his sister, and he bit his lower lip in worry. As he watched, Lesendal closed his eyes and turned away from them all, going to the door and leaving the room without saying another word. Salimen cursed under his breath and followed.

"That's not all," Dalzere went on, breaking the heavy silence after the door had whispered shut. He looked at Sasheer. "Somehow Kalern has also managed to reanimate the Raveners."

"Brilliant!" Sasheer muttered sarcastically, falling back on the bed and cursing.

* * *

Kellen sat at the breakfast table the next morning and barely touched his gruel. It was lumpy, lacked salt, and he was sure the milk had gone sour two days earlier. He stirred it unenthusiastically before pushing it aside. He eyed his drink, not certain anything in this tavern was edible, or even good for his health, and pushed that aside also. Only Ryland seemed to have an appetite, but Kellen assumed that was because the Haonian warrior drowned out the taste of the gruel with his black ale. He shuddered in reaction and looked at his silent companions. Lesendal was subdued—hung over—as he sat with his head resting on the table. Salimen didn't look much better, his blue eyes bloodshot, his cheeks paler than normal. It was depressing, and Kellen sighed, wondering what they were all going to do now.

"So what do we do today?" Lesendal asked, his voice weary as he lifted his head. He rubbed a finger over one brow and winced.

"I need to get back to the mainland," Sasheer said. "There is nothing more that can be accomplished here in the south. If you are interested, I would welcome your company."

"Of course I'm going!" Lesendal snapped angrily then raised a hand in mute apology. "I have to find Kessendra."

"The three of us want to go," Salimen said. "We started this together, and we'll end it together." His eyes briefly touched the silent Drow.

"Very well," Sasheer agreed. "Dalzere?"

"You need ask?" the other queried as he sat back with long legs stretched out. "I will always be at your side."

Accepting that, Sasheer turned to the Lancooti. "Peleyia, I'll need you to go back to GarFamita and warn Lasdajar about the Raveners."

"But," Peleyia raised pleading eyes, "I would rather go with you."

"I'm sorry, Pel, but she must be told."

"Then send someone else," Peleyia said unhappily. Sasheer just looked at him for a prolonged moment until the Lancooti sighed dramatically. "All right," Peleyia said, glancing over at Kellen, "Kell could come back to GarFamita with me."

"No," Sasheer shook his head. "It would be safer if he came with us."

Surprised and seeing that same surprise register on Peleyia's and Ryland's faces, Kellen scowled at the Ranger. He felt singled out and could guess what Sasheer meant by the word *safe*, under no illusion that the exasperating man was not implying he needed protection. Rather Sasheer would be referring to his potential for danger and his inability to control his emotions. It seemed he had a lot to prove before Sasheer would trust him again.

"If that is settled, then I think we should head down toward the harbor. I know a man there who would be willing to take us over to the mainland without any questions," Sasheer continued.

"Daljourne," Dalzere confirmed dryly. "He arrived in the harbor about a week ago and has been gambling heavily ever since. By now, I imagine he would jump at the chance of getting away from his creditors."

"Good." Sasheer pushed himself away from the table. "Let's collect our things." He gave Peleyia a half smile. "Remember to take *all* the Famita's horses back with you and thank Lasdajar for their use."

"Naturally," Peleyia grumbled. "As if I'd sell them."

"Sasheer, can a man like this Daljourne be trusted?" Ryland asked. "If he lives in this environment and is a known pirate, then will he not just sell us out to one of Kalern's spies to save his own skin or to repay his debts?"

"No, for he is governed by a higher authority," Dalzere answered as he stood and stretched to his full height.

"And what authority is that?" Ryland asked, his eyes going to Dalzere in distrust.

"Survival," Dalzere whispered, giving a wicked leer. "No one double-crosses a Drow," he ended, swiveling on his toes and following Sasheer out of the tavern.

"Damn Drow," Ryland complained as he got to his feet.

"Don't worry, my friend," Salimen placed a hand on his shoulder. "I feel this is going to be a very difficult and exasperating trip."

* * *

They made their way down to the seafront and fish markets. Despite the strong odor emitting from the place, it was crowded with buyers and hagglers alike.

Standing out of the way next to Peleyia, Kellen could understand his friend's reluctance to return to GarFamita, and he wished there were something he could do to help. To be a slave in any culture was not pleasant, and he believed Sasheer was being overly harsh in his judgments. Still, the Lancooti had not put up much of an argument, seeming to accept his given task, and Kellen wondered why he could not do the same.

Squinting at the dark-haired Ranger in the sunlight, Kellen bit his lip with a mixture of irritation and frustration. Sasheer refused to even look at him, let alone speak with him. How could Sasheer teach him to control his emotions if they could not even communicate without arguing? Glaring moodily at Sasheer's back, he let his gaze slide to the Ihovian prince, noting how Lesendal still looked paler than normal, as he shaded his eyes against the bright sunlight.

He turned away from his three silent and moody companions to look across the busy fish markets. He scanned the area for any sign of Ryland or Salimen. Or even Dalzere—although he was amazed that a Drow Elf could walk around so blatantly in daylight and not get accosted. Both Ryland and Salimen had insisted on accompanying Dalzere to arrange passage on the *May Queen*, the huge ship which was docked further along the harbor. They had been gone a good while, and Kellen was both anxious and frightened at the prospect of leaving the Southland. He cast another glance back at his silent companions and saw they were still ignoring him.

Scratching his head, he took in the color, noise, and numerous smells of the markets. The place was alive with activity, with stallholders quibbling, holding up huge fish, chickens, fruit and other items from far off shores. But the flavor of the market was lost on him as he battled with his own internal dilemma. So what was Sasheer planning to do with him once they left the Southland? He could not imagine Lesendal or Salimen taking much notice of his plight while they were searching for Kessendra. Maybe Ryland would worry, but what could the warrior do against Sasheer and his mystical powers? Or even against a Drow, for that matter? He chewed on a fingernail, casting his mind back to the previous night. Dalzere had painted a menacing picture when he had challenged Salimen, and he wondered if Sasheer would have stepped in if Lesendal hadn't ended the confrontation.

Glancing around when Peleyia touched his arm, Kellen saw Dalzere's approach. *Speak of the devil.* The Drow was weaving easily through the chaotic marketplace, and people hurriedly moved out of his path. His distinctive features were striking, his long overcoat as eye-catching as his amazing hair and startling eyes. Next to him was Salimen, who looked about ready to explode in a fit of rage; his expression dark. Bringing up the rear strode Ryland, who scanned the crowd warily.

"Well?" Sasheer demanded impatiently as the three drew level.

"No problem," Salimen answered gruffly, flicking a stray strand of blond hair from over one eye. "Your friend," the bowman indicated Dalzere with annoyance, "the Drow, *eventually* sweet-talked the captain."

"It would seem we can depart immediately upon the tide," Ryland elaborated, purposely moving to stand between the scowling Salimen and the brooding Drow warrior.

"Good. I would like to—" Sasheer stopped, as they heard a voice call out to them. A very loud, insistent voice that sounded female. The lady in question ended her call by swearing graphically as she came into view. She dismounted her exhausted horse in one movement to land on the cobbled road only feet from their position. Her face was set in an angry mask of determination, dust, and sweat stained her riding leather. Striding forward, she roughly thrust a merchant out of her way, toppling the unfortunate man backward, only to stop directly in front of the Ranger.

"Black stars, Watcher! But you are a hard man to track!" She cursed again. "I almost killed two horses searching for you!"

"Criz," Sasheer sighed, grinning in real pleasure.

"What are you still doing in this backward land, old man? And why can you never be where you are supposed to be?"

"A question I frequently ask also," said Dalzere wryly.

The woman raised her head at that, and impossibly, her snarl increased as she fluidly drew her sword. Raising an arm, Dalzere shoved Ryland and Salimen aside as she charged him, a battle cry leaving her lips in a strange tongue, its implications nonetheless clear. Getting his own blade up, Dalzere blocked her strike, grabbing her arm and twisting them both around before skillfully disarming her. They tumbled to the ground, knocking over two stalls before Dalzere ended up straddling her slender hips, a grin of pure, wicked triumph sweeping his features.

"So we meet again, Crizkerisomia, and it would seem you have still learned nothing," Dalzere taunted in false affection. "Until you sharpen your skills, you will never be accepted into the *Fe-ledrea*!"

"Get off me, you black demon!" she spat, slipping a hand free to slap him hard across the face.

Releasing her, Dalzere laughed, standing and sliding his sword away before stepping back. Her outrage was palpable, and Dalzere sent Sasheer a merry grin that lit up his entire face.

Crizkerisomia climbed to her feet and glared at the Drow, swiping her sword off Sasheer as the Ranger came over and took her elbow. He steered her skillfully away from the amused Drow.

Gaping at her in amazement, Kellen was shocked by the intense yet swift battle between the two. He stared openly at the woman and realized that she was Elven. Only she was white. Around him, he saw that Lesendal, Salimen, and Ryland were realizing the same thing.

"Criz," Sasheer started again, moving them all away from the furious stallholders as other fights broke out over smashed and scattered belongings. "What are you doing in the Southland?"

"Looking for you," she said again as she massaged a sore wrist.

"Why?" he pushed.

She cast her gaze around the faces studying her before addressing Sasheer again. "That is for your ears only."

"I suggest we get out of the marketplace," Peleyia said, pointing toward the local law enforcement officers who were flooding the area.

"Good idea," Sasheer said turning toward Ryland and Salimen who were loosening their weapons. "We'll head down toward the *May Queen*," he said decisively.

Following, Kellen cast a look back, seeing chaos as numerous people fled the area to avoid arrest. In front, Peleyia called his name, and he quickened his pace, navigating the busy dock area until they reached the anchorage where the ship was docked. Sasheer called a halt, indicating for the female Elf to now explain. She still looked unconvinced, and she turned her back deliberately on the Drow. That only increased Dalzere's grin.

"Criz, they are friends, involved in this dispute with Kalern. So you can speak freely," Sasheer said.

"Karczag sent me to find you."

"Karczag?" Sasheer's brow climbed as he briefly met Dalzere's worried gaze over her shoulder. The Drow's smile abruptly vanished.

"Who's Karczag?" Lesendal asked.

"A colleague of mine in the west," Sasheer dismissed as his expression turned serious. "How did Karczag find you?"

"I was passing through Sanctuary, and he pressed me into aiding the Brethren," she said.

"I see." Sasheer turned away and slowly sat down. "What is the message?"

"He said to tell you this war is a diversion." She took a deep breath, suspiciously eyeing the Ihovians and the Haonian. "While you have been watching Kalern's army here in the south, Kalern went secretly east and raided the tombs of Mitthsombaine."

"What?" Sasheer snapped, outraged.

"But how?" Dalzere broke in as he stepped forward. "They are blood sealed and can only be breached by the blood of the past."

Crizkerisomia slowly settled her eyes on the Drow, glaring at him for a moment before turning to face Sasheer. "Kalern killed Cornithia and his Shade. Then with their blood, he breached the ancient seals and took the Book of Spells."

"No . . ." Sasheer exhaled, paling as his eyes changed to an inky black. "So that is how he reanimated the Raveners."

"Not only that," she continued, "but he has resurrected the old protection spells around North Ridge. It will not be long before he starts the genetic experimentations on all those slaves in the caverns under Gerthwin."

"There will be war," Dalzere predicted in a hushed voice.

"It cannot be stopped," Crizkerisomia agreed. "Karczag said he needed you to return to the Keep."

Standing, Sasheer dragged a hand through his hair before turning to the Lancooti. "Pel, I need you to ride to GarFamita immediately. The tribes must be warned and prepared."

"Forget it." Crizkerisomia shook her head.

"Why?" Sasheer asked in a sinking voice.

"GarFamita is gone. Kalern has already neutralized it, and he is heading this way," she lifted a brow. "I suggest we leave immediately, as the Southland is lost."

CHAPTER THIRTEEN

Kellen stood at the prow of the pirate vessel and enjoyed the cold rush of wind as it swept his hair back. The exhilarating climb and dip of the boat as it rode the waves gave him the feeling of flying-free as a bird, watching the waves crash against the hull, occasionally getting sprayed with the icy sea. He had no idea that the life of a sailor could be so wonderful, so uninhibited, and he turned a little to observe the big Nezkernan men who manned the sails and rigging. It did not look too hard, though the previous evening, Ryland had said that the men of Daljourne's ship were from the White Cliffs and bred for this sort of task, making it look simple and easy. Still, the ocean views were spectacular and the rush of wind invigorating.

Three days they had been at sea, flying across the deep blue ocean as the cooling winter winds filled the huge sails, making the great mast groan. Lesendal and Salimen had spent the first two days ill below decks. Even Ryland had looked pale, not wanting food or ale, as he stationed himself near the stern. Sasheer had also kept to himself, having stayed below deck to question the white Elf, Crizkerisomia, in detail the first night. Only Dalzere and Peleyia showed no concern over their rapidly changing circumstances. In fact, Kellen noted that Peleyia was openly delighted, regardless of the shocking news concerning GarFamita. He imagined this now constituted Peleyia's freedom.

Closing his eyes and stretching out his hands, Kellen let himself absorb the feeling of the wind hitting his face, reveling in the sensation.

"Be careful, or one strong gust will throw you over the edge."

It was so softly spoken, and so close, that Kellen jumped then reached down to grab the wooden railing before turning to look at his visitor. Everyone had left him alone over the last few days, so now he was surprised to have his solitude broken. Of course, it was the Drow.

"I am being careful," he said, elated and awed by the Elf's presence.

Next to him, Dalzere leaned down and rested his elbows on the railing, closing his eyes. "The wind against your face is so refreshing and stimulating, don't you think?"

Trying to relax, Kellen nodded, a little apprehensive as he eyed the man beside him. "I have never seen the White Sea before. I had no idea it could be so beautiful. Or so big."

"Beautiful. Yes, it is here. But go further west or east, and it is a different story."

That made him frown, and Kellen let his glance sweep the horizon, seeing little. Just a dark blue line that merged into nothing. "How?"

"East of us are the Sailwreck Islands." The Drow opened his eyes to a slit and smiled. "They are aptly named, as wrecks litter the coral reefs and treacherous channels surrounding them. Only an experienced captain with detailed maps navigates those waters and gains access into the Black Sea."

"Why would anyone risk it, if it is so dangerous?" Kellen asked curious, amazed that the Drow appeared so normal, acted so *human*. Amazed that Dalzere would even consider talking to him.

"For profit," Dalzere answered, one shoulder giving a delicate shrug. "There is a lot to be earned in trading goods into the Eastlands."

Absorbing that, Kellen looked out again over the deep blue swells ahead. "And west of here?"

"About 150 leagues west of here are the shoals, or rapids. They give this sea its name, as all you can see are white waves continuously crashing into each other for leagues."

"Is there any way through the rapids?" Kellen asked.

"Not by boat," Dalzere assured. "And it would be too dangerous by foot. Mostly it is avoided—politically admired from afar by the good people of Engleton." He gave a half smirk. "It cuts down on legitimate trading and allows piracy to thrive."

"Oh," Kellen said, trying to give the impression he understood all the concepts involved. *The life of a pirate; it wouldn't be too bad, would it?* Not if you listened to Peleyia. "So where are we going now?" he asked, watching the deep swells.

Gesturing ahead with his chin, Dalzere turned slightly to meet his eyes. Long dark hair and the glistening golden eyes that seemed only to laugh gave the Drow an air of destructive mystery. "I imagine, we'll put down on one of the sand strips along the mainland of Sennovia."

"Sennovia?" He had heard Sasheer use that name before.

"It is the Elven name given to the entire continent."

"How big is it?"

"Compared to your kingdom of Ihova?" Dalzere mused. "It would be like this sea, and Ihova was a single drop."

Eyes widening, Kellen swallowed as he cast another look toward the northern horizon. But he could see nothing. Nothing except for an indistinct, dark line where the water and sky merged. "So we will land at a harbor? Is it like Engleton? Or like GarFamita?"

"Neither. Being a pirate vessel, I would imagine Daljourne knows many hidden coves, so he will put us down on a deserted beach. There are no natural harbors along this coastline, unless you travel either west or east past the Sailwreck Islands or beyond the shoals." He shrugged. "It is probably for the best, as the natives who control the sand strips which border the White Sea are a bit uncivilized."

Trying to visualize it, Kellen frowned, keeping his gaze on the distant horizon. *Natives? Uncivilized? But then the term uncivilized could mean anything to a Drow warrior*, he pondered silently, his eyes glazing over in a mixture of speculation, excitement, and fear. "These natives, are they like the Lancooti?"

"No. The Lancooti may be nomadic, but they are not barbaric. The tribes living over here are, I suppose, distant cousins to the Lancooti, though none will admit the connection. They are called Kizer. They dwell in filthy mud holes and are totally engrossed in religious rituals involving blood and sex."

He felt his cheeks color a little at the blatant way Dalzere spoke, and Kellen tried to brush it off. *Surely Dalzere did not mean sex as in 'sex,' did he?* "So I take it, they don't like visitors?"

"They kill all intruders who invade their lands, sacrifice any who desecrate their sacred sites."

Kellen's mouth fell open, and he stared at the Drow Elf. Forgotten was the tantalizing horizon; now he was focused solely on the man at his side who talked of death so matter-of-factly. "Kill..." he swallowed and tried again, "they kill travelers?" He saw Dalzere nod, saw how his eyes crinkled up in amusement. "Can we avoid them?" he had to ask. "Or better still, can't we just keep sailing until we reach a real seaport?"

"We don't have the time," Dalzere replied, turning his eyes on Kellen. "As long as we avoid all sacred sites, we should make it through Kizer territory."

"Sacred sites," Kellen repeated, far from appeased. "I take it you can tell which sites are sacred, can't you?"

"Sometimes," Dalzere said.

"Sometimes?" Kellen's voice rose an octave. "There must be some way of knowing."

"Yes," the Drow nodded calmly. "You know when you are being strung up over a fire and a witch is poking you in the ribs with a very sharp stick," he answered in a deathly tone.

Alarmed, Kellen turned away from the strong wind, pushing his hair out of his eyes as he studied the other man. He waited until the Drow looked at him. Then he saw how serious Dalzere was, and he shivered despite himself. "You can't be serious."

"Let's not dwell on what might and might not happen." Again Dalzere gave him one of those unreadable looks before standing and stretching. "By the way, Sasheer says he wants to see you in his cabin below deck." He lifted a pointed brow. "He mentioned something about discussing your future?"

Groaning, Kellen dropped his head into his hand, imagining the worst. When he looked up again, Dalzere was gone, and he was alone at the rail. Only now he cast an apprehensive look at the ever-changing horizon.

* * *

Going below deck a short while later, Kellen eyed the polished brass fittings and carved wooden banisters. The craftsmanship of the vessel presented a rich atmosphere, and he tried to dwell on that and not on what Sasheer was going to say to him. Since that day in the desert when the Ranger had amazingly drained his energy, neither had spoken about the incident. He now dreaded restarting the conversation.

He lifted a hand and knocked on the door to the room Sasheer had taken. He took a deep breath, calmed his nerves, and found he was subconsciously preparing himself for a fight.

"Come!"

Twisting the polished handle, he opened the door and entered the compact, yet inviting, cabin. Sasheer was sitting at an old wooden table, staring at a manuscript. His eyes flickered over Kellen, then he was rolling up the manuscript and tying it with a cord.

"Good. You are finally here," Sasheer said. "I was just about to send Criz up to get you since you seemed to ignore Dalzere's message."

"He's only just told me," Kellen protested. This was not starting off well, and he clamped his jaw and settled for glaring at Sasheer instead.

Sasheer gave a small smile. "Do you like him?"

"I don't know him," Kellen cut back just as swift.

Sighing, Sasheer indicated for Kellen to sit. "So defensive already? At least wait until there is something worth arguing about."

"Sasheer, what do you want with me?" he asked, sick of the bickering.

"I want your cooperation."

"In what?"

"In helping you."

"But I—"

"You don't need help. Yes, I have heard your protests, Kellen. They have assaulted my senses from the moment we met in Ihova,"

Sasheer finished for him, gesturing impatiently for him to sit down. "But we both know you are out of control."

Swallowing, Kellen got a mental image of the rage and wild anger he had almost unleashed on the other man. He had not intended to hurt Sasheer, and Sasheer had somehow dispersed that fierce energy with so simple a touch. With that thought, he sat.

"Kellen, I was never in any danger from you," Sasheer said quietly.

Lifting his head, Kellen realized the other had been reading his thoughts again, and he felt his resentment rise anew. "Stop reading my mind!"

"I'm not," Sasheer said. "Reading your mind would take patience, and I rarely possess that at the best of times," he settled back in his chair and studied his new young charge. "I was reading your emotions. And those are what you have to learn to control. Otherwise an enemy will outthink you, manipulate you, and kill you with little effort."

Taken back by the frankness, Kellen blinked in the candlelight and regarded the Ranger, desperately wanting to believe him. "All right," he whispered, "what can you teach me?"

"I can teach you what it is that you fear. I can teach you how to overcome that fear and see beyond to what is possible. But mostly, I can teach you basic control, so that you don't hurt yourself, or others," Sasheer said. "The ability to understand is as much a gift as the raw ability you have of tapping into the earth's currents and using them to amplify your will. Once you have control, then you can start to learn how to use the Gift you have."

"Gift," Kellen repeated. "You've said that before. How can it be a Gift when it kills?"

Abruptly Sasheer's face creased in worry, and then he was reaching over and brushing his fingertips gently over Kellen's forehead. "Tell me what happened."

The memory still hurt, but somehow the pain was not as acute, and Kellen found he could actually recall that wet day back in Ihova with no guilt. Was that Sasheer's doing, or . . ."I got angry then scared." He licked his lips. "The Black Guard killed Bains for no reason. And I wanted that guard to pay. Then all of a sudden . . ." he stopped and focused his gaze on Sasheer, looking deep into blue eyes. For the briefest of moments, he saw past the cynical attitude and into the world of this unusual man. He *saw* an ancient city; he *saw* war banners; he *saw* death—and Kellen rocked back in his chair and broke the connection between them. He blinked rapidly, exhaling hard. "I—I . . . I don't know what is happening to me anymore. I killed a Black Guard simply by touching him and willing his heart to burst. I now see images in my mind that confuse me. I hear voices whispering in my dreams." He lifted his gaze and cautiously met Sasheer's patiently waiting eyes a second time. Gone were the images, and he relaxed a little. "Am I cursed?"

"No," Sasheer said. He slid down in his seat a little more and stared at Kellen for a long while. "Tell me, Kellen, what did you feel inside when you killed the Black Guard?"

"Panic," Kellen said truthfully. "I ran—"

"After that," Sasheer prompted. "When you stopped running?"

"I was horrified," Kellen said. He closed his eyes tightly, remembering the gut-wrenching despair and fear that had overtaken him. Only being with Ryland and the Ihovians had kept him sane those first few days. They had kept his mind occupied.

Sasheer nodded, satisfied. "I can teach you how to stop that from ever happening again. I can teach you how to protect yourself—to use your will wisely. So that when you feel the currents, you will be able to ignore them without killing or harming a soul." He leaned forward, forcing Kellen to meet his gaze. "Do you understand what I am saying?"

"I think so." Kellen nodded, not liking this feeling of uncertainty.

"It is not all bad, Kellen. You aren't doomed to be despised—rather, you just have to accept it and then learn to live with this new aspect of your personality. It is neither good nor evil. It is just a tool, a new skill, if you will. An extension of your mind, and your emotions will determine its use."

"But why me?"

Raising a hand to his face, Sasheer brushed his fringe out of his eyes and sighed. Kellen saw a flicker of compassion cross the Ranger's face before he spoke again. "Remember the history I told you? Remember old Mitthsombaine?"

"Yes."

"This Gift is an echo from that time. Many of those who survived the destruction of Mitthsombaine fled into the four lands. Some of those who fled were Mage Gifted."

"Mage Gifted!" Kellen interrupted, shocked, even though he had been asking about the Mageborns. It was still a shock.

Briefly narrowing his eyes in annoyance, Sasheer stifled a groan. "This is one trait of the Southland I despise. This narrow-minded belief and inability to accept anything that hints at magic." He lifted his hand and glared at Kellen. "I know what Ryland thinks of me, and I know how stubborn Salimen can be. Can you, Kellen, think beyond their beliefs and petty concerns?"

Cautiously, Kellen watched as the blue eyes darkened to black, a sure indication of Sasheer's irritation. "I can try," he offered.

"Good! Because I have very little patience when it comes to persuading my students to accept past events as fact," he growled somewhat ungraciously. "I've lived through them once, and I am not overly fond of reliving them again. I can teach you, but you have to want to be taught. Can you do that?"

Meeting the direct gaze, Kellen hesitated. *Lived through past events,* impossible. Yet what had Sasheer said about the impossible? And if that were true, then how old was this man? "I need to learn to understand this power. But I still do not trust you entirely."

If anything, Sasheer's expression softened, and his smile was one of delight. "You should not trust me. Trust comes with knowledge and association. Rather will you accept my help? Accept my teachings?" Holding out his hand, the silent invitation hung between them.

Considering the offer and then the other's encouraging smile, Kellen slowly reached forward and gripped the warm fingers in his own. He closed his eyes as the warmth from Sasheer's hand tingled through him, making him doubt his decision already. But for now he was committed.

For good or bad. Only time would tell.

* * *

The next two days passed swiftly, and Kellen's mood was dampened by all the colorful descriptions from the sailors on the *May Queen* concerning the barbaric practices of the Kizer. Their stories echoed the sinister darkness Dalzere had hinted at, and Kellen grew alarmed at the prospect of seeing the coast of Sennovia.

It was only Sasheer's calm, coupled with Dalzere and Crizkerisomia's lack of worry, which settled the rest of the company, but still Kellen's uneasiness continued. As soon as land came into sight, he spent most of his time scanning the barren-looking coastline. Compared to the pristine, undulating sand dunes surrounding Engleton, this was positively desolate. Gray and brown foliage covered the slate gray coast, lines of black froth edged the dunes, and even the waters lapping the beach appeared muddy in color.

Disliking this land, Kellen turned apprehensively when he heard the heavy anchor drop. A small rowboat was lowered and a ladder thrown over the side. He stood at the rail watching Crizkerisomia climb nimbly down the rope ladder and settle in the boat. Hearing his name called, he reluctantly followed Peleyia as Dalzere motioned them over.

"I have a bad feeling about this," Kellen whispered to his friend. In front of him Ryland swore before descending into the rowboat below.

Peleyia turned and raised a single brow in amusement. "Now you are starting to sound like Salimen," he teased.

"Now I am starting to understand him," Kellen quipped.

"Kell," the other admonished. "What could go wrong? We have Sasheer and two Elves with us. So who would be stupid enough to challenge them? Not to mention your friend Ryland, and the argumentative Ihovians. And I'm not entirely useless in a fight—you just witnessed an unfortunate incident in Engleton."

"Unfortunate? We were almost killed."

"Ah, now you are thinking negatively again," the Lancooti grinned.

"I am not," Kellen defended. "I'm just stating the facts."

Peleyia released a breath and looked sideways at his friend. Like the rest of them, he now had his hair tied back, and his colorful leathers had been replaced with green brown tracker's clothing.

"I just don't like the look or feel of that coastline," Kellen explained in a reasonable tone, watching Sasheer hand Daljourne a money pouch.

"I have never been here, so for me this is an exciting adventure," Peleyia answered, his eyes taking on a dreamy quality. "But then I have never been free before either, so maybe my judgment is lacking."

Watching his friend, Kellen felt a pang of regret at his harsh words, remembering that Peleyia may have just lost everything he had ever known. "Pel . . ."

"Shh . . ." The other grabbed his arm. "We had better move before Sasheer leaves us behind."

"Now there's an attractive thought," Kellen muttered as he helped his friend climb over the rail and grab on to the rope ladder.

* * *

Once on land, Kellen reluctantly following Peleyia up the gentle slope with one final glance at the departing rowboat. His legs were unsteady on solid land, and he slowed to rub his thighs. He noted that the rowboat wasted no time in returning to the pirate vessel, and he scowled harder. His excitement had diminished, and he disliked the fact that their only escape from possible trouble was about to sail away. Rapidly.

"Are you ill?"

Kellen glanced sideways and met Dalzere's curious stare. Those yellow eyes reflected a mischievous twinkle, yet he got the impression that the Drow considered everything seriously. He saw Dalzere cock a brow, and he sighed, shaking his head in answer to the Elf's unvoiced concern. He had no idea how to explain his misgivings to the other man, no idea how to verbalize why a sick dread churned in his stomach.

So instead he moved away from the ocean's edge and hurried to catch up with Dalzere. Despite what Salimen said, he liked the dark Elf and found Dalzere to be far more informative and friendly than either Sasheer or Lesendal, regardless of his skin color. Stopping next to Dalzere, he stitched on a half smile. "So tell me more about these Kizer?" he asked, wanting to take his mind off his inner fears.

"Such as?"

"Their land," he began, gesturing to the dirty-looking grass around them. "Is it all like this?"

"No," Dalzere said. He started them moving, following the other members of the company across the dirty sand to the tangled undergrowth of weeds and tough grass. "This expanse of coast is positively pleasant."

"Really?" Kellen snorted, blinking around at the uninviting, windswept coast.

Dalzere gave a lopsided grin that vanished quickly. "Further inland, there are mud springs and underground cave formations. The region is very marshy, and except for snakes, some hunting hawks and carnivorous spiders, very little apart from the Kizer, inhabit these muddy dunes."

"Do they look like the Lancooti?" Kellen asked, his eyes briefly going to Peleyia.

"They are shorter in stature, dirty, and lack the imagination of color. But I suppose that is because their environment doesn't produce the vibrancy the Sandlands do." He frowned. "Try to remember that the Lancooti as a people have embraced life. They live in the visible world and are unable to resist a profitable challenge. Peleyia is a perfect example of his people's adventurous nature," he said, gesturing to the Lancooti. "While the Kizer, on the other hand, are introverted, living in the invisible realm of spirits and curses, navigating a system of intricate castes and punishment levels. They are extremely territorial, even of the different factions within their own culture, shunning active involvement with any other race."

Absorbing all this, Kellen glanced around, more apprehensive than before. "They fight amongst themselves?"

"Continuously. The ruling faction usually has the strongest witch. The strongest blood magic."

"Witch?" Kellen uttered incredulously.

"Don't be so narrow-minded."

Staring at Dalzere, Kellen closed him mouth, thinking that over. "So which tribe or faction is dominant at present?"

"I last heard that the Kizer-Dalicak controlled the largest portion of territory," Dalzere said after a thoughtful moment.

"Kizer what?"

"Da-li-cak," he repeated, putting the correct pronunciation and accent on the name. It sounded like a curse. "It is the name given to their current spirit which leads them in ritual worship."

"And these ones are particularly bad . . . because . . ." Kellen trailed off, not sure if he wanted to know. It didn't help when he heard Dalzere chuckle.

"They are the largest tribe, but not necessarily the nastiest. There are worse factions, like the Kizer-Horigan or the Kizer-Telicxon."

"And these are worse, why?"

"They are . . ." Dalzere paused, his eyes narrowing as he searched for the correct wording, "more imaginative in their punishments. More vengeful. Bloodthirsty. But fortunately small in number, as the other factions ritually cull them." He gave a sick, slightly twisted grin that turned his features feral. "As I said, not a pleasant race to be born into. Or to encounter as a traveler."

Feeling a prickle of goosebumps travel down his spine, Kellen suppressed a shiver. "I imagine not," he agreed. He looked around. "So which faction lives in this area?"

Taking a deep breath, Dalzere squinted up at the cloudy sky. "I'm not sure. We are at the narrowest point in the Kizer territory, and when I last came through here, I found no sacred sites to indicate a territorial staking or ownership."

"How long ago was that?"

"About a year ago."

"A lot can happen in a year," Kellen said, refusing to let his imagination conjure the worst. "What if one of those nasty factions you mentioned has moved here?"

"Don't borrow trouble, Kellen," Dalzere whispered, but his eyes took on a wary look. "There is no reason for the Kizer to alter set practice."

"I hope you are right."

"Unless it is for a—" Dalzere stopped, his gaze becoming distant.

"What?"

But the Drow just shook his head, refusing to elaborate. "I will keep watch for sacred sites," he concluded.

Not liking the look in the golden eyes, Kellen worried at his bottom lip as he cast an uneasy glance around. *Sacred sites? What would signify as a sacred site? A temple? A cave?* He had no idea what a culture like the Kizer's would deem as religious. "So," he breathed, hurrying to catch up with Dalzere's long strides, "so these sacred sites you mentioned are . . . ?"

"Holy areas for their spirits. Markers of their boundaries."

"Is there any way to know what they look like?"

Dalzere considered the question for a long moment. "Usually they are decorated with a cross-weaving of grass under a small mound of black rocks."

"Usually?" Kellen asked. *Not a building? A tree?* "Just rocks?"

Dalzere smiled wryly, his characteristic mischievousness returning. "That is if the hunting birds have not disturbed the area and thieved the weavings." Kellen looked at him in dread, and the Drow explained further, "The birds use the weavings for nests. They at least are not stupid, even if the Kizer are."

"A weaving?" Kellen's heart plummeted. "Not even a sign? A clearing? A lamppost? Just a grass weaving?" Fear welled in his chest, and he swallowed his nervousness. "Please tell me these weavings are large." He gestured with his hands to describe how large.

Dalzere's grin widened. "Mostly you cannot tell what is sacred and what is not."

"Then this is suicidal!" Kellen proclaimed, appalled by the very idea of the risk involved. "There must be a safer way to get to this Keep where Sasheer wants to go."

"Unfortunately there is no other way to get into the Westlands except through Kizer territory. This strip of muddy land stretches for over 1,600 leagues along the coast and is bordered by the wide Calmen River. The only way around it is if we had gone west into the Sandlands and then found a barge capable of transversing the Calmen land bar."

"And that would have meant—"

"Going through Kalern's advancing army," Dalzere finished for him.

Letting the silence stretch, Kellen started to imagine shadows everywhere. "So how long will it take to reach this river?" Now he wanted to get out of Kizer territory as quickly as possible.

"Two days," the Drow said, appearing far from concerned. "We will probably stop on dusk, for it is not wise to travel after dark. By lunch tomorrow, we should reach the river and buy passage across."

"But you just said no one but the Kizer live here, so how will we buy passage?"

"Along the Calmen River—on the opposite bank—there are numerous fishing villages. It is not hard to find some fisherman willing to risk carrying passengers for a price." He placed one hand on Kellen's bony shoulder. "Try not to worry, as worrying will not help."

Wanting to heed that advice, Kellen still worried, scrutinizing everything around him, from the unappealing scrub undergrowth to the slate gray ground and stripped, dead tree stumps, to the sparse wildlife. It was a depressing place, and his fingers strayed to his small hunting knife without conscious thought. But as time passed, he forced his mind to dwell on other things. One of which had been bothering him since Engleton. He turned to look at Dalzere and voiced his question. "What can you tell me about Criz?" he asked.

If anything, the Drow's reaction to the query surprised Kellen as the other gave a soft, affectionate laugh, his eyes sparkling. "She would have come across the Calmen land bar over a thousand leagues west of here. Then she would have ridden east to Engleton," he assured.

"I meant, you and her?" Kellen clarified delicately. "That fight . . ."

Again the Drow's face lit up into an amused, wicked grin. "That is nothing. She has been trying to kill me for the last twenty-five years. It is a game we play." He shrugged, totally unconcerned. "One day I will have to let her believe she has won, only so that I can have some peace."

Eyeing the Drow, Kellen found his respect for this unusual man increased. Looking ahead, he spied the woman in question. She was in the lead with Salimen, and the two appeared to be talking. Her hair was mostly short, only one long, narrow braid of silver hair trailed down her back, the rest feathering around her delicate features. She wore a type of men's pale hunting leathers, and at her hips hung ornate knives, with two more protruding from the tops of her laced boots. She was tall, as tall as Dalzere, and he noticed how Sasheer kept the two Elves separated. Studying her, Kellen was fascinated, recalling her reaction to Dalzere in Engleton, and her deep-seated passion for attacking the Drow at every opportunity. "You both must have been very young when you started this strange game," he observed.

Dalzere just leaned down and whispered the words in gentle amusement. "We are both older than we look, Kellen. You must try and learn to look at things with not only your eyes, but also with your other senses."

Mulling over that, Kellen felt Dalzere drop back to scout behind, and he raised his eyes, trying to understand what cryptic clues Dalzere had been attempting to tell him. Looking again at Crizkerisomia, he wondered what else he was supposed to see, and suddenly, without realizing it, he found he was studying Sasheer's uninformative back.

CHAPTER FOURTEEN

Water dripped rhythmically behind him. The chill in the cavern made him shiver, and a deathly coldness seeped into his bones. Around him, he could hear faint echoes, voices raised in despair. Torchlight flickered off to one side, throwing patches of brightness that barely penetrated the inky gloom, and he sensed rather than saw a deep pit of blackness loom before him.

He dragged in a deep, calming breath, the icy air burning his throat, as he slowly glanced down at his torn, bloodied hands and flexed his fingers. He reached out with his fingers, touching the cold stone under him, edging closer to the encroaching pit of blackness to see if anything was beyond. He reached the lip of the pit and peered over the edge and saw nothing except a blackness that stretched endlessly on. A bottomless pit cut into the rock floor, an abyss which sucked in all signs of life and all the warmth from the meager light. It was like a beckoning force that he was helpless to ignore, mesmerized by its presence.

"Control."

The word whispered up into his mind, almost hypnotic. Then laughter followed the word, the sound mocking. Taunting. A familiar sound that was always in the back of his mind—in his dreams, in his waking—driving him insane as Kalern's compelling voice haunted his every thought.

"Lose control. Fly with your emotions and shatter its heart. Lift your eyes, Kellen, and look at your destiny."

No. He closed his eyes tightly, refusing to lift his head and answer that powerful persuasion. He did not want to look. To perceive. He did not want to see the stone of power.

"Just reach out for the stone, Kellen. Reach out with your mind and embrace all Lichien's desires. You know you want to."

No! He shook his head, denying the suggestion, denying Kalern's compelling words, denying Kalern's presence and existence. This was just another nightmare, and he forced his mind to focus on something else, to mentally dismiss what Kalern was so artfully constructing in his subconscious mind. So he centered his thoughts on Sasheer, remembering the lessons Sasheer was teaching him, visualizing the exercises Sasheer instructed him to perform, remembering the way Sasheer induced calmness. He had to think, think, think.

But it was already too late, and Kellen shuddered, feeling his tormentor's arrival more keenly. Sasheer's voice diminished, and he was again dragged mentally down into Lichien's world. Into darkness. Into the unrelenting cold.

He hit the damp floor with a jolt and snapped his eyes open to see the abyss looming before him again—hungry in its insidious silence.

A faint breeze stirred his wet hair, and he reared back from the abyss' edge—and hit something hard. Cautiously he reached back, his fingers encountering velveteen robes, and he raised his eyes, dreading what he would see. He inhaled sharply when Kalern's profile was seductively outlined in the torchlight. The shadowed lord was the vision of perfection: immaculately dressed, jewels adorning his gloved fingers, stitched into the fabric of his clothing. Beautiful.

Then Kalern crouched to meet his searching gaze, heedless of the dirt, heedless of the damage the dirty water would do to his stunning robes. Sheer beauty, and it took Kellen a moment to tear his eyes away from Kalern's face and to focus on the hand held out before him. From the lord's gloved hand hung a delicate, hand-crafted pendant of purest gold, and at its center sat a green diamond, which shone brightly in the firelight.

"Reach out with your mind, Kellen," Kalern whispered temptingly. "I know you want to. Just reach out and touch Lichien, and then you can have this small trinket. You can have anything you want, if you just open your mind to me. Relax your will and touch Lichien."

"No!" Kellen jumped, being woken from a fitful sleep by a hand clamped over his mouth. It took him a prolonged moment to reorientate himself, and then he sagged back against his bedding and blinked up at Salimen. He watched the bowman lean closer and slowly raise a finger to his lips to indicate silence. Kellen nodded and sucked in a deep breath when Salimen released him.

"Are you trying to wake the entire continent?" Salimen hissed, rocking back on his heels to glare at him.

"What did I do?" Blinking sleep from his eyes, Kellen wiped the perspiration from his face, recalling little of the nightmare as he woke properly.

"Shhh!"

It was just on dawn, and Kellen sat up as Salimen shook Peleyia awake before moving away to gather up his few belongings. Around them, he could see Ryland carefully checking over his huge sword, while Lesendal rolled his pack together.

Their urgency was infectious, and Kellen scrambled out of his sleeping pack and found his small dagger. He hastily rolled everything together, paying little attention to neatness. At the far side of the camp, Dalzere was a blur of darkness, and Kellen stopped what he was doing to study the Drow. Dalzere was crouched over a pile of stones, his fingers searching the tough grass. Of Sasheer and Crizkerisomia, there was no sign.

Picking up his travel pack, Kellen crept over to the prince. He watched Salimen and Lesendal strip down some sticks they had collected the previous evening and assemble crude arrows.

"Lesendal?" Kellen whispered.

The prince just shook his head, as Salimen wrapped twine around the ends of each projectile. Ryland walked over to them, his face grim as he handed Kellen another longer knife. "Dalzere found the remains of what looks like a holy site, or something just as absurd, over by that round rock," Ryland said, his brow raised in disbelief. "Just looked like a pile of small black pebbles to me, but Sasheer was concerned."

Remembering what Dalzere had told him the previous day, Kellen understood the implications, and he felt his muscles tense. He looked around in dread, feeling Peleyia edged closer to his side. "Where is Sasheer now?" Kellen whispered, discerning the surroundings a little better as the misty light of dawn increased.

"He and Criz went to scout the immediate area. They should

be back very soon," Salimen answered, lifting his chin to indicate the Drow's approach.

"We have to move. Immediately." It was a harsh whisper, matching Dalzere's dark mood.

"I say we wait for Sasheer," Lesendal decided, not even looking at the Drow.

"We don't have the luxury of time. We have to go now before it is too late."

"We wait," Lesendal cut back, an edge coming into his tone.

"Then we die."

"Now, listen here," Ryland interrupted as he turned toward the Drow, seeing both the strength and the menace in the man.

"The Kizer will know we have been here," Dalzere pronounced in a flat, deadly tone. "Our only hope is getting out of this immediate area before their hunters track us."

"We wait," Lesendal insisted. He lifted his eyes and glared at the Drow.

Even in the pale light, Kellen could see Dalzere's nostrils flare in anger while those dangerous eyes narrowed to slits. "No doubt the Kizer hunters will appreciate your stubbornness, but I do not. Sasheer has probably been led away by false trails. That is what the Kizer do to prey. We go now."

Each sentence was clipped, conveying urgency as well as restrained anger, and Kellen wanted to do nothing more than obey Dalzere's voice.

"No," Lesendal growled, refusing to listen. "We stay."

Kellen stared at the prince in disbelief.

"What's that?" Peleyia broke in as he made a grab for Dalzere's arm. He swung around. "I thought I heard something."

Dalzere's finely shaped brows arched down as he searched the area again.

After a tense moment, Ryland released a loud breath as his grip slackened on the hilt of his massive sword. "It was probably only a ground rabbit."

"There are no ground animals in this region," Dalzere corrected darkly, continuing to scrutinize the area.

"Maybe we should do as the Drow suggests," Salimen said, his own expression mirroring Dalzere's concern. "It is too quiet," he whispered, "we should go."

"I still say we wait for the others," Lesendal snapped, his tone and expression reflecting his hurt that Salimen would side with the Drow. He reached down to snatch up his pack then balked and swore as a spear whistled past him and ripped the pack from his grasp.

"By the gods!" Ryland exclaimed as he drew his massive sword and started toward the bush where the spear had originated. He gave his clan's war cry and charged.

"Ryland! The rest of you, down!" Dalzere spat as he pushed both Kellen and Peleyia behind him. "You two into the bushland over there!" He pointed toward the line of squat trees now visible in the pale dawn light. Then Dalzere was drawing his fine blade and moving to help the southerners.

"I want to fight," Peleyia started but got no further as Dalzere swung around and glared at him. That look invited no arguments.

"Go!"

It was precise, powerful, and to the point, and Kellen took his friend's arm and dragged Peleyia over to the meager coverage. Risking a glance back, he saw a dozen darkly-colored small men swarm into the camp, throwing themselves at Lesendal and the others, not even trying to defend themselves or even fight. Their strategy was insanely simple as more little men jumped into the attack, calling out in a strange, rhythmic language as they trapped the big Haonian warrior by sheer numbers, binding him in twine. They pulled down Lesendal next until only Dalzere and Salimen managed to avoid the twine and stay upright to fight.

"We've got to help them," Peleyia said, his eyes glistening in anger. Then before Kellen could stop him, the Lancooti sprang from their concealment with his short blade raised, going to Lesendal's aid.

Agreeing with Peleyia, Kellen watched horrified as Lesendal was bound in twine and then as Peleyia was clubbed from behind. The Lancooti fell hard. Angered, Kellen drew the blade Ryland had just given him and charged the smaller mud men who were dragging Peleyia into the center of the clearing. He hacked at the twining and kicked the frenzied Kizer hunters aside as he tried to free his friend. He could feel hands reaching for him and slapped them aside in desperation, using his long knife to stab at the bodies crowding him, struggling to break free of the sticky twine thrown over his head. He managed to cut his way out, fright and excitement driving him, and a moment later, he felt the unmistakable tingle of energy sweep up his legs answering his silent call for help. He tried not to panic, knowing now that his biggest problem was not the Kizer, but controlling his emotions, and the fact that he could unwittingly kill not only the enemy, but also his friends.

He backed away, tripping over some stones and rolling to one side as one of the ugly, dirty little hunters made a grab for him. He kicked out, shoving the grunting man away, managing to escape for a moment. Around him dust obscured the fighters, the morning light identifying just how much trouble they were in. The numbers of mud men seemed endless, and Kellen swore in frustration. So what should he do? He had promised Sasheer that he would not initiate anything without the other's guidance. Would not, or should not? *It's all irrelevant*, he decided as he pushed the power back into the ground beneath his feet, choosing instead to use his knife to defend himself from a crazed attacker. *Sasheer be damned*, and he gritted his teeth, swinging at the advancing Kizer—only to be seized from behind and confined with that sticky, netlike twine.

He was disarmed, a hand grabbing his hair to wrench his head back as a blade was pressed against his neck. Warm blood ran down his throat, and he froze, obeying his attacker and moving when he was pushed forward. His eyes watered, his breathing accelerated, and his scalp felt on fire from the savage grip, but he still obeyed. He tried to swallow, his mouth dry as he was shoved harder. He almost stumbled a few times, would have fallen if his captors had not gripped him tighter. He stepped over numerous bodies, seeing how the scowling Kizer clear a path for him until they dragged him to a stop at the edge of the clearing. A deathly silence fell over the area. Then as the dust settled, and the early-morning light kissed the barren clearing, he realized he was standing in front of a very angry Elven warrior. Dalzere.

The tall Drow was breathing hard, his face fierce and primal as he was covered in blood and dirt, his eyes reflecting a type of deadly madness. Then even as the Drow raised his gaze and met Kellen's fearful eyes, the Kizer took down Salimen by entangling the bowman in the webbed twine. The sticky fibers hindered Salimen's movements, so that he could be disarmed and pinned to the ground with a spear pressed to his chest. The bowman was cursing, shouting at Dalzere to do something.

Behind him, Kellen heard his captor growl something unintelligible in a harsh accent at the Drow, the words emphasized by the knife at Kellen's throat, biting in further. Slowly, Dalzere calmed his breathing, sanity returning to his vivid, golden eyes, and he straightened from his fighting crouch.

Still the filthy Kizer repeated his demand in a louder, more urgent voice, and Kellen watched as Dalzere glanced around before tilting his head slightly in defeat and dropping his fine blade. The sword hit the dry earth with a dull thud, raising more dust, and Kellen breathed a sigh of relief, glad when the knife at his throat moved to rest against his collarbone.

Five Kizer hunters approached Dalzere in obvious apprehension, all with spears leveled at the Drow's chest. When close enough, they started to jab him with their spears, drawing blood and hissing unintelligibly at him. Then they rushed him, and Kellen lost his view of Dalzere as his captor turned him and bound his hands roughly with sticky twine that itched against his skin. He could not flex his fingers when they were finished, the restraint limiting his upper body movements.

He swallowed, his throat raw and sore, and he tried to turn his head to see what was happening to his friends. That earned him a slap to the head before his captor grabbed his hair a second time and pulled his head back. Words were hissed into his ear—words he didn't understand—but the tone was ugly in a way he would never have imagined words could be. He wanted to protest, to fight back, but couldn't, and he gasped in pain as he was thrust forward only to fall face first into the fine black dirt. He spat out a mouthful of dust, shaking his head to clear the dizziness, not protesting when he was lifted, and forced to march toward the dense tree line. Of his companions' fate, he had no idea. He could neither see nor hear them, glimpsing only the deformed faces of his captors.

* * *

Time seemed to crawl, the cold morning turning into a hot day as Kellen's entire world became focused on the task of breathing. His captor had a perverse sense of humor, he decided, for the filthy little man insisted on dragging him along by his hair. It was awkward, painful, and degrading. His scalp was numb, and his throat felt dry and sore. All he saw of the frightening journey was the cloudless sky and the high branches of the few stunted trees they passed under. More unnerving was the fact that in those branches hung numerous spiderwebs and wicked-looking nests. From the indication of all the webs he had seen, he was definitely in no hurry to witness the size of the spiders.

Then the terrain around him changed. He started to see some vague designs of dark drawings on a few boulders they passed. He was even beginning to smell wisps of burning wood. Then as they moved further inland, he saw that they were moving closer to a rock formation. The boulders became more frequent and larger in size until they were all he saw. Gone were the trees and long sharp grass; now the ground under his feet was harder, even slippery in some areas. More paintings decorated the boulders, and then abruptly the air became tainted with the smell of foul, rotting flesh mixed with decay and rank woodsmoke.

He tensed, struggling against his captor as he was marched through a rock opening and into a large clearing of stone and dirt. He sensed movement all around. Voices, numerous voices greeted him, and he heard a chant start off to his left, drowning out the confused babble of voices. Slowly, every voice took up the hypnotic chant. His hair was released, and he lowered his head, his neck cramping in pain. Around him, a sea of faces swam into view. Ugly faces, scarred by cuts and by bone piercing, and he recoiled from them as they leaned in close, sniffing and licking his face before snarling curses. He closed his mouth, not wanting to inhale the putrid stench. He was herded forward then forced to sit on the ground under a burnt-out tree stump. He sat against the old tree and stared around the Kizer camp in disorientation, moving his shoulder and neck to ease the cramp.

The clearing was huge. A lifeless, barren area devoid of all imagination or color. It was sheltered by a jagged rock formation on all four sides, locking in the insane frenzy of the Kizer people as they chanted and jumped around in a crazed dance. He shrank back from the madness, his eyes being drawn to the huge fire that burned fiercely in the middle of the dusty camp. He could see a dark cave entrance beyond the fire. The sides of the cave were decorated with star-shaped symbols painted in some black tarry substance and guarded by three twisted tree stumps. Numerous webs hung between each stunted plant, their webs sparkling an eerie gold in the overcast sunlight.

Alarmed, Kellen jumped when a body hit the ground next to him, and he turned to see Peleyia. Blood covered the Lancooti's temple, but he appeared to be alive, if unconscious. Relief flooded through him, and he inched closer to his friend, softly calling the other's name. He got no reply. Then more of the hunting party returned, and he watched, anxious, as Lesendal's unconscious body was dropped to the ground just as unceremoniously, while Salimen was forced to kneel next to Peleyia. The bowman snarled his defiance, and one of the Kizer leveled a spear at his chest in warning. Fury was stamped across Salimen's features, blood crusting on his lower lip, yet he still kept his glare fixed on the filthy Kizer. The Kizer hissed something vicious then shoved Salimen backward before walking away.

Kellen exhaled in relief. He glanced around the busy camp and saw that there was no sign of Dalzere or Ryland, and he returned his attention to his injured friends.

A piercing cry had Kellen swinging back to the main body of the camp, seeing a shorter Kizer mud warrior exit the cave formation near the raging fire. This Kizer yelled something in a coarse language and brandished a staff, its end decorated by bones. This Kizer took up the chant of the earlier song, his accent harsh, his inflections guttural as he stamped his feet in time to his words. All the other Kizer started to imitate his actions and song, the ripple of sound dreadful as a heavy oppression settled on the encampment.

Step by step the leader drew closer to his trapped position, and Kellen was shocked to see that this ugly man was actually a woman. Her face was twisted into a mask of pure hatred as she shook her staff over them, her mouth devoid of teeth, and her skin wrinkled with age. Again she chanted a rhythmic litany, and then she moved to stand in the center of the camp before the raging fire. Once there, she raised her staff and hissed a single word. Utter silence fell over the encampment, and all the Kizer stopped dancing. Kellen shivered, suddenly feeling very apprehensive as to what was about to happen. Foreboding hung in the air, the crackling of the fire loud and the scent of incense overwhelming. The woman repeated the hissed command twice more, and a ripple of excitement rushed through the congregated Kizer tribe as an image started to appear in the smoke circling over the central fire.

"Cursed bones," Salimen breathed as he too saw the image grow in the swirling smoke.

Inching back, Kellen almost forgot to breathe as the apparition took on a hideous form, its skin transparent, showing something undulating down its grotesque body as it coalesced. It grew even larger, and all the Kizer dropped to their knees, intoning two words over and over again. *"Nar'Karnrd Horigan! Nar'Karnrd Horigan!"* They raised their hands, petitioning the evolving creature within the smoke.

Kellen stared at the conjured image with wide, disbelieving eyes. It was not a man, yet not an animal—a monster like nothing he had witnessed before. Huge, with a hideous face, broad shoulders, rippling-muscled bulk, and hoofed feet. It pawed the dirt impatiently, sending a shower of hot ash over many of the

Kizer. Fire licked up its limbs, highlighting the growing skin and fur which covered a rapidly solidifying body. Then abruptly, it stepped out of the smoke and fire to stand on real legs, and Kellen whimpered in terror.

He had never seen anything like this—never imagined anything like this—and he gasped as the evil creature's hoofed steps echoed around the rock enclosure. Then it tilted its head down and looked at them, its eyes a blood red, its smile grotesque. One of its hands passed through the hot flames, and it captured the burning brightness, trailing the angry fire in its wake. It cupped the flames in one blackened hand then flung it at them, and Kellen instinctively flinched, trying to back away. Hot, fiery ash showered them, and he bit his lip hard, drawing blood and refusing to cry out as he was burned. He heard Salimen exhale a hissed obscenity.

The old woman shook her staff, slowly standing with arms spread as she beckoned the creature. Fire demon. *"Nar'Karnrd Horigan! Nar'Karnrd Horigan!"* She repeated her call twice more before the unholy monster turned and regarded her with baleful eyes. She held up her staff high and shook it, repeating her chant. *"Nar'Karnrd Horigan! Nar'Karnrd Horigan!"* She then turned and strode over to her tribesmen, shaking her staff in a frenzy, making the prostrating Kizer moan in religious ecstasy.

Abruptly a path was cleared, and a group of Kizer warriors appeared. They advanced between the parted worshipers, dragging a captive. It was Dalzere. His arms were bound behind him, his lips swollen and bleeding. He was propelled roughly forward to stand before the fire demon. The old women moved in front of the Drow, hitting him across the chest and legs with her staff then, to Kellen's amazement, ripped his bloodied tunic from his body. Dalzere bared his teeth, and the Kizer warriors drove him to his knees while the frenzied witch intoned another litany, striking the Drow repeatedly. Ugly welts and cuts adorned the Drow's body, but Dalzere uttered not a word, and then the old woman lifted her bloodied staff triumphantly before turning back to her conjured demon and respectfully bowing.

"Gar Nakrid."

The creature growled out a word, the sound of its demonic voice vibrating through the ground, shaking the entire area. Kellen gasped, watching with a mix of horror and awe as more incense and more wood were thrown onto the raging fire. The air filled with a new putrid scent of decay and death.

Trying not to inhale, Kellen was unprepared for the hands that reached for him and dragged him and Salimen over to Dalzere, thrusting them hard onto the ground beside the Elf. He chanced a look up, and saw Dalzere's pain-creased face, then he looked and saw the undisguised hunger in the demon's red glowing eyes. He shuddered. "Dalzere," he whispered then grunted in pain as he was kicked from behind.

"Let them go."

It was Dalzere's voice, his tone so commanding and frighteningly calm that Kellen had to look twice at his friend. Dalzere looked fierce, and he appeared to be in total control despite his position, and at that moment, Kellen could see what a true Drow creature looked like: the ultimate in deadliness and darkness.

The old witch woman spat at him, screaming something in her harsh language before beseeching her master again. "*Kar nakrid gar dern Plarzid.*"

"I said, let them go! *Dern kaznerd, Horigan!*" This time Dalzere's words matched hers in pitch and volume as he growled something in their own harsh language. His words must have been shocking, because the old witch took an involuntary step back before her Kizer tribesmen swiftly wrapped thick twine around the Drow's throat to shut him up. They jerked him down, forcing him to submit.

The witch then clubbed him with her staff over and over, her face twisted in anger and spite, screaming words that sounded like curses before switching her fanatical gaze to the patiently waiting demon lord. The demon smiled in wicked delight, hot-fire ash running from his mouth as he reached out a clawed hand to touch her staff. The thick wood burst into flames, burning a brilliant blue before subsiding, causing all the Kizer gathered to cry out in a type of ecstasy. Then the witch stepped closer to the demon and ripped open her meager clothing to reveal her naked, withered breast. She dropped her filthy coverings on the ground, stripping completely, and Kellen gagged as the demon lord reached for her.

"Enough!"

The single word hissed around the enclosure and seemed to feather down over the entire encampment, startling everyone, and Kellen struggled to see from where it had originated.

The witch swung around sharply, bones dangling from her pierced nipples as she snarled. Behind her, the demon's clawed hands caressed over her filthy shoulders like smoke, and she seemed to grow in both stature and power. Angry ripples appeared under her flesh as the demon clawed down her naked body. The pleasure and pain of his touch twisted her ugly face into an abhorrent mask.

"I said—Enough!"

Again the word cut the atmosphere, and suddenly Sasheer stepped out from behind a boulder. He walked casually into the mist of the camp unmolested, as all the Kizer stared at him in disbelief and apprehension. Behind the Ranger was the silver-haired Crizkerisomia, her weapons drawn as she scanned the waiting Kizer, and on her left was a very bloodied, and very angry, Ryland.

"You!" The snarled word was pronounced in Kellen's own language, making him blink, startled, and he glanced back at the old woman, seeing how she was torn between rage and fear. Her raised staff started to glow a deep red, like that of spilled blood, and it dripped fire that turned to scolding ash as it hit the ground. "Horigan will kill you this time, Watcher." It was obviously an effort for her to form the words and speak them, and the demon pressed closer to her body. Then he opened his mouth and sank blackened teeth into her neck, forcing and sliding his way into her squat frame, merging, to take complete control.

Sasheer looked sad as he shook his head. "I warned you last time what would happen if you forced my hand," he said, his voice soft, and Kellen had the impression Sasheer was addressing the demon rather than the Kizer witch. "Vengeance will be your downfall; even your own people's prophecy foretold that fact. So be it," he said, resigned.

Then Sasheer lifted one clenched fist, and Kellen felt a vast summoning of power spiral around him, his mind stalling in disbelief as he suddenly pictured the other man clearly in his mind. His inner vision narrowed until he saw a very different Sasheer. *Dark hair, unbound, curling in a power-storm as Sasheer turned his face and looked toward the heavens. He lifted a hand and summoned the elements, controlling them, looking ageless and menacing. A being that did not belong to a single time or place.*

Shocked by the image, Kellen battled to stay conscious as he experienced the draining effect of the gathered energies, trying to close his mind off to its seductive pull. The potential of what Sasheer was creating was so vast that the ground shook violently before the Ranger unclenched his fist and threw that summoned power at the demon. The release of energy took the form of a brilliant fire dart, and Kellen gaped in shock. Then he blinked, utterly bewildered, as he saw a fire-red dragon appear behind Sasheer's rigid body. The dragon hovered in the air before vanishing into nothing, and Kellen fell back, awed and stunned. Then his eyes darted to the demon.

The magical fire dart pierced the old woman's chest, and she screamed, while the demon inside her struggled to break free, climbing through her skin, shattering her bones as it tore from her body to step back into the safety of the fire. But the force caught it midway, devouring it, holding it in the unstable joining as the swirling smoke vanished, and the fire was abruptly extinguished to leave no escape. Shrieking in pain and loss, the witch clutched at her spirit lord, begging for survival as the thrashing demon pushed her carelessly aside and dived into the cooling embers of the fire pit.

Then silence descended on the entire camp as the Kizer worshipers stared in shock at the cold charcoal logs and the old woman's mutilated carcass. A heart-beat later the Kizer were moving, superstition and fear sending them scattering into the surrounding foliage and caves. Within seconds, Kellen found the area deserted, and he sucked in a deep breath as Dalzere raised his head slowly to look through his hair at Sasheer.

"What took you so long?" the Drow asked mildly, his voice hoarse.

"I had baggage," Sasheer said offhandedly, his eyes flickering toward Ryland. Then he grinned and knelt down beside the Drow to untie the sticky twine.

Crizkerisomia untied Kellen and then Salimen before attending to the prince and Peleyia. Salimen massaged his raw wrists then went to Lesendal's side as the other sat up and blinked owlishly.

"What happened?" Lesendal raised a hand and touched his bruised temple.

"It's all right, Dale. Can you stand?" Salimen asked as Ryland handed them back their weapons before reaching down to lift the unconscious Lancooti.

"Pel?" Kellen asked in worry, but Crizkerisomia shook her head.

"He will wake with a headache." She then turned from him to eye Dalzere from head to foot. "Just know this, Drow—I would have waited until the old crone killed you before rescuing the others."

"Your concern warms me," Dalzere said as he wiped blood from his mouth. "We should probably move, as the Kizer-Horigan will not stay spooked for long, and then they will be back with renewed vengeance."

"Agreed," Sasheer nodded as he went over and took Kellen's chin in his hand to examine his bloodied throat.

"I'm ... umm ... fine," Kellen said, surprised by Sasheer's concern and also overwhelmed by what he had just witnessed. Magic. Real magic. Sasheer was Mageborn, of that fact he was now positive. So what did that make him? And what of the fire dragon he had glimpsed? He eyed Sasheer in a mix of awe and mistrust, not sure what he was expecting, or what he had assumed a Mageborn would look like. He had imagined someone old and wise, yet Sasheer was nothing like that. He was young, impulsive, irritable, and sarcastic. *Maybe he's a reject?* Musing over that, Kellen watched how Sasheer helped Dalzere clean the worst of his injures before offering some of his own clothing to the Drow; and Kellen's brow drew down further in confusion and speculation.

"What were the Kizer-Horigan doing here, in this part of the mudflats?" Sasheer asked as he finished helping Dalzere.

"I don't know. I had assumed that the Kizer-Dalicak had wiped them out five years ago in that last war," Dalzere said disgruntled.

"That witch had invoked a blood-vengeance curse—"

"You don't need to remind me," Dalzere cut him off and then raised a hand in apology. "I had believed her line dead and the curse broken."

Laying a hand on the other's shoulder, Sasheer nodded then turned to the others. "We had best head west, toward the cliff," he gestured toward the hazy blackness of distant mountains. "The passes are our only hope."

"Wouldn't it just be easier to go straight to the river? It's only a half day's march." Salimen said.

"Normally I would agree," Sasheer said in a tired voice, his eyes briefly going to Salimen. "But with the Kizer-Horigan hunting us—and they will hunt us—that will be the first route they follow." Sasheer looked at each member. "With an incomplete blood-vengeance curse, the remaining tribesmen are morally obligated to sanctify their witch's death with the death of her attackers," he explained when he received only blank stares in return. "They will be outcast and killed by the other Kizer factions if they do not avenge their demon's dishonor. It is a powerful reason to hunt us."

"Oh great," Salimen complained as he wrapped one of Lesendal's arms around his shoulders to aid his cousin. "I just love being chased."

"Our best alternative is the cliffs. It is a three-day hike west of here and will take us into safer territory. We then will be able to cross the Calmen River by the footbridge."

"Will they not just be waiting for us there?" Ryland asked, his thick accent more pronounced as he grimaced in pain, clearly shaken by what he had seen.

"The cliffs are called the Death Peaks and are Drow occupied. All Kizer fear the area," Crizkerisomia said, resheathing her weapons and glaring at Sasheer. "We should move, old man."

Nodding, Sasheer indicated for her to lead. "I'll disguise our tracks," he offered.

Salimen and Lesendal fell in behind the female Elf, and Kellen followed, exhaustion eating through him. At his back was Ryland, carrying the unconscious Peleyia, leaving Sasheer and Dalzere at the rear of the group. The latter two were talking quietly, and Kellen would have given anything to know what was being said. He was positive that old woman—witch—had known Dalzere, and that he and the others had just been incidental to the ritual.

Turning away, he saw a flicker of movement off to his right and squinted into the sparse undergrowth of rocks and stunted trees. He saw a second blur of amber before the animal disappeared. It was not so much the idea that an animal could survive in the desolate country surrounding them, rather it was the *feel* of this animal. Just like the familiar feel of the fire dragon. How had he known to look? He was positive no one else had seen the dragon.

He shook his head to clear the puzzling thoughts. For just a moment, he would almost have sworn the signature presence he had felt was that of Terrica. But she was human, and this was animal. Yet did he truly know what she was? And why would she follow him? Then another thought hit him, and he hesitated, hearing Ryland call to him from behind.

"Lad, are you injured?"

"No," he shook his head and forced his legs to move. If Terrica could change forms—be human then animal—what of the evil entity that had tried to kill him in Ihova? What form would it take next?

CHAPTER FIFTEEN

The constant traveling, weaving in and out of muddy dunes and avoiding the treacherous mud springs, had them all exhausted and filthy by the end of the third day. Sasheer and Crizkerisomia had forced them to keep moving, even during the dangerous hours of night, risking the chance of stumbling across another tribe's sacred site. They had found a number of Kizer-Horigan sites, proving that a lot had changed within the last year. The Kizer-Horigan had obviously pushed for supremacy and warred with the other factions inside the intricate peer castes of their society. The reclaiming of old lands and the numerous sacred sites indicated that they might even have toppled the Kizer-Dalicak tribe. It was a disquieting thought, and one that both Sasheer and Dalzere worried over. For the only way such a brutal minority faction could have defeated the larger Kizer-Dalicak would have been with outside help.

Sweeping dark hair out of his eyes, Kellen glanced around, seeing no change in their surroundings, even if Crizkerisomia did say they were getting close to the passages leading to the Death Peaks. She and Dalzere were continually scouting the area, finding Kizer-Horigan trackers and dealing with them, while the main body of hunters continued to slowly close in around them. It was nothing obvious, but they all knew it. They could feel it, knowing that other Kizer factions watched and waited for the outcome of the vengeance chase. He glanced back at Ryland and saw Peleyia walking behind the big Haonian warrior. His friend was still pale and more subdued than normal, the adventure souring for them both.

Stopping, Kellen looked around before turning to watch Salimen's approach. The Ihovian had offered to lead the group behind Dalzere's scouting, and to his surprise, the two were getting on very well. At the moment, the lean blond was repeating in a whisper to Lesendal and Sasheer what the Drow had told him, and Kellen leaned closer.

"The passes are not far, but it seems the Kizer have anticipated our move and are rushing to block our path." Salimen drew a small map in the dirt. "Dalzere says he will lead them away from this small obscure passageway here and pretend to head for the larger passageway over here. That should give us time to get into these passes."

"Time, but maybe not enough," Sasheer said. The others all looked at him, and he explained. "The large path and this narrow path all converge at the same point, just before the cliff face. Only the larger pass gets there faster. Granted the narrow one might be safer, but..." He left the rest unsaid.

"So it is a race," Lesendal finished.

"Yes," Sasheer agreed. He stood and scanned the desolate area, frowning, searching for something. "We will have to try, for we cannot risk another night out here. Most, I imagine, will follow Dalzere, but there will still be some that might find our trail. That is the danger."

"Dalzere also said to tell you that he's found tracks," Salimen continued in a quiet voice as he looked at Sasheer. "Horse and wagon tracks."

"There are no large animals within Kizer territory," Sasheer said to no one in particular, as he considered this new information.

"He also said to give you this," Salimen pulled out a clasp from his belt and handed it to the Ranger. "He found it near the wagon tracks."

Running his fingers over the smooth metal, Sasheer turned the odd-shaped disc over to read the markings engraved on the other side.

"What is it?" Kellen asked.

"A key," Sasheer said, frowning.

"It's a very odd-shaped key, if you ask me," Lesendal snorted. "Can you read the inscription?"

"The runes are in the old tongue. They are the number 5."

"Five?"

Sighing, Sasheer glanced around. "It's a Slaver's key. The Black Guard—" He stopped, and sighed. "I doubt you'd understand. I am going to have to do something about the educational standards in the south."

Lesendal glared at him. "More fairy tales?"

"No," Sasheer snapped then sent Lesendal an amused look. "The Black Guard, as you know, are made up of three separate units. The Warrior Class, which you have seen in action within the borders of the south. The other two units are the Pen Masters, who run the Ice Cliffs and Gerthwin Caverns, and the Slavers, who roam the mainland collecting subjects for Kalern's experiments or candidates for his army."

"So you think these Slavers have been here and have taken the Kizer-Dalicak prisoner?" Salimen asked. "That could explain why the Horigan tribe is prominent again, I suppose. With their natural enemies removed, the little bastards would flourish."

"That is one explanation," Sasheer nodded.

"With no Kizer-Dalicak hindrance, the Horigan will be . . ." Lesendal trailed off as he glanced at his cousin. "You're right, Sal; we're in trouble."

"Let's just get to the pass," Sasheer said.

"How narrow is this passage where the two passes converge?" Ryland asked. "Maybe we could get through, then I could stand and block these mud demons until you are all safe, and the Drow has met up with me."

Sasheer raised a curious brow.

Ryland shrugged, looking a little embarrassed. "I would hate to lose the Drow now," he explained gruffly. "He is a skilled warrior—a member of this company—and we may have need of his skills if we are to enter Drow territory."

Sasheer laughed. "Very well." He looked to Salimen. "Sal, can you wait here for Criz and tell her what we are doing and then catch us as quickly as possible?"

"Fine," the Ihovian grinned. He gripped his cousin's hand hard in parting then slowly went back the way they had come.

Watching him go, Kellen felt a pang of apprehension as Sasheer led them forward again. The pace was fast, and he found himself almost running at times to keep up. Next to him was Ryland, and he cast his old friend a questioning look. "Do you really think we will get through?"

"If you had asked me that two months ago, I would have said no, but now . . ." He left the rest unsaid.

"Things have really changed," Kellen voiced the unspoken words. "Do you still think the Mageborns are a myth?"

The big man gave him a reproving glance before settling his eyes on Sasheer's slender frame in the lead. "I think the subject is best discussed at another time."

Taking the rebuke, Kellen frowned. "And Dalzere?"

Sighing heavily, Ryland gave him a pained answer, "What do you want me to say, lad? That everything Lesendal, Salimen, and I have been taught is wrong? That we are narrow-minded and stupid, just as Sasheer says?"

"No," Kellen said, contrite. "I don't know what I want you to say."

"There is more going on here than just saving the Southland and maybe finding the Princess Kessendra. I think you and I have stumbled across something that is far more dangerous than anything we can imagine, or understand. The ways of the folks who live on the mainland are not our ways. So it is probably best to keep our heads down and just watch and listen. Eventually things should become clearer."

"I just hope you are right."

"So do I, lad. So do I."

* * *

Sasheer called a halt in the early afternoon, waiting for everyone to catch up. Lesendal handed around the water pouch.

"Just ahead is the entrance to the narrow passage. I have seen no evidence of the Kizer-Horigan, but that does not mean they are not around. Once inside the passage, I want everyone to stay close, no dropping behind or detouring into side paths. Avoid talking, as the sound echoes. And stop when I indicate for you all to stop."

They all nodded.

"What of Sal and the white Elf?" Lesendal asked.

"We will wait for them before the junction. It will also give Dalzere time to catch up," Sasheer said.

Accepting that, Lesendal reshouldered his pack and followed the Ranger as the other silently crept through the low scrub. Close on his heels was Peleyia, followed by Kellen, both imitating the prince. Ryland guarded the rear. At the edge of the scrub, the ground became even more desolate, and they faced dark sandstone ridges and huge boulders leading to a steep, looming rock wall.

"That's it?" Lesendal whispered in skepticism. "So where's this passage?"

"See that opening over there?" Sasheer pointed to a spot a distance away.

Squinting, Lesendal shook his head in disbelief. "That's just a crack in the rock face; you can't be serious."

"Trust me," Sasheer smiled then studied the ground. "These tracks look to be a few hours old, so we may be in luck, and Dalzere's plan might just work." He turned back to the group, his expression grave. "Now remember, stay close to each other, and don't put your fingers into any curious holes you find in the rock face."

"Why?" Kellen asked.

"Because there are other things deadlier than the Kizer or even Drow in this region."

Wishing Sasheer would elaborate, Kellen felt far from happy when Sasheer turned away and slowly parted the low bushes. Beside him, he felt Peleyia brush his side and saw the other give him an encouraging grin. "You still think this is an exciting adventure?" he asked in a soft voice.

If anything, the Lancooti's grin only widened. "Ask me when we reach the other side."

"If we reach the other side," Kellen said, watching Peleyia move away. He glanced back one last time and shivered.

They followed Sasheer across the open strip of black sand to reach the looming rock wall, each squeezing through the tight crack of sandstone and awkwardly sliding between the two narrow rock faces. The sheer stonewalls went up so high that no light touched the dark crevice. It was damp and cramped and claustrophobic and seemed to go on endlessly. The narrow passage of icy stone was covered with patches of slimy, spongy fungus, and Kellen grimaced, shuddering in reaction to the smell of the passage, so glad when a faint light haloed the approaching exit. Only Ryland had serious trouble navigating the narrow gap, needing to stop and struggle out of his armor and weapons. When he emerged, his face and hands were scratched and bleeding, his tunic stained green from the moss.

Once on the other side of the narrow gorge, they all breathed a sigh of relief, glad of the sunlight and warmth. Ahead was another narrow passage, but it was marginally wider and not so dark.

"Gods . . ." Ryland released a heavy breath. Sasheer frowned at him, shaking his head before the Ranger unsheathed his sword, using it to brush away low-hanging spiderwebs as he entered the next section of passageway.

Cringing as the broken, sticky webs feathered down on top of them, Kellen also took his short blade out to clear away the remaining webs. He no longer felt curious as to what might be in the many odd-shaped holes and crevices which dotted the dark walls. He tried to keep from touching either side of the narrow passageway. The deep gloom of the twisting passages did not help his imagination, and a coldness started to seep into his bones.

Occasionally, they came to wet stone as water slowly ran down the high rock faces, making the floor slippery and the walls damp and moldy. A crusty fungus flaked off with just a touch, clinging to their clothing and hands as each tried to get past the wet places as quickly as possible. The sound of their footsteps echoed, creating an eerie sound that only added to the unwelcoming feel of the mountain. Entering a new section of passageway, they encountered a steep, winding track and low archways where more than just hideous webs hung.

Holding his breath as he hastily ducked under one archway behind Peleyia, Kellen almost cried out in alarm as one huge spider fell from the low, overhanging ceiling to land on Peleyia's back. Its long hairy legs were the same color as the surrounding rock, and two long antennae waved over the Lancooti's shoulder as it slowly inched its way toward his neck.

Horrified, Kellen just stopped himself from stabbing his friend in the back as they both scooted out from under the low, overhanging ceiling, Peleyia jumping up as he felt the creature's weight.

"Get it off! Get it off me!" He swung around, trying to knock the creature off his shoulder.

"Turn around!" Kellen told him urgently, forgetting to keep his voice down as Peleyia's natural panic infused them both. "Pel, turn, so I can kill it," he grabbed his friend's tunic, pushing him into the rock wall even as Ryland came up from behind. Both Lesendal and Sasheer stopped ahead and returned.

"Stars! Kell, get that thing off me!" Peleyia dropped his pack, instinctively trying to shake off the creature.

"Hold still," Kellen admonished even as he saw the cruel-looking spider slide from the Lancooti's shoulder to his forearm as Peleyia slapped at it. But the spider hung on, jumping abruptly and latching on to his slapping hand with a swiftness and grip that was terrifying.

"Ugh!" The Lancooti gasped in pain as the spider bit him, its antennae going rigid for a prolonged moment. He crashed into Lesendal, desperate to get away from the huge creature, beginning to shudder in pain and reaction from the venomous bite. Kellen gasped as the hideous spider suddenly leaped from Peleyia's hand right onto his left leg.

Without thinking, he mirrored Peleyia's actions and slapped frantically at the advancing spider with his knife, but it seemed to have no effect on the creature except to make it more agile.

"Stand still, lad," Ryland ordered as the big man reached for the creature with his steel-clad hand.

As confined as they were in the gloomy passage, Sasheer pushed

Lesendal aside, only giving the Lancooti a brief glance before using his sword to stop Ryland from touching the spider. "Be still, Kellen!" he hissed, his voice penetrating the panic.

Trying to comply, Kellen stilled, gripping Ryland, as his eyes never left the advancing eight-legged creature as it crawled its way over his belt buckle on to his leather tunic. It was twice the size of his own hand. "Sasheer, if you are going to do something, please do it now," he pleaded.

"These are *siacon*, a Drow-created pet," Sasheer explained, his tone conversational. "They sting their victims, paralyzing the muscles while they then go and call the rest of their nest, so all can eat in peace. They can usually consume a whole horse within hours. And the worst part is that the victims are usually conscious until the end."

"Lovely," Kellen breathed wryly.

"Sasheer, enough of the history lesson. Just kill it," Lesendal ordered as he held Peleyia's shivering body.

"Hold very still, Kellen," Sasheer whispered, leaning closer and pulling out a short knife.

Swallowing, Kellen shut his eyes as the spider sat heavily on his chest. Its long antennae tickled his chin, and he tried to ignore its deliberate advance on his neck.

Sasheer balanced his knife. "If it thinks I am going to reach for it, it will bite you, just like it bit Pel, so you have to deceive it." Then with a twist of his wrist so fast, it could barely be seen; he flicked the knife at the spider, catching it in the side and sweeping it off Kellen's chest to be pinned against the stonewall. "There," he said as Kellen sagged heavily against Ryland.

Reaching forward, Sasheer pulled his short knife free of the soft stone, letting the evil-looking spider slide down the wall in an oozing mess.

"Are you sure it's dead?" Ryland asked, using his huge sword to stab at the creature a second time.

"Yes," Sasheer assured in mild irritation. "But we had best move, before others from its nest show up."

"What of Sal and the Criz?" Lesendal asked. "Won't they have problems if more of those things live here?"

Muttering under his breath, Sasheer considered that then took his knife and scratched a symbol on the wall.

"What does that say?" Ryland asked.

"A warning for Criz." Turning away, he went over and took Peleyia's chin in his hand, seeing the effects of the paralyzing poison already seeping through the slender Lancooti. "We'll have to carry him."

"Let me," Lesendal offered as he stripped off his pack, tossing it to Kellen.

With an accepting nod, Sasheer squeezed past them again to take the lead. "Remember—touch nothing," he hissed and then beckoned for them to hurry.

Juggling his extra burden, Kellen also picked up Peleyia's discarded pack. He studied his friend in worry, noting Peleyia's flushed face and expressionless eyes. Peleyia's hand, where the bite had occurred, was gray, with an inky black bruise that spread up the Lancooti's bare arm.

"Come on, lad," Ryland encouraged, as he glanced at the walls nervously, holding his short dagger in one hand and his battle-axe in the other.

* * *

They made their way along the narrow passage, the late-afternoon gloom deepening the shadows before Sasheer called another stop.

Lowering the injured Lancooti to the ground, Lesendal flexed his stiff muscles before following the Ranger to the next junction. He drew his sword as he crept forward, crouching down as Sasheer pointed something out to him.

Curious, but not having the energy to follow, Kellen collapsed next to his friend and took Peleyia's slack hand in his own. He carefully examined the vicious bite. Beside him, Ryland lowered his pack also, going back to check on the path behind, muttering that he had heard something.

"Stay here, lad. I just want to make sure we are not followed."

"Pel," Kellen started softly, looking away from Ryland to study his unresponsive friend in worry. "It's going to be all right; you'll see. Soon as we are out of these passes and reach this Keep of Sasheer's, he will get you a healer. Then you'll be back to normal," he encouraged. The other did not even twitch, his light eyes just staring ahead into nothing. Even his colored hair appeared dull and dead. "I promise," Kellen whispered, leaning in close and making it sound like a vow.

Behind him, Ryland returned, and with him were the white Elf and Salimen. The Ihovian looked worse for wear, cradling a splinted arm protectively.

"Look who I found," Ryland sounded pleased. "I thought I could hear someone following us, and I prayed it was you two and not some Kizer mud men."

"What happened to your arm?" Kellen asked as Salimen stepped over him.

The bowman gave an awkward shrug, his smile typical as he regarded first Kellen and then Peleyia. He crouched down. "I ran into a few angry Kizer-Horigan. What happened to Pel?"

"He got bitten by a Drow pet, or so Sasheer said." Kellen shuddered in remembrance. "Ugliest looking spider I have ever seen."

"Is the Drow here?" Salimen asked, standing up again. All he saw were Ryland and Crizkerisomia talking with Sasheer and Lesendal.

"No."

Nodding, the blond made his way over to the others.

Watching them at the junction, Kellen rested his head against the cool rock wall, glad that the area was not as narrow and the wall not as high, giving more light. Releasing a breath, he tried to relax, slowly going over everything that had happened since leaving Engleton. He wondered if the seaport was still there, or if Kalern and his dark army had captured the city.

Kalern. It was a name he had never heard before meeting Sasheer, but it was a name which resurrected a surprising amount of loathing and resentment deep inside his mind. Like a buried memory, bringing an image into his head of a cold, dark cavern with an abyss. It was like a twisted dream. But why he should despise this lord so much, particularly one he had never met, baffled him. Yet the hatred was there. He could feel it welling inside his chest until all he could think about was . . . and he gasped—*reaching out he stripped the green diamond pendant from Kalern's grasp. The Eye of Jade—a pendant so precious, so coveted for its elemental ability to make its wearer invisible. Its qualities of suggestion, of artful manipulation, of seduction were legendary. A magical heirloom of his family. A gift from—*

Jolting upright, Kellen found he was sweating, and he ran a hand over his face. From where had those images come? Was it a dream or nightmare? Had he been asleep, or had be been awake believing he was asleep . . . or had he just imagined the whole thing? "The Eye of Jade," he whispered the name as his mind continued to whirl in chaotic circles. He was so focused on his own problems that he didn't see Ryland's return until the big man shook him gently.

"Come on, lad," Ryland said, "we have to leave."

Jumping, Kellen glanced up quickly, seeing Ryland's serious face. "What?"

"We have to go, as Criz say some Kizer-Horigan's are behind us, and the passage at the junction is clear." He shook his head. "We cannot wait any longer."

"But . . ." Kellen climbed to his feet. Next to him, Lesendal hauled Peleyia's unresisting body up and swung the lean youth over his shoulders. "But Dalzere—"

"As much as I want to help the Drow, Sasheer is right. We have to move while we still have the light, and while we have the advantage."

Not liking it, Kellen nonetheless fell into step behind the prince, shouldering the three packs as they exited the narrow passage into a wider and well-used trail. Ahead, the path climbed, and the wind picked up, a cold blast of air hitting his hot skin. In the distance, he could see a dark mountain range looming ominously.

CHAPTER SIXTEEN

They reached a steep gorge just as the sun started to set. Before them was a very narrow wooden bridge, which hung over the wide, rushing Calmen River at the bottom of the gorge. Looking in both directions, Kellen could see the river stretched for leagues. The sound of the water below and the whistle of the wind in the surrounding rocks were almost deafening, but it was here Sasheer called a stop.

Pulling his tunic tighter, Kellen reached down and liberated his cloak from one of the packs, wrapping it around his frame as the winter chill laced the strong wind. The others did the same, each eyeing the swaying bridge which spanned the treacherous river below. It was a very long way down into surging water.

"What now?" Lesendal called, the wind snatching his words away.

"We cross one at a time," Sasheer instructed, holding up a finger. He then touched Crizkerisomia's arm, indicating for her to go first.

She gave him a chilling grin then shouldered her pack and stepped onto the unstable bridge. It swayed under her weight, the old wood creaking and shifting.

Watching her careful progress only made Kellen feel worse, knowing as he did that she, out of all of them, was the most nimble and capable climber.

"Oh, isn't this just wonderful?" Salimen snapped sarcastically. "It's going to take us all night to get across," he complained loudly. Then cursed when Sasheer ignored him. "I'll go and check the pass behind us. Just in case those Kizer-Horigan are smarter than we thought."

Letting him go, Sasheer turned to the prince. "You go next

with the Lancooti. We'll strap him to your back, as you'll need both hands to navigate the bridge."

Helping Sasheer tie the paralyzed Lancooti to Lesendal's back, Kellen tried again to reassure his friend before Lesendal set out across the swaying bridge. He received little response and settled for just trying to close Peleyia's partially opened eyes. It was too unnerving, having those vacant eyes stare at him.

"Kellen, you to go next," Sasheer said, before he walked over to Ryland. "Go and find that crazy bowman and bring him back here. And hurry!"

"But . . ." Kellen started as he watched Ryland nod and then disappear around the corner of the rocky pass. Locking his eyes on Sasheer, he stepped back when the Ranger swept past him bad temperedly. He sighed, resigned, then picked up the three packs and slung them over his shoulders, securing them as best he could, balancing their weight, and watching Lesendal's slow progress. He doubted Sasheer would listen to anything he had to say at present.

"When he is about three quarters across, I want you to start," Sasheer instructed, his tone impatient. "By the stars! Where are those southerners?"

Raising a questioning brow, Kellen frowned. "But you said only one was to cross at a time—"

"I know what I said! You don't need to remind me; just obey," Sasheer snapped, his eyes piercing.

Kellen glared back for a long moment. "All right," he returned evenly, refusing to let Sasheer anger him.

"Good. I think we have just about run out of time, options, and luck."

Waiting until Lesendal was more than halfway across, Kellen hesitated then stepped onto the moving bridge. Immediately he clutched the side rails for balance, horrified to find they were made of only entwined rope. They pushed out, and he almost fell forward, losing his stability. The wooden bridge swayed dangerously. He could feel the vibration of Lesendal's footfalls far ahead, but he concentrated on his own plight, sliding his feet over the old wooden slats. He tried not to look down, focusing on the bridge ahead, his fear of heights reasserting itself. Swaying, he juggled the packs, getting hammered by the wind as he left the sheltered area of the pass behind, feeling the ropes burn his hands as he used them to pull himself along.

Every muscle started to ache as he fought the wind and the uneven sway of the bridge beneath his feet. He could hear the turbulent waters, far below—and tried not to think, not to panic. About halfway across, he felt the wood under him shudder, and he chanced a look back, groaning as he saw Ryland step onto the flimsy structure and send shock waves along the slatted wood. Quickening his pace as much as possible, he felt sweat drip from his face, his hands raw and sore, as ahead Crizkerisomia beckoned for him to hurry. Gritting his teeth, he battled on, relieved when Lesendal grabbed his cloak and dragged him to solid ground, his legs giving out on the solid rock floor.

After gathering his breath and settling his nausea, Kellen glanced back at the treacherous bridge. Close behind Ryland was Salimen, and as he peered across the expanse in the darkening gloom, he saw Sasheer start on to the bridge then turn back as Dalzere suddenly appeared out of the pass behind. The Drow looked to be running as he pushed the Ranger back toward the bridge, swiveling in one fluid motion to block the advance of some Kizer-Horigan with his sword. Throwing caution to the wind, Sasheer then threw something at the rock face, causing the whole mountain to shudder slightly, dirt and smoke flying everywhere.

As the dust cleared, Kellen could see Salimen had been thrown over the side of the bridge by the blast, and the bowman was now hanging by only one hand. His good hand. He swung helplessly in the buffeting wind while the old bridge swayed dangerously. On the bridge, both Dalzere and Sasheer were headed toward him, running, while behind in the smoke-filled pass, numerous rocks continued to slide down the stone face, blocking the narrow gorge.

"Sal!" Lesendal started to go back for him but stopped, contending himself with helping Ryland to safety.

Reaching the stricken Ihovian, Dalzere leaned down over the side of the wooden planks, gripping the blond's arm. The two swayed with the motion of the bridge. Under Dalzere's grip, Salimen twisted around as another gust of wind caught him. One arm was hanging useless, and his pack slid from his shoulder falling straight down into the churning, angry river below. Then Sasheer reached the duo, and lay on Dalzere's right. Sasheer reached for the Ihovian also, trying to pull him up by his clothing. Only Salimen lost his grip, and the Drow just caught the bowman before he fell.

Kellen held his breath, watching Dalzere and Sasheer battled to get a firm grip on the struggling man. He looked at the others and saw their concern, then gasped as he abruptly got a very bad feeling about the entire situation. A blanketing sensation of doom seemed to settle over him, blocking out all other sensations. An icy coldness, a dread, *death*—then without warning, something caressed his face, snapping him to awareness as he realized what he was feeling and sensing.

The invisible, evil entity.

He cursed and glanced around, desperately trying to pinpoint the creature's location. He focused his mind, his will, on the wicked little creature, wanting to force it into his reality and hold it captive long enough so his friends made it across the bridge. If he could force the mischievous Terrica to appear, then he was certain he could force this wicked entity to materialize.

Using some of the techniques Sasheer had started to teach him, Kellen summoned the energy consciously for the first time. He allowed the exhilarating rush of power to wash up his legs and into his chest. Like a well of hot, liquid fire, his mind exploded with the potential he felt gathering in his palms—only before he could release the power, he was interrupted, distracted by Ryland as the Haonian yelled a sharp warning.

Centering his gaze on the three men trapped on the bridge, Kellen saw what was happening on the far side of the pass. The Kizer-Horigan had somehow managed to break through the rockslide and were preparing to storm the bridge. And he saw that Sasheer, Dalzere, and Salimen were completely oblivious to the danger.

"I'm going back—"

"No." Crizkerisomia laid an arm across Lesendal's chest to bar his passing. "Any more weight on that bridge, and the whole thing will go. We can't risk it."

"So what are we to do?" Lesendal cut back. "Just watch my—our—friends die?"

"No," the Elf said as she pulled out Salimen's bow, which she had been carrying for the injured Ihovian. "I intend to fight." Leveling the crossbow, she prepared to fire.

"In this wind, no arrow will make it across that distance," Lesendal judged.

"I know."

"Then why—" Lesendal stopped as the arrow flew. It landed very close to Sasheer.

"To warn them," Crizkerisomia said.

They saw Sasheer lift his head and then saw Dalzere half turn also, both glancing back at the Kizer-Horigan behind. Letting go of his anchor, Dalzere reached over with his second hand and grabbed the Ihovian, hauling him up with brute strength.

Then the unthinkable happened. A savage gust of wind caught them, and all three went over the edge of the narrow bridge. Dalzere just managed to stop his dangerous slide with his legs by hooking them over a rope rail. Sasheer was not so lucky, and he went over, catching Salimen's injured arm and falling heavily against the blond Ihovian. The two swung in the cold wind. Using his leverage, Dalzere slowly hauled first Salimen up, so that the other could grab at the rope and then helped Sasheer climb back onto the wooden planking. By the time they had the Ihovian back on the bridge, two Kizer-Horigan had started charging toward them with spears raised.

"Come on," Crizkerisomia said, getting all the others moving along the widening path. "We have to leave, get to the ledge before the Kizer reach us," she insisted, pushing Lesendal ahead of her. "When we reach the ledge, remember to stay only on the left side."

Not wanting to go, Kellen reluctantly followed Ryland, glancing back often. He could still sense the dread in the atmosphere around him and wondered what traps this vindictive entity had in store for him and his friends. The energy he had summoned was still there but tempered now with control and understanding, and he knew he could release it whenever he wanted. It was a relief to know he could contain the volatile powers, and he knew he would eventually have to thank Sasheer for his basic teachings.

He was also no longer in any doubt that something had been piling obstacles in his way since that fateful day back at the old farmhouse in Ihova. Bracing himself for almost anything, he wanted to warn the others, and he turned with the words on his lips only to see Salimen's wearied approach. Behind him were Sasheer and Dalzere, and Kellen relaxed, his face breaking into a grin. Now he could start to believe that disaster would be diverted.

Letting Salimen pass him, Kellen waited for the Ranger and Drow to reach his side. "Are you okay?"

Sasheer just gave him a small smile as he looked over at the others. "The Kizer are right behind us. Our only chance now is to get past the ledge and into the peaks."

"Will they not follow us there?" Ryland asked.

"No," Dalzere answered, his smile devoid of all warmth. "They fear the Drow more than they fear their own curses."

"Let's go," Sasheer said, moving forward to take the lead.

"It's good to see you," Kellen murmured.

Dalzere only smiled before pushing him forward.

* * *

Approaching the ledge, Sasheer did not stop to instruct them. Instead, he increased the pace, urging them on with a hissed command. They could see the Kizer-Horigan trackers bringing up the rear, could hear their war cry as the squat mud men brandished spears and knives. Breathing hard, Kellen followed Ryland, keeping his back to the wall as he stepped out onto the foot-wide protrusion.

The narrow path was nothing more than a ledge cut into the rock face. Below was a drop straight down into the green foliage of a forest far beneath them. Above was just more smooth rock—

high and formidable, seemingly endless. It was at least half a league's distance either way, and he bit his lip, sliding his way along the rough stonewall. He tried not to look down, thankful for the fact that the wind was mild, skimming across the surface of the rock, sliding over them in a rush. He did glance out once and gasped, feeling his heart pound as he forced himself to keep moving along the narrow lip. Only the fact that he had Ryland in front, and Dalzere behind kept him going. He just had to trust them.

Evening was slowly descending, the sun sinking behind the impressive peaks of the Drow homeland, and Kellen prayed they weren't still on this precarious ledge come dark. He moved as fast as he could, needing to hurry but scared of slipping and plunging down into the gloom below. He felt hot, his palms sweaty as they slid over the hard rock as he searched for handholds—and then to his horror, he saw a small group of Kizer-Horigan trackers appear round the first bend. They shouted in victory.

"Don't look at them!" Dalzere hissed, and Kellen dragged his eyes away. He ignored the frightening sight and concentrated on maintaining his balance.

"Just move," Dalzere encouraged. "We are more than halfway across. Very soon we will be off the lip and safe."

Nodding, Kellen tried to move faster, shifting his feet over the ledge's surface, kicking chipped rock aside, slipping on the loose stones. He hugged the wall harder, swallowing his nausea and fear as he heard the loose stones rattled down the rock face into the gloom below. Looking ahead, he watched Sasheer step off the ledge and turn to help Crizkerisomia. Unable to help himself, Kellen glanced back and was stunned at how the Kizer literally ran along the narrow lip. *NO!* His heart started to pound in panic, and he almost fell. That froze him and he stopped, battling his fear and wanting to shrink into nothing when he suddenly felt the unmistakable touch of icy fingers wind around his throat. The wicked, invisible creature had returned, and its cold touch cut through all his defenses.

"Kell?"

He swayed forward in a total daze and then gasped as Dalzere's hand slapped against his chest and slammed him into the rock wall behind. He shuddered in pain and surprise, risking a look at the Drow and seeing his concern. Behind Dalzere were the Kizer with their demonic, painted faces—and everything around him seemed to slow down as he was given a glimpse of the evil creature's true agenda.

Death.

Its purpose was simple. It was there to kill him. Underneath the cold mask was a hatred so strong that nothing else existed for this creature. Hope was an alien concept, an emotion outside this creature's scope of reasoning, as it existed in perpetual grief.

Shocked, Kellen lifted a hand, feeling pity, and was rewarded for his compassion by a hard blow to the stomach. He slid down the wall and gasped in pain, then glared at the space around him, willing the creature to appear. :*WHY?:* he snarled mentally. :*Why are you doing this to me?:*

He got no answer, and he clamped his teeth, focusing his will on the area before him. He saw nothing, but he could *feel* the creature, and he tried to outthink his opponent. Then time returned to normal, and he became aware of Dalzere at his side, aware of the wind, aware of the faint tremors within the heart of the mountain.

He braced himself against the wall and stood, glancing up, not believing his senses. *Not possible,* but his eyes widened in perception. The wicked entity would kill them all to destroy him—and he reached out for help, calling silently to the second entity.

:*Terrica!:* he pleaded, sending out his thoughts, praying it was possible to banish one entity with the other. Silence greeted him, and he sagged against the rock wall in defeat as he heard devilish laughter tickle his ears. It was a taunting challenge, and he balled a fist, willing up the energy he had gathered earlier.

"Kellen! No!"

Sasheer's shout startled him, and he turned to look at the Ranger, meeting those dark blue eyes and seeing fear reflected there. *Fear?* That puzzled him, and he slowly blinked, catching sight of Terrica hovering behind the Ranger's back. Only this time she did not resemble the sensual female form he had last seen. This time she appeared as a small fire dragon. He stared, stunned.

"Kellen?"

Dalzere's voice brought him back to the present, and he turned to look at his Drow friend. Dalzere uttered a curse in a strange language, searching for a handhold along the ledge as the mountain started to shake.

"Another quake? Here? Impossible!"

Dalzere sounded shocked, and Kellen looked beyond the Drow and saw one of the leading Kizer-Horigan topple from the ledge to fall and crash against the wall below before disappearing into the dense forest. His scream drifted up eerily, causing his tribesmen to hesitate. It was surreal, and Kellen blinked, wondering if this was another waking nightmare.

"Kell?" Dalzere called.

"Get away from me, or it will kill you," he said, knowing it was the truth. He reached out and shoved Dalzere away, even as they both were showered with dirt and loose stones from above. Then a second, stronger tremor shook the mountain, and he didn't know if he wanted to laugh or cry at the perverse creature's sense of humor.

"What will kill me? What are you talking about?" Dalzere barked, grabbing Kellen's arm and trying to shelter him.

"No—it's me, don't you see?" Staring at the Drow, Kellen saw only mild annoyance as Dalzere glanced around in worry.

"This whole ledge is about to go." Dalzere warned then jumped back and caught Kellen as the ledge beneath their feet gave way. He clutched at Kellen's wrist, holding him fast as Kellen slide down the rock wall. He crouched, trying to haul the younger man to safety, even as more of the ledge broke away, sending the Kizer behind them plummeting to their deaths.

"Let me go," Kellen said. He lifted his eyes and met Dalzere's gaze, amazed and comforted by the intensity of the Drow's fierce determination to protect them both.

"What?"

"It's the only way," he said, praying Dalzere listened. "If you let me go, then the tremors will stop." He understood the game now—understood that all along this invisible, manipulative, evil entity had wanted him dead, risking everyone around him to obtain its goal. Was this his punishment for killing the Black Guard commander?

"Have you gone mad?" Dalzere hissed as he raised an arm to shelter them both from the falling debris.

Hanging, with his face against the cold rock, Kellen knew Dalzere could not hold him forever. He closed his eyes for a moment, absorbing the coldness of the rock into his body. Then he glanced up and smiled at Dalzere, seeing Dalzere's confusion, seeing how his friend was filthy and bedraggled. It was only then that he realized how extensive the damage to the ledge was—only then that he saw how doomed Dalzere was. This unusual Drow would die because of him. And what of the others? He could not see them, and the idea that this vindictive creature would kill everyone around him, made him very angry. To chase him was one thing, but to kill his friends was totally unacceptable.

Cursing in anger, he shouted out his defiance. "I won't let you do this!" He knew the creature had heard him as he sensed its gloating laughter in his mind. "I will fight you!"

"Kellen?" Dalzere looked at him in concern. "Who are you talking to?"

"You will not win!" Kellen hissed, tears of rage blinding him as he reached up to grip what was left of Dalzere's ledge. Then focusing his mind, he deliberately searched out the evil entity's energy lines, homing in on them before lancing his gathered energy and anger directly into the creature. He heard its squeal of pain and surprise, before the creature tried to dart out of reach. But he held it—wanting it dead—wanting its protective armor destroyed. He poured all his rage and despair into the entity and felt part of its armor crack. He briefly got a glimpse of tarnished white scales and large silver eyes before the creature whimpered in pain and vanished.

Then the stone ledge he was clinging to broke away, and he was sliding uncontrollably down the cliff face.

CHAPTER SEVENTEEN

Cursing as he lost his hold on Kellen, Dalzere quickly glanced over at Sasheer and the others, seeing their shock. He locked gazes with Sasheer in silent communication, sending his partner a dark grin.

Then he purposely stepped off the narrow ledge. He knew in his mind that there was a faint possibility Kellen would survive the fall if he slid the length of the wall, and if the packs he wore cushioned his fall. He prayed he was right and that he had made the right choice as he bumped and slid his way down the rough surface, seeing Kellen disappear into the foliage below.

Night was rapidly approaching, and night was the time of the Drow. His first priority would be to locate Kellen and then make sure all the Kizer-Horigan were dead. After that he would scout for hunters. Drow hunters.

CHAPTER EIGHTEEN

Lifting his head with effort, Kellen coughed out dirt and water as he glanced around, amazed that he was still alive. Then another thought struck him. If he had survived, then what about the Kizer-Horigan?

He climbed to his feet and ran hands over his sore, bleeding body, feeling where his leathers had torn in numerous places. He assessed the damage, and apart from a few nasty grazes, nothing was broken, and he sighed before studying the gloomy surroundings, unable to see anything substantial. He lifted his eyes to squint up into the blanketing darkness of the thick trees canopied overhead but could see nothing, not even one of the large luminescent moons.

Limping over to the rock wall, he placed his hands on the icy stone and tried to look past the overhanging branches, but only darkness greeted him. He turned away, leaning against the rock, and pondered what he should do. Or even could do. Very little in the dark, and he sagged against the cold rock in defeat. Not only had he lost his friends, but he had also lost the three packs with all the vital supplies, and he groaned in frustration.

"Damn," he inhaled sharply and moved away from the wall, wincing in pain. "It's that stupid creature's fault," he complained, running a hand over his leg and encountering warm stickiness. "Oh great, I'm bleeding again," he continued, glaring around at the darkening forest.

Still favoring his sore leg, he hobbled back to where he had landed, hoping to find the remnants of at least one pack. He searched the ground, scowling, but saw very little as night rolled over the land. He sank to sit on the cold, damp ground and considered his options. He had none until dawn, and he cursed, reaching out with his hands to explore the cold grass and slippery leaves. It was a useless exercise, but he persisted for many moments until common sense told him that it was probably for the best that he remain in one place rather than stumble around in the dark. Especially in this forest.

Trying to ignore his apprehension at the idea of meeting an unfriendly Drow, he wrapped his arms around his aching chest and lay down. He listened to the echoing sounds of the night creatures, knowing that sleep was impossible.

* * *

Coming awake with a start, Kellen immediately reached for his dagger, feeling restraining fingers hindering his attempt. He panicked, opening his eyes wide and staring up. Dalzere's face swam into focus. He released a shuddering breath of pure relief as he recognized the other man in the orange light of dawn.

"Dalzere! Am I glad to see you!"

"Hush . . ." The Elf reached down to touch his lips with a warning finger before he turned to study the area.

"Dalzere?" Kellen whispered, sitting up, his fingers seeking the blade at his belt.

"I saw the tracks of a Drow patrol not far from here, so we must be careful."

Digesting that, Kellen looked at the heavily treed area with wide eyes. Then he noticed something strange. "Where are the others?"

"I imagine somewhere up in the winding passes. It will take them days to get safely to the other side of the peaks and then down into the moors."

"Oh." Kellen relaxed, remembering the windswept fissures and the urgent dash they had made across the rope-twine bridge, only to end up on the dangerous ledge with fanatical Kizer mud men chasing them. All because of a Kizer blood curse; he never had found out the true reasons for the curse, and he looked again at Dalzere. Then he remembered something else: the evil entity. It had attacked him deliberately, attacked him and his friends. "I'm sorry I made you fall—"

"You didn't," Dalzere dismissed. He stood, reaching down to offer a helping hand.

Accepting the offer, Kellen winced as he tried to put weight on his injured leg. "What do you mean?" he asked, puzzled. "You had to fall. I saw the ledge—"

"Let me see your leg," Dalzere interrupted, turning Kellen around so as to inspect the wound. It was only then that Kellen saw the other man's cut hands and chin. "We'll wash the injury in a stream."

"Dalzere?"

The other just looked up and raised a questioning brow as his usual self-mocking mask fell effortlessly into place.

"What do you mean, you didn't fall?" Kellen insisted, ignoring the look in Dalzere's eyes.

"I am a Drow. Falling is not in my nature," Dalzere stated then gave a small lopsided grin. "I chose to follow you."

Kellen stared at him in a mixture of gratitude and relief. "You chose?"

"It was a good possibility you would survive the slide down the rock face if you stayed against the wall," Dalzere said with a shrug, his tone easy as if he were discussing the weather. "I did not like the idea of you wandering through Drow territory alone."

"Thank you," Kellen replied, though it seemed so inadequate. He watched as Dalzere waved the words away and wondered why the other man shied away from gratitude.

Lifting a hand, Dalzere just ruffled his hair. "My pleasure. Can you walk?"

"Yes," Kellen nodded, taking in Dalzere's bedraggled appearance and imagining his own. This was the first time he had seen Dalzere as less than immaculate, and he smiled, speculating on how long it would take the Elf to fix his appearance.

Over the long weeks of travel, that was one of the things he had noticed about all his friends—their traits and idiosyncrasies. Salimen liked to argue for the sake of an argument, while

Lesendal was the diplomat, the one who worked at keeping the peace amongst them all. Crizkerisomia was highly strung and seemed intent on waging a personal war against Dalzere, while the dark Elf preened under her angry glare. Dalzere took pride in his appearance, was strikingly handsome and knew it. Whereas Sasheer didn't seem to care what he looked like, or what he sounded like, as he came out with some of the most amazing yet sarcastic explanations. There was a wealth of knowledge hidden, wrapped in so young a body, and that intrigued and bewildered Kellen.

The only members of the group he was truly comfortable around was Ryland and Peleyia. Ryland, because the man said what he believed and was honest and straightforward—a true warrior with a heart of gentleness. And Peleyia because the Lancooti was fun and adventurous, and someone his own age.

His smile faded as he recalled how ill Peleyia was, and he glanced over at Dalzere, wondering if he would tell him more about the Drow creations, and noticed how the Elf was already repairing his ruined leathers.

"We'll go this way," Dalzere announced. "I found the remains of a pack over here. We should try and find them all and hide them before a Drow patrol returns, otherwise we will be hunted."

"What of the Kizer-Horigan?"

"Dead. Or at least the two bodies I saw were."

"Do we bury them also?"

"No, we leave them for the Drow." Dalzere gave his normal, wicked grin. "A raid by a Drow-hunting party in Kizer territory usually restores the balance in their perverted society. I should imagine the Horigan faction will be almost extinct by the time both the Drow and other factions exact vengeance."

A little shocked by the harshness of those word, Kellen said nothing as he slowly followed Dalzere back through the trees. Maybe Dalzere's mask of viciousness was not a mask at all.

* * *

By midmorning, they had found the remains of all three packs and managed to put together enough supplies to fill one pack and then buried the rest.

They ended up by a small fast-flowing stream, and Kellen watched as Dalzere caught a fish with his bare hands, taking his catch and cooking it over a small contained fire. While the food cooked, Kellen went into the stream and washed his leg, bracing himself against the cold, as the icy water stung his numerous abrasions.

"You might as well have a proper bath while you're at it," Dalzere called as he carefully turned their breakfast over.

Straightening, Kellen glared at the other man. Just because Dalzere was vain didn't mean he had to risk life and limb just to be clean. "I'll catch pneumonia in here as it is, and you want me to get wet all over?"

Laughing, Dalzere shook his head. "A little cold water has never hurt anyone, least of all a healthy child like you."

Leaving the stream, dripping wet from the hips down, Kellen stood over the seated man and glared at him. "I am not a child."

"You are to me," Dalzere said. "Now if you are not going to wash, sit over there and dry off. The fish is almost done, and I imagine you are hungry."

Finding he could not stay annoyed for long in the face of such reasonableness, Kellen sat, favoring his leg and wincing. The sun warmed his chilled skin, and he slowly relaxed, enjoying the silence and the smell of cooked food. "So how old are you?" he asked, watching Dalzere, fascinated by everything this man did.

"In your years, probably about eighty."

"What?" Amazed, Kellen felt his jaw drop. "You don't look that old."

"Thank you."

"Do Drow always live that long?" he asked. "Or are you a special case?"

Dalzere snickered, his smile positively wicked. "And how long do you think a Drow should live?"

"Well," Kellen hesitated, not missing the mischief which entered those amber eyes.

"I'm not old. In fact, I'm still considered too young," Dalzere told him. "You just said I do not look old; now you are assuming I am about ready to fall over dead."

"No, it's just . . . I know so little about, your kind."

"As a people, Drow can live as long as five hundred years. I hope to match that record."

"Five hundred years?" Kellen repeated. "Wow. I once knew a man who lived to be sixty-nine in Ihova, and we all thought he was old."

"Different races, different rules," Dalzere shrugged as he picked the cooked fish up and tossed it onto a large leaf, blowing on his fingers. "I hope you like your fish burnt."

"It's food, and I'm starving, so I'd probably eat it raw at the moment," Kellen replied as he eyed the sizzling meat. He watched, enthralled, as Dalzere, swiftly and with little effort, gutted and stripped the bones from the tender white meat. Then those long fingers neatly divided the fish.

"No need to be barbaric," Dalzere said. "This species of freshwater fish has worms. Remember, it is always best to cook something unless you know for sure it is safe."

"In Ihova, our freshwater fish didn't have worms," Kellen informed him loftily then grinned as the Drow handed him one half of the cooked fish. "How'd you learn all this anyway? You know all about my land, the Kizer, Jorean's movements, Lichien's plans—everything. Is it a Drow thing, or can I learn it too?"

Giving a small laugh, Dalzere tasted a piece of the cooling white meat. "Anyone can learn. Even Peleyia could learn how to survive without thieving, if he tried."

"Pel . . ." Hearing the name, Kellen remembered his friend's injuries and his earlier questions. "He was bitten by a spider in one of those passageways," he said, putting his food down as he anxiously stared at Dalzere. "Will he recover?"

"He got bitten by a *siacon*?"

"Big gray eight-legged thing with long hairy eyelashes, or

something," Kellen described, holding up his hands to indicate size, watching as Dalzere frowned.

"A *siacon*," Dalzere judged. "Everything was so frantic in the pass; I had not noticed. Was he paralyzed?"

"Yes."

"Then I should imagine Sasheer will try to get him to the Healers, either in Sanctuary or the Keep, as quickly as possible."

"And they are where?"

"On the other side of these peaks." Dalzere gestured to the mountains behind them.

"So he'll survive?"

"Maybe."

Finding he had lost his appetite, Kellen just stared at the food before him, worried sick for his friend. He should have killed the spider as soon at it had jumped on Peleyia's back. He should have stabbed it.

"Eat, Kellen. You cannot help Peleyia at the moment. His best chance is with Sasheer. And trust me when I say, Sasheer knows what he is doing." Dalzere's eyes were direct and for once devoid of humor and teasing. "We have a long way to go before dark, and I want to make sure all our tracks are covered."

Nodding, Kellen picked up his meal and ate, hardly tasting the fish. He had so much to learn, so much he wanted to ask, to understand, that at times he felt so lost in the confusion of his new life. He looked up as the tall Elf pushed his long hair back, and he tried to give the other man a brave smile. He finished his meal and sighed, deciding to worry about only the things he could control. "How can I help?" he asked softly, silently offering Dalzere with his eyes, his willingness to do anything. "How long will it take us to get to the other side of these mountains?"

"About a week, if we're lucky."

"A week?" Kellen repeated, horrified, as he glanced back up at the tall peaks in question. "Do we go around or climb back up?"

"We go through."

Kellen's brow disappeared into his hairline as he stared at Dalzere in disbelief. "But aren't these mountains the home of all

Drow? As in underground caves filled with seasoned killers and such?" Kellen asked as he eyed the Elf standing before him. Dalzere was Drow, yet for some reason he had a hard time thinking of him as Drow. Not that he knew any Drow to make such an assessment, but he had heard stories. He viewed Dalzere like he viewed the Ihovians and Ryland: as family. He even thought of him as human, *at least more human than Sasheer*—and he frowned over that thought, amazed at how swiftly his thinking had altered in the last few stressful weeks. "Aren't the Drow just a little paranoid about visitors, particularly with you being one of the good guys?" He frowned harder, puzzled by Dalzere's amusement. "You are one of the good guys, aren't you?"

Resurrecting his wicked laugh, Dalzere's grin increased, his eyes bright with mirth. "Are you scared?"

"Should I be?" Kellen asked, a sudden fluttering of nervousness overtaking his breathing. It was like Dalzere had abruptly expanded in size to look menacing, and for a long moment, Kellen was not sure what to do, or what to think.

"Scared—yes," Dalzere breathed, stepping closer, his eyes narrowing to slits. "But not of me. I am, as you say, one of the good guys."

Kellen released a breath he had not even been aware of holding and asked another question. "Do you have a family inside the Drow society?"

"No," Dalzere hesitated. "Kellen, remember it takes much more to being a Drow than just being born looking like a Drow."

"How?"

Shaking his head slowly, Dalzere ignored the question as he started to clean the ground, removing any item that might hint at their presence. "Maybe I'll tell you along the way. Now bury that fire. Do it like Ryland showed you."

* * *

Two days later, Kellen was reeling from the experience of living life on the run as he and Dalzere avoided any contact with the

Drow patrols. He finally was able to see for himself the differences between Dalzere and his kin, and Kellen realized it was not just the other's clothing or attitude which set him apart from his race, but his entire personality.

Dalzere took pleasure from life, regardless of his twisted humor. Dalzere enjoyed the sun and forest around them, talking constantly, making everything a learning experience for him, and Kellen came to understand the land and to respect the many different creatures. This was Dalzere's philosophy on life, his upbringing reflecting his life as a Ranger—where the normal Drow as a race were locked into severe restrictions, into duty, existing in a world of religious hatred that stemmed back many thousands of years.

Kellen shuddered as Dalzere described the Drow home, picturing the Drow as living a bleak existence, regarding everything as an obstacle to be defeated. There was no argument about their skills and abilities as hunters or as living weapons, yet learning about them, Kellen felt a deep pity for them.

Later, when he had told Dalzere about his observations, the other had just chastised him, saying that the Drow as a race deserved no pity. That they freely chose their own destiny and should be given no advantage in a fight.

"Banish any compassion you may feel, Kellen, for it is wasted on a Drow. It will make you hesitate, and that is all the opportunity a Drow hunter would need to cut you down. To kill you."

Trying to understand Dalzere's serious words, Kellen still wished the other would tell him why the Drow were like that. What had happened to taint an entire race of people? Was it innate? And if so, then why was Dalzere so different?

Working through the baffling questions, Kellen kept silent as he followed Dalzere's long-legged frame through the thickly treed forest. He listened as the Elf told him that these woods extended for almost three hundred leagues into the western ring, bordering the desert plains and harsh grasslands.

He found that all the childhood stories he had heard years ago now paled in comparison to the truth. The expanse of the land, the beauty of the forest, and the intelligent deadliness of the Drow, all combined to show him how isolated his life had been in Ihova, and how narrow-minded the people of the Southland were. In that at least Sasheer had been correct. Thinking about the Ranger, he wondered how the others were doing.

"Dalzere?" he whispered, catching up with the Elf's graceful gait. "Why do some people call Sasheer a Ranger, while others call him a Watcher?"

Shrugging, Dalzere kept his eyes focused on the surrounding forest. "They are one and the same."

"And the Brethren? Criz mentioned that they had sent her to find Sasheer."

Dropping his gaze, Dalzere frowned. "Why do you ask?"

"They are all the same, aren't they? The Brethren, Rangers, and Watchers?" Kellen pushed, starting to see and understand the pattern. "And you are?"

"I am Sasheer's traveling partner. Nothing more," Dalzere said. "Now we had best move. This is not the safest place for such a discussion."

How long had they been traveling partners? Kellen pondered, wanting to ask, but holding the question back. Instead he inspected the immense trees around them, contemplating Dalzere's soft words. Then quite suddenly, he realized that he could no longer hear the sounds of birds or crickets in the forest around them. All animal noises had vanished, and he cast a nervous glance around at the towering trees. It was an oppressive quietness; a hushed stillness that had descended on the ancient forest—death's malignant touch—as if the entire area was devoid of real life. "Dalzere," he whispered cautiously, his hand automatically straying to his short blade.

"The closer we get to the Drow fortifications, the less creatures you will find," Dalzere explained as if reading his mind.

"Is that because they hunt the animals here?" he asked.

"No." Dalzere turned, and Kellen could see his face crease in disgust. "It is because the animals fear the area."

* * *

It took them just over a day and a half to track through the dead forest and reach the black ridges of the huge mountains and peaks—Death Peaks—and Kellen wanted to ask how they had come to bear the name. But he didn't ask, didn't disturb Dalzere. Rather, he concentrated on keeping up with the Elf's long stride as Dalzere led them to an accessible opening in the dark range. It was on dusk when they arrived at the narrow cave entrance, but Dalzere refused to camp in the area and insisted that they continue.

They entered the cave, and Kellen was amazed to discover it was an old disused mine shaft. "Is this safe?" he asked, awed.

"This old shaft has been here longer than records show. It predates the Drow. Is a sacred place for them and therefore avoided. None outside Drow society even know of its existence."

"So how do you know about it?" Kellen asked. He received an amused and smug grin, but no explanation, and he scowled, quickening his step to keep up with the agile Elf.

"So this is not a Drow mine," Kellen continued, catching up to Dalzere and willing his eyes to adjust to the muted gloom. "Then why . . ."

Dalzere's voice dropped to a whisper. "It is feared and untouched by Drow, layered in superstitions because it was here long before the Drow came. Abandoned. Some say, haunted. Most avoid it."

Most? Kellen's eyebrows climbed. "So who used to work this mine?"

"No one knows for certain. Although some of the markings along this first chamber's wall suggest it was possibly Dwarven. But no one is sure. And no one has ever stepped forward to claim its contents."

"A silver mine?"

"Gold," Dalzere corrected.

Kellen stopped, immediately interested. "Gold," he repeated. The soft metal was a rare commodity, highly valued, and sought after. He had believed the only mines producing gold were hidden in the Northlands.

"Yes, gold." Dalzere stopped also and turned back to look at him in the darkening gloom. He reached out, took Kellen's arm, and pulled him along. "This mine's lower caverns are said to be laced with gold, but the Drow make sure those caverns remain hidden. Now come, as there will be patrols in the area soon, and I want to be far down the old primary shaft before then."

Kellen complied, his eyes searching the blackened walls for any sign of the yellow gold. He saw nothing.

"And, Kellen," Dalzere added dryly, "promise me you will never tell Peleyia about this place. Otherwise I'd be forced to kill you."

Kellen swallowed and almost choked, not sure if Dalzere was joking or serious.

CHAPTER NINETEEN

It took over a day to travel down the old wooden shaft, and Kellen's eyes slowly adjusted to the dim light, forcing him to rely on Dalzere's help when they entered the pitch-black tunnels. They stopped there for a drink and some food before Dalzere took out a small pouch from his belt and tipped some powder into his palm. He then mixed in a little water, and the powder glowed a muted orange in the inky blackness.

They continued down to the lower levels and reached an old wooden platform that led into cramped tunnels with stale air. Not a sound could be heard; everything deathly still, silent, and enshrouded in utter darkness. Dalzere had told him they were still ten levels above the main tunnels and caverns of the Drow city, adding that Drow patrols should be minimal in these disused chambers. Still, he worried as the Elf tied a length of leather rope around his waist and then attached it to Kellen's belt, just so they did not get separated.

Around him, the walls were cold and damp, yet smooth to his fingers, and Kellen tried to keep up with Dalzere's pace. His footsteps echoed faintly, yet he could not hear Dalzere, and he tried to imitate his movements. The Elf was a complete blur of darkness in front of him, only his unusual golden eyes reflected in the mute orange glow when Dalzere turned to check on his progress.

Far off in the distance, he could hear water dripping, its sound becoming rhythmic until it faded into the background with all the other intermittent echoes that sounded deep inside this living mountain. Occasionally, he would bump into his companion as the other man stopped to listen, but as his eyes grew accustomed to the darkness, he started to distinguish his friend's outline in the near blackness.

* * *

Time slowed in this womblike environment, totally enshrouded in an impenetrable blackness, and Kellen felt his legs grow numb, his body aching in exhaustion. He had no idea what time it was, or even what day it was as he concentrated solely on the silent man in front of him. He stopped abruptly, discerning Dalzere's raised hand. Silence, a heavy, oppressive silence greeted his ears as he sent out his senses to detect any noise. But there was nothing, yet still Dalzere did not move.

Then the unimaginable happened, and Kellen sucked in a breath, startled. He heard a scratching sound off to his left. The sound lingered, and Kellen held his breath, jumping in shock when a louder sound shattered the silence. It was the echo of a large machine starting up, and the location of the strange noise seemed to be in front and under him, a vibration shaking the tunnel floor. Dust showered down on him, and he reached out, moving closer to Dalzere.

Touching the Elf, he found a measure of comfort, and he tried to listen, very aware of Dalzere's slow, measured breaths and complete stillness. So what was Dalzere hearing or sensing? Kellen knew that his senses were not as finely tuned as Dalzere's, and that his judgments were next to useless in this darkness. So he waited, trying to imitate Dalzere's legendary patience. Then just as swiftly, the deep, grinding sound stopped, and utter silence settled over the tunnel once more.

"We will rest here for a while," Dalzere said eventually. He spoke the words and then moved off into a smaller hidden tunnel. "It should be safe enough for each of us to take a turn at sleeping."

Stunned by the fact that they were so close to another tunnel, Kellen studied the wall, never even having picked out the opening in the gloom. "What was that sound?" he whispered, feeling for a place to sit. "You don't think the Drow have started mining the gold again, do you?"

"No. It is just one of the huge hydraulic pumps, I should think. The Drow mine many minerals deep inside these peaks. And those pits are far below even the city levels."

"So how far in are we?" Kellen asked in the same hushed voice. He felt safer and warmer when Dalzere mixed some of his florescent powders together to create the orange glow. The faint brightness illuminated the tiny tunnel and highlighted Dalzere's sharp features eerily.

"Probably only near the First Posting."

"And that is?" Kellen waited for the rest.

"A spacious chamber or guard post. There are six Postings within these mountains, and they are spread out over a great distance. We need to get above the Third Posting, which will lead us into the moors and marshes of the Brethren."

Picking up on that word as he recalled their last discussion about 'Brethren' and Dalzere's avoidance of the topic, Kellen nodded. "That's where this Keep is."

"Yes."

Wishing the other would elaborate, Kellen sighed. Glancing up, he saw Dalzere take out some of the dried meat he had cooked before they had entered this tomb of darkness. It was then he realized he was starving, and he accepted the food gratefully.

"We must try and make our supplies last. It will probably be another three or four days until we can exit these twisting tunnels."

Chewing on the tough meat, Kellen considered that. "So what does the Drow City look like?" he asked, hoping that was a safe topic of conversation. Dalzere had seemed to change over the last few days, to focus inward, becoming almost sullen. "Is it all in darkness like these caves?"

"No," Dalzere shook his head. "It is well lit, with immense fires that burn constantly, their glow reflecting off the crystals decorating the cavern's roof, which is over a league in height. The crystals hold the firelight, hold warmth, and bathe all below in soft light. The city itself is massive, a vast network of caves, caverns, chambers, and tunnels."

"Does it have a name?" Kellen asked, hesitant to interrupt but compelled by curiosity to try and penetrate the mystery behind this man and the Drow people.

"Sethesthovaln," Dalzere breathed, giving the name life and

body. "Its original meaning was 'life and freedom.' A magnificent jewel, forever hidden from the eyes of the outside world. It should have been a celebration of achievement and laughter but..."

"But what?"

"It turned into a celebration of hatred and death as they took up the service of a false, twisted master." There was bitterness in his tone.

Uncertain as he heard the barely concealed anger in Dalzere's soft words, Kellen searched for something to say, wondering if it was wise to continue. But he wanted to know, and it was obvious Dalzere cared and had been to the magnificent city. He looked at the man crouched opposite him and speculated on what Dalzere's reception had been in this city. What his people had thought of him. "So they were not always evil?"

"No," Dalzere breathed the word. "Once..."

"Once... what?" Kellen prompted. "I have only ever been told that the Drow are born evil. That's not true?"

"Oh, it is a very long story, Kellen, and I don't want to bore you with my people's sordid history."

"But how will I learn to understand, if you will not teach me?" Kellen whispered into the strained silence which followed. He watched the glowing powders slowly dim and knew in a short while they would go out altogether. Taking advantage of what light was left, he studied Dalzere's face, seeing a mixture of torment and longing as the Elf pushed his overlong hair out of his eyes. *Drow*, a creature forever young, never appearing to age, to wither and die. Were all the Drow the same, or was Dalzere the exception to the rule? Or was he just like Sasheer? "I want to learn," he whispered.

Dalzere lifted his gaze, his eyes direct and hard. There was no emotion in his gaze for a long moment, and then he slowly relaxed and nodded. "All right, I will tell you of the Drow's fall, but only briefly, as there is so much pain involved." He leaned forward as if to compose his thoughts, and Kellen watched, fascinated, as Dalzere then drew a strange symbol in the dirt between them with a long finger. "A protection spell, to safeguard us from searching Drow ears."

Swallowing, Kellen shivered despite the warmth in the cave, feeling the hairs on his arms rise in apprehension. "We are being watched?"

"I am not sure, maybe not yet, but it is inevitable. But this is a safeguard against the mountain itself, as the Drow story will attract the spirit within its heart."

"I see," Kellen said, really not understanding at all. But Dalzere's nervousness was contagious.

"A very long time ago, after the Coastal Mages had been defeated, a lot of their captives were freed from Mitthsombaine to return home. Of this group were a small peace-loving minority of Elves who had been slaves for centuries in the caverns beneath Mitthsombaine." Dalzere spoke softly, his voice taking on that musical quality Kellen adored. "These Elves were no longer strictly classified as 'Elves' because the Mages of Mitthsombaine had altered their genetic code during some vile experiments. Their skin pigmentation was forever changed, stained: their hair, eyes, and that special quality that made Elves so beautiful—their magic—had been bred out of them. They were defenseless—different and despised by their ancestors—hunted and killed by the Sun Elves who had once been their kin."

Kellen stared at Dalzere in awe. "Are you saying that the Drow are descendants of the white Elves?"

"Blood kin," Dalzere hissed. "Once loved, now hated. Feared because they were different. Shunned because the Sun Elves feared they would infect and destroy Elven society. So the defenseless were cast out of the Elven city of Capliarkia one fierce winter. Forced into the desolate marshes where many died of hunger and cold." Dalzere lifted his gaze to meet Kellen's wide eyes. "Hunted. Bludgeoned. Treated like animals that needed to be killed."

Dalzere dropped his head forward, and Kellen could see his strange eyes glisten with tears in the dying florescent light. "Capliarkia?" Kellen questioned.

"The perfect city of the Sun Elves. It sits high in the Glass Ranges, its battlements face west toward the sea. Sheer beauty, forever bathed in golden sunlight." Dalzere's voice softened even more. "A jewel forever denied to all Drow."

Kellen wanted to see it, imagining this Sun City and getting a flashed image of perfection and brilliance in his mind. "Go on," he encouraged.

"War was inevitable. The Sun Elves sought to wipe out the impurity of their race. Calling it a 'holy' duty. This cleansing drove the dark Elves further into the mountains as they searched for protection. Many were brutally murdered or butchered, yet still the Sun Elves formed hunting squads, which later became known as the greatly lamented *Fe-le-drea*."

"*Fe-le-drea*? Like Criz?" Kellen interrupted again in a whisper. All these names and places held a familiarity to him, a memory of another time that he felt fluttering in the back of his mind. He had a glimpse of darkness, of war, of grief—the memories a force deep within his mind that wanted to break free—and he shut his senses on the impulse to invite the images, scarred by the promised power behind the unknown force. It was frightening, and he stared wide-eyed at the Elf opposite him, barely seeing Dalzere's outline.

"*Fe-le-drea* . . . no, not like Crizkerisomia. She could never be *Fe-le-drea*, her heart is too pure." He glanced up, his smile lopsided. "Real *Fe-le-drea* are special Elven warriors, honored among all the Sun Elves—a high distinction and ranking within their society. They kill without compassion." Dalzere sighed, the sound barely audible, as the small glow vanished, casting them both into complete darkness. "I dare not light more powder."

"I know," Kellen acknowledged, closing his eyes as the oppressive warmth of the small tunnel pressed in on him.

"The *Fe-le-drea* were trained to kill the dark Elves—the abominations, as they were called. It was a one-sided war, with the Sun Elves slaughtering innocent kin. A war that lasted for over one hundred years, and no one could mediate a solution. Not even the respected Brethren," Dalzere said in disgust. "Then the few surviving dark Elves found a way into the forbidden—sacred—caves and mine shafts of these mountains. They ignored the curse—battling to survive in the dark, barren tunnels. They starved and died but were left alone by all the other nations. Abandoned. And so a bitterness started to consume their souls, leaving them vulnerable and open to a different type of coercion."

When Dalzere stopped to take a breath, Kellen was not sure if the other wanted to continue. "Dalzere," he whispered, wanting to prompt him as he barely made out the other's outline.

"That was when the true Drow was born." Dalzere's voice was hard, cold, and bitter. "The Drow were not created by the Coastal Mages, nor twisted by war, famine, and disease, but rather shaped by their own kind, created by the *enlightened* society of Sun Elves."

Kellen didn't know what to say, shocked by the viciousness in Dalzere's voice, enthralled by the story. Again, it was so different to what he had heard whispered in Ihova. "Were they enslaved again?"

"In a way, but not in the physical sense. They stumbled across a dying man deep within the old mining tunnels west of here. Or at least they thought he was dying," Dalzere added with a gruff laugh. It sounded cynical. "Within his hands, he cradled a living stone, a stone of wondrous colors and great magic. This man did not judge them, rather he offered them magic, he offered to restore their stolen Gifts. He also offered protection and a way to kill the Sun Elves—if they helped him."

"A living stone?" Kellen repeated, remembering the fantastic and unbelievable story Sasheer had spun for them many months ago. It could not be true? *Could it?*

"An evil stone," Dalzere hissed. "It offered them revenge. It offered retribution. It offered them the true meaning of the word 'hate.' Then for two hundred years, it instructed them, corrupted them, mutated them, and changed them into heartless killers," he spat the words. "When the Drow left the confines of the old mining shafts centuries later, they emerged killers and the slaughtered the Sun Elves, teaching them the true meaning of carnage."

"By the stars—" Kellen gasped, suddenly remembering something else which he had also heard whispered, which Sasheer had insisted was true. "Kalern. That dying man was Kalern."

"Yes," Dalzere said. "And so the legends began, and every Drow is cursed by the history whether it applies or not."

Not breaking the silence this time, Kellen just sat there, numb, his mind running in circles as more pieces fell slowly into place. Maybe Sasheer's story was more fact than fable. It was a scary concept. "And you escaped from the curse, how?"

"I was not born within these peaks," Dalzere said. "I was not indoctrinated. My mother was a Sun Elf who had been raped by a Drow hunter and left for dead. Fortunately, she was found and nursed back to health, until they discovered she was with child, then she was cast out as cursed. I am told she abandoned me in the forest soon after the birth, leaving me for the wild animals as a gift to the Elven gods as a sign of her purity, so that she could return to her people with a clear conscience." Dalzere paused for a long moment, his voice raw, his breathing loud in the darkness. "I was saved by—" he stopped.

Opening his mouth, wanting to know more, Kellen blinked as Dalzere reached across the space between them and covered his lips with a quieting finger.

"That is enough for one night," Dalzere said in a firm tone.

"But—"

"No, I have finished telling. Now get some sleep. We have a long way to go. I will keep the first watch."

Not knowing what to say or how to say it, Kellen just shut his mouth as the Elf stood and walked soundlessly away. Stunned by what he had learned, Kellen knew that to thank Dalzere for what he had shared would be inadequate—and probably unwanted. Yet he felt sorry for what the Drow as a nation had endured in the past. But now? How could the injustices of the past balance out the wanton bloodshed of the present?

Frowning, Kellen stared at the place he knew Dalzere had gone, trying to make out his friend's outline in the darkness. He could see nothing. Then another realization hit him. *Dalzere was part Sun Elf!* Found—and probably raised—by a Brethren. *By . . . Sasheer?* Was that why the two men now traveled the lands as partners? Like mentor and student, or father and son? Chewing on his lower lip, he recalled Dalzere's earlier words while in the forest beyond the peaks and remembered that Dalzere was eighty years of age. So it was unlikely that Sasheer had found him. Because the Elf might not age, but Sasheer was human. At least he *hoped* Sasheer was human—Mageborn. Did the Mageborn age?

With his mind swimming in circles, he slowly lay down, doubting he would get much rest. Instead he listened to the deep echoes of the mountain around him.

* * *

Waking as something soft and warm touched his face, Kellen rolled over, encountering damp, cold stone. He just caught himself from speaking as memory came flooding back as to where he was—inside the Death Peaks with Dalzere—and he relaxed. He turned slowly, looking for Dalzere, assuming it was the Elf who touched him.

Sitting up, he blinked around, waiting for his eyes to pick out objects in the darkness, scanning the tunnel with his senses, expecting to pick out Dalzere's crouching form any moment. But he could sense nothing, and he rubbed his eyes. "Dalzere?" he called softly, jumping when a warm, furry creature leapt on his chest and used its paws to cover his mouth.

"Shhhsshhh!"

"What the mmyph—" He found his words cut off as the little creature leaned into his face and shook its head furiously.

"Shhhh . . . shshshh," it seemed to stutter at him, and Kellen could just make out its dark eyes in a mass of dull whiteness as the creature blinked. "Will . . . not . . . hurt . . . white-thing."

Stunned by the sudden appearance of a creature in these barren tunnels, Kellen stared at the animal in surprise. It felt warm, smelled damp—yet it could talk. Was it another exotic Drow creation? He closed his mouth and was relieved when the animal took its paws from his lips.

"White-thing . . . good."

Only seeing its pale outline as the warm body jumped off his chest to stand beside him, Kellen shook his head, wondering if he was still dreaming. Then even as he watched, the single creature seemed to multiply into two white shapes, then three moving white shapes. He rubbed his eyes again, but the animals remained. They were the size of a fat desert rodent, and he tensed as they came closer and sniffed him.

"What—" Again he got no further as the first creature pinched him on the leg in reproof.

"Shhh . . . shhhssh!" it chattered at him urgently, making a curious scratching sound before it climbed up onto his chest a second time. "Must . . . not . . . alert . . . nasty . . . dark-thing."

"Drow," he whispered then jumped as a different creature bit him on the hand. He snatched his hand away and glared at the animal responsible. He was not sure he liked this situation.

"Nasty . . . dark-thing . . . around . . . corner."

"There's Drow around the corner?" he asked, worried suddenly for Dalzere. He pushed up and went to approach the corner.

"No . . . no," the first creature grabbed his tunic and swung up off the ground, clutching onto him as he stood.

Removing the claws from his chest, Kellen winced, peeled the creature off his clothing, then he peeked around the corner, worried for Dalzere. But he could see absolutely nothing in the blackness.

"Come . . . back!" the creature pleaded, making Kellen look down into the small white face, seeing those dark eyes blink at him in the paleness of its fur.

"What are you?"

"Called . . . Dart . . . want . . . to . . . save . . . white-thing."

"Dart," Kellen repeated, trying to understand all this.

"Me!" Dart squeaked, pleased. It jumped at its own excitement and scrambled up Kellen's arm to sit on his shoulder and hide behind his loose hair.

Grimacing as Dart's sharp claws dug into his skin, Kellen was about to protest when he felt another of the small creatures scratch his leg while stretching against him.

"You . . . must . . . come . . . with . . . us." Dart whispered in his ear as Kellen reached down to liberate the creature from his leg before his leathers were torn further. He couldn't believe this; he was talking to white fluffy rodents. It had to be a dream. "Listen, Dart..."

"I ... am ... Scratch," the second creature said boldly as it scrambled over his wrist and up his arm.

"It fits," Kellen decided, feeling the first creature wrap a long warm tail around his throat. He unwound the hot tail and wondered if he was going mad.

"White-thing ... come ... with ... us ... now?" Scratch asked.

"Where?" Kellen whispered, deciding to play along with his nightmare. Then he saw two more furry white creatures appear on the floor and walk toward him. He groaned.

"Away ... from ... bad ... dark-thing ... of ... course."

"Drow?" he asked and saw Scratch nod furiously. "You know a quick way out of these tunnels, to the marshes and moors?" *Now I'm humoring myself in my own dream!* But his question again got furious nodding from his strange companions. Then he felt something bite his ankle through his leather boot, and he hissed out a curse. *That could not have been a dream!* He glared down and saw one of those fluffy white animals sitting on his boot.

"That ... is ... Bite. She ... is ... irritable." Dart sounded almost apologetic. "You ... come ... with ... us?"

"I have to find my friend first," Kellen corrected, determined either to find Dalzere or wake up.

"Another ... white-thing?" Scratch asked, his dark eyes getting larger.

"No," Kellen shook his head, holding up his arm and cradling the one called Dart as the small creature wiggled off his shoulder. "He is a Drow, but a good one," he ended hastily as he felt Scratch twitch nervously. The animal's hind leg automatically started to scratch against his tunic. Lifting the creature away, Kellen crouched down and placed both animals on the floor next to the rodent called Bite.

"No ... good ... dark-thing."

"Just one," he reassured, stopping as he saw, first Bite then Dart, scramble away. Scratch clawed its way behind him.

"Kell?"

It was a soft sound, Dalzere's voice, and Kellen sighed in relief as he just made out the other's dark outline as the Drow seemed to detach himself from the rock wall. So he was awake, and this was real, and he stifled a laugh. He sighed gratefully when Dalzere moved toward him and crouched. He could just make out the Drow's features.

"I heard a noise; are you all right?"

"Fine." He grinned at the other man. "I seem to have found a new set of friends," he said as he dragged Scratch reluctantly out from behind him.

"Eeeekkkkk," the small creature squealed.

"Lexsii," Dalzere laughed.

"You know these creatures?"

Reaching out a hand, Dalzere tried to touch the squirming animal. "They used to live in the regions of the old cave system, but I had thought them extinct, as the Drow hunted them extensively." He moved his hand away from the distressed animal. "They are basically harmless but love to eat through rock, unwittingly disrupting the mining projects. Many consider them a pest."

"They look adorable."

"You say that now, but just wait until they eat all your food, bedding, and supplies."

"Do . . . not . . . like . . . dark-things!" Scratch declared as it clung to Kellen's arm.

"I will not hurt you," Dalzere returned. "I am not from Sethesthovaln."

"But . . . you . . . are . . . dark-thing!"

"I have no love for either the white or black Elves. You have my word."

Unwinding himself from Kellen's hand, Scratch marched up to Dalzere and sniffed him. "You . . . still . . . look . . . like . . . dark-thing . . . but . . . you . . . smell . . . different."

"You can trust him," Kellen assured. Glad when the other Lexsii came out of hiding. Bite just walked up to Dalzere and bit him on the leg, and to his surprise, Dalzere picked her up and tickled her belly. She started to chatter at him, squirming in delight as the other Lexsii approached the Elf.

"They say they know a quick way to the moors," Kellen said.

"They may at that," Dalzere conceded. "It has been years since I transversed these passages and chambers. And if it helps us avoid patrols, I'll try anything."

CHAPTER TWENTY

Three days later, Kellen was no longer sure the Lexsii understood what the meaning of the words 'short cut' meant. Because if anything, they had traveled deeper into the heart of the dark, malevolent mountain.

Crawling on his hands and knees, following Dalzere's lithe form, Kellen stopped to brush water out of his eyes. They had been fortunate so far in avoiding the infrequent Drow patrols, but he wondered for how much longer their luck would hold. The Lexsii had led them into a very narrow and wet—*extremely wet*—old water conduit. An underground passage that was centuries older than Sethesthovaln, or so Dalzere had judged when he had inspected the old rusty machinery and the numerous shafts. They had found themselves four levels above where they had originally started, and Dalzere had laughed in wonderment, amused when Dart had told him that the Drow had no idea this tunnel existed. The Lexsii had assured him that it was no accident that the Drow were ignorant.

The small intelligent Lexsii intrigued Kellen, and he listened with interest to Scratch's story about how the Lexsii had gone into hiding after the Drow, in their usual competent way, had tried to exterminate the species. The Drow had very nearly succeeded, and now the Lexsii were careful not to let the Drow see them, preferring to stay in burrows created by water runoffs and narrow connective crevices and passes. One of which they were currently navigating and which was supposed to lead to an exit from Death Peaks.

Utter blackness surrounded him, and Kellen tiredly got his limbs moving faster as he felt the rope between him and the Drow pull.

"Are you all right?"

The question came out of the darkness immediately in front of him, and Kellen stopped just in time as he made out Dalzere's vague outline. "Could you open your eyes or something, so I can at least see you?" he asked, his tone wearied.

"My eyes are open," Dalzere replied without heat. "Would you like to stop and rest?"

"I want dry clothes, a hot drink, and real food," he grumbled.

"Soon."

"You've been saying that for days!" he complained, knowing it was not the Elf's fault, but he could not stop the words. "I'm so waterlogged that I don't think a month in the sun would dry me out."

"I can't predict how long these tunnels extend. But they must get us out on the west side of these mountains somewhere," Dalzere said. "Your friend Scratch is a little vague with distances and locations."

"Tell me about it," Kellen grumbled as he collapsed to sit in a cold puddle. Water splashed around him. He lifted a hand and tried to see his fingers in the oppressive gloom. "I bet we both look like shriveled prunes."

"I hate to think what we look like. But at least we are not short of water."

"Oh, very funny," Kellen muttered. "You are a laugh a minute. You know that?"

Sitting with his back to the wall of the cramped tunnel, Dalzere started to laugh softly.

"What's so funny now?" Kellen asked, indignant.

"We should hear ourselves," Dalzere explained, amusement lacing his words. "Against all odds, we have managed to avoid all contact with the Drow, rediscover the Lexsii, and find a safe, secret—if damp—route through Death Peaks," he sighed, his tone light. "Do you know how fortunate we are?"

"We're not out yet," Kellen replied, but the sting had gone from his words.

"Granted, but I doubt your new furry little friends would let anything harm you."

"Us," Kellen said.

"You," Dalzere repeated. "They still don't really trust me. With good reason," he added with a touch of dry humor. "And as I remember it, Bite thinks you're cute."

"I just wish she'd stop nibbling at my clothing," Kellen said, finding that it was very easy to relax in Dalzere's company.

"Regardless," Dalzere continued, and Kellen could see his teeth as the other smiled, "they will lead us out. Just where is the question."

Resting his head against the cold wall, Kellen closed his eyes and tried to remember what the sun and sky looked like. It seemed like an eternity since they had seen any real light. "I wonder if it is night or day."

"Early morning."

"You know or guess?" Kellen asked, impressed.

"I can feel it in my bones when the sun sets and rises. It is early morning."

Storing that interesting fact away, Kellen slowly nodded to himself, wondering what day it was. "I imagine the others would be breaking camp. Unless . . ."

"Unless what?"

"Would they have reached the Keep by now?"

"Maybe." Dalzere shrugged. "By tomorrow morning, definitely."

Kellen sighed as he eyed what he could see of the man opposite him. He felt undeniably close to Dalzere in the darkness, almost as if he understood the Elf. Or as much as you could understand another person. "Dalzere, can I ask you a personal question?"

"It depends."

"You don't have to answer if you don't want to but," he paused, sucking in a deep breath, "but—did that witch back in the Kizer-Horigan camp know you?" He felt the other move away slightly, and he reached out a hand in apology. "It just seemed strange the way she singled you out. The more I think about it, the more curious I get."

"Then think about something else," Dalzere cautioned, his

tone offering no answers. "That is past. Of no concern any longer," he ended in a quiet voice.

"Dalzere!" Kellen admonished, getting exasperated. "I just felt that her actions were personal—"

"Kellen," Dalzere growled in warning.

"Tell me I am wrong," Kellen challenged, so sure of what he had seen and sensed. So many images were still etched in his brain, and he wanted answers.

"You are very perceptive," Dalzere whispered after a lengthy pause. "Sasheer is right about you. You possess a rare Gift."

Feeling his brows climb with that, Kellen was amazed. "Sasheer has talked to you about me?"

"Only briefly. When he told me Wyran had died."

Wyran. His whole universe jolted to a stop as he remembered his brother, and Kellen shuddered. He had not thought about Wyran for weeks, not since leaving the Southland, and abruptly he felt a pang of guilt. "You knew my brother?"

"I knew of him," Dalzere corrected.

Digesting that, Kellen thrust the image of his brother out of his mind, not wanting to think about his death, not wanting to dwell on the mystery surrounding Wyran and the Ranger. *Ranger, Watcher, Brethren . . .* Somehow he believed the three were the same. "What is a Watcher?"

Snorting in amusement, Dalzere did not answer at first as he studied Kellen's face in the gloom. "Again?"

"I want to know," he shrugged, unapologetic.

"Why?"

"I have heard them call you a Watcher," Kellen explained. He was determined to learn the truth somehow.

"Heard who call me that?"

"The Lancooti."

Dalzere shook his head and laughed again. "I should have expected that. I am not a Watcher."

"And Sasheer?" Kellen pushed, knowing the other was trying to evade his questions. Again.

"As I have told you before, that is one name used."

"What is he, Dalzere? And why the secrets?" Kellen asked, moving a little closer to the Drow and pleading silently with him to answer. "Please?"

"I suppose you will find out soon enough for yourself anyway," Dalzere sighed, resigned. "Sasheer just wanted to have you in the Keep before you discovered the truth."

"What truth?" Kellen pinned Dalzere with his gaze.

"Sasheer and a few others like him are Mages."

"Mageborns," Kellen whispered, having already come to that conclusion.

"Just Mages," Dalzere corrected gently. "They dislike the old term," he said. "They are from the Eastland. A group of very old men who have appointed themselves as guardians over the four lands. Hence the name, Watcher."

Feeling his jaw drop, Kellen said nothing as he felt the knowledge seep into his mind, realizing it was true, as everything seemed to click into place. Old, they were old—from the east. *From Mitthsombaine?* "He is one of the original twelve—" Kellen said, awed, his mind in shock. He didn't need Dalzere's answer to know the truth. He felt the rightness of it, yet it was so incredible. "But he looks so *young*," he stressed the last word in disbelief, remembering Sasheer's youthfulness. Yet he also remembered the man's eyes, those mesmerizing blue eyes which seemed to hold the answers to everything. Such age and such cynical humor. "He's so juvenile."

Dalzere just stifled another laugh. "I wouldn't advise that you say that in Sasheer's presence."

Feeling Dalzere's damp hand on his arm, Kellen smiled also, imagining Sasheer's instant flare of anger. "I can feel the truth, feel the knowledge. How, I don't know, but it scares me, Dalzere," he admitted softly. Honestly. "It is like a waking dream, or is it a nightmare? I don't know any longer," he shook his head and looked away from his friend. "In this dream I am . . ." He hesitated, not wanting to invite the images that hovered on the edge of his waking mind.

"Kellen?" Worry now colored the Elf's tones, his fingers biting into the damp fabric and firm muscle of Kellen's arm.

"*He* is here. Right here," Kellen breathed, suddenly *feeling, smelling,* and *tasting* Kalern's presence, *seeing* his dark cavern, *seeing* the abyss open before him. The tunnel around him faded to nothing, and he shuddered, trying to move away from the lip of the beckoning abyss that had become his bane.

"Who?" Dalzere asked, his gaze narrowing as he studied Kellen's fearful expression. "Who do you see, Kellen? Who is here with you?"

Blinking owlishly, Kellen felt his perception shift completely into that darker universe. Swirling around him was the presence of evil, and he *saw* and felt—*a long black flowing cape feathered down over his legs. The silken fabric caressed his bare legs, making him shiver in a mix of fear and desire. Panicked, he tried to brush the fabric aside, pulling away from the hand holding him as he stared blindly forward, hearing a hissed breath against his ear.*

"He . . . he crouches before me like a thoughtful adviser, inviting me closer, commanding my obedience," Kellen whispered, reliving the nightmare. He pressed back into the muddy, damp wall behind, shying away from any contact with Kalern's hands. "He whispers to me constantly, offering friendship, offering me love. He entices me forward until I can almost see and touch the—"

"Kellen!"

Dalzere's voice cracked loudly in his sluggish mind, but Kellen could not focus on it. All he could see was Kalern's dark, hypnotic eyes and the shining brightness of Lichien, which sat on the opposite side of the abyss. The lure to obey was getting stronger, and his resolve was weakening. He lifted a hand to touch the beckoning stone and felt his fingers captured and held in a firm embrace.

* * *

"I want you to come back!" Dalzere hissed, realizing what was happening. He held Kellen's searching fingers, dragged the younger man closer, and shook him hard, desperate to break the deadly spell in which Kellen was entrapped—a powerful, dark enchantment of evil magics. But whether it was of Drow origin or of . . . and Dalzere faltered, not wanting to think of the alternative. Hastily, he muttered an elemental banishment, using his own innate powers to break the mental entrapment. He felt Kellen shudder and groan as if in pain, and he said the first thing he could think of. "Concentrate on the Lexsii."

"Dalzere?"

It was uttered with such pain and loss that Dalzere paused. He stared at the younger man then moved, kneeling in front of his friend and seeing Kellen's trancelike state.

"One will come of the bloodline and challenge for control. That one will touch a lost soul and shatter a divided heart. If the soul is restored then innocence will be sacrificed." Kellen recited blindly, tonelessly, his eyes vacant as he sat passively against the cold wall.

Shocked by the whispered words of so ancient a prophecy, Dalzere reached over and slapped Kellen's pale face hard, needing to wake him. He got no response, and so he slapped him again, hearing Kellen gasp.

He glanced fretfully around the muted darkness, knowing that he had to move them. He was scared for them both, knowing what the aftereffects of such powerfully invoked words would have on the evil that lived within Death Peaks. The echo of Kellen's voice lingered in the air, seeped into the cold rock, whispered in the darkness, and he knew the tainted spirit of the mountain would awake. He also knew there was no power or protection spell that could reverse the damage Kellen's uttered words had caused. They were dead unless he got them moving. "Kellen!" he growled, shaking his friend then slapping him a third time.

* * *

Jolted by the stinging pain across his face, Kellen snapped awake. "I . . . Dalzere? What did you hit me for?"

Releasing a heavy breath, Dalzere glared at him. "You were sleeping," he said, his eyes meeting Kellen's searchingly.

"Sleeping?" Kellen's voice rose in disbelief. "How can I have been asleep when you were just telling me that Sasheer is a Mage?" Kellen eyed the tense Elf and then raised a hand to rub his sore cheek. "You should learn to relax, Dalzere."

"You remember talking about Sasheer?" Dalzere questioned.

"Yes," Kellen frowned. *Why is Dalzere acting so strange?* "You said he was one of the original twelve, and I was telling you how I sometimes can sense weird images inside my mind."

"I see," Dalzere said very evenly, placing a hand on the cold wall beside him, as if feeling for sounds. His scowl deepened, his fingers searching out the soft dips in the damp rock wall.

"Sasheer says it's a Gift," Kellen continued, puzzled by what Dalzere was doing. It looked like the Drow was attempting to merge with the wall, his pupils huge in his yellow eyes. Frightening.

"It is," Dalzere agreed absently, his concentration centered entirely on the damp stone under his fingers.

"A Gift?" Kellen repeated unhappy, feeling better as they fell back into the old pattern of comfortable conversation. "More like a curse."

"It may appear like that at times."

"And what of you?" Kellen asked again, concerned about his friend's detached attitude. "Dalzere? Are you all right?"

"Me?" Dalzere raised his head, confusion and consternation in his eyes. He looked around as if he sensed some trouble, his brows drawn down.

"Yes, you were going to tell me why that Kizer-Horigan witch wanted you dead."

"Oh, that," Dalzere said with heavy emphasis.

"Sasheer said it was a 'blood-vengeance curse' or something," Kellen persisted, hiding his grin when Dalzere winced at his choice of words. No doubt the Elf had hoped he had forgotten about this subject.

"You should not eavesdrop, as it is not polite."

"I didn't eavesdrop," Kellen defended. "I was standing right next to him when he said it."

"It is over."

About to protest, Kellen stopped midbreath as he felt the arrival of the Lexsii.

"Stop... so... soon?" Scratch jumped up onto Kellen's leg to avoid the water, shaking his small body to dislodge the wet droplets.

"Scratch!" Holding up his hands to block the spray, Kellen swore. "And I was just starting to dry out!"

"Not... far... to... go... but... must... hurry... as... dark-things... have... somehow... discerned... your... presence."

"What? In the tunnels?" Dalzere asked as he immediately moved into a crouch. He cursed with venom, angry that he had ignored his basic instinct.

"Yes..." Scratch told him.

"And you, my little friend?" Dalzere asked.

"We... will... have... to... wait... and... see... but... you... must... go... for... nasty-things... will... not... rest... until... you... are... killed."

Stroking the little creature's shoulder, Kellen thanked him before scrambling to catch up with the fast-moving Drow.

* * *

Kellen had to really push himself to keep up with Dalzere's boundless energy. He lost all track of time as he battled the old narrow tunnel system, sliding at times down steep drops to land in pools of deep water.

Spluttering to the surface after one particularly nasty drop, Kellen was very glad when Dalzere hauled him out of the deep well and up onto the ledge.

"Thanks," he breathed. "I never did learn how to swim."

"I was more concerned about the noise you were creating with all the needless splashing," Dalzere said.

Eyeing the Elf, Kellen scowled then glanced around. Behind them, four narrow tunnels branched off into different directions, and he turned, crouching down next to Dalzere and trying to see into the darkness. "Which way?"

"The one on the left does not feel right."

"How can you tell?" Kellen asked, fascinated. He squinted into the gloom, slowly becoming aware of the warm air circulating from that tunnel.

"Trust me. It could be blocked or . . ."

Not liking the sound of that second option, Kellen turned to look at the other three narrow outlets. "And these?"

"We take the one second on the right. There is a slight draft."

Lifting a hand, Kellen felt nothing on his wet skin and raised a skeptical brow. "There is?"

He never got an answer, as a sharp sound of steel against rock froze them both.

Moving, Dalzere touched one of the walls, resting his ear against it for a long moment before pushing back and shoving Kellen into the tunnel with the supposed draft.

Scrambling to his knees, Kellen found himself sliding and half-rolling into the tunnel as Dalzere followed behind. The Elf was silently urging him to move when that sharp sound of steel on stone echoed behind them a second time.

Throwing all caution to the winds, Kellen crawled as fast as he could along the rough surface, sweeping pebbles and dirt out of his way as he rounded numerous bends. Breathing hard, he could just make out Dalzere's bulk behind, and he skidded around another bend to feel the first welcome touch of a breeze. *Dalzere's right!* Relief washed through him, and he tried to move faster, starting to feel cobwebs stick to his face as the darkness lessened.

He swept the webs aside, his eyes and mind now wholly focused on the tunnel ahead. The tunnel lightened further, and he briefly wondered about the possibility of *siacons* living in the watercourse but dismissed the thought as he stumbled and fell face first into chilled, foul-tasting water.

"Dalzere," Kellen spluttered as he struggled to rise.

"Hurry. I think they have broken into the Well Room behind us."

Not needing to be told twice, he splashed his way around another corner, squinting his eyes shut as bright sunlight flooded the tunnel's downward spiral. Feeling his purchase on the walls decrease, he was abruptly sliding uncontrollably downward. He tried to gain some purchase, but the grit and stones cut his fingers, and he was hurled violently along with the rush of damp dirt and water. Then he was falling, utterly weightless, airborne, before hitting a warm body of water, flat on his back. He grunted in pain and shock.

He tried to open his eyes, but the bright sunlight burned. Instead, he heard Dalzere's muttered curse, and he moved, given only a moment to save himself before the Drow came flying at him. Dalzere landed next to him, splashing more water over him, and Kellen gasped for breath, feeling as though he was drowning a second time.

"Bright stars . . . we're out!"

"But not safe," the Elf said as he stiffly got to his feet. He bent down and dragged Kellen up, cutting the leather tie between them. "We are going to have company very soon, so I suggest we run."

Groaning with exhaustion, Kellen squinted once more up at the opening in the rock face and wondered about the Lexsii. "Scratch and the others?"

"I imagine they will block off the tunnel leading to the well. Don't worry. Just move."

Getting his sore muscles to work, Kellen held a hand up to shade his light-sensitive eyes as he hobbled after the Elf. He really believed that things could not get any worse.

* * *

After the first hour of careful cross tracking, Kellen stopped to lean against a tree, breathing out deeply. He was exhausted and hungry. His eyes had adjusted, but his fingers and knees were torn and sore. "How far behind do you think they are?"

"Not far enough," Dalzere's tone was bleak. "We have come out further northwest than I would have liked. We are probably closer to the Fifth Posting."

"Is that good or bad?"

The other shrugged. "Depends. If the Drow hunting us are from the Fifth and have called for reinforcement, it is bad. If they are not from the Fifth, then it is better. We should be able to get into the marshes and disguise our trail."

"And how far are these marshes?" Kellen asked with a sinking feeling.

"Half a day's travel. Now move, Kellen."

CHAPTER TWENTY-ONE

Hours crawled by, and Kellen did not believe he could muster any more energy, wishing they could stop and rest. He stumbled forward, surprised as a noise whistled past his ear, and he glanced up, stunned to see a small black dart embedded in the bark of a dead tree. He stared stupidly at the unusual dart, even as Dalzere whipped around and roughly thrust him out of the way. He fell heavily to the ground, rolling over and catching a glimpse of a dark shape as it leapt over a rotting tree stump. A Drow hunter.

Startled by the sudden attack, Kellen managed to catch his balance and back away from the hunter and Dalzere. He had not even suspected they were still being followed, his mind too numb with exhaustion. Slowly he pulled his short blade free and gasped, horrified and enthralled by the deadly battle, wishing Dalzere strength and luck. They were evenly matched, so alike, yet also so dissimilar, Dalzere's long hair and traveling leathers softened his features, while the hunter's severe haircut, numerous weapons, sparse clothing, and skin markings highlighted his savagery.

He saw Dalzere throw the Drow onto his back before the hunter agilely rolled to his feet then warily danced around Dalzere. The Drow warrior spat something in a cruel language, the words indistinct, but his expression was full of hatred. Then the hunter removed a wicked-looking, curved blade from his belt and swiveled it in his hand, the blade rotating as if by magic. Amazed, Kellen sagged back against his tree and watched, scared for Dalzere as his friend blocked the swift stroke of the blade with his knife. Then Dalzere lunged, his hands a blur as he swiftly stunned and disarmed his challenger.

Impressed by the skill, Kellen suddenly noticed out of the corner of his eye a second Drow hunter homing in on Dalzere from behind. His eyes went to Dalzere, but the Elf was oblivious to the new danger, so acting on instinct, he raised his own small knife and threw it at the second Drow with all his might. The knife cut through the leaves, giving the second hunter a small warning, allowing him to just brush the knife aside before his demonic, painted eyes locked on him. A slow, evil smile touched the hunter's lips before he advanced.

"Oh, bright stars," Kellen gasped, diving through the bushes next to him, rolling away from his attacker as the second hunter reached his position. In haste, he got to his feet and ducked behind another tree, watching the skilled Drow stalk him. He debated what he could possibly use against such a proficient killer. A surge of adrenaline spiked through his system as he was forced to evade the Drow's mock attack. He knew the other was taunting him, playing with him, and he hiccupped on a breath.

Not bothering to wait for the hunter to tire of this game, he turned and ran through the trees, stopping when he came to a small clearing. He was breathing hard now, desperate to escape but knowing it was useless. He turned and watched the hunter pace toward him, mesmerized by the red paint decorating his face and body, seeing the contempt on the Drow's face, and he braced himself for the worst as the hunter flicked his wrist and produced a weapon as if by magic. In the Drow's hand was now the same razor-sharp, curved blade that the other hunter had produced. He stared at it, hypnotized by its polished blade and wicked-looking spike. He lifted his gaze to meet the Drow's cruel gaze, trying to read what this creature would do next.

The honed weapon was leveled at him with the spike prominent, and he panicked, sensing instantly what the other was going to do. He guardedly backed away from the tree on his left and forced himself to drop to the ground even as the Drow threw the strange-looking weapon. The tree behind him split in two, the blade missing him by inches. Surprised he was still alive, Kellen struggled to his knees, searching for any weapon and grabbed a sturdy tree branch. Confusion clouded his thinking, and he was at a loss to try any of the lessons Sasheer had taught him, so instead he used brute force and swung at the Drow, ignoring the snort of laughter his actions produced. He swung again, noting how the Drow hunter stepped so gracefully away, only to slide under his defenses and rip the curved blade from the fallen tree behind. Then the Drow grinned with deadly intent.

In a show of bravado and defiance, Kellen raised his branch threateningly and stepped backward. His opponent mumbled something, then followed, and Kellen swung his branch, hitting the Drow squarely. But the hunter merely grabbed his branch and ripped it from his grasp. A moment later, those same cold fingers were locked around his throat, choking him.

He gasped for breath, stumbled, falling to the ground and pulling the hunter down on top of him. He bucked, gripping the wrist holding him and felt the Drow lean forward and whisper something in his ear. The words were snarled, ugly, while those golden eyes held nothing but pure malice and hatred. His eyes watered, and he struggled for air, watching in horror as that wicked, curved blade again began to swing down in a death stroke toward his chest.

Expecting sharp pain, Kellen gulped in fear, shocked when he was abruptly released. He sat up, gasping for air, only to find Dalzere cutting the second hunter down with a similarly curved hand blade. Dalzere gripped the dead Drow around the neck for a moment longer before dropping the body with distaste.

"Are you all right?"

"I will be in a moment," Kellen answered in a hoarse voice. "How did—" he glanced past Dalzere, "you . . . is the other one."

"Dead." Dalzere did not sound happy. His face was set in an angry scowl as he threw the weapon he held on the ground, and then he cursed in the same language the Drow hunter had used.

It was disconcerting, and Kellen slowly stood, fingering his throat before he approached the uncommunicative Elf. Dalzere was stained red with blood; a vicious cut above one eye bled sluggishly. "What is that thing?" He indicated the evil-looking, curved blade that was sitting on the grass, covered in bright blood.

"A *cuxsia*." Dalzere spat the term. "A bespelled Drow instrument of death," he added in a calmer voice. "I had hoped never to use one again."

Hearing the anger and disgust in the other man's voice, Kellen looked for a way to defuse the emotions surrounding Dalzere. He had never seen the Elf so angry, or so *changed*, and he looked away. "Will there be others coming?"

"If not others, then a patrol."

"So we had best move," Kellen decided as he reached over and touched Dalzere's arm. The Drow flinched. "You need to lead us out of here," he coaxed, willing his mild-tempered friend to return.

Lifting his head, Dalzere seemed to consider him for a strained moment, before nodding once. Crouching down, he pulled a second longer blade free of the dead Drow's weapon belt. "Here, take this. You might need it."

"But it's a Drow weapon." Kellen held his hands away from the offered sword. "Didn't you just say they are bespelled?"

"The *cuxsia*, yes, but this is just a simple, crafted sword." Dalzere held it up again, his eyes bright with anger. "Take it. It may save your life."

Kellen accepted the sword, hesitant, and held it up, feeling its lightness and even balance as he looked down the straight blade. "Something so evil should not look so beautiful."

"The good or evil intent can only come from the user."

Hearing the echoes of Sasheer's words in his mind, Kellen fell into step beside Dalzere as the other went back to the first dead hunter and stripped items from the body. This painted Drow warrior had been beheaded, and Kellen looked away in abhorrence. He hated the sight of death and did not want to see what his friend took from the dead. He only wanted to escape this gruesome sight and was glad when Dalzere walked away. He followed, finding that he had to run in order to keep up with Dalzere's punishing pace. Only this time he did not argue.

* * *

Not wanting to break the heavy silence which had fallen after leaving the two dead behind, Kellen kept quiet, following Dalzere's tall frame as the other led them down a number of different tracks. It seemed like hours since the encounter, and the dread of it faded in his mind. Now he was able to start and take notice of the forest surrounding him, and he saw minute changes in the vibrancy of the trees. The landscape altered subtly as evening descended across the land, and it was not until he started to smell a foul odor that he realized they must be approaching the marshes and moors.

"How much further?" he asked, his voice still husky, his throat sore and bruised. Beside him Dalzere continued to brood.

"The marshes are off to our right," Dalzere said, his tone harsh. "We will go into the woods near Sanctuary's borders and spend the night there."

Glancing off to his right, Kellen wondered why they were not going straight to the Keep. "How far is this Keep?"

"Not far."

"Then why don't we go straight there?" He quickened his pace, so that he matched the Elf's long strides. "It would be safer than the woods, especially if other hunters come after us," he tried to reason and heard Dalzere grunt in acknowledgment. "Well, wouldn't it?"

"No Drow will violate Sanctuary's woods."

Dalzere sounded so sure, yet Kellen could not imagine a race like the Drow respecting anything. "Why not go to the Keep?" he pushed.

Sighing, Dalzere stopped abruptly and turned to Kellen in exasperation. "Because we would not get there before dark, and the marshes and moors are guarded by wolves. It is safer to wait in the woods."

Raising his hands in mute apology, Kellen said nothing further as Dalzere stalked off again, an angry blur of darkness in the evening gloom. *What danger could wolves be when compared to Drow hunters?* he asked silently, wishing he could voice that question aloud. He had grown up with wolves in Ihova, and they were not that fierce. But at present, he didn't trust Dalzere's chancy temper.

Biting his lip, Kellen frowned after Dalzere's figure, noting how the Elf did not slow his pace. It forced him to lengthen his own stride just to keep up with the irritated man, and he muttered a curse. His annoyance was soon replaced by awe as Dalzere led him into a beautiful, dense pine forest. Everything about the place smelt clean and fresh, pure in a way he had not experienced since leaving the old woodlands of Ihova. It almost felt like home, and he was grinning without knowing it.

The air was a little warmer under the trees, and he inhaled the scent of the forest around him. He could hear the crackle of pine needles under his feet, taste the crispness of the air, and it soothed his soul, especially after his last few days of being wet and trapped in putrid water. Thinking back on that, he hoped the Lexsii were all right, and that their carelessness had not put those little creatures in danger from the Drow.

Sighing again, he noted that the forest cut away into numerous valleys and hills, and he slowed his pace, enjoying the feel of place, and he stopped as a new sensation washed over him. He glanced down at his feet and frowned. He squinted harder but could see nothing unusual, yet he felt something wash over him. Not a presence, but a pressure, a flow of heat that swept around him brushed his skin and swirled between his ankles. Like a breeze . . . It was baffling, and he turned, trying to discern what it was he could feel yet not see.

"What is the problem?"

Jumping at Dalzere's growled question, Kellen turned to look at the Elf. He lifted a hand, not sure how to explain the strange sensations, and stopped as he stared down at his hand. The thrill was there again, like a wash of warm water over his fingers. Restful. "I feel . . ."

"The currents," Dalzere finished for him in a bored tone. He stopped and braced his weight on one hip before he sighed and rubbed his face in exasperation. "I had forgotten that this would be new to you."

"Currents?" Kellen questioned. He raised his second hand, trying to cup the strange rush of invisible warmth and giggled when it just seeped through his fingers, tickling his senses. "Magic?"

"Where is Sasheer when I need him?" Dalzere complained, piqued, before he half-glared at Kellen. "No, the currents are not magic. They are harmless, neutral, and without intelligence. They flow across certain sections of the mainland of Sennovia—a remnant of old energies that spill from Mitthsombaine to weave across the earth. Most never feel their touch unless they are Gifted." Dalzere gave a snort of false laughter. "Can you play later?" he asked pointedly as Kellen laughed and spun around in the gathering flow of currents. "Stop teasing them, and they will go away."

"What?" Delighted, Kellen grinned at the scowling Elf. "It feels wonderful."

"They are not a plaything, Kellen," he growled. "Ignore them." Then Dalzere swiveled on his toes and walked away.

Stunned, Kellen stared after Dalzere. *Plaything?* He glanced down again at his fingers, enjoying the touch of the seductive currents and reluctantly stepped away from the pool of sensations. Immediately, the rush of warmth diminished to merely brush his feet, and he sighed. He looked after the Elf and wondered if Dalzere would calm down soon, so he could get a full explanation of this amazing phenomenon. Because facing Dalzere in a snit was definitely better than asking Sasheer in any mood.

Casting one last look of longing at where he had stood, Kellen rushed to catch up with his uninformative friend. Everything felt different in the forest, and as he left the gully, he felt the flow of heat lessen until he could feel nothing. *The currents lived in pockets?* Speculating about that, he picked up the pace to catch Dalzere.

Ahead, he could see Dalzere's bedraggled form, and he glanced down at himself, knowing that even Ryland would have a hard time recognizing him. His hair was mostly loose and filthy, his leathers torn beyond repair. His skin and clothing were stained by constant soaking in black water and by crawling through polluted tunnels—not to mention the blood which now covered the Elf. And he laughed, feeling fantastic, even if he did look half dead. It was an amazing feeling.

Putting his foot down on more pine needles, he felt the ground give way suddenly under him, and he reached out to grab hold of a tree but missed. Arms windmilling uselessly, he slid backward down a damp, grassed slope into a gully below.

He landed with a thud, coming to an undignified stop, and just lay there, then he groaned out a disbelieving breath before gingerly feeling the new lump on his forehead. There was no rush of heat or pressure around him, and he sighed, disappointed at not feeling a new swell of currents in the ditch. *There goes that theory.* Dropping his head down, he rested flat on his back, realizing how exhausted he was now that he was lying down. He could fall asleep, and he lifted his lashes to find a sword hovering a few inches from his nose.

"Just stay very still and keep your hands away from that Drow blade."

It was a sharp warning from somewhere in the vicinity of his feet, and he did not even bother to raise his head as he complied. Stretching out his arms, he waited for his captor to come closer, so he could see him.

"Good."

He felt a foot prod his boots, searching for other weapons.

"What is your name?"

The accent was weird, yet he understood the words and grunted in reply when his boot was kicked and the question repeated.

"Answer me!"

"Kellen," he said, deciding he didn't feel up to a new fight. If they wanted to kill him they could.

"That is your whole name?"

"Yes," he tried to raise his head, but the sword swam closer. "And you are?"

"Where are you from?"

It was a demand, and he exhaled in a loud rush. "I'm not going to hurt you."

"Where are you from?"

This time the question was in a higher pitch, and he hid his smile as he realized his captor was a woman. *Salimen would kill himself laughing if he ever heard of this!* "You wouldn't know it if I told you."

"I'll decide that, so just answer the question."

"Ihova."

There was silence for a long moment, and he waited, getting a little annoyed.

"A southerner?"

Impressed, he nevertheless swiftly swiped the fine blade point from his face and sat up. "Look, I've had a really bad day, week. Okay—a bad few months," he corrected as he held up a hand to ward off a blow. "I'm in no mood for games. If you intend to kill me, just do it, otherwise, I am getting up because this ground is cold, and where I've been lately, that is the last thing I need." Standing slowly, he kept his hands away from the sword at his waist as he stretched sore muscles. Cautiously he eyed his assailant, noting her slender frame and very competent stance as she kept the fine sword leveled at his chest. "And you are?" he asked.

"None of your business," she said, her eyes traveling over his disheveled frame.

"Fine," he shook his head. "What happens now? Do we stand here all night talking in circles, or do you let me go? Better still, can you take me somewhere where there is hot food and drink? And maybe a soft bed?"

"You are in no position to give me orders," she cut back, her face hardening a little as she swept her eyes over him again. "If I take you back to my elders, they will probably hang you for trespassing!"

"Really?"

It was a new voice, and Kellen let his smile grow as Dalzere stepped from behind a tree.

The Elf regarded them both with amusement before leaning back against the same tree and folding his arms, his scowl sullen. "So tell me, Tich, have the councilors in Sanctuary taken to imitating the Drow's tactics just to win an encounter?"

"What are you doing here?" the female named Tich asked darkly as she turned her glare on the Drow.

Curious at her reaction, Kellen noticed that she showed no surprise at Dalzere's appearance or comments. If anything, she relaxed.

"Just passing through," Dalzere said. "But before I go, I need this one. So are you finished with the dramatics?"

Lifting her chin, she became even more indignant. "Are you going on to Sanctuary?"

"No," Dalzere shook his head, walking straight past her. "I am going to the Keep."

"I have just come from there," she said. She swung her eyes between both men and frowned. "All is not well. Do you know Cornithia and Breeze are dead?"

"Yes," Dalzere growled.

If he were feeling charitable, Kellen would have warned her to drop the questions. But he wasn't. Instead he winced when she persisted in following Dalzere and rattling off more questions. But to his amazement, Dalzere stopped and sighed, resigned.

"Just tell me if Sasheer is at the Keep?" Dalzere asked at last.

"Yes. He did not mention you to me," Tich returned.

Ignoring that, Dalzere turned to look at Kellen in the darkening gloom. "We will make camp here then go on to the Keep in the morning."

Glad that a decision had been made, Kellen raised his hands again when Tich lifted her sword in his direction. "I'm just going to collect some firewood, okay?" he almost snapped at her, disgruntled at how she seemed to have broken Dalzere's bad mood when he had been unsuccessful all afternoon.

Backing away and grumbling about her distrustful behavior and Dalzere's grouchiness, he kicked out at a few fallen branches. It was obvious the two knew each other very well, and he felt left out. He stamped into the forest and took out his mood on a couple of unsuspecting trees. Then laughed at his over-reaction, gathering up the fallen wood and starting to envision a warm fire. With luck, Dalzere would find food, and then he could sleep for the first time in weeks, warm and with a full stomach.

He lifted his head at the sound of footfalls in the pine ground cover, and stifled a groan as he saw Tich approach. This was all he needed, and he turned his back on her.

"We did not get off to the best of starts," she said. "I now feel that you do not like me."

"Understatement," Kellen muttered, still keeping his back to her. "That usually happens when someone points a sword in my face."

"Kellen . . ."

He stopped, listening to the way she pronounced his name, her accent making it sound soft and appealing. Bracing himself, he waited for her to speak.

"Dalzere has said that you can be trusted, that you have fought with him and proved worthy of honor," she continued in a gentle tone as she walked around his rigid frame to see his shadowed face.

"That's nice." But silently his mind was reeling. He was stunned and amazed that Dalzere would think so highly of him. Or that Dalzere would speak so openly of his feeling to this stranger. Who was this woman?

"I am sorry if I offended you," she said, regarding his stubborn expression. "My name is Tich, and I am a Healer. I live in Sanctuary, and I treasure these woods. It is just that we get so many trappers, spies, or slavers infesting our home lately that I . . . by the look of you, I just . . ." She shrugged, her eyes drifting down his lean body.

Getting a little self-conscious about his appearance and her assessing gaze, he swallowed and stood straighter to cover his nerves. "I'm not exactly at my best."

"No," Tich agreed. "Those leathers are ruined. In fact, they are almost nonexistent." Her face lit up into a teasing smile. "You might as well go naked, for what they hide. Or should I say don't hide?"

Feeling himself blush, Kellen pushed past her, going back to camp and preparing the fire like Ryland had taught him, wishing she would go away—go back to this Sanctuary.

Eyeing Kellen in curiosity, Dalzere raised his head as Tich followed Kellen into the small camp area with a smile plastered across her pretty face. "I take it you will return to Sanctuary in the morning?" he asked.

Kellen waited for her answer, praying it would be in the affirmative.

"No, I think I'll accompany you back to the Keep," Tich decided then added seriously, "besides, I have a sick Lancooti there who needs my help."

CHAPTER TWENTY-TWO

Feeling uncomfortable and not understanding why, Kellen took to fidgeting with his belt. He adjusted the strap, securing his new sword for the tenth time as he walked behind Dalzere and the female Healer from Sanctuary.

He had been the last to wake that morning and had found to his chagrin that both the Elf and Healer were already up and talking while Dalzere cooked a small rabbit over the rekindled fire. Both had stopped midsentence when he had groggily raised his head and both had stared at him with mirroring expressions of interest before Tich had grinned, and Dalzere had raised his customary brow.

Thinking about it now, Kellen was still disconcerted, especially as he felt he was missing a vital clue. Though breakfast had been the best thing, he could remember eating in weeks. His only misgiving was the Healer. Dalzere seemed to take no noticeable offense at her blunt appraisals, but he found her frankness just a little too personal, especially when she had tried to drag out every piece of information about him from birth onward. It had left him reeling, especially when she had given him a sweet smile before promptly turning away to pick up her pack.

Being the last to move, he had kicked out the fire, then trailed the two obvious acquaintances out of the small valley. Somehow he never did manage to catch the pair as they exited the pine forest and entered the stagnant marshes and moors.

Sighing, Kellen unconsciously pushed again at the straps holding his sword to his belt, raising his eyes to watch the large birds he could see hovering way out over the land ahead. With the putrid smell and low, bushy undergrowth covering the moors, the land looked very unappealing and desolate.

"Are you sure anyone lives out here?" Kellen asked as he squinted up at the warm early-morning winter sun.

The Healer turned toward him with a superior expression on her pretty face. "Of course they do! The Keep is only a half day's march away. Don't you know anything, southerner?"

"I've never been here before," Kellen reminded her, banking down on his temper.

"That's obvious," she said indignantly.

"I only meant..."

"Don't comment on something you know nothing about," she advised loftily, ending it with the same sweet, false smile.

Closing his mouth, Kellen tried not to glare at her as he let his eyes swing to Dalzere's straight back. But the Elf was either ignoring the exchange or oblivious to it, lost in a world of private thought. Letting his eyes go back to Tich, he tried to decide if it was just irritation or extreme dislike he was feeling as he moodily studied her slender frame.

She was shorter than he was, petite, *which is one advantage*, he decided begrudgingly. She looked nothing like Crizkerisomia, who towered over everyone. The Healer's hair was a mousy brown color with just a hint of red showing through in the sunlight, and she had it tied in a loose braid with white ribbons trailing down her back. *Her skin is the color of summer,* he mused, his eyes losing focus as he studied her. He blinked and scowled, lifting his gaze and catching her arched glare before she turned away. He decided her eyes were hazel—deceitful—as they danced in mischief every time she looked his way.

He shivered, feeling sweat start to trickle down his spine. Her elegance, her clothing—and he studied her long, straight smock that was slit to the waist, seeing her soft leather britches underneath. Swallowing, he looked away, trying not to think about her body. Yet she fascinated him, despite her superior attitude, and he snorted at his own wayward thinking. Even her voice, her laughter was a tantalizing sound that thrilled and excited him.

He exhaled hard and forced his eyes away from her narrow waist. He needed to concentrate on other things, and he deliberately searched for the circling birds overhead, watching how they glided in the warm air columns high above.

Unfortunately, the birds did not hold his wandering attention for long.

* * *

By midmorning, Kellen was about ready to collapse in overheated weariness. The marshes exuded a stifling humidity that sapped his energy. It seemed to him that they were walking in aimless circles, although Dalzere refused to comment. Tich had informed him earlier, in a very annoying manner, that this was the only safe trail, as all other paths led to quicksand and dangerous pits. Never liking to be reprimanded, and especially by someone he didn't know and who was a *girl*, Kellen had kept silent. He felt far from communicative, and so he swung his pack onto his other shoulder, amusing himself by idly swatting at the tiny gnats, which infested the foul-smelling moor.

"At last," Tich called. "There's the Keep, southerner. And look, they are opening the gates for us."

Watching Tich as she swung around to smile at him in triumph, he tried to show some enthusiasm as he climbed the gentle rise, thinking this fabled Keep must either be very small, or be underground for them not to have seen it long before now. For the moors, although smelly and dotted with numerous pits, were relatively flat in nature.

Stopping on the top of the rise, Kellen followed Tich's pointing finger and felt his jaw drop, getting his first good look at the Keep. It defied description. It was massive, with huge spiraling towers and battlements. He absently raised a hand to rub his eyes as he stared at the huge stonewalls, amazed that so large a structure could hide in plain sight.

Speechless, he cast his eyes over the surrounding area, noting the moot and small gardens outside the main gates. Slowly, he started to comprehend that unless he looked directly at the towering structure, its outline blurred and seemed to vanish. He glanced to his left, staring at the Keep out of the corner of his eye and gasped when the solid structure vanished completely. He turned back and stared at the castle. *Magical?*

"Close your mouth, southerner. Or you will attract even more gnats," Tich said before hurrying down the slop to catch up with the silent Elf.

Locking his jaw, he sent her a look of annoyance before moving also, deciding it was probably best to stay with the others just in case the massive Keep suddenly relocated when he was not looking.

He was the last through the massive iron gates, and Kellen eyed the four guards in apprehension as they shut the gates with a resounding clang. Around him, in the open courtyard, numerous people could be seen, all clad in colorful garments. None took any notice of them; and none seemed concerned that they were living in the middle of a swamp.

Flustered, he stared around the paved courtyard, realizing that the awful smell of the stagnant water had also vanished, and he glanced back at the huge gates. *What is this place?* He turned in a slow circle, letting his senses read the atmosphere and found he was relaxing, his fears were evaporating, and that this structure *felt* welcoming.

The architecture of the Keep was stone, the people all dressed in long, flowing robes, and he could sense the age of the place gather around him. It was addictively appealing, and he had to stop himself from reaching out to embrace a cold stone pillar. *Magic.* He could feel it—could almost taste, and he laughed in delight. This was pure and simple magic, and it permeated every fiber of his being.

"At last!"

Abruptly seized from behind and wrapped in a warm bear hug, it took Kellen only a startled moment to realize it was Ryland who held him. The Haonian set him down then held him at arms' length.

"You had me worried, lad. You had us all worried," Ryland grinned then clapped him on the back. "When I saw you slide down that rock face, I thought we had lost you for good. Until that unprincipled Drow stepped off the ledge in your wake."

"I thought I had lost it too, for a while," Kellen said, his smile growing in delight at finding his friend. It was so good to see Ryland. "What happened to everyone else?"

"Sasheer drove us at a demon's pace through those ridges. It was possibly for the best, as snow started to fall just before we descended into these moors." Ryland gave a disgusted look. "He and that white Elf got us all through. They even managed to keep Peleyia alive long enough to get him here."

"Pel? How is he?" Kellen asked urgently, wanting to go and find the Lancooti, appalled that he had forgotten about Peleyia over the last few stressful days.

"Better," Ryland replied. "Some sassy little Healer is treating him."

"Figures," Kellen mumbled, picturing Tich in his mind.

"And you, lad?" Ryland asked as he eyed the bruising showing around Kellen's throat. "What happened here?"

"I ran into the wrong end of a Drow," he replied flippantly, wanting to forget the incident and just go see Peleyia.

Frowning, Ryland's gaze slid briefly to Dalzere, who had been stopped by an older looking man in a thick, long cloak.

Smiling a little, Kellen shook his head as he surmised what Ryland was thinking. He glanced also at Dalzere, noting his friend's troubled expression. "Wrong Drow," he told Ryland. "The one I encountered had absolutely no sense of humor, and even less dress sense." He gave a small smile, seeing Ryland blink at him in growing understanding. "In fact, if it hadn't been for Dalzere, I would have died that first day in Drow territory."

"Then we owe him our respect."

"We owe him more than that, Ryland. He deserves nothing less than our complete trust."

Ryland paused, his eyes flicking over Kellen to the Drow. "A lot has happened in the last few months," he said with an assessing gaze. "You have matured since leaving Ihova, lad."

"I haven't had much choice," Kellen said. "So much has happened since you rescued me from the Black Guard. It feels like a lifetime ago."

"I know what you mean," Ryland said.

"I sometimes wonder how much of our homeland is still there."

"From the little I've heard since arriving here, it seems this is not the first time Kalern has tried to destroy the Southland. He has never succeeded before, so I doubt he will succeed this time."

"But why?" Kellen asked, bewildered. "Why does he want to destroy the Southland in the first place? Isn't his kingdom far off in the north country?"

"That I do not know. But," with a slight tilt of his hairy head, Ryland indicated to the man over by the stone well, who was talking with Dalzere, "the Brethren all say that—"

"Ryland! Kellen!" Salimen interrupted the conversation as he bounced to a stop and eyed the younger man curiously. "Lords! You're filthy, Kell. What have you and that Drow been doing?"

"We went through Death Peaks," Kellen said.

"Through?" Ryland's eyebrows climbed as he looked shocked by the news.

Lifting a hand, Salimen interrupted the bigger man. "It will have to wait. Sasheer has asked that we all congregate in the main library now that Dalzere and Kellen have arrived. He is anxious to see you," he paused, giving the younger man a very hard glance. "But maybe you should wash first, Kell, as you reek of something long dead."

"Thanks," Kellen muttered before following the unrepentant bowman to the massive stone steps that led up into the castle.

* * *

By mutual consent of everyone within the company, both Kellen and Dalzere were forced to bathe before joining the others in the Keep's antiquated library on the second floor.

Brushing his overlong, damp hair and tying it back, Kellen put on some new leathers which had been left out for him. Fastening the laces, he glanced around the spacious bedchamber before stepping out into the richly decorated corridor.

The Keep was unbelievable, delicate carved statues lined the walls, while gold-inlayed paneling decorated the ceiling and floors. Deep, rich colors assaulted the eyes in a pleasing mix of splendor. Even the thick, lush tapestries added a sense of age to the wisdom infusing the atmosphere of the place. Battles, buildings, and people of a time long dead were depicted in the tapestries, while canvassed paintings hung in the stairwells and widening entranceways. Jeweled lights protruded from the walls, with ornate candles lit, highlighting the wealth and magnificence of the Keep. He was stunned.

Up until that moment, he had always believed the white marbled palace in Ihova, which was renowned throughout the Southland for its extraordinary beauty and grandeur, to be the wealthiest building in existence. *But now . . .*

Shaking his head, awed by the elegant splendor surrounding him, he made his way back down the wide staircase to the second level and found most of his friends were already waiting inside the massive library, along with numerous other people. The library was another place of magnificence, of awe-inspiring splendor and beauty. He had never seen so many books, been entranced by so many pictures of far-off places, and so captivated by the maps which hung on the walls. Every book in creation seemed to fill the room, lining each wall from floor to ceiling.

In the center of the library stood Sasheer, and Kellen stopped to stare at the Ranger. Sasheer still looked impossibly young, if disgruntled, as he waited, his frown darkening. For once Sasheer's hair seemed tamed, his clothing clean, showing him to be almost a different man until the Ranger impatiently motioned for him to approach, and he sighed. Little had changed.

He pretended not to notice Sasheer's instant scowl and the narrowing of those changeable eyes when he ignored the invitation. Instead, Kellen cast his eyes around the room to try and pick out one of the Ihovians. If he could find Salimen, then he was sure Sasheer would leave him in peace awhile longer. He saw all his friends, except for Dalzere and Peleyia.

Even Crizkerisomia was present, and Kellen watched her lean

over a very detailed, three-dimensional map, which rested on a long table in the middle of the room. She was tracing the point of her knife gently over the blackened ridge that represented Death Peaks. Curious, Kellen took a step toward her then stopped when a tall man, who was dressed in one of those flowing robes, went quickly to her side and removed the knife from her grasp. To Kellen's surprise, Crizkerisomia didn't even flinch, which was extremely unusual behavior for the proud Sun Elf.

"Kellen!"

Sasheer's voice startled him, and Kellen found his arm imprisoned in a firm grasp. He was unceremoniously dragged away from Crizkerisomia and over to a group of gentlemen of varying ages. Then Sasheer was introducing him.

"This is Tattlier and Tanish."

"Nice to meet you," Kellen responded politely. He looked at both men, taking in their similar attire. One was old, and the other was of average height with thick, dark hair and sharp, clear eyes. He pondered their connection to Sasheer and glanced back at the Ranger, and to his amusement, he saw that Sasheer looked a little uncomfortable. He was restless, as Sasheer's long fingers pulled at the collar of his exquisite robe.

"Likewise," the dark-haired and sharp-eyed man returned, his tone bored. He reached forward to take Kellen's hand and shook it in welcome. "I am Tattlier, and Sasheer has told us all about you."

Not quite knowing what to say, Kellen was spared from answering when the tall man, who had liberated the knife from Crizkerisomia only moments ago, joined the group. He went and stood between Tattlier and the older man—Tanish.

"Sasheer! I wish you would civilize your friends before you bring them home." The tall man held up a small deadly, elvish blade to show his companions. "She was rearranging the landscape on the center map with this, would you believe?"

The older gentleman of the group reached forward, took the knife from the new arrival, and carefully felt along its edge. "A fine weapon. Probably 150 years of age, if I am reading this hilt correctly. Probably a birth gift."

Amazed, Kellen became even more impressed when he realized that the older man, Tanish, was blind, his eyes totally white as he stared sightlessly ahead. But his grin was warm and inviting.

"Stop showing off, Tanish," the tall man said. He swiped the knife off his grinning colleague and settled his gaze on Kellen. "So—this is the young trainee. He is shorter than the last one you brought home, Sasheer."

Sasheer sent the speaker an irritated look before introducing him. "Kellen, this is Dybellia."

Nodding, Kellen was not sure what to make of these three men. They seemed old, yet so impulsive, certainly not acting like the elders he was used to seeing in Ihova. He glanced around the group, not missing how their ages ranged from Sasheer's youthfulness to Tanish's elderly appearance. *Is it all a lie?* For he knew Sasheer was older than he appeared. So how old did that then make the blind Tanish?

"Dalzere tells me you have been asking questions about Drow history and other things from the past," Sasheer said as his eyes fell on Kellen.

Kellen swallowed nervously, distracted by the way Sasheer seemed to be ignoring Dybellia's snort of amusement.

"Maybe it is time I gave you the answers you seek?" Sasheer finished musingly. "If you are interested in learning."

"Of course he's interested," Tanish stated in mild reproof. He turned his sightless eyes on Kellen and smiled. "Welcome to the family, young man."

"Family?" Kellen repeated, puzzled. "I think you assume I already know what you are talking about, but I don't. I don't want to sound ungracious, but what's this all about?"

"Kellen," Sasheer said sharply but was stopped when Tattlier broke in with feigned shock and mock outrage.

"Don't tell me you haven't told him yet? Oh, by the Towers, Sasheer, when are you going to loosen up and learn?" Tattlier turned to Dybellia. "How many has he lost now because he insists on keeping the secret for the sake of the secret?"

"Too many to count," Dybellia agreed. Kellen saw the man glance at Sasheer then add, "Kalern knows what we are doing. Why you persist in keeping the silence, I'll never fathom."

"He was not the firstborn, so I have not had the opportunity, or time, to instruct him properly," Sasheer defended hotly. "Besides, with the amount of promise his older brother showed, I looked no further down the line."

"He's the second son?" Tattlier asked, his eyes going back to Kellen in cordial interest only.

"His older brother died carelessly," Sasheer said.

"You lost another one?"

"Dybellia," Sasheer growled in warning. "Do you want me to throw you off the battlement a second time?"

"Once every thousand years is enough," Dybellia grumbled peevishly, shuddering slightly. "You have no sense of humor, Sasheer."

"I thought it was funny," Tattlier commented. "It could have been worse. Sasheer at least waited until the lake was flooded before throwing you off the battlement," the sharp-eyed man said. "That was considerate, if you ask me."

"Well, I wasn't asking you," Dybellia shot back. "You try inhaling black swamp water."

Raising a hand, Tanish silenced them all with a stern look. "Enough! You are confusing the poor child."

"Tanish, I—" Sasheer tried again.

The blind man just sighed as he reached over to touch Sasheer's wrist briefly. "My friend, you are a little impatient, I have found, when it comes to teaching the young."

"More like tactless," Tattlier judged.

"Remember what he did to poor Aquiletta?" Dybellia reminded as he looked at Tattlier.

"That was not my fault!" Sasheer protested.

"You upset him and frustrated him to the point where he almost brought the roof down on us all," Tattlier said. Next to him, Tanish sighed and rubbed his eyes in exasperation.

"Aquiletta showed no common sense. No discipline or ability

to reason out problems!" Sasheer said, folding his arms and glaring at his accusers. "I cannot believe you would resurrect this subject."

"Do we have to argue about this now?" Tanish asked in a reasonable tone.

"But Aquiletta died," Dybellia emphasized.

"That was only because he was too puffed up with his own self-importance to accept my warning and advice." Sasheer's clipped tone invited no argument. "I don't know why you insist on blaming me for his death."

"We don't," Tanish soothed. "You blame yourself."

Frowning, Sasheer turned away and mumbled something that sounded suspiciously like a Drow curse.

Lifting a hand, Tanish reached out with firm accuracy and gripped Kellen's shoulder. "Come, lad, let's go over here, away from this rabble, so I can answer those questions I know are in your head."

Feeling his mind spin in confusion, Kellen numbly followed the older-looking man. Who was this Aquiletta? And why had he died? Coming to a stop by a large etched window, Kellen saw it overlooked a small hanging garden. The beautiful garden seemed so odd, especially as just a few feet from its edge was the Keep's stonewall and beyond that a desolate moor. It seemed easier to dwell on that peculiar oddity than on what he had just heard. On what he had just witnessed.

"Youngling?"

Refocusing, Kellen turned to the other man, seeing the milky white unblinking eyes watch him with such an assessing expression that he was left with little doubt that this man could 'see' him on some obscure level. See him, or read his thoughts? Like the Lancooti had tried? "Well, can you?" he asked, watching Tanish frown.

"Read your mind?"

"That, I suppose, is answer enough." Kellen sat down heavily on the soft, velvet, padded window seat. Around him the room seemed to dim as people were ushered out. He saw both Ryland and Salimen give him a worried glance before they were escorted from the warm library. Turning, he looked again at the older man, his gaze narrowing as he sensed a tangible warmth, an inquisitive presence, press around him. *This man is like Sasheer. Mageborn.* His frown deepened, and he slowly sucked in a breath as he realized what it was he was feeling. The tangible brush of an invisible entity. *Not again . . .* he concentrated on the feel of this entity, comprehending with a shock that it was not Terrica or even the evil, sadistic creature from the past that he was reading. Rather it was a new entity. *A third creature? How many invisible entities are there?*

"I read your feelings, sensed your emotions. That is different to reading your mind. Sasheer must have explained that much to you at least, youngling," Tanish said, breaking into Kellen's chaotic thoughts, as he sat beside Kellen and touched his knee. "You are confused."

"I used to think I knew who I was, but now—" Kellen paused and lifted a hand in mute helplessness, not sure where to start asking his questions. Then he decided to start at the beginning. "How did you know my brother?"

"Wyran?" Tanish asked then sighed. "I knew of him, having never met him. That was Sasheer's task, to assess all firstborns."

"Firstborns?"

"A concept from our old ways. A failing, I know. But we find it hard to think past so many ingrained concepts, even if it is for our own sakes."

"I don't understand," Kellen said.

Lifting a brow, Tanish slowly nodded. "You probably don't, at that. Ignorance is one of the educational drawbacks of living in the Southlands. Let me see if I can explain."

Not sure if he was being insulted, Kellen sat back and shook his head. "How old are you?" he asked, not wanting to believe in the impossible.

"How old do you think?" Tanish answered with a question of his own.

Considering the blind man seriously, Kellen let his mind caress over Tanish's aura and abruptly he gasped—awed and stunned. "You are one of the original twelve," he said. The impression and knowledge was very clear in his mind, shockingly plain and daunting. "As is Sasheer," he whispered, remembering back to the firelight story Sasheer had woven for them all. Only it wasn't a story any longer. "And those other men, Tattlier, Dybellia—"

Tanish's face lit up, delighted. "You heard or sensed?"

"Sensed," Kellen mouthed, barely making a sound.

"Good, very good," Tanish replied, pleased. He carried on, ignoring Kellen's shock, "Yes, I am one of the original twelve who fled Mitthsombaine over four thousand years ago. I and eleven brothers of my heart, whom I trusted implicitly."

"You are four thousand years old?" Kellen asked in disbelief.

"Give or take another few thousand," Tanish shrugged nonchalantly.

"And Sasheer?" he asked, picturing in his mind the youthful-looking man.

"Younger," the old Mage said. "He and his twin, Serine, were the youngest of our group. The most impulsive, inexperienced and, I might add, the most talented. Sasheer's appearance belies his true self."

"But . . . but—" Kellen shook his head, lost for words. *Sasheer has a twin?* Then he recalled the images he had glimpsed months ago while in the Divide. Images of Sasheer and another man who was injured—dead. "How is it possible?"

"It is all connected to our Gift."

Gift. Kellen was getting sick of hearing that word.

"Or talent, if you prefer. It can be very beneficial," Tanish said. "For once, you learn to control your mind's wild mental sendings, and your potential power is mastered, then with that control, you'll find you can conquer almost anything, including your body's ability to age."

"But Sasheer looks so young."

Tanish chuckled. "In Sasheer's case, I think his vanity played a major part in his rash decision to stop aging so young. For now, he wishes he had chosen the matured look of wisdom above physical youthfulness, if only to gain respect from those in the Southland."

"But couldn't he just," Kellen gestured around obliquely, "change?"

"No, once the process is halted, then the Mage will stay at that outward appearance for the rest of his existence."

"So can you die?" Kellen asked, ghoulishly fascinated.

"Of old age?" Tanish considered that seriously. "I have never known a Mageborn to die of old age. To fade away in boredom, yes, or be killed. All too many of my friends have been murdered. But none have died of extreme age."

"Then your population must have been limitless and old," Kellen surmised.

"An old race, yes, but not numerous," Tanish corrected. "Not everyone had the potential, and those that had it did not always make it to adulthood. You see, the Mage ability was highly prized in our society, bringing instant nobility for the entire family," he explained, his voice soothing and instructive. "Then there were the caste levels within the Mage circles, which thinned the numbers even more. Mostly only the firstborn males received a proper education. Then depending on their benefactor, they led a protected life until they could defend themselves adequately."

"Protect themselves?" Kellen frowned.

"Just because they had the Mage Gift did not ensure they were not killed by powerful families in order for another to be chosen. It was a difficult and dangerous time for any young candidate. Many died before reaching the second year of training."

Remembering how Sasheer had said that Mitthsombaine had been evil, Kellen suspected the Ranger had not told half the truth of the matter. He looked at Tanish. "What if others, younger brothers or sisters in the family, had the same Gift?"

"Sadly, their talent was either blocked by the College of Magery, or they were sent to temple for discipline. Or they were killed," Tanish said. "Mostly they were killed because it was the cheapest alternative."

Appalled, Kellen eyed the old man, searching for the truth. "That's barbaric."

"I agree. That is one of the reasons why we left Mitthsombaine," Tanish replied. "We fled, not only to save the four lands, but also to save our own lives and the lives of our families. Yet in doing so, we brought down the ruin of our beloved home. It was a very hard decision to make, and one which we labored long and hard over."

"Why destroy the city then; why not just the corrupt leaders?" Kellen asked. He sensed an age-old pain behind Tanish's words.

"My people, sadly, had reached a point where science was no longer a tool designed to aid, but rather to mutate and destroy. They had lost all sense of conscience, evolving into haughty creatures that I no longer recognized. Mitthsombaine as a city housed too many dark secrets. It had to go," he replied philosophically.

"So you destroyed your city's defenses with this created stone?" Kellen summarized. "Sasheer said it was a power stone."

Tanish nodded in answer. "It was a magnificent stone, for it held all our personal Mage focus gems." He cupped his hands, indicating its size. "An extraordinarily intimate creation, reflecting our very souls in its pure heart. An instrument of justice, yet in a single instant, the unthinkable happened. Its pure heart was cracked by Mitthsombaine's vengeance, turning it into our worst nightmare."

"Lichien," Kellen whispered, remembering Sasheer's haunting story months earlier. Even then it had seemed unreal.

"'Lichien' is the Elven word meaning *mind darkness*," Tanish said. "An insidious creature, which uses its knowledge to destroy all that surrounds it," he added. "Lichien has used the memories trapped within our personal focus stones as a weapon to destroy us one by one."

"So this stone is a part of you?" Kellen asked, confounded.

"It is the essence of twelve minds melded into one consciousness, forever mad, turned insane by the wickedness of Mitthsombaine."

Kellen stared at Tanish. "Then since it knows you all so well, doesn't that make fighting it hard? Doesn't that make you vulnerable to it or something?" Kellen asked as he started to imagine the convoluted problems involved.

"Extremely. That is why we have lost half our brotherhood, with Cornithia being its latest victim."

Remembering hearing that name, Kellen frowned. "Sasheer said this Cornithia was in the east. At some old ruins."

"Yes," Tanish nodded, irritation coloring his tone. "I don't know what possessed him to go near the old ruins of Mitthsombaine, but somehow Lichien must have lured him there, probably with an archaeological artifact, for Cornithia was always chasing grubby-looking pieces of stone and pottery. It was his passion, his hobby." Tanish suddenly looked old and tired as he rubbed a hand over his blind eyes. "Cornithia would have died knowing what Lichien wanted."

"And that was?"

"A sacred book. A powerful remnant of Mitthsombaine's evil magics. It was bound and locked in an old burial tomb deep beneath the surface, locked and sealed with the blood of old. The only way Lichien could break the seal was with the blood of an original Mage from Mitthsombaine."

"So the stone killed one of you," Kellen said, now starting to understand more of the history Sasheer had tried to teach him. It still seemed so unreal, but looking at Tanish, he was slowly accepting the truth of it. He reached out instinctively and squeezed Tanish's hand in sympathy. "So how many are left of your . . . brotherhood?"

"Six of the original twelve," Tanish said, a heaviness entering his tone.

A little shocked, Kellen studied the older man's face, experiencing some of his pain. "I'm sorry. I don't mean to pry."

"You are not. It is just hard to think that Cornithia will never again return to the Keep. That after four thousand years, he will never bore us again with his little trinkets of old pottery and volcanic stone." He sighed, looking troubled. "It is a shocking blow to us all. For now it has placed every living soul within the four lands in danger, because Lichien, through Kalern, has the cursed Book of Spells."

"Lichien is a stone, and Kalern was a guardian?" Kellen left the sentence hanging.

"Lichien is the mind and heart. Kalern is the body," Tanish clarified. "They are one and the same."

"And they will use this magic book to do what?"

"The Book of Spells is a cultural history of Mitthsombaine. It contains within its pages every imaginable spell and experiment that was conceived and carried out, in meticulous detail. Anyone with the Mage Gift could access the book's protection locks and then release its horrid secrets upon the four lands a second time," Tanish said angrily. "It would bring back the original evil, the original power of Mitthsombaine, and enslave the surrounding races."

"So if you are right, and Kalern has this book, then surely you must get it back," Kellen stressed, not liking the implications of what Tanish said.

"If only it were that simple," Tanish agreed. "We cannot get near Lichien. In the past, Lichien has picked up on our presence through the connection it holds with us. That is how it has picked us off one by one over the long centuries of fighting. And now, with the Book of Spells in Lichien's possession, it can weave so many protection spells around its castle in North Ridge that no one could ever get through."

"So what are you going to do?"

Tanish shrugged. "That is what we are here to decide, why all the surviving Brethren have been recalled to the Keep." He glanced up and looked unerringly straight at Kellen. "Besides, there is always hope—for the prophecy has not yet been fulfilled."

"Prophecy?" For some reason that word roused something so deep inside Kellen that a shudder ran through him. A nightmare flash of darkness loomed in the back of his mind. "What prophecy?"

"A prophecy of ancient times and a possible future."

"What does it say?"

"Sasheer has told you all about Kalern, I take it."

Nodding in answer, Kellen forgot the other could not see him and rushed to explain. "Yes. He told us how Kalern was killed then brought back to life by the stone."

"Simplified but essentially correct," Tanish nodded. "Kalern was one of two sets of twins from a single bloodline. The younger twins. Kalern's brother was Aserties, and they were identical in every way." He paused, as if considering what to say. "Just before Aserties was killed," he went on, "he brought down a blood curse on Lichien. A curse so powerful that Lichien used Kalern to wipe out his family's entire bloodline just to prevent its fulfillment."

"Did Lichien succeed?"

"He tried," Tanish assured him with a grin. "But things did not go to plan for him, which is one of the reasons why he is so obsessed to this day with destroying the Southland."

"I have been meaning to ask about that."

Tanish nodded, a small smile playing about his mouth. "About fifty years after Mitthsombaine was destroyed, a warlord called Byront took his people and went to settle in the Southland. And with him went a number of refugees from Mitthsombaine."

"Yes, I have heard the history of Byront, and how he isolated the Southland from the rest of the four lands as a safeguard to his people." *A topic Lesendal is overly passionate about,* Kellen added silently.

"His reasons went beyond that. For among those refugees of Mitthsombaine were Aserties' daughter and Kalern's only son."

"Kalern had a son? Are you saying that the people of the Southland are descendants of Kalern—of Mages?" It seemed so incredulous, so unbelievable.

"The refugees were not all from the Mage bloodline, some were just innocent victims of the war," Tanish explained. "But Kalern's son and Aserties' daughter chose to flee to the South, where they lived in safety before they had a son."

"They had a son? Together?" Kellen's brows climbed incredulously. "Cousins?"

Tanish shrugged. "It has happened before, and I imagine it will happen again."

Considering that, Kellen then tried to remember the dates involved. Tried to remember what Sasheer had told them all. "That would have been . . . after fifty years they would have been too old, wouldn't they?"

"For normal society, yes," Tanish agreed. "But they were from old Mitthsombaine and so were blessed—or cursed, depending on your point of view. Despite their age, they had a son and were afraid Kalern would learn of his existence and take him from them. They named their son Azzeryes, which means *great sight*, because this child at a very early age demonstrated an enormous potential," Tanish said softly, describing the time so clearly that Kellen was left with little doubt in his mind that the other had experienced the events described so vividly. "Angered by this setback, Kalern went and searched out his grandson, thinking that to kill him would end the curse, but instead he made matters far worse."

"How?"

"He tracked down his son and used him as bait to force his grandson, Azzeryes, out of hiding. Then Kalern slaughtered his son before Azzeryes and the congregated throng."

Horrified, Kellen listened, enthralled. "And Azzeryes?"

"As I said earlier, he was greatly gifted, and one of the facets of his Gift was the power of prophecy. So when he went to meet Kalern, he took along both scribes and warriors from Byront's clan, so that the meeting would be accurately recorded."

"And Kalern allowed this?"

"He tried in vain to change the course set but was held by forces stronger than his own." Tanish shook his head. "Azzeryes was no older than you are now, a child, yet old in knowledge, for he knew what would happen to him if he ever met his grandsire in battle. He had seen his fate in his dreams, from infancy onward. Yet he still bravely confronted Kalern."

"How could you let him do it? If you knew Kalern would kill him, why let him go?" Kellen asked in a subdued whisper.

"It was ultimately his choice; we only aided him as we could," Tanish replied softly. "As it was, in a fit of rage, Kalern killed Merrdian—"

"Merrdian?" Kellen questioned, getting lost in all the ancient names.

"One of the twelve. Merrdian had been Kalern's beloved mentor and uncle before Lichien had been created. So by killing his son and then his teacher, Kalern symbolized his break with Mage tradition and law," Tanish sighed. "He then took my sight as punishment and went after the remaining Brethren."

Kellen stared wide-eyed at Tanish, finding it so hard to think of Sasheer in terms of 'old.' Or in terms of having been involved in such momentous events in the past. No wonder the man was so jaded and cynical.

"In the end it was only young Azzeryes' words and calm which saved the situation, as he repronounced the original curse and added to it, creating a prophecy so strong it bound and limited Lichien's life span. I am sure that, even to this day, Lichien and Kalern have trouble sleeping."

Kellen's mind spun as Tanish's words slowly registered. Kalern killed his twin brother, then killed his son, and killed his uncle. Then attacked Tanish who was his mentor and threatened Azzeryes his grandson. Were they all related? "And Azzeryes?"

"He died that cold winter morning on the battlefield of Dwaye, near where the capital city of Dalisen is today."

"That's in the Southland." Kellen blinked, shocked, knowing of the place. It made the impact of the story so real. "Kalern killed him? Like in his dreams?"

"Yes."

Looking around, overwhelmed by the old man's soft words, Kellen wondered if he could have been as brave—*or is it suicidal?* Then he remembered his own nightmares. He shuddered. *No.* "Why do I get the feeling that's not the entire story?"

"Because when Azzeryes died, he left an infant son." Tanish resurrected a brief smile. "Hidden and protected in the Southland."

"Kalern must have known . . ."

"Naturally," Tanish agreed. "Always remember, Kellen, when you stand in his commanding presence that he was well trained in Mitthsombaine, well trained in temple lore, and that he is a very dangerous opponent. He can pull knowledge out of your mind with a single glance if you let him."

Nodding, Kellen silently vowed never to get close enough to

test the theory, never to go anywhere near the insane lord and his evil stone.

"Byront's family took the infant and his mother into his own clan and hid them. Then when Byront's royal line expanded, his descendants, with our help, divided up the land to make twelve realms in order to confuse Kalern and his numerous spies. Infrequent wars plagued the south until finally the Twelve Kingdoms cut themselves off from the rest of Sennovia." Tanish shrugged, thoughtful. "It did work, to some extent, but Kalern still unerringly seemed to track the bloodline, never quite destroying it completely. Until now."

Feeling a dread build inside him, Kellen was not sure he wanted to hear the rest. "Until now?"

The old man reached over with that same unnerving accuracy and took his shoulders in a strong embrace. "Yes. For now, with the Southland destroyed, and the Book of Spells in his hands, I am afraid you are the only surviving descendant of that bloodline. Our last hope really."

Those words froze him instantly, and Kellen could only stare at the blind old Mage. Inside, his mind reeled as he fought the knowledge, feeling its truth in every fiber of his being but wanting to deny it fervently. "No . . ." It was more an expression of sound than an actual word.

"It is true," Tanish assured him in a gentle whisper. "The genetic traits are far too strong in Azzeryes' line, breeding unerringly true about every seventh generation." He sighed as he released Kellen's rigid shoulder. "We have been watching for one with potential. Only we had been watching your older brother and his cousin."

"Cousin?" It seemed so unimaginable that he should have a cousin. Then he remembered Sasheer admitting as much months ago while traveling the Divide.

Sitting back, Tanish frowned, debating how best to explain. "Your father was one of twins," he said soothingly.

"Twins," Kellen only mouthed the word, not believing he was hearing this. Why had his mother never told him any of this? Why had Wyran never told him about Sasheer?

"As I said, the firstborn's line always breeds true. Then about sixteen years ago, your father and his brother were tragically killed in a strange hunting accident. To this day, Sasheer does not believe it was an accident. So he moved your mother and her sons to Ihova and your cousins to Olvaronia."

"I had family in Olvaronia . . ." he echoed, just trying to absorb all this.

"For a while," Tanish said evasively. "Everything seemed to be going well, until your mother died, and Wyran started acting erratically."

"He fell into bad company," Kellen quipped a little sarcastically, remembering the military recruiters who had visited the holdings. Wyran had been so taken with their stories.

"It happens, I suppose, but it was a pity, for he showed all the correct characteristics." Tanish moved, turning away a little as he cast a slight, guilty look in Kellen's direction. "I'm sorry, but we did not assess you, for you were second born. As I said, a great failing of our society."

Considering that, Kellen thought of his brother, remembering Wyran's cocky attitude and teasing smile. "Did Wyran know this prophecy?"

"Some of it," Tanish answered honestly.

"Did he know about our father's suspicious death? About our cousins?"

"Yes," Tanish said.

Closing his eyes, Kellen tried to calm his racing pulse. *Why?* he wanted to scream. Why had Wyran not confided in him? Had his brother hated him so much?

"Youngling?"

"You all knew more about my family and my brother than I did," he said angrily.

"It may seem that way, I know, but Wyran wanted you protected."

"Protected!" Kellen cut back. "He left me for dead! He ran off the first chance he got and left me behind."

"Kellen, please don't judge us or your brother harshly for what has happened. Sasheer tried to safeguard your family, but he was taken out of Ihova when Kalern's forces captured your cousins. And Wyran was a rule unto himself. No one could have predicted what was going to happen, and when we found out, we tried to get aid to Sasheer," Tanish said miserably. "I am just thankful that Lesendal found you before Kalern did."

Thinking on all this, Kellen did not know what he was feeling, so he just sat there mutely. Should he be angry, sad, or relieved? "And these cousins who were captured, are they dead like Sasheer said?"

Tanish said nothing, just nodded.

"I see."

"You are special, Kellen."

"Now, yes. But not before Wyran or my unknown cousins were killed."

"I know it sounds like that, but—"

"It is the way your culture is structured. I know," he finished bitterly. "You told me. So what would Wyran be doing now, if he was here instead of me?"

"Kellen . . ."

"I know Sasheer would have brought him here."

"He would be taught, and his potential would be assessed properly," Tanish answered. "There are no guarantees he would have survived the journey. There were other," he hesitated, "obstacles, he had to overcome first."

"I can imagine."

"Kellen, I feel the Gift in you, without even testing you. I can feel the turmoil and the rigid barriers you have wrapped around your emotions because of the power you are scared of touching."

"I—"

"It is normal to be scared. Now you are here; we will show you how to contain it, how to control that energy inside your mind." He placed a gentle hand on Kellen's knee. "Sasheer has started the process; now let him finish it."

Resting his head back against the cold glass-window paneling, Kellen closed his eyes, not believing any of this. What was real, and what was imagined? What would have happened to him if he had been born in old Mitthsombaine? Would he have been killed or sent to the temple to be a guardian? Dismissing the troubling images, he closed his eyes. What was he going to do?

"We are your family."

A family murdered. "And this prophecy?" Kellen asked.

"It is real. It states that—"

"One will come," Kellen cut him off dryly. "Yes, I've heard it," he ended in a clipped tone.

Startled, Tanish faltered, visibly thrown. "You have heard the prophecy?"

"Yes," he answered unhappily. "In meticulous detail."

Pursing his lips, Tanish battled to cover his shock at that. "Who told you this prophecy?"

"I can't remember," Kellen frowned, looking over at the older man and seeing his suppressed tension. "Must have been either Sasheer or Dalzere."

"You . . . are probably right," Tanish said. "How do you feel about this prophecy?" he continued carefully.

"How do you think?" Kellen snarled back, getting angry suddenly. "Thrilled by the prospect that because I am now the last of the bloodline, you will force me to face Kalern!" he said indignantly. "How am I suppose to stop him when his own brother and grandson, with help from the rest of you, could not slow him down four thousand years ago?" he demanded. "And back then, there were twelve of you. Now there are only six!"

"Kellen, we do not expect you to run off and face Kalern," Tanish said, aghast. "Whatever else you may think of us, we are not monsters."

"No, you are just manipulative!" he snapped at the blind old man, his tone a little harder than he intended. "A very old culture that seems to be a reflection of your fabled city, Mitthsombaine. Oh, by the gods!" Kellen stood and paced away as another realization fell into place. The library around them was now silent, dimly lit, and warm. "I must have sounded so pathetic to Dalzere. And stupid," he said, remembering back to his time inside Death Peaks.

"To think he followed me down that rock face, not really for my benefit, but because I was the last of the bloodline, and he had to make sure I arrived here in one piece!" He rubbed a hand over his tired eyes. "He has probably already told you every silly little question I uttered over the last two weeks."

"Kellen, you have it all wrong."

"Do I?" Kellen swung around. "Would any of you have really cared what became of me if Wyran or my unknown cousins were still alive?"

Tanish sighed as he sat back.

Just standing there, watching the old Mage, Kellen shook his head in denial of what was unfolding around him. This was not what he wanted, not what he had dreamed about as a child. This was making his life a mockery, dishonoring his friend, who had died for nothing. Turning away, he walked quickly toward the huge library door, just wanting to get out of the stifling room—just wanting to get out of the entire place. He needed to sort out his mind.

CHAPTER TWENTY-THREE

As Kellen withdrew, Tanish sighed again before raising a hand to stop Sasheer's hasty departure, as the other man stepped from behind a huge tapestry. "Let him go."

"But Tanish—"

"No," the old man broke in firmly. "Let him go for the moment. You would only make it worse now if you chased him. He is angry, and I do not blame him for that anger."

"Then you should not have been so honest with him. A little deceit can calm the waters, Tanish," Sasheer grumbled.

"I would rather have the truth in the open now, than have him learn it later. And trust me when I say that he will learn it, for he has a very strong talent. It pulled even at me."

"I know," Sasheer said. "I've had to mentally squash him over a dozen times during the last few months. His potential is staggering; the simplest acts backlash through him."

"Then let's follow Karczag's advice for once, and let the child do the running rather than smother him in our ways."

"We may lose him that way," Sasheer warned as he held out his hand to Tanish, helping the other to stand. "Like we lost Wyran."

"Wyran was bespelled before we could intervene. You spent far too much time trying to redeem what was already lost, when you knew Lichien had already taken his soul at infancy," Tanish admonished, gripping Sasheer's hand.

"It was his appearance," Sasheer whispered, sounding vulnerable. "He looked so much like . . ."

"I know," Tanish soothed. "Kellen is Aserties' mirror image also. But he is more like Serine in personality than Wyran could ever have hoped to be."

"Don't—" Sasheer held up a hand as he swallowed, feeling defeated.

"I understand how hard this must be for you, my friend, but you must not let his looks or traits drive you to distraction. We need him more than ever now," Tanish implored, reaching out with confidence to touch Sasheer's cheek.

"I just wish," Sasheer left the rest unsaid as he closed his eyes. "I do not want to get involved with him. It will mean his death. I have *seen* death in the visions—"

"Not even you, with your Foresight, can predict that with a firm certainty," Tanish replied.

Sasheer tried again to dissuade the older man. "But what of his dreams?"

"Those we will have to watch."

"And the warning Dalzere gave us?" Sasheer continued. "What if Lichien has already reached out and taken Kellen's mind? For that is the only way he would have learned of the prophecy in full, and you know it."

"True," Tanish conceded. "But his mind is untarnished. There are no shadows in him. Yet."

"It may still be too late," Sasheer said stubbornly.

"I doubt it."

"And what if he runs too far out of our reach?" Sasheer asked, searching for any reason to convince his elder not to condemn him to be Kellen's teacher. "What if he runs unwittingly straight into Kalern's hands?"

"Then it will be your responsibility to pull him back."

"But I failed with Wyran! I failed with Aquiletta and Cabell. I even failed with my own brothers! With Serine and Aserties," Sasheer said in exasperation. "I am too close to the problem. You and the others have said that before. It is too personal for me."

"Sasheer, it has to be you," Tanish answered.

"But why me?" Sasheer asked irritably.

"Because his blood calls to you, my friend, so, therefore, ultimately he will become your obligation, regardless of how much you both fight against it."

"Oh, I can see this will be fun."

CHAPTER TWENTY-FOUR

He was angry—seething—and Kellen quickened his pace when he caught sight of Ryland's worried face. He didn't want to explain, didn't want to talk—period. He just wanted to escape this old castle and its dark, nasty little secrets. He hurried forward, heading directly for the large iron gates.

Once there, he stopped and tried to slow his anxious breathing, needing to control his temper. He could already feel the surge of responsive energy flush up his body, could feel a wash of power caress his legs. *The invisible current,* and suddenly he understood what it was he had felt in Ihova, only to a lesser degree. What he had felt most of his life.

Stopping in front of the massive gates, he dared not turn, not wanting to talk with anyone at that moment, and was grateful when a guard stepped out of the gatehouse and, without questioning him, opened a small door in the massive iron structure. *Have the guards been given instructions to leave me alone?* Nothing would surprise him about the Brethren.

Stepping through the doorway, he found himself facing the uninviting marshland, and he breathed a sigh of pure relief. He stalked away toward the first rise he could see and found a squat tree to sit under. He kept his back to the Keep, not even wanting to think about the last few hours. Instead he stared ahead into nothing.

But predictably, his mind kept returning to the old library and what Tanish had told him. The worse part of the entire encounter had been that he could sense Tanish had been telling the truth, that Tanish expected him to just accept and possibly even show gratitude.

At present, he didn't even know who he was. It had been bad enough to be cursed with destructive emotions, and then to add insult to injury, he was supposed to believe it was a Gift? That was laughable. A Gift he had to learn to control. *As if*... Then within the very next breath, Tanish had shattered his foundations—his identity—by telling him so bluntly that he was a direct descendant of Mitthsombaine's evil Mage society. From Kalern's line, no less, *bright stars!* He was doomed. His Gift had to be evil, so how could he control something like that? Something from Mitthsombaine's evil heart? He shivered. Even the name was enough to inspire nightmares.

So where in the scheme of things does this leave me? If it was true, and he had no reason to doubt Tanish, then *what* was he to do?

Thinking hard on that, he bit his lip until it started to bleed, his mind dissecting everything that had been said. He understood that Tanish really believed he was from Kalern's line and, therefore, the answer to the prophecy. And that Tanish was... Sasheer was... *old*. He closed his eyes tightly and swore under his breath. The destruction of ancient Mitthsombaine and the creation of Lichien had nothing to do with him! This was not fair! No wonder his brother had disobeyed Sasheer and run off to join the army. *Maybe Wyran wasn't so stupid after all.*

Exhaling hard, he dropped his head onto his raised knees and berated himself for thinking so badly of his brother. *If only Wyran were alive*... Calming his agitated thoughts, he went over all of Tanish's explanation again. The old Mage had stated that the Brethren did not expect him to confront Kalern, so that only left... *stars! They'll force me to marry!*

He sat bolt upright as that unpleasant thought sank in. They probably already had a wife picked out for him and were going to shove him off to some corner of the Keep to breed. He dragged in a frightened breath, his eyes darting around the area in panic. *Who would they pick?* Some old female Mageborn, or someone like—Tich? He swallowed, both alarmed and excited that it might be the argumentative Healer. Now he was flushed for a different reason.

The concept of marriage seemed far worse than the idea of confronting Kalern and Lichien. He'd rather die. Rather fall down that abyss from his nightmares than marry . . . and he stilled, remembering what Tanish had said about Azzeryes and *his* nightmares. The abyss. *Is the dream real or just a dream?* Yet even awake, he could picture Kalern's lair, could *hear* the shadowed lord's voice whisper to him seductively. If he closed his eyes he could even imagine himself leaning over the edge of the abyss to—*feel the rush of hot wind against my face*—and he jumped, falling backward and staring around the moor in shock.

He didn't want to think about Kalern. Or about Lichien. Or even his nightmare. He didn't want to marry, either—*so what other choice is left?* He sat up and cast a glance over his shoulder, back toward the Keep. The castle was still there, and he half-wished it would vanish, so he was spared this confusion. If only he had known all this in Ihova, he would not have willingly followed; he stopped and considered that idea. No wonder Sasheer had wanted to get him to the Keep before he learned the truth. Salimen was right; *Sasheer is a crafty bastard.*

"No!" He stood up and spat the word at the silently waiting Keep. "No, I will not let you manipulate me. I will not become your puppet in a war which . . . which—" He faltered, lost for words. *In a war that has no end*, he realized, a war that was still raging after four thousand years.

He wiped the tears of useless rage from his cheeks before clenching a fist in anger. Turning away from the Keep, he fled, heading deeper into the marshlands, running blind, and disregarding all the warnings he had heard concerning this dangerous land. He no longer cared. He just wanted to escape the madness which was consuming his life.

* * *

Coming to a halt a long while later, Kellen leaned forward, hands on knees, bracing his weight as he drew in ragged breaths. His muscles ached, but now it was a different type of ache. His heart was pounding in his chest from the vigorous exertion of his irrational run, but even that felt good.

He lifted his head and pushed long damp hair behind his ears before he glanced around and realized he was lost. Well, that had been the idea, *hadn't it?*

He felt better; his anger had abated, and he started to take serious note of his surroundings. He had the faintest suspicion that his rash departure from the Keep might not have been too wise—but he pushed that thought aside.

The area around him was thickly covered in dull gray woody bushes and tough grass. The smell now registering on his senses was foul. Turning full circle, he walked up the nearest rise and searched the area, seeing nothing that looked or felt familiar. He could not even sense the invisible ebb of currents. *Great!* Not only was he lost, but now the Mages would think him stupid as well. At this rate, they would grant him no freedom to do anything.

He collapsed onto one damp mound to contemplate his sorry life, and laughed at the mess he was in. It could not get any worse, and he sighed, tensing a moment later when he felt a tentative touch on his arm. He glanced around and peered into the bush beside him. But nothing moved, and he dismissed the oddity, knowing his judgments were as jumbled as his life.

He felt numb and deceived by all around him. Especially by Dalzere, for he had trusted the Elf. He had really liked and respected him—had cherished Dalzere's offer of friendship—yet the Drow had betrayed his trust to Sasheer. Then there were Lesendal and Salimen. How much did they know? How involved were they with Sasheer? What of Ryland? *Gods! Peleyia!* The Lancooti was an old associate of Sasheer's and had openly stated that he liked the Drow and the Ranger. He groaned, feeling a headache start behind his eyes. And Crizkerisomia? She knew all the Brethren, so he doubted she would question Sasheer's word.

Raising a hand, he rubbed at his temple. He wasn't sure who he could trust anymore. His home was captured, his family dead; even Bains was dead. A pang of guilt sliced into him again with that memory. *Bains* . . . All escape routes had been blocked.

Around him the temperature dropped, and he lifted his head

when he felt the first few drops of rain on his hot skin. *Even the weather turns against me*, he bemoaned dejectedly.

Never having felt so depressed, he just sat there, staring off into nothing, letting the rain wash him. In his mindless state, it took him a long while to realize that he was *not* alone. The awareness was nothing substantial, just a feeling at first of being watched, and then he became conscious of an insidious danger. With care, he focused his mind then studied the rain-soaked area.

Off to his left, within the ground bushes, there was a sluggish, but erratic, movement. Just faint activity, as if a small creature was trapped, hiding, or perhaps just sheltering from the rain. Curious, he brushed the rain from his eyes and watched the bush. For long moments nothing happened and he sat, waiting, watching—the marshlands around him were shrouded in misty rain—then he relaxed as the foreboding presence dissipated. The bush beside him vibrated anew, and he smiled. He could not see the animal, but he imagined it was some small rodent trapped within the labyrinth of twisted branches.

Moving forward, he extended a hand, trying to offer no threat as he gently parted the scrub bush to see the small creature. The first thing he saw was a tail, and he blinked at the animal's sooty darkness. The tail flicked out and touched his hand, producing a thrilling tingle of goosebumps up his arm. *Magic!* The creature was blanketed by a variation of the invisible currents.

Despite the thrill, he still felt compelled to assist the creature. Careful not to touch its smooth, scaly skin a second time, he took his knife from his belt and cut through some of the entwining branches.

He saw the creature crawl away, and he watched, fascinated, as it hissed at him. Interested in what type of animal it was, he stood and tried to get a better look at the animal before it disappeared into the surrounding scrub. But all he saw was a sleek, scaled back and a long, slender tail, and he snorted, disappointed when it disappeared.

Resting his chin in his hand, he glared around at the bleak environment, speculating on why the Brethren had chosen this desolate place in which to live. Did it reflect their perverse personality?

The more time he had to think, the more he realized that running away was not the answer. He needed to learn, and he needed to tell Sasheer and Tanish that he would not be manipulated—that he would not marry—although he was in two minds about that.

Coming to a decision, he stood up, stretched, and was abruptly engulfed in a web of power. He cried out in shock, as a sinister swirl of emotions—a taint of evil, so great an evil and so cold—wrapped around his body. He swung around to defend himself, knowing it was the evil entity. Then just as swiftly, the intensity and dark malice vanished. It happened so fast that he was not even sure he had experienced the shocking jolt of anger and hatred, and he looked around the marsh. He saw movement out of the corner of his eye and lifted his knife, then hesitated as he saw—was mesmerized—by a glimpse of silver, of brilliance, before the strange creature ducked behind a squat tree stump. Startled, he crouched down and put his knife away, then stretched out his hand to entice the animal out. It was the same creature he had rescued.

"I won't hurt you, I promise." He was not sure if the animal understood his tone, so he sat down again and just waited. His patience was rewarded when he saw the animal peek out from under another bush. He got a better look at the creature this time, noting its long, square head which was covered with scales layered over its nose. Keeping very still, he studied it, enthralled, never having seen an animal like this before, and seeing how its ears were pinned back in fright.

It was the size of a small hunting hound, yet so much more refined. It had short legs, a long sleek body and tail, and its skin appeared to be covered entirely in delicate, enfolding scales. Added to that, it was the strangest color—translucent—with an inky blackness that penetrated every fiber of its body, but which also looked so out of place. Like a contamination.

He felt compelled to help the animal, and he raised a hand, keeping his gaze trained on the large silver eyes observing him.

Assessing him, studying him, and a shiver of apprehension touched him before the animal blinked and broke the strange connection. Then all fear was gone, and he held still as the creature crawled forward until it sat before him. Then it stood on its hind legs and sniffed the air.

Taken back by the strangeness, he waited, not moving, as he noted that this animal was far more intelligent than he first believed. Even more intelligent than the Lexsii, and his senses tingled in a silent warning of danger. As if inviting danger—an image flashed into his mind with vicious ferocity, and he felt swamped by a hatred so deep it was stifling, making him sag in blinding pain—then the images cleared, and he was left blinking, dazed, shocked, and trembling.

What is that . . . ? He scooted away from the animal, wiping a hand over his face, not sure of what he had seen or experienced. On instinct, he gathered in his own energy lines in readiness to fight, but could no longer detect an actual threat. He stared again at the animal. The large silver eyes opened and shut with such innocence that he began to doubt his senses. Maybe he was just overtired?

Frowning, he shook his head. In front of him, the animal shrunk back and closed in on itself before shivering in fright. It represented no threat, and he reached over to touch the scales. The animal was cold under his fingers, the scales soft, almost silky, and he gently brushed his thumb between those large silver eyes.

"Hello," he whispered as he felt the animal lean toward him, seeking shelter from the rain. Without thinking, he offered shelter, thinking how adorable the animal was, and how overworked his imagination was. "Are you lost too?" he murmured then squinted up at the sky. Dark, pendulous storm clouds were rolling in, and they promised a nasty evening of weather. "Looks as if we had better find shelter," he decided.

He stood and, with tentative care, reached down to lift the shivering animal, amazed at how light it felt in his arms. The animal made no move to fight him, just burrowing into his shoulder, its claws sharp.

He scanned the bleak surroundings, feeling unusually protective of this strange creature and decided to stay by the squat trees. He sat under them, curling his shoulders in to shelter them both. "I think we had best wait here until the storm passes." He let his eyes go back to the animal and wondered what he was to do with the creature after the storm. It obviously must have a home somewhere in the marshes and moors.

"Ccccold..."

Astonished by the soft, raspy word, Kellen looked down again and saw how the animal blinked at him in mute appeal.

"Ccccold..."

"You can talk?" Kellen asked, shocked, recalling the intelligence he had seen in those eyes. Then a gust of wind hit them both, and the animal's trembling increased.

"Hhhave learned words."

The words were hissed, distorted by the animal's shivering, and Kellen felt a tingling of danger lick along his senses a second time. He glanced down but saw nothing. The animal in his lap appeared helpless, and he relaxed his muscles, chastising himself for his hasty judgment. How could a little thing like this be dangerous? The *Lexsii* could talk, and he had not questioned their motives.

"Ttthank you fffor helping me."

Drawn by the softer words, he released a tense breath, puzzled by his own overreaction. Maybe the danger he felt was the current across the moor? "I am glad I could help. Do you live around here?"

"Nnnooo."

The little creature shivered again, and he could feel every flex of muscle in the cold body under his hands. Lifting one hand, he trailed a finger down the animal's bony head, marveling at the delicate scales.

"I cccome from far away. I was rrrunning from the hunters."

"Hunters?"

"Tall dark-skkkinned hunters," it answered with growing confidence. "With short curved blades."

"Drow," Kellen supplied, suddenly understanding the animal's fear. That was probably what he was picking up—the animal's fears, rather than a personal attack.

"They kkkill. I am all alone."

"They killed others like you?" Kellen asked, but already he imagined the worst. He raised a protective arm when the rain fell harder, attempting to shelter them both.

"I am all alone," the creature repeated in a defeated voice.

Understanding that emotion, he wondered if there were any more like this animal in a different part of the marshlands. He wanted to ask but couldn't as the wind suddenly whipped in strongly, and thunder crashed over-head. The storm descended heavily across the moors, and Kellen huddled over the animal, offering what warmth he could while he waited for the worst of the rain and wind to settle. The storm did not last long, and soon the heavy clouds passed into the mountains behind and the atmosphere warmed, becoming humid as the late-afternoon sun broke through the remaining clouds.

Saturated, Kellen slowly sat up, wiping water from his face. He hated being wet, and he laughed, remembering how wet and filthy he had been two days ago. He stopped with that thought, stunned. Was it only that morning he and Dalzere had arrived at the Keep? It seemed a life time ago.

He stood, lifting the animal and feeling it wind its tail around his arm for balance. He got an abrupt glimpse of a larger creature—of a powerful, mystical dragon—in his mind, but it faded almost instantly. Disconcerted, he dismissed the unease and glanced down at his new friend. "I have to return to the Keep."

"No!"

Shocked by the tone and strength behind the word, Kellen stilled, watching as the animal coyly blinked at him.

"I do not think ttthat is wise," the creature added gently in a soothing tone.

"The Keep is safe. They are friends," he said, wishing with all his heart that it were true and his suspicions were wrong. He needed them all, even Sasheer. "They will not harm you."

The animal shook its head. "They will kill me."

"I promise they won't."

"They are bad. You are good."

Kellen smiled. "They won't hurt you. I will protect you," he said as he rubbed the soft scales under the animal's chin. "Trust me."

"You, I will trust. But no one else."

Shaking his head, Kellen tried to think of something else to say to reassure the little creature.

"I am dead if I am found. Please do not let me be found. Please."

Moved by the earnest words, Kellen felt saddened for the little animal as it clung to him, its tone pleading. "All right, I will hide you. I will not tell the others about you."

"I trust you to keep your word," it sighed. "I will go with you and repay your loyalty with my own."

The words were so solemn, so like a vow, that Kellen could not believe he was actually having this conversation with an animal. What was he getting himself into? "Do you have a name?" he asked.

The creature seemed to consider him before it released its hold on his arm and floated up in front of him. It took him a stunned moment to realize that the animal was flying, that those long silky scales across its back were really wings. "What are you?" he mouthed softly.

The creature flew around him before coming back to face him, its expression softening in pleasure. "I am Shard. An outcast. I have no family as you think of family. I am alone, and terribly lonely. I am tired of running, of hiding. Can I be with you for just a little while?"

Wanting to help this beautiful and enchanting creature, Kellen found he could not turn away from Shard. "I would like that," he found himself saying with genuine sincerity. "My name is Kellen, and I will help you in any way I can."

* * *

He was very aware of Shard as the animal hovered next to him. Very aware of the looks Shard gave him as he started back in the direction of the Keep. "So what are you?" he asked in conversation, noting with dread that evening was fast approaching. He wanted to find the Keep and talk with Sasheer. He wanted the Ranger to know that he was not Wyran, and that he would not be exploited.

"I do not remember the name of my kind," Shard said. "There were so few of us to begin with, that very few now remain. But I think that once I was a snow dragon."

"You live in the mountains?"

"No. I have no home."

Lifting his gaze, Kellen found it hard to comprehend. His senses were curiously blank, as if there was nothing of Shard to perceive, just an emptiness, a void in his mind, and that oddity niggled at him. He was so tempted to reach out with his mind to probe the creature, but he was not sure how the animal would react, if Shard would retaliate, so he resisted the urge.

"You are not from around here, are you, Kellen?" Shard asked, his words more a statement than a question.

"No. I am from the Southland. Or at least what is left of the Southland," Kellen said. "And I am also alone."

"No family?" it pushed, tone curious.

"No. Apparently they have all been killed. Even cousins I didn't know I had were killed in the war. I am apparently the last of my line," he said, peevish, remembering Tanish's words. It still annoyed him.

"Ah," the creature almost purred as it flew on ahead, a peculiar glow lighting its silver eyes. "Then it is lucky we have found each other. Yes?"

"Yes," Kellen repeated, bewitched by Shard's unusual beauty.

"So why go to the Keep? We could go away together." It swung back and pinned him with a coaxing expression. "I could find our way out of these swamps and take you somewhere where you will be free. Utterly free. Think of that, Kellen."

Tempted by the seductive words, almost hypnotized, Kellen did not answer immediately, feeling his mind clear of any doubts.

He shook his head and glanced away from Shard before risking another look at the mystical creature and its bright silver eyes.

"I know a place far in the mountains, away from here, where you can become whatever you desire. Where no one can control you."

It sounded so good. So enticing. So much like what he had been thinking about before he had discovered the creature. *Is Shard reading my thoughts?*

"Kellen!"

Startled by the abrupt call, Kellen turned, recognizing Dalzere's voice. He breathed a sigh of relief and regret. Regret that it had been necessary for the Elf to search for him, and relief he had been found. About to call out, he gasped in shock when he felt Shard's cool wings brush over his face. He staggered back, thrown off balance by the creature's unexpected closeness.

"Think, Kellen. If you go back to the Keep, you will lose your freedom. They will devour you."

"But they are my friends . . ." *aren't they?* He felt a potent wave of mistrust and suspicion assault his mind.

"I am your friend," Shard hissed in encouragement.

Meeting the bright silver eyes, Kellen wanted—desperately wanted—with all his heart to do as Shard suggested. Then he heard Dalzere's call a second time, heard the urgency, the unmasked fear behind the Elf's call, and his mind threw off the suspicion. "I have to answer him," he whispered. "He is my friend."

"He is Drow. Evil. His kind will kill me. Death. Think on that, Kellen. He is death. Remember how he killed. Remember how he betrayed you."

"No—" Kellen shook his head. He struggled to say the word, to deny the overwhelming desire to flee. "No," he repeated, stronger. "Dalzere is not evil." Then in an instant, the reluctance passed, and he saw Dalzere in his mind, a clear image of the friend who had risked his life to save him. "No."

"Kellen, I cannot go with you. Will you now condemn me to eternal loneliness?"

"Come with me," he said, his mind starting to function again, his senses becoming alive as a prickling of apprehension ignited in his chest.

"I can't!" It was a pain-filled whisper as the creature seemed to dissolve in front of him, disappearing into nothing.

"Shard!" Kellen called, frightened and bewildered by the creature's self-enforced banishment. Yet a prickle of danger remained.

"Kellen!"

He was seized from behind and turned before being enfolded in a fierce hug. Then Dalzere was pushing him back and glaring at him in an effort to cover his relief.

"Why didn't you answer me?"

Not sure how to explain, Kellen glanced around, but he could see no trace of Shard. Nor could he sense the creature.

"You had me so worried." It was spoken more in the Elf's usual growled tones as those golden eyes assessed him. "And to my amazement, you are drenched yet again."

Meeting Dalzere's gaze for the first time, Kellen sighed and attempted to smile. "I'm sorry, Dalzere. But I needed to think. Alone."

"Did you have to wander so far to think?"

"Apparently," Kellen muttered, seeing Dalzere's lip twitch up into a reluctant grin.

"Are you finished thinking?"

"Probably."

Dalzere threw his hands up and sighed long-sufferingly then cursed in his native tongue. But his grin belied his actions. "Southerners, and their need to brood."

Smiling despite his circumstances, Kellen waited for Dalzere to look at him again. "You know, that curse you use is the same curse I heard Sasheer use."

"And where do you think I learned it?"

"Really?"

"No—I am not teaching it to you."

Kellen stared at the Elf, his smile fading. "I want to go back to the Keep."

"Good." Dalzere said. "With your talent for trouble, I am encouraged by the fact you haven't yet fallen into a mire."

"I'm not that lucky." He fell into step beside Dalzere, just casting one last look at the undergrowth and stunted trees. But Shard was gone.

"I had not noticed this death wish of yours before," Dalzere said dryly.

"I had not talked to Tanish before," he cut in as some of his original resentment returned in full force.

"I see," Dalzere said slowly and patiently.

"Did you know?" he asked, halting the Elf and forcing Dalzere to look at him. Was he as alone, as Shard intimated? Should he even tell Dalzere about Shard?

"About your heritage?" Dalzere asked. Kellen nodded. "Yes," the Elf said.

"So that is why you followed me down the cliff," Kellen surmised.

"No," Dalzere's answer was swift. "That was my choice. I took the risk with no other motive, other than finding you," he said without hesitation. "I would've done the same for Salimen or Peleyia. Even Crizkerisomia."

Wanting to believe that, Kellen searched the golden gaze locked on him. "I had started to think—"

"You started to doubt. To mistrust."

"I don't know what to believe."

"Regardless of who you are, Kellen, or what you might one day become, my actions would not have changed. You're one of my companions, a valued member of our group. And a friend. I have all too few of them to allow any to die needlessly."

Dropping his gaze, Kellen frowned and studied his feet. His eyes slid to the Dalzere's dark-skinned hand where it gripped his arm. The long fingers looked delicate, yet he knew they were strong. He knew they offered friendship and trust, and Kellen released a hot sigh. "I shouldn't have questioned your motives. I'm sorry, Dalzere."

"Ask, youngling. I will answer. Don't let doubt fester into something worse."

He forced himself to meet those golden eyes. "Can I ask you something personal?" he ventured, waiting until Dalzere nodded in consent. "Why were you so angry after killing the Drow hunters?"

Opposite him, Dalzere took a step back, a hissed breath escaping his lips, and he closed his eyes briefly. Then the Elf dropped his head, considering his response before his eyes darkened, and he pinned Kellen with a fierce stare.

"I hate the emotions such ones resurrect in me. I hate the blood lust," Dalzere whispered, his tone flat and his eyes unguarded. "That is a . . . part of my life I have battled to subdue."

"Your Drow instincts?" Kellen questioned.

Dalzere shook his head, his long dark hair almost twitching in mute testimony to his unhappiness over the encounter with the Drow hunters. "My white Elf heritage," he corrected, his eyes narrowing. "It is their viciousness I fight, their ruthlessness and ambition to win, coupled with the Drow cunning and blood hate imbedded in my genes. Sometimes I forget who I am."

Stunned, Kellen held his breath, slowly starting to understand the abhorrence and anger Dalzere had expressed after the killing. He reached out in comfort and touched Dalzere's shoulder, amazed when the Elf barely suppressed a shudder.

"That is behind me now. In the past."

Nodding, Kellen dropped his hand, a little uncomfortable.

"Promise that next time you feel confused, you will talk to Sasheer," Dalzere asked. "Don't alienate yourself from the comfort of friends."

"But I'm not what Tanish—or even Sasheer—believes. Or wants," Kellen protested. "I am not Wyran. I am—" he searched around for the correct word, "second born."

"You are what you are, regardless of birthright," Dalzere stressed. "That is all any of us can ask."

"Yet Wyran—"

"The past is lost to us all. If you must focus on it, then focus on the fact that your brother died because of who he was," Dalzere instructed, his words carrying a passion that was infectious.

"What if I fail?"

"Kellen, if you try to learn, then you have not failed, regardless of the outcome. Only by walking away will you fail." Dalzere leaned in closer as his voice dropped to a whisper. "And that is what Kalern wants you to do."

"But he is so powerful," Kellen uttered, finally verbalizing the fear deep inside. "How can I possibly do what Tanish wants?"

"He and the others want nothing more than your continued survival."

"So they'll marry me off and count the days until I produce an heir," he said, a little downheartedly.

Stifling a laugh, Dalzere shook his head. "What gives you that idea?"

"It's just a feeling I get," Kellen returned indignant. He sneaked a look up at Dalzere's amused face.

"I doubt you'll be married for a while, so relax. At the moment, the Brethren are more concerned with the fact that Kalern has the Book of Spells. They'll be working on a way to counter its affects. Or to get it off him. So there will be little time to arrange a betrothal."

Relieved, Kellen frowned. "They are going to try and get the book from Kalern?" He had thought, from what Tanish had said, that they were resigned to its loss.

"It is imperative." Glancing up when a wolf's cry cut the cool evening air, Dalzere's expression sobered. "We had best move."

Kellen glanced around, never having heard such a mournful cry before. How big were these wolves?

"This way," Dalzere indicated. "Hurry."

Managing to keep up with the agile Elf, Kellen raised another question that had been bothering him. "So what will the Mages do with me?"

Dalzere sighed. "Nothing, except teach you. I realize there is nothing I can say or do which will make you believe me, but please, Kellen, just trust in those around you, as we mean you no harm. I vow to keep you safe until you are willing to believe in your own heart and instincts."

Not knowing what to say, Kellen just stared wide-eyed at Dalzere, feeling both comforted and lost. How could he have doubted Dalzere? He would accept Sasheer's teaching for the present and learn all he could. "I really want to understand."

"That is a start," Dalzere murmured as he picked up the pace.

Behind them a wolf cried again, this time closer. Its eerie call sent a shiver down Kellen's spine.

"Now hurry."

Not needing to be told a third time, Kellen ran on, keeping his eyes centered on his friend's leather-clad back. Behind him the sun sank.

CHAPTER TWENTY-FIVE

After being admitted through the dark gates of the Keep, Kellen breathed a heavy sigh of relief and sagged against the cold iron. Dalzere said something to one of the guards before he turned back to Kellen.

"Go and change into something dry. When you are ready, I'll be in the library with the others."

"And Pel?" Kellen asked, reaching forward to stop his friend with a hand on Dalzere's arm.

"He is resting in a room a few doors from your own."

Letting the other go, Kellen made his way back inside the castle, glad for the dim lighting as he climbed the magnificent staircase and found his room. He stopped at the old wooden door, letting his fingers brush the cold wood and looked down the spacious hallway toward the other rooms. Dalzere had said Peleyia was close to him, and he really wanted to see his friend. If anything, the Lancooti's perceptive observations and humor would help put his own thoughts into some order.

Hesitant, he walked past a number of rooms, their doors open, and he peered into the darkened areas, seeing nothing. The fourth door was closed, and he faltered, glancing along the hallway before lightly tapping on the heavy door.

Nothing happened, and he just stood there, debating whether to knock again or to just go and do as Dalzere had suggested. About to turn away, he took a step back when the wooden door opened soundlessly, and he came face to face with the Healer from Sanctuary. She stared at him in dubious concern.

"My, if it isn't the southerner," Tich said. "Haven't you found the energy to bath yet? Or is washing not a custom in your homeland?"

Casting a look down at his appearance, Kellen pondered if it was just bad luck, or bad timing that kept him running into this female whilst in such a bedraggled state. Or if she was just normally irascible. "I had washed. I simply went for a walk."

"In the rain?" she asked incredulously.

"It wasn't raining when I started my walk," he snapped, getting annoyed. She seemed to bring out the worst in him.

"Did you ask the guard at the gate about the changeable moor weather before starting your walk?"

"It must have slipped my mind," he growled through clenched teeth.

"You're not very intelligent, are you?"

"Look—"

She cut him off again, "I take it you are here to visit the Lancooti? Just try not to drip all over the bed coverings. I don't want him catching a chill." Standing back a little, she indicated he could enter the warm room.

Deciding that this had probably not been his most prudent move, Kellen nevertheless entered the room and glanced around, feeling the heat from the open fire hit his damp face.

"Use this."

Turning at the Healer's voice, he caught the towel thrown at him. He scowled at Tich and was flustered by the pleased little smile she sent him.

"If Peleyia needs me, I'll be in the library. Can you remember that?"

Refusing to comment, he nodded, watching her go, liking the way her heavy braid swung down her back before the view was lost when the door shut.

"Kell?"

Wiping his face, Kellen dismissed Tich from his mind and grinned in relief as he saw Peleyia. He walked over to the enormous bed and sat on its edge. Peleyia was propped up with numerous pillows, looking pale and drowsy. Then the Lancooti was pushing himself up, battling the covers.

"They told me you had arrived after breakfast, but . . ." Peleyia started as he took in his friend's wet appearance. "Kell, what have you been doing?"

Biting his lip, Kellen shook his head. "Dalzere and I got in before lunch. Then Sasheer dragged me into the library. After that . . . things happened, and I had to get away from them all for a while."

"Away?"

"I would have visited sooner," he frowned, trying to see past the confident smile plastered on Peleyia's face. He didn't trust that expression. "I was so worried, Pel. Are you—"

"I'll recover, or so the Healer tells me." Peleyia pulled a face. "I wanted to go to the library this evening since there is supposed to be this *big* discussion on what should be done next. But she forbade me."

"I doubt you'll miss much."

Peleyia snorted. "What happened to you?"

"Nothing." Kellen shook off the ill mood and used the towel to wipe his face a second time, avoiding Peleyia's shrewd gaze. "I'm more interested in you, after that spider bite. Do you remember any of it?" he asked, not wanting to discuss his misgivings just yet.

"Everything. I remember everything." Peleyia shuddered. "I couldn't move a muscle, but I could hear every word that was spoken. Knew everything that was happening. It was awful. All I wanted to do was help but couldn't. I was a burden."

"It wasn't your fault."

"I shouldn't have panicked."

"I almost did the same."

"But you didn't," Peleyia reminded him. "I feel so childish."

"No one thinks that." Kellen placed a hand on his friend's arm. "No one could blame you."

"No, they are all very polite," Peleyia said on a tight breath. "Lesendal is so wrapped in his own personal little drama that I doubt anything could get through his mental armor except, maybe, his lost sister. And Ryland is so mystified by all that's been happening; he is finding it very hard to adjust his beliefs. Then there's Criz—I don't know if you have noticed, but she is one very angry Elf. She seems determined to kill everything in sight. In a way, she is almost as fanatically focused as Sasheer." Peleyia grunted in mock humor, "I have never seen Sasheer so irrational. He drove us through the passes at a deadly pace. I was strapped to Lesendal's back for most of the journey, so I had a lot of time to watch and listen to them all. Of them all, only Sal made any effort to talk with me, to encourage me."

"I'm sorry," Kellen whispered, wishing he could have been there to help his friend. "I wish . . ."

"And you were gone," Peleyia gushed. "I had no idea what had happened to you, or Dalzere. I panicked—"

"It's over now," Kellen said, seeing the pain in Peleyia's wide eyes.

"Maybe." Peleyia gulped in a breath.

"We survived."

Peleyia sighed and he pushed further up the bed. "I get the impression that Sasheer wants to go after this Kalern. Or is it Lichien? He was so angry, first from what Criz had told him and then by what happened in the Pass with the Kizer."

"He's a Mage," Kellen whispered, glancing around to make sure they were alone in the warm room. The darkened chamber made him feel paranoid.

"I know."

"You know?" Shocked, Kellen frowned, the words turning into an accusation.

"Calm down," Peleyia soothed. "Of course I know. He's a Watcher, and all my people know what they are. I just hadn't realized the full implications of his abilities until I was paralyzed and forced to watch him day and night."

Mollified a little by those rapidly spoken words, Kellen's scowl lightened. He debated telling Peleyia the truth about Sasheer.

"Just say whatever is on your mind, Kell," Peleyia urged.

"I heard something earlier."

"What?" Peleyia breathed the word, while Kellen glanced around the room. "It's all right, Kell, we're alone."

"Are you sure?"

"Positive."

"I . . ."

"What?" Peleyia demanded in an excited whisper.

"I learned that Sasheer was one of the original twelve," Kellen replied in a hurried and hushed tone.

"Original twelve?" Peleyia repeated in a puzzled voice.

"The original *original* twelve," Kellen stressed slowly. "From Mitthsombaine."

"Oh." Understanding dawning on him, Peleyia's face first lit up with fascination, then burning curiosity. "That's old."

"You're telling me," Kellen agreed. "There are others here who are even older, and I got the impression Sasheer was one of the youngest."

"He looks young."

"But he's ancient. He's older than the Southland," Kellen said. "That's frightening."

"That would explain why he is so obnoxious," Peleyia murmured, his eyes narrowing in calculation.

"Why? Because he's frightening? Or because he is older than dirt?"

"You just said he's the youngest," Peleyia clarified. "He is probably at the bottom of the pecking order of Mages. I know in GarFamita what that's like—to be the youngest and at the lower end of the food chain," he said. "This would explain his rapid mood swings and temper."

"But can he be trusted?" Kellen asked, not sure if there was an answer to that question.

"If you can't trust him, then who can you trust?" Peleyia returned. When he saw Kellen's skeptical look, he continued, "I get the feeling that he has been hurt badly. I'd say it happened a long time ago. And now everything that happens to him is outside his control. Because of that one event."

"So?" Kellen frowned. "Doesn't mean we can trust him."

"He wants this Kalern dead. And for that reason alone, you can trust him."

"You know or think?"

"Feel." Giving a small half smile, Peleyia turned his wrist over and gripped Kellen's icy hand. "Remember, my people are trained to feel," he shrugged. "We read minds, emotions, and feelings. It helps to manipulate our buyers."

Nodding, Kellen remembered the young girl—Tontie—in GarFamita. She had tried to read his emotions and thoughts.

"I don't condone the practice, but sometimes such strong images scream out at me. And in the passes, I had a lot of time to watch and read Sasheer."

"Does he know you did this?"

"I hope not," he snorted. "If he does then he will not let me go with him when he goes east."

"He's going east?" Kellen asked, shocked. This was the last thing he had expected. "But why?"

"I heard Tich discussing it with Sal earlier when they thought I was asleep. That was why I wanted to go to the library tonight, to find out more. Gods, Kell!" Peleyia sighed in frustration. "I don't want to be sent back to the Sandlands. I think I would rather face these evil Raveners that everyone talks about with fear and awe, than go home."

"They won't send you home," Kellen told him.

"I want to go to the library," Peleyia insisted.

"Pel," Kellen said, unsure as he saw his friend push back the covers.

"I'll be fine," Peleyia gave a forced smile. "Don't you have to go there?"

"Well, yes," he said with some reluctance.

"Then go change out of these soggy leathers, and come pick me up on your way down. I'll dress."

"You can't!"

"Kell, I've been stuck in this room for the last three days; I need to get out. And besides, I want to find out what's going on."

"You already know more than me," Kellen said, wondering why Dalzere had not mentioned that small fact about heading east earlier. Getting up off the bed, he met the Lancooti's bright, smiling gaze and nodded once. "All right, but if that Healer has a go at me about this then I'll . . . I'll—"

"Don't worry; I'll deal with her," Peleyia soothed as he pushed the bed covers aside and got out of bed.

CHAPTER TWENTY-SIX

Kellen returned to his own room and washed sketchily before he dragged on fresh clothing, fastened his leathers, and combed some order into his hair. What Peleyia had told him had intrigued him—excited him—and he wondered if the Mages were serious about going after Kalern and the fabled Book of Spells. Would something that old still be legible? Tanish seemed to believe so.

He shook his head, thinking hard, and tied his long hair out of his eyes. He then sat on the edge of his huge bed to pull on clean, dry boots. He knew so little about magic, about how it worked, about the currents, about what was possible and what was impossible. What had Sasheer once said to Salimen, about it being all in your point of view? Was that true? Dismissing the troubling thought, he still found it unbelievable to think that he was from Kalern's line. The last of the line.

Then another thought hit him hard. Was that *why* he had been continually plagued with premonitions of disaster and death? Why all around him had been destroyed—because Kalern wanted him dead? Was Kalern the evil, cold entity?

Frozen in place as that eerie comprehension sank in, he shuddered. He felt suddenly ill, sick to his stomach with dread.

"Kell?"

A soft whisper behind him had Kellen turning to see Peleyia by his bedchamber door.

"Kellen!" With a worried look on his face, Peleyia hobbled over to him and gripped his arms. "What's wrong?"

"I've just realized—"

"What?" Peleyia demanded.

"It's my fault," Kellen answered, not bothering to hide his fear and self-loathing.

"What's your fault?"

"All the accidents."

Lifting a brow in bafflement at the ambiguous words, Peleyia tried to read behind the tone. "How have you come to that conclusion?" he asked. "Did Sasheer say that?"

"No." Kellen shook his head, breathing in deeply to banish the uneasiness. "I was forewarned. But I ignored it."

"Forewarned?" Peleyia blinked at him, puzzled.

"I didn't know. The dreams—"

"Stop! Stop right there," Peleyia instructed, his confused expression turning into annoyance. He moved closer to his friend and glared at him. "Not knowing is not a crime, Kell. Neither is not understanding."

"But I should have known."

Peleyia snorted in reply before he limped away to lean on Kellen's bed. "You know," he said, "I believe I finally understand what your problem is. You think too much." He softened the words with a cocky grin. "You should just stop, disengage that overactive imagination of yours, and go with your feelings. And right now, my feelings are telling me that *we* are missing some vital information by staying up here in your room discussing ancient history." He leaned forward and peered at his friend. "We should go downstairs and eavesdrop."

Not being able to stay serious when Peleyia grinned at him like that, Kellen gave up. He threw his hands in the air and exhaled hard. "Fine," he said. "But what do you think they will be discussing?" he asked. "Ancient history?"

"Ah, but that's even more ancient than your history. And that is useful information. In the right circles, it could make us very rich."

Kellen stared at his friend then started to laugh.

* * *

The two quietly entered the large old library and tried to stay out of sight. Kellen suppressed a shiver, remembering his last visit to this library, and he glanced around at the people present, not seeing Sasheer or Tanish. The large drapes were now drawn, and soft lamps lit the spacious room, warming the atmosphere. The lamplight softened the walls of books and manuscripts to create an intimate environment. It felt inviting, and Kellen dragged his gaze away from the allure of the library to take note of the numerous people either seated or standing around an oval desk. In the middle of the table was the three-dimensional map that Crizkerisomia had been rearranging with her knife earlier that afternoon, and he gave a soft chuckle in remembrance.

Then Peleyia was touching his arm, gesturing to the far side of the room. Kellen squinted in that direction and saw Sasheer. The Ranger stared at him—and for an instant, he didn't *see* the Ranger, rather he saw a young scholar—then he blinked, and the image was gone. In its place was Sasheer glaring at him. He returned the glare, just imagining what uncomplimentary thoughts were going through Sasheer's head.

"Don't aggravate him," Peleyia advised as he leaned close and whispered the words. "Or he'll turn you into a toad."

Kellen swung around and looked hard at Peleyia. "He can do that?"

Peleyia shrugged. "I don't know. But my point is, do you want to take that risk?"

Musing over that, Kellen let his eyes skim over Sasheer one final time then moved out of his line of sight and focused again on the table and its gathered assemblage.

To one side of the massive map structure sat five men in high-backed chairs, their robes a richness of color. He recognized them as the Mages he had been introduced to earlier, only now they looked stern rather than jocular. He knew they each possessed a great number of years—were old beyond his imagination—yet appearances suggested they were merely of a mature age when compared to the other occupants seated around the table.

Two old Dwarves, in particular, looked age worn, and Kellen blinked at them, noting their unusual mail tunics of silver and their long white beards. There were a number of distinguished-looking men and women, all dressed in similar clothing to the Brethren, so Kellen assumed they were residents of the Keep. There were also other men at the table who looked like neither the robed Mages nor the well-dressed lords, but who appeared curiously ageless. He studied them before sliding his eyes to the members of the table he did recognize—namely Dalzere, Ryland, and Lesendal, all of whom were listening attentively to a tall lord Kellen had never seen before.

"Come on. You'll never hear anything of interest if we stay in the doorway."

Feeling the tug on his arm, Kellen turned and watched Peleyia move away. Debating his choices, he decided to follow the Lancooti and skirted the edge of the table until they were in a better position to hear the discussion. Movement at his side caused him to suck in a breath, until he saw Crizkerisomia move from between two bookcases and cast him an assessing look. Then her eyes flickered away, briefly touching on Dalzere before she crossed her arms and melted back into the dimness of the shadows.

"What are you doing here?"

Startled by the feminine voice in his ear, Kellen whipped around and came nose to nose with Tich. He glared at her, wishing that her disproving scowl didn't seem so appealing. Then Tich was lifting a finger and pointing to something behind him. He followed her gesture and saw Peleyia inching closer to the table, the Lancooti's eyes alight with inquisitiveness. Typical.

"I expected you to at least have more sense than to drag him here tonight." Her hissed words were full of annoyance and displeasure.

Stung, Kellen drew himself up to his full height and was about to reply when he saw Peleyia grin over at them in mischief, then the Lancooti was approaching, his smile unrepentant. Kellen glowered at him.

"You are more skilled than you give yourself credit," Peleyia whispered persuasively to the Healer. "My recovery is almost complete," he tapped his chest in emphasis. "Rather I would say it is Kellen who needs your expert care. I believe he developed a cold while out in the rain."

Choking on a startled breath, Kellen glared at his friend when Tich settled her assessing gaze on him.

"He does look a bit flushed, I suppose."

"I'll leave you two to discuss it then," Peleyia offered before winking at his friend and slipping past the Healer.

Not believing Peleyia would do this to him, Kellen glared at his friend's back then jumped when a cool hand touched his brow.

Tich raised one curious eyebrow. "You wash up very well. And look! You actually have white skin under all that dirt. Very nice white skin at that." Her grin was wicked. "I'm so glad I didn't take you back to Sanctuary. All my friends would have devoured you."

Not liking the tone of her teasing, Kellen pushed her hand away and regathered his lost composure and dignity. "I'm fine. Really," he stressed. "But thanks for your concern."

"You looked ill. Maybe I should take your temperature."

Getting exasperated, he frowned harder at her. "No—"

"Children, please be quiet."

The voice was hissed from behind, and Kellen stilled, feeling Crizkerisomia brush soundlessly past them. Now he was embarrassed, and he settled his annoyed gaze on Tich.

"We'll discuss this later," Tich mouthed. She ran her eyes over his frame one final time, then sniffed, swiveled on her toes, and walked away.

Finding himself alone, Kellen seethed. His eyes narrowed, and he stared at the Healer's back until she disappeared from view. Only then did he stop to consider where he was. He turned back to look for Peleyia. His friend was almost standing at the edge of the table, looking for all the world like he was an invited member of this distinguished company. How he did it, Kellen couldn't fathom, and he sighed, letting his frustration go. Checking around the room anew, he decided to move closer, so he could hear the discussion.

He could pick out most of the words, but some of the replies remained lost until he was able to stand within a few paces of one of the high-backed chairs. He raised up on his toes, glimpsed the map in its full glory, and gasped. The torchlight threw prism shadows across the surface of the detailed map, turning the rippling contours into a velveteen carpet of mountains and valleys. It looked real, magical . . . just like the faces of those who sat around the huge oak table.

At the head of the table, one of the Mages was speaking, his voice sedate, encouraging, yet compelling. He appeared to be middle aged, but then age was a deceiving factor—but he had a commanding presence, a short well-trimmed beard, and shrewd eyes. Dark eyes. His robes were obviously ceremonial, as was the staff at his side, which held a huge gemstone that sparkled in the muted glow.

Studying this Mage, Kellen got the impression that . . . *something* . . . something else was sitting on the chair behind the Mage. A presence, a tangible imprint on his senses, and Kellen frowned, focusing his eyes and his senses on the invisible entity. It didn't feel like Terrica, or like the evil creature he'd first encountered in Ihova. This entity felt carefree, joyous, a gentleness across his senses.

Perplexed, he lifted his gaze to watch the Mage, thinking hard. *How many of these strange creatures are there?* Scanning the room, he tried to pick up Terrica's signature but could not find any trace of her. He frowned. Maybe she had not followed him, and he remembered he had not sensed her since before his fall in Death Peaks. Then maybe Peleyia was right, and all his concerns really were no more than his overworked imagination. Sighing, he flicked his gaze back to the speaker and decided to concentrate on the conversation.

The second speaker was tall regal, also in his middle years, with a touch of gray in his beard. His eyes, sharp and bright, holding a vast knowledge. And his voice was deep and commanding.

"—given all those facts, then I strongly recommend we remove the Book of Spells from Kalern's grasp before he learns how to resurrect more abominations from the past," the speaker said, glancing around the table. "Are we all agreed?"

"The old enemies, legends, have already come back to life, Karczag," one of the Dwarves said, his voice a deep, gruff sound. "The Raveners now roam at will. They have crossed the Dead River and have been seen in the Ice Cliffs. None of us are safe."

"Many have died, Councilor, to bring this news," the second Dwarf added, his expression solemn.

"I am sorry, my friend," the one named, Karczag, replied. "That is why we sent word to you and your clansmen, Roargan. Because we knew it was inevitable that Kalern would resurrect the Raveners as soon as he held the Book of Spells in his possession."

"Among my people, it is fable that an oracle existed once which blinded the senses of the Raveners," Roargan said. Next to him, the other Dwarf nodded in agreement, his gaze hard and unflinching. "It was told to me by my father, and is still told to the young today, that one of our forefathers—Toar—created the Oracle and used it to penetrate Mitthsombaine's lower sanctum and bind the Raveners' hunger."

"That is true," Karczag said, his tone gentle as he regarded the two Dwarven lords. "Toar was instrumental in the Oracle's formation. He gave it as a gift to the Magus. He took it back when war came, but I believe he lost the crystal in the pits beneath Mitthsombaine. That was on the eve of the city's destruction."

"I don't recall anyone actually attempting to find the crystal," Dybellia interjected. "Toar wanted to go back into the ruins and remove many of the magically enchanted objects. But with the trouble in the south—"

"Lichien's formation occupied our time," Tanish clarified. "None of us thought about returning to Mitthsombaine for the Oracle. The Book of Spells was hidden, the Raveners neutralized, and the city buried."

"Then Toar died," Karczag said in order to end the debate, sending a private smile in Tanish's direction.

"So the Oracle is still in the underground caverns of Mitthsombaine? If we could find it, then . . ." Roargan let the rest hang, and Kellen noted how Karczag sighed and rubbed his eyes, how Tanish nodded, how Dybellia frowned and Tattlier rolled his eyes before glaring at Roargan. "I understand your distaste of the ancient evil, but the Raveners need to be stopped. The Oracle is one option."

"Granted," Karczag agreed, holding up a hand to stop Tattlier from commenting. That earned him a glare from his opinionated brother. "Later," Karczag admonished softly. Then he turned back to look at the Dwarves again. "We have heard of your people Roargan—the Hammer Clan—but what of you, Blaine? What of the Silverglow Clan?"

Blaine scowled at Karczag miserably. "We lost a third of our young men when the pits collapsed last spring," he growled. "Many blame the curse. Blame Kalern for bespelling the tunnels. So we have tried to stay completely clear of anything to do with the old city. King Hamblin respects the law."

"Good," Karczag sighed before answering. "Venturing into Mitthsombaine's tombs via the tunnels will only bring the Stone Ghouls. It is a cursed placed."

"But we have to live with the curse."

"You don't have to risk lives," Tattlier said then sighed as the Dwarven lords scowled at him. "We explained to you months ago why traversing the old tunnels was not recommended."

"Let's not dwell on what was decided last council," Karczag advised, raising a hand when other members around the table started to murmur in agreement and displeasure. "The question now—what we should do with Lichien and Kalern?"

"I still believe that if you want the Book of Spells returned, then you will need the Oracle. Can the Oracle be retrieved another way, without going into the tunnels?" Roargan persisted. He searched the faces around him. "I've heard it said that the Oracle would hide from the user of the Book of Spells. Is this true?"

"Essentially," Tanish said, settling a hand on Tattlier's arm to prevent him from snapping at the Dwarf. "It is doubtful Kalern would have found the Oracle. If it still exists and is whole."

"Then I say we find it. It is our best defense against Kalern," Roargan declared. Numerous others agreed.

Karczag exhaled hard, gesturing for the noise around the table to settle. After a few more muttered comments, all complied, and he slowly sat back, meeting each concerned gaze squarely. "I understand your concern, but—"

"Karczag," Sasheer interrupted by stepping forward. "Roargan does have a very valid point. If the Oracle is still in the old library, hidden beneath the city, then I am willing to go and look for it." He kept his eyes pinned on Karczag, ignoring Tattlier's scowl. "If I can find it, then that means we can slip into North Ridge without alerting Lichien."

"It is an unnecessary risk," Karczag counseled.

"A risk, yes, but maybe our best opportunity also," Sasheer said. "Lichien will be so taken up with having Kalern search out the book's protection locks that its attention will be divided, allowing me to slip in and catch it unaware."

"Even if you do manage to find the Oracle, Lichien will still feel your presence. It will still feel your approach and be able to anticipate your every move. It won't need the Raveners." Tanish pointed out, supporting Karczag's reasoning. "You won't get the Book of Spells, rather it will just give Lichien another opportunity to kill one of us. And there are so few of us left, Sasheer."

Licking his lips, Sasheer gave a small secretive smile. "Let Lichien think I am coming for the book." Sasheer lifted his lashes, his blue eyes extremely dark and deadly. "I just want to get close enough to cast the fragmentation spell—to destroy it—to shatter its evil heart and break it into the twelve original components."

Utter silence greeted that comment as every eye locked on Sasheer's tall frame. Then Karczag cleared his throat and stared at his friend and brother. "To cast the spell would mean your death. You know that, Sasheer." His tone was grim.

"I am willing to die, if it means killing Lichien and releasing Kalern's body from the stone's possession."

Again silence followed Sasheer's passionately hissed words, and then Tattlier coughed, breaking the tension.

"Sasheer is right," Tattlier offered into the strained stillness. "As much as I hate to admit it, this is the best opportunity we've had in over three thousand years. The seal to the underground caverns is now broken. So if we can find the Oracle—then use it to get into North Ridge—Sasheer can cast the fragmentation spell, and Lichien will die. Kalern will be free, and the Book of Spells will be nullified. That will break the spirit of the Black Guard, and the war will end before it starts."

"And the Raveners?" Blaine asked as he stroked his long beard in thought.

"With the Book of Spells under our control, we can lock them away forever," Tanish reassured. He leaned forward in his chair, the lamplight highlighting his sightless eyes. "Karczag?"

"I just abhor the idea of losing another brother to Lichien," Karczag said, his eyes still locked on Sasheer, their expression searching, compassionate, and understanding.

"It is my place to do this, as you well know," Sasheer reminded him.

"I know," Karczag sighed before glancing back over at the two elderly Dwarves. "Can you both speak for your clan kings on this matter?" he asked, and both Dwarves nodded. Taking a deep breath, Karczag cast one final questioning look at Sasheer, then nodded gravely. "It is decided then," he declared formally. "Sasheer will go to Mitthsombaine in search of the Oracle. Blaine, since the Silverglow Clan is closest to the underground labyrinth of the city, can you assist?"

"We are at war, as you know, with our cousins. All our warriors are committed to stopping Torank, Damklin, and Kasarn from breaking through the fortifications around our silver mines and taking our deposits for Kalern's growing army." Blaine shook his head sadly. "I fear we will be unable to offer much aid."

"If you send word to the Sun Council in Capliarkia, I am sure the Elven elders will gladly send aid," Crizkerisomia interrupted.

"We had anticipated such an act, and I carry a prepared proposal for the Sun Council," Blaine answered with a roguish grin. He lifted his eyes to the old Mage. "What of the south? Should not word be sent to Hersoford, to the lords of the South Sea? Lichien concerns all four lands."

Considering that, Karczag glanced around the table at his colleagues and friends. "Before we drag the armies of Hersoford into this situation, I would like to know more of what is happening in the south."

"I could travel down to Hersoford," a tall ageless, weather-beaten man said. He was dressed in traveling clothes.

Karczag's eyes sparkled with displeasure, but he agreed. "Rhys can sound out the men of Hersoford and inform them of what is happening in the north."

"Kalern is targeting only his old rivals at present, and I think we should try to avoid another great war," Tanish said. "The last great war almost destroyed the entire continent of Sennovia."

"Agreed," Roargan said gruffly, "but if the Elven and Dwarven armies fail, there will be nothing to block Kalern . . ." he trailed off, not needing to explain the very real dangers to the others around the table.

"I will have messengers sent to the Elven Council," Tanish promised as Karczag nodded. Even Tattlier and Dybellia looked concerned. "When you arrive at Danchern's Junction, send us an assessment of the current situation."

"Thank you," Roargan acknowledged. "We may not be able to help directly in your journey to ancient Mitthsombaine, but I believe King Darchain has a clansman living in Sanctuary who would make a perfect guide into the tombs beneath the dread city."

Karczag raised a questioning brow.

"Gralvin Broadhammer," Roargan said, the name rolling off his tongue. "He is cousin to the king and comes from a strong line of expert tunnelsmiths."

Accepting the offer, Karczag turned to look at Sasheer. "There, my friend, if you still want to go through with this, then I suggest you go to Sanctuary first and ask Gralvin Broadhammer for his assistance. For you will need him outside Blackstone Pass."

"I know Gralvin; he is a good man and perfect for our needs.

Who else may I take?" Sasheer asked as he glanced around the other members of his Brethren. "Seaton?"

"We are all committed to our own tasks, Sasheer, I am sorry," Tanish replied.

"I have to go north anyway, so I will look out for you and let you know how the land feels," Seaton, offered. He appeared only slightly older than Sasheer, with fair hair, a tanned face, and a warm smile. "The Gully Gnomes have been suspiciously quiet these last few months."

Sasheer lifted a brow and then squinted over at the others seated around the table.

Lesendal cleared his throat as he hesitantly leaned forward, speaking up for the first time. "I am not going to pretend and say I understand all you have discussed here, but if you are going north, then I want to go also. I am impelled to go. I must find out what happened to my people and to my sister. I must learn the truth, for my honor and for the honor of the Southland."

"I thought you might say that," Sasheer said, looking pleased. Then his gaze slid to the big Haonian warrior. "Ryland?"

"I have come this far; I am now curious to meet this Kalern," Ryland said, nodding his assent.

"That is not something to be wished for lightly," Dalzere said as he stepped into the light. "I also will accompany you—if there had ever been any doubt of my involvement."

"None, my friend." Sasheer smiled.

"I want to go—" Peleyia broke in, stepping forward into the circle of light. His gaze was direct as he forced Sasheer to take his request serious.

"Peleyia, the journey will be taxing," Sasheer started.

"I will not let you down," Peleyia promised.

About to dissuade the Lancooti, Sasheer paused when Dalzere's hand rested on his shoulder.

"He is a skilled and experienced thief. A useful talent for when we enter the tombs," the Drow stated matter-of-factly. "Let him travel with us back to Sanctuary. If he survives that trek, he can accompany us east."

"Practical Drow logic," Tattlier said sarcastically before grinning unrepentant at the tall Drow warrior. "Your levelheadedness has been missed inside these walls, Dalzere."

"It is nice to be missed," the dark Elf said, inclining his head in respect.

"Very well," Sasheer agreed with little enthusiasm, giving the Lancooti one final, raking glare before glancing at the silent Sun Elf. "Criz?"

"I have no pressing engagements at home. Nor have I ever been that far east," she said concisely as her eyes slid to the Drow. "It will be an experience."

Ignoring her, Dalzere's golden gaze traveled around the rest of the members at the table. "That is six in the party, Sasheer."

"The smaller the number the better," Karczag said. "Plus you will have Gralvin. That gives you a guide, a hunter, a tracker, a thief if he makes it," he quipped as he glanced over at the silent Lancooti. "And two southern swordsmen. Who else would you need, Sasheer?"

"Oh, I was hoping for a bowman," Sasheer left the rest unsaid as he turned to look into the shadows behind. "Salimen? Are you still awake back there?"

Dalzere's lips twitched up in amusement when he heard an explosive sigh answer Sasheer's taunt. He turned in time to see the tall blond Ihovian walk into the light and scowl at them all.

"Lesendal, have you lost your mind?" Salimen snapped, outraged.

"Sal, I have to go, you know that," the prince petitioned his cousin, his tone diplomatic and calm. "If there is only a hope of finding Kess, then I have to go."

"Is she worth your life?" Salimen asked, his tone harsh.

"Yes." Lesendal raised his chin, refusing to back down.

Grumbling under his breath, Salimen cast a disgruntled look at the Drow and then at Sasheer. "All right, Ranger, you win."

"Good, now our company is complete," Sasheer ended, pleased. "I suggest we start in the morning by meeting down in the—"

"I would like to include one other," Dalzere broke in, feeling all eyes settle on him. Sasheer stopped in midsentence and sent him a warning glare.

"No." Sasheer cut him off, knowing exactly what Dalzere was going to suggest. "Absolutely not."

"I think Kellen should accompany us," Dalzere continued as if Sasheer had not spoken. He avoided his partner's fierce stare, instead training his eyes on the young man in question and silently challenged Kellen to protest.

Meeting that direct provocation, Kellen's fists balled at his side as he felt others turn to look at him. He did not want to go off exploring the country east of the Keep. In fact, he wanted to go nowhere until he sorted out his mind and his jumbled life. He definitely did not want to go chasing after some mythical crystal in Mitthsombaine—that was a bad idea all round. Even Karczag didn't like it. "I think Sasheer might be right in this instance." Kellen found his voice, and cleared his throat. *Am I actually agreeing with that infuriatingly arrogant Mage?* That was a novelty.

"Really?" Tanish spoke up. All the other Mages looked at him in disbelief when he took the Drow's side. "I think Dalzere is right."

"It would be too dangerous," Sasheer hissed back, furious. "We need him here. He must be taught, Tanish!"

"I thought we had this discussion earlier." Tanish raised his head and looked in the direction of the fuming Sasheer. His eyes were milky white, but his smile was all-knowing. "You must teach him," his tone blunt, "and if you think running off to Mitthsombaine relieves you of that responsibility then you are sadly mistaken, my friend." He moved his head to take in the others. "Don't you agree, Karczag?"

Karczag looked uncomfortable, and he let his eyes travel around the other Brethren, each giving a silent answer to the wordless question he asked. He sighed and let his gaze settle back on Sasheer's tense frame. "He goes with you. You can leave him and the southerners with Gralvin Broadhammer at Delheck's Reach after you exit the tombs of Mitthsombaine. That is, if it would be acceptable to King Darchain?" Karczag asked politely.

The old Dwarf mumbled assent. "The King, I imagine, would

be delighted to offer shelter." He lifted his gaze to the White Elf. "By then, our allies the Sun Elves will have helped us secure the pass into Delheck."

Crizkerisomia just nodded.

"There, Sasheer, the boy will not be in danger. He will never enter the North so the prophecy will be safe. Are you happy now?" Karczag asked.

"No. I still believe it is a risk. But if this is the Council's decision, then we had best get moving before all the Dwarven Clans fall to Lichien's dark army," Sasheer grumbled, then swiveled on his toes and strode out of the library.

* * *

Shocked and angry, Kellen marched from the room. *Boy?* Now the head of the Mage Council was calling him *the boy*. It was so degrading!

Breathing out deeply to dissipate his anger, Kellen watched Sasheer stalk off in the opposite direction and decided it was time they had their talk. Going after the temperamental Mage, he was stopped by a hand on his shoulder. Turning, ready to snap a cutting remark at the Healer, he closed his mouth when he met Salimen's angry gaze.

"Kell, we are having a meeting in Dale's room. I think you should attend."

Shrugging Salimen's hand off his shoulder, Kellen tried not to glare at the Ihovian, already too disgruntled. Instead, he carefully considered the request. "What is the meeting about?"

"This stupid venture. What else?"

"Stupid?"

"I think it's suicidal, but that is just my viewpoint." The bowman took a measuring breath, trying to control his own temper. "Come to Dale's room. In half an hour."

Kellen stared after Salimen's stiff back, not believing how complicated events were becoming yet again. He could understand the other man's concerns, and knew that both Salimen and Lesendal disagreed more often than agreed on varying topics. At times it was amazing they were still friends.

Glancing down the hallway, Kellen frowned, recalling all that he had learned in the past few amazing, yet stressful months. Despite Sasheer's mulishness, he admired the Ranger. Liked him even. So what was he to do? *Tackle Sasheer first,* he decided. The Ihovians could wait.

Finding Sasheer was harder than he first imagined. The Ranger was not in his room, the secondary library, or the courtyard and Kellen looked through another half-dozen rooms before giving up. He wandered the lower levels and realized he was starving when he caught the aroma of hot food. He followed the smell and found the kitchens, and to his amazement he also found Sasheer sitting at one of the long tables, drinking ale and being his usual antisocial self.

Homing in on the irritable Mage before the man could disappear again, Kellen grabbed an apple on the way past and went to sit with his unsmiling mentor. "We need to talk," he announced as he straddled the bench across from Sasheer.

Sasheer looked up with no surprise, his gaze far from inviting. "It was not my idea to include you in the company."

"Then reverse the decision," Kellen suggested.

"It is not that simple."

Biting into his apple, Kellen glared back at the man watching him, a sudden intense rage building inside him. "You want me to learn control? Well, how am I going to do that while dodging the Black Guard? Or helping you search some old ruins? Or being left behind with the Dwarfs? Or watching helplessly while you run off to die on some stupid quest?" Kellen ended in a rough, hissed tone. Where the pain had come from, he did not know, and he glared harder at Sasheer, daring the other man to deny his words.

Blinking, startled, Sasheer was speechless, then astonished, before he closed his eyes. "To face Lichien is my decision, Kellen. My responsibility," he said, his tone resigned.

"But why is it your responsibility?" Kellen pushed. This was not the argument he had envisaged having with this intriguing man, but now he found it was more important to stop Sasheer dying than to find reassurance for his own insecurities. "That older Mage, Karczag, said you would die if you tried to destroy Lichien."

"Yes." Sasheer nodded. "But so will Lichien." He lifted his lashes and smiled gently. "You see, in order to destroy Lichien I need to touch the stone. But in doing so, I will be trapped in the volatile magics of the spell and be consumed. It is an acceptable risk—as Criz would say."

"I don't care what anyone says!" Kellen shot back, incensed. "Surely there must be another way to destroy Lichien other than giving your life?"

"Kellen, we have been trying for thousands of years to destroy Lichien, and believe me when I say nothing has worked. Instead, Lichien has picked us off one by one. Destroying our families. Killing friends. Killing my students," Sasheer said, holding Kellen's gaze for a long moment before he cast his eyes down. "I am tired of the constant battle. So tired. And now Cornithia is dead. And with his death we are given a rare chance to get into old Mitthsombaine and find the Oracle. Roargan is right. With the Oracle I can penetrate the fortress at North Ridge and confront Lichien. One way or another, I must finish this. I must end this travesty."

"But to die? Willingly?"

"My choice."

"But what about this prophecy Tanish speaks of?"

"Tanish is a historian," Sasheer said wearily, slumping a little further in his chair. His clear eyes darkened. "He sees things in a different way to the rest of us. In a different reality. He has faith—"

"And you don't," Kellen whispered, starting to understand. He got a faint glimpse of Sasheer's haunted memories and pulled back his senses, giving the Mage privacy.

"My faith died a long time ago, Kellen."

He had never expected this outcome, nor the pain behind Sasheer's softly uttered words, and on instinct he leaned closer. In the back of his mind he could hear Peleyia's words of earlier... *'I get the feeling that he has been hurt badly. I'd say it happened a long time ago. And now everything that is happening is outside his control'* . . . "And the prophecy?" He breathed the question, almost dreading the answer, "do you believe in the prophecy?"

Lifting his gaze, Sasheer stared at him with utter frankness. "I have seen many of your bloodline die because they believed they were the instruments of this prophecy. I do not want that to happen to you. You deserve to live, not die facing Kalern or Lichien."

"But I thought—" Kellen stopped, confused, "I don't know what I thought."

Sasheer gave a small, self-mocking laugh. "Kellen, I want you to live, to learn, and to help the Brethren. I wanted that for Wyran, but I failed him." He took a steadying breath. "They need new blood and new ideas in these old walls."

"But," Kellen said at a loss, "the prophecy says—"

Sasheer cut him off. "It says very little, if you think about it. And what it does say, is cryptic. *'One will come and challenge.'*" Sasheer emphasized the words snidely. "All who have been born from Aserties' line have challenged. All, Kellen. And all have died!" Sasheer snarled. "Then the prophecy goes on about *'to save a lost soul'*? What is a lost soul? Or what is innocence for that matter?" He shook his head mockingly and let out an explosive breath. "The prophecy could be talking about a life or a belief. It could be talking about a symbolic innocence or literal purity," Sasheer said, pushing his goblet away. "The words are not specific."

"Sasheer—"

"No," Sasheer cut him off again, warming to his theme, a cynical bite coloring his tone. "Tanish is a romantic. I, on the other hand, believe Lichien will only be destroyed by direct magical intervention. Not by mystical words."

Kellen just stared at Sasheer, dumbfounded.

"I have disillusioned you, haven't I?" Sasheer asked with a tight grin.

"No, not really," Kellen said. "But where does this leave me?"

"You?" Sasheer frowned. "After we leave Mitthsombaine, you

and the others will return to the Keep. From there, I think Karczag will probably take over your training."

"But I want you to train me." Kellen took a shuddering breath; suddenly knowing he had accepted all Sasheer had been forcing him to face over the last few months. Accepting for the first time who he was and what he had to do. Coming to a decision, he locked gazes with the unpredictable Mage and grinned. "You, Sasheer, are my teacher."

"Kellen . . ." Sasheer warned.

Hardening his resolve, Kellen shook his head and reached over to grip the other's cold fingers. "You offered me help and training months ago, and I accepted. I will not break our pact now. So, if you insist on going to North Ridge, then so will I."

"No!" Sasheer pulled his hands free. "You will stay with King Darchain."

"Like you said, it is a matter of choice." Kellen smiled sweetly as he saw the other's eyes narrow to dangerous slits. "To accompany you will be my choice," he ended, folding his arms and daring Sasheer to argue. Sasheer said nothing for a strained moment, and then he was cursing, using the phrase Dalzere often muttered. Listening carefully to the pronunciation, Kellen wondered if he would ever deliver the same curse with as much dedication as Sasheer was currently doing. For the first time in months he felt completely in control.

CHAPTER TWENTY-SEVEN

The next morning Kellen found himself back on the moors, walking behind Peleyia as they headed toward the distant woodlands and the fabled township of Sanctuary.

The events of the night before still seemed so unbelievable. Out of everyone present, he had been the only member of the group not allowed to make his own decision. Even after talking with Sasheer, he still felt angered and frustrated by the way things had turned out. It was not because he was forced to go to Mitthsombaine, but rather, it was because no one had bothered to ask his opinion. It seemed so unjust the way he and Peleyia were treated. He was not a child, regardless of his age, and neither was Peleyia.

He frowned then squinted up at the early morning sunlight, seeing clear skies. If it weren't for the putrid odors emanating from the marshes, the morning would be pleasant, and *no* . . . he would never agree with Sasheer and believe you could get used to the stench of the moor and marshes.

Thinking about the contrary man, Kellen let his gaze touch Sasheer's back before turning his attention to Dalzere. After leaving Sasheer the previous night he had run into Dalzere. The Drow had been searching for Sasheer, and Kellen had taken the opportunity to express his annoyance for a second time. But Dalzere had just smiled in that wicked way of his, only stating that he believed Kellen would benefit from the journey to Mitthsombaine.

The injustice of the situation had infuriated him more. So he had stalked off to his room and sulked, totally forgetting about Salimen's invitation to discuss the proposed journey. It wasn't until

Peleyia had bounced into his room later that night that he remembered. The Lancooti was excited, looking forward to the journey, and at that stage Kellen had told the jubilant man exactly what he thought about the proposed journey and the various members of its company. If anything, Peleyia had just laughed harder, telling him it was only another adventure and that he should learn to enjoy life while he could. Then the annoyingly cheerful man had bid him good night, which had left him feeling worse than ever.

An adventure? How on earth could Peleyia think that the last few months had been an adventure? He would never understand his friend. What could possibly be so horrible back in Peleyia's own homeland that it would drive the likeable Lancooti to do everything possible to avoid any hint of returning to the Sandlands?

Bemused, Kellen had settled in the large bed and found his thoughts went in full circle, until he remembered the vulnerable little creature he had discovered on the moors earlier that afternoon. *Shard.* That had cheered him up, because if anything, this journey would give him a chance to find the little animal.

Keeping that motive in the back of his mind, Kellen studiously watched Sasheer, who was in the lead. He carefully worked it so that he could drop back in the group until only Ryland was behind him. Ahead, they had a few extra members who needed to return to Sanctuary, one being the Healer and the other being Karczag, so both Sasheer and Dalzere's attention was divided. Smiling, Kellen glanced back at the Haonian, judging his chances of walking behind the big man, and saw Ryland shake his head in mild reproof. Were his motives that transparent?

"What are you doing, lad?"

"If you must know, I am trying to avoid the Healer," Kellen lied smoothly. Ryland cocked his head to one side and gave him a grin.

"She is a nice lass. A little high-strung, but honest-hearted. You could do worse."

Stunned, Kellen sent Ryland a horrified stare. "I'm not trying to do anything," he protested. "Just looking for some peace."

Ryland chuckled, his eyes showing that he didn't believe a word. But he said nothing more.

Kellen's eyes went to the Healer before he forced himself to look away from her attractive frame. *No*—he was not even going to think about her. He forced himself instead to remember what Peleyia had told him at breakfast.

"So who is Karczag?" Kellen asked, sampling the apricots and sweet melon he was given for breakfast.

"He is the head of Sanctuary. Or so I've heard," Peleyia whispered conspiratorially. "Apparently it's a secluded village or city or something—high in the mountains, and this Karczag lives there. He rules the township." The Lancooti shrugged. "I'm not totally sure, but I also heard that Karczag is in-charge of the other Mages. Head Mage. He has some outlandish title . . . Magus or something . . . and makes all the major decisions. And once he makes a decision he never changes his mind. While, on the other hand, I hear that your friend Tanish—"

"He's not my friend," Kellen protested.

Peleyia waved his words aside. "Tanish has a title something like 'the Keeper of the Histories'." He wiggled his brows at Kellen in amusement. "Whatever that means!"

"Where do you hear this nonsense?" Kellen asked, not sure if he wanted to believe it or not.

"I have my sources."

"But you have only been here—what four days?" Kellen calculated. "And you were bed-bound for three of those days."

"It is all in how you approach someone," Peleyia advised.

Studying his friend, Kellen scowled. "You've been using your Lancooti Gifts, haven't you?" he accused. "You've been reading people's minds—"

"No," Peleyia cut in, hurt. "I haven't. Besides, Lancooti can't read minds as you say. We read intentions. Can sometimes influence another's desires. That's all." He sniffed, offended. "I was just being friendly to the kitchen staff," he added. "You should try being friendly sometime."

"I am friendly." Kellen didn't miss how Peleyia snickered. Relenting, he smiled. "So what else have you heard?"

"Something very interesting," Peleyia said, leaning in closer. "It seems that Sasheer spends very little time in the Keep; is only here when one of the other Mages drags him back. It is said he chooses to live with outsiders rather than his own family and brothers."

Puzzled, Kellen asked nothing more and Peleyia offered no further information as they both sat at the large breakfast table and cast Sasheer surreptitious glances.

Bringing his mind back to the present, Kellen again looked at the fascinating Mage. *What is Sasheer's secret?* Peleyia's words had given him a little more insight into the complicated world of the Watchers. Watchers, Rangers, Brethren, Mageborns—and their creation—Lichien.

* * *

The morning passed slowly, the humidity and smell of the marshes stifling, and Kellen found it hard to believe that this gnat-infested, steamy swamp was the same dreary marshland of yesterday where he had been caught in a thunderstorm. Cautiously he scanned the area for Shard. It was weird, but he longed to see the strange creature—had an overwhelming urge to check on the animal's safety.

Against his better judgments, he found he was reaching out with his mind—*seeking, searching, needing, wanting*—and he felt the brush of an invisible entity. It wasn't Terrica, nor was it the evil entity. It wasn't what he was hunting either, and he sucked in a fearful breath. The presence was toward the front of the group, a hovering substance hidden in shadow and light. He tried to discern what it was then caught a brief glimpse of a large hunting owl. A bird with an immense head and large unblinking, shrewd eyes. Then the image vanished, and he staggered back.

"Easy, lad. The ground is a tad uneven."

Ryland's voice grounded him further, and Kellen hastily shut down his sense, berating himself for being so rash and stupid. *What am I thinking?* He'd get himself killed that way.

Picking up the pace a little, he thanked Ryland but maintained a silent vigil for Shard, keeping silent as they exited the marshlands and entered the thick pine forest on the northern edge of Death Peaks. It was now late morning, and the overhead sun was lost in the entwining branches. The temperature rose as they ventured deeper into the pine forest.

* * *

"Are you all right, lad?" Ryland asked a few hours later.

Kellen was jolted alert by Ryland's deep voice, and he turned to regard his friend. "Fine," he mumbled, catching a glimpse of the other's growing frown.

"I have not had the leisure to talk with you properly since your return to the Keep, and I am concerned that you may be disappointed with my failure to prevent your slide down that mountain's ledge."

Startled by the sincere words, Kellen berated himself for not anticipating Ryland's feelings. "Ryland, how could I blame you?"

"You have been avoiding me since your return," Ryland said, his eyes still showing doubt and hurt.

"Not intentionally." He did remember turning away from the big man the previous day, and he winced. "What happened to me was no one's fault except my own," he explained. "Then at the Keep, I heard a few things which . . ." *angered, infuriated, frustrated . . .* "shocked me, and I just needed to get some air." He looked at the warrior in apology. "I am sorry, Ryland, if it looked like I was trying to avoid you."

Appearing only mildly reassured, Ryland laid a steel-encased hand on Kellen's shoulder and squeezed gently. "The four of us from the Twelve Kingdoms must stick together."

"What about Peleyia?" Kellen asked when he realized the Haonian had not included the Lancooti.

"His people are from across the Divide and are a bit strange. He is not from one of the kingdoms," was all Ryland said. "Always remember, Kellen, that whatever may happen to us here in Sennovia, we are still southerners, and our primary concern must be to remember our heritage and to help Lesendal find his sister and other captives from this war. We will return home and help free the south from Kalern's offensive rule." It was almost a vow. "We cannot afford to get too involved in these Magery politics—"

"But you, Lesendal, and Sal, agreed with Sasheer last night," Kellen complained. "You decided to go east."

"Lesendal has to learn his sister's fate, so he, Salimen, and I discussed it last night after the council. You were invited to Lesendal's room, so you should have attended," the big man chastised. "If Sasheer can rid the land of Kalern, then that is good, but there is also a strong chance that Sasheer will fail or die. Then we will still be faced with the same problems, but with one less ally."

Bewildered by that attitude, Kellen wondered why both Lesendal and Ryland were so narrow-minded. Was it a trait of the Southland, or were they right in their assessments? Had he been like that? Or had he changed—grown? Yet to stop Kalern, and the stone, would surely be more beneficial to all the four lands.

Seeing that Ryland was still watching him, Kellen nodded, keeping his thoughts to himself, not understanding any of this. Was he betraying his friends?

"Good, lad," Ryland said, pleased. "I am glad we had this chance to talk, but now we had best pick up the pace before that Drow comes looking for us."

That Drow? Even more shocked, Kellen blinked, wondering what had really happened over the last few days to make his friend so negative toward Dalzere again. Then Salimen approached them, and he was not given the chance to pursue the topic.

"Dalzere recommends we stop at the brook ahead for a quick lunch. The forest after that becomes dense, and the track narrows before reaching the lake village of Sengold."

"Sengold?" Kellen asked.

Salimen shrugged. "A small fishing village from what Karczag says. We need to go into the village in order to find the road to Sanctuary." He shrugged a second time.

"That's a bit odd," Ryland frowned.

"Odd?" Salimen scoffed. "Everything we've seen since leaving Ihova has been odd, so why should this seem any different?"

Used to the blond's cynical humor, Kellen still scowled as he listened to the exchange.

* * *

After a very brief lunch of cold meats, cheese, and bread, the group filed out again into the dim gloom of the blanketing forest. Amazingly, Kellen found himself behind the Healer this time and was apprehensive when she turned to offer him a long sturdy stick.

"Here, this will help with the trek ahead."

Accepting the knotted branch, he mumbled his thanks. "So what is this forest called?" he asked, remembering what Peleyia had said over breakfast. Maybe if he copied the Lancooti's attitude, he would learn more.

"It's a Drow name. One you wouldn't understand," she replied, not bothering to turn.

"Oh, right, how stupid of me to ask," he muttered sarcastically.

She did turn and glare after that. "It's called *Seldarveion* if you must know."

"Meaning?" he shot back, not letting her get the upper hand in this discussion.

"A place of fear," she returned just as fast, her eyes hardening in challenge.

"So I take it you speak, Drow," Kellen continued, seeing her shoulders tense. "You seem to know an awful lot about them. A lot about Dalzere."

"I know many things, southerner."

"If that were true, then you would know that your assessment of me is not entirely accurate," he replied in a mild tone. He was pleased when Tich hesitated then swung around to glare at him anew. Biting his lower lip in order to cover his smile, he waited for her to ask, while he tried to perfect the look of innocence his brother always accused him of using during one of their arguments.

"What's not accurate?" she asked in a mixture of annoyance and curiosity.

"I am not a southerner. Not by heritage." If anything, her eyes only narrowed further. "I grew up in the south, granted, but it now seems my origins are more eastern." Unable to hold his smile back as her expression mirrored only blank incomprehension, he grinned at her charmingly.

"Eastern . . ." she began, confused.

"Yes," Kellen said, starting to enjoy this game. "At least according to Tanish."

With that, her expression changed, and her eyes widened. She stared at him unblinkingly for a long moment. "You're a . . ."

"What?" he asked, a little wary when her attitude changed so suddenly.

"Damn him!" Tich spat angrily as she turned away and marched off.

"What did I say?" Wondering what he had done now, Kellen hurried to catch up, hearing her mutter a string of strange words that sounded suspiciously like more Drow profanities. Throwing caution to the winds, he grabbed her arm and forced her to look at him again. "What's wrong?" he demanded.

Sucking in a large breath, her eyes drifted over his shoulder to the others behind before she met his dark gaze again. "I should have known by the look of you that you just had to be from *his* line. That explains everything! It's my own stupid fault; I should have guessed!" Pulling her arm free, she backed away, refusing to say more.

Wanting to know what she meant, he was not given the opportunity to ask, as she squeezed past first Peleyia then Lesendal to walk behind the Sun Elf. *His line* . . . as in Kalern's line? Was the resemblance that strong? He blinked after her. *Now she hates me,* and he sighed.

* * *

Not managing to get close enough to question Tich further

until they entered a small fishing village, Kellen squinted up in the bright afternoon sunlight as they emerged from under the dense forest canopy. It was a relief to be out from under the trees' oppressiveness. He gazed out with wonder at the two huge mountain ranges that surrounded the town, and at the massive lake which faced him. The small village was nestled in the protective embrace of towering rock, dense forest, and tranquil waters. Picturesque and beautiful.

"Wow."

He heard Peleyia whistle behind him as the other shaded his eyes to take in the magnificent surroundings.

"Imagine living here," Peleyia said. It was wistful.

"So this is Sengold," Salimen said as he pushed his blond hair out of his eyes. "Some simple fishing village."

Sasheer approached them, his scowl still firmly in place. His emphatic blue eyes scanned the Lancooti, looking him up and down almost clinically. "How are you feeling?"

"Fine," Peleyia said, plastering on a confident smile. Kellen got the impression Peleyia would say that even if he were dying.

It appeared Sasheer was under the same impression. "I'll have one of the Healers check you over when we get to Sanctuary." He looked around and pointed at one of the wooden structures ahead. "We'll rest in the inn overnight then continue on to Sanctuary in the morning."

"How far is it?" Ryland asked.

"About half as far again. We should reach it by lunch tomorrow," was Sasheer's curt response. He then walked away, refusing to answer any more questions.

Left alone, Kellen shared a puzzled look with Peleyia, hearing Salimen start to mutter more uncomplimentary observations about Sasheer's character.

CHAPTER TWENTY-EIGHT

He barely slept that night, surrounded by strange night sounds that didn't resemble any animal he had ever heard before. So by morning, Kellen was exhausted, his eyes sore and red, and his mood as dark as Sasheer's.

After washing and repacking his belongings, he went in search of Peleyia. The early-dawn light was a golden orange that tracked a path of molten glory across the still lake. Beautiful; and he made his way to the docks. He found Peleyia by the old wooden structure, watching the men of the fishing village glide their boats out over the lake. The scene was relaxing and tranquil, easing his tension.

They stood there in shared silence until the last golden tracks of sunrise had abated, and then they reluctantly climbed to their feet and returned to the inn. Kellen cast one final glance back at the exquisite setting behind before joining the others for breakfast.

Karczag called farewell to the old innkeeper and then led them through the small sleepy village. Only a few residents nodded good morning. Large nets hung over racks, drying out in the warm sun as a couple of men cleaned out huge wooden bins. It was comforting to see such simple tasks, to know that not all in the world was strange, and Kellen dragged his gaze away from the activities, feeling homesick, and almost bumping into Peleyia's immobile form.

"Kell!" the Lancooti chastised, as he peered up at the massive ornate gates.

Looking up also, Kellen studied the odd structure, noting how the four armor-clad guards standing by the gates appeared so out of place in contrast to the sleepy village behind. Had he just believed this village was ordinary? *Bright stars . . .* The guards' armor gleamed in the morning light, a curious design stamped on their chest plate that matched the design on the gates and on the banding of their spears.

Karczag spoke to one of the guards, who glanced over the party then bowed before indicating the gates should be opened. The unusual gates swung inward soundlessly, revealing on the other side a wide paved road amid a mass of greenery and ferns.

It was such a difference—Sengold, this gate, and the forest beyond—that Kellen glanced back, mystified, before stepping under the archway and entering a tropical woodland.

When all the company had passed the four guards, the gates swung magically shut, blocking off all view of the village and lake beyond. Even the sounds from the village vanished, and they were suddenly surrounded by the hum of the forest, by bird noise, and insect buzz.

He walked forward in amazement and stared around wordlessly, liking the feel of this place. The airiness, the calmness, and tranquility of this forest. He turned to share his observations with Peleyia and found Tich standing beside him. Debating what to say, he attempted to give her a seductive smile. "Are you talking to me again?"

"Don't try and charm me."

"I'm not," he said with a snort, dropping the smile. He believed he was starting to understand her tactics, and debated ignoring her. He glanced ahead and was about to make another attempt at conversation, when he noticed something peculiar. In front, on the wide paved road, he could see Sasheer and Karczag walking side by side—both obviously lost in some discussion. What was strange was the creature—*or is it even an animal*—that walked next to Sasheer. The animal resembled a hunting cat, and Kellen wasn't even sure he was seeing right. He stared, watching how the cat's tail flicked. It looked to be wild, with dark, almost-burnt red fur, white paws, and black-tipped ears. Had to be wild, but then why was it walking next to Sasheer?

He turned to see if Tich had noticed and found that the others around him were staring curiously at the creature also. Salimen even had his crossbow loaded and aimed at the animal.

"Tich," Kellen said very slowly, his own hand creeping to the fine Drow blade at his side.

"Yes?" She looked at him and then frowned as her gaze followed his stare.

"What is that?" Kellen raised a finger and pointed at the creature. "It looks like one of those vicious moor cats."

"Do southerners always overreact?" she asked in mild exasperation as she reached over and pushed Salimen's crossbow down. "It's just a Shade."

"A Shade?" Salimen beat Kellen to the question as he edged closer. "What's a Shade?"

"You mean . . ." she trailed off, her eyes going first to Salimen then Kellen in a disbelieving glance. "You really don't know, do you?"

"No I . . . we don't," Kellen shook his head.

"All Mages from the old time . . . Sasheer really hasn't told you?" She peered closer at him, skepticism written clearly on her pretty face.

"Sasheer never tells me anything." Kellen assured her a little louder than necessary. In front of them, the Mage in question turned and scowled at him.

"Okay," Tich sighed, raising a hand to calm the situation and stifle her grin. "From what I know, I can tell you that any Mage who originated from Mitthsombaine has a Shade."

"That's not . . . a real animal, is it?" Salimen asked incredulously. "That's just another," he waved his arm disrespectfully in the direction of Sasheer, "another magical thingy that Sasheer does?"

Tich laughed, then covered her mouth as she saw Sasheer stop and start to walk back, those blue eyes clouding over in temper. Then Karczag was gripping his tunic and dragging him forward away from the group behind. "Let me see if I can explain," she offered.

"This should be good," Ryland muttered as Salimen snorted in agreement.

"Long ago in Mitthsombaine, all trainee Mages had to perform two tasks to qualify for a position in Mitthsombaine's wealthy, ruling society."

"You know or guess?" Salimen asked.

Tich glared at him. "Will you shut up, so I can explain?" she grumbled. "I read this, and if you had education in the south, you would know this also. If you prefer to ask Sasheer, then be my guest!" She lifted an arm and indicated that Salimen could go after the Mage.

Salimen bared his teeth, and Lesendal placed a hand on his chest. "Easy." Then he looked at Tich. "You explain it."

"I do know that none of the Brethren will willingly discuss Mitthsombaine. Not even to correct the history books," she said.

"Why?" Kellen asked, puzzled.

Tich sighed and dropped her arm, and Kellen saw Salimen glare at the Healer stubbornly. "I don't know, Kellen. All I know is that none of them will talk. All I know of Mitthsombaine is what is recorded in old manuscripts."

"So these old manuscripts say that trainee Mages had to perform two tasks—to achieve what?" Lesendal asked, bringing the Healer back on topic.

Sending the prince a grateful glance, Tich nodded. "To qualify, or leave their training halls, I assume. I don't know. During their academic training, they needed to first create a focus gem of rare value—"

"Oh, and we all know how that turned out! Don't we," Salimen said caustically.

"Sal," Lesendal growled then indicated for Tich to continue.

"The second task, and far more dangerous, was to create a shadow," she said.

"A shadow?" Kellen questioned. Ahead, both Karczag and Sasheer had stopped by a large tree, and it looked like Karczag was expressing something pointedly while Sasheer rubbed his temple. Off to one side stood Dalzere, looking bored. *He probably is bored . . .* Kellen mused. Then he turned his attention back on Tich.

"A shadow, or more commonly termed, Shade. A familiar," she clarified patiently. "In essence, all that means is that the Shade is a projection of the Mage's personality—a second pair of ears and eyes. It is a protection for them when sleeping, hunting, or casting spells, an extension of their egos."

"So Sasheer's ego is a moor cat?" Salimen asked incredulously, before he started to laugh. "Figures."

"No," Tich shook her head. "That image is what the Shade chooses to display. The Shade could choose any image, but usually they will choose to represent an animal that best helps them to blend in. Its real form is far more elemental."

"Elemental?" Kellen repeated, baffled.

Tich let out an exasperated breath and glanced around at the five men surrounding her. "Each Mage has his own strength within the elements. Their Shades represent those strengths. For instance, Sasheer's power is strongest in the element of fire, which goes a long way to explain his quick temper," she added. "His Shade mirrors that strength, so her color is that of fire. In her elemental form, she is even redder. And like her master, her temper is quick and hot, so I suggest you treat each and every Shade with respect."

"So they can think independently?" Lesendal asked.

"Yes." Tich nodded, relieved one of the southerners was taking her words seriously. "You know, I'm amazed that this is the first time you have seen her." She frowned. "You have all been traveling with Sasheer for months, and normally his Shade is very curious."

"Trust me, if it had appeared before, we would have noticed," Salimen answered. "So what about Karczag? Does he have one of these Shades?"

Tich pointed upward to the trees above, and they all craned their necks to see a ghost image floating above the high branches. "Karczag's strengths are in the air and light. His Shade is called Silver, and he enjoys taking the form of a wood owl, even in direct sunlight."

Kellen blinked up, seeing the owl and recognizing it as the one he had sensed on the moors. That entity was a . . . Shade? Then his mind stalled. *Could the evil entity be a Shade?* If so—then *who* among the Brethren was trying to kill him? Or maybe it was Kalern's Shade? But Kalern was not a Mage . . . and Kellen closed his eyes, confused.

"So why are we seeing them now?" Peleyia asked in a subdued voice as he stared upward. "Why have they both just appeared?"

"That's because we have passed the bespelled protection gates leading to Sanctuary," Tich answered. They continued to stare blankly at her, and she released another long breath. "Don't tell me, no one has explained what Sanctuary is?"

They each shook their heads.

"Don't you have any knowledge of the histories of Sennovia in the south?" she asked, shocked.

"In the Southland, we are taught to avoid contact with the nations across the White Sea," Salimen said.

"Then you are more primitive than I thought," she said, stopping five sets of protest by holding up her hands. "All right, I'll give you a brief rundown, as you'll probably need it. If you want to know more, then I suggest you take the time to visit the libraries in the Collegia," she advised. "Sanctuary was created by the twelve Mages after the Great War. It is a spell-protected area, designed to shelter the weak and deformed who escaped Mitthsombaine's cruel genetic-experimentation laboratories. None may enter the borders of Sanctuary except through the gates, and then those who enter will find their concealment spells stripped away. If visitors are at all uncomfortable with this, then they may leave before passing under the second gate, which is not far from here."

"What happens at the second gate?" Kellen asked, fascinated.

"It is a more powerful, bespelled area, warding against those with strong magics and ill intent. No cast spell will work past those gates. Any hint of Mage power will instantly alert the guards."

"Does it affect a Mage in any other way?" Kellen asked, curious, thinking of his own explosive feelings. Dwelling on that, he realized that he had not once felt out of control since arriving at the Keep. Maybe those exercises Sasheer had showed him were actually working.

"No," Tich shook her head. "There is a huge difference between being Mage Gifted and casting formulated spells. It is the same with my talent. I am a Healer; it is also a Gift. No Gifts are blocked, just formulated spells, the casting of spells and concealment spells are forbidden. As I said, it is a protection for the people who live here and who are sensitive to such displays of power."

Absorbing all that she said, Kellen looked again at the owl overhead and then at the slinky moor cat sitting obediently beside Sasheer. It had to be the same cat he had glimpsed in Kizer territory. Had she been scouting the land for Sasheer? "You said these Shades are intelligent," he said, getting the funny feeling that the cat was laughing at him.

"Extremely," Tich nodded. "I suggest you all stay away from them, for a while; they may be an extension of the Mage's persona; they also have the instincts of the creatures they choose to resemble."

"Point taken," Salimen muttered.

"So the owl is named Silver," Peleyia indicated the creature partly hidden by the branches above Karczag's head. "And the cat?"

"She is mischievous and should be called pest," Tich said with affection as she looked back at the animal in question. Its red gold eyes stared back unblinking. "But her name is Terrica."

Feeling his stomach sink into his boots, Kellen's jaw dropped as he stared at the creature in question. *Terrica!* No wonder she felt familiar. "Bright stars," he gasped in realization as another thought hit him hard. If Terrica was an extension of Sasheer's senses, then that would mean that, back in GarFamita, Sasheer would have been the one trying to warn him. It also would mean that the manipulative Mage would have known everything he was thinking and feeling right from the very beginning. *That bastard . . .*

* * *

Having left the second gate behind hours ago, the beautiful forest around them captivated Kellen as the road continued to wind upward. The trees were alive with birds, which sang and darted from treetop to treetop. Then as afternoon descended, the serenade of birdsong quieted. On evening, they rounded another corner and came to another set of ornate gates, only these ones were wide open in welcome.

Again guards greeted Karczag, Sasheer, and Tich warmly, ushering them all inside just as firelights were being lit around the town square. Kellen could see little of the township in the decreasing light, but what he did see looked inviting. The main square near the gates was cobbled, with gardens and a well in the center. Surrounding the gates on both sides were large dark-brick structures, with lanterns hanging over the doors and shutters on all the windows. On the far side of the square was an inn, and Kellen had to laugh when Ryland instinctively marched toward the establishment.

"I'll settle you all into the Hunters Inn for the night," Karczag said. "It is a comfortable place with good food and lots of ale. First thing in the morning, I'll call a council and invite Gralvin Broadhammer and his clan to attend. Until then, my friends, good night." Karczag backed away then stopped and called to Sasheer. "Would you accompany me to the Collegia?"

Being left alone, Kellen followed the others into the spacious inn, noting its cleanliness and homely scent. It made a change from the other inns he'd seen in Engleton. Ryland pulled a disgusted face.

"This is unnatural," the big man complained. "There must be something terribly wrong with their ale for a place to look this clean."

"Look on the bright side, my friend," Salimen advised, his smile firm. "You can go to bed sober for a change."

Ryland grunted.

Lesendal strolled up to them and grinned. "It seems we're expected." He gestured to the innkeeper. "Everything is on the house. Rooms are already prepared upstairs, and dinner will be ready within the hour."

"I think I could like this place," Salimen decided.

Feeling as if everything was sliding back into place with his friends, Kellen glanced around and found that Tich and Peleyia were missing. Curious, he went back to the main door and peered out into the darkening evening. But except for the few guards on the other side of the square, the town of Sanctuary was quiet. Unnaturally so.

"Kell?" a voice called from behind.

Leaving the main door, he went back into the room, seeing Salimen's questioning look. "I was just trying to find Peleyia," Kellen said.

"I'm sure he'll turn up," the bowman replied. "Now the innkeeper says we should get cleaned up before dinner. Are you coming?"

* * *

Halfway through dinner, both Healer and Lancooti returned. Tich looked happy, but Peleyia looked dissatisfied.

"What's wrong?" Kellen asked as the other man sat next to him, accepting the plate of hot food offered. Tich had declined to join them, going instead to speak with the old innkeeper.

"She won't tell me if she's going to allow me to continue on to Mitthsombaine," Peleyia said disheartened.

"Why? What did she find?"

"Nothing! Absolutely nothing."

"Okay," Kellen soothed, picking up his fork again. "Try and relax. I'm sure she'll let you go."

Peleyia stopped eating to look at his friend in speculation. "Kell, you could ask her for me."

"What makes you think she'd tell me," he asked.

"Because she likes you . . ." Peleyia left the rest unsaid as his smile widened into a grin.

Almost choking on his food, Kellen knew he was blushing, and he glared at his unrepentant friend. "I don't think so."

"'Course she does; that's why you both keep arguing about stupid things, and why she keeps looking this way now."

Hunching down more in his chair, Kellen tried to look everywhere but at the bar. Suddenly he was very aware of eyes on him. "Don't be ridiculous!"

"I'm not," Peleyia said then boldly waved to the Healer.

"Pel!" Kellen hissed, not believing his friend would do that.

"Sit up, Kell—she's looking again."

"Stop it!" Kellen said in a strangled voice.

"Surely you must have had girlfriends in Ihova?" the other asked teasingly as he saw the dark-haired man squirm.

"I—"

"Kell?"

"I never got around to it."

"Oh." Peleyia frowned, his smile vanishing, then he brightened again almost immediately. "I'll tell you what, after dinner, just go up to her and ask her to show you around town."

"At night?" Kellen asked in a shocked and slightly higher-pitched voice than normal.

"Best time," Peleyia wiggled his eyebrows in suggestion.

Feeling his cheeks burn, Kellen studiously avoided looking at his friend or at the bar. Even his food no longer appeared appetizing.

"Now behave, Kell, because here she comes," Peleyia whispered as he leaned closer.

Panicking, Kellen reached for his ale and knocked his glass over just as Tich stopped beside the table. The dark brew stained the tablecloth and splashed onto Tich's smock, and he made a clumsy grab for the glass before it rolled to the floor and smashed. Feeling like a fool, he chanced a look up and saw her delicate brow crease down in disapproval. "I'm sorry . . ." he stammered.

She ignored his words and fingered her smock. "I was going to say that if you like, I'll show you around the town."

Opening his mouth, Kellen realized no sound was coming out

as Peleyia nudged him hard in the ribs. "What? Now?" he croaked lamely.

"No, in the morning," she snapped, her frown returning in full.

Totally disgusted with himself, he sank back in his seat as Tich left the inn and Peleyia started to laugh. Then he became aware of the others all watching him in amusement, and he wanted nothing more than to be able to slip under the table in embarrassment and die.

CHAPTER TWENTY-NINE

Again Kellen had difficulty sleeping, despite how exhausted he felt. His mind kept going over everything Peleyia had said to him during dinner. Did Tich like him, or was the Lancooti only teasing? Could she like him? And wouldn't he have noticed by now if that were really the case? Maybe he should have just ignored Peleyia. Then again, maybe she *did* like him. And it was not as if he wasn't interested, because he was. She was different from the girls in Ihova, GarFamita, and Engleton, and certainly very different from Crizkerisomia. The white Elf both attracted and repulsed him, and he was very aware that the Elf only took an interest in him when Dalzere was present. So what did this all mean?

Tossing in the narrow bed, laying awake watching the first rays of dawn touch his small window, he found the butterflies in his stomach returned in full force. *What am I to do?*

By breakfast he had changed three times, tied and untied his hair, cursed, and vowed to get it cut short. So much had changed over the last half year, and it scared him to think about what could be happening back in the south. The foliage on the trees outside his window were turning a bronzed yellow, while back in Ihova, the trees would be covered in a light layer of winter snow. It was so easy to lose track of time. To forget.

Straightening, he glanced at his reflection in the polished silver, lifting a hand to feel his chin and wondered when he was going to get whiskers. But his face still felt smooth, and he recalled how, even after Wyran's nineteenth birthday, his brother still hadn't developed facial hair. Was he doomed to look like his brother? Then he remembered having never seen either Sasheer or Dalzere put a razor to their faces during the long journey from the Southland—or Peleyia, for that matter. Was it a trait of the Mage society? Of Elven society? But then how did that explain the Lancooti?

He snorted, dismissing the speculation, remembering that Karczag and Tanish both sported full beards. Maybe it was just vanity—or an age thing? He turned away from his reflection and took a deep breath, calming his erratic thoughts before leaving his room.

Outside the inn there were people everywhere, the open spaces full of wheeled tables as goods were sold and bartered, a teeming marketplace of activity. Even the cluster of shops next to the inn was busy. He glanced over at the buildings by the ornate gates and realized they were barracks surrounded by tall trees that blended into the forest behind. He stared around, captivated by the mix of cultures, colors, and races that seemed to coexist so peacefully in this mountaintop village.

"Did you sleep well?"

Startled by the question, he turned and found Tich watching him. Next to her were three other females, all similarly dressed as the Healer in silken britches and shimmering, soft overblouses.

"Very well, thank you," he replied politely, even as his heart sank. Tich was intending to show him around with a group of other friends; there went his fantasy and Peleyia's theory.

"Kellen, this is Natash, Liani, and Sariah. They are Healers like myself," Tich introduced.

Kellen nodded in respect to each young woman. "It's a pleasure."

"Tich has told us *so* much about you," the young lady dressed in a combination of soft greens said, her smile playful.

"Sariah!" Tich stood on her friend's foot.

"Don't be shy, Tich, as that is not like you. He's gorgeous," the Healer beside Sariah said. Her clothing also reflected the greens of the forest, the shine of the material changing as she moved.

"I can see it was a mistake to introduce you all," Tich informed them as her frown faltered. "Besides, he is from the Southland. Remember?"

"So?" The other Healer grinned.

"Liani," Tich warned.

"It's not forbidden to broaden our experience and taste a different fruit occasionally. Is it?" Liani countered.

"I don't believe you just said that," Tich breathed, shocked.

"Stop acting so modest," Natash snapped good-naturedly. "Take him around, and if you run out of things to show him, just call us."

Tich's eyes narrowed suspiciously. "What are you lot up to now?"

"Nothing," Sariah said innocently. "But I hear there are three more southerners at Hunters Inn. Grown men who are far from home."

"And hopefully lonely," Liani finished, giggling.

Watching them hurry away laughing, Kellen was not sure what to make of them, his senses tantalized by the clothing they wore, especially by the pale yellow smock Tich was wearing. He cleared his throat and tried to look unaffected.

"I tried to warn you about my friends at the Keep."

"I remember, vaguely," he said.

"So would you like a tour?"

"I'd be delighted."

"Good." Holding out her hand, she lifted a brow in silent question, challenging him to deny her.

Hesitating only briefly, Kellen took her hand, feeling her warmth and sensing her smile, as her light brown eyes sparkled in pleasure.

"Let me show you the markets first and then the Collegia."

* * *

Sitting down on an old stone bench in the gardens behind the huge Collegia, Kellen was amazed by all the different races that lived, or had lived, inside the borders of Sanctuary. Each race was represented on a huge tapestry in the foyer of the Collegia, as a tribute to all who had survived the Great War of the four lands. It was a history, honoring those who had died, honoring those who had been shunned because of their deformities. Some of the genetic mutations still existed, proof enough of the reason why Lichien and Kalern could not be allowed to keep the Book of Spells.

Having learned more than he wanted to admit, Kellen let his gaze travel around the massive gardens, seeing numerous groups of people gathered under the shade trees. "Thank you for showing me around," he said sincerely, having enjoyed Tich's company. Regardless of what Peleyia had hinted at last night, he had found the tour enlightening, despite the fact that he had sacrificed breakfast for it.

"I enjoyed it also," Tich said, none of her usual bite behind the words.

Taking a gamble, Kellen asked a question that had been plaguing him all morning. "Do you know much about this war between the Brethren and Kalern?" he asked, believing that with her knowledge of history, she could give him an unbiased answer.

"Oh my. What a way to start a new conversation," Tich smiled.

"All this," he gestured around, searching for the right words. "All this was built because of what Mitthsombaine did to innocent people. The Brethren guard this place, from what you have told me. So Kalern must know what you do here. This stone must know."

"I know that Kalern is evil, and that he must be stopped from getting control over the four lands. And I know that the Watchers, the Brethren, are diminishing in number. That eventually even they will fail, will be hunted and killed, and then we will be defenseless against Kalern and Lichien's manipulations."

"Even here?" Kellen asked.

"Even here," Tich said. "For without Karczag's influence, without any of the Brethren's help, the protection spells will fail, and all who shelter here will be vulnerable."

"So Kalern has to be stopped," Kellen said more to himself than to his companion, recalling Ryland's passionate words to the contrary. "And Jorean."

"Jorean?" Tich questioned.

"Oh, he was just the figurehead of Kalern's forces in the Southland," Kellen explained as his mind worked over the facts.

"I hear that the south is almost certainly lost," she said, leaning forward to watch his face. "I'm sorry."

"Maybe it can still be saved," he said, praying that were true. "If Sasheer can destroy Lichien, then Jorean's power and influence will fail. The Deathwalkers will disintegrate."

"Deathwalkers?" Tich repeated, horrified. "They have been used in the Southland already?"

"Oh yes," Kellen assured her. "I think they must be like these Raveners I keep hearing about."

"No, they are two different things," she said.

"In what way?"

Tich looked at him for a long moment then sighed. "The Deathwalkers are reanimated corpses who are impervious to any sort of pain or injury. They are already dead. Kalern uses them because the sight of a dead loved one demoralizes people."

"Yes, I've witnessed their effect on warriors," Kellen whispered, remembering all too clearly the campsite in the Ihovian Mountains.

"The Raveners are living, mutated Drow."

"Drow?"

"They are the ones from Mitthsombaine. They are some of the first abominations created by the Coastal Mages, altered by hideous experimentations, which mutated the genetically created Drow, making them living wraiths. They are neither living nor dead. Nothing can kill them, and just a single touch can drain a full-grown warrior of his life's energies. They smell a living soul from over a league away. And it is said that they become frenzied when they devour their victims."

"Nice," Kellen muttered, just suppressing a shudder. "So that's why Sasheer is so adamant that we find this Oracle in the tomb below Mitthsombaine."

"Without it, he will never get into North Ridge. Legend says that the Oracle is the only thing which can deceive a Ravener's senses," Tich said.

"He's dead either way, according to the council," Kellen

reminded her sourly. That was still an issue he hoped could be avoided.

"Yes," she said, "I know. But at least he is doing something. Not like the other Brethren who are too frightened to face Lichien a second time."

Hearing the disquiet behind her words, Kellen, paused as another elusive piece of the puzzle slid into place. "They've tried before to destroy Lichien?"

"Yes, and failed. But you won't find that in the history books. Actually, you'll find very little in the history books."

Kellen frowned over that. "Why is that?"

"I really don't know," Tich frowned. "It is just the way things are. No one asks. All respect Karczag's silence," she shrugged. "I suppose none of it is recorded because we still have six of the original founding Mages alive. They are the living history. When they are gone, then it will be recorded."

"But how can you record something if you don't know the truth?"

Tich sent Kellen an amused smile. "You are starting to sound like Sasheer."

Kellen snorted, not sure if that was a compliment or insult. "So tell me, how is it you know so much if it is not recorded in the history books?"

"I grew up in the Keep. I heard things as a child."

"You're Karczag's daughter?" Kellen asked.

Tich looked at him, stunned, then laughed. "Of course not. Whatever gave you that idea?"

"Oh . . . I just assumed."

"Well, you assumed wrong," she said, still smiling.

Enjoying the sight of her smile, he grinned back. She no longer resembled the scowling, sword-wielding woman of the forest; now she looked approachable and sexy. "I have to leave in a day or so . . ." he said softly.

"I know. If you don't retrieve the Book of Spells then Lichien will eventually send his Raveners to the Keep. Then when that is destroyed, they will violate Sanctuary, destroy all our defenses, kill the forests before crippling the four lands."

For the first time, Kellen realized how serious the threat was—how deadly—and he shook his head in dismay. Ryland, Lesendal, and Salimen's objectives faded into nothing compared to the bigger picture. Lichien would unleash madness and death on them all, would trample the other races and finish what evil Mitthsombaine had started four thousand years ago. It would create a slave world, full of horrors and darkness and ugliness. He could not let that happen, and for the first time, he understood Sasheer's desperation. "Sasheer—"

"What about Sasheer?" Tich asked as she leaned closer.

Not realizing he had said the name out loud, Kellen coughed then decided to ask his question anyway. "Do you know much about him?"

"Like what?" Tich asked.

"Like—does he return here often?"

"In that respect, I suppose he is like Seaton," Tich replied. She saw Kellen's instant puzzlement and explained. "Seaton was the fair-haired Mage at the council," she said. "The one not dressed in formal robes," she added and saw Kellen nod. "Seaton spends most of his time north, watching Kalern's movements and assisting the Dwarven Clans, while Sasheer has attached himself to the south for much the same reason."

"And his twin?"

"What?"

"What happened to Sasheer's twin?" Kellen had to ask.

"Serine," Tich breathed the name in soft reverence. She closed her eyes. "He is only a . . . memory."

Kellen stared at Tich, trying to understand her meaning. He knew the Mage was dead, but from everything that had been half-said and whispered about the man, he had assumed that Serine's death was a recent thing. "A memory?" he prompted. "How long ago did he die?"

"Three and a half thousand years ago," Tich breathed, opening her eyes to meet Kellen's shocked gaze. "Don't ask me how, because I don't know. All I know is that he was the fifth Mageborn to die, and that he died at Kalern's hands when he tried to destroy Lichien. It was somehow linked to an ancient prophecy."

Prophecy, there was that word again, and Kellen recalled Sasheer's haunting words in his mind—*I have seen a lot of your bloodline die because they believed they were the instruments of this prophecy.* He blinked, wondering if Serine had taken one of the bloodline to face Lichien and Kalern. Or had Serine's attack been more personal, like what Sasheer was attempting now?

"If you want to know more, then you should ask Tanish," Tich suggested.

Shaking off the strange memories, Kellen refocused on Tich's pretty face. "Why Tanish?" he asked, fascinated.

Glancing around, Tich made sure they were far enough away from other collegia students. "It is rumored," she whispered, "that Tanish went after both brothers when he learned of Serine's plan to destroy Lichien. But he only managed to bring Sasheer back alive."

"I wonder what happened," Kellen murmured.

"I don't know."

"Did Sasheer try to confront Lichien and Kalern?" he asked, looking at Tich, wishing he could read people like Peleyia could. "Did he fail because of his brother?" Was that why Sasheer was so determined to face Lichien now?

"None who have faced Lichien have survived," Tich breathed the words so softly that they barely carried. "None, Kellen." She licked her lips nervously. "Whatever you do, promise me you will not bring the subject up with Sasheer." She pinned him earnestly with her gaze.

His frown deepened. *None . . .* So Sasheer had never faced Lichien. "Why?" he asked slowly.

"The last trainee who questioned Sasheer about his twin, died messily."

Shocked, he could not help but ask, "Was that, by any chance, Aquiletta?"

"Yes. How did you know that?"

"Oh, just a lucky guess," he replied flatly. "Tich, what else should I know before embarking on this journey to old Mitthsombaine?"

"I don't know," she took a deep breath then grinned at him in appeal. "But I'm thinking that if you kiss me, I'll escort you to the council chambers for the meeting Karczag has organized."

Abruptly, all thoughts of Raveners, death, and ancient prophecy vanished from his mind, and Kellen found his eyes were instantly homing in on Tich's moist, kissable lips. His heart hammered in his chest as he leaned closer to her tempting form. Even his stomach stopped growling, and he decided he could definitely do without lunch.

* * *

After the council meeting, at which it had been decided that Gralvin Broadhammer would accompany the group to the old ruins, the party met once more inside the Hunters Inn for dinner.

"This is just unnatural," Ryland mumbled again while he watched the sedate drinkers sit around the bar.

"What's unnatural?" Salimen asked. He stretched back and relaxed, enjoying his ale.

"No inn should be this peaceful," Ryland said sourly. "There should be fights, arguments, loud conversation, and drunken behavior."

"A bit of blood splattered on the walls as bodies fly through windows," Salimen mocked.

Glaring at the blond Ihovian, Ryland looked over toward Lesendal. "Can I hit him?"

"It won't do any good," the prince said, "in fact, I think he enjoys it."

"Gentlemen, please," Sasheer stressed, his blue eyes darkening in irritation. "Show some courtesy," he then gestured Karczag and Gralvin over to their long table. "We have to decide our route east."

"Horses," Gralvin said gruffly even before he sat down. The Dwarf glanced around at the faces staring back at him. "I'm not walking all the way to Sunset Ridge, so we need horses."

"We could buy some from Lord Cohlen at Crystal Gaze Castle," Dalzere suggested. "Apparently the plains of Maltros are plagued by wild herds."

"Maybe so, Drow, but I hear all is not well in the peaks of Crystal Gaze," Gralvin cut back.

Lifting a brow, Dalzere turned to Karczag.

"It has been rumored that Rock Trolls have moved into the ranges bordering the castle," Karczag said. "Last we heard from Lord Cohlen was at the beginning of autumn. A fever had broken out in his subjects, and he needed medical supplies. He needed them urgently as he was planning to remarry before winter."

"Remarry? Again? At his age?" Sasheer asked, aghast.

Karczag ignored him. "Now that I think about it, we have not received word since we sent the supplies. But with all that has been happening within the Keep, I may have missed the messenger."

"Nothing came back," Gralvin said bluntly. "He either got the supplies and has been too occupied with his new bride to notify you, or the Rock Trolls intercepted the shipment." The Dwarf took a healthy swig of his beer. "Or the trolls got your messenger." Gralvin belched. "Either way, no message came back."

"Then we should check," Dalzere said.

Karczag rubbed his beard and nodded. "I think I'll send along a contingent of guards with you to Crystal Gaze, plus more medical supplies and a Healer, just in case those shipments never made it through." He looked at Sasheer. "Just send the guards and Healer back if everything is all right."

Nodding, Sasheer glanced around the silent group. "Any questions?"

"How far is this castle?" Lesendal asked.

"About a week's march," Gralvin answered for Sasheer. "It borders the eastern wastelands."

"Sounds inviting," Salimen muttered.

"That's the easy part. From there, it's a two-month ride across grasslands and desert, Blondie," Gralvin told the Ihovian bowman. "If our mounts survive the ride, then we'll enter the old Pass of Deceit which lies beyond Sunset Ridge and rings Deception Cove.

Then we are within the influence of the decaying ruins of Mitthsombaine." He belched again. "That's if we make it that far."

"I can't wait," Salimen said from between his teeth, his glare never leaving the Dwarf's hairy features.

"Which reminds me," Sasheer interrupted. He placed a hand on Salimen's shoulder to settle him, and glanced over at the unusually silent Lancooti. "Peleyia, Tich has given you leave to accompany us to the castle. Then, depending on the Healer's judgment, you will either stay on at the castle and assist Lord Cohlen, or return to Sanctuary."

"I'll be fine," Peleyia stated.

"Wait until you see the gorges and then decide." Gralvin grinned at the Lancooti before calling out loudly for another ale.

* * *

Kellen said nothing until after the party broke up. He sat next to Peleyia and was as dumbfounded as his friend over Sasheer's attitude. He could not understand why Sasheer was so reluctant to have Peleyia accompany them east.

"I'm going to bed," Peleyia said before he stood up. He sent a hard glare Sasheer's way then leant down and wished the other good night. "See you in the morning, Kell."

Nodding his good night, Kellen just continued to sit there, watching all the different members of the group slowly get up and depart for their beds. Only the dwarf remained with the two Mages. The three of them were sitting by the open fire drinking ale.

Studying Gralvin, Kellen was not sure if he liked the Dwarf. The man's disposition was gruff to say the least, even Salimen was riled, which was unusual for the bowman. The Dwarf was short and thickset, with curly hair covering his head, face, and forearms. His clothing was a mix of leathers, metal, and wool, and a heavy, short-handled pickaxe hung from his wide belt. His stance was confident, and Kellen was left with little doubt that his man could look after himself in a fight.

Disgruntled, he threw off his moody thoughts and pushed his glass aside, deciding to go to bed. He wondered if he would see Tich before he left, or if she would even want to see him again.

"Why so sad?"

It was a friendly voice at his side, and Kellen glanced up, meeting Karczag's wide, assessing gaze. So far he had been adept at avoiding the older Mage.

"I'm tired," he covered his surprise.

"May I sit and talk with you a while?"

Lifting a hand, Kellen gestured to the seat across from him, as a nervous panic started in his gut. *Where is Dalzere when I need him?*

"I know Tanish has spoken to you, so I assume you understand that we need you to survive and come back to the Keep. Alive."

"Yes," Kellen nodded.

"So I am asking you now to heed all that Sasheer and Dalzere tell you. That when you arrive in old Mitthsombaine, no matter how exciting the adventure may seem, you must return with Gralvin to Sanctuary." Karczag pinned him with his icy blue eyes. "Do you understand?"

"You don't want me entering North Ridge," Kellen said dutifully. He had already heard this from Sasheer and had told the man his feelings on the subject.

"For good reason, Kellen."

"Because I am the last of the line—"

"No, more importantly, because you have not been trained," Karczag corrected softly, his eyes kind. "Training takes years."

He had not expected this, and Kellen just stared at Karczag, thinking that the old Mage wasn't that frightening.

"There will be more than just you returning to Sanctuary. Hopefully all will return, except Sasheer and Dalzere."

Knowing that was the plan, Kellen nodded. He lifted his lashes and carefully studied the man across from him. "Is it true that Sasheer will die if he tries to destroy Lichien?"

"Yes," Karczag's tone was grave. "In the instant, he casts the spell to defragment the bindings holding Lichien together, he will be vulnerable to the backlash of energies released. It will destroy them both."

Biting his lip in thought, Kellen frowned. "There must be another way."

"I have searched for another way for over three thousand years. Unfortunately, it is the nature of the spell."

"But won't Kalern—or Lichien—know this?" Kellen asked, remembering what Tich had told him—*that none who had faced Lichien had survived.* "Won't Lichien have a defense against this spell?"

"We created Lichien in our own misguided stupidity, and only we can destroy it. It has no protection against us, except to kill us one by one before one of us manages to get close enough and formulate the spell. It knows. We know."

"All that have faced Lichien have died," Kellen repeated the words, watching Karczag and noting how the Mage showed no surprise at his recital. "How many have tried, and how many have died by accident like, Cornithia?"

"Lichien sent Kalern to intercept them all. None, but one, of my brothers has ever made it into Lichien's presence," Karczag said, his tone reflecting his sadness and regret. "This time Sasheer will have the Oracle, and he will have an advantage. This time we have a chance."

A chance . . . and Kellen looked away from Karczag's concerned face. They had a chance to right a wrong, yet no matter what the outcome, Sasheer would die. Troubled by that, Kellen frowned, not sure what to say. Then something else occurred to him. "What about Peleyia?"

Puzzled by the question, Karczag raised a dubious brow. "What about him?"

"Why is Sasheer doing everything possible to stop Peleyia from traveling east with us?" Kellen asked. "Is he really that ill?"

Releasing a breath, Karczag rubbed his clipped beard. "No. I would hazard a guess and say that it is because Sasheer has *seen* something which bothers him."

"Seen something?" Kellen began, confused. "Like what?"

"Like others in his family line, Sasheer is Gifted with Foresight. I believe it is an unsettling Gift."

Feeling his jaw slacken, Kellen suddenly understood and realized that Sasheer was trying to protect the Lancooti rather than victimize. Only Sasheer had little tact. "Then we have to stop Pel from going."

"Leave it, Kellen," Karczag advised, a touch of steel entering his tone. "You must not interfere. It is the Lancooti's choice."

"But—" Kellen objected.

"No. You must never interfere in matters like this."

CHAPTER THIRTY

They left the peaceful city of Sanctuary and traveled through the tranquil woodlands to exit via a different gate, north of Sengold. That gate had led to similar pine forests, which bordered grasslands, and their progress was steady.

Gralvin, and the four guards who accompanied them from Sanctuary, took the lead as they exited the grassy slopes two days later. The Dwarf guided them down into a series of small valleys and foothills until their path became sparse and rocky. From there, the trees became fewer, and the reedy streams all but disappeared. What water they found was bitter, and at night, the temperature would drop, reminding them all that winter was fast approaching. Each day the countryside grew bleaker until they no longer saw trees or grass, but past into the drab brownness of rock and crumbling sandstone platforms.

All in the party viewed the new surroundings with wary apprehension, Salimen grumbling the loudest about the continuous cold. He would reminisce about Ihova, about how beautiful the forest would be now that summer would be touching the Southland. The reminder had brought a dazed look to Lesendal and Ryland's eyes, and Kellen had felt a pang of homesickness—until he had remembered that the small isolated kingdom of Ihova had not even been his place of birth. He had no home, no family, and no future.

* * *

By the ninth day after leaving Sanctuary, Kellen was willing to believe that things could not get any bleaker. It was early afternoon, and he squinted up at the sun, trying not to think about Ihova and his complex life.

Gralvin led the company, guiding them through a huge valley of colored sandstone and unstable ledges. It was beautiful in a bleak way, but dangerous, and Kellen breathed out deeply, wishing for the simple pleasure of just resting under the shade of a tree. But they hadn't seen a tree in days, or tasted sweet springwater, and he was starting to hate this barren, desolate land.

He glanced ahead and saw Sasheer. The Ranger seemed unconcerned about what fate awaited him at the end of this journey, and he started to think Sasheer felt nothing at all, not even fear of death, and then he reminded himself how old Sasheer really was. That had to account for the Mage's jaded attitude.

Thinking on what Tanish had told him about old Mitthsombaine, he tried to speculate on what Sasheer's life might have been like, the magnificence, the decadence, the horrors, the hardships, and the wars. He thought about the anguish and pain Sasheer must have endured over the last four thousand years as he watched friends, lovers, and family die; the haunted memories he must have of races and cultures long gone; and the fear of watching new societies crumble. *No wonder the man is neurotic and bad tempered*, Kellen decided. Yet now, Sasheer was willing to sacrifice all that, all his knowledge, his very life to save the people of the four lands. A people who would never thank him, or even know him, or even understand why he died. That puzzled Kellen, and he shook his head in wonder, admitting that Sasheer's determination—his capacity for love and hate—was staggering.

Startled by this new perspective, he glanced up a second time at the impossibly young-looking Mage. There was so much more to Sasheer than he first believed, and he started to understand Dalzere's loyalty. If a Drow Elf could change and learn to embrace life through association with Sasheer, then what could he learn from Sasheer? Silently, he vowed to try and suspend some of his mistrust concerning the Mage. Instead, he decided to turn his mind to the problem of finding another way to destroy Lichien without risking Sasheer's life.

Releasing another deep breath, Kellen pushed the puzzling thoughts aside and looked around at the barren valley and wide gorges ahead. They were surrounded on both sides by tall peaks as one desolate valley led into the next. According to Gralvin, this was the only route to Crystal Gaze Mountain.

His mood mirrored the depressing wilderness, and he glanced back at Peleyia. That was another dilemma weighing on his mind, and he turned away before the Lancooti caught him staring. Did he want to believe in Foresight? But then he would not have believed in the currents if he hadn't experienced them. Nor in the Lexsii, or the magic of the Keep unless he had seen it. Or in the mystical Shades. He frowned, knowing deep down that what Karczag had said was truth, but he didn't want to believe it. So was Peleyia fated to die?

Not if I can help it, he vowed, making a fist and studying his white knuckles. So all he had to do was prevent Fate from taking Peleyia, and save Sasheer. *Easy . . .* and he swallowed his nervous bubble of laughter. *Obviously insanity is hereditary*, he mused. He just had to look at his legendary, numerously great, grandfather who had defined the term 'insane.' He was as mad as Aserties.

He released a tense breath and tried not to think about Aserties, about Kalern, about all the others who had died—rather he squinted around at his desolate surroundings, allowing his eyes to fall on Tich. She plagued his mind as well and made him uncomfortable, in a different way.

To make matters worse, she had volunteered to accompany the group to Crystal Gaze Castle. Her presence made him nervous, which she misread as uncommunicative—causing them to argue sporadically for five days straight before Dalzere had purposely separated them. The fact that Dalzere had interfered puzzled him, because he would have expected Sasheer to chastise them. But the Mage kept silent.

So now, on the ninth day after leaving Sanctuary, Kellen found himself walking behind Tich for the first time in two days. She was purposely ignoring him, and he scowled at her, rubbing his nose and wondering what the scent was that kept wafting past his nose. It was sweet—*a sweet, addictive scent of flowers and spice*—and eventually he narrowed it down to the ties in her hair. Hating the awkward silence, he decided to offer an apology. He quickened his pace until he was beside her. "I'm sorry I snapped at you." There, he'd said it.

"And I'm sorry I shouted at you," she replied after a strained moment then glared at him from under her lashes. "I don't understand you at times."

"I don't understand me either," he offered as inoffensively as possible.

"I thought you would have been happy to have me along on this trip."

"I am," Kellen defended, wondering if they were going to start the same argument yet again. Why his life had turned so complicated after just one kiss, he would never comprehend.

"You sure don't show it."

"I've just got a lot on my mind."

"Oh, please, don't start with that Peleyia nonsense again," she said, her voice rising an octave. "That's all you've talked about for the last week!"

Kellen tried to sound reasonable. "But it bothers me." He sucked in a resigned breath when he saw Dalzere turn to eye them both.

"I am the Healer, Kellen, you should let me decide if Peleyia is fit to travel. As far as I'm concerned, unless he falls down a gully and breaks his neck, he's healthy enough to go with Sasheer," she said, lifting her chin determinedly.

Rubbing his eyes, Kellen debated saying more then thought better of it—but Tich continued, only warming to her theme.

"What is your problem, Kellen? I thought you liked girls."

"I do," he said, chancing a look at her doubtful face. "I do, Tich. I like you—very much—I just heard something in Sanctuary which concerns me."

A little appeased, Tich reached out and took his hand, squeezing his fingers. "So let's talk about something else," she suggested.

"Something completely different, like where you think you might be living when you return from Mitthsombaine."

Frowning, Kellen barely heard her words as he caught Dalzere's warning scowl. *Why is Dalzere so annoyed?* It was so unlike the Elf.

"Kellen?"

He felt her squeeze his fingers harder than necessary, and he looked at Tich, seeing her displeasure. Obviously she hated to be ignored. "What do you know of Dalzere?" he asked instead.

"Dalzere?" Tich repeated, frowning. "When did we start talking about him?"

"He keeps glaring at me."

"Just ignore him," she said. "Like I do."

"Were you told what happened to us after we crossed the White Sea?" he decided to try a different angle. His eyes touched Dalzere briefly before he centered his attention on Tich, giving her a charming smile. It worked, as he saw her relax.

"No," her tone dubious.

"We landed in Kizer territory and were ambushed by the Kizer-Horigan tribe. They are a vicious faction in their society," Kellen explained, refusing to drop the topic.

"Really?" Tich said, uninterested.

"They set a trap. I think they were hunting for Dalzere specifically." He licked his lips in thought, slowing his pace and forcing Tich to slow with him, so that Dalzere moved out of earshot. He prayed the Drow's hearing was not as good as Sasheer's. "Would you know why?" he asked, sensing Tich's discomfort with the question.

"How could I? I wasn't there."

"But you still know, don't you?" he pushed, seeing how Tich avoided his eyes. "Please, Tich."

"Dalzere does not like to talk about personal things," she evaded.

"You've known him a long time, haven't you?"

"Yes," she said, stepping off the path when Salimen and Lesendal approached. The Ihovians sent them a curious glance but kept walking.

"The Kizer were hunting him, weren't they?" Kellen pushed.

"It's a long story," Tich said and then tried to walk away.

Kellen refused to release her hand, pulling her back. "Tell me," he pressed.

Ryland stopped behind them and coughed. "Pick up the pace, you two. I, for one, do not want to spend one minute longer out here than I need to," he grumbled. "And keep your eyes open. The guards think the Rock Trolls may try to set a trap."

Kellen kept his hold on Tich and started them walking. "Talk to me."

"Kell," she sighed.

He was manipulating her he knew, by leaning in close as he spoke, and squeezing her hand. He wondered if she was aware of the manipulation. "I saw what they did to him," he said, coaxing her. "Now I need to know why."

"Are you always this persistent?" she asked, not quite covering her exasperation.

"Always," he assured her. Then he grinned again.

"You are so . . . bad," she paused then glanced over at Dalzere in slight apprehension. "It was a long time ago. Before I was born—but I think he must have been scouting the area when he was captured by one of the Kizer factions and given to the witch."

"Go on," Kellen encouraged.

"Because he was Drow, the witch believed—I'm not sure—but I think she believed that in sacrificing him to their demon in some barbaric, erotic ritual that they would gain victory over the other tribes," Tich said in a rush. "The Kizer have very complex beliefs."

"What sort of ritual?" Kellen asked, remembering how ugly and how haggard the Kizer witch had appeared, how she had taunted Dalzere before inviting the demon into her body.

Tich gave a short laugh. "If you use your imagination, I'm sure you can come up with the type of erotic rituals I'm talking about."

"Oh . . ." Kellen felt himself blush. *Those type of rituals*, and he remembered how Dalzere had warned him of the Kizers' perversion on the *May Queen*. So the Drow had been speaking from experience. "So what happened?"

"Sasheer got him out," Tich said. "End of story."

"There has to be more." He gazed into her eyes and saw her relent.

"After Dalzere healed, he went back into Kizer territory and butchered most of the tribe."

"He—what?" Kellen asked in disbelief.

"You asked," Tich warned.

"I know, but—"

Tich cut him off and held his gaze. "But nothing. Don't judge, Kell. You weren't there. It was a long time ago."

Understanding that, but wanting to know more, Kellen nevertheless kept his questions to himself. He could feel Tich scowling at him, and he nodded, wordlessly promising to drop the subject and was rewarded a moment later with her pleased little smile. It was a beautiful smile, until she frowned. "Tich?"

"Did you hear that?" she asked. She released his hand and let her fingers stray to the hilt of her short blade.

Alerted by her action, Kellen also reached for his sword as he saw two of the six guards draw their weapons.

"Rock Trolls!"

Kellen heard Gralvin hiss the words from behind before the stocky Dwarf pushed past him.

"Tich, come on." Kellen held out his hand and urged her forward. Behind him, Ryland and two guards protected the trail.

"Typical," Gralvin muttered. He squatted down next to Lesendal, Crizkerisomia, and Salimen. "They always attack on sunset. Unimaginative bastards." He gestured to the crumbling sandstone that surrounded them. "This sort of barren valley would suit them perfectly." He drew a rough map in the dirt. "We are here, and the road leading up to the castle is here."

"So we need to get around here," Salimen mused, tracing a finger over the route.

"Can't do, Blondie." Gralvin shook his head. "The only safe path is this one."

"So we fight," Crizkerisomia said in a deadly whisper.

"That would be my advice," Gralvin agreed. He glanced up at Sasheer. "We'll need a scout," he said, and Sasheer nodded.

Closing his eyes, Sasheer concentrated for a second, and a ruddy mountain cat appeared on the ledge above him. Terrica. The cat's coloring blended in with the surroundings of red brown stone, and she crouched, her ears back, teeth bared before she looked down at Sasheer with golden eyes. "Rock Trolls, love, you know what to do," Sasheer said softly.

With only a flicker of her tail, she was gone, bounding off up a steep ridge and disappearing from sight.

"Is that wise?" Ryland asked. He frowned then stared at Sasheer.

"She will buy us time," Sasheer shrugged. He then looked toward the horizon. "We have only a short while before it gets dark."

"Will Terrica be all right?" Salimen asked even as Lesendal stared after the animal, bemused.

"She'll be fine," Sasheer assured. "Dalzere, check the trail behind. Criz, can you scout ahead?"

Both Elves complied without a sound, going in their separate directions.

"I see you still need to keep them apart," Gralvin quipped, walking up to Sasheer. "You should just let them fight it out. Let them clear the air, so you can sleep at night."

Sasheer ignored the comment and got them all moving forward with the Sanctuary guards leading the way. Crizkerisomia's warning call when it came gave them only a small advantage. Sasheer stepped back and indicated he wanted both Kellen and Tich behind him.

Abruptly, on the ridge above, dark, deformed shapes appeared, huge shapes that defied belief that blended in perfectly with the desolate area. Rock Trolls. Their faces were hidden in shadow as the trolls loomed over the company. The silence held for a prolonged moment, and then one Troll gave a barked cry and as a group, the trolls jumped from the ledges.

Drawing his Drow blade, Kellen gave no thought to his own safety, charging from behind Sasheer and attacking the nearest Rock Troll he could find. He stabbed at the creature, finding the point of his blade deflecting away as it bounced off hard flesh.

"What the—" Kellen was given no chance to try a second lunge as a thick arm swung down and backhanded him across the face. He was thrown backward, catching a glimpse of Lesendal's sprawled form next to him before Salimen loosed a rapid volley of arrows. Wiping his mouth, Kellen tasted blood, and he grinned.

Gralvin seemed to have the right idea as he chopped the legs out from under his Troll, bringing a shout of triumph from the guards as one massive creature tumbled to the ground. The guards followed his example.

"Go for the legs," Salimen spat as he ducked a vicious swing from one Troll. He discarded his crossbow, and drew his short blade.

Getting up, Kellen drew his dagger also, feeling Lesendal at his back. Another of the giants approached them. Behind him, he heard Sasheer murmur some incantation, then the gloom lit up briefly, and one Troll ignited. Flames blanketed the screaming creature, and it staggered away in fear and panic.

That seemed to unsettle the Trolls, and the travelers pushed their advantage. Peleyia leapt from a high rock to straddle one troll and start to hack at the monster's neck with his blade. Seeing the giant reach back to seize the Lancooti, Kellen knew a moment of utter fear, wondering if this was what Sasheer had seen, but Dalzere stepped in and joined forces with Salimen to bring the Troll down.

"Watch your head, Kellen," Lesendal snapped as he blocked one Troll's lunging advance. Helping the prince, Kellen stabbed at the Troll's legs with his knife, thinking how useless his sword was when the big Troll's foot just crushed everything in sight. Then the creature was stamping after him, forcing him to scramble away. Ducking behind a boulder, Kellen gasped as the giant's foot crashed down beside his head, showering him with rocks and dirt. He clamped his eyes shut, stretched forth his hand in protection, and felt the familiar swirl of invisible currents dance between his fingers. That gave him a moment's pause, and he lifted his head to stare at his hand. This was the first time he had felt the currents since leaving the forest around Sanctuary, and he purposely gathered them toward him. They came readily, sliding up his arm and starting a tingle deep in his chest.

He could not believe how easy it was, and he glanced up to find the massive Troll snarling at him. Then the creature picked up a huge rock and hurled it at him. Diving behind another rock, Kellen felt the force of the boulder hit the ground to his left, and he scrambled to his feet.

Down in the gully, he saw Peleyia thrown to the ground, saw how his friend lay unconscious in the dust as one large Troll raised a bolder to crush the Lancooti.

No . . . urgently Kellen glanced around but saw Salimen and Lesendal struggle to aid Dalzere—saw Sasheer ignite another Rock Troll. The brief flare of fire was blinding, and he turned away and saw Crizkerisomia and Gralvin were also occupied. No one was aware of Peleyia's danger.

"No!" Kellen hissed, letting his fear surface, and he dragged in the currents, gasping in shock as he was filled with unbelievable raw energy. It heated his body, tickled his nerves, and he struggled to contain his panic. He had to hold it, had to control it, and he focused his eyes on the Troll who was standing over Peleyia. He felt charged with so much energy and raised a hand before baring his teeth, challenging the Troll, "Come on! Fight me! Come to me!"

The Troll turned sluggishly, as if drawn against its will to face him, and then it was rushing toward him, unbelievably fast. It shoved him back with one hand and pinned him to a sandstone wall. Dirt and dust enveloped him, and Kellen exhaled in shock. He gripped the Troll's cold fingers, which pressed into his chest, and focused all his wavering attention on the massive body before him. Surprisingly, he felt little pain, felt little of anything as he concentrated on channeling the energy of the currents into the Troll.

Nothing seemed to work for a frightening moment, and then the Troll's eyes widened. Heat burst out of Kellen's hand and sliced into the Troll's toughened flesh. The Troll's skin reddened, and the monster's lips peeled back in pain before the creature let out an anguished cry. The heat intensified, turning the Troll's body a molten red, and within a heartbeat, Kellen was blasted with hot fragments of dust and stone as the Troll disintegrated into nothing.

Stunned, Kellen staggered forward, then fell to the ground. His surroundings blurred and sound distorted, and the last thing he saw was a really strange view of Sasheer's feet, then the pain deep inside his mind blinded him to all else. Vaguely, in the background, he could hear trumpets, but they were drowned out by his own erratic heartbeat, as blackness descended like a curtain, and he lost consciousness.

CHAPTER THIRTY-ONE

"Kell . . . Kellen . . . Kellen?"

A soft, coaxing voice intruded into his pain-filled mind, and he forced his heavy eyes open only to see the blurred image of Tich's smiling face.

"Kell?"

He opened his mouth, trying to speak, but he couldn't connect the words. Then more voices feathered over him in a jumble of sound.

"Is he going to be all right?"

"Shhh!"

"I'm sure she knows what she's doing."

"Did he hit his head?"

"Kellen?"

"He's got a pretty hard head, I've noticed."

"He did obliterate that big bastard."

"Will you all be quiet?"

He wanted to reassure his friends, but his head hurt too much, and he found his eyelids closed traitorously.

* * *

Waking a second time, Kellen heard the faint chatter of birds, the hum of bees, and he slowly forced himself to wake. He groggily opened his eyes and blinked his surroundings into focus, seeing pale walls decorated with masks and tapestries. Disoriented, he moved his head and looked down at his toes. He was whole and warm, and he noted the bright sunlight that streamed across his bed.

Bed?

"Good. You're finally awake."

Lifting his head, Kellen groaned as a sharp pain knifed through his skull. *Where in the ten levels of hell am I?*

"Here, drink this. It will help your headache."

The voice sounded like Tich, *yet* . . . opening his eyes wider, he blinked, watching her face swim closer. She was frowning and appeared very serious. Opening his mouth to say something, he almost choked when she tipped bitter fluid into his mouth. He sat up, coughing hard and clutching his head as the pain behind his eyes increased tenfold. Wiping his mouth, he sucked in a breath and squinted around the room before settling his eyes on the scowling Healer. "If you treat all your patients like this, it is amazing they recover," he muttered. He saw how she scowled in annoyance, and he closed his eyes. "So—where am I?"

"Better than, 'who am I,' I suppose," Tich snapped in irritation.

He risked opening an eye to glare at her.

Tich exhaled hard then gestured around the room. "We are at Crystal Gaze Castle. We arrived last night. You've been unconscious since late yesterday afternoon."

"I have?" he croaked.

"Do you remember anything at all?"

He frowned harder. He cast his mind back to the last thing he could remember clearly and got an image that was familiar, yet alien. It was of Peleyia, and he looked shrouded in darkness. That shocked him, and he opened his eyes wider.

"We got attacked by Rock Trolls," Tich explained. "Then you decided to vaporize one before passing out."

"I did?" he asked, amazed. Vaguely, his memory was returning.

"You expended too much energy. Killing the thing would have been sufficient, Kellen," she chastised before touching his brow with gentle, assessing fingers.

Her touch felt nice, and he grinned at her, feeling oddly giddy. "So how did we get here?"

"Terrica alerted the castle, and Lord Cohlen sent his knights down to clear a path for us."

"How considerate," he mumbled, wondering what else he had missed. "And the others?"

"All fine, except for a few cuts and bruises. You were the only casualty this time," she said. "Want some breakfast?"

Shaking his head as the thought of food made him nauseated, he contented himself with studying the spacious room. "So where is everyone this morning?" he asked as he went to push the covers back.

Tich stopped him. "Oh no," she said. "You are staying in bed at least until lunch."

Glancing down at himself, Kellen prudently pulled the covers back up, stretching them to his chin when he noticed he was embarrassingly lacking in clothing. He hoped he wasn't blushing.

"The others are all watching Lord Cohlen and his new wife, Lady Deirdre, hold court in the state room," Tich continued as she poured him a mixture of herbs and water.

"You don't sound too happy," he observed. He'd learnt her various moods and expressions fast over the last week.

"I just cannot understand some of the barbaric customs people adhere to," she explained. "I mean, take Lord Cohlen, he is a very old man, with no heirs, yet he goes and marries a young woman, with no references, from the Eastlands. And he marries her in the hope that she will give him a son to inherit his title."

"So?" Kellen asked. It seemed a sensible plan, and he could see nothing wrong with that arrangement, but then he remembered Tich had a more liberal attitude toward marriage. "Sounds reasonable."

Tich glared at him. "Reasonable? Kellen!"

"What?" he asked, wishing she wouldn't shout.

"He should have just entered into a bonding agreement with her, then if she ends up barren, he will still have the option to bond with another. Such an agreement is beneficial for both, because if she falls with child then she can demand a betrothal. Most marriages in the civilized world are not celebrated until after the birth of the first child! And in some cultures, it has to be the birth of a male child!" she stated with passion. "Don't you agree?"

Not really following her logic, Kellen just dropped his head back on the pillows and gave a weak nod. If he pretended compliance, she just might go away. "Sounds practical, I suppose."

"Mind you, the Lady Deirdre apparently already has three daughters to another marriage, so I imagine she is fertile," Tich carried on, her tone peeved, "and if you listen to Salimen, the daughters are extraordinarily beautiful," she ended with a sarcastic bite. Looking back at Kellen, she noted his relaxed sprawl and bit her lip in worry and indecision. "I really think you should avoid the three daughters, Kellen," she added, glancing over at the door when it opened. She saw Peleyia pause on the threshold and then amble confidently into the room.

"Why should I avoid the daughters?" Kellen asked; he then raised his head when he saw the Lancooti. He couldn't help it; he grinned in welcome.

"Tich," Peleyia nodded in greeting. He stopped beside the bed and smiled. "Sasheer said something about needing your services in the state room," he informed the Healer.

A flicker of displeasure passed over her face before Tich gave a resigned nod then picked up her cloak. "Don't let him get out of bed," she instructed before leaving.

Waiting until the door had closed, Peleyia grinned and sat on the edge of the wide bed. "So how are you feeling?"

"Confused," Kellen said honestly. "What's going on?"

"Not much," the Lancooti shrugged. "This morning, Lord Cohlen's knights are currently using the Rock Trolls for target practice. It seems he had no idea the problem was so bad down in the valleys. He'd just assumed people no longer wanted to visit," Peleyia said in disbelief. "Imagine that?"

"He is a lord. They have funny ideas."

"I know. And he is amazing. Especially being so old. A little misguided and definitely under the influence of his new wife and her daughters, but still amazing," Peleyia mused while his eyes narrowed in thought. "I don't know, Kell, but I think there is something strange going on inside the castle."

"What could be stranger than not knowing you had Rock Trolls living on your doorstep?" Kellen said tiredly.

"True," Peleyia acknowledged. "But there have been a number of unexplained deaths recently within the castle as well. And not just the elderly have died."

"There has been a fever here. Remember? Karczag told us that," Kellen said, more asleep than awake. Peleyia was silent for a long minute, and Kellen opened his eyes to see if Peleyia was still there and got a glare in return

"Do you always have to be so . . . so . . . logical?" Peleyia accused as he gestured around impotently.

Grinning, Kellen stifled a weak laugh.

"All right, I'm probably just paranoid," Peleyia amended sourly. He folded his arms and raised one brow in displeasure. "But I still believe there is something sinister about Lady Deirdre's daughters," he finished, not meeting Kellen's eyes for a long moment.

Elbowing himself up the bed a little, Kellen continued to study his friend. It seemed the only things he had heard about since waking were the lord's adopted daughters. "Tich said Sal thinks they're beautiful."

"Sal's right," Peleyia said. "But that is not the problem. I don't like the feel of this castle. For one thing, Lord Cohlen's new wife does not look old enough to have three grown daughters. It's weird. And get this, they're triplets."

Raising a brow, Kellen looked harder at his friend. For Peleyia to speak like this had to mean something was wrong—off—and he made the effort to listen. After all, Peleyia was gifted in reading auras. "Have you told Sasheer?"

"What could I say?" Peleyia asked, then he was shrugging and rubbing his face. "Tich is probably right. You should just stay away from the daughters," he concluded, giving a small smile.

"Me?" Kellen asked, stunned. "What about Sal, or the others? Or you?"

Dropping his head to one side, Peleyia just gave him a teasing look. "Because you're the one who always gets into trouble."

"I do not!"

"Trust me. I'm the expert on trouble. Remember?" Peleyia informed him with a grin.

"Why am I always banned from all the fun?" Kellen griped in a sulking tone.

"Kell, have you looked in the polished silver lately?"

"What are you talking about now?" Kellen asked, confused again.

"I'm talking about you!"

"Me?"

"Kell, you're tall, extremely good-looking, have an intriguing southern heritage which any female would love to add to her family crest. And you fill out a set of leathers better than I do. What does that tell you?"

"That you think too much."

"That you should avoid obvious trouble. And the three daughters are just that," Peleyia ended with a laugh. "I don't know, but I think you and Salimen are going to be the death of Sasheer."

* * *

Kellen was allowed out of bed after lunch, and he migrated as far as the outside balcony. He was feeling much better, even though he still ached all over. Tich had warned him that the bone-deep lethargy would ease with proper food and rest. Around him, birds played in the potted shrubs, bees moved from bloom to bloom; the scent of the flowers sweet, just as the breeze was light and the sun warm. A perfect terraced garden which overlooked the vastness of the plains at the bottom of the mountain. Gone were the drabness, the barren sandstone, and red earth; now he was faced with an awe-inspiring view of the land east of the mountains.

The effects of winter were far removed in this castle paradise, and Kellen let himself become mesmerized by the tranquil beauty of the place. He was happy for once to obey Tich's instructions and not move, to soak up the peacefulness of nature. He didn't even rouse himself when he heard the door open behind him, imagining it would only be Peleyia to come and share some new gossip with him.

When the Lancooti didn't speak, Kellen roused himself enough to open one eye, then jumped, startled, seeing Sasheer peering at him cynically. It was the last thing he had expected, and he forced himself to sit up straighter. "Sasheer . . ."

Sasheer waved him to silence and simply hooked a second chair closer before sitting down. He glanced out at the view and then sighed, settling his changeable gaze on Kellen. "I have come to see if you are ready to talk."

It was an abrupt statement, and Kellen swallowed a little nervously. "Talk about what?"

"Kellen . . ." Sasheer growled in warning.

"Okay," Kellen breathed, his mind once again in a chaotic spin. Gone was his state of utter relaxation.

"Yesterday. What were you thinking?" Sasheer snapped.

"I was fighting Rock Trolls!" He snapped. For some reason, Sasheer always brought out his stubborn insolence.

"Fighting?" Sasheer snorted in disbelief. "You were playing! Or maybe just trying to give me heart failure! Your control was gone. Your focus haphazard at best. And if you can't learn how to regulate the energy wisely, you will be killed."

"Killed?" Kellen asked. "I thought you said this thing was a Gift?"

"It is!" Sasheer shouted, effectively shutting the younger man up. Kellen stared at him, before he turned away to stare out over the balcony. "It is a sixth sense—a Gift," Sasheer went on, calmer. "And one, if strong enough and unchecked, will devastate your life. It will take you over, consume you, and control all your other senses. It will blind you to reason and eventually burn you out."

"Some Gift," Kellen muttered snidely.

Sasheer ignored the comment. "But when trained, you will be able to use the same Gift, the same energies to influence all around you. If you don't learn, don't listen—then you will die."

"How will I die?"

"Ignorance kills, Kellen. Or haven't you comprehended that fact yet?" Sasheer returned in irritation. "You will die by ignoring those exercises I've tried to teach you."

Kellen leaned his head back and closed his eyes. He could easily visualize the boring meditation exercises that Sasheer was talking about. "I have been practicing."

"But not enough," Sasheer informed him. "This power, or potential, may feel limitless right now. It may feel malleable, but eventually, it will use you as a conduit, and you will not be able to stop it. Then you will die from something as simple as exhaustion," Sasheer explained. "Your mind may assume a task is possible, where in reality it is physically impossible, and you will either pass out unconscious or die trying to achieve the unachievable."

"Like what sort of task?" Kellen asked in apprehension, wondering how close to the line he had already stepped.

"So far you have done things which are instinctive, easy to accomplish through anger and need. You have not attempted to plan ahead and formulate strategies. For instance, let's use the example of the Rock Troll you killed. You could have simply wished him dead from a wound inflicted. But no, you went ten steps further and converted him back into his basic dust elements. That was unnecessary and extremely dangerous. Dangerous because you put your entire mental strength behind that one act, causing yourself to pass out from overexertion. Now if you had been alone, another Troll would have just walked over and killed you."

"So I overextended and left myself vulnerable."

"Yes," Sasheer said. "And that is one of the things you need to learn. Not just how to access the full extent of your energies, but also how to pull back and stop an action."

"All right," Kellen conceded. "You've made your point. I will concentrate harder on the meditation exercises."

"I'll devise some new mental exercises for you. Something a bit more challenging, to stimulate your interest."

Kellen groaned, not missing how Sasheer mocked him deliberately, and remembering the last series of exercises the Mage had come up with. He had been given the task of holding a glass sphere with a tubular hole through the center, then balancing a drop of water in the middle of the conduit while Sasheer sent periodic images of Kizer mud men to distract him. Very frustrating, confirming his suspicions that Sasheer had a twisted sense of humor. "I imagine this exercise will have Trolls in it?" he ventured, seeing the cynical smirk Sasheer sent him. Then the Mage glanced down, his smile dying as he sighed, looking suddenly old and defeated, and Kellen blinked, sitting forward. "Sasheer?"

"What I ask, is important. These basic tasks will order your thinking and help you to focus your thoughts during times of stress. They will stretch your mind," Sasheer explained. "I can devise more complicated exercises for you on the way east, as Lord Cohlen is selling us some horses."

Getting that trapped, sinking feeling again in the pit of his stomach, Kellen looked down at his hands. He didn't want to think about Mitthsombaine, didn't want to think about what awaited them at the end of the journey. So instead, he asked a different question: "What are the currents?"

Sasheer lifted a brow and sat back in his chair, as his smirk returned. "I was wondering how long it would take you to ask. Dalzere said you felt them in the woodlands."

"I wish you and Dalzere would stop discussing things behind my back," he grumbled, sick of feeling manipulated.

"Maybe if you were more approachable—"

"Me?" Kellen gave a harsh laugh. "You're the one who has scowls that turn rain to ice. Not me." Sasheer was silent for a moment, and then he laughed, his whole face changing as he slid down in his seat. Kellen stared at him, furious, amazed by the years that seemed to fall away from Sasheer with so simple a gesture. "All right, so maybe I have been a bit difficult," he admitted, watching how Sasheer's eyes stayed a warm blue and how he nodded in acceptance.

"You have been no worse than I was at your age. In fact, you are probably better mannered," Sasheer said. "The currents," he continued, stopping Kellen from commenting or asking personal questions. "When Mitthsombaine of old was a very young city, it was charged with so much energy that it was necessary to find a way to release that energy, or risk destroying the balance within the Magii Towers. So the ruling Magus of that time and his council found a way to channel the energy they did not use. They channeled the currents into the city, gave it to the people in the form of lighting, heating—creating a beautiful, functional city. The jewel of the east. Every dwelling was run by the currents—and as I recall from my history, those were settled years, happy years, young years filled with learning and peace," he shrugged, his face thoughtful. "Centuries later, after the war when the Towers had been destroyed and the central well sunk into the earth, the energy lines didn't vanish as we had all expected. Rather the energies found a new route, bubbling up out of the foundations of the old Towers to spill across the earth. And now it flows like a never-ending river— a current—across Sennovia. It is a continuous flow from the center of Mitthsombaine to the oceans. No one is certain, but many have studied the phenomenon. Some believe the current circles back from the ground to sea to underground caverns and back up through Mitthsombaine."

"The currents are magical?" Kellen asked.

"No," Sasheer shook his head. "At least not in the way you are imagining. They are pure energy. But those with innate ability can draw on their abundant supply of energy so as to enhance their talents."

"And they have been flowing across Sennovia for four thousand years?"

"Yes." Sasheer nodded. "They run in concentrated strips— hence the name. They glide over the earth and always take the most direct path to the nearest shoreline. Most people never feel their passing. It is only those like yourself, like the Elves and certain wildlife that have adapted and learned to thrive off its energy."

"Is it evil?" Kellen asked, remembering how wicked the old city of Mitthsombaine was.

"No." Sasheer shook his head. "They reflect what the user feels. Like those currents you pulled in order to kill that Troll— your fear, your excitement, your desperation—marred them. As they flowed on from you, a trace of who you are went with them, and any Mage who was following behind could have read your signature in them."

"Could the currents be used against me?"

"Oh yes," Sasheer said, his voice lowering. "That is how Lichien hunts."

"That's frightening," Kellen said in disgust. "Lichien could follow my every move, my every thought."

"That is why I advised caution," Sasheer reminded him. "Certain parts of the ground have been stained with dark magics. This is from a continuous use of dark powers concentrated in one spot for centuries—or from a single act so vile that nothing can remove the taint. In these areas, you cannot access the currents and hope for a good outcome. The darkness in the earth will automatically turn your thoughts and intentions bad."

Not liking the sound of that, Kellen made a mental note to try and think before he reached out and played in the addictive currents in future. "I wish I had known this sooner."

"Would it have stopped you?"

Not liking that perceptive question, Kellen glared at Sasheer from under his lashes, studying the Mage. He saw the other man sprawl back in his chair, saw Sasheer's easy appraisal, and had to concede that the Mage was right—again. "Probably not."

"Sometimes trial and error is the only way to learn."

He grunted in acknowledgment. "Even if your student dies trying?" he asked irritably.

"That would depend on your level of stupidity," Sasheer said conversationally. "Only stupid students die. But then with you, I suppose the possibilities are endless."

"Thanks a lot. I think."

"You're welcome." Sasheer grinned, this time it made him look incredibly mischievous. "Now that we have had this heart to heart, I had better go and check on the Ihovians. They are almost as impulsive as you," he said, pushing himself up. "Must be something in the Southland water supply."

"Can I ask you another question? A personal question?" Kellen asked softly, stopping Sasheer from leaving. He felt the Mage pause at his side and waited for what type of response he would get this time.

"You can ask."

There was no promise of an answer in the remark, and Kellen turned in his chair to look up at Sasheer. He met those perceptive blue eyes that had seen so much, and which reflected the Mage's mood eerily. At present, Sasheer's gaze was curious, so he decided to risk his question. "Terrica."

"I thought Tich had explained the Shades." Sasheer frowned. He reached out and pulled his chair over then sat and considered Kellen seriously. "What is it you want to know?"

Startled by Sasheer's abrupt willingness to discuss the mountain cat, Kellen dragged in a breath and ordered his thinking. "You've had her for—?"

"Over four thousand years," Sasheer answered. "Creating Terrica was my final achievement before I was thrown out of the Towers by the ruling Magus."

Thrown out of the Towers . . . Kellen's mind boggled, and he wanted to ask more, but something in Sasheer's tone warned him to be careful. "You must have been very young, when you created her."

"Age is relative," Sasheer gave a humorless smile. "Although in our case—my case—I had a lot to achieve in a very short time."

Kellen studied him, noting the hasty correction, reading under the words, realizing that Sasheer was referring to his twin, and guessing that something unexpected or even catastrophic must have happened them both. He remembered what Tanish had said about Sasheer and his brother being the youngest, and he wondered just how old the Mage had been when he was 'thrown' out of the Towers. How old he had been when he had chosen to stop the aging process. Or even how old he had been when he walked away from Mitthsombaine to help destroy her. "What age were you when you started your training?" he asked instead, and was abruptly hit by an image so strong that nausea rose up into his mouth. He gagged, hearing a child scream, then . . . *saw* . . .

"You are pathetic! You think—believe—you are ready? You think you are entitled to a place within the Magii Towers?"

A tall man dressed entirely in black paced around the outskirts of the room. His cloak dragged across the damp cobblestones, his posture angry, his eyes hard and unrelenting. He stopped at the old wooden door and turned to scowl at the child sitting on the floor, a young child, no older than six or seven, a child who was struggling not to weep.

"You will have to prove your worth, otherwise I will return you to your family. You will be disgraced, and they will banish you from the city." He growled, his lips curling back in a sneer. "They will give you to the Ghouls. Do you want that?"

The child shook his head, his eyes remaining lowered and respectful. The Mage's gaze narrowed, then he lifted one hand and negligently gestured toward the lamp. The flame flickered, then went out, throwing the room into darkness. Only the meager light from the shadowed moon left a trail of silver across the child sitting defenseless and trembling in the center of the room. "I will return at first light. Be prepared!"

The door slammed shut, and the child hiccupped, dragging in a frightened breath. He looked up after a while, the large blue eyes filled with pain and aching hopelessness as tear tracks lined his cheeks, until he scrubbed them dry. Then he turned and crawled to the wall under the window. With care he reached out to a bundle of rags, turning them over to reveal a second child. This child had blood on his forehead, blood staining his lips as he sluggishly opened his eyes.

"Go. Leave me—"

"Never," the first child said as he gathered the second child in his arms and stroked his hair. "I won't let him kill us," he hissed the words, his eyes darting to the closed door. "I promise, Serine. I won't let him kill us!"

"I ... was very young," Sasheer breathed, his face pale as his hands gripped the sides of the chair in a death grip.

Stunned, Kellen pulled back for the powerful vision and blinked. That had been Sasheer and his brother. Serine. What shocked him the most was the fact that even after all these years, thousands of years, Sasheer was still so bruised by this memory. "I'm sorry..."

"Don't be. It was a long time ago," Sasheer said, his color returning. "So what were we discussing?"

"Terrica," Kellen answered, still shocked.

"Yes, my relationship to the Shade. She is my eyes and ears when traveling. She protects my back when sleeping. She is an elemental; her focus is fire, and unfortunately, like all Shades, she has a mind of her own. And a temper to match," Sasheer said.

Accepting that some topics were off-limits, Kellen concentrated on understanding one thing at a time about Sasheer. "Do all Mages have a Shade?" he asked instead and was rewarded when Sasheer sent him a brief smile.

"All who were trained in Mitthsombaine do."

"Can a Shade be killed?" Kellen asked.

"Yes," Sasheer said slowly, his eyes darkening as he assessed Kellen. "Why do you ask?"

"Just curious . . . and I heard about Cornithia's Shade," Kellen defended. "If Terrica is killed, what happens to you?"

"Insanity, most likely," Sasheer muttered dryly.

"So they are a liability," Kellen concluded as he looked at Sasheer with more understanding and respect. "That's dangerous."

"Thank you for pointing out the obvious."

Hearing the sarcasm, Kellen sighed, noticing how Sasheer's eyes twinkled in wicked humor. "So, will I be able to create a Shade?"

"I do not know," Sasheer said. "It has not been done successfully outside Mitthsombaine. I imagine that it will depend."

"On what?"

"On you. On how well you learn your lessons and practice your exercises."

Kellen pulled a face.

"Those exercises strengthen your mind, stretch your ability, and they are extremely important. Because once you reach a certain point in your life, your flexible mind muscles will stop evolving, and then your ability will be locked."

Feeling the hairs rise on the back of his neck in apprehension,

Kellen said nothing for a very long moment. "So my ability will be decided by what I do now?"

"Yes." Sasheer nodded, sitting back in his chair and stretching a little. A pleased look entered his eyes, making them lighten in color.

Clearing his throat, Kellen stared at Sasheer. Why had no one told him this vital piece of information before? Then he remembered *why* most of Sasheer's students had died in the past, and he scowled at the Mage, not missing the patented smirk. "Terrica—"

"Terrica?" Sasheer repeated, a little puzzled.

"Did you send her to me in GarFamita?" Kellen asked pointedly. He had to know. Had to know if Sasheer was playing mind games with him.

"She visited you in GarFamita?" Sasheer asked, shocked. His smile vanished, and he scowled at the space next to him. "Is it true? Terrica?" he demanded.

Seeing the action, Kellen was amazed when the mountain cat swiftly appeared as if from nowhere, realizing he had not even sensed her presence. A Shade could mask its presence? He had to remember that. Then the cat was casting him a guilty look before leaning against Sasheer in coy appeal.

"You saw her like this?" Sasheer asked. He reached down and absently stroked her head with one hand.

"Well, not . . . exactly," Kellen started. "She . . . umm . . . looked more female."

"Terrica!" Sasheer demanded. The Mage scowled at her, and she pinned her ears back and purred, blinking up meekly. Then she lifted one paw and placed it on Sasheer's leg.

"So you didn't know," Kellen finished lamely.

"Of course I didn't know!" Sasheer snapped bad temperedly. "What did she say to you?"

"She just warned me about the Lancooti." He stopped deciding it was probably best not to describe the earlier encounter in the Southland woods.

"Is that all?" Sasheer asked suspiciously.

"That's all," Kellen stressed firmly, trying to give Sasheer a sincere look.

"You are not to interfere," Sasheer told the cat, chastising her softly. She wiggled closer to his side and rubbed her head on his thigh. "And stop trying to pretend innocence."

Clearing his throat, Kellen hid his smile, watching the obvious affection between the two. It was the closest he had come to believing Sasheer had a gentle side.

After a comfortable length of time, Sasheer looked back up at Kellen. "There is something else we need to discuss—a more delicate subject."

"What?" He asked, tensing as he read wariness in Sasheer's expression. Without meaning to, he automatically went on the defensive.

"Tich," Sasheer said.

"Tich?" Kellen frowned, his eyes going from Sasheer's shrewd gaze to Terrica's auburn unblinking stare. Now it was his turn to squirm uncomfortably.

"I—we—have all noticed how," Sasheer paused, "close you both have become. And I don't think it—"

"You don't think it is a good idea," Kellen finished for Sasheer. He crossed his arms in annoyance and glared at the Mage. The fact that he had not thought beyond just seeing Tich, was inconsequential. What infuriated him was the fact that Sasheer had the audacity to tell him who he could and could not associate with.

"Not at the moment. No."

"Not ever, if I understand anything of what Tanish told me back in the Keep," Kellen added gruffly. Sasheer was at it again, manipulating him already.

"That is not for me to say," Sasheer said carefully. "At present, it is not advisable. Because Tich is of..."

"Of what?" Kellen asked belligerently.

"Mixed heritage. With Gifts of her own. Plus she is far older than you might think. Although she is undoubtedly a lovely-looking woman," Sasheer added as an afterthought.

"She would not be good for the bloodline," Kellen said, glad when Sasheer's eyes widened in surprise. So for once he had outguessed the crafty Mage. "So how long before we leave this castle?" he asked in the most irritating tone possible, wanting to annoy Sasheer. It worked.

"A day or two." Sasheer exhaled hard, his brows drawing down in harassment. He clicked his fingers, and Terrica obediently vanished, her presence lingering for a moment before dissipating completely. "It seems some refugees from the Southland have escaped Kalern's Slavers. They were taken in by some of Lord Cohlen's Herders down in the village of Maltros."

"You think some of the survivors are from Ihova?" Kellen asked, forgetting his anger and thinking only of Lesendal and his desperate search for his beloved sister.

"Maybe. I don't know," Sasheer said. "Dalzere and Ryland have taken Lesendal down to the village to check over the survivors. They should be back later tonight."

Wishing the prince success, Kellen sat back in his chair and contemplated what would happen if Lesendal found Kessendra. Then the prince would leave the group and return to Ihova, as would Salimen and Ryland, maybe even Peleyia which would leave him all alone. He frowned, brooding, glancing up when he felt a hand on his shoulder. Sasheer was standing beside his chair, those strong fingers squeezing his tense shoulder muscles before releasing him.

"We will stay in Crystal Gaze as long as Lesendal needs to stay."

Stunned by Sasheer's soft comment, Kellen sat still, staring ahead even long after Sasheer had departed. Would he ever understand the unpredictable Mage? Or would they ever have a conversation that did not end in an argument?

CHAPTER THIRTY-TWO

After dinner, Kellen joined Salimen, Crizkerisomia, Peleyia, and Gralvin out on the huge balcony that overlooked the magnificent courtyard of Crystal Gaze Castle. Dinner had been bizarre affair, and he almost wished he had opted to eat in his room. But he had wanted to meet the new lady of the castle and her three charming daughters. He had to agree with Salimen; they were beautiful—and identical in every detail, making them even more bewitching.

Of course, Tich had not been amused. The Healer had kicked him under the table numerous times. It was getting to the point where he was no longer certain what to expect from her. They had kissed once, and he did like her, but that didn't mean she owned him.

"Kell?"

Hearing her voice, he turned away from his friends as Tich approached. He paused for a moment to study her graceful movements. She was indeed lovely, but he knew with a painful certainty that Sasheer was right. The Brethren would not encourage their friendship. They had another future for him, and despite his protests, he was anxious to move forward and discover what it was.

"I just wanted to let you know that I'll be returning home with the Sanctuary guards at first light," Tich said, a little downhearted.

"Is it safe?"

"All the knights seem to think so," she replied. "Besides, I have a few urgent messages Sasheer wants me to give to Councilor Karczag."

"What about?"

"I don't know. I don't read personal mail," she said tartly.

"I wasn't suggesting . . ."

"You're spending too much time with Pel. I can see that his bad habits are starting to rub off."

"Tich," he petitioned and was rewarded with a teasing smile. He could hear Salimen laugh behind them, and he glanced back, wondering what the joke had been.

"Are they still discussing the attributes of the triplets?" Tich asked, arching one brow.

"Well," he started evasively.

"You're disgusting, Kellen," she snapped, anger abruptly coloring her words. Then she swiveled on her toes and marched away.

Blinking at her retreating form, Kellen was at a loss to understand her rapid mood swings and just stepped back, narrowly avoiding an irritated Crizkerisomia as the white Elf also growled something in disgust before leaving. Ambling back to the others, he just caught the end of the discussion as Salimen and Peleyia argued with Gralvin about the Lady Deirdre's possible age, compared with the age of her well-endowed daughters.

Sipping his wine, Kellen stretched, enjoying the company and the cool night breeze. In all honesty, he was not interested in the triplets, his mind too crowded with more immediate concerns, like Mitthsombaine, or Sasheer and the glimpses he'd seen of the past, or even his training . . . and the fearful knowledge that Fate could claim Peleyia at any moment. He shuddered. Then there was Lesendal's mission to rescue his sister, and Salimen's discontentment with his cousin. Not to mention Crizkerisomia and Dalzere's continuous bickering and sporadic sword fights. He snorted into his wine; his companions were far more interesting to watch than a dozen Lord Cohlen's and his three stepdaughters. Exhaling hard, he tuned in to the conversation around him.

Gralvin belched and studied his wineglass with dislike before standing. He stopped next to Kellen. "I think I'll go and see if I can find something stronger. Something with a bit more bite to it," he slurred before staggering away.

Watching him go, Kellen smiled whimsically and glanced over at the blonde Ihovian. "When will Lesendal get back?"

"I don't know," Salimen said, unusually subdued.

"Why didn't you go with him?" Kellen asked, watching the other man fidget with his glass.

Pulling a face, Salimen shrugged. "Dale will be fine without me. Besides, I would just get in his way." He glanced up, not quite meeting Kellen's curious gaze. "He wouldn't even know I was there."

"But aren't you betrothed to his sister?" Kellen asked, having remembered Ryland telling him that once. "I would have thought you would have wanted to find Kessendra more than Lesendal."

"No," Salimen said. "It was an arranged marriage." Again Salimen tried to sound unconcerned as he leaned forward to look over the balcony. "It won't happen now, and I think that is the only good that has come out of this war."

Intrigued, Kellen speculated on what Salimen wasn't saying. Did he not want to marry the renowned beauty of all Ihova? "But I thought—"

"Kell, leave it," Peleyia advised, moving to lean against the cold railing, his light eyes briefly touching the Ihovian's closed face. "So tell me, Salimen, how long have you and the prince known Sasheer?" he asked, changing the conversation.

Raising a brow, Salimen glanced at the Lancooti and grinned, obvious relief in his tone at the change of subject. "I first saw him when I was about eleven years old, I think. Lesendal's father asked him to aid in a delicate border dispute between two old barons."

"Why would the king ask for Sasheer's help in a matter like that?" Kellen questioned, puzzled.

"The two old barons were from Kalhorn and had settled across our border. King Arikaines wanted to avoid a war," Salimen explained, waving away further questions. "It was a long time ago, and I don't remember all the details, only that Sasheer had reluctantly intervened and was very annoyed with Lesendal's father."

"Sounds about right," Peleyia muttered.

Salimen spiked him an amused look. "And you?"

"And me, what?" Peleyia cut back.

"Sasheer introduced you to us as an old acquaintance."

"Oh." Peleyia cast the bowman a harassed glance.

"Yes, how did you meet Sasheer?" Kellen repeated, having wanted to ask that question for a while.

"Like Sal, I met him when I was a child."

"And?" Kellen pushed, pinning his friend with his eyes.

"And . . . he rescued me."

"Rescued you? From what?"

"I—" Peleyia's eyes grew impossibly wide as he searched for a way to explain. "It's not easy to talk about."

"Pel?" Kellen moved closer to him, worried by the look in the other's eyes.

Sighing, Peleyia sent Kellen an annoyed glare. "I was traded by my father to the Famita for payment on an old debt and well, the . . . umm . . . duties they gave me, or wanted me for, were rather unpleasant." He said, challenging them to comment. "Not long after the trade, Sasheer came across the Famita's camp one night and was appalled by my . . ." he wavered, "by what he found. He took me out of their hands, fixed me up, and then delivered me into the care of Lasdajar's house. She owed him a favor, so things were slightly better." He took a deep breath. "And for that I owe him."

"You are a body slave," Salimen said, aghast. "I can't believe things like that still happen in the Southland."

"I *was* a body slave," Peleyia corrected, hearing Salimen's self-righteous tone. "If GarFamita fell to Kalern's forces like Criz predicted, then I am now free."

Confused, Kellen blinked firstly at Salimen then turned back to Peleyia. "What's a body slave? Is that something like a manservant?"

"Not . . . quite," Peleyia said, avoiding his friend's searching eyes.

"Pel?"

"You should have rebelled," Salimen decided, looking appalled by what the other described.

"It was not that easy," Peleyia shot back in defense. "Rebellion meant death and dishonor to my tribe. Besides, death is a permanent condition. Where there is life, there is at least hope."

"But you were our guide?" Kellen whispered, still puzzled.

"I learned how to do other things," Peleyia defended, getting upset. "I learned anything that would get me out of GarFamita, for even a few days."

"Hey," Salimen lifted a hand in apology. "I'm sorry, we have no right to judge or question your actions."

Letting his gaze briefly sweep over the blond, Peleyia turned his attention back to Kellen. "I am not that person anymore. I struggled to make a life outside GarFamita. And now, by a twist of fate, I am free. I just want to enjoy life."

By a twist of fate . . . the words sounded ominous, and Kellen winced. Somehow he had to find a way to warn Peleyia without making matters worse. *But how?*

"At the rate we are going, you are more likely to get killed," Salimen quipped.

"At least I will know I was alive before I die," Peleyia replied curtly.

"Excuse us, but can we take in the night air with you?"

Startled by the quiet question from behind, Kellen turned, seeing Salimen and Peleyia do the same. Before them stood three golden-haired women. Each was identical in appearance with long hair spilling over their bare shoulders. Their skin was flawless, pearl white, and their throats were adorned with emeralds and rubies, with each wearing a dress that was cut to emphasize their feminine charms. Their eyes promised many pleasures, their perfume tantalizing—and Kellen found he was leaning closer without realizing it.

"Umm," Salimen was the first to break the heavy silence as he stood straighter and cleared his throat. "My ladies . . . the balcony is yours if you wish for us to depart." He got no further as the woman nearest to him reached out a hand and lightly touched his arm, her fingers then skimming up to caress his cheek.

"Please stay," she whispered. "Or better still, walk with me to that seat over by the enclosed garden."

"It would be my honor," Salimen assured, his expression changing from puzzlement to devotion so swiftly that it startled them all. Lifting an arm, he accepted her hand, leading her away.

Kellen stared wide-eyed after Salimen then backed up a step when warm fingers touched his hand. He looked at the lady before him.

"Maybe you would care to walk with me?"

Her voice was as beautiful as her appearance, and he nodded without thinking. He didn't want to offend; yet he was apprehensive of denying her request. Then she turned her full attention on him; her eyes trapping him, and all his resistance melted away.

CHAPTER THIRTY-THREE

Stunned by the blatant display, Peleyia frowned after Kellen and Lord Cohlen's step-daughter, watching as she so artfully lifted a hand to brush the hair from his friend's face. It was a well-practiced maneuver—a deliberate act—and he was about to intervene when he felt gentle hands cup his own face. There was strength behind those hands, and he gasped as she turned his head; and he met the gaze of the third step-daughter.

"You are Peleyia? Yes?"

It was a sweet voice, filled with a strange thrill, with power, and Peleyia found his scowl darkening. Many had tried to play this game of seduction with him in the past, and he had grown immune to the manipulations of sex. "I don't like games, so just tell me what you want," he said in a harsh whisper.

"Shhh," the female covered his lips with her fingers before she stepped closer, her expression showing a flicker of irritation that was swiftly covered. She slowed her breathing and leant even closer, so that her perfume assaulted his senses, hitting him like a potent intoxication. It dulled his responses and hampered his thinking.

"I want your company."

Lifting his lashes, Peleyia watched her in disgust as he felt her fingers creep insidiously down his chest before he managed to grab her hands and halt their progress. He glanced away from her beautiful, bewitching eyes to scan the gardens for his friends. Salimen was a blur behind some hanging plants, while Kellen looked flushed and bewildered, his leather jerkin already undone as his seducer pushed him backward to sit on a low bench—and Peleyia groaned, understanding the sudden danger.

"Peleyia?"

The soft voice drew him further into her spell, and he avoided the enticing lips that tried to capture his mouth. Her voice was poison, her words echoing in his mind, and he realized with a jolt of panic that she would kill him unless he could . . . could . . .

Marshalling his mental talents, he forcefully pushed her insidious voice from his mind, just as he pushed her clinging warmth from his body. The cold night breeze hit his limbs, and he gasped in a breath of clean air then turned his gaze on the woman—witch—in disgust. She was no lady; she was a parasite, and he shook his head, clearing the fog from his mind. "Who are you?" he snarled.

"Let me taste you, and maybe I will let you find out."

"Never!" he spat. She came at him then, and he battled to untangle himself from her embrace, wanting, needing to warn Kellen and Salimen before it was too late.

His Lancooti-trained senses prickled with unease, the taint of her hunger now a putrid stench on his senses. His initial impressions had been right, and he closed his eyes, attempting to reach out with his mind to feel Kellen and Salimen's distinctive personalities. His own latent, telepathic abilities were weak compared to this woman's powerful mind, but he still tried.

Salimen was blocked to him, but Kellen . . . In desperation, he flung his thoughts at Kellen, feeling the witch's blanketing awareness recoil from his fleeting mental touch. Then for a brief instant, he connected with Kellen and felt Kellen's repulsion and shock. He latched to those feelings, forcing the fragile link between them to widen, struggling to give Kellen the aid he needed to push the witch away. It worked for one glorious moment, and clear thought flowed between them, and then the link collapsed—and he screamed in silent agony.

He snapped his eyes open as real pain lanced into his body, feeling himself lifted. Then he was falling, falling backward, flying through the air to land with a shuddering jolt in Lord Cohlen's picturesque gardens far below.

CHAPTER THIRTY-FOUR

Surrendering to the pleasure of the seductive kiss, was easy, and Kellen barely knew where he was or how long he had been sitting on the cold stone bench, with his lips tingling in hunger. The overpowering scent of sex enveloped him, filling his lungs, warming his blood until he could think of nothing except that hot mouth which caressed his own. Then, unthinkably, that wonderful mouth pulled away, and he shuddered in agony, begging for the connection to be renewed. He clutched at his seducer, loving the texture of her silky skin, firm breasts, and moist lips. He wanted more, wanted everything.

Her name eluded him, but that didn't matter. Her voice whispered continuously in his head, promising so much pleasure that he followed blindly.

Then slowly, insidiously, the timbre of her voice changed, and he no longer could hear her gentle words of love—rather he started to discern a new voice under her words. Only this new voice was screaming for attention, like an annoying buzz in the back of his subconscious, and it took him awhile to find the energy to concentrate on who the new voice belonged to.

Peleyia . . .

He frowned, his pleasure diminishing as he homed his sluggish senses on Peleyia. His friend was screaming at him . . . It was disturbing, then abruptly, he glimpsed an image of the Lancooti in his mind and saw Peleyia writhe in agony before seeming to fly through the air.

He gasped, instinctively thrusting his lover away, horrified by the raw hunger and malice which instantly flooded his system in reward. He stared at the step-daughter in abhorrence, no longer seeing her beauty or flawless skin, rather he saw her true appearance, that of a hag, wrinkled and weather-beaten, with matted hair and rotten teeth.

He recoiled from her, doubling over as pain lanced into him, consuming him, rushing through him to cripple him. He pushed her back with one hand—then fell to the cold floor, striking his head on the way down, and losing consciousness.

Gradually awareness returned, bring with it fleeting, disturbing images, and he struggled to understand what was happening to him. Trying to remember . . . to remember why he was lying on the floor of Lord Cohlen's balcony. He felt drained, heavy limbed, and aching all over. In his mind, he saw ghoulish images of a grotesque creature—but they no longer frightened him. Instead, he was utterly captivated by the hands caressing his body, by the song that was floating through his mind.

A song he had never heard before, but which was thoroughly fascinating. It bewitched him, occupied his every thought and fed his every need. With the song came an alluring voice, a voice that whispered to him, that pleasured him and turned his blood to fire. This voice promised the fulfillment of all his darkest fantasies.

Kellen!

The call was from far off, and he frowned.

Kellen!

Abruptly, the song stopped, and he was shaken. Pain cramped his limbs, nausea curled in his stomach, and he vomited up his dinner. He coughed, hissing in agony as a headache started to pound behind his eyes. He heard someone call his name again, and he groggily focused his eyes, seeing Dalzere. Only this was not his friend; this was an angry Drow warrior.

"Kellen, answer me!"

It was not a request, and he blinked with difficulty. He felt disorientated and ill. His memory was fading, as the pain in his body seemed to intensify.

"By the gods, if he and Salimen are damaged, I swear I will rip this castle apart and kill those wretched whores, and their mother!"

"Calm yourself."

Someone murmured—*Sasheer*, and Kellen felt warm fingers

touch his temple, assessing him. A mental probe darted straight into his mind, and he gasped. Then just as swiftly, Sasheer's signature vanished, leaving him stunned and shaking.

"Put him to bed, and we will see how he is after the effects have worn off," Sasheer said.

"She could have killed him!"

"Dalzere . . ." Sasheer's voice sounded oddly reasonable and seemed to come from afar. "I will deal with it. You put him to bed."

Wanting to protest and tell them he was awake, and that he could put himself to bed, Kellen found the words would not come. An instant later he was lifted by strong arms and carried. He tried to voice his opinion again, but nothing happened, and he dropped his head back, feeling deathly tired.

He grunted when he was lowered onto a soft bed and tried a third time to reassure . . . his rescuer . . . Dalzere, but by the time he managed to lift his head off the pillow, Dalzere was gone. He blinked around the room and found it was an effort to sit up. What had happened . . . ? He willed his memory to fill in the blanks—and then it all came rushing back like a torrent. One of the triplets . . . *her kiss, her scent, her touch, her hunger, her hypnotic reptilian song and transformation,* and he convulsed in revulsion.

Then he remembered Peleyia, and tried to struggle out of bed. His friend needed help . . . but his body wouldn't obey him, and he shivered, sweating from the exertion, falling back onto the mattress, exhausted.

He remembered now. Remembered all of it, and felt, polluted by the stench of the grotesque creature. He wanted to reach out and strike at the vile creature . . . but lacked all energy. Instead, he tore off his clothing, tears of rage marring his face—and promptly passed out.

* * *

Waking with a start when a hand brushed his shoulder, Kellen instinctively lashed out and heard Tich's startled cry. He turned over and blinked at the Healer. "Sorry."

"That's all right. I should have taken care before waking you."

He sat up, still feeling bone weary and sore. He also had a headache that refused to ease. He rubbed his eyes. In all honestly, the last person he wanted to see was Tich. He would have preferred Dalzere, just so he could learn what had happened to his friends, because if one of the triplets had attacked him, he was sure Salimen and Peleyia were in similar peril. And Peleyia had tried to help him—he had an image in his head of the Lancooti flying through the air. Dropping his hand, he saw that Tich was studying him with a hesitant expression.

"I heard about what happened," she said, her eyes traveling over his sprawled form in worry. "Pel is a mess."

"He's alive?"

"He dislocated a shoulder from the fall."

A fall . . . maybe the image was real. Feeling acutely self-conscious under her assessing gaze, he dragged the covers up and leaned back against the pillows. *If I never kissed another woman again, it will be too soon,* he decided.

"Sasheer is furious."

Sasheer is furious? He had thought that had been Dalzere. But then he remembered that Sasheer very rarely showed his true feelings.

"Kell?"

He knew he was scowling, but he couldn't help it. He felt angry, useless; an impotent fury churning inside him. He wanted to exact his own punishment on the witch, wishing he had done something—anything. He glanced around the room, wondering where the others were and noticed that Tich had only lit two candles, leaving the room bathed mostly by moonlight. He focused on that, his frown increasing. "Tich, what are you doing here?" he had to ask. She was still studying him in worry, and that made him feel even more self-conscious.

"I couldn't go back to Sanctuary without seeing you one final time. Especially after the way we parted on the balcony earlier. I'm sorry if I shouted at you."

He smiled weakly at her, suppressing a bubble of nervous

laughter, not believing they were having this conversation. There were more pressing problems to deal with.

"We need to talk, Kell."

"Talk?" he repeated, mystified. Irritated.

"Yes," she took a very big breath and moved to sit closer to him on the bed. "I—" she faltered, "I have never felt like this before."

He squinted at her, realizing suddenly just how dark the room was. Maybe he should suggest they light some of the bigger lamps?

"Kellen, I want to bond with you," Tich finished on a fast whisper.

His scowl returned and he said nothing as he eyed the disappearing space on the bed between them. Something was wrong here, and he lifted his eyes, trying to read behind her words. So what else had he missed while unconscious? "Bond . . ." Hadn't he heard that term somewhere before? He had a bad feeling about this. "Tich—"

She cut him off. "I know what you are going to say. I know this is a bad time to discuss anything. I know you have to do this thing with Sasheer, and that is fine. I know you have to learn all that he has to teach, and I realize that could take years. And I know you want to go back to the Southland."

Startled, Kellen just nodded at each point, not having really considered any of them. All he had been going to say was that he didn't feel up to talking. Chancing a look at her expression he could tell she was serious, and he didn't want to upset her further. "Tich—"

"Kell, let me finish." She leaned in close and cupped his face with a warm hand. He pulled away, and she sat back and sighed. "All I ask is that you return to Sanctuary in one piece after you have visited the old ruins. I don't want you going anywhere near North Ridge."

"That would not be my first choice," he whispered. He shifted a little further away from her, his skin hypersensitive to touch. He took her hands in his own and squeezed them in reassurance and apology, before releasing her completely.

"I think we would make a good team. You and me," she said, her tone softening as she gained in confidence. "And being a Healer, well, I can . . . umm, sort of predict the outcome of any union between us. The ceremony in Sanctuary when you return would be routine. Then if you wanted to go back to Ihova . . . we could." She paused and looked at him through her lashes. "Yes?"

"Ceremony?" Kellen muttered, frowning. *What ceremony?* If he returned to Sanctuary then it would be because Sasheer was dead, and that was not something he wanted to celebrate. "Listen, Tich—"

"Bond with me."

"What?" he snapped, then relented as he saw her crushed expression. He held up a hand and closed his eyes. "My life is nothing but a confused mess."

"Then let me help you."

It sounded so reasonable, yet in the back of his mind he remembered Sasheer's warning. "Thank you, but there are things no one can help with."

"I thought we were friends?"

"We are," he stressed, his headache returning with a vengeance.

"I thought we were more than friends."

He hesitated, his mind immediately recalling the vile creature that had tried to suck the life out of him. Only Tich was not vile, she was most definitely lovely, and he remembered the kiss in Sanctuary. Looking down, he exhaled hard. "We are." Her smile was reward enough, and he grinned also, thrown a moment later when she laughed and flung herself at him, wrapping him in a warm hug. He tensed, expecting pain, but found that her touch and smell lulled him and even eased his aches. Very slowly he returned the embrace.

"You mean it?"

Hearing the breathy words in his ear, he nodded, glad that one disaster had been adverted, and that somehow he had managed to please this flighty little Healer.

"Oh, Kell, I do love you!"

Stunned by those words, he opened his mouth in protest,

then frowned, not sure what to protest about. She moved away and then he found himself pressed back against the pillows, and in his arms was a very warm and very sweet-smelling young woman, and he relaxed, deciding not to argue. Her eyes were bright, her smile full and uncomplicated, and he reached up to brush hair from her face. *Maybe Sasheer is wrong . . .* he mused, watching her. She looked beautiful in that instant, and he dragged her closer, initiating a gentle kiss. Her breath was sweet—and then the kisses were no longer soft, but a demanding and full of passion.

CHAPTER THIRTY-FIVE

Kellen came awake with a start and sat bolt upright in bed. Twisted dream images from the previous night lingered in his mind, and he blinked around in a daze. Raising a hand to his temple, he grimaced, his head starting to pound as the dawn light stung his eyes. He felt like he had been drugged, or beaten senseless, at the very least drunk on wine. On the edge of his thoughts was a disturbing memory about . . . something, and he shook his head, not quite about the capture the images.

"You have a headache still?"

He jumped and almost landed on the floor before he caught a look at the person stretching awake next to him. It was Tich, and she was *naked*, and his mouth fell open. *In the same bed . . .* Then the Healer threw back the covers and reached for her clothing. He swallowed hard, and lifted the sheets and saw that he was just as naked. He blushed. *Had they . . .* he swallowed. Problem was, his mind was curiously blank.

"Drink this. It will help your head."

He squinted at Tich and relaxed, seeing she was dressed in her usual attire. Should he ask? That option didn't seem polite, so instead he took the glass she offered and gulped the bitter herbs down without protest. He fervently hoped his memory would return when his headache settled. He risked another look at her and caught the smile she sent him. *Oh, yes, I'm in trouble.*

"I have to go," Tich whispered. She leaned across the bed and lightly kissed him on the lips. "I don't want Dalzere to find out I'm here, even though I think Peleyia walked in on us last night." She wrinkled her nose at him, her grin full of mischief. "You'll have to talk to him, convince him to keep his big mouth shut."

Speechless, he remembered to close his mouth and just nod. He could not believe this was happening, or that he couldn't remember. Then he recalled Sasheer's stern words and decided that shutting Peleyia's mouth was a very good idea. He lifted his eyes and looked again at Tich. She was gorgeous in the pale sunlight, her hair a mess and her smile infectious. Beautiful.

"I will wait for you in Sanctuary. So just remember all that we talked about and all that you promised," she said. Then she stood and picked up her pack, waving to him one final time before rushing from the room.

He sat and stared at the closed door, then pinched himself. "Ouch!" He rubbed his leg, cursing, repeating the Drow phrase he had heard Dalzere use so often. Somehow it seemed apt, even if he didn't know exactly what it meant. So what had he promised Tich?

* * *

Splashing water on his face, Kellen tied his hair back and finished dressing. He wondered if he should just come right out and ask Peleyia to tell him about last night, or ignore it completely.

"Kellen?"

He spun around guiltily and saw Dalzere standing in the doorway of his room. *What had Tich said about Dalzere?*

"How are you feeling?"

"Umm . . ." Kellen cast around for something appropriate to say. Something ambiguous.

"Confused? Light-headed? Sick?"

That about summed it up, he decided and nodded in reply, thinking Dalzere was being very reasonable about the whole thing, especially if he'd seen Tich.

"Salimen looks even worse than you do," Dalzere said with a grin.

Salimen? When had Salimen entered his fantasy? He was sure he would have remembered the bowman's presence in his room, even if he couldn't remember most of last night.

"Kellen?" Dalzere sounded worried, then the Elf walked over and held up a small vial of fluid. "Drink this. Tich said that you may feel ill for most of the morning."

"Tich—" Kellen started, feeling as though he was going to pass out.

"Yes. I spoke to her at breakfast. Before she left for Sanctuary." Dalzere frowned and grabbed Kellen's arm when the other swayed. He steered him back toward the bed.

"Gods!" Kellen groaned. It couldn't get any worse. "About last night—"

"You have no memory of it, I know," the Drow said gently.

Glancing up, Kellen hesitated before meeting the amber eyes. "I have some memory."

The Drow raised a brow. "Salimen is the same."

"Sal?" Kellen repeated, puzzled. Now he felt uncomfortable as well as ill.

Sighing, Dalzere gave him a cocky half smile. "You, Peleyia, and Salimen were entrapped last night by three very old and very nasty witches."

"Witches?" Now he was confused. That had not been what he was thinking or worrying over, although now that Dalzere mentioned it, he could sense the truth of those words . . . and see an image of a grotesque creature at the peripherals of his mind. *Bright stars!* He bit his lower lip and risked another look up at Dalzere, meeting the Elf's searching eyes. Maybe this had nothing to do with Tich. Holding up a hand, Dalzere halted his questions. "The triplets," he explained. "It seems they are from the White Cliffs of Nezkernan. They bought passage on a mercenary ship to the east and then killed the mercenaries before meeting up with Lady Deirdre—who is also not as young as she appears," he added in an angry growl. "The witches enhanced Deirdre's appearance, for a price, and then traveled with her as her daughters, helping Deirdre marry into a succession of wealthy households in isolated communities. Then between the four of them, they slowly devoured the life forces of each household, acquiring wealth, before moving to the next isolated village."

"Until they got here."

"Yes. We arrived just in time, otherwise Lord Cohlen and this entire community would have died out," Dalzere said, furious. "The witches even lured the Rock Trolls here to keep visitors away."

Stunned, Kellen just blinked at the enraged Drow.

"Their plan might have worked to some degree. Thank the heavens for Peleyia's strange moral code."

Absorbing all that Dalzere told him, Kellen found parts of his memory returning, and he raised a hand to his mouth, feeling suddenly very ill.

Removing the top on the vial, Dalzere held it up. "You're as white as washed bones. You had better drink this before you're sick. I've had enough of that this morning with Salimen being ill everywhere."

Forcing the fluid down, Kellen wiped his lips and looked doubtfully at the other man. "So where are these witches now?"

"Gone," Dalzere spat, angry again, his voice dropping to a dangerous growl. "By the time we checked you and Salimen, they had vanished. Sasheer went to Cohlen. He did manage to stop Deirdre's hasty flight," he said with a grim smile. "Then Sasheer stripped away her facade, revealing her true age, story, and appearance. It kept us busy for most of the night. But I did send Pel to check on both you and Salimen. The others went with the knights to search the Herders' village in Maltros in case the witches fled there." Dalzere flexed his fingers in annoyance. "Cohlen has Deirdre in the dungeons at present—deciding her fate."

Feeling his nausea settle with the herbal medicine, Kellen did not know what to say or think.

"Finish dressing, then come to the dining hall," Dalzere instructed. Those deadly eyes studied Kellen's face for a long moment. "By now Criz and Ryland should be back from their second sweep of Maltros. So we will need to discuss our next move."

* * *

Kellen entered the dining hall and was relieved when none of his friends questioned him about the previous night. Salimen was sitting next to Lesendal, who looked angry and worried. The bowman appeared pale and subdued, as he traced circles in the dampness created by his glass on the polished wood. Watching him, Kellen went and sat next to Ryland, glad when the big warrior reached out and gripped his shoulder in silent reassurance.

"Every time I turn my back, you end up in trouble, lad. I hope this practice is not habit-forming."

The gruff comment was laced with affection, and Kellen gave the Haonian a grateful smile before he hesitantly raised his eyes to look at Peleyia. Since talking with Dalzere, he had remembered more of the previous evening, especially Peleyia's part in it. But the Lancooti's attention was elsewhere. Giving up for the moment, Kellen glanced around when Sasheer swept into the massive room. The Mage looked incensed.

"Cohlen has sent messengers to the other affected holdings in the grassland region, calling for any who want to attend Deirdre's trial."

"Will she be killed?" Peleyia asked, an uncharacteristic note of viciousness coloring his tone. Kellen stared at his friend, noting for the first time the bruising which covered his face and throat.

"There will be a trial," Sasheer said, his sharp gaze briefly touching the Lancooti. "I have sent a message to Sanctuary, so I imagine Karczag will send someone suitable to oversee the trial."

"What about those other three vile creatures?" Ryland growled.

"Spellcasters," Sasheer spat the word with distaste. "Practitioners of the lowest form of magic. They meld the currents and use dark spells to achieve a kill."

"Just tell me you have them," Ryland cut in. The big warrior was fully dressed in his armor, helmet and all, and he looked intimidating.

"No," Sasheer said curtly, "they escaped. For the moment at least," he added. "But they won't stray far from the Black Sea region. I imagine they will delight in adding to the chaos the Black Guard have started."

"You know them!" Lesendal accused.

"I've had the pleasure of seeing their handiwork first hand, in the past," Sasheer said with a note of disgust. "And if I had the time, I would track them down and end their sorry existence. But I don't have the luxury of time." He exhaled hard, his eyes darkening ominously. "I need to get to North Ridge before Lichien releases the Raveners on the Dwarven community."

"The grassland and desert expanse are larger than the entire Southland combined, Sasheer," Gralvin reminded. "Those witches could be hiding anywhere, lying in wait for us. If they trap us, it will not matter what Kalern does."

"Thank you for making that point so perfectly clear," Sasheer replied testily. He glared at the Dwarf, who just shrugged, unconcerned.

"Your funeral, Mage."

"So what do we do now?" Lesendal broke in as he glanced around at the other members of the group. "Can we go on, or should we go back? Some of the Maltros Herders told me that other southern refugees may have escaped Kalern's slavers and could be hiding in the grasslands stretching east." He looked up at Sasheer. "They could become targets for the witches."

Slight pity touched Sasheer's expression, and he sighed, pushing hair behind one ear. "If other captives escaped the Slavers then the Herders will find them. The Herders will also send word to warn other communities about what has happened here. It will make staying in the grasslands near to impossible for the witches," he explained gently, his eyes never leaving Lesendal. "There are always ways to deal with parasites like them. Besides, we will only be crossing the northern edge of the expanse, so I'm hoping to avoid most of Kalern's forces."

Slumping in his chair, Lesendal nodded, not looking happy. "Kessendra has to be out there somewhere. I have to believe that."

"If she is, then she will be found," Dalzere assured.

"Cohlen has given us horses," Sasheer said. "It is a long way east and with winter fast approaching," he shrugged, his eyes touching each member, "I think we should leave. I would like to get through the open grasslands before the cold really hits."

"I agree," Dalzere said. "The Herders report frost already, and I think we will be hard pushed to reach Sunset Ridge before snow."

"If the weather does turn on us, then we will be lucky to make it at all," Gralvin interrupted. "Kalern's guard, his Slavers, and the witches combined will be the least of our problems, and you know it."

"So we'll travel down to the Herders' village this afternoon," Sasheer said, ignoring Gralvin's glare with ease. "Dalzere, help Salimen with the supplies."

CHAPTER THIRTY-SIX

They slept that night in the Herders' camp at the base of Crystal Gaze Mountain. While Dalzere and Crizkerisomia scouted the area, the others went and visited the southern survivors. None were from Ihova, and none had heard of Kessendra, but each survivor told a different story of atrocities witnessed at the hands of Kalern's Slavers. Tearful accounts of how loved ones were turned into Deathwalkers in order to drive villagers from their homes, so that the Black Guard could slaughter them in the fields.

Of those who escaped, half died on the journey here from the cold and dehydration. Other survivors told stories of hideous creatures called Mindwipes who crippled the elderly or very young. Those crippled, the Slavers would purposely leave behind for the desert scavengers to feed on at night. Their cries had echoed for leagues and caused despair among the captives. Still others told cruel tales of how the Slavers buried victims alive, leaving them for the Blu-kin ant. They were left as object lessons for runaways.

Appalled by the horrific stories, Kellen hardly slept that cold night. He stared into the dying embers of the fire, picturing in his mind how terrified and how desperate those refugees must have felt. Kalern had to be stopped, and he promised himself that he would find a way.

The next morning dawned clear and cold. All in the makeshift camp were subdued, and Kellen noticed that Crizkerisomia was unusually quiet. She said nothing to anyone, then before they left the Herders' village, she marched over to Dalzere and stood braced before him. Her jaw was clenched, her fists resting on her hips, but she did not draw her sword. Rather she stared at Dalzere then spoke, weighing her words carefully. "I have discovered, against my beliefs, that there may be a worse abomination plaguing this land than you."

Turning, Dalzere gave her a narrowed glare as he folded his arms and waited.

"So, until I track and kill this abhorrent demon called Lichien, I vow to delay your execution."

"I'm touched by your concern for my welfare," Dalzere said snidely, giving her a mirthless grin. "You do your unjust *Fe-le-drea* proud."

"Beware, Drow," she whispered dangerously, "or I may change my mind."

* * *

Getting painfully reacquainted with the joys of horse riding, Kellen grimaced when his gray mare broke into trot. He had never enjoyed the sensation of riding, and this was only reminding him why, as he bounced up and down in the hard saddle. The others around him displayed no discomfort, and he just gritted his teeth, glad when the horse's motion changed into a smoother stride. He hoped he would pick up the knack of handling this spirited horse quickly, dreading to think that it was going to take two months of continuous travel to cross the vast grassland and desert expanse.

Two months! And that was as long as nothing bad happened along the way. Glancing sideways, he saw Peleyia lean down into his mount, saw the scowl of pain which marred his friend's pale face, and he bit his lower lip in thought. Debating how to open the conversation, he gripped the reins harder and tried to imitate the other's competent riding style. He had not spoken properly to Peleyia since leaving the castle, and he was conscious of the fact Peleyia was avoiding him. Because of Tich—or because of the witches?

Thinking of Tich, he shook his head. She was the nicest thing that had ever happened to him, and he just wished he could remember more of their night together. As it was, he promised himself that he would sit her down and talk to her next time they met. When he returned . . . *if* he returned.

He glanced again at the Lancooti, vaguely recalling how Peleyia had touched his mind. How Peleyia had spoken to him in mental communication. He pondered if the mental link could be re-established a second time. He spent an number of hours thinking about it, and discovered to his surprise that he'd relaxed in the saddle, and so long as the horse didn't do anything but gallop, he was fine. For the moment.

That new burst of confidence gave him the courage to try and reach out to Peleyia, and he concentrated on picturing the Lancooti in his mind. It was harder than he expected. He frowned over his inability and employed some of the exercises Sasheer had taught him to search out that place in his mind which held the imprint of Peleyia's touch. Suddenly, in a rush of sensations, he was flooded with all the Lancooti's emotions. He gasped, tightening his hold on the reins when he felt Peleyia's shock vibrate down the mental link.

Delighted by his accomplishment, he spared his friend a grin then reinforced the pathway before mentally projecting his friend's name. :*Peleyia* . . . :

Peleyia straightened in his saddle then stared at Kellen wide-eyed and startled, before a look of fear, then resignation colored his gaze.

Curious as to what Peleyia would say or do, Kellen waited for Peleyia to acknowledge him, willing his friend to accept the connection. He sent his thoughts along the mental channel a second time. :*Are you angry with me?*:

:No.:

The answer was immediate and honest, and Kellen blinked amazed, comprehending that it would be impossible to lie via this means of communication, because each thought carried with it the emotions, the hidden motivations—stripping away all pretenses. It was a shock, and he chose his next question carefully. :*Then why do you refuse to talk with me? Is it because of the witches, or Tich?*:
Instantly, he sensed Peleyia's discomfort and hesitation, and he

held his breath, wondering what the Lancooti was feeling from him via the mental link. He risked a glance around and saw how Peleyia frowned. *:Pel?:*

:It was unethical.:

A little stunned by that reply, he bit his bottom lip in thought. With that one sentence, Peleyia had answered all his questions about the previous night.

:A Gift is a blessing. It should not be abused. I just don't—can't—approve of what Tich did. Regardless of her motives.:

The depth of Peleyia's emotions rolled over him just as Peleyia's words echoed in his mind, and Kellen seriously considered what the Lancooti was saying. Then before he could formulate an answer, Peleyia blocked the connection between them and pulled away from the link. It was not severed or broken, rather just silenced, and that gave him hope. At least they were still friends. *Unethical?* He had such hazy memories of Crystal Gaze Castle that he couldn't pinpoint why Peleyia believed Tich had acted unethically.

* * *

By late afternoon, Kellen was getting sick of seeing nothing but monotonous rolling slopes of endless grass swaying and dancing in the gusty wind. Out there, somewhere, were Slavers and Black Guard with southern captives. People he might know who were being herded toward northern slave pits. Or killed, or even worse, left alive to be slowly eaten by the grassland predators. What would be worse, Deathwalkers, Mindwipes, or being eaten alive? Shuddering, he glanced back at the Dwarf and wondered what he might know about these carnivorous creatures.

Gralvin rode behind him. Kellen noted that, if anything, the Dwarf looked as awkward on horseback as he felt. He hid his grin and slowed his mount, waiting for the gruff Dwarf to draw level with him.

"What is it, child?" Gralvin asked. He never glanced up, his entire concentration centered on the rider in front.

Startled by both the forward question and insulting epithet, Kellen hesitated.

"You pulled back," Gralvin explained in exasperation. Then he looked at Kellen from under bushy brows. "Now I know you feel all out of sorts by what happened up in Crystal Gaze Castle, and if you have a query about them witches, then you had best ask Sasheer, for he knows far more than any other about the subject."

"No, it's not about the witches," Kellen assured, a little taken aback by Gralvin's words and obvious admiration for Sasheer. "I was just going to ask what you knew of these Blu-kin ants."

"Ah," the Dwarf gave a grimace. "Ugly creatures, and vicious."

"Ugly?"

"Huge ugly mutations. Another remnant of perverted Mitthsombaine," Gralvin said, indicating their size with his fingers. "Flesh eaters. They live far out in this barren expanse, in massive sand nests or mounds. Their head is bright blue, which gives them the name, and they feed off the wild herds."

They were created in Mitthsombaine? "They hunt?" Kellen asked, appalled by the idea.

"Not as in chase down," Gralvin corrected, "but they never miss an opportunity to feast," he said. "I once saw them kill and eat a proven Dwarf warrior. He had made the stupid mistake of smashing one of their nests while drunk, but before he could move more than six paces, they swarmed over him." Gralvin shook his head in distaste. "Brought him down like a bull, within seconds, and there was nothing any of us could do to help him. Because once they start to swarm, they engulf everything within range. One of his kin threw an axe and took his head off before he suffered overly long. It was a sour experience."

Alarmed, Kellen stared at the Dwarf in dismay. He glanced ahead at the benign-looking grasslands then back at Gralvin. "Are these nests recognizable?"

The Dwarf gave a gruff laugh. "Just keep that stubborn animal of yours on the trail behind Sasheer, and you will have no problems."

Not feeling terribly comforted by Gralvin's words, Kellen urged his mount to catch up with the others.

* * *

That first night under the stars, surrounded by nothing but swaying grass, made Kellen restless and anxious. He shivered as the temperature dropped, and he squinted into the inky darkness, apprehensive about what awaited them. Black Guard, Blu-kin, Raveners, even Deathwalkers. He hated not knowing.

The wind had picked up, and he wrapped his arms tighter around his chest. He glanced behind, seeing the thin tents pegged against a gentle slope. They were crammed in together, even the horses, because Gralvin predicted an icy change, and Sasheer listened to the Dwarf.

Kellen swept his gaze over to the fire and noted that Salimen had taken over the cooking while Crizkerisomia and Dalzere skinned the six skinny hares. He watched the Elves, baffled, because they were working together. It seemed an unnatural relationship, especially as he was so used to seeing them fight. They drew their knives on the other more often than on any attacking enemy, and this civility was off-putting. He found himself holding his breath, waiting for the calm to break. But Dalzere remained cordial, and Crizkerisomia answered in polite aloofness. Salimen had even started a betting pool to see how long the truce would last. That had infuriated the female Elf, and Sasheer had been forced to curtail Salimen's fun in order to stop the bloodshed.

So now the bowman kept his comments to a minimum, muttering continuously while he worked over the deep fire pit he had prepared.

Kellen switched his gaze to Lesendal and frowned. He could tell something was terribly wrong with the prince, and he speculated on what it might be. Lesendal had changed since returning from the Herders' camp, a haunted look clouding his normally clear eyes, a depression that not even Salimen's dry humor seemed able to penetrate. He got the impression Sasheer knew what was going on behind Lesendal's stare, but as usual, the Mage kept all knowledge to himself.

Then there was Peleyia. The Lancooti was still refusing to speak with him, refusing to acknowledge he was hurt, and refusing to unblock the link. It was frustrating, and at present there was nothing he could do but wait Peleyia out. Only Ryland and Gralvin seemed untouched by the strangeness infecting the other members of the group, and he cast them a searching look. The Haonian warrior was grinning, pleased with himself as he conversed with the brazen Dwarf, neither man paying any attention to the disquiet surrounding them. Kellen shook his head. There were only so many tales about battle that he wanted to hear.

Sighing, he had the impression that the next few months were going to be difficult for all of them. He bent down, picked up the sticks and grass tufts he had found earlier, and approached the unhappy bowman. Salimen was still muttering to himself while he helped Dalzere and Crizkerisomia skin and clean the animals.

"I've brought some more dried grass for the fire."

"Fine, just leave it over there," Salimen instructed, not even bothering to glance up.

"Is everything all right?" Kellen asked, willing the other man to talk to him. He crouched down and eyed the Ihovian across the fire. Out of all his friends, he trusted Salimen to give him an honest answer.

"That depends on your definition of 'all right,' I suppose," Salimen muttered sarcastically. "If charging headlong into danger is classed as normal behavior, then I would say we are all perfectly sane." He lifted his head and gave Kellen a forced, humorless smile. It never reached his eyes.

"I see." Turning away from the bowman, Kellen's mind stalled. He had definitely missed something vital. *But what?* Stepping away from the protected area, he picked up his cloak and wrapped it around his frame then went to stand at the edge of the camp. He stood facing into the wind, letting the icy fingers of night wash over him and scatter his jumbled thoughts. The moon was shadowed, so only a little light escaped the clouds to illuminate the vast plains, which stretched for thousands of leagues. Even the sound of the wind in the grass was like a moan of desolation.

Without thinking, he stepped away from the camp and walked down the slope, feeling the grass tangle around his thighs. For an instant, he just wanted to escape the turmoil of unhappiness behind, escape the uneasiness and find . . . find—

Anger, resentment, betrayal.

Kellen shook his head to banish the abrupt wave of confusing emotions and found that they vanished as swiftly as they had arrived. He swallowed and stood trembling for a prolonged moment, before becoming aware that he was no longer alone. Slowly he turned, apprehensive of what he might find and blinked, stunned, when he saw a cute little snow dragon hover above the grass only a few paces away. He reached out, palm up, and was instantly rewarded when the dragon flew closer and caressed him with its velvety wings. He laughed in delight. "Shard!" He exclaimed in a soft voice, genuinely pleased to see the strange little animal. "What are you doing here?"

"I . . . I followed you."

"You followed me, how?" he asked, not moving when Shard moved closer and pinned him with a dark, unblinking stare. "I looked for you on the moors but couldn't find you," he said.

"I watched you go into the secret place. Into the magic place," Shard whispered. "So I waited for your return."

Secret place? Magic place? "You mean Sanctuary?" he asked and saw the animal nod. He relaxed and let his fingers trail over Shard's icy nose. The little dragon looked adorable, and he was so glad they had met up again. "Do you want to come into the camp?"

"No!" Shard said vehemently, flying back out of reach. It hung there, silent for a moment before it explained. "Death in camp."

Assuming that Shard was referring to Dalzere, Kellen exhaled and shook his head. "Dalzere will not harm you. None of them will. I give you my word."

"Why do you go into grasslands?" Shard asked instead, ignoring the offer of help. It flew back to Kellen and softened its tone. "Why?"

"We are going to the ruins of old Mitthsombaine." Kellen shrugged, unconcerned by Shard's evasion.

"Why go there?" the dragon questioned. "There is nothing but death in that city."

Smiling at the way Shard settled on his outstretched arm, Kellen stroked the animal's head, enjoying the dragon's company. *At least Shard isn't irritable, uncommunicative, or bad tempered,* he decided. "Sasheer wants to—"

"Sasheer?"

Kellen stopped. "Sasheer is a . . . Ranger," he said at the last instance, trying to soothe Shard's agitation. "It sounds worse than it actually is."

"You trust Sasheer?" Shard inquired as it turned its head and leaned closer to Kellen, its voice taking on a strange quality. Almost wistful.

"Yes," Kellen said and realized that he actually meant it. Regardless of what Sasheer said or did, he found that he liked and respected the cantankerous man. "Sasheer needs to go to Mitthsombaine," he explained.

"No one goes to Mitthsombaine," Shard stated. "No one sane."

Relaxing and finding Shard's words mirrored Salimen's thoughts on the subject, Kellen sighed. "He is looking for an oracle that will help him get into the Northlands."

"How . . . interesting," Shard hissed.

The hissed reply alerted him to a new, developing tingle of danger, and Kellen studied the small creature, fascinated by the slight shift in colors under its scales. Instinctively, he pulled his cloak tighter, and glanced around them, but saw nothing. He looked again at Shard and was immediately captivated by the dragon's large eyes, enchanted by the moonlight that seemed to pass through the animal, fascinated by the inky blackness of its scales that turned the dragon almost invisible. Disturbingly beautiful, magical, and he tried to mentally probe behind Shard's façade.

Then within a heartbeat, he was engulfed by swirls of powerful madness and wicked desire, and he staggered back, away from Shard. He tripped and fell into the long grass, sinking further into a mental mire of darkness. The grass became alive, animated, as it smothered him, imprisoned him, and he gasped, battling the tangled web of clinging coldness, feeling crushed into the ground. He struggled to his feet and then was pitching forward, rolling down the slope, and hitting a knot of dark, unnatural currents. His mind froze, and his skin instantaneously chilled to near death.

This was nothing like the currents he had felt previously, and then he remembered the warning Sasheer had given him about polluted, stained threads of old magics and power that dotted the earth. A swirling energy field of whispering malice surrounded him. He tried not to invite the current into his body, tried to crawl out of the current's embrace, and managed to get on his hands and knees—then stopped.

The grass faded to nothing, and he lifted his head to find that he was kneeling on cold, dark stone. Firelight flickered behind him, and the stench of incense filled his nostrils. Slowly he raised a hand and pushed hair out of his eyes and saw . . .

Kalern . . .

The Dark Lord was crouching in a pool of silken robes, magnificent to behold, deathly beautiful, and Kellen dragged his eyes away from the Dark Lord only to see the abyss. It beckoned.

"No . . ." he hissed, refusing to play Kalern's games. "You are not real!"

"*I am your destiny.*"

Kellen shook his head and backed away then fell—

He tumbled further down the slippery slope only to land sprawled in tufts of long icy grass. He stared around, disorientated, and saw the cloudy sky above, heard the wind moan through the grass and knew he was back on the plains. He stretched out his hand and saw his skin was whole, and that the dark currents were gone.

Warily, he stood and stared around, brushing grass from his cloak. Shard was hovering to his right, and he marched up to the little dragon and glared at it. "What just happened?"

The dragon ignored his ire and hardened its tone. "You will go with Sasheer to North Ridge," it stated, the words hissed with deadly menace. "You must. It is preordained. Fated . . . you will . . . will . . . will . . ." The dragon's tone faltered, and it started to shake violently.

The change alarmed Kellen, and he watched the dragon in suspicion, relenting when he realized the animal was in obvious distress. He reached out and gently rubbed his finger over the ridge of Shard's brow. "I will take you back to camp," he said. "If you are in trouble, then Sasheer can help."

"I can't . . . can't . . . can't . . ."

"Can't what?" Kellen asked, reaching out and grabbing Shard. He looked into those dark, inky eyes and saw a flicker of compassion, a trace of real color—a glow of pure silver that softened Shard's features. It was striking.

"He will kill you if you go north," Shard whispered urgently, then the dragon pulled free of Kellen's warm hold and disappeared into the surrounding darkness of night.

Numb, Kellen held still and looked at his hands. *He will kill me? Who? Kalern?* Did Shard know something about Kalern's plan? How . . . and he frowned, not sure what to make of the strange encounter, or of Shard's personality change. For a brief moment, Shard had felt like a Brethren's Shade, and Kellen scanned the vast grasslands wondering if he was sensing Terrica, or something else. But he saw nothing—sensed nothing. Even the knot of unnatural current was gone.

"Kellen?"

Shaking himself of the ill feelings, he turned when he heard Ryland call a second time. The big warrior was standing on the top of the slope, and Kellen made his way back up the grassy hill.

"There you are," Ryland muttered. He placed a hand on Kellen's shoulder and steered him back into the light. "Sasheer says to stay inside the circle of firelight tonight. He said something about darkness increasing the power of evil. Increasing the dangers."

Dangers . . . The word echoed inside him, and Kellen pushed the images of Kalern from his mind. Somehow he didn't feel it was necessary to inform Sasheer about his strange visions, or about Shard. They were his problems, and if he was being haunted by an evil Shade then he was determined to prove to Sasheer that he could survive as a student.

"Come. Dinner is ready," Ryland added, his smile growing. "If Salimen's cooking is anything like his sick humor, then it could be an interesting meal."

CHAPTER THIRTY-SEVEN

Winter hit them with a savage blast within a week of traveling the desolate grassland plains, chilling them all to the bone as rain and ice slowed their progress. They come across only one Black Guard patrol, and all of them had charged into attack before Sasheer could prevent the encounter, each member of the company needing the physical outlet of a fight to burn off the disgruntled energies. The small group of guards had not stood a chance against the unleashed aggression, with none escaping alive to report their presence. Sasheer fumed over their stupidity, while they each checked the other for injuries. But after the altercation, the mood lightened, and traveling became easier.

* * *

One late afternoon a week after the encounter, Kellen sat astride his mare and tried to concentrate on mastering the current lesson Sasheer had taught him while scouting for wood three evenings ago. He glared at his palm, willing the small spark of flame to appear, drawing on the energy within his body and shutting out the currents so temptingly close. Using them was considered by Sasheer to be cheating, and he found it was harder than he thought possible to formulate such a simple mental command. Watching Sasheer do the exercises was one thing, quite another to do them, and he was still in awe of the Mage's abilities. Sasheer made things seem so effortless, but then his young appearance was also a façade, belying the man's age and experience, masking his amazing wit and sharp humor. He was seeing another side of the man now that they were away from the Keep—an approachable side.

He glanced up to make sure he was not falling behind the group and saw Gralvin studying him. Hastily, Kellen rubbed his palm over his tunic and sent the Dwarf an innocent smile. At present, he had promised to keep his lessons with Sasheer secret because the Mage feared some unseen menace could target him. He couldn't comprehend Sasheer's explanation, so had agreed.

Turning away from Gralvin's shrewd gaze, he scanned the grasslands ahead. Tall silvery gray salt grass appeared to roll across the gentle slopes, hypnotizing in its strange beauty as it reflected the sun's glare. He shifted in the saddle, by now used to riding and paying scant attention to his mount. Ahead of him were the others, with only Ryland at the rear, and he blinked when he realized that Gralvin had slowed his mount in order to ride beside him. He slouched down in his saddle and contemplated his predicament, knowing the Dwarf would probably ask personal questions. Questions about his odd behavior around Sasheer, or even what he was doing staring at his hands. The Dwarf's forwardness was disarming. Chancing a look to his left, he saw Gralvin's grin, and clear gaze that reflected the Dwarf's amusement.

"While in Maltros, I noticed that you were sweet on Dalzere's daughter," Gralvin started, his voice low, his tone nonjudgmental, yet his eyes were assessing. "You plan on bonding with the Healer?"

He sat bolt upright in his saddle and opened his mouth then closed it just as fast, feeling gut punched as he turned to stare at the Dwarf. *Dalzere's daughter!* "I—I . . . what?"

Gralvin laughed, a rolling gruff sound. "I was only going to advise that you seek Dalzere's permission before you pursue the Healer. Things are done differently here as compared to the south."

"Bond . . ." The word sent a terrifying sense of dread tingling through him, and he shuddered. He had a vague recollection of Tich mentioning that word to him, more than once. "Tich is . . . I didn't know, Dalzere, was married."

If anything, Gralvin's laugh deepened. "Married?" He grinned, truly amused. "As I recall, that never came into it," he said, lifting a hand to stroke his beard in thought. "The Kizer witch who bore his daughter was insane. She had our Drow friend tortured and left for dead after her demonic ceremony. If it weren't for Sasheer, he would have died. Even so, it took Dalzere months to get back on his feet, and when he did, he returned to the Kizer territory despite Sasheer's warnings and slaughtered most of the tribe. He then brought his daughter to Sanctuary." Gralvin paused, his eyes serious as he gazed at Kellen. "Walk carefully, Kellen. No Drow is to be taken lightly regardless of their civilized veneer."

Stunned, Kellen stared after the Dwarf when Gralvin moved his horse away. *Tich is Dalzere's daughter? Is part Kizer and Drow?* No wonder Sasheer had said she was of mixed bloodlines. No wonder Dalzere had refused to talk about the blood-vengeance curse. Digging his heels into his mare's flank, he hurried to catch up with the others.

That startling news occupied his thoughts for the rest of the week, until they saw a faint outline of dark shapes against the distant horizon. Within days, the shapes took the form of a looming mountain range, and the closer they got, the more the landscape improved. Grass gave way to stunted trees, small bushes, and stagnant ponds that dotted the countryside. Several large anthills dominated the eroding riverbeds, and twisted trees gave meager shade to the few large animals they had seen watching them nervously from a distance. Even the days got colder.

It took two weeks of constant riding to reach the foothills of the massive range Gralvin called Sunsway. After reaching the foothills, Gralvin led them to the narrow trail, and they labored up the uneven and disused track. Eventually they reached the plateau named Bernum's Passage and were able to stop and rest. The platform was a clearing, a natural formation of smooth rock that led to a massive overhang, a ledge known as Sunset Ridge.

* * *

Kellen stood on the rocky ledge of Sunset Ridge and gazed down in wonder at the open plains below. They stretched for as far as the eye could see, and he found it unbelievable to think that they had just crossed that desolate country. By Gralvin's reckoning, it was three moons since they had left the security of the Herder's village in Maltros. It seemed much longer, but the Dwarf was rarely wrong, or so Dalzere said.

Far below, the light slowly receded across the grassed plains, and Kellen watched the sun dip behind the majestic range at his back, an impressive, magnificent sight. He was mesmerized by the shimmering colors of the grass, by its silky appeal as it swayed and danced in the wind.

"Breathtaking, isn't it?"

The quiet question startled Kellen, and he half-turned to see Sasheer standing next to him, tall, remote, and strangely haunted. Those dark eyes were looking far away, seeing things long dead, making Sasheer appear old, contrasting with the youthfulness of his face and body. Sasheer was a confusing picture of wanton beauty wrapped in a shroud of loneliness, and Kellen wondered how often the Mage had stood on this ledge to survey the land below. "I have never seen a sight like it," he whispered, awed.

"Nor will you again," Sasheer said, an edge of regret coloring his tone. "This was where the armies of the four lands massed, where they fought and died. Time has rotted their bones into the ground, yet when I stare out at the expanse before us, I still see their gleaming armor, and their war banners which stretched for leagues in every direction."

Frowning, Kellen squinted at Sasheer and then at the grasslands, trying to imagine such a sight. Almost four thousand years ago. Ancient people from all nations had rebelled against the injustices caused by the Coastal Mage Society. So this was where they had gathered. This was where they had died. It was staggering. "You watched the war from up here?"

"It was required training. I had not finished qualifying for a place in the Great Hall of Magus. So with others like myself, we were compelled to watch, while senior members from the Towers gave cruel object lessons to unfortunate soldiers. It was more a sport than a war, as I recall."

The disgust in Sasheer's voice was tangible, and Kellen experienced some of Sasheer's anger as the Mage's emotions escaped his tight shields. Then Sasheer was wrapping the cloak more tightly round his slender frame, his shudder visible. Astonished that he was seeing this side of the normally closemouthed Mage, Kellen realized another amazing fact. "This is the first time you've been back to Mitthsombaine. Isn't it?"

"Yes," Sasheer said after a prolonged moment. "Unlike the other members of the Brethren, I find returning too painful," he stopped, taking a deep breath and then turning away from the dazzling sight below. "I wanted to speak with you about something else."

Kellen raised a brow, not sure what to expect. So far, during the long and often wet weeks of travel, he had found Sasheer to be surprisingly good company, if a little moody. He was a very complex individual, not prone to personal revelations—but a rather talented teacher when it came to explaining different facets of Kellen's Mage Gift. He no longer saw Sasheer as arrogant or harsh, or as the infallible, wise man Crizkerisomia described. He now understood that Sasheer was just a man, an incredibly old man, but still only a man who was tormented by the past, and who was trying to right the future.

"Tomorrow we will descend into the lower tracks which will lead down into the outskirts of the ruins. Once inside the walls of the old city, I ask that you do not touch anything. It is very important."

"Why?" Kellen asked.

"I will explain more later over dinner to the entire group, but for now I just need you to trust me. It is very important."

Licking his lips, Kellen gave a small nod. "I trust you," he said and found to his total amazement that Sasheer grinned at him. An uncomplicated grin.

"Thank you," Sasheer returned, and he reached over and gripped Kellen's shoulder. "I know this has been rather confusing for you, but during the next few days, I will need you to do everything I say without question and without hesitation." His changeable eyes darkened as he pinned Kellen with a searching look. "Can you do that?"

Curious as to where this was all leading, Kellen just nodded again.

"Good." Sasheer gave him another rare smile. "Now, have you mastered control of that last exercise I showed you?"

He had expected the question earlier, and Kellen hid his smile, thinking Sasheer was becoming predictable. He didn't comment, instead he lifted his hand and held his palm up, then exhaled, calming his erratic thoughts. He could sense Sasheer watching, both physically and mentally, as he tried to block out all distractions as he struggled to control his doubts—and produce a pure, focused image. With a spark, a flame materialized in his palm, buffeted slightly by the breeze, and he sought to curb it. Picturing it in his mind, he perfected its streamline silhouette until he had deliberately changed the flame's color from a warm orange to a deep blue. It flickered then sat absolutely still, floating above his hand, a pure blade of light and power.

"Very good," Sasheer whispered. He reached over and captured the flame in his fingers before extinguishing it. "You are learning fast to block outside influences. That is encouraging."

Preening under the praise, Kellen could not help his grin from spreading at the sense of accomplishment.

"Now let's see how you control an outside threat," Sasheer said, moving his hand in an arc and creating a ripple of fire that hung in the air and flickered from an invisible wind. Kellen stared at the trail of fire, drawing his brow down and meeting the challenge set.

"Calm the agitation without extinguishing the flame. When you have mastered that, the flames will extinguish, and you may return to camp." Sasheer gave a lopsided smirk. "Try not to take too long, or you will miss out on whatever new concoction Salimen has created for dinner." Then Sasheer turned on his toes and walked away.

"Great," Kellen muttered, his eyes never leaving the dancing flames. He reached out and found his mind was suddenly filled with silly distractions. The relaxing breeze was now too strong, a bird he had admired was now chirping too loud, a gnat bite from last night was starting to itch, and he gritted his teeth in annoyance.

* * *

Sitting around the fire later that evening, Kellen cupped a warm brew between his hands. He had failed Sasheer's test, too caught up in 'thinking' as Sasheer termed it, to actually solve the puzzle. In the end Sasheer had taken pity on him and returned to extinguish the flames, and Kellen knew the exercise was just postponed, not forgotten.

At present, he was savoring his supper while listening to Gralvin as the Dwarf drew a map in the ground by the fire. The map detailed the inner part of the old city. Unlike Sasheer, the Dwarf and many of his clan before him had on occasion returned to Mitthsombaine on behalf of Karczag and Tanish in order to check on activities in the area.

"As far as I know, the archway is still standing, and the tunnels leading to the chambers beneath the Great Hall are intact." The Dwarf glanced up at Sasheer, a frown creasing his wide forehead. "I have never actually been into the tunnels below, but they were built by Dwarven slaves, so they should still be passable. Very little else has been disturbed, and for some reason, few animals and very sparse vegetation survive in the heart of the old ruins," Gralvin finished, his stick thumping the ground in emphasis.

"I'm not surprised," Sasheer said. "The place is cursed."

"Just how far does this curse extend?" Crizkerisomia asked. Oddly, she was seated beside the Drow, her finely shaped cheekbones highlighted by firelight and making her appear fragile and feminine. "I have heard that the curse affects only those with evil intent."

Dalzere scoffed, not even glancing at her slender frame as he leaned forward, his bright eyes lifting toward Sasheer. "No. The curse is real and touches everything."

Clearing his throat, Sasheer's gaze traveled around the entire group.

Mirroring the Mage's actions, Kellen also let his eyes study the other members of the group, trying to picture what Sasheer saw. He noted Salimen's curiosity, Lesendal's determination, Ryland's bafflement, and Peleyia's speculative interest. He also saw that Dalzere was still watching Sasheer while Crizkerisomia scowled at the Drow's leather-clad shoulders. Only Gralvin seemed disinterested.

"This curse was placed over Mitthsombaine thousands of years ago by the leading Magus of the Great Hall," Sasheer said, his eyes settling on the Lancooti. "The Magus cursed the city before he died, making everything from the smallest pebble to the largest marble statue a vivid reminder of the carnage that had occurred inside her walls. A living curse."

"So what exactly does that entail?" Salimen asked.

"It means that if you pick up anything inside the walls of Mitthsombaine, or try to remove anything, you will die."

"Die?" Peleyia repeated as he sat up straighter. "As in a Black Guard appearing out of nowhere and killing you—or as in just dropping dead from some old magic?"

"As in just dropping dead, you little thief," Gralvin replied bluntly.

Salimen laughed, seeing the Lancooti's unamused expression. "This could prove to be your undoing, Pel."

Dismissing the laughter around him, Sasheer never took his eyes off the Lancooti. "You must touch nothing. Remove not a single object. Do you all understand?" He waited until everyone soberly nodded in acceptance. "Peleyia?"

"I get the message," Peleyia grumbled.

"Good. Now let's get some rest. I want to get off this ridge as soon as possible." Sasheer muttered, suppressing a shiver and turning away from the company to vanish into the surrounding darkness.

Kellen stared after the Mage then looked to Dalzere and saw the Drow's worry. Slowly he picked up his blanket, apprehensive of what they would find inside Mitthsombaine, scared of what would happen to Sasheer. Then he glanced over at Peleyia and heard the Lancooti mutter a curse. Was this what Sasheer feared? Was this what Sasheer had seen with his Foresight? Was Peleyia going to die because of his insatiable curiosity?

Troubled, Kellen settled for sleep, wondering how he could protect his friends. The tentative link he shared with Peleyia was still present, but silent due to the fact Peleyia refused to acknowledge its existence. *Just another problem*, and Kellen frowned. Between his own nightmares, Peleyia's refusal to talk about Tich, Sasheer's increasing remoteness, Lesendal's depression, and Crizkerisomia's strange behavior—he was amazed they had survived this long.

Sighing, Kellen rolled over in his blanket and looked into the fire's dying embers, trying to imagine what the old city of Mitthsombaine must have once been like. *A jewel*, was the way Gralvin described it. It had clearly been a commanding empire, the center of the known world, rich in wealth, beauty, and power, yet so evil at heart. Then he remembered Sasheer's words of earlier— *I find returning too painful*—and Kellen wondered how he would have reacted if given the choice of betraying his home, his family, his friends, against saving a land that would never thank him. Could he have done what Sasheer did? Could he have walked away from security into the unknown?

Then there was Serine, and he speculated on what he had been like. The name held allure, a secret that he wanted to unravel. He guessed that both brothers had probably stood together on the ledge overlooking the grasslands far below. He tried to imagine what had gone through their minds. Were they similar or vastly different? Opposites, like Wyran and himself?

The fire blurred before his eyes, and Kellen tried to picture what Serine might have said to Sasheer, wondered about his temperament, his motivations—and how he died. It was puzzling and he blinked, lifting his head to see if Sasheer had returned. He glanced around the quiet camp and saw no evidence of Sasheer, then realized that Dalzere was gone also.

* * *

Something dark and sinister teased his mind, and Kellen snapped awake, lifting his head to stare around the cold, dark chamber. Utter silence greeted him, except for the faint, rhythmic dripping of water somewhere deep beneath him. He was cold, deathly so, and he flexed cramped fingers, feeling heavy iron chains cut into his skin. He glanced down and realized he was shackled to the wall.

Nothing seemed real, and he turned his head, trying to avoid looking at the beckoning pit before him. The abyss was his doom—he knew it—could feel it in every fiber of his being. Yet . . . yet there was still hope.

"Hope."

The word swam up in his mind, whispered seductively, and Kellen closed his eyes tight, trying to deny that persuasive voice, that corrupting tone.

"There is always hope, Kellen, always hope."

The compelling words continued, touching him deeply, intimately, and he found he could not evade their meaning.

"Just reach out with your mind, and this nightmare will end . . . just reach out and embrace your future. You know you want to. I can feel it inside you. I can feel your desires . . . your needs . . . your strengths."

NO! The silent shout echoed inside his head only, and he battled to hold the powerful being out, knowing he was losing the battle. NO, please! He raised his hand to ward off the invisible fingers that reached out to caress him, to stroke his cheek, to imprint on his senses.

"Please . . ." The voice breathed the word. "I have not heard that plea since . . . since Serine sat where you are now sitting."

Gods! Was he doomed to relive Serine's fate? Opening his eyes wide, he tried to find his tormentor in the gloom, barely catching a glimpse of pale skin when the Dark Lord turned. Kalern clicked his fingers, and a small flame sprang to life in the lamp beside him. He jumped, then yanked on his chains, watching how Kalern grinned at him in wicked delight, watched as the faceted edges of the jade pendant Kalern wore captured the firelight.

"Kalern—" Kellen hissed, spellbound—by the man's grace, by his elegance as the Dark Lord glided over to his side and cupped his face in strong hands. He forced his captive's face up into the light, his thumb tracing a pattern over dry lips.

"I will not submit," Kellen stated, wishing his voice were stronger, wishing he were not trapped—helpless and so alone.

"I don't want your submission, my pretty child. I want your fire, your passion, your hatred."

Confused by those words, he searched those magnificent eyes which commanded attention. Where had his resolve gone? His control? Then Kalern leaned forward, and he was overwhelmed by the Dark Lord's powerful aura. His knees started to shake, and he groaned as panic rose in his mouth like hot vomit.

"That's it . . . you are almost there. Almost mine. Just reach out with your mind."

"Kell?"

Waking with a start, Kellen gulped in a violent breath and backed away from the hands touching him.

"Kell?"

He battled to refocus his eyes, blinking the darkness clouding his vision away and homing in on Peleyia's anxious face. The lavender-haired Lancooti was leaning over him, one plait falling heavily over a leather-clad shoulder. "Wha—what?"

"It is dawn, and Sasheer wants us to leave. Remember?" Peleyia sounded unsure as he studied his friend's face. "Another nightmare?"

"I . . ." Trying to gather his composure, Kellen did not meet the questioning gaze. He still felt too vulnerable and exposed. It was as if the nightmares were becoming reality. The twisted images were becoming real.

"Kell?"

Breathing out hard, Kellen shut his eyes and willed the lingering shadow away. "Just give me a moment."

"These dreams are getting more frequent, maybe it is time you told Sasheer about them."

"And what could he do?" Kellen asked. He rubbed a hand over his face. He was damp and sticky from perspiration despite the morning chill.

"I don't know, but you can't go on like this."

"I'll be fine."

Unconvinced, Peleyia just gave him a skeptical look before standing and picking up his pack.

Frowning, Kellen watched Peleyia walk away, then he moved, hastily rolling up his blanket and following Ryland from the campsite.

* * *

They led the horses down the winding trail, catching tantalizing glimpses of the green fertile land below and the brilliance of the ocean in the distance. By evening, they were just over halfway down the steep track when Sasheer called a stop. It was another old disused campsite and overhang, another plateau. All of them were drawn to the spectacular views, only made more breathtaking by the magnificent spectacle of the burnt orange glow of sunset on the ocean's horizon. The winter winds around them could be heard whistling through the mountain's narrow passes, and Kellen let his gaze linger on the tall ruins bordering the coastline below. Mitthsombaine.

"They sing songs and tell tales of Mitthsombaine's splendor, but few, I feel, appreciate those song and tales, until they see the sights."

Turning, Kellen let his eyes study the dark Elf beside him, seeing the proud stance, the dark leathers and long black hair that hung to Dalzere's waist. He looked unearthly. "I can only imagine what it must have looked like before the Mage War," Kellen murmured.

"Sunsway Mountains protected the valleys below," Dalzere offered in a soft tone, his fingers pointing out the ruined splendor. "They hid its beauty from the rest of the world until the nations rebelled. And by then, neither the mountains nor the sea could save Mitthsombaine's long overdue destruction."

"But the nations had cause," Kellen said. Looking at the peaceful setting now, he found he was starting to doubt all that he had heard concerning this city. He gazed down in wonderment at the tall gleaming marble walls, at the broken spires that reflected the golden rays of sun so exquisitely. The city looked innocent.

"Never doubt that," Dalzere whispered. "In a way, the old city is still as seductive and as evil as it was back then."

"How?"

Dalzere took a breath and straightened his shoulders. "Four thousand years may have passed since its demise, yet Mitthsombaine still kills. More have died simply exploring the ruins than by the brutal and bloody Mage War."

Shocked, Kellen again let his eyes travel over the ruins before him, still marveling at the charm it radiated. "But it seems so . . ."

"Harmless?" Dalzere supplied, a small smile gracing his lips. "Do not be fooled by appearances."

"I am not anymore," Kellen said, lifting his eyes away from the city to look at the sparkling ocean beyond. "I am learning to see past disguises."

"Good." Dalzere gave a lopsided grin. "Then I can count on you not to be swept away by awe when we enter the ruins?"

Looking at Dalzere in suspicion, Kellen raised a questioning brow. "Dalzere, what are you and Sasheer playing at? He said something similar to me yesterday then refused to say more. Is something bad going to happen to one of us? To Pel?"

"Pel?" Dalzere's brows climbed in curiosity. "What could happen to Peleyia, except the fact that one day he will get caught thieving, then not even I will be able to save his mischievous carcass?"

"Oh, nothing," Kellen shook his head. "Just something I overheard."

"I see," Dalzere said after a breath, thinking hard. "Eavesdropping again?"

"So what do you and Sasheer want me to do now?" Kellen asked, ignoring the slur on his character.

"Stick close to me, and whatever you do, touch nothing," Dalzere said then just winked at him. "And just keep an eye on Peleyia for me. All right?"

"Dalzere!" Kellen spluttered then smiled when he saw the Elf grin. He nodded his willingness, not being given a chance to question the Drow further when Crizkerisomia walked up to them. She was clad in her usual light tan leathers, a total contrast to the Drow's menacing black outfit. They made a striking picture.

"That disgusting bowman just told me to go and do something useful," Crizkerisomia said, a little perplexed. "So I was curious as to whether you would be interested in scouting ahead with me, Drow. To see if there are any interesting surprises awaiting us below."

Giving her a civil look, Dalzere turned and saw Sasheer was watching him. He begrudgingly accepted her invitation, frowning, and muttering something before he grabbed his cloak and led the way down the trail. "We can go as far as the Nook. Any further in the dark would be pointless."

Surprised that Dalzere would accept the offer, Kellen cast Sasheer a glance, but the Mage was scowling at Lesendal. He would have liked to have accompanied Dalzere, but he got the firm impression that Crizkerisomia would not have welcomed his company. So instead he went over to Ryland and helped the Haonian prepare the fire. He had a funny feeling it was going to be a long night.

CHAPTER THIRTY-EIGHT

Midmorning two days later, the group stood outside the high walls of Mitthsombaine.

"I don't want to hear any arguments," Sasheer started as he stripped off his cloak and placed it over a low stonewall. "We all must wash and change, remove anything that is stained with blood. And clean all your weapons."

Kellen stared at Sasheer, watching how the man scowled, how he pulled off his tunic and undershirt. It was the first time Kellen had seen so much of the man, and he was amazed at how finely muscled the Mage's body was. What he had expected, he didn't know, but Sasheer never ceased to surprise him. Then Kellen noted that Dalzere was also stripping, dark, flawless skin replacing the dark, supple leather. When Crizkerisomia followed suit, stripping to her undergarments, and he turned away, reluctantly dropping his pack and undoing his cloak.

"Why?"

It was Salimen who predictably had to ask, and Kellen sighed. In the mood Sasheer had been in over the last few weeks, he didn't think it was wise to antagonize the Mage any further. But Sasheer just lifted his gaze, and his expression effectively shut Salimen up. Then Lesendal reached over and touched his cousin's shoulder.

"I suggest we just comply," the prince said. Next to him, Ryland grunted gruffly then dropped his armor to the ground. It hit with a dull thud.

"There's always one who's got to argue," Gralvin snorted in amusement, as he started to strip the horses of their saddles. "You want me to set these beasties free?" he asked the Mage.

* * *

After they had changed, discarded bloodied items, set the horses free in the valley below, and then assured Sasheer their weapons were clean, the group proceeded through the open gates of Mitthsombaine. The outer, fortified wall stood intact, the destruction hardly noticeable from outside the gates, yet inside was a different story. The city looked like it had been torn apart from within. Tall buildings, statues, and huge marble columns lay where they had crashed against the inside walls, their perfection shattered as if by a great force.

Stepping around fallen objects, each stared around in astonishment and silent awe, realizing how very little had been left untouched on that fateful day almost four thousand years ago. A thin layer of strange green moss covered everything like an insidious infection, from the enormous stone statues to the broken china that littered the paved streets. It was eerie and fascinating, compelling and gruesome all at once. All mixed in with the broken marble was human bone; bones, which littered the road, and shone silver white in the winter sunlight. Some of the bones appeared to be half-eaten, swallowed by the earth itself. *Looters*, or so Gralvin muttered, the Dwarf only giving the splintered bones a momentary glance as he concentrated on keeping Salimen from straying too far off the road.

Turning, Kellen glanced back at the massive gates that hung open. This was not what he had expected of Mitthsombaine. Then he spied Peleyia stopping by a large toppled column, gazing at something in rapt interest. Going back to him, Kellen tried to see what he was studying so hard. "What is it?" he asked, curious despite himself.

"I don't know," Peleyia frowned. "That's what I'm trying to work out. I thought it was a sword at first, but look at the end of the thing. It could be a scepter. See the gold coloring under the moss?"

Following the Lancooti's pointed finger, Kellen frowned harder. The object Peleyia was studying was mostly concealed by a fallen statue of two entwined lovers. It was covered in green moss, and the only bit that showed any real color was the edge of the thing as it reflected the pale sunlight. Dropping his head to one side, Kellen glanced away, seeing the other members of the company disappear behind a fallen building. "We had better go—"

"It's gold; I'm sure of it!" Peleyia said in excitement. Then, before Kellen could stop him, the Lancooti had stepped over the fallen statue and was reaching for the object.

"No!" Grabbing him, Kellen held Peleyia's wrist firmly, stopping his friend from touching the object. He saw Peleyia's outstretched fingers hesitate only a dozen inches from the enticing artifact. "Remember the curse," he whispered, tightening his hold around Peleyia's wrist. Yet oddly, now that he was closer to the object, he could almost swear the intriguing artifact was pulling at them—whispering to them both in an undertone. He sucked in a startled breath when the moss-covered item suddenly turned, moving toward Peleyia's outstretched fingers.

"Kell?"

Kellen felt Peleyia start to tremble with exertion, and he found that his own hand was frozen in place on Peleyia's wrist. His skin had turned an unnatural color and was cold, while his fingers remained locked. He released a forced breath and tried to marshal his own thoughts as he felt Peleyia try to jerk his hand away from the beckoning object. But nothing happened, and Kellen's eyes widened when the half-concealed scepter moved again then turned slowly upward, unwinding from its bed of destruction. As it turned, the vile green moss slid from its surface to reveal a gold handle that was decorated with colored gems.

"Kell, I can't move my hand, or my arm." An edge of fear colored Peleyia's hushed tones, and he tried to jerk free a second time. "It's as if I'm locked in place. And that thing is moving!"

Again the object turned, its rotation taking it even closer to Peleyia's vulnerable, outstretched fingers. The movement was made more sinister by the tempting way the sun reflected off the precious stones.

Closing his eyes, Kellen tried to think, feeling a heavy constraint cover both his hand and arm. It secured him in place, kept him bound to Peleyia, and through their close proximity, he could easily sense the Lancooti's agitation and powerless struggles to pull free. "Don't," he breathed. With a new clarity, he understood how their panic just drew the cursed item closer. It seemed another of Sasheer's lessons was finally paying off.

"What?" Peleyia asked, panic marring his tone.

"Just relax," Kellen told him, forcing calm and wondering if he could relax Peleyia enough in order to work his plan. "Just relax; clear your mind. Think of water."

"Water?"

"Yes, water," Kellen repeated, struggling to dampen down on his own fears.

"Kell, are you crazy?" Peleyia demanded.

"No!" Kellen snapped in anger then bit back on the uncontrollable emotion when he saw the scepter continue to turn, like a screw loosening. "Just try and do as I ask."

"Kell, how the hell is water going to help us now?"

"Pel, will you just shut up and stop fighting me," he snapped again. "Trust me. Close your eyes and think of water."

"What damn water?" Peleyia started and then gulped in a fearful breath, as the object quickly closed the inches between them. Its clean gold crown gleamed enticingly only an inch from his fingers.

"Any damn water!" Kell hissed back. "The cursed sea for all I care! Just do it!"

"But—"

"Pel," Kellen broke in, suppressing his exasperation with difficulty, remembering how Sasheer had once told him that it was harder to formulate a specific direction for magic, than to simply react. *Sasheer's right.* "Please," he petitioned, purposely lacing calm into his words, forcing the other man to trust him. "Just think of cool, soothing water. Sink your mind into the image of the sea."

"The sea?" Peleyia whispered in panic.

Feeling and hearing the other man's fears clearly, Kellen took another deep breath. "Yes, the relaxing calm of the sea, of our journey across White Seas," he encouraged, fighting to bury his own terror and capture Peleyia's turbulent emotions within his own aura to mask the Lancooti's fear and deceive the object.

"Kell, are you—"

"Just do it!" he hissed, a hard edge cutting his tone. "Close your eyes and concentrate on the calmness of the ocean." The object lifted further, and it would only be a matter of moments before its seductive embrace latched onto Peleyia's hand. He felt Peleyia swallow a nervous breath, and he let his own lashes fall, conjuring an image of the trip over on the *May Queen*. Slowly, he felt Peleyia's mind open to him through the link . . . *gentle rocking of the big boat. The soothing sounds of water lapping at the hull, stilling his fears for his homeland. Setting him free to live.*

Kellen felt the hot rush of energy flare deep in his chest; he also felt the currents swirl around his ankles, but he dared not use the seductive energy they offered. Dared not mix his magics with anything from Mitthsombaine. He concentrated on his goal and sensed how Peleyia's consciousness fell into tune with his own—and then sensation abruptly returned to his cold fingers, and he wrenched them both free. He fell backward, the momentum carrying them over the fallen statue to land on their backsides in the middle of the cobbled road.

Glancing around wide-eyed, each looked down at their hands then back up at the object still glistening in the afternoon sun. It hissed and shook with bitter resentment before sinking back into the earth.

"Kell?"

"Yeah?"

"I . . . umm . . . think I now know how this curse works."

"Me too." Kellen returned Peleyia's half smile.

"Thank you."

"Don't mention it." Watching him, Kellen frowned, feeling Peleyia mentally withdraw from the link. To know and understand someone so intimately was frightening, yet also addictive. "Pel, about this thing . . ."

"Yes?" Peleyia questioned reluctantly.

"How strong is it? I mean, will it work over a great distance?"

"I don't know," Peleyia said. "It is not supposed to work like this at all."

"It's not?"

"No." Peleyia shook his head. "Linking is a technique my people use on difficult traders. Usually it only works after the victim has been sedated with a drug in his food. It is supposed to make them receptive to certain ideas—it shouldn't be a two-way flow of emotions. Then after the connection is broken, the subject never remembers the mental touch."

"But I did," Kellen breathed, staring at the Lancooti and seeing his discomfort. "I remembered even after the witch's drugs wore off."

"Yes," Peleyia agreed. "That shocked me."

"I know." Kellen grinned then elaborated when Peleyia stared at him astounded. "I felt your shock when I called you outside Maltros. Remember?"

Peleyia nodded. "I don't know how to break the connection between us."

"Do you want to?" Kellen asked.

"No . . ." Peleyia hesitated, "but this could be dangerous."

"Why? Because there can be no secrets? Because I might learn too much about you?"

"No," Peleyia said very slowly, pushing a length of stray hair out of his eyes. "I trust you with my life. It is only—"

"It just saved our lives," Kellen defended, gesturing toward the now-silent object behind them. Then he frowned as his head started to ache.

"Yes. It saved our lives today. But later, it might distract and kill us."

"Maybe."

"Which reminds me, how did you know how to break the curse?" Peleyia countered, a frown pulling down his brow.

"I honestly don't know," Kellen shook his head. "It just suddenly came to me. Like a forgotten memory." He raised a hand to rub his temple.

"And now you have a headache," Peleyia finished. He raised a hand to his own temple, his frown mirroring Kellen's scowl. "I share it."

Thrown by that admission, Kellen said nothing, just studying Peleyia's face as the other man stood and brushed off his leathers before offering a hand up. He did not want to think about the complications of the linking, dismissing his own concerns as he reached for his pack.

"We had probably better catch the others before Dalzere comes looking for us like a miniature thundercloud." Peleyia gave a small smile, trying to lighten the experience.

"Pel?"

"Yeah, I know." The Lancooti let the apology hang between them. "I promise not to get distracted again."

CHAPTER THIRTY-NINE

With a prickling of apprehension, Dalzere glanced around at the group behind, sensing the discontentment and exhaustion of the southerners. He wanted to offer them aid, words of support, but their distrust made it difficult. Instead he narrowed his gaze and looked past the weary men to the growing shadows which heralded the approach of evening.

"Which way do we go now?" Ryland asked, breaking into his thoughts. Ryland had his sword out, and Dalzere could see by the way he held it that it was more for comfort than protection. "There is death in the air. I would hate to get lost inside these walls and be forced to spend the night here."

"Believe me, none of us want that," Dalzere muttered. He walked over to speak with his silent friend. Sasheer was pale, his dark eyes sightless as he stared up at what was left of the once-magnificent Great Hall.

"I have never wanted to return . . ."

Hearing the whispered words, Dalzere glanced up at the old building. "The past is gone, my friend."

"Is it?" Sasheer murmured, dropping his eyes to stare intently at the Drow. Dalzere looked at him in compassion for a prolonged moment before Sasheer sucked in a breath and visibly pulled himself together, marshaling his own control.

Dalzere turned away from the ruined building to find the southerners staring at him nervously. At the back of the group, he saw Kellen and Peleyia hurry forward, and he muttered a curse. He had tried to keep an eye on the adventurous duo but was distracted by Sasheer's unnatural hesitancy. This was a complication he had not expected, and he looked back at the subdued Mage with trepidation. He had forgotten his partner's fears of the old hall, although he had heard most of the horror stories concerning Mitthsombaine. He had also lived through many of Sasheer's neurotic nightmares. "We should probably try to find the tunnels before the sun begins to set," he said, reaching out to lightly brush fingers over Sasheer's shoulder.

"Of course. Just give me a moment," Sasheer shuddered and then pulled his eyes away from the hall. Dalzere followed his gaze, seeing the pale faces behind them. Sasheer's eyes turned toward Kellen before resurrecting a small smile. "I am surprised we have had no casualties."

Suppressing a grin, Dalzere said nothing.

CHAPTER FORTY

Kellen watched Sasheer walk toward them; the Mage's expression was grim as he took the large sword out of Ryland's hand without comment. Then Sasheer used the sword to draw a map on the moss-covered cobblestones.

"We are here, and as far as I can remember, there are two entranceways into the tunnels below the city. One is here, and the other is over here," Sasheer said, marking each area with the sword tip.

"This one has been blocked by a quake," Gralvin informed him gruffly, touching the map with his boot.

"Then we will not bother with it and head for this entrance here," Sasheer decided.

"What if it is blocked also?" Salimen asked, raising a skeptical brow.

"Then we unblock it."

"What if we can't?"

"Then we die," Sasheer growled, not bothering to hide his impatience before he handed the big Haonian his sword back.

"I had a feeling you were going to say that," Salimen said.

Kellen frowned, seeing Sasheer level an annoyed glare on the bowman. Then just as swiftly, the anger in his gaze changed to tired frustration.

"After dark, this place reverts into a death pit as the Stone Ghouls come out to hunt the living," Sasheer warned.

"Stone Ghouls?" Lesendal asked. "What are they?" The others around him asked similar questions.

"Ancient abominations which normally live only in stone. Living rock," Sasheer added, in a more reasonable tone.

"So why," Salimen spoke up, "why are we safer underground? Because—I may be wrong here—but isn't there more rock underground than up here?"

"Yes." Dalzere nodded. "But up here is the remembrance of blood."

"And that matters because?" Salimen asked again. "I can tell you I'm liking this excursion less and less."

"Because they are drawn to blood," Sasheer snapped before Dalzere could explain. "And the fresher the blood the better."

Kellen jumped at the sharpness of Sasheer's verbal rebuke, his eyes going to Salimen and noting how the bowman glared at the Mage. They were all stressed, and he forced a deep breath, worried by the way Sasheer's irises had darkened to an almost black. Then he saw Dalzere closed his eyes before the Drow reached out and stepped in front of Sasheer, placing a palm on his chest.

"Time," Dalzere murmured. "We don't have time."

Sasheer nodded, covering Dalzere's hand briefly before moving away. "The sun will set in two hours. I suggest we hurry," he said, his eyes lightening, before he turned and walked away.

Salimen's scowl didn't ease, and he turned his annoyance on the Drow. "Dalzere?" he asked expectantly.

Kellen didn't relax even when Dalzere sighed, the Drow's yellow eyes tracking Sasheer's progress before the dark Elf glanced back at the other members of the group.

"You deserve an explanation," Dalzere agreed, gesturing for them to follow him. "The Stone Ghouls were created hundreds of years before Mitthsombaine fell. They were originally created to protect the passageways underground. Placed like sentries to stop the Dwarves from invading the city."

Gralvin grunted and rested his huge axe over one shoulder. "They did claim many lives, or so the histories tell."

"After the Mage War, or during it, I'm not sure," Dalzere continued, "the Ghouls were released from their restrictive environment in the deep underground tunnels and allowed to roam at will anywhere within the city's walls. Above ground or below. Normally it would take a spilling of blood to call them, but up here, in the old city, so much blood has been spilt that the ground is actually stained. So the Ghouls gather here every night to feed on explorers or animals who stay after sunset."

"Without any blood being spilt?" Peleyia asked with morbid curiosity.

"Yes," Dalzere confirmed. "And in the dark, or at night, their sense of smell is strongest."

"How strong?" Kellen asked, fascinated. "And will they hunt us in this place where Sasheer wants to go?"

Dalzere hesitated, obviously composing his thoughts, before he continued, "Somehow the Ghouls can sense a warm-blooded being and rise out of the earth to pull their prey down. But from what I have read, and heard, we are definitely safer underground at night."

"Are the Ghouls, by chance, linked with this magical curse?" Peleyia asked.

"Yes." Dalzere nodded. "Every item within these walls acts as a lure for the Stone Ghouls."

Kellen exchanged a horrified look with Peleyia, just realizing how close they had both come to being pulled down.

Dalzere was still talking, his eyes sliding to the Dwarf. "Your ancestors died because they returned victorious through the tunnels with blood on their clothing and weapons. They unwittingly dragged the Ghouls into the surrounding Dwarven communities. That is why the Magus of the Great Hall allowed your people entry to the city. By doing so, he sacrificed a few soldiers, mostly temple guards and some civilians, while on the other hand, he wiped out the entire population inside the prosperous Dwarven silver mines."

"So he could then claim those mines for Mitthsombaine," Gralvin said in sudden understanding. "That bastard! My people had often wondered what happened to the clans living under Sunsway Mountains. All written records were lost, or destroyed."

"It is only my guess, as I have no proof," Dalzere cautioned. "It is what I have heard discussed by some of the Brethren."

Gralvin grunted. "They are a closemouthed lot, I have found."

"So blood draws them," Salimen broke in, dragging them back to the initial subject. "I want to be perfectly clear about this point if we are going into the dark tunnels. Is it just fresh blood or any sort of blood?"

"Any sort," Dalzere confirmed. "That is why Sasheer made us change clothing and clean our weapons before entering the city."

"I've noticed he dislikes explaining anything of importance," Salimen ended sarcastically.

"So these Ghouls will feed on the surface, regardless if we bleed or not, but only feed underground if we bleed," Lesendal clarified.

"Yes," Dalzere said. "Since the war, it is now safer underground."

"That is not common knowledge, Drow," Crizkerisomia said softly. "Maybe a sign should be posted to warn of the dangers at night. It would save the deaths of so many explorers."

"No."

It was Sasheer's voice, and Kellen jumped again, so lost in the imagined fear Dalzere's words had produced. He turned and found Sasheer was standing beside a toppled marble column, partially hidden from view. How long he had been listening to their conversation, Kellen didn't know. But he suspected Sasheer missed very little of anything.

"There are too many secrets still hidden deep within Mitthsombaine, and those secrets need to be protected. I think—regardless of how cruel it sounds—that the Stone Ghouls are a necessity." He cast a dark glance around them all. "Now unless you want to experience that necessity, I suggest we move a little quicker."

* * *

They climbed and slid over fallen columns, walls, and general rubble for over an hour until they arrive at a dim chamber that was still partially protected from the cold weather by a massive roof. A part of the roof was caved in, but enough remained intact for them to crawl through.

"This way. Hurry," Sasheer muttered. He led the way forward, his movements quick and graceful.

Outside, the sky was darkening, and all the evening sounds faded into an eerie stillness. The atmosphere became heavy, oppressive, like the entire city was holding its breath in preparation for night—in fear of a dreadful, encroaching hunger.

Some of the old hallways were damaged beyond repair, and Sasheer hesitated, muttering to himself before he led the way down curved stairs. Kellen studied the steps, imagining how once they must have been immaculate, majestic, and he ran his hand lightly over the old tarnished banister. The wide staircase took them to a lower level, and Sasheer pushed past fallen doors and half-toppled walls to get them into a wide chamber. It looked to be an old banquet hall. Spacious. Kellen could see broken crystal lights hanging from the ceiling. Ripped and decayed tapestries festooned the walls, while under his feet, the floor was pure, solid marble, filthy, mostly covered, but if he rubbed at the dirt, he could see the brilliance.

The magnificence of the place astounded him, and he had to hurry to keep up with the fast pace Sasheer set. The Mage never stopped to examine anything, leading them lower still, to other halls and massive rooms. Kellen stopped at another set of ornate stairs and fingered the blackened silver, amazed by such traces of beauty in so deadly and wicked a city. No wonder explorers risked entering Mitthsombaine—only to be captivated by the exquisite beauty of the treasures hidden within the old city walls and then to die at night, locking those secrets away until the next explorer arrived. He shook his head, appalled and awed.

At the next level, they had to struggle around a collapsed roof and broken statues. Everything lay exactly where it had fallen thousands of years ago. A tomb of death, of pain, and destruction—and Kellen even glimpsed a dust-covered crystal glass, still intact as it rested against a skirting board. Perfectly preserved, and he paused, tempted to go and pick it up. Then Sasheer glanced back, the Mage's expression grim, almost desperate, as he pushed a heavy door ajar.

"Quickly now. Everyone, down the stairs. Dalzere, light one of the lamps while I secure this door," Sasheer said.

Turning away from the glass, Kellen obeyed, shivering when a ghost breeze teased over him. He half-turned and squinted back up the narrow steps to see the others and was glad when Dalzere lit the lamp. Then he saw Sasheer drag the door closed and wave his hand over it. A tingling feathered over him, and Kellen tensed, not sure he would ever get used to how easily Sasheer evoked a spell. He made it appear so effortless.

They continued down the narrow winding steps until they reached a dark lower level that was devoid of the magnificence like those of the rooms above. Here all the furnishings were smashed beyond recognition, the walls covered in soot, and the air laced with the smell of charcoal. Sasheer never touched a thing, moving past each of the party to join Dalzere in the lead. He led them through long hallways and then stopped when they reached an inaccessible section of corridor. Here the roof and the walls from above had caved in.

"What now?" Dalzere whispered, lifting his torch higher to get a better view of the destruction and blocked passage.

"This is the only way through," Sasheer muttered as he glanced around. "The entrance to the lower tombs and tunnels is just beyond this point. On the other side of this section is a lever which releases the trap doors and secures the doors behind us from physical intruders."

Stepping forward, Ryland attempted to move one of the large blocks littering the dusty floor.

"What about using magic?" Salimen asked, lifting a hand to gesture at the stone and marble blocking the way. "You know, like make the stone disappear or something."

"This city is magic cursed," Sasheer explained softly, his smile curling when the other's seemed to brighten at the idea. "And what that means is that all forms of spell casting are useless, except the most basic enchantments. But even those are dangerous, because they will draw the Ghouls."

"Lovely," Salimen muttered.

Kellen stared at Sasheer, remembering the enchantment he had seen Sasheer use on the doors. Remembering the knowledge, the deep, intrinsic magic he had used to free Peleyia on the surface. *We're doomed.*

"Is there no other way?" Crizkerisomia asked. She checked her knives and glanced down the darkened corridor behind them.

"No," Sasheer said as he raised a hand to rub his eyes. "Our time has almost gone."

"Time for what?" Salimen asked again.

"The Ghouls," Dalzere said, his voice a hiss.

"But we're underground," Salimen protested.

"Not far enough," was all Sasheer said.

"Oh great!" the bowman spat as he pulled out an arrow and loaded his bow. Lesendal drew his sword also and turned to watch their backs.

"I cannot move this," Ryland grunted before intensifying his efforts to shift the fallen blocks. Gralvin moved to help him.

"What of that?" Crizkerisomia asked. She pointed upward toward a small gap in the fallen rocks. Ryland went over to it and started pulling rocks aside.

"Well?" Sasheer asked impatiently.

"It is indeed a gap, but not big enough for us to get through."

"Maybe not all of us, but I could get through," Peleyia offered. "What does this lever look like?"

Blinking at the slender Lancooti, Sasheer took a deep breath, his dark eyes considering the thief. "It is a narrow trigger built into the side of the left wall, about halfway down. You will have to search for it with your fingers and push it in."

"If it is there, I will find it," Peleyia assured.

"Opening the trap door may dislodge all the rubble. You may get crushed when the ceiling falls," Sasheer warned.

"It is a risk I'm willing to take. Especially as the other choice is being devoured by Ghouls," Peleyia said, giving a cocky grin. Stepping over the fallen statues and sections of wall, he climbed up next to the big Haonian and eyed the narrow gap.

"Be careful, lad," Gralvin muttered, and he helped to hoist

the thief up into the narrow crevice. "And remember, don't bleed, or . . ." He left the rest unsaid.

Struggling between the cold blocks of stone, Peleyia said nothing as he peered into the darkness beckoning him.

* * *

Biting his lip, Kellen kept his eyes firmly trained on the small opening, wishing he knew how Peleyia was getting on. He was nervous, and he debated trying to open the link between them, but that might just distract the other man, and he didn't want to do that. So he just stared at the rock, flexing his fingers impatiently, willing himself to feel something. Anything. "Shouldn't he be through by now?" he asked again, knowing Sasheer was standing close behind him.

"That would depend," Sasheer said after a pause.

"On what?" Kellen glanced back at the pacing Mage.

"On how easy it is to get past the fallen section of ceiling, I would imagine," Sasheer's reply was tart.

"What if he doesn't make it?"

"Kellen." It was a warning growl.

"I mean, what if the Ghouls get here first?"

"There is no point in discussing the worst possibility."

"What if he cuts himself and is bleeding?" Kellen asked, his imagination supplying the worst possible scenario.

"Kellen!"

"He might already be dead," Kellen continued, warming to his theme. "The Ghouls might already be here and we—"

"Kellen!" Sasheer grabbed his arm and shook him. "That is enough! Between Salimen's persistent 'what ifs' and you, I—" he growled, exasperated then released the other man and stepped back. "I am not cut out for this," he muttered as he glanced at the ceiling. "Tattlier is right; I do not have the patience to competently train a student."

"Sasheer?" Kellen started again.

"What?" The word was snapped, and then Sasheer was glaring at his young charge.

"If something were to happen to Pel, you would know. Wouldn't you?"

"Yes," Sasheer said with firm emphasis.

"And you would tell me?"

"Yes. I would tell you."

Accepting that, Kellen turned and stared at the narrow opening in the rubble. He didn't want to think about Karczag's solemn words regarding Peleyia's fate, nor about Sasheer's Foresight. Rather he had to trust Sasheer like Dalzere did. Taking a deep, calming breath, he realized he was chewing his nails—again—and forced himself to relax.

"Sasheer?"

"What now?" Sasheer snapped in annoyance when Ryland walked over. The big man had a scowl plastered across his face.

"I think you should take a look at this," Ryland called before he pointed toward the two Elves. Both were standing by the rockslide, inspecting the damage. Next to them, Gralvin stood peering into the small opening, softly calling Peleyia's name.

Muttering to himself, Sasheer marched over to the two Elves. "Well, what is it now?"

Dropping the piece of stone she was holding, Crizkerisomia lifted her eyes to meet the darker ones of the ill-tempered Mage. "This slide only happened a few months ago," she said. "It is new, as the stone fragments are fresh compared to the rest of this ancient disaster."

"Are you sure?" Sasheer asked, his anger abating as he looked over toward Dalzere for confirmation.

"Positive." The Drow nodded. "It looks like it was deliberately brought down to block the tunnel's entrance."

"Kalern," Crizkerisomia said before a hard, unpleasant smile graced her lips. "We know he came here to get the Book of Spells, so it is possible he brought this section of roof down to stop any other member of the Brethren returning for the Oracle."

"It is possible," Sasheer said, then he closed his eyes and sighed. He rubbed his face then stared at his hands and shook his head. "I should have anticipated this."

"Which means there will be other traps in the lower levels," Dalzere said.

"More than likely," Sasheer agreed.

"If we get to the lower levels," Crizkerisomia reminded him.

Dalzere sent her a glare, about to reply when the floor beneath their feet trembled. "Ghouls or—"

"Get back!" Sasheer hissed, as he pushed the two Elves to safety before grabbing the Dwarf and Ryland and shoving them back. Then Sasheer took a pace back and watched the floor. His eyes were intent and bright, before a small smile tugged at the corner of his mouth. He took another measured step back when a crack appeared in the stone floor—then abruptly the debris was falling, leaving a gaping hole in the middle of the passageway.

They all coughed as dust obscured the confined area. Dalzere raised the torch higher, so they could see when the atmosphere cleared. Most of the collapsed section of wall and ceiling had gone, and they could see the far wall. Immediately in front was a dark hole that led down into a silent tomb of blackness.

"The trap door," Crizkerisomia muttered in wonderment.

"He did it!" Gralvin grinned moving toward the opening.

"Peleyia?" Sasheer called softly, following the Dwarf.

Kellen hurried after Sasheer, shivering in the sudden chill that tinged the air. He glanced around and then settled his eyes on the pit. It looked like an abyss. "No," he whispered, bumping into Sasheer and feeling the Mage's gaze on him. Troubled, he lifted his lashes and met those blue eyes, seeing firelight reflected eerily in the dilating pupils. Breaking the connection, he swallowed and looked away. Was this his nightmare?

"Pel?" Dalzere carefully stepped around the trapdoor's edge, using his light to see into the shadows beyond, breathing a sigh of relief when he heard a hoarse cough. "Peleyia?"

"Here," came the faint answer.

Lifting the torch higher, Dalzere gave a smile, making out the Lancooti's outline in the darkness. The slender thief was wedged between the wall and a broken statue.

"Are you all right?"

"Oh fine, if you mean do I liked to be crushed every day," Peleyia complained. He pulled himself clear of the dust-covered artifact and limped to the edge of the hole. He gazed down into the darkness, brushing the dust from his leathers. "Some trapdoor. The old Mages didn't do anything by half, did he?"

Sasheer ignored that observation and gestured toward the darkness. "Quickly, all of you, down the stairs." He pushed Lesendal and Ryland to the front as the air around them frosted, and ice started to form on the walls.

"What stairs?" Salimen asked as he was also pushed forward. He glanced back. "Why the hell is it getting so cold?"

"Don't ask," Gralvin muttered, moving past Salimen to rush down the treacherous steps. "Come on, Blondie."

"Dalzere, quickly! Our time has gone!" Sasheer hissed.

Taking the hint, the Drow agilely jumped down into the open pit, landing on his feet and lighting the way into the tunnels.

Each member followed as fast as possible, climbing over the remains of the debris and following Dalzere's beckoning figure. Behind them, they could hear a faint wail. The sound was like a moan of loss, of death, and no one asked any questions. Each needed no second reminder, and they rushed down the steps and into darkened tunnels.

The further down they went, the colder the atmosphere became, and Dalzere lit a second torch, handing it to Gralvin when the various sets of steps became slippery with mould and water. The moans of hunger had faded behind them, but none of them relaxed or spoke.

Deeper and deeper into the underground caverns they traveled. The walls were smooth and icy to touch, the atmosphere heavy, the air stale as their hot breaths frosted around them. Dripping water echoed in the distance, the smell of decay all around as the tunnels went on endlessly.

It was with a sense of relief that Kellen entered the first huge underground room behind Lesendal, the sudden vastness easing his panic. In the gloom, he could just make out pale statues and enormous carved pillars. Firelight reflected off the statues' stern faces, highlighting the chiseled stone, the stark whiteness of the marble, the sightless eyes and cold lips. Each statue rested on an oblong platform that was inscribed with a spiraling script.

Approaching one statue, Kellen ran his hand over the raised script, feeling its texturing, absorbing the coldness of the stone. These statues were old—*very old*—from a time beyond reason, from a time of death, and he sucked in a shuddering breath before looking up when Peleyia stopped at his side. The Lancooti eyed the gold-embossed statue.

"It's magnificent," Peleyia said in whispered reverence. He folded his arms resolutely so as not to reach out and touch anything. "I bet this would be worth a fortune."

"Fortunately it won't fit in your pack," Salimen said as an aside, stepping around Peleyia's discontented figure.

"What is this place?" Lesendal asked in awe. He stopped next to Gralvin and inspected another similarly decorated statue.

"Mitthsombaine's tomb," Gralvin stated.

"A tomb?" Lesendal questioned. "This is where they buried their dead?"

"No," Sasheer answered for the Dwarf. "This is the tomb of the High Maguses only. And most were buried alive in order to preserve their status of Magus before the title was passed on."

"That's . . . barbaric. Horrid," Salimen said in disgust.

"The whole city was horrid," Sasheer reminded him. "Now come, and remember to touch nothing."

"What's ahead?" Peleyia asked.

"The old treasury, library, and a few other practice chambers and prisons," Sasheer listed then looked at the Lancooti.

"I know, I know," Peleyia muttered sourly. "I won't touch a thing."

"Prisons?" Crizkerisomia asked, her gaze narrowing. She glanced briefly at Dalzere before turning to Sasheer. "Elven prisons?"

"Yes," Sasheer said, his tone neutral. "Where some of the genetic experiments were carried out."

Dalzere shuddered before he pinned the Sun Elf with his angry gaze. "This is where my people were born. This is why you slaughtered my race in the Second War."

"Dalzere, please." Sasheer placed a hand on his arm, making sure he stood between the two Elves. "That is the past. We are all friends here."

"Drow is still a curse," Crizkerisomia hissed, her hand straying to the knife at her belt. She drew it swiftly, sidestepping Sasheer to place the blade at Dalzere's throat.

"Not as much as your people were a curse when they slaughtered the innocent," Dalzere said, no fear in his eyes or voice.

Kellen stood frozen and watched, fascinated and shocked when Dalzere moved in a swirl of black leather and long silken hair. The Drow's actions so precise, so elegant—utter deadliness overlaid with enchanting beauty. Seductive. Then Dalzere had Crizkerisomia pinned against one of the old marble statues, her blade falling uselessly to the stone floor—and Kellen remembered to breathe. The move had looked so basic, yet Kellen had seen Crizkerisomia fight and knew that she was the equal of any warrior. *Any fighter that is, except Dalzere,* he reminded himself. Both were so proud, one dark and one white yet identical in appearance. He then glanced at Sasheer in worry and saw how the Mage ran fingers through his hair in agitation before looking to the ceiling for inspiration.

"You kill what you do not know," Dalzere breathed the words, his smile nasty as he shoved Crizkerisomia harder against the cold statue, until she grunted in pain. "Your people only know how to murder."

"My people do not murder!" Crizkerisomia spat, refusing to back down. "Drow hunt. Drow kill. Drow are the evil which walk the land!"

"Please!" Sasheer broke in. He pushed between the two and glared at them both. "Many races were cruelly destroyed within these caverns of the past, and many more will die in the future unless we find the Oracle," he stressed, waiting for acknowledgment to flash in both Elves' eyes. "We need rational thinking. I need both of you," he said. "I need you working together."

Dalzere was the first to back away. He unclenched his fist, released Crizkerisomia's leather tunic, and then walked away, not saying a word.

Watching him go, Sasheer gave the female a harsh smile. "My advice to you is: don't provoke him."

"What of me, old man?" Crizkerisomia asked. "He started it," she added. "You always take his side."

"Dalzere is not your enemy," Sasheer snapped and then relented when she sagged against the statue and pouted. "And don't pout at me," he said, as her eyes narrowed in anger. "If you took the time to understand Dalzere then you would know why I take his side in this senseless bickering," Sasheer informed her. "Now go. Watch the rear door. Make sure the southerners don't stray." He waited until Crizkerisomia complied and then looked for Dalzere. But the Drow had disappeared into the surrounding darkness. Muttering an uncomplimentary Drow curse, Sasheer settled his eyes on Kellen. "Don't tell me you have an opinion as well?"

Holding up his hands, Kellen shook his head and turned to study the wall.

CHAPTER FORTY-ONE

The next two chambers were much like the first, deathly cold, with massive tombs and sculpted decorations lining the walls. Little was damaged, making Kellen feel as though time had simply stopped. Images of the past—frozen, captured in perfection, breathtakingly stunning—were everywhere he looked. The air was frigidly cold, dust hanging in the firelight, shadows dancing on the gold-inlaid walls, subduing their excitement and fascination. They all filed through the chambers in silence, none willing to disturb the rest of the ancients. Of ghosts.

The fourth chamber was massive. The huge ornate door swung open without effort or sound when Sasheer's fingers brushed the stone latch. Gralvin lit the massive lamps by the doors, and the flare of brightness lit the entire chamber. Warm firelight reflected off the treasures stored in the expansive chamber. Gold glistened all around them; the floor piled waist high in coins and jewelry, precious plates, goblets, and ornaments. Gold-lined trunks lay open, full of rare gems and diamonds the size of melons, with some littering the floor and surrounding shelves. Splendid framed pictures of imposing men leaned against walls, and trunks of all sizes were stacked beside the doors. All a silent testament to an agelong dead—an age of wanton riches and limitless wealth.

Resting a hand on Peleyia's shoulder, Salimen steered the younger man straight ahead, refusing to let him stop and marvel at the beautiful objects, while Dalzere led them through the dazzling chamber of riches to the opposite doors.

Kellen had never imagined so much wealth could exist in just one place and was speechless, glancing back at the gorgeous items. He trailed behind Crizkerisomia, picking up the pace when she hissed his name. He stepped away from the awe-inspiring brilliance and stopped dead—his wonder quickly turning to revolt when his eyes fell upon the gruesome remains of a body spread before them in welcome. He gagged at both the smell and sight.

"Oh gods!" Salimen said, as he turned away.

Lesendal said nothing, covering his mouth and nose with his sleeve and allowing Ryland to pass him as the other man moved closer, inspecting the gruesome sight. Dalzere stood by the body and raised his torch. He shook his head sadly before glancing back at Sasheer, who walked slowly forward.

The body was partially decayed, the skin shriveled, eyes sunken, mouth wide open in what looked like a scream of horror. The hair was dark, thick, and matted, indicating that the victim had been of a young age. Blood stained the shrunken skin, stained the ripped clothing and stone tabletop. With a grim expression, Sasheer reached forward to remove the pendant resting on the corpse's chest.

"Sasheer?" Crizkerisomia whispered as she walked closer. She pointed to the dried blood that adorned the massive doors behind the corpse. A star was painted across the seal, the golden handles caked in old blood. "Why?" she asked as the others moved closer.

"This room and the one adjoining are bespelled," Sasheer whispered, his eyes losing focus. "The Ghouls are forbidden to enter this area. It is sensory locked against them."

"So," Crizkerisomia started, "we are safe here?" She glanced around, her knife in her hand.

"Yes," Sasheer said. He gazed despondently at the pendant in his hand, the gold chain slipping through his fingers to dangle so lifeless.

"Cornithia." Dalzere spoke the name at last, his expression grave.

Sasheer only nodded, his finger closing over the pendant before he closed his eyes. He said nothing for a long moment then looked up at Dalzere, his gaze beseeching. "A message for me—for the Brethren—Lichien knew we would come." He looked again at the remains of the dead Mage. "This was so unnecessary. Cornithia had no interest in fighting Lichien. All he enthused over was finding artifacts from the past to teach the children of the present. This was a senseless act." Sasheer stopped, his anger rising as he studied Cornithia's body. "He did not die easily."

"Sasheer?" Gralvin called, holding his torch over another, smaller body. It looked to be the remains of a hunting fox. The animal's fur was pale, the body sunken and decayed, and blood covered the tiny creature from throat to groin. Its legs had been tied cruelly, and its jaw wired shut.

"Breeze." Dalzere swallowed as he moved over to crouch next to the magical Shade. "She's been gutted."

"For Kalern's amusements no doubt," Sasheer snarled before he turned away. "Kalern and Lichien will be accountable."

"What should we do with them?" Lesendal asked. "They deserve a decent burial at least."

"We leave them," Sasheer said without hesitation.

"What?"

"We leave them," Sasheer hissed louder, a hard edge entering his tone. He slipped Cornithia's pendant into his pocket and turned away. "In this room, their bodies will be preserved and act as a living warning. Now we must find the Oracle—or their deaths will have been for nothing!"

Tearing his eyes away from the partially decapitated corpse, Kellen watched Sasheer push the bloodied door open. He remembered hearing how the room could only be breached with the blood of old, and his eyes went again to Cornithia, then to the small dead Shade. He could imagine the fear the Mage must have felt, knowing he had failed his brothers, knowing he had died helping Lichien. The grief he would have experienced, the pain as he watched his Shade butchered.

Pulling his cloak tighter around his chilled body, Kellen entered the magically enchanted room, feeling his own anger rise. He was starting to understand why Sasheer was willing to die if it meant destroying an abomination like Lichien.

The bespelled chamber was spacious, like the previous treasury and ancient tomb halls. Massive. Only this chamber didn't hide gold and silver, or statues and tombs—this chamber held books. The walls were lined with charts, maps, and glass jars containing scrolls, while the floor was littered with books and sheets of paper. In the center of the room were rows upon rows of shelves, all loaded with books and documents. It was dusty, stuffy, and stank of mould. Looking around, Kellen's eyes fell on a large engraved case which lay smashed in one corner of the room, glass scattered across the threadbare carpets.

"Kalern was not pleased," Dalzere muttered as he inspected the destruction of the library.

"No," Sasheer agreed dryly. "He obviously couldn't find the Oracle."

"So if he couldn't find it, then how can we?" Salimen asked, glancing around also.

"No one can find it; that is the charm of the Oracle," Sasheer said, flippant, softening the comment with a half smile.

Staring at the infuriating Mage, Salimen frowned, confused. "So if it can't be found, then why are we here?"

"To get the Oracle," Sasheer said, seeing Salimen open his mouth.

"But you just said . . ."

"Sal," Lesendal interjected as he grinned at his cousin. "Remember, Karczag said the Oracle should find us. It was designed that way as a protection."

"I must have missed that bit," Salimen admitted in poor grace.

Ignoring him, Sasheer cleared a space on the library floor and sat cross-legged, closing his eyes.

Kellen focused on Sasheer, feeling tense and uncomfortable. Something about this room was more unsettling than anything he had seen so far in Mitthsombaine. Only he didn't know what it was. So he worked on relaxing his stance, deliberately releasing his death hold on the hilt of his Drow sword. He was shaken after seeing Cornithia's body, but now, standing inside this old room, he could feel the power, could feel how the energies within the chamber slowly built. It made him nervous, and he looked to Dalzere for a clue as to what was happening. But the Drow ignored him, so he centered his gaze on Sasheer. Why was Sasheer sitting on the floor?

Nothing happened for a long time, and Kellen felt himself relax. Behind Sasheer's still form, Dalzere paced, the Drow's long strides distracting, and Kellen tore his eyes away from Sasheer to study the other members of the party. Gralvin was removing a book from Peleyia's inquisitive fingers; Salimen was glaring at the seated Mage while Lesendal rubbed his eyes. Ryland was standing guard at the door, his battle blade out and held ready, his expression challenging. Only Crizkerisomia seemed unconcerned as she rested back against the far wall, her eyes trained on the pacing Drow. Kellen shivered when he followed her gaze and met Dalzere's predatory scowl. *What is going on between Criz and Dalzere?*

Deciding to ignore all the charged emotions circling the room, Kellen dropped his gaze once more to the seated Mage and willed Sasheer to explain what was happening. Around him the oppressive energy levels increased—he could feel it, like a tangible pressure that swirled around him. It made him dizzy, breathless—*something tainted, something pure*—and then he started to hear words, in his head, whispered words in an ancient dialect that was seductive, inviting, and forbidden. The words sank deep into his mind, and the room around him started to fade.

Scared, he tried to step closer to Sasheer, and found that he stepped into a web of powerful magics. *Suffocating, entrapping, chilling*—and he saw a ghost rush past him, an image from the past that vanished into nothing.

He stared, amazed, and saw the room around him change. Mutate. The firelights turned into bright lanterns; the threadbare carpets became vibrant, plush wool; the maps and tapestries uncurled to show splendid pictures and designs, and all the books scattered across the floor disappeared to become arranged in perfect order on pristine shelves. The change was stunning, and he scanned the room, turning in a full circle. Gone were his friends; gone was the stench of age—now he was standing in a room that was warm, inviting, and so alive.

Slowly he started to discern voices, and he stared at the space before him, seeing four men slowly materialize. Each man was dressed in a long flowing blue robe, and each had dark hair intricately braided with red gold emblems. The men looked young, and they were whispering amongst themselves, obviously searching for something hidden on one bookshelf. *Students?*

He watched them curiously then gasped when a new figure entered the room and brushed past him. He stepped back and stared at the man who had entered. This new arrival was older, his presence commanding immediate attention, his eyes hard and cruel as he glared around the library at the four students. He said nothing, but his stance and clothing identified him as a man of importance.

Moving to one side, Kellen assumed this one was the teacher. *The Magus?*

Then the four students turned obediently and bowed respectfully, before one of the students started to speak—protest—about something—and Kellen tried to understand the strange language, tried to make out the meaning of what he was witnessing. The Magus sent the complaining student a nasty, condemnatory sneer, and Kellen shivered in dread, taking another step away from the tall imposing figure.

He didn't know what had been said, but he didn't need a translator to understand that the student was in dire trouble. He switched his gaze back to the student, and to his shock and amazement, the student didn't flinch under the Magus' glare, rather the student just folded his arms and lifted his chin defiantly. Stunned, Kellen stared at the brash student before turning his eyes on the Magus.

The Magus seemed to expect this defiance, for he raised a hand and pointed a finger at the unrepentant student. Power curled around his finger like a poised snake, the promise in his stare frightening. Then a second student hastily rushed forward and started to speak pleadingly.

Intrigued, Kellen watched—the words washing over him, and slowly he started to comprehend the language. The meaning.

"Curi^ion vr'anon thi^lem of the Oracle, master," the second student said, bowing his head in submission. The student held that pose for a moment then risked a glance up, his eyes disturbingly familiar, and Kellen blinked. The eyes, the expression, the pose—it looked eerily like *Wyran*.

Taken back, he stared at this Wyran look-alike, seeing his brother's face perfectly. *Yet this could not be Wyran; it was impossible,* and he turned to stare at the first defiant student trying to identify him. Then as if his vision had suddenly cleared, Kellen's mouth fell open as he identified the first student. Sasheer. A very young Sasheer which would mean that the second student was Serine.

Shocked, Kellen staggered back a pace and stared at the two brothers, taking in everything he could about Serine. Watching him, seeing Wyran—then looking at Sasheer and seeing how the young trainee challenged the Magus.

"Very good, Serine," the Magus hissed, his eyes hard and demanding. He lowered his hand, the power arching down to crackle around his magnificent robes. His face was ageless, but his eyes were old and cold as he sent a warning glance around the room. "*As Sasheer has so kindly pointed out, the Oracle will not appear while the Book of Spells is present,*" he snarled at Sasheer, who remained perfectly still, with his arms folded insolently. "*You should have removed the Book of Spells, Sasheer. Then your task would have been achievable.*"

Hearing the suppressed venom behind the softly spoken words, Kellen shuddered, and he risked a look at Sasheer. He saw how the younger Sasheer paled but held his ground. "*But to touch the Book of Spells means death, Master,*" Sasheer answered politely. "*So my task was doomed to fail, which you anticipated. This cannot be a proper test—*"

"Do not tell me what is proper and what is not!" the Magus roared in anger. "Or I will have you entombed as an object lesson for others!"

Kellen felt all color drain from his face, and he instinctively moved away from the volatile Magus. He backed into the far wall and stared at Sasheer, silently begging the trainee not to provoke the Magus. *Please, be silent* . . . But the young Sasheer didn't heed his pleas. Instead, Sasheer kept his chin up and his eyes direct, refusing to flinch. Then Serine broke Sasheer's defiance by stepping in front of his brother and raising his hands in appeal to the Magus a second time.

The Magus immediately struck Serine with a bolt of Magefire. He threw the helpless young trainee across the library and slammed him into bookcases, toppling the shelving and showering Serine in books and scrolls.

"Never side with your brother, Serine! Never! Or you will take his place in the tombs," the Magus hissed, then he turned back and advanced on Sasheer. "I fail you, Sasheer. Next time you fail a class of mine, I will have your soul, regardless of your sponsor's status!"

Shocked, Kellen tensed when the Magus swiveled on his toes and walked directly toward him. He panicked and cried out when the enraged Magus slammed into him and walked right through him—the shocking experience throwing him back into the present. He stumbled, dropping to his hands and knees, breathing out hard. Slowly he opened his eyes and stared down at the threadbare carpet, at the dust covering his fingers, before lifting his head—only to meet Sasheer's smoldering blue eyes. Eyes so old and so haunted in a face that was forever young.

"I passed the test. Now which one of us is entombed?" Sasheer asked, raising a brow in challenge as he opened his palm to display a vibrant, glowing crystal orb. The Oracle.

Sickened and appalled by what he had just seen—witnessed—Kellen stood up and backed away from Sasheer, only to run into Ryland's solid bulk. He jumped, feeling the Haonian's hands settle on his shoulders.

"Easy, lad."

Swallowing, he hiccupped and nodded, looking away from Sasheer's commanding gaze. He met Dalzere's eyes and saw the Drow's concern. That steadied him, and he felt his heart start to slow.

"That will get us into Kalern's fortress?" Lesendal asked, reaching out to lightly touch the object.

"It will get Dalzere and I in. The rest of you must return to Sanctuary," Sasheer corrected before he stood in a fluid motion. "But, yes, this crystal is powerful. It can blind the senses of the

Raveners and hide us from Kalern's searching eyes. But only within a certain sphere."

"What sphere?" Crizkerisomia asked. She moved forward and fingered the glowing orb. The light it generated was dazzling.

"Like all magical protectors, it has limitations. The Oracle's power will only be effective within a circle no bigger than four arm spans in each direction."

"So we need to stay close," Lesendal ventured determinedly.

"What a nice cozy group we'll make," Salimen muttered.

Sasheer glared at the Ihovians.

"I suggest we get out of here and argue the finer points later," Dalzere advised. "Which way do you want to go?"

"Past the dungeons and into the old tunnels that lead north toward the old deserted silver mines," Sasheer said. Nodding, Dalzere turned back toward the doors.

"I have heard tales of such passages and mines," Gralvin grumbled. "But have never seen them. Numerous songs tell of glorious battles and victories against the Coastal Temple Guards."

"Yet many of your people died in the tunnels before the end of the war," Sasheer told him. "It was a bitter time, as I recall."

* * *

With the Dwarf by his side, Sasheer led the way out of the catacombs. The Mage hardly spoke, as he placed the Oracle inside his cloak pocket. They backtracked through the treasury and into one of the old tombs again before entering a system of broad tunnels. Numerous galleries and chambers branched off from the spacious passageway until they entered an immense cavern.

A dark lake sat to one side of the underground cavern. Down one wall was a crevice where water trickled, while overhead more water dripped from dark cracks. The sound of trickling water echoed throughout the chamber, a rhythmic pattern of sound that lulled them into calmness. The roofline seemed to disappear into the darkness overhead, and the only visible vegetation were sporadic, colorless plants that clung to the protruding black rocks like fungus.

Their footfalls sounded overloud in the cavern, and none of them spoke as they crossed a narrow bridge that spanned the dark lake. Small ripples appeared on the lake's surface, and Kellen wondered what animal could possibly survive in the cold, dark environment. Looking away when the ripples grew nearer, he decided he did not really want to find out and hurried to catch up with the others.

On the far side of the lake, they found the remains of numerous old weapons. They lay were they had fallen scattered across the dirty floor: huge spears and silver axes, bound with perishing leathers and silver twine; helmets and chain mail armor covered in dust and strange pale vegetation. It was a gravesite.

"Dwarven," Crizkerisomia said needlessly. She paused to turn an axe blade over with her foot.

Gralvin had stopped also and was studying some of the designs on the partially concealed blades and spears. "These old weapons look to be part of the ancient Hammer Clan." His voice was filled with awe and wonderment as he gazed around.

"They have probably lain here for thousands of years," Crizkerisomia said, walking over to another pile of silver mail.

Inspecting some of the insignias on the decaying weapons and chain mail, Gralvin swore in disgust. "Drow teeth! There are teeth marks on the silver mail. It looks like something ate the dead."

"Or dying," Crizkerisomia added.

Gralvin glanced up and glared at her. "It is a disgrace to the dead."

"It was most likely some water creature," Ryland said, glancing back at the silent lake behind them. He fingered some of the intricately woven chain mail, marveling at the design. "I would guess that it was something very large."

"From the lake?" Crizkerisomia asked, her eyes also going to the lake before she gave the Dwarf a sympathetic look.

"This is not helping us get out," Sasheer said as he stopped further up the slope.

"But these warriors could have been my ancestors," Gralvin whispered the words wistfully. "My history states that the three greatest clans combined during the war against Mitthsombaine. One clan went under the mountain; one went over the mountain, and one went through the outer walls on that final day of battle. But until now no one knew which clan did what. Yet, here are my ancestors. They went under."

"Gralvin," Dalzere said, "it was long ago. This entire city is a memorial to the dead of all races." His tone and words mirrored those spoken earlier by Sasheer.

"I know. It is just so humbling to stand in the presence of so many great heroes from our history, to actually see their burial site. I wonder if the great Durin Silver Hammer lies here somewhere?"

"If you listen to the songs of legend, my friend, you will know he survived the war and went on to establish the biggest silver mine in the northeast mountain range," Dalzere said lightheartedly as he too studied the numerous chain-mail shirts littering the stone floor.

"That is what the songs say, yes. But according to the history of my clan," Gralvin added, "it is believed that Durin died, and it was his son who founded the northeast mining operation in his father's name."

"Can we discuss history later?" Sasheer asked somewhat impatiently as he motioned the others forward. "I, for one, would like to get out of these passageways before next month. We are running out of time as it is."

Hiding his smile, Dalzere clapped the old Dwarf on the shoulder then preceded the Sun Elf out.

* * *

Sighing, Gralvin took one final look around at the old burial site before following also. It was a haunting sight. The discolored chain mail shone a dull green in the torchlight, the bodies long decayed, or eaten, and leaving only empty armor husks. Stepping over one such husk, Gralvin froze as his torch picked out the details of the Hammer Clan's insignia lying on the ground. It was an old clasp, the kind worn long ago by the clan Elder. Bending down he picked it up, rubbing off the dirt and tracing his fingers over the chiseled emblem of two crossed axes. Tears welled in his eyes, and he recognized it as belonging to the line of the great Durin Silver Hammer, Elder and Chief of the united clans, the last great war leader of his time. Clasping it tightly, he hurried to catch up with the others, knowing how precious this clasp would be to his people when he returned it to the Great Hall.

* * *

Glancing back once more, Kellen saw Gralvin catch up with the group, and he relaxed. Sasheer had told them that this tunnel was the final stretch that would lead them to the surface on the other side of Sunsway Mountains, leagues from the corrupt city of Mitthsombaine. He could not wait to breathe clean air or feel the sun on his skin.

"What's ahead?" Salimen asked, lengthening his stride to catch up with the Mage.

"We should exit into the valleys and river system that leads down into The Delheck." Sasheer said, not slowing his pace.

"And what is the Delheck?" Salimen pushed.

"The home of the Silverglow Dwarven community," Sasheer said after a moment. "Where the journey, for you, will end."

Stopping, Salimen stared after Sasheer's back and shook his head. "Great. And I suppose this community lives underground as well."

* * *

Time blurred for Kellen, as he was forced to march at a fast pace, half-running on occasions to keep up with the seemingly tireless Mage. Sasheer was driving them hard, and Kellen was not sure if it was because of the Stone Ghouls or because of the time factor, or if it was from another harsh memory that ancient Mitthsombaine inspired inside the Mage.

He shuddered, remembering the last glimpse he had experienced of Sasheer's past. The more he learned, the more he felt drawn to Sasheer, intrigued by his life, and the more he respected and feared the man. That last glimpse had shown him that Serine had loved his brother—while *his* brother Wyran had despised him. *Why?* He still didn't know why Wyran had hated him so and still didn't know how Serine had died or why Sasheer had trouble facing the memory.

Musing over that, Kellen slowly became aware of how the tunnels were changing around him. They were getting narrower and colder. The walls were no longer man-made, rather they looked to be a natural formation of uneven rock, with the floor changing from stone to hard, compacted dirt. In some areas, the tunnel was only wide enough for a single man to pass. It slowed their progress, and Kellen took the opportunity to rest.

Ahead of him were Sasheer and Dalzere, with the two Ihovians and Peleyia. Behind him were Ryland and Crizkerisomia, with Gralvin guarding the rear. No one spoke, and the only sound echoing around them was their labored breathing and the fall of their feet against the unforgiving ground.

Minutes turned into long, painful hours as the tunnels went on and on, winding up steep inclines and then down into damp gullies, until Kellen was not certain they were making any progress. It seemed endless. Then, for some reason—he glanced back. The atmosphere around him was changing again, turning cold, and he felt the prickling of danger whisper along all his nerve endings. He glanced at Sasheer, wondering if the Mage felt the icy change, but Sasheer appeared to be locked in a world of his own.

Unsettled, he wondered if this was a tainted section of earth—if it were simply the currents he was sensing—but again the feel was different, he acknowledged after careful consideration, like a heaviness that whispered of a spell. Yet Sasheer had not invoked anything, and he paused, shivering as the air around him dropped to freezing. His breath started to frost the air, and he saw tiny bubbles of ice form on the cave walls. A prickling of panic surged in his chest, and he looked back again seeing Gralvin stop and thrust out his hand. Then a look of pure horror crept over the Dwarf's features. Alarmed, Kellen stopped and let Ryland pass while he extended his senses to try and work out what was wrong.

"Lad?"

Jumping when Ryland's voice sounded so loud in the eerie silence, Kellen just pointed back into the dimness to where the Dwarf was outlined. Crizkerisomia stopped also and drew her knife when Gralvin started to swear and curse in obvious horror.

"Gralvin?" Ryland called, preparing to go back and aid the Dwarf.

"No," Crizkerisomia cautioned, resting a hand on Ryland's arm to prevent him from approaching the Dwarf. "I sense a danger."

Gralvin held the torch high in one hand, while in the other, he held out a silver object. Dropping the burning torch to the dirt floor, he tried to shake then pry the object free from his hand—his cursing taking on a note of desperation. But the silver medallion would not budge, and Gralvin stumbled backward as if pulled by a strong arm.

"We have to see what the problem is," Ryland said, his frown deepening.

"What is that thing he is holding?" Crizkerisomia asked. She held the Haonian back and indicated to Kellen to move away. Behind them, the others returned.

"Kell?" Salimen reached him first. "What's wrong?"

"I don't know," Kellen said. He gestured toward the Dwarf. "One minute he was fine, and the next it looks like he is fighting an unseen force," Kellen said just as Gralvin let out an anguished scream of horror.

"By the stars!" Sasheer cursed. "Go! Run now!"

"What?"

"Run! Run as fast as you can." Sasheer ordered.

"But we have to help him," Ryland protested.

"I dare not. Now run!" Sasheer hissed.

Gralvin screamed a second time, his pleas chilling as the silver object in his hand bit deeply into his pale flesh, ripping his hand apart. Blood welled, running down his arm and fingers before dropping to the cold ground beneath his feet. It sizzled on the ground for an instant, and then within a heartbeat, the air froze, and an invisible wind swept past them all. It heralded death. It caused the dirt around Gralvin's feet to lift and engulf his boots, sucking him down into the ground and trapping him in living rock.

"Run!" Sasheer snarled, pushing them all away from the unfolding horror.

Hiccupping in panic, Kellen glanced back one last time and wished he hadn't. What he saw made his blood run cold. Around Gralvin, the rock lifted, literally reaching up, molding around his legs and hips, brutally crushing his struggles. The dwarf yelled, his cries weakening as he fought against the living rock as it devoured him inch by inch, smothering him whole to pull him into the hungry earth. *Stone Ghouls* . . . and Kellen swallowed his fear.

Then Sasheer grabbed Salimen's bow and loosened an arrow, killing Gralvin's tortured cries, ending the Dwarf's agony, and dropping them into a chilling silence. "Now run!" Sasheer hissed.

Kellen ran, terror driving him, the oppressive silence overwhelming.

* * *

They ran until exhaustion made them stumble, and even then, they continued on, not speaking or looking at each other as Sasheer led them forward, the Mage's expression grim and unapproachable.

Then just when he thought he could go no further, Kellen pushed past thick vegetation to exit the dark, wet tunnel, and he fell, stumbling down the wet, grassy incline.

He was on a hillside, surrounded by tall tress and facing a small tranquil brook. He lifted his eyes and stared at the pale blue sky, letting the early-morning sun caress his face for what seemed like an eternity. Behind him loomed the mountain range of Sunsway, and he closed his eyes, wanting to cry. Against all odds, they had made it out alive, yet they had lost a friend and valued companion. Mitthsombaine had claimed another life. How many more would die, he didn't know. Feeling ill, he threw-up, giving in to the combination of fear, fatigue, and grief.

"This is the Delheck Range. The home of the Silverglow Dwarven Clan," Sasheer said. Then the tall Mage walked past them all and went down to the brook to wash his hands and face. He never once looked back.

CHAPTER FORTY-TWO

A heavy depression lingered over the group as they each followed Sasheer to the brook's edge. Then without conscious thought, they stripped and bathed in the icy water in a futile attempt to wash away the memories of the previous night.

Sometime later, as the early-morning sun warmed the air, they sat huddled around a fire while Salimen handed around their remaining dried meat. They ate in silence, no one willing to broach the subject of why Gralvin had died. Or even discuss what they had each seen during the long, dark flight from Mitthsombaine.

"So this is the Delheck?" Salimen finally asked in a quiet voice. His hair was still damp from his wash, one errant lock falling down over his eyes when he looked up from shaping new arrowheads.

Glancing around the subdued group, Sasheer did not say anything for a prolonged moment, seeming to assess the mood of each member. "This stream is part of Danchern's River chain. We will follow it upstream toward those peaks you can all see. They are called the Delheck and are home to Hamblin's Silverglow Clan." He paused briefly then added, "From there, most of you should be able to get safe passage back to Sanctuary."

"That is if Kalern's army has not taken the Dwarves' ancestral home," Crizkerisomia said.

"There is that possibility," Sasheer agreed. "But by now, hopefully, your people are aiding Darchain's Clan in stopping Kalern from advancing past the narrow gorge at Heaten's Reach."

"How long before we get to this gorge at Heaten's Reach?" Lesendal asked.

"You are not going to the Reach," Sasheer said frankly. "It is far too dangerous, even without Kalern's army. Rather, it will take us a week to reach the stronghold King Hamblin holds inside the Delheck. That is where you are going."

* * *

Five days later, they were still making slow progress up into the densely treed mountains. They followed the river's winding path northwest, where it widened out from a stream to a full-flowing series of rapids and falls. It was picturesque, but cold. They camped each night away from its banks and feasted on fresh fish. The forest surrounding them was quiet, unnaturally so, and their fears grew. Crizkerisomia's warning days earlier about the abandonment of the Dwarven mines seemed prophetic, and Kellen half-expected to see Black Guard patrolling the forest.

On the evening of the fifth night while Kellen was gathering twigs and small sticks for the cooking fire, he was delighted to find the little snow dragon sitting on a tree limb.

"Shard!" he called with genuine pleasure as he reached up and stroked the small animal's face. "I looked for you on Sunset Ridge. Where did you go?"

"I could not go into the old city," Shard whispered. "I did not like its feel."

"None of us did," Kellen acknowledged in a somber tone. He turned and glanced behind, lowering his voice when he heard Ryland's laughter echo through the hushed forest. "This forest is not safe either," he warned, caressing the small snow dragon. "Dalzere found tracks. It looks like the Black Guard are in the area. Maybe you should travel with us."

"Why? Where are you going?" Shard asked, its eyes blinking in innocence.

Sensing nervousness, Kellen sent the small animal a genuine smile. "You can trust me," he promised. "I want to help you." He reached out, but the snow dragon moved, avoiding his fingers.

"Where are you going?" it repeated.

Kellen studied the animal then sighed. "Sasheer says the Silverglow Clan lives not far from here. So we are going there.

Then a number of the group is returning to Sanctuary. You could go with them," Kellen added, watching how Shard dismissed that comment.

"And the Oracle?" Shard asked instead. "Did you find it?" The question was slightly hesitant—reluctant even.

Frowning, Kellen searched Shard's wide eyes, troubled by what he saw. He wanted to trust the animal, wanted to believe it was defenseless, but he also got the strong impression that something else, something sinister was motivating Shard's responses. A spell? A ruse? Or just a fear? "What is unsettling you?" he asked instead.

"The Oracle, Kellen," the snow dragon hissed, a hard edge coloring its tone. "The journey to Sanctuary will be unsafe without the Oracle," it added.

Mildly reassured by that reasoning, Kellen nodded. "Sasheer has the Oracle. But I doubt it will be needed to get you to Sanctuary. You will be safe, I swear." He reached out again to touch the small creature, but Shard shied away from the touch. Scared—and then its expression softened and it stood, spread its wings; the inky blackness of its gaze fading to be replaced by a silver glow—a whiteness—like the moon's reflection on a pond. Mysterious. The change was startling, and the concerned expression that fleetingly touched the dragon's eyes was worrisome.

"You should leave," urgency colored Shard's tone, a softness that had not been present before. "Go away. Far away. Back to the Southland and hide. Change your name and marry a wench."

"What?" The words were said so passionate, so serious that Kellen stared at the creature mystified.

"Leave this forest. Do not go to the Silverglow Clan, because if you continue to follow Sasheer, you will die."

"Shard?"

"Do not follow him into death!"

Taken back by the fervent warning, Kellen blinked at the agitated dragon, watching how the animal shuddered, then mutated before him, turning black. Slowly the gleaming flecks of silver dulled in Shard's eyes, and the little dragon shook violently, battling the transformation. "What are you?" Kellen asked, taking a step back when Shard's large eyes once again resembled the inky blackness of despair.

"A lost soul . . ."

Shocked by the familiar words, Kellen instinctively reached out with his senses to read the creature, and his mind was flooded with an image of a cloaked figure. The same figure he had first glimpsed in Ihova, and he gasped, stunned. Darkness enshrouded the figure; slowly, very slowly, the cowl lifted, and Kellen watched the light penetrate the shadows to infuse the apparition and he saw . . . *he saw a young face, a beautiful face . . . a male face . . . Wyran's face . . . only it wasn't Wyran, because Wyran had never smiled at him like that. Had never appeared so untroubled . . . so approachable . . . so likeable . . . so . . .*

"Stop that!" Shard screeched.

Kellen blinked, and the image immediately fracturing into a million tiny pieces and dissipating around him. "Who was that?" he breathed, fascinated, looking at Shard, noticing how the snow dragon had fled to hover a dozen paces away. The animal was trembling, and Kellen cautiously walked toward it and held out a calming hand. Shard felt like a Shade—*the evil Shade?* Impossible. Yet Sasheer had warned that nothing was impossible. "Let me help you."

"Trust no one!" Shard hissed, incensed. "Nothing is as it appears!"

"I trust you."

"Especially not me!" It screeched.

Refusing to accept that, Kellen waited with his palm up but was not surprised when the animal swirled in a blur of darkness then vanished into thin air. He cursed and searched around, knowing Shard could not have gone far. He had the impression that if he could breach the barrier between them, then he would learn what terrible secrets the snow dragon was keeping. "Bright stars! Shard?" he called, stepping around a tree and coming to an abrupt halt. Dalzere was standing there, watching him, assessing him with a shrewdness that was unnerving.

"What are you doing?" the Drow asked in a quiet, controlled voice. "Shard? Who is Shard?"

"You saw," Kellen trailed off, remembering how scared the

little dragon was of the Drow. Maybe that was why the creature had acted so strange? Maybe that was the darkness he sensed? He eyed Dalzere a second time, taking in the elegance and unearthly beauty of the Elf, and shook his head. Dalzere was not evil.

"I saw you running through the wood. You were making far too much noise," the Elf chastised.

Meeting the unblinking, knowing gaze, Kellen marshaled his erratic thoughts. "I'm sorry. I thought I saw something... strange... in the trees."

"Like what?" the Drow questioned.

"It is hard to describe, but it is gone now," Kellen knew his response was lame, and he turned away, disliking the fact he was deceiving his friend. But for some reason, he could not betray the little creature just yet—even though he knew Dalzere would not condemn Shard. It was almost like a compulsion not to speak. Dalzere's eyes narrowed, his stance relaxed, but Kellen knew the Drow did not believe a word of his explanation.

"We had best return to the camp before it gets dark."

Glad Dalzere did not pursue the lie, Kellen released a deep breath and walked dutifully beside his friend. He kept his eyes down, refusing to meet Dalzere's astute gaze.

"Tell me, Kellen, are you still plagued by dreams?"

Startled by the soft words, Kellen stopped dead in his tracks and found he was staring at Dalzere in panic before he realized it. "How?" was all he could manage, before he stopped the question.

A smile played across the Drow's lips, and then Dalzere was beside him, touching his cheek with gentle fingers. "I have seen your troubled sleep."

"The dreams are nothing," Kellen mumbled. If Dalzere knew, then he was certain Sasheer knew, and his heart plummeted. So why had the insufferable Mage not questioned him personally? No... he remembered that Sasheer always sent Dalzere to do his dirty work.

"Do you see the same dream over and over?"

Swallowing, Kellen tried to dismiss the topic, not wanting to think about the nightmares. "Yes and no. I... it progresses."

Dalzere said nothing for a moment, his gaze lingering on Kellen before he sighed. "You should talk with—"

"No." Kellen shook his head. The last thing he wanted was another lecture from Sasheer.

"Kellen?" Dalzere laid reassuring hands on his shoulders and held him still.

Forcing himself to meet Dalzere's golden gaze, he exhaled hard. How could he tell Dalzere that half his visions were of Sasheer, and that the nightmares were of an abyss deep in some cavern? He wasn't even sure if the nightmares weren't just part of Sasheer's horrific memories. "I can't, Dalzere. Don't ask me to. Besides, I think he knows exactly what I see. I think he's lived it. Is still living it," he said, relieved when Dalzere said nothing, showed no shock, and did not judge him. "How can he function with such shocking memories?"

"He survives the best way he can. As we all do. As you will," Dalzere offered softly. "Don't isolate yourself."

"I won't," Kellen promised, warmed by the Drow's genuine affection and support.

Then Dalzere released him and sent him a cocky half smile that lit up his face. "Come," Dalzere encouraged. "I think we are having fish again for supper."

Waiting until Dalzere had walked away and was safely out of hearing, Kellen sighed. "Thank you," he whispered after the remarkable Elf, meaning it sincerely.

CHAPTER FORTY-THREE

Three days later, they encountered a Black Guard patrol and were forced to fight.

Instinctively, Kellen drew his Drow blade and charged the leading guard with Lesendal at his side. He was not as proficient as the prince, but what he lacked in technique, he made up for in sheer desperation, as he drove the guard to the ground.

Ryland dragged two of the Hoindrite Black Guard from their horses, while Salimen shot three with his crossbow, using them for target practice. Once on the ground, both Elves displayed why their race were known as ruthless hunters, disposing of each guard efficiently and with minimal effort.

Concentrating hard on his dismounted Hoindrite guard, Kellen grinned, enjoying the challenge. His opponent was already bloodied and sported a head injury from his fall, and Kellen smiled when the man staggered and then stumbled over a tree root. He was really starting to enjoy the sword contest, putting into practice all the lessons Ryland had given him, and he skillfully blocked the Black Guard's lunge. He thrust his own blade forward, his grin widening when he encountered soft flesh, and he heard his opponent hiss in a pained breath.

Then the Black Guard snarled and tried to swat him in annoyance, and he danced back, waiting for another opportunity to attack the Hoindrite's vulnerable side. The Black Guard's arm went up, and he moved, lifting his sword tip and lunging—only to have the guard abruptly pitch forward and fall face-first into damp leaves. Dead.

Shocked, Kellen looked up from the dead guard to see Crizkerisomia, and he glared at her. "Hey!" he protested. "That was my Hoindrite!"

Crizkerisomia sent him an amused glance, wiping her knife negligently on the dead guard before walking away.

Miffed, he kicked the dead guard and hurried after the Sun Elf. The fighting around him was over, with Ryland and Lesendal already gone to round up the horses.

"What a nice afternoon," Ryland grinned when he returned. "Good exercise and fresh air, what more could you ask for?"

"A little less activity would be nice," Sasheer suggested, as he stepped over a dead guard. "Is everyone more or less intact?"

"Fine," came the answer from all, and Kellen stared around, feeling cheated of his fun. He lifted his chin and addressed the female Elf. "Next time, Criz, I'd appreciate it if you'd let me finish off my own guard," he declared, upset by her actions. "I can fight. I am not a child."

"You are to me," she replied, unconcerned by his anger. Insouciantly, she went around and collected her knives, inspecting their edges.

About to protest even louder, Kellen stopped when Dalzere laughed.

"Never mind, lad," Ryland encouraged, placing a friendly hand on Kellen's shoulder. "I am sure we will have the pleasure of running into more guards before reaching this Dwarven stronghold."

"I sincerely hope not," Sasheer said as he marched away.

* * *

They located an old entrance to the Dwarven mines by evening. Sasheer knocked on the solid, impenetrable portal and waited until he was asked to identify himself. A very narrow door was opened, and they all filed into the dim interior under the scrutiny of grim-faced Dwarven warriors.

They were led into a low cavern, and their enthusiasm soured when a squat Dwarf informed them that it was a long, tedious journey underground to the main caverns of the Silverglow Clan.

"You are expected. Only we have been waiting weeks," the gruff Dwarf said then spat before wiping his bearded chin. "Leave the mounts. Follow me." Their horses were led away, and they could do little else but follow the ill-tempered Dwarven guide.

They must have traveled for leagues, or so it seemed, passing other Dwarves, all hurrying about their daily business.

"I hate underground tunnels," Salimen commented to no one in particular. "Surely there must be an easier way to reach this city than by traveling through the damn mountain?"

"I am not fond of tunnels either," Ryland said. "The area is cramped. Not enough room to make a decent sword swing if the situation required it."

"The situation will not require it," Sasheer muttered. "Nor is there an easier way into the underground city." He looked at the unrepentant Ihovian. "These mines are built like fortresses, which was beneficial during the early wars with Mitthsombaine. The only way to safely reach the Delheck is via these tunnels; otherwise, it is a very long journey around the entire range. A range crawling with Lichien's army."

"Long, maybe, but at least it would not be dark and cold. I hate not seeing what hides in the dark crevices," Salimen said.

"There are worse things inhabiting the dark then a few spiders," was all Sasheer said before turning away.

Salimen contented himself with glaring at the back of Sasheer's head and muttering curses.

* * *

By the time they reached the wider tunnels, numerous fires lit the way. They entered the caverns and connecting chambers, their eyes slowly adjusting to the brightness of huge inground fire pits, which warmed and illuminated the rooms. The caverns were spacious, clean, and neat, with designs carved into the walls, and intricate emblems decorated the ceilings and archway. The Dwarven warriors they encountered seemed confident and proud.

Eventually they reached the massive labyrinth of the underground city, and the magnificence, charm, and sheer size of the place stunned them all. It was full of inhabitants. They stared at the spectacle, all of them exhausted, and they gratefully accepted the offer of food, drink, and rest.

The area they were escorted to was a huge dining hall, filled with mouth-watering aromas that drifted through the archways from the adjoining kitchens. Children laughed and played, chasing each other around tables as older Dwarven women worked over massive pots and steaming tubs. It was busy, yet homely—the closest feeling to normalcy Kellen had experienced in months—and he drank in the noisy atmosphere and welcoming peace. Relaxing back on his bench, he saw Sasheer stand when two older Dwarves approached.

"Welcome, Sasheer," the first Dwarf said, his eyes warm and welcoming. "King Hamblin wished to make you feel at home. Though we can give you little good news."

"How goes the war?" Dalzere asked. In response, the Dwarf glanced at him then frowned.

"This is Dalzere," Sasheer introduced. "My partner. I am sure you have heard of him."

"Yes, the Drow who fancies himself as a Watcher." The Dwarf gave a crooked smile. Dalzere nodded in brief acknowledgment. "Forgive my rudeness, but Kalern is using Drow and Gully Gnomes to undermine our defenses. Having you within the mines may cause some . . . unpleasantness," he explained before turning back to Sasheer. "Please eat then freshen up. Groman will escort you to the main halls when King Hamblin returns."

* * *

After they had eaten their fill, they were shown to a series of guest rooms, which led to hot-spring tubs, and for once, none of them needed urging to wash and change into clean, dry clothing and leathers.

It was hard to tell what time it was, but Kellen roused from the edges of sleep when the old Dwarf named Groman came to escort them into the main hall. Inside the vast chamber, many Dwarven warriors lounged. Huge fires sat deep in the floor under grates. At the far side sat a carved bronze and silver throne, and behind it were tapestries that depicted the vibrancy of the land outside.

King Hamblin sat on a raised dais, his expression dark, brooding while he waited for Sasheer to approach. "I wish I could say it is a pleasure to see you, Sasheer, but as you well know, war is the only time the Brethren grace these halls."

"Sad, but true," Sasheer acknowledged.

Kellen eyed the king then looked at the two younger Dwarves who were standing beside the throne. Neither looked pleased by Sasheer's presence, and each scowled at the tall Drow.

"What news do you bring?" the old king asked. He stood and gestured for Sasheer to follow him away from the raised dais to a more private chamber behind the throne. Curious, Kellen trailed behind Dalzere.

Many weapons lined the walls of this secluded room, and Kellen found maps, books, and armor piled on the floor. He studied them, seeing Salimen and Lesendal tentatively inspect some of the ancient blades.

Sasheer sighed, going over to a table and fingering the scrolls. "I see you have been studying the old histories."

"Anything to gain an advantage over Kalern. Anything to understand his mind," the king said then indicated the two younger dwarves who had followed them into the private chamber. "My sons."

Sasheer nodded to the younger warriors then set his gaze on the king. "Hamblin, you cannot comprehend Lichien's mind—to try is perilous."

"I have to do something before he takes my mine," King Hamblin said, his eyes showing the seriousness of the threat. Then he looked away from Sasheer and turned his attention to the wearied group behind the Mage. "You seem to be missing a member."

Sasheer nodded. "We lost Gralvin Broadhammer in one of the old passageways under the Mitthsombaine."

"That news is disheartening," King Hamblin said, his eyes reflecting genuine sorrow. "Roargan will be saddened. I believe Gralvin was a distant relative."

"Fourth cousin," Sasheer confirmed. "So, tell me about Lichien's army."

"It is not good," Hamblin admitted as he glanced around again to make sure they were not overheard. "I have had to pull back most of my clan in order to stop the Black Guard from taking this mine from behind. That has seriously weakened our forces against Kalern's frontal attacks. I feel we are running out of time. Fast."

"And King Darchain?"

"He was injured, last I heard," Hamblin said. "Not fatal, from what the messenger reported, but enough to make him bad tempered." He gave a faint smile. "The Sun Elves have arrived, but even with their skill, we are losing ground. All three silver mines at Heaten's Reach are taken, and they are now fighting at Danchern's Junction for Darchain's silver mines. If that city falls, then there will be nothing to stop Kalern's march into the Delheck. He will then take this mine from under us, and nothing will be left of the proud Dwarven community." The king's gray eyes met those of Sasheer's. "You and that Oracle are our only hope, I fear. Darchain and I have not spoken a word to the Dwarven Council about your mission."

"Thank you, my friend," Sasheer said. "Dalzere and I will need to get through the fighting. Is there a way?"

"By river maybe," the old king mused. "Kalern is so sure of his conquest; he has not tried to dam the river yet, so a small vessel may get through the battle lines and past the Junction without being seen."

"Can it be arranged?"

Glancing at the others in Sasheer's party, Hamblin gave a slow nod. "Just you and the Drow?"

"Just the two of us," Sasheer confirmed. "The others must get back to Sanctuary."

"That is impossible for the moment," Hamblin said. "They are welcome here with my clan until I have scouts to spare. Or you can try and get them to Darchain. One of the Elves may be able to help them get through to Maltros."

"Sasheer, I want to go with you," Lesendal broke in anxiously, stepping up to the Mage and the elderly king.

Salimen groaned and rolled his eyes then grabbed for his cousin's tunic. "Dale—"

"Lesendal, where I go, I do not expect to return. You, on the other hand, have a chance of returning to Ihova and reuniting the Twelve Kingdoms," Sasheer advised.

"But what of Kalern's armies in the south?" Lesendal asked.

"Mostly returned," Hamblin confirmed, eyeing the blond prince. "Even as we speak, they march across the eastern front. In another six months, maybe less, there will be nothing left south of here to protect. Nothing to stop Kalern and Lichien taking control of the mainland."

"They have left the Southland?" Lesendal asked, shocked. "And the kingdoms?"

"Gone," Hamblin said. "I am sorry, but the Southland no longer exists."

"Then we have nothing left to go back to," Lesendal whispered.

"The prince has a valid point," Crizkerisomia broke in as she eyed the silent men. "With the south gone and the Dwarven mines under threat—all that is left is the western quadrant. My people." She looked at Sasheer in growing fear. "You know Lichien will destroy Capliarkia. He will do it using Drow."

"He already has allied himself with the Drow," Hamblin spat in disgust then looked apologetically at Dalzere.

"They are not my people," Dalzere assured before turning to Sasheer. "When Kellen and I passed though the Death Peaks, I must admit there was very little activity in the Postings."

"It was expected that the Drow would back Lichien. I just had not believed it would be so swift," Sasheer agreed, not liking the information. "I must get to North Ridge quickly."

Hamblin agreed, "Kalern had already infiltrated our clans with Mindwipes by the time Roargan and Blaine returned from the Keep. So he knew of our alliance with the Sun Elves. Because of that, Kalern was able to have his forces waiting for the Elves, east of Heaten's Reach."

Rubbing his eyes tiredly, Sasheer sighed. "Does Karczag know of this?"

"We have sent messages, but I cannot say if they are getting through," the king said grimly.

"It might be safer for us all to go to Danchern's Junction," Dalzere suggested, his eyes going to Sasheer's set face in gentle persuasion.

Kellen held his breath, poised, awaiting Sasheer's response, and saw how the Mage first looked at the old king and then turned to glare at Dalzere. But the Drow never flinched, and eventually Sasheer sighed and muttered something that brought a ghost smile to Dalzere's mouth.

"All . . . right," Sasheer consented begrudgingly. "We'll make for the Junction. Have you any scouts you can spare?"

"I will give you my son, Harkon," King Hamblin said and placing one large hand on his son's shoulder. "He is the best scout I know and will get you safely through to Darchain's Silverglow Clan."

* * *

They all returned to the private guest chamber—all except Sasheer. Kellen nothing of the Mage's absence, and noticed that Dalzere was uncharacteristically moody. Then he took a better look around and realized that not only was Dalzere imitating something dark and menacing, but that Salimen was pacing the floor and scowling at Lesendal. Bewildered, he was about to ask Ryland what he had missed when the Drow strode from the room in a swirl of black deadliness. It was so unusual for Dalzere to show such strong emotion that Kellen stared after the Drow, shocked. He looked immediately to the Sun Elf and wasn't surprised when Crizkerisomia muttered something in the Elves' musical lilt before pursuing the unhappy dark Elf. Intrigued, he was about to follow but stopped when Salimen let out an explosive breath and practically yelled at Lesendal.

"Gods!" Salimen spat, rubbing his eyes, hardly slowing his pacing as he glared at Lesendal. "Have you utterly lost what little mind you have left?" he demanded, stopping in front of the motionless prince.

Absolute stillness hit the room, and Kellen held his breath. Then Salimen swung away and commenced pacing again. It was Ryland who eventually broke the harsh silence. "I think we should look around the outer chamber. Maybe find the food halls again," the big warrior said aloud before he grabbed both Kellen and the gaping Peleyia and shoved them out of the guest room.

Afire with curiosity, Kellen glanced back, thankful when a couple of Dwarves engaged Ryland in conversation. He politely excused himself and walked off in the opposite direction then backtracked swiftly, returning to the guest rooms. Once there, he hesitated, checked the connecting passageway, and pushed gently on the closed door. A hand landed on his shoulder, and he jumped, spinning around, and he came face to face with Peleyia. The Lancooti was shaking his head in amusement.

"Not that way, over here," the Lancooti whispered as he crept away.

Burying his smile, Kellen followed, finding Peleyia was, as usual, correct in his assessment. They stopped at a vented opening behind the fireplace, and he was amazed that he could hear every word and every breath both Ihovians took. Salimen's voice was agitated, the sound carrying perfectly, and he raised a suspicious brow at his friend.

Peleyia shrugged and grinned, unrepentant. "I've had lots of practice," he mouthed. "How do you think I learn so many secrets?"

Turning his attention to the intensely private conversation unfolding in the private room, Kellen shoved his guilt aside and listened. He briefly wondered where he was picking up all these bad traits—but that pang of guilt was squashed when he heard Lesendal's reasonable reply to Salimen's accusations.

CHAPTER FORTY-FOUR

Hardly noticing when the others left the room, Salimen continued to glare at Lesendal, incensed beyond belief that they would now be going to the worst place imaginable.

"Sal—"

"Don't even try lying to me!" Salimen spat as he leaned forward. "I know you too well, remember."

"Sal—"

Salimen cut him off again. "Did you hear what King Hamblin said? The Southland is lost! The kingdoms destroyed! By the stars! Dale—we should go home!"

"We can't. To save the south, we have to stop Kalern. We must help Sasheer. I can't go home."

"Won't!" Salimen corrected harshly. "Kessendra is dead. I just wish you would accept that fact and let her go. We are needed at home. . . . We are next to useless here in this war. Even Sasheer says we should go home! Our own land needs us—needs you, Dale. You are Arikaines' only heir; the people need you to pull them back together and give them hope."

"No," Lesendal said and stood up to face the other man. "Kess is alive. I can feel it, and I am not following an empty dream like you and Ryland believe. She is alive."

"Even if that were remotely true, then surely she is lost to us. Probably insane."

"No," Lesendal said again. "I wish you wouldn't hate her, Sal. Can't you try to forgive her?"

Salimen snorted. "Forgive?" he asked sarcastically. "Even if I could—I wouldn't." He shook his head. "Not after what she did to—" he heaved a great sigh and started again. "If you really knew her, you would not ask this of me."

"I need you both in my life."

"God, Dale! Don't do this!"

"Kess is alive. I can almost sense her confusion, taste her fear."

"Stars!" Salimen exhaled in frustration, rubbing at his face in fury. "Dale, please listen to me!"

"I can't explain it, Sal, but please trust me. I have to follow Sasheer." He gave a small smile, seeing the other's scowl deepen. "Besides, you are of royal blood yourself. You could take the throne in Ihova just as easily as me."

"Never," Salimen snarled. "I have denied that part of my heritage all my life. I do not want it. I despise it!"

"But someday you may not be given a choice," Lesendal whispered. "Look at Ryland. He has never said anything of his heritage, yet I recognize the insignia on his sword hilt."

"Yes, I too," Salimen said. He cast an angry look at Lesendal. "He is a proud man."

"No more than you," the prince quipped then dropped the smile as he studied the other man. "I go with Sasheer."

"But why?" Salimen demanded. "And please don't give me any more nonsense about Kessendra!"

Lesendal shrugged, falling back to sit on the narrow bed.

"He goes to North Ridge." Salimen protested in exasperation.

"I know."

"You heard Karczag! Sasheer will die if he faces Lichien. That will mean no escape from North Ridge."

"Sal..."

"Even Dalzere is unhappy with this plan!" Salimen half-shouted in frustration. "You can see it written all over his face. He goes out of loyalty!"

"Sal, I know why Sasheer wants us to return to Sanctuary," Lesendal cut in, capturing Salimen's complete attention. He waited for Salimen to look at him. "And Sal—it's not because of the Southland, or for our safety, or because he is going to die."

Raising a curious brow, Salimen licked his dry lips and considered this new point. "Then why?"

"Because of Kellen."

"Kell?" Salimen asked in a puzzled voice.

"I know you all think I have lost my wits over these last few months."

"That's an understatement," Salimen said sourly.

"I haven't. I've been listening very carefully to everything that has been said."

"And?" Salimen asked impatiently.

"I heard Tanish and Sasheer discussing Kellen's birthright in the Keep library, the morning after we showed up. They didn't know I was there."

"So?"

"Well, haven't you ever thought that Kellen looks just a little un-Ihovian?"

"Gods, Dale," Salimen cursed, "next you'll be saying I remind you of Sasheer!"

"Only in temperament."

Pushing his long fringe back, Salimen glared at the other man. "So Kell doesn't look like a classical Ihovian. So what? Many have migrated across our borders."

"Remember that first day we found him?" Lesendal asked. "Tell me, how did he manage to escape from four of the Black Guard, and steal a bag of white gold?"

"Luck?"

"I don't think so," the prince said. "No one is that lucky."

"Dale," Salimen sighed long-sufferingly. "Where are you going with all this? Because next, you'll be telling me he's a Mage or something." He ended on a half laugh.

Lesendal gave a small smile. "From what I overheard, it seems young Kellen is of Kalern's direct line and poses more danger to that evil lord's plans than a hundred oracles combined. Somehow *he* can destroy Kalern. The only problem is, Kellen is fighting against his heritage."

Salimen just stared at Lesendal, speechless, not sure if he wanted to laugh or curse. It took him a long moment to realize the other man was deadly serious. "Sasheer said that?"

Lesendal nodded. "Kellen has some gift, which is unpredictable. Magery—probably, which would explain how he escaped the Black Guard in Ihova. Or how he survived that slide down the mountain."

Staring at Lesendal, Salimen just blinked, stunned.

"Sasheer is supposed to teach him control or something," Lesendal went on. "And I have been watching them the last few months. All the heart-to-heart discussions, all the arguments, all the times Sasheer took Kellen scouting..."

"You're not making this up. Are you?" Salimen asked.

"Of course, I'm not making this up!" Lesendal snapped in a hurt tone. "There is a more dangerous game being played here than we have been told. I, for one, would hate to be in Kellen's boots."

"Hell," Salimen sighed. He sat down and considered the idea. "I don't blame him for rebelling in that case. I'd fight against that sort of responsibility."

"You already have," Lesendal reminded him.

"I didn't have much choice!" Salimen returned just as seriously, before raising a hand in apology. "You are the heir, not me." He stopped short. "So what do we do?" he asked. "And who else knows about this?"

"Dalzere."

"What a surprise," Salimen muttered sarcastically.

"Probably Peleyia," Lesendal shrugged. "He and Kell are fairly close."

"Nothing would surprise me with that little thief," Salimen agreed. He lifted his eyes and met Lesendal's pale blue gaze that matched his. "So Sasheer wants us to go back to Sanctuary because we are..."

"Babysitters," Lesendal finished for him. "Remember, Sasheer did not want Kellen on this journey."

"He didn't want Pel either."

"For different reasons, I'd say. The Lancooti attracts trouble like a magnet," the prince said. "No, Sasheer wants Kellen back in that magically protected city of Sanctuary before Kalern's forces march west."

Accepting the logic of that, Salimen asked a different question. "So why didn't you tell me all this earlier?"

"I couldn't until I had sorted all the mixed signals out myself," Lesendal said. "I've been watching them. It's confusing. Sometimes I think Sasheer and Kellen are so alike."

"They argue," Salimen shrugged. "It's only natural."

"Like us," Lesendal grinned at him. "I also didn't tell you because you have been angry with me for the last few months."

"That's because this was the last place I ever wanted to go," Salimen said, then he shook his head and released a deep breath. "Okay—so what now?"

"Now? Now I suggest we go and have a look at this map King Hamblin wanted to show Sasheer. I think we're going to need to know the layout of North Ridge."

CHAPTER FORTY-FIVE

Refusing to open his eyes and address the silence that had fallen after, both Ihovians had left the private guest room, Kellen waited for Peleyia to yell, to ask why he had not told him about his connection to Kalern sooner. But nothing happened, and he carefully lifted his lashes to see if the Lancooti had left in disgust. It was what he expected. But Peleyia continued to sit across from him, watching him, weighing him up in silence. It reminded Kellen of the first time they had studied each other. So long ago. Now Peleyia no longer looked so flamboyant; his hair was tied back, his worn leathers a respectable brown—but the eyes were the same.

"Why didn't you tell me about Kalern?" Peleyia asked, with no judgment or allegation in his tone.

"I couldn't. Didn't know how to. I didn't want to believe it. Then after . . . I just couldn't work out how to bring the subject up," Kellen said, needing truth between them.

"And Sasheer?"

"You do know that he's been teaching me?"

"Yes," Peleyia nodded. "You have Mage ability. But I have always known that about you," he said. "But what is Sasheer teaching you to do? To die? To fight Kalern?" he asked with a touch of anger.

"No." Kellen frowned. "What Lesendal said is true. Sasheer has never wanted me near North Ridge or Kalern." He glanced up again, meeting Peleyia's furious glare. "Nor does he want you there."

Peleyia raised a curious brow then exhaled, thinking hard. "After what I've just heard, I am almost too afraid to ask why."

"Because you will die. As will I," Kellen said. He felt the link between them pulsate, and he let Peleyia sense the seriousness of his words. "One of Sasheer's Gifts is Foresight," he explained, noting how Peleyia didn't cut off the link but let it flourish. "He saw the future. He saw our deaths."

"We . . ." Peleyia gestured between them with his hand, "you and I will die if we go to North Ridge? Sasheer saw this? No . . ." He frowned, reading Kellen's turbulent emotions through the link and closed his eyes in sudden understanding. "No—Sasheer has predicted this," he corrected softly.

"Yes and no."

"Which is it, Kell?" Peleyia asked. "I think it could be important."

Reaching forward, Kellen captured his friend's anxious gaze with his own. "In my nightmares I . . . I fall into an abyss. I see it over and over. No matter how I try to avoid it, the abyss is always there, beckoning. It is my doom." He licked his lips. "With you—Sasheer has predicted your death," he confirmed.

"Then we both must return to Sanctuary," Peleyia decided.

"It's not that simple."

"No." Peleyia gave a sly smile. "It never is."

"In the past, every Brethren that has faced Lichien and Kalern has died. I don't want Sasheer to die," Kellen said. He gave a tight, nervous smile. "If he dies, I think we will all die. All the lands. So there has to be another way. I just don't know what it is. Yet."

Peleyia said nothing for a very long time, and then when he did speak, his voice was subdued and quiet. "I think," he swallowed, "I think we should not mention this to anyone. We should go on, and if—and I mean—*if* we end up in North Ridge then we make our own destiny." He liberated his short knife from his belt and deliberately sliced open his palm, watching the blood well up before he continued. "We make a pact now, Kell. To safeguard each other and cheat the destinies. Can you accept that?"

Nodding, Kellen took the knife from his friend and cut his own palm, pressing their hands together to seal the promise. "I can," he breathed, meaning it with every fiber of his being.

* * *

The next morning dawned cold and frosty, the gray light giving everything a deathly hue. Exiting from another small concealed tunnel, Kellen glanced around at the dense woodland, his boots sinking into damp grass. He tried to shake off the ill feelings of trouble. He had not slept well, and he noticed that the other members of the company were subdued also. He looked back again at the two Ihovians, seeing Salimen's worried expression and Lesendal's resigned determination.

Sasheer was in the lead, and the Mage seemed unconcerned by the change in plans, accepting the idea of going to King Darchain's mines. Everything was normal—except, the previous night he had walked in on the tail end of an argument between Sasheer and Dalzere. His presence had ended the heated words, but he could feel the anguish and anger in the room, then Sasheer had disappeared for most of the night, while Dalzere had brooded. Not even Crizkerisomia's presence had pulled the Drow warrior from his deep meditations.

Crizkerisomia. *She is another worry*, Kellen decided. The knives might have been put away, but it was obvious the war between her and Dalzere was far from over. It was an intricate dance of wills, almost as deadly as their physical encounters, yet with this new silent battle of wills, Kellen was not sure which side was winning.

The awkwardness of the group only worsened with the inclusion of a new member—Harkon. It was obvious the Dwarf did not share his father's views, and the young prince made it clear he did not want to leave the Delheck. To make matters worse, Harkon openly disapproved of Dalzere.

"We will go down through the woods to the river's edge and then cross over. It is safest to travel on the northern side of the river, regardless of the Hoindrite patrols," Harkon said in a harsh tone. He eyed each of them with mild discontent, then he lifted his own pack and threw it over a broad shoulder.

Glancing over at the squat Dwarven guide, Kellen's frown increased.

"We will follow your lead," Sasheer said, gesturing for Harkon to show them the way.

Falling in behind Salimen, Kellen found himself again in the middle of the group. He turned to look behind and saw that even Lesendal was trailing him. He found it infuriating, and he scowled at Peleyia, glad when the Lancooti quickened his pace to catch up.

"Something wrong?" Peleyia asked as he measured his strides to match Kellen's.

Nodding, Kellen spied a look up at Sasheer and then glared at Salimen's back. "I just wish they'd stop treating me like a child."

"They worry. Remember?" Peleyia gave an impish grin.

"I feel like a piece of useless baggage again."

"Will you relax?" Peleyia whispered. "Ignore it. Besides, what do you think of our new guide?"

"Harkon?" Kellen whispered back. He let his eyes settle on the Dwarf's partially obscured figure and studied his squat frame. "He's spoilt. And he distrusts outsiders."

"I think it's more than that."

"Like what?" Kellen asked, cutting the words off as Salimen glanced back at them and indicated for silence.

:*I don't know. Yet.*: Peleyia sent silently down the link before falling into step behind Kellen. :*Just . . . something.*:

CHAPTER FORTY-SIX

He was cold and wet. So cold that it took effort to raise his shaking fingers to wipe the moisture from his lips. The tangy taste of copper and salt flooded his mouth, and he stared at his fingers, numb, seeing fresh blood. He couldn't remember what had happened—his mind was blank—and he sucked in an anxious breath then glanced into the enveloping darkness. Nothing visible, yet he knew, felt, that something unimaginably evil was haunting his steps.

He let his lashes fall, willing his heart to stop pounding in fright as he pressed into the damp stonewall at his back. All his thoughts were confused, circling frantically, and he banked down on his irrational fear. He knew—remembered—that Kalern wanted to break the prophecy, that Kalern had discovered a way to taint and destroy the bloodline, by giving him to . . . to . . .

The memory was elusive, and he sobbed in a breath, clamping his teeth together and denying the dread and nausea that blossomed in his stomach. So what had he forgotten? What diabolical plan had Kalern set in motion? He couldn't remember. He opened his eyes and focused on his hands, and a vague memory resurfaced. A disturbing image of hands.

Female hands. Soft hands. Persuasive, cunning hands that entrapped him, caressed him, aroused him, stripped him, and imprisoned him.

No. He wanted to banish the memory, gagging as he recalled how those same hands had forced him to drink a bitter mixture. That was when his world had turned upside down, and he had been . . .

Wrenching his mind away from the ominous memory, he stared down at himself and saw he was naked. Naked and covered in blood. Panic loomed in his mind, and he pushed away from the cold stone, stumbling down the narrow tunnel. Lost. So lost and confused. Yet he knew he had to find Sasheer? Had to warn him. Had to tell him to trust no one.

"Kellen?"

Lashing out with a fist, Kellen came awake with a gasped cry and nursed his sore hand. He struggled out of his bedroll and backed away from his attacker.

"Cursed stars! Kell, what are you doing?" Salimen demanded in annoyance as he sat up and rubbed his jaw. He glared at the younger man.

"Sal?"

"Who in the ten levels of hell did you think it was?" Salimen demanded as he stood.

Kellen glanced around, disorientated. The poignant dream images lingered in his mind, infecting his judgments, and he raised a hand to his head as a headache started behind his eyes. He closed his eyes, not wanting to think about his dream. Reality was mingling with fantasy, and he had no idea what was truth and what was lies. He opened his eyes and searched around. Ryland had stopped his packing and was staring at him, while Lesendal hurried to Salimen's side. Even the grumpy Harkon gave him a suspicious glare—then Peleyia was moving to crouch next to him.

"Kell, are you okay?" the Lancooti whispered as he pushed Salimen away. He gripped Kellen's shoulder and shook him. "Snap out of it!"

"I have—" It was an effort to talk, and he shrugged Peleyia off, struggling to his feet and staggering away. Everything was disjointed, surreal. Then he collapsed to his knees and shivered when a warm presence settled by his side. He opened his eyes and met Peleyia's worried gaze.

"Another dream?"

"Nightmare," Kellen corrected as he dropped his head down into his hands.

"What's wrong with him?" Salimen asked. He cautiously approached and crouched down. His eyes were direct and his tone less accusing.

Lifting his head, Kellen saw that he had an audience and just dreaded Sasheer's questions when the Mage got hold of him. Where was Sasheer anyway?

"Kell?"

Looking again at his anxious friend, he tried to give a reassuring smile. He could read the fear and worry in Peleyia's eyes and knew the Lancooti was as nervous as he was about going any closer to North Ridge. But they had agreed to see this journey through, agreed to help Sasheer. "I just had a bad dream," he explained.

"Understandable, considering what we have all witnessed over this last year," Ryland offered, his voice deep and gruff, but compassionate.

"Yeah, but I don't usually wake up swinging," Salimen protested.

"I'm sorry," Kellen said, finding a smile as Salimen stood up then reached down to offer a hand up.

Accepting the hand, Kellen got to his feet and noticed that neither Sasheer nor the two Elves were in sight. "Where's Sasheer?"

"We're getting close to the Junction," the normally uncommunicative Dwarf informed him. "Sasheer wanted to check on something down by the river. He was concerned that Drow might have breached the Junction's only accessible pass on this side of the wide Darchern River." Harkon shrugged, lifting his ax and swinging his pack over one shoulder. "They should be back anytime now. Be ready to move."

Raising a brow, Kellen looked over at Peleyia for a better explanation. The Lancooti shrugged, bending to pick up his own pack.

"I overheard Sasheer saying something about Gully Gnomes and Drow hunting parties that could be tracking us. We are so close to the Junction, that I'm amazed we haven't run into Kalern himself," Peleyia quipped, leveling a grin at the other man.

Kellen just suppressed a shudder at those words, a sudden urge to run swamping him again. He swallowed nervously and avoided Peleyia's gaze, hurriedly packing his few belongings, not wanting to think about North Ridge and its insane lord and master. Instead he thought about mundane things—about how difficult the trip had been so far. It had taken many weeks to reach this point along the Darchern River, and they'd been lucky to evade the Black Guard patrolling the southern banks of the wild, raging river.

Despite Harkon's sullen attitude, the Dwarf had kept his word and kept them safe, although Dalzere, and even Crizkerisomia, suggested they could be walking into a trap—a feeling Kellen mirrored.

Shivering in the early-morning chill, he glanced around at their surroundings. The seasons were changing again, as the land around started to show the first signs of snow after a mild, frosty autumn. It seemed like the cold, wintry season kept following them, like a rampant dog on their heels, chasing them slowly yet inevitably north. Which was the last place he had ever wanted to go.

Musing over that, he blew warm air on his cold fingers, trying to imagine what it would be like back in Ihova, far away in the south. It would be midsummer, and the forests would be full of small flowers, fresh new grass, and sweet blossoms. Shaking himself, he dismissed the daydream, focusing again on his immediate surroundings. Ihova was a lifetime away, a peaceful land destroyed by Kalern and his guard. By Lichien. He frowned, realizing that in each and every nightmare, he had seen Kalern, but never Lichien. *Why?* That puzzled him.

Hearing the murmur of voices around him, he dragged his mind back to the present and to the fact that they had to get across the treacherous river. He stood and stretched, then leant down to retrieve his rolled pack—and froze.

An annoying hum of sound started in his ears, a vague distraction, and he tried to shrug off the effects. But the sound held him frozen in place, narrowing his perception dangerously. He became acutely aware of the muted forest sounds, of the crickets, the bird song, then just as swiftly the mysterious sensations passed, and he was able to lift his pack and glance around. He scanned the forest in suspicion and let his gaze settle on the other members of the company.

Salimen was off to one side still rubbing his jaw and muttering to Lesendal. The two were almost identical in appearance, their leathers blending in perfectly with their surroundings. Peleyia was checking over some of his weapons, while Ryland stood very still, as if listening for something. The big warrior was fully encased in his own armor, a steel-clad hand resting on the hilt of his massive sword. Tufts of curly hair stuck out of his helmet, and his beard was speckled with snow, giving him a comical look—except for the shrewd eyes that missed nothing.

He squinted at the Haonian, letting Ryland's uneasiness wash over him, letting it infect his mood. Then Harkon kicked dirt into the dying embers of the fire, breaking the tranquil spell that had blanketed the campsite. Kellen breathed out hard and decided his edginess must be from the nebulous remains of his nightmare. Resurrecting a faint smile, he crouched down and gasped when a dart whistled past him to embed in the tree behind.

"Gnomes!" Harkon hissed, immediately dropping into a fighting stance.

"They must have waited until the group separated," Ryland snarled as he drew his huge sword.

The hissed sound of cold metal sent a shiver through Kellen, and he dropped his pack to rest his hand on his own Drow blade. And abruptly—weirdly—everything around him dimmed, darkened into a dreamlike illusion. Movement slowed to a crawl, and he blinked, trying to clear his sluggish mind. Sounds disappeared, and he felt himself stagger backward, catching the look of fear which filled Peleyia's eyes. *Fear?* The Lancooti was saying something to him, but the words were lost; and then he tumbled backward when a squat, dirty figure fell from the trees above.

The Gully Gnome, all pudgy eyes in a grotesque face, ambushed him. It all happened in a disjointed manner, and Kellen battled to draw his sword, shoving the damp Gnome from his chest. He saw Ryland and Peleyia kill half a dozen little Gnomes before Salimen made a dive for him.

Salimen? Was it really Salimen?

Puzzled, he dragged a hand over his face, wanting to wipe the fog from his vision. He blinked and again saw Salimen, only now the Ihovian was mutating into the shadowed darkness of Kalern—

the blond hair darkened; the light blue eyes turned utterly black, and the long mouth curled up into a sneer.

On one level, he knew it was an illusion, yet the image of Kalern inspired panic, inspired hatred, and he lashed out. He instinctively raised his sword, intending to kill Kalern once and for all, to kill the man rushing toward him. It was a programmed response—he knew it deep in his gut—but he was unable to halt the madness, unable to fight the compulsion. He extended his sword, his arm trembling, a hissed growl of anguish leaving his lips as he lunged forward. *No . . . no . . . no . . .* and he threw himself sideways, falling on his sword arm, begging sanity. The jarring impact hurt, and he grunted, feeling hands bruise his arms and haul him into a sitting position. Then he was being propped against a tree while fingers gently brushed hair from his vision. With the touch, reality returned, and he saw Salimen.

"Kellen!"

Salimen was shaking him hard, then pulling him to his feet, and Kellen wanted to protest, but he couldn't get his body or mind to cooperate. He could see the worry in the bowman's face, could taste his anger.

"Kell? Can you hear me?"

He was shaken again, then he watched, mesmerized, as Salimen turned away and swatted a Gully Gnome with the handle of his crossbow. Salimen was swearing colorfully, and Kellen collapsed to lean against the tree, wishing he could shake off the strange lassitude.

* * *

"Dale!" Salimen called, using his body as a shield to protect the dazed young man behind him.

"One of us has to let Sasheer know what's happening," Peleyia panted as he used the hilt of his sword to knock another Gnome senseless.

"Are you volunteering?" Salimen asked, using his crossbow like a club. He saw Peleyia's glance slid toward Kellen's slumped and motionless form.

"Kell?" Peleyia called but got no response.

"He hit his head," Salimen explained when he saw the Lancooti's shock. Then he grabbed Peleyia and shoved him clear of another Gnome, smacking the ugly little man across the face. "These Gnomes are like rodents. Not exactly deadly, just annoying," he mumbled, kicking a second Gully Gnome away.

Picking up Kellen's discarded sword, Peleyia used it to slap at the hands of a filthy little Gnome. "True," he said, "but they are surprisingly limitless. They also have us pinned down very efficiently."

"Understatement," Salimen muttered then glanced around at the others, trying to catch Lesendal's attention. "Pel, maybe you should go and find Sasheer."

Peleyia nodded, resigned, and then cast one final look at his dazed friend before stunning another Gnome. And instant later, he stepped behind a tree and disappeared into the misty forest.

Trusting the little thief to find Sasheer and the Elves, Salimen concentrated on cutting a clear path toward Ryland and Lesendal. Even Harkon had given up fighting on his own and had joined forces with the other two warriors in the center of the small campsite. Reaching back to grab Kellen, he managed to drag the unresisting man with him past two Gnomes before Kellen let out a blood-chilling cry. Salimen swiveled and just caught the look of terror and self-loathing which filled Kellen's eyes—then the younger man was gone, blindly running through the trees away from them. "Damn!" he cursed, and slashed at one Gnome in anger before taking off after the fleeing man.

* * *

Kellen ran heedless of the dangers, no longer knowing what was real and what was imagined. He didn't know if he was asleep, dreaming he was awake, or awake praying he was asleep. He hoped it was the former. Nothing made sense, from the appearance of the dirty, green-skinned Gnomes to the dark shadows overlaying his friends. So he ran—ran before he destroyed all that he loved.

He ran until his lungs felt like they would burst from the exertion, and then he was stumbling, falling, tripping over half-hidden tree roots, and hitting the ground hard. He slid in the icy snow, inhaling dirt and water and tangling in the underbrush. He got to his feet in a rush and exhaled hard, glancing around and brushing snow and leaves from his clothing. He was filthy—and utterly lost.

He turned in a slow circle and gradually became aware that the forest around him was deathly quiet and cold. He breathed out deeply, seeing his breath frost the air, and he raised a hand to wipe hair from his face. He spun around, apprehension prickling his nerves, and his hand crept down to his sword hilt—but his Drow blade was gone. All he had was a single dagger, and he drew it swiftly as he was washed in the aura of evil.

A cold, chilling caress of corruption swept around him. A seductive, lethal presence that he both craved and despised. Familiar . . . so familiar. This was the same presence which had haunted his every step in the Southland. The same invisible entity that had exposed him to the Kizer, that had forced him off the ledge in Death Peaks—and he spun around, raising his dagger to kill the creature—and came face to face with Shard.

He cursed, and lowered his dagger to stare at the small snow dragon. Images, places, and hidden understanding slowly and painfully fell into place, and he scowled at the deceptive creature. *He knew* . . . had always known on some intuitive level that Shard would betray him.

"Stupidity seems to run in your family," Shard hissed, hovering just out of reach, its black eyes veiled.

Narrowing his gaze, Kellen raised his dagger again, his fingers tightening around the warm hilt. "What do you mean?"

"I tried to warn you," Shard hissed in anger. But whether that anger was directed at Kellen, or itself, was not clear.

"Warn me about what?" He demanded. He watched as the animal shivered and changed color briefly before it once again resembled the inky blackness of night.

"I did not want to like you. I wanted to hate you. And I do . . .

hate you. You are weak, and you will make me weak." Shard accused, a flicker of fire frosting the cool air surrounding it.

"You deceived me. Tricked me," Kellen said, shaking his head. "Lied to me."

"I wanted to kill you.'

"But you didn't," Kellen returned, growing in confidence as he watched Shard shrink back in startlement and shock. It was like a shroud had been lifted from his mind, and he was allowed to see Shard for what the creature was. His mind tirelessly played over all the dangerous encounters he'd had with this contrary creature, and he lowered his dagger. "Even in Ihova, you would give me too much warning, making sure I survived."

Recoiling as if stung, the dragon belched flames at him, then flew a short distance before returning to glare at him, to hover close and snarl at Kellen's smiled of triumph. "I despise you!"

"You need me," Kellen said.

Even more taken back by that, Shard spat at him in a cruel language. "I will not submit to you!" the dragon hissed. "My true master will break you. Then he will kill you!"

"I know," Kellen whispered, suddenly understanding what all the nightmares had been about. Visions, warnings, promises—premonitions of the future. He swallowed, burying the fear deep, and looked at Shard through his lashes. "Tell me, what color were you originally?"

"What?" the dragon snapped, surprise in his voice.

"I understand now that Kalern has contaminated you. That you were not always like this. I bet you were once the purest of white, with silver eyes that would have glistened as brightly as sun-warmed snow."

Backpedaling, the little creature trembled in panic. It convulsed, falling to the ground to lie shuddering in the dirty snow. Snow as unclean as it had become. "To help you means death," the creature lisped. "Death to us both."

"You're a Shade, aren't you?" Kellen asked, dropping to his knees to gently turn the small dragon over. He ran fingers over stained scales, waiting for those large eyes to open and look at him.

He remembered the first time he had seen the dragon, touched it, the first time it had beguiled him so thoroughly on the moor. "You are half a soul. You mirror one of the dead Mages. But which one?"

"Enough!" Shard said, moving away from Kellen and shaking the snow from its wings. It wrinkled its nose in irritation. "You know nothing of what you speak. I would advise you to run—but even that would accomplish nothing. You are alone. Vulnerable. Defenseless. I have crippled you. So now I will take you to my master. To your new lord. To Lichien."

"Think again, demon!" Salimen called as he aimed his crossbow and fired an arrow at the hovering dragon.

"No!" Kellen cried, leaping forward to protect the little creature as the arrow passed through one of Shard's wings, causing the animal to screech in pain before it magically disappeared.

"What did you do that for?" Kellen demanded. He spun around and marched over to the blond bowman then punched him hard.

"Kellen!" Lesendal intervened, pulling the younger man off his cousin.

"You stupid idiot!" Kellen continued as he struggled out of the prince's hold. "I was just breaking through its conditioning! When you—"

"Me!" Salimen countered. "That's twice in one day that you've hit me! And might I remind you that whatever that 'thing' was—it is the enemy. Not me!"

Turning away, Kellen shook his head, not believing any of this.

"What was that thing, Kell?" Lesendal asked in a softer tone as Salimen swore behind him.

"An entity," Kellen said, tired. "A Shade."

"Oh great, another one," Salimen snapped, far from appeased. "Terrica's evil twin, I bet!"

"From Kalern?" Lesendal pushed, ignoring Salimen's outbursts. He walked over to Kellen and forced the other man to look at him. "Kalern has a Shade?"

Unsure, Kellen hesitated. "Maybe. It would seem so."

"Oh damn," Salimen said as he dropped his crossbow and

drew out his sword. "I think there's your answer," he trailed off, wiping blood from his split lip as he pointed toward a group of mounted Black Guard who materialized around them, like wraiths appearing in fog, silent, insidious, and deadly.

The leading Hoindrite guard dismounted and took off his helmet as he approached the three men.

"Stars! I always imagined Hoindrites were ugly, but that Hoindrite takes some beating," Salimen said in an aside. He raised his sword in preparation, studying the waiting guard. "This isn't looking good."

Lesendal did the same as he yanked Kellen between them. "Now we know why they wear the armor," he muttered in reply to Salimen's comment.

"Yeah," Salimen agreed, "to keep all that ugliness contained."

"I have five units of guard," the huge Hoindrite commander said in a thick, grating accent. "Surrender, or I will have you killed. Either way, I take the boy." Then as if to make his point, the commander raised a hand, and the clear sound of crossbows being loaded echoed through the forest.

Feeling insulted, Kellen glared at the ugly commander. "I am not a boy!" he spat, locking his jaw and lifting his dagger. He realized a moment later how stupid that must have looked and sounded.

The commander gave a grunt and half grimace, which might have been a grin, then drew his huge sword. It was even bigger than Ryland's, and Kellen stared at it, impressed. Even Lesendal and Salimen appeared impressed.

"If you want to die, so be it."

The challenge hung in the air between them for a prolonged moment, then Lesendal threw his sword down and indicated for Salimen to do the same.

"Dale—" the bowman growled.

"We have a better chance alive than dead," Lesendal said.

Not liking it, Salimen still complied and nudged Kellen to do the same.

"Good," the Hoindrite commander snarled. "I have always admired the southern intelligence."

CHAPTER FORTY-SEVEN

"Those imbeciles!" Sasheer fumed, almost beyond rage. "Of all the stupid . . ." he trailed off, uttering a string of Drow curses. Even his normally untamed hair seemed to stand on end, his eyes dangerously black and feral.

Dalzere studied his friend, lifting a hand to warn Peleyia away when the Lancooti held up Salimen's abandoned crossbow. On the ground next to where the crossbow had been found were two Ihovian swords and a small southern-made dagger. Sighing, Dalzere leaned back against a tree, his yellow eyes studying the forest, his expression uncompromising. Harkon had identified the boot print of a Hoindrite guard, and he estimated the Black Guard had been twenty in number by the amount of hoof indentations in the soft ground.

"They would have been badly outnumbered," Harkon said, his fingers testing the depth of the indentations. "There is no indication of a struggle." He glanced up. "Maybe those Drow by the river were a lure?"

Dalzere let his gaze flick over Harkon, remembering the fight at the river. It had been vicious, fast, and bloodthirsty. His sword had snapped under the impact of a Drow's dead weight, and he had been forced to take up one of his race's weapons, a *cuxsia*, the bespelled, wicked-looking, curved hand blade that all Drow carried. He'd won the challenge with the *cuxsia*, and now the tainted, magical blade sat snugly against his hip, whispering to him.

He fingered the blade, subduing his abhorrence and admiration for such a weapon. Not wanting it, yet finding it had molded to his hand lovingly, to become a part of him, claiming him, owning him. He closed his eyes, mentally refusing to give into the *cuxsia's* magical pull.

"Where do we go now?" Harkon asked, eyeing the enraged Mage and the distracted Drow warrior.

Dalzere snapped his eyes open and sucked in a breath, forcing his fingers away from the *cuxsia's* powerful appeal and glanced at Sasheer. There was an air of something terribly destructive encasing Sasheer, an impotent fury, and he could understand why no one wanted to disturb his rant. Should he? Then the question was moot as Sasheer turned and stalked toward him. He watched his friend battle with his temper, before the Mage let out a slow, measured breath, rubbing his eyes in frustration.

"Well?" Sasheer's voice was an angry growl.

Straightening, Dalzere considered his answer, considered his partner, accepting his anger and anguish. "I imagine they will be taken upriver to Heaten's Reach. From there, they could be thrown into the slave pens under the Ice Cliffs, but more likely they will be taken through Hoindrea to North Ridge."

"If they are alive!" Sasheer snapped.

"There is that small point," Dalzere agreed, his tone mild. "But I doubt they will be killed. That will happen when they reach North Ridge," he reasoned, reading Sasheer's hidden fears very well. "Otherwise we would have found Salimen and Lesendal's bodies here. The guard has probably been ordered to bring all southerners to Kalern—alive."

Releasing another harsh breath, Sasheer gritted his teeth. "You are undoubtedly correct."

Hiding his grin, Dalzere looked up when the others approached. He caressed his new weapon a second time and then met the Mage's smoldering gaze, offering silent support.

"So, do we go after them?" Ryland asked. There was a fierceness in his eyes that begged vengeance.

Sasheer turned to glare at Ryland.

"We are still on the north bank of the Darchern River," Dalzere offered, delaying a confrontation. "If we cut north into Coldan, we could avoid most of Kalern's forces and then turn south to Blackstone Pass. Kalern would not expect us to come across the Gerthwin Swamp."

"I would not expect us to navigate Gerthwin Swamp," Sasheer replied tartly.

"Remember, we have the Oracle," Dalzere reminded.

Sasheer just snorted in response.

"There are worse things than Raveners hidden within the swamp," Crizkerisomia said, lifting her eyes to touch the Drow. There was puzzlement, warring with respect and affection in her glance. "Will the Oracle protect us against those creatures?"

"To a point," Sasheer said. "As long as we stay within the Oracle's sphere of influence."

"I can deal with flesh-and-blood creatures. You just get us into North Ridge," Ryland uttered. "With or without the Oracle."

"Getting in will not be the problem," Dalzere said with heavy emphasis, not liking the plan or Sasheer's sudden silence. That always spelled trouble. "It is getting out that worries me."

"I'm sure I could find us a safe route," Harkon offered.

"No." Sasheer's scowl lightened. "You, my young friend, need to find Darchain and his clan and tell them what has happened here. Somehow get word to Karczag in Sanctuary, so that news can be sent to Hersoford. The men of the east would be more than happy to fight against the guards when they learn of Kalern's plans. Also ask the Elves if they can send a ship to Red Sands Inlet. To anchor behind one of the reefs in three months and wait a week. If we have not made the inlet by then, they should not wait any longer."

"All right," Harkon said slowly, sounding a little disheartened that he would not be going on the journey.

"It will be a long and hard trip north, Sasheer," Dalzere warned. "I doubt we will catch the guard."

"I know." Sasheer locked eyes with his friend and relaxed. "But by taking Kellen, Lichien has extended an invitation." He gave a small, cynical smile. "It's an invitation I can no longer refuse."

"Even if it is another trap?" Crizkerisomia asked, looking between the two men.

"An enticement," Dalzere corrected, letting a frown grow as he held Sasheer's gaze. "He will kill you before you reach the dais," he whispered softly.

"After four thousand years, that might even be a blessing," Sasheer said, then he looked away from Dalzere.

"Sasheer..."

Refusing to be drawn, Sasheer waved Dalzere's concern aside and turned to the Dwarf. "If you find Seaton, tell him about the Gully Gnomes. I am sure he will come up with a creative way to stall their advance on Darchain's underground tunnels."

"Not to mention the interference of the Drow," Dalzere reminded darkly.

Grinning now, Harkon nodded. "I will." He eyed the remaining company with what was the first show of friendship. "Good luck to you all."

CHAPTER FORTY-EIGHT

During his first few days of capture, Kellen had been defiant, even angry with the Black Guard. Sullen and uncommunicative as his wrists and ankles had been tied before he had been thrown over a horse and transported like a sack of dirty potatoes. It was as the days turned into a week, then one week into two weeks that his defiance had waned, and his desperation and fear had grown. His hope faded. For he had expected Sasheer or even Dalzere to magically step from behind a tree, or snow ridge to rescue him. To rescue the three of them

But it never happened, and as time passed, his apprehension grew, making him reckless—until he attempted his own escape.

The higher up into the bleak, snowbound mountain range they'd traveled, the less he was confined to a horse, and one morning, he found himself standing free with only his wrists tied. Instinct kicked in, and he bolted into the white maze of forest. His feet sank into soft snow, hampering him as he tried to run, and then he was plummeting into a deep ravine of snow. The soft, icy embrace restricted his movements as he landed face first in the cold wetness. He battled to breathe, to get free, as a deep chill numbed his senses and body, and it took him a long moment to realize hands were on him, seizing him and dragging him back to the trail.

There the commander waited, and Kellen shivered, as much from the chilling cold as from the expression on the commander's face. He expected to be punished, but the huge man only stared at him, a sneer curling his lower lip before the commander snarled a set of gruff orders. He tensed then watched horrified as Salimen was dragged forward and beaten until the Ihovian lay unconscious. Silence descended as red blood stained the snow, and Kellen looked away, not daring to meet Lesendal's eyes. *So like Bains' blood . . .* and he pushed the memory away, understanding the commander's silent threat very well. If he didn't cooperate, his friends would suffer the consequences.

After that, he was marched away to the front of the war party and tethered to the commander's huge horse. There he stood, cold inside and out, petrified for them all.

* * *

The journey through the treacherous Ice Cliffs took weeks, and during that time, they encountered other guards, all of whom told fantastic stories of victory over the Dwarves and Elves. It was disheartening, and Kellen despaired, worried about his friends, about the people he had come to think of as family. His only bit of security was in knowing that somewhere, out there, Peleyia survived. He could feel the Lancooti's life force via the mental link they shared, and the connection was his lifeline to sanity. He needed to believe that if Peleyia was alive, then Ryland and the others were alive also.

He clung to the link but refused to reach out and touch Peleyia, or even touch the currents or use what lessons Sasheer had taught him. His skill was unrefined, so he chose not to test his limits—until there was no choice left. That happened one night, in a moment of exhaustion and fleeting panic as he saw the guards mistreat Lesendal—he reacted on instinct and reached out with his mind to gather the currents and *fell . . .* fell into a hideous web of mental power and corruption.

Lichien. The dark, brooding, malicious awareness pounced on him in mental glee, and he caught a transitory glimpse of how it had waited, watched, and schemed on the periphery of his conscious mind. Anticipating the day he would lower his mental shields in order to help a friend.

Pain—incredible pain exploded inside his mind, and he screamed, dropping to his knees as he hastily tried to reconstruct his barriers. He succeeded to some extent, but it cost him his precious link with Peleyia. He remembered little after that, only knowing that the Black Guard had dragged him to his feet and forced him to walk.

After that . . . after that he didn't think, didn't dwell on hope as he welcomed the cold, welcomed its numbing effect on his mind and heart. He felt trapped, knowing Lichien waited, knowing that as soon as he reached out he was doomed. He lost touch with reality, with time, with faces—not sure any longer what sanity was.

Around him, the weeks turned into months.

CHAPTER FORTY-NINE

Exhaustion registered on his mind, along with the fact that he was filthy and hungry. But it was only now—now that he was inside the dank, gloomy tunnels leading to North Ridge—that Kellen allowed himself to become aware of his state. Now that the journey was almost complete, and his doom was at hand.

The abyss.

He shuddered when cold water splashed his face, jolting him back to his current misery. He lifted his lashes and ignored the guard's snarl; instead he looked up into the unlit blackness, imagining the kind of creatures that Lichien might have unleashed in this icy underground fortress. Everything unpleasant and deadly. Then he was dragged to his feet, and he couldn't stifle his gasp as he was shoved forward.

The problem was, he didn't want to think about what awaited him. He knew. He had seen the abyss and had rationalized his fate and hardened his heart against hope. Clamping his jaw to ward off panic, he forced his feet to move and misjudged another step. He went down hard, the impact driving a grunt from him. Cold, filthy water hit his hands again, and he didn't resist as the unsympathetic guard yanked him to his feet a second time. Then he was propelled forward, only to fall again from exhaustion and loss of coordination.

"Move!" the guard snarled, impatient.

He shook his head, idly watching dirty water drip from his long fringe, from his shriveled fingers. He glanced around, chancing a look back, and wondered what had become of Lesendal and Salimen. He saw nothing behind and wearily sucked in a tight breath. Then hands grasped his hair making him cry out as he was lifted, and he swallowed his curse as the guard pressed up behind him and hissed in his ear.

"If I have to carry you, I promise, you will not be only sorry, but extremely sore."

Not answering, he tried to catch his balance when he was pushed again, and he stumbled into the tunnel wall. He marshaled a glare, meeting the guard's menacing grin but refused to be intimidated. He forced his sore legs to work and staggered forward, the dark passageways dimming before his eyes as Lichien chose that moment to target his shielded mind. It hurt, and he tensed, drawing in a labored breath and blocking Lichien's dart of power. He was used to these sudden invisible attacks, even though they weakened him, tore at his confidence, yet he knew the game was almost at an end. Soon he would make a mistake, and Lichien would win.

"Bright . . . stars," he breathed as the attacked passed, leaving him light-headed and ill. He reached out with his fingers for support and encountered jagged stone. His feet were numb, his boots and clothing saturated, and he knew that only madness waited at the end of this tunnel, cunning evil wrapped in the cloak of beauty. *No . . .* giving in to his crushing despair, he folded and fell to his knees, willing release.

"Get up!" the guard snarled, kicking him.

"Just kill me," Kellen begged, his voice hoarse, "just kill me."

The guard gave a cruel, gruff laugh then lifted him off the floor to shove him forward into the darkness. "That pleasure is not mine," he growled, an evil grimace disfiguring his ugly face. "You are for the Master."

* * *

The dreadful labyrinth of wet tunnels eventually widened into a huge underground cavern, and Kellen shuddered, seeing his nightmares come to life. Before him rose a cathedral of natural stone and shuttered light that was both harsh and impressive. The roof of the cavern was lost to blackness, while dark, nebulous shapes drifted through the air overhead. A pool of still, coal black water lay off to one side, and he hesitated, getting shoved from behind.

He stared at the black water in apprehension, quickening his step as they came to a narrow stone bridge that spanned the still lake.

He wrinkling his nose at the unpleasant smell, seeing beneath the bridge how the water was murky, repugnant, with tiny bubble breaking the surface ever so often. Not a ripple disturbed the mirrored effect, and he lifted his eyes to the walls surrounding the lake. They were a confusing mixture of angles and shadows, decorated with small firelights that gave the gallery a sinister feel.

On the other side of the bridge, he noticed that half of the cavern was shrouded in darkness, with only a small area lit. Again, large fires sat along the floors to cast an inviting yet cold glow over the raised dais in front. Statues, blackened by more than age, sat to one side, eerie and grotesque, showing figures caught on the verge of fear or ecstasy. He couldn't decide which, and he tore his eyes away from them, concentrating on the dais ahead.

The platform was carved from white stone, the only contrast within the cavern, and he stared at it, fascinated by the fires burning beneath its lip. He was stopped before the dais by a large heavy hand on his shoulder, and he obediently complied. He never glanced back, his eyes lifting to fix rigidly on the throne that sat in the middle of the platform.

The throne was huge, carved from polished anthracite—black, flawless—and it dominated the entire dais, the polished rock shining in the flickering firelight, majestic and imposing. To the throne's left stood a pedestal, chiseled from the same polished anthracite. Nestled on top of this pedestal sat a magnificent, multi-faceted crystal. It glowed, radiant, reflecting shimmering colors over the raised dais. It was dazzling—hypnotic—and Kellen felt completely overwhelmed by its presence.

Lichien.

Tearing his eyes away from the luminous stone, he felt the weight of the stone's personality hit him squarely for the first time. He grimaced, dropping to one knee then panted out his shock when the stone abruptly released him. That surprised him, and he lifted his gaze, his eyes going from the stone to a beautiful woman who stepped out from behind the monstrous throne.

She was stunning, and he stared unashamedly. She was perfection: so pale, delicate, unblemished, and so out of place in this cavern. Her hair swung to her waist and was the color of spun gold, her skin as smooth and pure as milk, her eyes like living sapphires. Her dress was a simple frock of blue velvet, the bodice of fine, bleached white lace that covered her breasts, emphasizing her desirability. He followed her with his eyes as she walked around the throne, not sure if she was real or imagined.

"Kessendra? Kess!"

The shout jarred him, and Kellen turned in time to see Lesendal and Salimen struggle forward. Guards stopped them before either man could touch the dais, and then they were shoved to their knees beside him.

Kessendra—and he blinked as he realized this devastating beauty was Lesendal's sister. It would make sense for Kalern—Lichien— to use her to control the Ihovians. He shook his head and looked at his two friends, relieved and glad they were alive, but also scare for them all, knowing there were only alive because Kalern wanted to play a twisted game. It would be better that they had all died on the snow field at Danchern's Junction .

"Bright stars," Salimen snarled at the guard who held him. "This is all I damn well need."

Kellen breathed out slowly and dragged his eyes back to Kessendra. Beside him, Salimen was now cursing, and he remembered that there was no love on Salimen's side towards Kessendra. Why, he didn't know and he turned again to look at his friends, noting how bloodied and disheveled they both were.

"Are you all right?"

Blinking, he nodded then met Salimen's fierce and determined gaze. "Very glad to see you both," he said, meaning it. He glanced back at Kessendra and could not suppress his admiration. The sight of her gave him hope, and he raised his chin in defiance to Lichien.

From behind the throne, the darkness shifted, intensified, and then gloved hands were slowly, artfully traveling over the polished, coal-colored throne with loving concern, before a cloaked and hooded figure emerged. The figure was tall, wrapped in a shifting black fabric that rejected all light, giving the illusion of total darkness. This tall stranger moved to stand before the throne and raised a hand in Kessendra's direction.

She moved, turned mechanically, dutifully stepping forward and lifting her hands to push the cowl from the stranger's face. Kellen gulped, his eyes drinking in the man's appearance. His face was both sensual and elegant, his features stunning, his mouth curving up into a devilish, tormenting smile. It was a face that Kellen knew intimately from his dreams and nightmares, yet nothing could have prepared him for the reality, the magnificence of Kalern's appearance.

Then Kalern shifted his dark gaze. He turned his hand to cup Kessendra's chin, caressing her cheek in possession, his smile sly. Slowly, Kessendra swayed closer to the Dark Lord, her arms hanging lifelessly by her sides, her eyes unblinking. Kalern chuckled and turned to observe his guests, his movements graceful, his clothing designed to confuse the eye, a combination of dark midnight silks and jeweled leather.

"Captivating, isn't she?" Kalern purred, his voice a seduction, while his eyes darkened with depravity. He released her cheek, his gloved fingers trailing her throat before he moved away and smoothly descended the steps. His gaze brushed the prisoners, doing a full sensual appraisal of each man until finally resting on Kellen. "Welcome to North Ridge," he smirked.

Watching the Dark Lord, Kellen braced himself and suppressed a shiver. He wanted to deny this man, to deny Kalern the satisfaction of seeing him falter, yet his physical presence was overwhelming. Beguiling, and he locked his jaw until his muscles ached then glanced up, only to be distracted by a ghostly shadow that drifted down from the high roof. The ghost-shadow flew closer and landed to perch on the back of the immense throne, and he stared at it in utter disbelief. "Shard?"

Kalern snorted, both pleased and amused by Kellen's awe and discomfort. "I see you know my talented . . . pet."

Kellen bit back on his immediate response, ignoring Kalern

and concentrating with determination on Shard. He willed the dragon to look at him, and when Shard turned those large eyes on him, he growled his frustration. "Why?"

"Don't waste your breath," Kalern advised snidely. "That magical entity is now more corrupt than the original society which spawned it."

No . . . he would not accept that. Kellen shook his head, keeping his gaze locked on Shard and letting the small creature see his disappointment. The dragon flinched, spreading its wings and hissing in displeasure. Then Lesendal lunged for the dais, and Kellen moved, feeling guards grab him as four other Black Guard restrained Salimen and dragged Lesendal back to the floor and forced him to his knees. Once there, Kalern turned his glare on the Ihovians.

"What have you done to my sister?" Lesendal demanded in belligerence.

A slow, amoral smile graced Kalern's lips, the expression never reaching his eyes. He paced toward Lesendal and leaned down over the angry man, inhaling the prince's anger. His eyes shut for a moment, and then Kalern looked again at the prince, his pupils contracting until his eyes were the color of winter. "I've done nothing remotely interesting . . . yet," he whispered. "Why? Do you have a suggestion?"

Banking down on his rage, Lesendal fought against the guard holding him. "Touch her, and I'll . . ."

Kalern laughed. "You'll—what?" he mocked, his eyes slowly transforming to the dark lifelessness of his usual stare.

"Dale," Salimen whispered, horrified, as Kalern's expression mutate into something inhuman.

"Yes—Dale," Kalern mimicked. "Do as you're told, or I'll snap her in two." He straightened and raised a hand to gently rub his thumb and forefinger together. On the dais behind him, Kessendra swayed, like a doll blown about in the wind.

Seeing the action, Lesendal paled, then he exploded in fury, attempting to lash out at the monster standing in front of him. But the guards restrained him.

"Temper, temper," Kalern chastised, his long cloak swirling around his boots as he turned. "I see a lesson is in order," he said, his gaze going to Kellen briefly, before he pulled a knife from his belt and lifted it, so the prince could see it. He mouthed a few words over the blade then threw it in the air—and the blade vanished.

Mystified by the trick, it took Kellen a long moment to work out what had happened. Then he felt sickened when he saw Kessendra snatch the blade out of the air. She held it expertly, her expression never alternating, her fingers locking tightly around the carved hilt. Kalern laughed and gestured toward her with another murmur of words. Languidly, Kessendra responded by pressing the sharp edge of the blade against her smooth cheek. Blood blossomed on her white skin, running down the contours of her face to drip off her chin and stain her unblemished throat and lace bodice.

"Stop it," Lesendal pleaded, appalled by the demonstration.

Kalern ignored the pleas, watching her in pleasure as she never blinked, cutting deeper into her cheek. Warm, living blood stained the polished silver hilt, splashing onto the white floor. And still she continued to angled the blade in.

"Stop it! Please stop," Lesendal cried, begging Kalern to cease this torment. "You can't do this!"

Turning his back on the bleeding girl, Kalern again graced them with a smile that never reached his dead eyes, before clicking his fingers and removing the blade from her grasp. It vanished. "Obedient, isn't she?"

"What have you done to her?" Salimen asked.

"I've trained her to be submissive." Kalern shrugged, uninterested. "I've encased her in my will, bound her will. It's very stimulating actually." He sighed theatrically as he walked away from them. "You'll be pleased to know that I've left her mind intact, so she knows exactly what she is doing at all times. But I own her body." He grinned, in obvious enjoyment of the horror and fury on the Ihovians' faces. "She has no will. No power. No voice. She is locked inside her own mind, shrieking mentally at what I have made her witness, and do. It will eventually drive her insane—I think." He walked up the stairs and went to stand behind Kessendra's trembling figure. She was utterly passive, only her eyes showing her terror as Kalern traced a finger along her damaged cheek, whispering in her ear. The injury closed as if it had never existed. Only the blood staining her throat, bodice and floor testified to the event. Teasingly, Kalern kissed her golden hair, before laughing at Lesendal's dismayed and sickened expression.

"You're insane," Salimen breathed.

Raising a brow, Kalern grinned. "Why, thank you."

"Demented," Salimen continued, incensed by the power Kalern so blatantly displayed. Next to him Lesendal was gritting his teeth and staring at Kessendra.

"Depraved and—"

Kalern cut him off by a simple click of his fingers, choking the bowman with an invisible grip of power. "I prefer ingenious," he hissed as he faced the prisoners.

Salimen gasped, his mouth wide, his eyes bulging while Kalern's lips twisted in wicked delight.

"I find your flesh weak and fragile," Kalern said, releasing the invisible bonds. He watched Salimen gulp in air, then he lifted his hand and tossed the bowman across the floor and into the sidewall. The Ihovian hit the old stone with a thud, then lay there motionless.

"The Brethren will stop you," Kellen spoke up, deliberately interrupted Kalern's sport before he could kill both Ihovians.

"Ah," the Dark Lord breathed. He swiveled on his toes and pinned Kellen with an interested gaze. He seemed to immediately dismiss the two Ihovians from his concern and walk across the dais to stand before Kellen. "You can actually speak. Construct a sentence and look at me. I had started to worry. Started to imagine that the misguided Brethren had stripped away your independence."

Kellen willed himself to relax, lifting his lashes and meeting Kalern's powerful, hypnotic stare. It was like being sucked into a windstorm. "I know what you are, and I know what you want, but you will not succeed."

"And how could one so young possibly know what I want?" Kalern whispered sensually, deceptively. He skimmed a hand up Kellen's chest, hiding his smile when the younger man tensed.

"I have been told." Kellen swallowed, refusing to move. "I have seen . . ."

"You have seen only what that stupid misguided brother of mine wants you to see," Kalern corrected, then stopped as he saw Kellen's mystification.

"Brother?" Kellen repeated before he could stop the word.

"Sasheer hasn't told you our family's sordid little secret?" Throwing his head back, Kalern laughed. "How he and Serine, being first born, were chosen for the Hall of Magus, for the Magii Towers, leaving Aserties and I, as second born, condemned to Temple." He paused. "Surely this is a pet subject of his," he hissed, leaning forward until his breath hotly assaulted Kellen's face.

Kellen tried to ignore the blatant challenge, tasting Kalern all around him, watching the way those wicked eyes scanned him, read him, and tired to manipulate him. He gathered his composure and balled his fists. "No," he mouthed. He had started to suspect the truth, *but . . .* "He rarely talks of the past, to anyone," he said. "The past is dead, of no concern."

Allowing a predatory smile to grow, Kalern looked at Kellen through his lashes, refusing to move out of his personal space. "Really?" he asked. "We—that is, Aserties and I—were sent to temple to die. Regardless of our mage potential, we were condemned because of our talents. Surely you must understand my anger. Understand the stain of being second born?"

The whispered question echoed deep inside him, and Kellen fought to deny the implications, knowing Kalern was using his own inner feelings of betrayal and anger against him. "No."

"But Wyran was their first choice. You are nothing to them."

"No." Bracing himself when he felt the full force of Kalern's persuasive mind—Lichien's keen intelligence—focus on him, Kellen shuddered at the tantalizing taste of power that washed over him. He took a step back, feeling the guard at his back, and looked up to meet Kalern's stare. Those dark eyes were pools of desire, of enticement, and he shook his head, making it clear that he would refuse any offer the Dark Lord suggested.

"They would have let you die, Kellen."

The persuasive words feathered over his senses, causing him to shiver. "You killed Wyran," he countered, just managing to control his own wavering self-control and deserting strength. "And you killed your brother, Aserties. Not the Brethren. Not Sasheer. You!"

"You impertinent little—"

"And you killed Serine," Kellen continued, seeing Kalern recoil and stare at him. The Dark Lord's nostrils flared, his eyes changing color and turning a smoldering charcoal that boded destruction. Pushing on despite the build of power around him, he continued his verbal attack. "You couldn't even create a Shade. I bet Shard belonged to Serine, not you. You will never own him as long as a single descendant survives to defy you!"

"You understand nothing," Kalern hissed, saying the last word as a snarl before drawing back and glaring at the naive younger man. "I have the power. Eventually Sasheer will be forced to face me, and then I will kill him. His passions will betray him, just as they betrayed Serine." He calmed his anger and studied his captive with interest. "You are wrong about Serine. I was not the one who held the knife."

Not wanting to understand the implications behind those softly spoken words, Kellen avoided the fingers that reached out to skim over his face. "You lie."

"Ah . . . I see you already know the truth. Don't you?"

"Leave him alone!"

The shout broke the spell, and Kellen sagged when Kalern released him. He sucked in a breath and glanced over at Lesendal, seeing how the prince purposely distracted the Dark Lord. *No . . .* he shook his head, warning the prince. But Lesendal refused to acknowledge him.

Swinging around sharply, Kalern snarled and focused his attention on the Ihovian. He used his will to entrapped Lesendal with invisible fingers, then drive him into the floor repeatedly until the prince no longer had a voice to protest. When he was finished, he smirked in satisfaction and turned to level a challenging stared on Kellen. "I am tired of sparring words with you, child. You are blood of my blood. My challenger for Lichien."

"I want nothing but your destruction," Kellen answered, realizing suddenly how true Kalern's words were. He *was* a challenger... But that was not something he had consciously considered—until now. Lichien would choose the most powerful mind to inhabit, and he blinked, stunned. No wonder Kalern killed off every descendant at birth. No wonder the Dark Lord was driven by such vicious paranoia.

Then another disturbing idea slid into his mind—*Lichien had sent the nightmares, not Kalern*, and he turned to stare at the patiently waiting stone. Lichien wanted him to fight Kalern—and he met Kalern's dark eyes, seeing the fear of that in his unblinking stare. Suddenly he felt Lichien touch him, felt the stone's gloating encouragement which pushed, which wanted his fire and passion, which offered him immortality. The vastness of power on offer was suffocating, addictive, and so irresistible.

"You desire my destruction?" Kalern purred, his eyes narrowing to dangerous slits. "As have all my family. All my descendents."

"Yes," he breathed, finally understanding the true game being played out. With Lichien's help he could *kill* Kalern... and he shook his head to silence the stone's corrupting whispers.

"Ah," Kalern breathed. "I see the spark of awareness has finally hit you." He smiled knowingly, slinking closer to his victim. "You are a true child of Mitthsombaine. A true descendant of my beloved society."

"I am not like you."

Kalern chuckled, the sound playful. "No?" he taunted. "You have the drive, the viciousness, beauty, the fire, and the potential." He shook his head mockingly. "Sasheer must be annoyed that he has lost you," he paused, "but then, my deranged brother never really learned how to look after younger siblings."

Kellen stared balefully at the grinning lord.

"Do you know how many students he has... accidentally killed?"

"You don't know him," Kellen said, defending the Mage, remembering the visions and vulnerability that surrounded Sasheer like a cloak, that made the man so exasperating, so different to his peers. So human. "He is far better than you could ever hope to be." He breathed out hard, watching how Kalern regarded him in annoyance. "But then you wouldn't know what Sasheer is like, would you? You've never faced him. You have forgotten what true courage is—"

"Enough!" Kalern roared, silencing his adversary with invisible fingers of strength.

Kellen gasped, held immobile by Kalern's anger. Slowly, the Dark Lord regained his composure, his eyes clearing as he looked to the stone and then looked back at Kellen. He unclenched his fist, and Kellen sank to the ground, panting for breath.

"My brother is not the issue. It is you. So tell me, are you my lost soul in the prophecy?"

"I am your death," he spat hoarsely. He raised a hand and rubbed his throat, then glared at Kalern before looking at the silently waiting stone. Deep in his mind, he felt an ancient resentment build and explored it, realizing that the emotions were *not* coming from Lichien. That puzzled him, and he opened his senses to the alien feelings and discovered that they came from the cavern around him. From the lost spirits of the Mages who had died in this cavern at Kalern's hand. They were the voice of prophecy, a voice *far* older than Lichien. Thoughts and memories clicked into place, words rushed to his tongue, filling him, and he let those words guide him. Everything inside felt right, whole, and he resurrected a smile, one that mirrored the Dark Lord's.

Kalern hesitated. "You are so like Aserties."

"And like him, I will deny you," he whispered. Too well he understood that wanton look which passed across Kalern's handsome features. So like Sasheer.

"Pretty child," Kalern purred, his temper leashed with effort as he reached out to embrace Kellen's bony shoulder in a vicelike grip. "You are my curse and my salvation," he said as his fingers slid from Kellen's shoulder to skim up his throat. He gripped

Kellen's chin and forced the younger man to look at him. "It will be a shame to kill you," he mused. "You are almost my mirror image."

"No," Kellen hissed, sending the lord an insolent grin as he wrenched his chin free of the icy grip. "I have seen what you are—what you want—and I will not help you," he said. "I denied you in my dreams, so I will deny you in reality."

"Brave words," Kalern said, leaning closer. "Yet all I need do is kill you, and the prophecy is ended. What then?" he asked.

"Another will come," Kellen assured him. He had to believe that.

"Yes," Kalern uttered softly, intimately. "Even I cannot be sure that those insane fools living in the Keep haven't got another heir hiding somewhere. So there has to be an alternative."

"Nothing you do will stop the prophecy," Kellen vowed, feeling the words flow out of him naturally.

"Nothing?" Kalern asked. "Are you sure of that?" He lifted a strand of Kellen's black hair and studied it. "What does the prophecy say?" he asked, his eyes darting up to capture Kellen's gaze. *"'One will come . . . '* that's you," he acknowledged, his twisted smile returning. "And *'one will challenge.'* Will you challenge me?" he taunted. "And what about that part which says, *'of touching a lost soul, and shattering a divided heart?'* Would that be poor me?" he mocked. "But I especially like the bit which talks of *'sacrificing innocence.'* Are you innocent, young Kellen?" he snickered. "No, I think not," he said. "I think I will break the prophecy by getting you to give me an heir of my own. Someone who I can control."

"What?" Kellen gasped as he moved away from the seductive touch. He stared at his hair as it trailed through Kalern's fingers and suppressed a shudder before glaring at his tormentor in horror. "I won't help you."

"Yes—you will," Kalern assured, his tone reasonable. "Why do you think I went to so much trouble to bring you here?" he asked.

Watching him, wide-eyed, Kellen felt a prickling of fear run down his spine.

"You are young, very young. And so far uncorrupted by those idiots calling themselves the Brethren. You are a pawn, and I own you now."

"You will never own me."

"If I wanted you dead, I would have killed you at Danchern's Junction, or on the moors. Remember the moors and Shard's little display of helplessness?" he scoffed. "Or I could have killed you a dozen times before that. Maybe I should have taken you as a babe," he mused, "like I took Wyran. He was mine from childhood, and that fool brother of mine tried everything to save him." He laughed crudely. "And you think I don't know Sasheer. He is a woeful, sentimental idiot!"

Shaking his head, Kellen tried to block the words. *Wyran had been Kalern's since childhood?* He stared, dismayed. That was impossible . . . yet what had Tanish said? *Wyran is lost . . .* Shivering, he tensed as Kalern clicked his fingers, and he was seized from behind by guards, his wrists bound. Kalern patted him once more on the cheek in mock sympathy and then smiled sardonically.

"With the Book of Spells in my grasp, and with you as heir to the prophecy my prisoner—I will be invincible. All I need now is Sasheer charging in here, and all my dreams will be fulfilled." Kalern spun around, his cloak of darkness reflecting a multitude of shimmering colors as it danced around his long legs. Laughter followed him up the dais, where he turned and glared down at his captive in enjoyment. Then he beckoned Kessendra closer, smirking as she dutifully obeyed. "I hope Sasheer follows," he whispered, "for I have a surprise prepared for him."

Kellen bared his teeth, praying Sasheer heeded Dalzere's advice and stayed away, although he knew that was a vain hope. For now he understood. It had always been a trap, with him as the bait and Sasheer as the prize. Feeling ill, he considered reopening the link between himself and Peleyia to warn the Mage, but dismissed that idea as he chanced a look at Lichien. The stone still waited, and if he reached out, then . . . all would be lost.

He refocused on Kalern, desperate to work out a plan and froze—seeing Kessendra walk woodenly across the polished floor of the dais to stand within Kalern's embrace. The Dark Lord raised a finger and traced the bloodstained lace of her bodice while whispering in her ear. She said nothing, her expression never changing as she endured his fondling.

Beside him, Lesendal swore and he glanced down, glad the prince was alive, and he tried to warn Lesendal with his eyes to stay silent. For next time, he knew Kalern would kill the prince. Lesendal stared at him, those light blue eyes filled with anger and worry for his sister, and Kellen looked away before lifting his gaze to pin Kalern. If he didn't do something, then Lesendal would, and he wasn't willing to lose another friend. "You can't do this," he called, seeing how Kalern glanced at him in amusement. This was turning into his nightmare. It was now unfolding exactly as he had foreseen in his dreams, and he felt powerless to stop the inevitable.

"Kalern!" he called louder, stilling when he felt the rush of currents sweep past him as the Dark Lord invoked a spell. The currents were tainted with malice, with all things dark, and he couldn't suppress his shiver, *seeing* them, *feeling* them wrap around Kessendra's captive body. He opened his mouth to protest—but stopped as Kalern sighed in pleasure, releasing Kessendra from his grasp and stepping back, his snarl twisted in amusement.

Not sure what Kalern's spell was meant to achieve, Kellen remained still, his eyes locked on the Dark Lord. Then slowly, very slowly Kessendra started tremble. Her cheeks darkened in a flush, her breathing accelerated, and her expression became dazed.

"What have you done," he asked, scared of the answer, inwardly knowing the truth and despising both himself and Kalern for what would follow. *Lesendal . . . forgive me . . .* he sent silently, trying to back away as Kessendra turned and locked her hot gaze on him. "This is unnatural!" he hissed, hearing Kalern laugh. "I won't help you!" he cried in desperation, fighting the guards who held him.

Then Kalern was walking down the steps of the dais, his smile smug as he reached out and captured Kellen's chin in cold fingers. "Now, now," he shook his head in reproof. "I cannot have you injuring my vessel. Can I?"

Kellen braced himself as he felt the rush of more currents answer Kalern's wordless call, felt them wind up his body in a loving caress, felt them infect his mind, fill him with a hunger that was not his own. He tried to deny them, tired to use his own inner strength to push them away, but Kalern just call more darkness, just wrapped him tighter in the Dark Lord's bidding. The currents insidious energy dulled his senses, drained his power and turned his mind sluggish. He sucked in a breath and forced his eyes open, meeting Kalern's merciless gaze.

"There . . . that is so much better."

Wanting to struggle—to argue, to scream his protest—Kellen found he could do nothing. He tried to glare at Kalern and trembled instead, watching mesmerized as Kessendra slowly, provocatively walked to his side. Her eyes were filled with horror, with a terrible grief, until Kalern brushed her cheek a second time, and her expression went glassy and vague.

"At least you will die a happy man," Kalern mocked, then stepped away and laughed. He clicked his fingers again and the guard obeyed, dragging Kellen toward the far side of the dais. "Let no one say I don't have a sense of humor."

No! Kellen tried to shout, but no words came out. He was dragged backward by the Black Guard, across a small bridge and into a well lit tunnel. *No! I will not cooperate. I will not!* Whether he said it or merely thought it, he didn't know, only hearing Kalern's laugher echo in his mind.

I can fight this, he willed himself to believe in the impossible, as images from his dreams, his nightmares, turned into reality. He had *seen* this future . . . and he kicked out at the guards in panic. There hold was too strong—or he was too weak, he didn't know, feeling himself thrust into a small room. A cold room. He hit the floor, tasting dust as it flashed up into his face, then felt hands pulling at him, lifting him.

His responses were uncoordinated, his mind too fractured by the dark currents to concentrate, to formulate a plan, any strategy . . . and then he was being placed on a stone table. The coldness was a shock, and he lifted his head groggily, snarling at the guards who secured his hands with twine, who held him in one place.

"No," he hissed the word, turning his head in time to see Kessendra enter the small room. She was . . . bespelled, yet *so* beautiful, and he shook his head, trying to connect with the woman trapped inside Kalern's evil designs. But her eyes were dull, fixed, and unblinking. Then with trancelike slowness, she raised one hand and started to unlace her bloodstained bodice, pulling the delicate ties loose. He stared; he couldn't help himself, fear welling in his chest as she slowly revealed pale, soft, touchable breasts.

"Don't do this," he implored her, pulling away as she reached out and traced a finger over his dry lips, pressing a cup to his mouth. He turned his head, then felt her fingers in his hair, pinning him in place, forcing his compliance.

The sudden rush of a bitter fluid filled his mouth, and he spat it out, gagging. More fluid was poured into his mouth as his nose was held, and he coughed, choking, inhaling and swallowing the vile mixture. It burnt a trail down his throat; hit his stomach like hot ash, and killing all resistance.

He groaned, loosing all track of time, of place, of self. An insidious curl of pleasure blossomed deep in his loins, and he blinked open his eyes to see Kessendra. He focused on her with difficulty, realizing that she was no longer standing beside, but now she was straddling his hip. Her beautiful sky blue eyes were sightless, distant, and devoid of expression, and he watched as a single tear of grief run down her perfect cheek.

"Kessendra," he whispered, petitioning her, wishing he could prevent what Kalern wanted, wishing he could save her this anguish. She did not respond. Instead, she picked up a curved knife and ran the tip over his tunic.

He inhaled, unable to move, his eyes widening in alarm as he watched the progress of the blade as it traced down his chest to rest poised over his breastbone. She didn't do anything more for a strained moment, then she was slicing open his leathers, cutting through his cotton undershirt and exposing his skin to the chill air.

He gritted his teeth, wanting to deny her, to deny Kalern—Lichien—, but her perfume, her hot breath, her beauty, all mixed and he was helpless under her charms.

Kessendra—don't do this . . . fight Kalern . . . fight the currents . . .

Whether the words were spoken, he didn't know, it felt surreal, and he opened his mouth—a hissed groan of approval escaping his lips.

Then the blade slipped lower, slipped under the waistband of his breeches, and he shivered. Only this time it was not from the cold. He was a pawn in Lichien's world . . . and he screwed his eyes tightly shut. Somehow he had to think of a way to prevent Kalern's plan from succeeding. Somehow, somehow . . .

Then Kessendra put the knife down and stripped off her dress—and he was lost.

CHAPTER FIFTY

Lifting his head, Kellen glanced around the darkened room, disorientated and confused as to where he was, before memory slid unhappily into place. Rolling off the hard table, he knelt on the floor, not moving for a long moment as he dragged in painful breaths. Slowly he climbed to his feet, aching and bruised. Cramp locked his muscles, and he rubbed his thighs, blinking to clear his vision. He tasted blood in his mouth and gently touched his cut lip before grimacing in disgust. He was naked and cold, and he hugged his chest against unseen pain, feeling sickened as he searched around for a way out.

At the end of the stone slab, he found a pile of clothing. They were not his own, but they would do, and he dragged them on, disliking the idea of wearing what Kalern dictated. The color and sensual texture of the clothing was just another reminder of Kalern's subtle manipulation of his mind and body.

Once dressed, he investigated his prison. His fingers skimmed the surface of the damp rock, searching for anything that felt or appeared like a hidden lever. Vaguely he remembered all the different tricks Peleyia had shown him during their travels, and he wished the Lancooti were here. *No*, if Peleyia came to North Ridge, he would die.

Kicking the cold stone in temper, he refused to look back at the slab behind him, locking away the images of Kessendra and what they had done. It revolted him, and he swallowed, feeling physically ill as he too easily recalled the vivid details. He turned and leaned against the wall and shivered before sliding down to sit on the unswept floor. He muttered a curse, then repeated every curse he had learned from Dalzere, before starting his litany again. It helped to some extent.

Falling silent, he traced a pattern on the dirty floor, and caught sight of an indent in the wall by his hand. Bending lower, he studied the small indent and used his fingers to explore the oddity, then grinned as he found a leaver, hearing the telltale click before a small hole appeared in the wall to his right.

He hastily crawled out of his prison and into a dim tunnel. The tunnel was lit with torchlight, and he scanned the silent passages before choosing a direction. The tunnel widened, and he heard the echo of voices, and he glanced back. But nothing moved. He advanced a few more steps before coming to a sharp bend and saw four Black Guard. He swore, his hand automatically going to his hip. But he had no weapon, so he turned, and ran.

They yelled after him, and he ran faster, rounding another corner and slamming into another set of guard. He was subdued before the fight really began, then spun and marched back the way he had come, only this time, to his amazement, he was not returned to his stone prison but taken into the main cavern. Marshaling his defenses, he lifted his chin in defiance, straightening to his full height, not wanting to give Kalern the pleasure of seeing him defeated. He was going to die, he knew, but somehow he was determined to take Kalern with him.

On entering the vast cavern, he was shoved again, needlessly, just managing to stay on his feet, shrugging off the guard's hand. The cavern before him stretched out in endless dimness, the tunnel behind coming from a different direction to the last time he had been escorted from this chamber. He could see the dais and throne ahead as they walked past two dark, motionless pools of water. The walls bordering the pools looked slimy and wet from the constant trickle of melting ice, giving the impression that the dark stone was actually weeping. The atmosphere was heavy and damp—oppressive.

He stepped over a vine that covered the damp floor, and saw Salimen and Lesendal chained against the far wall. He relaxed, relieved that they were alive. Seeing them gave him hope, and he glanced around, studying the area. He searched for some advantage, and then his gaze locked on a large opening in the floor to his right—it was a pool of blackness that gave way to nothing.

An abyss.

Abruptly all the air vanished from his lungs, and he faltered, mesmerized, shocked, as the gaping pit registered on his mind. Ghost images feathered over him—and he shivered, turning away and closing his eyes. He didn't want to look, didn't want to see . . . and he was jolted from behind, forced to follow the path around the abyss. Fear filled him, the gaping hole a vicious reminder of his doom.

He was escorted to Lesendal and Salimen and chained to the wall with iron manacles. He didn't fight, didn't protest, just waited until the guard had left, before falling against the cold stone in despair.

"Kell?" Salimen called, softly, watching him.

He nodded, finding it hard all of a sudden to look at his friends.

"Kellen?" Lesendal whispered. "Did . . . did Kalern do what he suggested? Did he?"

Turning his head, Kellen lifted his face and let the prince read the answer in his eyes. "I'm sorry."

"Damn him!" Lesendal growled then swore.

Salimen looked from one man to the other with one brow raised. Lesendal just muttered another curse while the bowman sighed and sagged against the wall. "I missed most of that little interview," he started, turning to study Kellen, his eyes darkening in fury.

"Kell," Lesendal put no accusation into his tone as he chose his words with care. "What happened is not your fault. Don't let this bastard win. You can still defeat him."

"How?" Kellen snapped, not wanting compassion. "Kalern has the Book of Spells, the Raveners, Lichien, your sister," he stabbed an angry finger in Lesendal's direction, "and now, more than likely, an heir with which to destroy the prophecy! So how do you think I can—or we can—do anything to stop him?"

"Calm down," Salimen whispered, his eyes darkening in understanding. "I sure there must be something we can do."

"Sal's right," Lesendal agreed, glaring over at the vacant throne before looking at Kellen. "Two days ago, you had Kalern off balance—"

"Two days?" Kellen broke in.

Lesendal nodded.

He felt himself go pale, and when Lesendal reached out a hand to support him, he shied away from the contact. "Don't touch me," he hissed, as everything suddenly caught up with him.

"Kellen," Lesendal started, then hesitated, looking away. "I think it's been two days. It's hard to tell in this cavern with all the fires," he gestured around them. "Kalern and Kessendra," he said the name with effort, "returned only awhile ago, and . . ." he trailed off as Kellen looked away from him. "Kell?"

Regathering his composure, Kellen turned to meet the prince's searching gaze. He trusted both Lesendal and Salimen with his life, they were friends, and then he remembered what Dalzere had told him so long ago—*do not isolate yourself.* "I'm sorry," he said again.

Salimen was the first to offer a smile, his teeth very white against his dirty skin. "Things have been boring around here while you were gone," he said conversationally, gesturing with his chin toward the Black Guard who lounged near the dais. "Mr. Ugly returned a few hours ago," he said, deliberately changing the subject and injecting lightness into his tone. "He said something to Mr. Black-Leather-With-The-Bad-Attitude, which really put our host into a foul mood. I don't know, but I'd say it concerned Sasheer in some way." Salimen turned back to Kellen, his smile cocky. "After that, Kalern stormed out of here. I can tell you, they have not been generous with either food or water."

"If Sasheer comes here, Kalern will kill him," Kellen whispered, starting to remember earlier conversations. "In fact, Kalern wants him to come."

"Maybe," Lesendal agreed. "By the way, the guards have been moving into the tunnels; I'd say something important is going to happen soon."

* * *

The three of them sat silently for a long while. Each lost in private thought that none would willingly share, while the cavern around them remained relatively deserted and quiet. Only the fires crackled, the sound broken by the periodic rhythmic dripping of water somewhere behind them.

In fact it was so reminiscent of his nightmares that Kellen half-expected Kalern to appear from behind a dark shadow at any moment to taunt him with seductive words. But nothing happened. The Dark Lord's absence made him edgier, and his eyes traitorously kept going back to the enchanted stone nestled on top of the pedestal. It was beautiful, attracting him, especially now that he could hear its constant whispers in the back of his mind, like an enticing, melodic voice, vibrating deep in his subconscious, encouraging and promising revenge on all those who hurt him.

Captivated, he tore his eyes away from the stone, knowing logically it was just another perverted game, but somehow Lichien's charm outshone the dangers.

:*I am misunderstood . . . labeled evil by those who have not tried to see past my fear . . . banished before I could grow and help the twelve . . . hunted like a wild animal . . . outcast with a madman . . . condemned to live in seclusion . . . forced to aid Kalern . . . forced to survive in this prison.*:

Shaking his head, Kellen tried to clear his mind of the beguiling voice. He turned his eyes on the stone to glare at it. :*You are evil,*: he sent back in mental challenge, knowing Lichien would hear him. :*You are Lichien.*:

:*Yes . . . that is the name given to me . . . but how can I be evil when I am made up of such vibrant goodness from the twelve? . . . I fear they have poisoned your mind against me . . . I will be forever alone . . . forever lost within Kalern's madness.*:

:*No!*: Kellen wrenched his mind away from Lichien's seductive words, physically turning into the wall, so he could not even look at the dais and the corrupt stone. He would not be deceived. Tanish, Sasheer, and Dalzere would not have lied to him, would they?

:*You could help me, Kellen . . . please . . . *:

Screwing his eyes shut, he tried to ignore the plea, not wanting to feel the emotions behind the artfully phrased words.

:Please . . . take me away from here . . . I could help you and your friends escape . . . help you find Sasheer.:

:Stay out of my mind!: he hissed.

:You and I will be one . . . help me . . . please . . . :

"Kell?"

Salimen's voice breached the spell Lichien was weaving, and Kellen released an explosive breath, focusing on the bowman and seeing Salimen's anxious expression. "W—what?"

"Look. Isn't that—" Salimen stopped, pointing to the far end of the cavern.

"Sasheer," Kellen breathed the name, washed in a strange relief as Lichien's invisible velvet fingers slipped away from his mind. All of a sudden, he could think again, could see what was unfolding, and he glanced back at the now quiescent stone, a spike of apprehension engulfing him. *It is a trap! Lichien wants Sasheer—* and he stared at the stone, knowing how it waited patiently, malignantly. Its evil heart and seductive words only confirmed all of his worst suspicions.

Shaking his head, he opened his mouth to scream a warning, but his voice was cut off as Lichien invaded his thoughts with swift viciousness. This time the voice in his head did not plead—this time it roared, and he lost all connection with his surroundings.

CHAPTER FIFTY-ONE

Kellen tugged against the chains that kept him captive, knowing Salimen and Lesendal were doing the same. In the distance, he could hear the echoes of steel colliding with steel as Black Guard raced to the far side of the massive cavern.

"Come on, come on," Salimen muttered, attempting to get a better view of the battle across the lake.

Distrusting Lichien, Kellen cast a look over at the dais, wondering where Kalern was. He had his suspicions. He knew the Dark Lord had planned this, and his eyes went nervously back to Lichien. The stone was silent, the roaring gone from inside his mind, and he had the impression that Lichien now waited with fervent glee for the chaos that was about to descend. It wanted him to react; it wanted him to reach out with his Gift. Calming his turbulent emotions, he refused to give into the building temptation to call Sasheer, balling his fists and remaining silent.

Shouts echoed toward them, and he saw first Dalzere, then Crizkerisomia cut through the Black Guard blocking the tunnel. Sasheer came from behind them, and he blinked, stunned. It was the first time he had ever seen the Mage display his Gifts so forcefully, and at present, Sasheer presented a formidable opponent. The Mage swatted one guard out of his way, like a child swatted a bug, and never slowed his pace. He looked regal, elegant despite his filthy traveling clothes, with the energies surrounding him sparking with vibrancy, his midnight eyes blazing as he looked first to the dais and then to the chained captives.

Suppressing his initial delight, Kellen relaxed, banking down on his excitement, and willed Sasheer's angry gaze to find him.

When it did, he saw instant relief flash across Sasheer's face, and he felt both pleased and ashamed to know that Sasheer valued him so much.

Closer to the dais, a tremendous splash sounded, and it broke Kellen's concentration. He glanced away from Sasheer and swept his gaze over toward the enraged Haonian. Ryland was snarling and forcing three more guards into the murky black lake on the far side of the cavern. His war cry scattering the remaining few guards as he swung his massive sword. He was encased in full battle armor, his long cloak trailing down his back like wings as he pivoted, and swept another Black Guard off his feet.

"Gods, I love that man," Lesendal laughed.

"So long as he's always on our side," Salimen agreed.

Kellen held his breath, noticing how most of the guards had vanished, disappearing into the numerous tunnels surrounding the cavern, and his apprehension grew as he glanced around in mistrust. Then Peleyia was rushing across the narrow bridge to reach them, and he had to marvel at how the Lancooti looked every inch the seasoned fighter. Then Peleyia sent him a mischievous grin, darting into the tunnels beyond to check for guards.

"Pel!" Salimen called, impatient, as he held up his imprisoned wrists.

Swiftly, the Lancooti was back, and if anything, his grin was even cockier. He had blood on his face and relief in his gaze.

"Quickly," Salimen urged, lifting his wrists and begging the Lancooti with his eyes.

Across from them, the other members of the company were approaching the dais, and Kellen turned back to Peleyia when Salimen growled a complaint.

"Come on, Pel, will you hurry up!"

"Stop complaining and hold still," Peleyia snapped. He quickly took out a strange-looking steel clip, bending it with nimble fingers. Running his fingers over the lock, he cursed under his breath before pulling out a second clip from his belt and attacking the old padlock.

"What's been happening?" Lesendal asked, watching Dalzere and Crizkerisomia flank Sasheer as they stopped in front of the vacant platform on the other side of the abyss. Ryland engaged the remaining two guards and dispatched them easily.

"Oh, it's been a real holiday, first the barren wastelands, then the swamps. I don't think my sense of smell will ever be the same. Then there were the Raveners." Peleyia suppressed a shudder. "Have I told you how much I dislike this part of the country?" he asked sarcastically, pausing as he concentrated on the lock in his hand. "Sasheer's been unbearable, his temper chancier than ever. And if I were any of you three, I'd stay away from him for a while. Like a year or two."

"Will you stop yapping and hurry up?" Salimen said.

"Yeah, well it's nice to see you too," Peleyia shot back with a sigh, giving a genuine smile as he glanced up.

"Pel!" Salimen glared at him, about to say more when the lock clicked open.

"It's all in the quality of metals used, I think. Some locks are just so much easier to manipulate, depending on the purity of silver and—"

"Peleyia, save the lectures and get these off me," Lesendal ordered. Beside him, Salimen was massaged his wrists before moving away to check the silent tunnels at their back.

"No respect," Peleyia complained good-naturedly, undoing the second lock quicker. "Oh, by the way, Ryland has your weapons," he said, offhandedly.

Neither Ihovian commented. Salimen made a gesture with his hand indicating he would watch the tunnel while Lesendal went to get their weapons. It was a gesture so familiar that Kellen felt his mouth twitch in a smile. Then he looked at Peleyia and saw the Lancooti tense. Not moving, he waited and watched his friend, relieved and annoyed that Peleyia had broken their pact by traveling to North Ridge. Now they were committed on Fate's course.

"Kell?" Peleyia ventured, his eyes traveling over Kellen's attire. "What's with the morbid dress sense?"

Dropping his head down, Kellen closed his eyes then lifted his wrists, requesting silently that Peleyia not ask. He felt the other hesitate, felt Peleyia's uneasiness, his fear and his pain over the fact that the link between them was blocked. "I had to," he whispered, praying Peleyia would understand. "I never wanted you here."

"Do you seriously believe that I would leave?" Peleyia snapped. He attacked the locks binding Kellen's wrists. "That I could leave?"

"This place is death," Kellen whispered, begging his friend to understand. He met those expressive eyes and saw how Peleyia's pupils dilated, how the Lancooti accepted death despite his fear.

"You are my friend. I could not—would not—turn my back on you." It was almost a vow.

Not wanting the responsibility of another friend's life laid on him, Kellen glanced away then shook his head, admitting to himself that if their positions had been reversed, he would have done the same. *Peleyia is not Bains.* "Then hurry," he rushed, "because I feel . . ."

"What?" Peleyia prompted. "You feel what?" he repeated. "And while we're on the subject, why are you blocking me?"

Kellen shivered, feeling Peleyia's natural talents gently brush his barriers, and he deliberately strengthened his mental shields. "Because I will not drag you down with me." He exhaled hard, shocked by the turmoil he glimpsed behind Peleyia's expression; feelings that mirrored his own confusion.

"Together we can—"

"Lichien is playing with us. With me," Kellen hissed. His eyes went past Peleyia to the dais. It was easier than meeting his friend's perceptive gaze.

"Sasheer knows," Peleyia said, clicking the lock open.

"He knows? Yet he still came?"

"Nothing could have stopped him. Nothing could have stopped any of us," Peleyia said. He hesitated then reached out to touch Kellen's arm. "Kell, what's happened?"

He said nothing but let some of his fear, turmoil, and anger touch Peleyia and saw the Lancooti step back as if stung. Then Peleyia was fumbling with the sword at his belt, awkwardly sliding the beautifully crafted Drow blade free before offering it up.

"I have your sword. I found it and wanted to safeguard it for you."

Hating himself for treating Peleyia so coldly, Kellen shook his head and stepped away from the wall. "Keep it," he admonished, his eyes conveying his gratitude. He knew Peleyia was frightened, could sense it, and just wished he had the time to explain everything to his friend. But time was the last thing he had—the last thing any of them had. Deliberately he reached across the distance separating them and forced himself to cover Peleyia's icy fingers with his own, crushing his friend's hand around the hilt of the Drow sword. "Please, Pel, I can't explain now, but I want you to keep the sword for me."

"What are you planning? Kell?"

"Where I'm going, the sword is useless."

"Now you are scaring me," Peleyia whispered, urgent. "Our own destinies, remember?"

"Pel, promise me—whatever may happen here, you will stick close to Dalzere," he said, letting a little of his tightly held emotions escape. He saw Peleyia shudder and pale in reaction.

"I can't promise that."

"You must!" Kellen demanded, tightening his grip on Peleyia's hand. "Do not leave Dalzere's side. Promise me!" Those words cracked unexpectedly around them, and Kellen saw Peleyia jump, felt him tremble, then saw the realization of what was going to happen imprint itself on the Lancooti's senses. He released him abruptly.

"No!" Peleyia gasped, reaching over to grip Kellen's bare shoulder. "Talk to me! Please!"

"One of us must make it back to the Southland," Kellen said. Energy sparked between them, connecting them for an instant, opening the link wider—and then Peleyia snatched his hand away, flexing his fingers as if burnt. The Lancooti stared, stunned, and then slowly reached out with his hand, palm up, asking wordlessly for trust.

"Quickly!" Salimen shouted coming up behind both men and breaking the tension. "More guards are gathering in the tunnel behind, and we need to get across the abyss. Now!" he stressed.

Kellen avoided the offered hand and stepped back. The pain he saw flare in Peleyia's eyes hurt, but he would not place his friend in any more danger. "I know," he whispered instead, pinning Salimen with his eyes. "The guards will force us to the dais."

"You know?" Salimen demanded, stopping in midstride to eye Kellen. His eyes narrowed in worry. "Next you'll be saying, you know, Kalern's plans." He joked, but his words fell like lead weights into the silence. He rubbed his face tiredly, hearing Peleyia mutter something uncomplimentary, and he glanced between the two friends. "Kellen? Peleyia?"

Straightening, Kellen just gave the bowman an ironic smile. "Unfortunately, I do know."

"Know what precisely?" Salimen asked, starting to frown.

"Kalern's plans," Kellen clarified. He saw Salimen close his mouth in shock and felt Peleyia's unhappiness via the tentative link. He ignored it. "We had best get to the other side of the abyss," he said, taking control of the situation. "The guards will block this exit, like they have done with the other tunnels across the lakes." He indicated toward the far side of the cavern. "Lichien has been planning this moment for many centuries, so we had better not miss the floor show."

Watching Kellen walk away, Salimen stared first at the younger man's uncommunicative back, then at the tunnel entrance, and then finally at Peleyia. The Lancooti was speechless, his eyes dark and angry, before he shook his head. "What—"

"Don't ask," Peleyia said.

"He knows or guesses?" Salimen asked, regardless.

"Sal, what happened to him?"

Salimen said nothing for a prolonged moment, then he grabbed Peleyia's tunic and pushed him after Kellen's departing form. "You wouldn't believe me if I told you."

Kellen walked carefully around the abyss, keeping his eyes locked on the dais and refusing to give into his fear, to show Lichien any weakness. *The nightmares would not control his Fate, or Peleyia's—* he had to believe that, otherwise both of them were dead. Standing taller, he approached the others.

They were fighting the few remaining Black Guard, and out of the corner of his eye, Kellen caught sight of Dalzere casually pulling a knife free from one guard's chest and handing it to the Sun Elf. It was such an odd action that he was momentarily distracted.

He focused his attention on the tall Drow, watching the Elf's deadly dance of black leather, long back hair, and mesmerizing yellow eyes. Then Dalzere sliced a second guard nearly in two with a *cuxsia*, using the enchanted Drow weapon with competent efficiency, his movements pure grace. The wielding blade was like a part of his body, and Dalzere spun to block then pin the last guard with perfect accuracy. Surprised by the Elf's new weapon of choice and remembering the last time he had seen Dalzere use a *cuxsia*, Kellen wondered what had happened to make Dalzere revert to such means.

He felt a moment of disorientation then shuddered when Salimen and Lesendal brushed past him to hurry to Ryland's side. He sensed Peleyia at his back and knew the Lancooti intended to shadow him, and he let out an exasperated sigh. He closed his eyes and blocked all the conflicting emotions—searching mentally for Kalern and getting washed in the stone's anticipatory excitement. He could read Lichien's eager impatience, and he knew what to expect, snapping his eyes open a heartbeat later to see the impenetrable darkness solidify behind the throne to reveal Kalern's elegant form. Hiding his smile, he schooled his features, knowing his next move would be the hardest gamble he had ever taken in his life.

Stepping forward, Kalern snapped his fingers to dismiss the new guard who approached from behind and then walked toward the front of the raised dais with measured steps. He was dressed immaculately, his cloak now gone, to reveal styled leather and silk. He smiled down at Sasheer in gloating pleasure.

"Hello, brother," Kalern purred. His eyes swirled in color before turning black as they drank in the older Mage's less-than-presentable appearance. "My, my . . . not only have you lost all you value, but it seems you have also lost all self-respect."

Refusing to be intimidated, Sasheer braced his weight on one leg and glared at Kalern in irritation. He muttered something in a strange language then folded his arms and let his stance mirror Kalern's brash arrogance.

Blinking, Kellen was suddenly reminded of the vision he had witnessed in Mitthsombaine's old library. *A student defying his Master*—nothing had changed except the circumstances and style of attire. Sasheer's expression was the same, his attitude, his strength, and tenacity unchanged.

"My brother is dead," Sasheer replied coldly.

"Oh, how you wound me!" Kalern mocked, clutching his chest in mock pain. He snickered, then walked down a few steps and eyed the rest of the group. "After so many centuries, is that all you can say?" he asked. "Look at your followers; they watch in fear, hatred, and awe."

"I didn't come here to play word games with you."

"Maybe not," Kalern said, "but you will, won't you, brother?" he whispered emphasizing the last word. Curling his fingers around the gold chain of his pendant, he lifted the emerald and displayed it for Sasheer to see. "Look what I found nestled inside the protective cabinet with the Book of Spells."

Kellen blinked and saw Crizkerisomia cast a puzzled glance toward Sasheer. She was edgy, her hands gripping a sword and dagger in preparation for more trouble. Even Dalzere was still, silently waiting, standing only a few feet from Sasheer like a protective shadow.

Sasheer snarled at Kalern's taunt, his eyes changing color. "How—"

Kalern dismissed his protest. "The Eye of Jade. Stone of invisibility. Nothing can be hidden from me now. I can go anywhere, and you cannot stop me!"

Kellen stared at the dazzling stone, having seen it before in his dreams and knowing how perilous such a prize was in Kalern's hands. In Lichien's possession. He saw Sasheer's expression reflect the same fear.

"Don't tell me; I let you into North Ridge only to have your sullen silence as reward?" Kalern ridiculed, his lip curled up into a sneer. "Come now, dear brother. Let us relive old times."

He willed Sasheer not to react, wishing then that he had spent more time talking with the volatile Mage—suddenly envying Dalzere his intimate knowledge of Sasheer. He watched how Sasheer released an impatient breath, before the Mage stepped forward, and Kellen sucked in his own breath when he noticed how Dalzere tensed, how the Drow's eyes went flat, and one of his hands curled into a fist. And it took him a moment to understand why Dalzere was so upset, and then he knew. Sasheer was deliberately drawing Kalern's attention away from the other members of the group, and he wanted to scream at Sasheer. He knew what Lichien was doing, and he suddenly knew what Sasheer intended. It was frightening.

"What do you want?" Sasheer demanded. He held up a hand to stop Dalzere from following him.

"The magical question," Kalern laughed, delighted, his eyes following Sasheer. "What could I possibly want that you have not already delivered into my hands?"

"Delivered?" Sasheer asked, mildly, walking forward. Kalern was still on the top few steps, and behind him was the throne, and to his left, Lichien.

"I have your prophecy," Kalern whispered, lifting a hand and reaching out toward the silent figure of Kellen who was standing at the far side of the dais. Kalern curled his fingers, an evil smile spreading across his face, and Kellen flinched, feeling the invisible touch, like that of a knife piercing his chest.

"Seeing him and owning him are two different things, Kalern. But then you were never the brightest addition to the family, were you?" Sasheer cut back, his tone deadly, his eyes remaining focused on the Dark Lord. "Your grasp on reality was as weak as your potential. Or lack thereof," he added for insult. "For without Lichien, you are nothing."

Straightening to his full height, Kalern hissed in anger, madness flaring in the dead eyes before the Dark Lord slowly relaxed and released a soft laugh. "Very good. Very, very good. I have missed you, brother. I had forgotten that you were the one with the sick humor and devious mind, while Serine had all the brains. Where he excelled, you fumbled. When he pleaded, you killed. When he died, you lived." Kalern swept a hand out, and droplets of blood flew from his fingers to splatter Sasheer's face and clothing. "What were your last touching words to beloved Serine before you plunged that knife into his chest?"

"That memory no longer controls me," Sasheer said, wiping a hand over his face to remove the blood. "Have you finished with the showy theatrics?"

"I only want your loyal companions to see you for what you really are. A *murderer*," Kalern snarled the word.

"That will not work."

"But it already has," Kalern assured him. "One doubt, and he will be all mine," Kalern said, his smile triumphant as his eyes challenged Sasheer to deny the truth.

Shaking his head, Sasheer didn't turn to look Kellen. "He is smarter than the others. Smarter even than Serine," he said. "Besides, shouldn't you be worrying about Lichien, and its schemes?"

Momentarily taken back, Kalern stepped away and let his eyes briefly touch the stone in question. "My hold on Lichien is secure," he said with confidence, yet his frown deepened.

"How gratifying. For you," Sasheer answered, his smile never reaching his eyes.

"You will not trick me. I have everything you want." Kalern raised a hand, and a tainted, inky shape drifted down with soundless grace from the ceiling above. It circled the Dark Lord once before obediently settling on his outstretched, gloved arm. The simple action strengthened Kalern's arrogance.

Staring at the petite snow dragon, Kellen felt pity for the Shade. He noticed how Sasheer didn't react, yet the Mage's voice held an edge, a pain of excruciating acknowledgment.

"Shard," Sasheer shaped the name with care. "How did you manage to keep Shard alive when—" Sasheer stopped as the small dragon turned its head to blink at him in eerie familiarity. "It's not possible . . ."

"I thought you believed in the impossible," Kalern taunted. "You were fond of Shard, weren't you?" he added, reaching over to rub the Shade's chest. "Tell me, where is Terrica? I cannot sense her presence. Surely she would like to see an old friend."

"I left her behind. Protected," Sasheer said. "You're slipping, Kalern, becoming a liability to Lichien. You should have made certain she was with me before you let me near you."

"You give yourself too much credit!" Kalern cut back, an edge of fury lighting his gaze. "Besides I can always use Shard to hunt her down after your death."

"How did you subvert a Shade?"

"You never gave me due credit!" Kalern snapped. "I learned. I had a passionate drive to survive. It took killing five of the Brethren to perfect the skill of capturing a Shade."

Kellen felt ill, only now imagining what each Shade must have gone through. He remembered Sasheer telling him that for a Mage to lose a Shade meant madness. *What of the Shade?* He lifted his lashes and watched Kalern walk back toward his throne and place Shard on the armrest. Then the Dark Lord turned, his expression malicious, his gaze lingering on Sasheer before he walked over to Lichien and gently caressed the living stone.

"You have lost, Sasheer. Just admit your defeat," his whisper was silky.

"Never."

"I let you in here—with the Oracle..." Kalern trailed off, his gaze becoming speculative. "Show me the crystal." Sasheer said nothing. "Show me, or I will have your friends thrown into the abyss."

"You know the Oracle cannot be forced to show itself," Sasheer reprimanded. "And as long as we have it, your Raveners cannot touch us."

"Ah, my pet Raveners," Kalern nodded. "Thank you for reminding me." He grinned. "That brings me to another point of ownership. I believe you came for the Book of Spells." He left Lichien's side to march down the steps and stand before Sasheer, invading his personal space. "I know your pathetic plans!" he shouted, suddenly incensed. "How you and those disgusting old men want the book for yourselves! Well, to get it, you will have to kill an innocent!" he spat then raised his hand and snapped his fingers.

Abruptly, Kessendra appeared. The dress she now wore was of the purest white, like a bridal gown. Her hair was fashioned elegantly, with flowers entwined delicately through her golden curls. Her face was calm and beautiful as she glided forward with measured steps, and within her arms, she clutched the old leather-bound Book of Spells. She stopped at the edge of the dais to stand serene and composed.

"I am sure you know who she is . . . brother," Kalern sneered, his voice laced with venom. "My three other guests know her . . . intimately." He gave a wicked leer.

Behind Sasheer, Lesendal rushed forward only to be stopped by Dalzere.

"She is mine," Kalern said. "Mind, body, and soul. To reclaim the ancient book, you must kill her. Because she will fight you to the death for its possession." Kalern smirked. "And she is an excellent fighter."

"Let her go!" Ryland growled as he lunged forward and raised his massive sword. Sasheer raised a hand in warning, but Ryland ignored him, rushing up the steps of the dais.

Kalern turned from Sasheer, delight playing over his features as he extended a gloved hand and sent a bolt of fire into Ryland's chest, knocking the big man off his feet and sending him crashing into Dalzere and the Sun Elf. Ryland's chest exploded in flames, and he cried out in agony.

Reacting without thinking, Crizkerisomia threw a knife at the Dark Lord, her accuracy astounding—except Kalern caught the blade and disintegrated it with a muttered spell. Propelled into action by the abrupt chaos, Lesendal rushed up the stairs toward his sister, grabbing her by the arm and trying to drag her away from Kalern. To his surprise, she resisted.

"No," Kellen whispered, feeling locked in place, isolated from the confusion unfolding around him. He watched, knowing Lichien was orchestrating the events. Only Sasheer remained utterly still, his gaze locked on Kalern. "No," he murmured again, wanting to move, watching how Dalzere struggled to get the molten breastplate off the injured Haonian. The Drow was cursing in his native tongue while Salimen rose from Ryland's side to stare at his cousin, torn between aiding Lesendal attempt to drag Kessendra down the steps or to help Dalzere. Only Crizkerisomia seemed to have a plan as she stalked the Dark Lord, throwing a volley of deadly knives that fell broken at Kalern's feet.

Then Peleyia swore and pushed past him, and Kellen made an attempt to grab him, but Lichien interfered. *NO!* Kellen screamed in mental fury at the stone, dreading the outcome of this chaos. Closing his eyes he tried to focus on Sasheer, to warn him, reaching for Sasheer with his mind—and froze as Lichien's voice sliced through his thoughts.

:Reach out and claim your birthright, Kellen.:
:No.: He shook his head.
:I can feel your acceptance of what must be.:
:No.: He snarled the word at the stone.
:I can feel your desire.:
:No.: He turned his face away, refusing to listen.
:You will replace Kalern by my side.:
:Never.: He denied, even as his anger faltered.
:Together we could build a new world.:
:You only destroy.: He said.
:But with you I can create.:
:I can't.: He hesitated.
:Shall I prove myself?:
:How?: He had to ask. Felt compelled to ask.
:I can give Kalern to Sasheer. For revenge.:
:Revenge will not provide redemption.: Yet it was tempting. So tempting.
:Trust me.:

"NO!" Kalern's screams of denial shattered the noise in the cavern, and the Dark Lord turned to stare at Kellen before swinging around and centering his eyes on Lichien. "No!" Kalern screamed again.

Jolted by the Dark Lord's fury, Kellen shuddered. Instantly the connection Lichien had forged was gone, and he was again alone in his own mind. He gazed up at the enraged Dark Lord, reading Kalern's murderous intention. The games was now over; it was time to claim ownership, and he watched Kalern raise both hands and wrap the currents' vibrant energy into twin fireballs.

"You dare challenge me for control? For ownership?" Kalern snarled aiming his words solely at Kellen.

Raising his chin, Kellen steeled his nerves, hiding his thoughts and allowing his instincts to take over, willing the old knowledge to resurface from deep within his mind. *This evil has to be abolished*, Sasheer was right about that; and he took a step back, away from his friends and toward the abyss. Kalern followed, and he felt Lichien's interest follow Kalern, the stone focusing on both of them, encouraging them to fight.

He did not want to win ownership of the stone—and all of a sudden, he blinked in stunned amazement as the meaning of the prophecy clarified in his mind. It was a riddle. He was not the one to fulfill the ancient words—that was Sasheer's task. *Blood of blood—not blood from the bloodline . . .* Burying that painful realization deep in his mind so that neither Kalern nor Lichien glimpsed his awareness, he stood straighter and snarled at Kalern in defiance. Months ago, he had vowed to aid Sasheer in any way in could, and he intended to keep that promise—even if it meant going into the abyss in order to give Sasheer the chance he needed to destroy Lichien.

He nodded to himself coming to a decision, and then took another step backward, hastily recalling every lesson Sasheer had laboriously taught him and praying it was enough to trick Lichien. He braced his weight and called the currents, feeling their tainted darkness swirl around his ankles, feeling the evil of this cavern darken his thoughts. He ignored the danger and focused again on Kalern, putting all his defiance into his challenge. "I dare!" he hissed, sensing Lichien's gloating satisfaction.

Numerous sensations flooded him in that instant: Sasheer's shock, Dalzere's fear, Peleyia's dread, Lichien's delight—and he blocked them all, keeping his eyes fixed on the Dark Lord. Kalern was livid, releasing mage bolts of energy, blackening the damp floor around him, but never touching him. He sent the enraged lord a twisted smile and held his ground, knowing Lichien protected him—and making sure Kalern understood his favored position. The irony was not lost on Kalern, and the Dark Lord charged down the dais and thundered toward him in a murderous rage.

At last, and he prayed Sasheer took the opportunity to defragment Lichien. He held his ground making Kalern come to him, ducking Kalern's first wild swing, feeling strangely detached. He wasn't scared any longer, instead he felt flushed with confidence. The Dark Lord lunged at him again, and they rolled across the cold floor. In that instant, he felt pity for Kalern as he saw past the madness and into Kalern's world of loneliness, past betrayal and pain—and he wondered if these true emotions were the remnants of the lost soul Kalern had once been.

"I will kill you," Kalern hissed, almost incoherent with rage as he lifted a hand and placed it over Kellen's forehead, summoning power—vast power that could drain the essence out of a hundred souls.

"Stop!" Dalzere abruptly intervened, yanking Kalern off his captive and standing poised between the two. The Elf's eyes went frantically from Kalern's face to Sasheer's, but both ignored him. Then an invisible hand struck him, knocking him sideways and pinning him to the ground.

Kalern howled, releasing Dalzere and returning his attention to Kellen. "I will break your spirit and consume your being then twist your heir into something that will destroy all it touches!" he vowed, shoving Kellen backward.

"And I will watch as Lichien's heart is shattered," Kellen whispered, as he fell to his knees at the edge of the abyss.

Startled, Kalern paled, torn between killing his challenger and going to Lichien. Seeing the realization flood Kalern's eyes, Kellen reached up and dragged the Dark Lord down. Holding him fast, and using the currents to tether Kalern to his will.

Kalern's eyes went impossibly wide. "You distracted me purposely . . ."

Giving a harsh laugh, Kellen nodded. Behind them, Lichien began to shriek in outrage and fury, and he sent his final answer to the corrupt stone. *:You will cease to exist.:*

"You will die—" Kalern gasped, his fingers reaching out to lock around Kellen's throat.

"Yes," Kellen gasped. "But so will you."

Knowing real fear for the first time in thousands of years, Kalern threw Kellen off and reached out a hand toward Lichien. But it was too late, as Sasheer worked the ancient incantation, entrapping Lichien in the original spell and using his blood to break the evil stones power.

Kellen gasped as white energy exploded across the dais, knocking him to the ground, destroying the darkness inside the vast cavern. Lichien shrieked, its scream of rage tearing round the walls, shaking the mountain's foundations. Then Kalern was grabbing him, strangling him, and he fought to breathe, feeling the Dark Lord thrust him back until he hung over the edge of the abyss.

"I will entomb you," Kalern promised in a deadly whisper. "You have seen your Fate, just as I have, so you know you will never leave this place alive!"

Kellen snarled at the Dark Lord, even as his boots slipped on the loose stones. Reaching out he clutched at Kalern's silk vest, collecting the jeweled pendant in his grasp, and using it to pull the Dark Lord closer. "If I fall, you fall," he said, watching as Kalern's eyes widened in understanding.

"I'm already dead," Kalern mouthed, then thrust Kellen over the edge.

He gasped, teetering on the edge of nothing. Weightless, and for one glorious moment secure as gripped the emerald stone, using Kalern's weight to balance him. Then even as he watched, he saw Kalern disintegrate into ashes, saw his magnificent clothing crumble—and then he was falling, disappearing into the beckoning darkness of endless silence.

CHAPTER FIFTY-TWO

"NO!"

It was Peleyia's voice, but Sasheer's anguish.

Sasheer pulled his attention momentarily from Lichien to see Kellen fall—then turned to the stone with renewed determination, seeing the minute hairline fracture which had appeared within the stone's heart. He could not stop the unfolding spell, because to falter now would change the complexities, and kill them all.

The stone shimmered under his assault, then fractured, its destruction imminent as the volatile energies binding the twelve focus stones burst free. He raised an arm to ward off the effects, feeling the invisible awareness known as 'Lichien' rant before going berserk. It was to be expected, and he prepared himself for the final part of the casting that would kill the evil intelligence and suck him into the death spiral.

He exhaled hard and stretched out his arm, the energies flowing easily from his fingertips—when suddenly a section of the roof above him came crashing down. He gasped, driving to one side as the black throne was crushed. He climbed to his feet and muttered an old Mitthsombaine curse at Lichien's diversion tactics. He glared at the fragmenting stone seeing how it no longer resembled a ball of energy.

"*You have failed, Sasheer!*" Lichien hissed the words in a raw guttural voice. "*I have broken your spell.*"

Refusing to answer, Sasheer continued his casting, layering a new entrapment into his wording. Then the floor beneath his feet started to shake, and he swore again as Lichien howled in crazed desperation.

"For Aserties," Sasheer whispered, reworking the spell and hurling it at the evil madness. "For Serine. For Cornithia. For Kellen!"

Searing power engulfed Lichien, constricting it, dazzling the eye with many colors as its screech of anger echoed off the walls. Then the unexpected happened—Kessendra ran forward, her face streaked with tears as she lifted the Book of Spells in her grasp and smashed it over the dying stone.

"NO!" Sasheer shouted, but it was too late, and he watched as the princess turned and looked at him, recognition clear in her eyes as she shuddered in reaction.

"I . . . had to," she said. "Its' voice was in my head . . . always in my head," she sobbed, raising a hand to her head.

On the pedestal the dying stone exploded, the energies arching out, hitting the old book clutched in Kessendra's hands—and Sasheer's eyes widened in shock. The old book burst into flames, the blue fire-storm engulfing Kessendra. The awareness shrieked; the backlash knifing into the Book of Spells, consuming the princess held immobile inside the flames. Then a small part of the fire-storm bounced off the book, hitting the pedestal and throwing the twelve individual focus stones from the dais.

Climbing to his feet, Sasheer watched as the flames around Kessendra petered and died, leaving the princess unblemished as she gasped for breath, her mouth opening in horror, only no sound came out. Tears of sorrow and pain streamed down her smooth cheeks as she continued to pant for breath, then she convulsed, shaking like a rag-doll. The book remained in her hands and she lifted it to her chest where it lit up in brightness, scorching every corner of the cavern.

Sasheer slowly backed away from the ruins, swearing and not believing what had happened.

"Kess!"

Lesendal's call gave him a moment's warning, and he made a grab for the distraught prince, pulling him away from the evolving princess. "She is gone."

"Leave me alone!" Lesendal shoved Sasheer aside with determination. Then he was rushing over the fallen section of roof and climbing up onto the shattered dais to reach his sister.

"Damn him," Sasheer hissed, glancing around and seeing Black

Guard rush into the cavern. Under his feet, the tremors were getting stronger, and he didn't like any of their chances. Then he heard Lesendal gasp and look back at Kessendra.

The princess was changing, mutating into a creature that wore the face of loveliness but housed a heart of stone. Pure evil. "Dalzere?" Sasheer called, ignoring his own exhaustion as he saw the black lakes start to bubble and spill their banks as the earthquakes continued. It was only a matter of time before the entire cavern collapsed in on itself.

A cry of pain pierced the silence, and he glanced around, just catching sight of Shard as the small elemental snow dragon plunged down from the darkness above and plucked something from the ashes of Lichien's destruction. "Shard!" Sasheer called, but the Shade ignored him, as it flew past him and disappeared over the lip of the abyss. Running to the edge of the abyss, he shook his head, seeing nothing. Then swore as huge ice formations fell from the ceiling high overhead to crash into the cavern floor, showering them all in ice.

"The entire chamber is going to collapse," Crizkerisomia said needlessly, stopping to help Dalzere to his feet. "Sasheer?"

Sasheer barely heard her. His eyes locked on the shattered stone fragments rolling across the dais and under Kessendra's feet. They were the original mage focus stones, and he desperately wanted to collect them, but then his eyes lifted to Kessendra, seeing that her transformation was almost complete. "We have to leave. Now," he decided. "Get Lesendal."

He backed away from the abyss, glad Dalzere went to the prince and dragged him away. Kessendra's pure white dress was slowly darkening to an inky black. Her beautiful, golden hair mutating into tresses of black silk; even the flowers in her hair had wilted and died, with the delicate petals dropping like ash to the floor. Her pale complexion altered, her skin turning ebony—then she opened her arms, and the scorched Book of Spells fell to the floor with a sickening bang. Its impact raised dust around her feet, and she tilted her head to one side, lifting her lashes to reveal pitch-black, feral eyes.

The ground shook again, and Sasheer grabbed Dalzere's arm to stop him from going after the Book of Spells. "It is too late. Far too late. We have to get out of here," he stressed.

"But—" Dalzere let his gaze travel to the silent princess. "Lichien?"

"Lichien has a new host," Sasheer said. "And we need to go before it wakes fully."

"Kessendra . . . ?"

Hearing the pain in Lesendal's tone, Sasheer gritted his teeth and pushed Dalzere away. "Get the others moving," he instructed before going to Lesendal's side, understanding his anguish. Around them, the Black Guard were in a state of confusion, their will broken by the death of their lord and master, and he wanted to take full advantage of their dazed state. "Lesendal . . . there is nothing you can do for her now."

"I can't—"

"We must leave," Sasheer said.

"But . . ." Peleyia protested. "What of Kell?"

Burying his pain, Sasheer shook his head. "Let's not make his sacrifice worthless."

"I won't—can't accept that!" Peleyia shouted, only to be stopped and shaken by Crizkerisomia.

"He is gone. We all saw it. Your eyes do not deceive." Her voice was soft. "Now go. His memory will live in your actions."

Peleyia went where he was pushed, stumbling and falling to the ground. His hand landed on a shimmering object, and he picked it up, half-turning to watch Sasheer, horror in his eyes. Then Crizkerisomia was drawing him away, and he numbly pocketed the glowing orb.

Moving closer to the destroyed dais, Sasheer took the opportunity to search the debris for his focus stone, for any stone, but could see none of them.

"Why not just kill her now?" Crizkerisomia asked, taking out her remaining blade.

"You can't do that!" Lesendal protested.

"She is no longer your sister," Crizkerisomia reminded him, preparing to throw the blade.

"I won't let you," Lesendal rushed in front of the Elf.

"It can't be killed with an ordinary blade," Sasheer said. "Like the stone before, this host will also be impenetrable. Lichien's only weakness was the original formation spell. Now I don't know what we can do. It will be twice as dangerous."

"Only twice?" Dalzere questioned.

"All right, a hundred times more dangerous," Sasheer admitted with poor grace.

"Still, let us see if it bleeds," Crizkerisomia said.

"No," Lesendal said again. He pulled away from Sasheer and rushed to his sister's side. He approached her carefully, touching her blackened cheek with his fingers. "Kess? Love, it's me. Remember? Your brother."

She blinked and focused her eyes on the prince with a swiftness that was inhuman, her mouth twitching into a small smile that was both sweet and beautiful. "Bro—bro—brother?" her voice was husky, deeper than before.

"Yes," Lesendal encouraged, his relief plain as he turned to look at Sasheer in triumph.

Kessendra waited for him to look back at her, then she raised a hand and muttered a few words. Instantly, Lesendal's dagger appeared in her hand, and she examined it, a small frown pulling at her perfect brow.

Noting the sudden appearance of his knife in her hand, Lesendal gentled her. "Kess, love. Let me have that—" He got no further as she moved with frightening speed and buried the silver blade to its hilt, in his chest. There was no remorse in her eyes as she studied his paling face before pulling the blade free. She then thrust him away and lifted the blade to examine the warm blood, before tasting it with her tongue.

Appalled, Salimen was the first to react, rushing to the edge of the ruined dais and turning Lesendal over. His hands went to the gaping wound as Lesendal gasped for breath, blood staining his lips as his eyes dulled in death. "No," Salimen breathed, shocked, before he looked up at the princess. "You—you . . . bitch!"

Dalzere grabbed the bowman and pulled him away from creature that wore the face of an angel, thrusting him at Ryland. The big Haonian nodded and held the bowman fast.

Tears of rage stained Salimen's face, grief and loss hampering his struggles. "You perverted, bitch!" he yelled. "He loved you! Loved you unconditionally. Even after you betrayed him. Even after you—"

"Leave it," Dalzere stressed in an unwavering hiss, pushing them all toward the tunnels behind the throne. He glanced back at Sasheer, seeing how the Mage watched Lichien reawaken in this new body. "Sasheer?" he called.

"You . . . cannot . . . leave," Kessendra said, blankly.

"Take them and go," Sasheer instructed, waving Dalzere away. He dragged in a breath and ordered his thinking, preparing to meet Lichien's challenge. He looked from Kessendra to the still power-charged pedestal as it continued to fuse itself into the shattered dais. Something was not right, and he frowned. Not all of Lichien had gone into the princess, and he wondered how that would affect the future, how it would affect Lichien, how it would help him kill this abomination.

Kessendra dropped the bloodied knife and delicately, with exquisite femininity, lifted her skirt and stepped over Lesendal's dead body as she followed Sasheer. Her face creased into a knowing smile as she stopped on the top step of the dais and raised a slender finger to point at Sasheer. "You . . ." she paused, frowning. "You I will kill."

Sasheer watched her, not trusting her, and inhaled sharply when she glanced down and lifted her skirt a second time. At her feet were two of the Brethren's focus stones, and his heart plummeted. Slowly, and with great precision, Kessendra raised her foot and stepped on one glowing gem, crushing it ruthlessly to powder. Then she did the same to the second gem.

Dismayed, Sasheer felt ill, and he scanned the area around the pedestal, desperate to find any of the remaining ten focus stones. There were none, and he backed away, knowing he had precious little time.

"I shall kill you . . . Sasheer," Kessendra murmured, stepping on another focus stone and grinding it into the cold floor. "I shall take great pleasure . . . in killing you."

Around them, the cavern shook with a stronger quake, and Sasheer took advantage of chaos to make a dash for the narrow bridge while it still remained. He ran across to the other side of the lake, seeing Dalzere and Crizkerisomia scatter the few remaining Black Guard. He knew North Ridge would fall into pandemonium until Lichien was functioning properly again, and he patted his pocket to make sure the Oracle was still safe, and then started to plan mentally their route back to the Keep. The council needed to know of this new evolving evil.

"Stop!"

The command was laced with power this time, and Sasheer swore. He had hoped it would take Lichien a little longer to readjust, obviously he was mistaken. He gritted his teeth and turned just as a bolt of mental fire hit him and tore through his mind. The intense savagery of the attack spun him around and slammed him into a cold stonewall, and he lay where he fell, limp, unable to breath, amazed at the strength behind Lichien's sending. Not enough to kill him outright just yet, but enough to cripple him. He tried to sit up and glanced at the ceiling above then looked at Kessendra. She was advancing slowly toward him, but her expression was one of perplexity, as if she did not remember why the cavern shook.

He could use that, he decided, and he wove a new spell. He sent the working magics up into the darkness, masking his intent, and winced in genuine agony as he was hit with a second mind bolt. It would not be long before she came to gloat, and he studied her through his lashes, watching her approach, satisfied that he would at least entomb them both. It had to be enough. He sagged back against the wall and shut his eyes then jolted awake when hands dragged him up. Dalzere was there, his face creased in worry and fury.

"Here . . . take the Oracle . . ."

"Shut up, Sasheer," Dalzere growled, lifting the Mage and carrying him to safety. Behind them the cavern shook again, only this time it was stronger, bringing down larger sections of roof and cracking the foundations. They fell to the floor inside the tunnel, and Sasheer laughed weakly while Dalzere cursed.

"You idiot," Sasheer breathed, bracing his ribs with a hand as he inhaled. He had broken a number of bones and suspected he had other internal injuries and lacked the energy needed to push the dark currents away. They sucked at his remaining strength. "I will slow you down. Here, take the Oracle and head south in these tunnels," he wheezed the instructions. "I have already sent the spell that will ensure North Ridge is buried deep—"

"I'll take you and the Oracle," Dalzere said, stopping for a moment and using his Drow healing talents to assess the injured Mage. "You will live," he said, then deftly ripped a long strip of leather free from Sasheer's ruined cloak and began binding it around the Mage's chest. "This should help with some of the pain until we get out of here."

"I have to stay," Sasheer protested, seeing the other members of the company appear out of the dusty haze in the tunnel. They all looked shell-shocked and defeated. "To make sure . . . Dalzere, Lichien will send—"

Dalzere cut him off again. "I know." He tied off the makeshift bandage tightly, causing the Mage to wince in reaction.

"I—I . . . I can stop her."

"You are barely conscious," Dalzere said as he stood, motioning Ryland closer.

Glaring up at the tall Drow, Sasheer was about to protest, when Ryland lifted him. The sensation of movement made him swoon in pain, and he just caught the Drow's grin before he passed out.

CHAPTER FIFTY-THREE

Seeing Sasheer lapse into unconsciousness, Dalzere called Crizkerisomia, giving her the Oracle and setting her in the lead. He wanted them to stay close, to follow the tunnels until they found daylight. The mountain around them still shook, and more of the ceiling caved in, entombing the cavern behind. Dirt and dust obscured the air, and he glanced back in apprehension, knowing that pursuit would be swift in coming.

* * *

The tunnels seemed endless, filled with dust, the tremors lessening the further away from the cavern they traveled. At the rear of the company, Dalzere glanced back often into the darkness, not liking the feel of the atmosphere or unnatural silence. They were being tracked—he could feel it—and not just by Black Guard, but by hungry Raveners. Crizkerisomia was still in the lead, and she was doing a competent job of navigating a way out. He had to admire her skill, beauty, and attitude, although he would never admit it. Not even if they survived and made it to the surface before nightfall.

Dismissing his worries, he flicked his gaze over Crizkerisomia a second time. He was not sure he could keep the others moving without her, not sure they would trust him enough to follow his lead. *The curse of being Drow*, and he gave a small self-mocking smile. He would let Crizkerisomia deal with the southerners as he had other more pressing concerns, one of which was Salimen's grief-stricken silence. He understood Salimen's feelings of betrayal and his need for vengeance; it was an attitude he was intimately familiar with, and at any other time, he would help the Ihovian seek his revenge. Only circumstances were beyond his control, and the anger he felt at Lesendal's unnecessary death were overshadowed by Kellen's fall into the abyss. A loss he refused to consider—refused to believe—until after they were safe outside the labyrinth of North Ridge.

He frowned and found he was looking at Peleyia, and he gave an inaudible sigh of irritation. The normally exuberant Lancooti was dazed, disillusioned, and distracted. His stare was blank as he moved woodenly behind Ryland, and Dalzere found he had to push the thief forward more than once. He realized that infusing a spirit of optimism back into the group was going to be hard—near impossible—and he gritted his teeth, not wanting that task. That was Sasheer's Gift, not his, and he tightened his hand around the curved hilt of the *cuxsia*, glancing behind into the insidious gloom again.

He didn't like their chances of survival, especially with Sasheer drifting in and out of consciousness. For that reason alone, he knew Terrica could not be trusted to act rationally; her fear could do them more damage than good. He prayed Sasheer would recover, and he had to admit that he had no reserves left beyond his own cunning and instincts. And right now, all his instincts and senses were telling him that they were being herded into a trap.

"Criz," Dalzere called, stopping the white Elf. She turned and looked at him, one brow raised in question. "This does not feel right."

She glanced into the darkness beyond and then placed her fingers gently against the cold tunnel wall. "What are we to do, Drow?" she asked, with no challenge or bite in her tone. "If it is a trap, then maybe we can surprise our captors. Kill them first."

Dalzere let his grin grow in rueful acknowledgment, liking her assessment and the way her mind worked. "You and me, yes. But not the others."

"Agreed," she nodded, mirroring his smile.

"Now wait just one damn moment!" Salimen hissed in anger as he glared between the two Elves. "I am not going to stand back and watch while—"

Dalzere cut him off. "I need you to guard Sasheer."

"Ryland can watch him!" Salimen snapped, unfazed by the calm logic. "Or even Pel, for that matter!"

"Salimen . . ."

"They just murdered Dale and Kellen!" the bowman continued in a tight voice, unable to hide his fury. "So how can you ask me to stand back? How can you stay so calm and impersonal?"

Placing a hand on the bowman's arm, Crizkerisomia ignored his vicious glare when he shrugged her off. "We cannot argue," she stressed, her delicate brows drawing down. "Although Salimen does have a point, Drow. Our only strength is in remaining firm and focused."

"I want to fight," Ryland growled, shifting the Mage's weight onto his other shoulder. The semiconscious man groaned.

"You are injured, so they will take you and Sasheer out first," Dalzere said, knowing their enemy's tactics all too well. "And we need Sasheer alive if we are to make it back to Sanctuary."

"It is a moot point now," Crizkerisomia warned, nodding toward the four Black Guard who came around the corner from behind them. She had her sword out and was ready to fight even as Salimen charged into their ranks.

"No!" Dalzere warned, unable to stop the Ihovian as he caught a glimpse of a Ravener hovering behind the guard. This is what he had been afraid of. "Stay within the protection of the Oracle!" he hissed, shoving Peleyia back into Ryland and glaring at Crizkerisomia before going after Salimen. He vaulted over one guard and thrust a foot into the second guard's chest, sending the hapless man reeling backward into the Ravener's embrace. The guard screamed a blood-curdling cry of utter agony, but Dalzere never spared him a look, concentrating on killing the last two guards with swift efficiency.

Chaos added him, along with the flickering torchlight, which lay abandoned on the floor, and Dalzere watched dispassionately as the guard's dead husk dropped from the Ravener's spiderlike hands. The sight distracted the last guard, and he seized that advantage to hook a hand in Salimen's belt and yank the bowman away from the fight. He propelled the startled Ihovian into the safety of the Oracle's influence then turned to grin at the last remaining guard. The large guard slapped the flat of his blade against his chest, muttered an oath, then charged. Dalzere lifted his long blade to block the first stroke, but the force of the blow sent him reeling backward, and he pulled his *cuxsia* free, utilizing the tainted magic to slice under the guard's defenses.

The guard fell dead to the floor with a heavy thump, and Dalzere stilled, disliking the sudden unnatural silence which fell around him. He glanced back and saw Crizkerisomia and the others standing a dozen paces away, and he held up his hand to stop their approach. On the floor, the touch light dimmed further, and he narrowed his eyes, searching the pockets of darkness along the tunnel wall. He knew the Ravener was close; he could taste the lingering evil in the air, the stench of death catching at the back of his throat, and he backed away from the ill gloom. He indicated for the others to flee further up the winding tunnel. To his relief, they obeyed.

Then before he could take another step, four more guards materialized out of the darkness and prevented his retreat. For such armor-encased warriors, they moved with so much skilled silence that Dalzere had to admire their proficiency. He walked to the narrowest point in the tunnel, blocking their path and bracing himself for a new attack. Only nothing happened for a prolonged moment, and then the guards parted, allowing the Ravener entrance. It ghosted out of the darkness, old rags hanging from its emaciated frame to trail along the cold floor, as its presence sucked all warmth from the air.

Swearing under his breath, Dalzere saw Crizkerisomia rush toward him, and he shouted a warning. "No! Go! You must leave!" he snarled and lunged forward to disable the front guard and block the man's massive downward thrust. He needed to buy them time... he needed... time. "Find Karczag—" he gasped, getting no further as two guards charged him.

Both guards were better skilled in the sword, and he took pleasure in the challenge, outmaneuvering both men with practiced ease. Around him, more Black Guard arrived, and he risked a glance behind, relief flooding him when he saw that Crizkerisomia had obeyed his command. He let his mouth curve up into a nasty grin. If the guards wanted him dead, then they would have to work hard for the pleasure. Again he used the enchanted *cuxsia*, disarming his opponent with expert precision and then blocking another cutting stroke. He focused fully on the fight before him, his movement flowing without thought, reacting on pure instinct as he killed those in his path. He was master here, his race the skilled fighters, killers, assassins, and Lichien would not take him easily.

He parried low, spinning around and slicing open another guard, dropping him like a dead weight to the floor. But still they came. His style was well suited to the narrow tunnel, and he soon lost track of time and of the number he had killed. He ignored his own cuts and bruises, concentrating only on the contest of wills, on the dance of skill.

Inevitably they forced him backward, maneuvering him into a wider section of tunnel, and he found himself surrounded before he could kill more than three guards. They were swift to subdue him with swords held crossed at his throat, stripping him of his weapon and forcing him to his knees. He waited for the killing blow, lifting his chin in defiance and hoping he had bought the others enough time to escape.

"So you are the lamented Drow who fights for the Brethren," one guard snarled, moving aside as the Ravener drifted nearer. The creature's breath was foul, its eyes hungry and feral, before it muttered a single cursed word. He imagined it would now be his turn to be embraced by the Ravener's seductive, depraved hunger, to be sucked dry of all his knowledge as his living essence was used to empower the evil creature and aid it in the hunt for his friends. But the Ravener never touched him. Instead, it moved past the guard and disappeared into the dimness of the tunnel, following the same path Crizkerisomia had taken.

Watching the evil creature move out of his line of vision, Dalzere growled in anger, attempting to fight his way free and was clubbed from behind. He hit the floor, tasting blood in his mouth, feeling more warm blood run down his throat. Then a hand in his hair yanked his face up, and he saw a huge Hoindrite guard step forward.

"It seems you have a reprieve, Drow. Lichien wants one of you alive," the guard said.

Surprised by that, Dalzere hid his wince as his hands were tied, and he was dragged to his feet and shoved back toward the destroyed cavern.

CHAPTER FIFTY-FOUR

Crizkerisomia hesitated for only a moment then made an instant decision, understanding Dalzere's sacrifice as he valiantly blocked the passageway and prevented immediate pursuit.

Making the others run on, she dared not relent, dared not stop to study the tunnels branching off the main route. She was not certain which way they should go, but since Dalzere's passionate command, she had neither seen nor sensed any pursuit. The Raveners were still around; she could feel them waiting, feel their hunger as they searched with unseen eyes, but so long as she held the Oracle, they were protected from the unseen hunters.

Escape was their only chance, and as much as she hated to admit that a Drow could be right, she knew that Dalzere had not lied. She understood his decisions and closed her eyes briefly—still seeing in her mind his magnificence eyes, his heroic stance—and she knew his death would tear at her heart. He was worthy of honor, and she would see that he was honored when she returned to her people.

A noise behind had her snap alert, and she turned to listen. A tapping sound deep in the mountain echoed up, and she shook her head at the unvoiced questions she could see in Salimen and Ryland's eyes. She did not understand why the guards had changed their predictable tactics, and she wished Sasheer would revive, so he could guide her in their choices. But the Mage was drifting in and out of consciousnesses, his responses not really coherent enough to understand, and she had simply shaken her head and pushed on. She would obey Dalzere's last command until Sasheer regained his senses. If he regained them. That was just another problem, and she looked grimly ahead, increasing their pace.

"How much further?" Ryland puffed. He winced and shifted the Mage's dead weight. His armor was blackened from Kalern's lightning bolt and his face covered in sweat.

"Not far," Crizkerisomia assured him. "I taste a freshness in the air."

"Let me take him for a while," Salimen offered, stopping and forcing them all to gather around the big warrior.

"Are you sure?" Ryland asked, panting for breath. "He may look skinny, but he is not light."

"It is the least I can do to help," Salimen said, easing Sasheer off the Haonian's shoulder and over his own. "Stars," he sucked in a breath, "he's as heavy as a horse."

"I know," Ryland agreed with feeling, stretching sore shoulder muscles.

"We should not rest. Not here," Crizkerisomia warned as she looked from one man to the other. "It is not safe."

"Is it safe anywhere?" Ryland asked, his usual fearless attitude blanketed by the loss, making him sound as depressed as the others.

Studying them, she had no time for comforting words, only too aware of their fragile advantage. She wished again that Dalzere were present to soothe the bruised egos and sore spirits of the exhausted men. Tact was not one of her virtues. "Dalzere said we must continue. We must escape."

"Dalzere is dead," Peleyia said.

Looking at him, Crizkerisomia's frown deepened. "We do not know that."

"Oh, please!" Peleyia snapped as he turned away both in defeat and disgust.

"The guards are not following like before, so maybe he survived," she said, not believing those words either.

"Criz," Salimen said, his tone dejected. "He is dead. Just like Dale and Kellen. And Gralvin before them. And all the countless others that perverse entity had killed."

"I am sorry for your loss," she answered. "But we have to get out. Don't you see? This will surely bring war to the entire four lands. Lichien will not stop because it has killed Kellen, Dalzere, or even Lesendal. This is bigger than all of us, and we must warn the Brethren. For your Twelve Kingdoms, and for my people. For the Eastland, and the Dwarven Clans. For all the races," she stressed, petitioning them to see the bigger danger. "I know Lesendal was your . . ." she hesitated, her eyes sinking into Salimen's and reading the truth within his gaze, "he was your brother?"

Glaring up at the Elf, Salimen did not deny the claim. "My half brother. We shared the same mother," he broke off, pain bright in his eyes, "and we have never been separated. Until now."

"I knew it," Ryland said, allowing a little smile to enter his voice. "That is why you did not want to marry Kessendra, yes?"

"Do we have to talk about that . . . about her?" Salimen didn't bother to keep the disgust out of his tone.

"Then for your brother's sake, and for the sake of your land, you need to escape. As heir to the throne of Ihova, it will be your task to organize a defense against Lichien."

Taken back, Salimen said nothing. "The Ihovian throne is the last thing I want."

"Dal . . . zere . . ."

The disjointed word came from the semiconscious Mage, and Crizkerisomia quickly checked Sasheer over, seeing him hover on the edge of wakefulness. Blood stained his lips, old blood from an injury not visible, and her face creased in worry. "We have to move," she said, taking hold of Salimen's arm and pulling him forward. "Everyone stay close as I still sense the taint of Raveners."

"Charming," Salimen muttered, but he obeyed.

CHAPTER FIFTY-FIVE

Choosing to guard the rear of the group, Peleyia glanced around, unable to shake his depressed mood. It was not that he disliked the female Elf, just that she showed no emotion and assumed they should all do the same. But he could not. He was shrouded in guilt over Kellen's senseless death, having believed they could break the curse if they stayed together—stayed strong. When he had first seen Kellen chained to the wall, he had known then that something bad was going to happen, had seen the shadows in Kellen's eyes and read it in Kellen's aura. But he hadn't wanted to acknowledge the fear. But he *should* have, and that was what pained him now.

His hand drifted to the hilt of the magnificent sword attached to his belt, and he buried his grief. This was not the time to mourn, or to seek revenge like Salimen wanted. *Later* . . . later he would find a way to kill the evil that had taken over Lesendal's sister.

Releasing a deep breath, his lifted his head and centered his gaze on Ryland's massive back. They were only five now—with Sasheer's recovery in doubt. So he had to survive to keep Kellen's memory alive, to keep . . . *gods! Dalzere*. He did not want to be the one to tell Sasheer about the Drow's fate. Regardless of the Mage's irascible nature, he knew the Drow's death would hit the ill-tempered ancient very hard.

His eyes slid down Ryland's back, and he caught sight of a slender object falling from Ryland's belt loop. Curious, he stopped and picked the object up to study it. It was a small dagger, and he recognized it as Kellen's. He shuddered in reaction, battling to deny the instant rush of tears. He wanted revenge.

Contemplating vengeful thoughts, he lifted his head and saw how the others had moved away. He sucked in a shocked breath and hurried forward, stilling a moment later when he felt hissed breath curl around his ears from behind. Dread crept over him, and he forced himself to turn, his eyes darting into the gloom of the dark tunnel at his back. With every inhale, he could now taste the putrid decay of death, and he battled his innate fear as his eyes fell on a Ravener. It hung on nothing, the creature's deformed appearance abhorrent, a parody of what it had once been. A mutated Drow warrior—a wraith of shrunken skin and protruding bones. The black sackcloth hung limp from its bony shoulders, covering twisted limbs as the creature floated weightless, lacking any noticeable substance from below the waist. It made him ill just to look at it, and he backed away, sensing that the Ravener wanted him to run—to flee.

Swallowing nervously, he lifted Kellen's old dagger, never taking his eyes off the grotesque creature. Its blood red gaze pinned him; its lips curling back to reveal blackened teeth, and Peleyia shuddered. To touch a Ravener was death, and he knew that each Ravener was driven by an insane hunger for living flesh. Its clinging embrace could kill within a heartbeat, and nothing could stop them. Nothing could kill them—at least nothing tangible.

Taking another step back, he gagged when the creature drifted closer, playing with him, knowing it had him, and he knew it too. What had Kellen told him? *"Sasheer has seen your death with his Gift."* Again he took another step back, feeling for the wall at his side as he rounded a corner, praying the others had escaped.

"Pel . . ."

Hearing Ryland's voice filled him with hope and fear, and he hesitated. If this was his Fate then he wanted none of the others to die, yet he wanted to believe that he could cheat death. So he risked a glance and saw Ryland, saw how the big warrior had his sword out and was rushing to aid him. Hope flared in his chest, and he turned back to the Ravener, a smile forming on his lips. He would make it; he would survive, and he would live up to his promise to Kellen. *"Make my own destiny."*

Confidence infused him, and he took another step toward freedom, knowing he would be within range of the Oracle's protection within moments. Then strangely, Ryland stopped his charge. The Haonian stopped and stared, horror reflecting in his eyes, and Peleyia stumbled into the wall at his back, looking at his friends in shock. Ryland was standing with his mouth open, his eyes fixed on the darkness beyond, while Salimen and Crizkerisomia where assisting Sasheer to stand. He blinked in confusion. *Sasheer is awake? So why are they stopping?*

Not understanding, he turned just in time to feel the first sick touch of the Ravener's breath creep across his face. Then it was too late—far too late—and his last coherent scream was lost within the creature's wretched embrace.

"Kellen!"

CHAPTER FIFTY-SIX

Shaking his head, Sasheer awoke to see Peleyia being stalked then entrapped by a Ravener. *Why* the young Lancooti was outside the influence of the Oracle, he did not know, but he could feel the Lancooti's terror as the vile abomination enclosed the screaming man within its hungry embrace.

Not thinking, only reacting, he snatched the Oracle off Crizkerisomia and issued the first spell that came to mind—throwing both Ravener and human into the far wall. They hit with a jolt, the spell freezing them in a single instant of time and then ruthlessly pushing them deep into solid rock. Merging them, the living and the dead and encasing them in cold, lifeless stone. Like water sinking into sand.

"Oh by the gods..."

The horror and disbelief in Salimen's tone was unmistakable, and Sasheer turned to look at the bowman. He had no logical answer and glanced around for Dalzere, trusting the Drow to protect them all. Then he was collapsing back into unconsciousness.

* * *

It was early morning the following day when the group escaped onto the cliffs overlooking the cold northern seas. They simply stood there for a long time, paralyzed and exhausted, silently contemplating the last few harrowing days. All were in a state of utter shock, overwhelmed by despair at the friends they had lost.

Sasheer was conscious but uncommunicative, and they wearily kept moving until dusk, waiting for an attack that never came. They found shelter and fell into a set routine of gathering branches for a small fire and dividing up what food they had left. It was a bleak night.

* * *

The morning dawned clear, bright and cold, and they all gazed out in silence at the ocean far off into the distance. Small dots could be seen reflecting off the water's glassy surface, and Crizkerisomia judged they were Elven warships. But even that gave them little hope.

The Sun Elf found a trail—a narrow, treacherous gorge that led down the salt cliffs to the sheltered bay below. None of them spoke about what had happened, and each kept a silent vigil for pursuit. But it never came.

By late afternoon, they had reached a small gully that would offer shelter for the night. Crizkerisomia guessed it would take a further two days of hard traveling before they reached the tiny strip of beach and could safely alert the Elven ships. None of them wanted to think about having to cross the desolate plains of Gerthwin a second time if they failed to reach the inlet.

* * *

Sasheer sat in front of the meager fire knowing he should move, but he didn't have the energy. They were in a sheltered gully, and he was very aware of the nervous looks each member of the company cast his way. Especially Salimen. They had all changed, matured since leaving Ihova so many fateful months ago, but none more so than the talented bowman. Sighing, Sasheer dragged his attention back to the present and winced. He was sore, but Dalzere had initiated a healing, and with time, the pain would ease. *Dalzere . . .* and he closed his eyes to deny the pain. Deny the knowledge that he had failed again.

"Sasheer?"

Salimen's voice startled him, and he lifted his gaze with

difficulty, finding it so hard to remain positive. He focused on the bowman and regarded the Ihovian's somber expression.

Clearing his throat, Salimen voiced his question. "Sasheer, what did you do to Pel?"

Peleyia . . . so many lost. Gone. Vanished into the blur of memory. He stared at the bowman and then flicked his gaze over to Ryland and Crizkerisomia. This was all that was left of their company.

"Sasheer?" Salimen repeated, a glimmer of distrust and worry entering his light blue eyes. "Peleyia. What did you do to Peleyia?"

The persistent question brought vivid images into his mind, and Sasheer recalled seeing Peleyia being blanketed by the embrace of a soul-seeking Ravener. He knew he owed them an explanation, but it was just so hard to remember exactly what he had done. His mind was fogged with pain, his memories jumbled, and immediate thoughts became lost as he tried to come to terms with Dalzere's loss. After eight decades of being together . . . "I reacted . . . I—" he stopped and rephrased his words. "I wanted to protect him. To stop his death."

"But you pushed him and the Ravener into a stonewall," Salimen said.

"It was all I could do," Sasheer said, feeling beyond tired. His energy was gone, and too many people had died—people he felt acutely responsible for. *Gralvin, Kellen, Lesendal, Dalzere, and Peleyia . . .* "I saw his death while at the Keep," he whispered. "I tried to prevent his inclusion in the company, but Peleyia was stubbornly insistent."

"Yes." Ryland nodded, lifting his gaze, a warning in his eyes as he looked over at Salimen. "We cannot blame each other. That is false guilt. Each of us had a choice, including Peleyia. He lived life impulsively. We should remember them all with fondness. Otherwise, we tempt Fate's hand anew."

"I did try to save him," Sasheer said, more to himself than the others.

"How?" Salimen asked, ignoring Ryland's look. "Being taken by a Ravener means instant death."

"No," Sasheer said, his mind sluggishly recalling all the horrific facts. "Of that, I am sure. Or at the very least, I saved him from a painful death."

"Are you saying that the Ravener didn't kill him—but that your spell did?" Salimen asked, aghast.

"It's hard to explain."

"Try," Salimen growled.

"Sal, leave it," Ryland warned.

"No," Sasheer sighed, "he . . . you all have a right to know the truth." He let his gaze settle on the Ihovian, seeing Salimen's determination and fire. *He will make a good king given time. A strong leader.* "The spell I cast through the Oracle stopped the Ravener from killing Peleyia by violent means. But," he added hastily, seeing Salimen open his mouth to protest. "But—it may not have killed him. It should have. Painlessly, I might add. By entombing him with the Ravener inside solid rock." He frowned. "It more than likely did."

"So he's dead?" Salimen clarified.

Sasheer shrugged.

"He's either dead, or he's not dead. Which is it?" Salimen asked confused.

"I don't know," Sasheer said with honesty. "I didn't have the time or energy to find out if he survived the spell."

"Are you saying Pel may have survived? That he may be trapped—alive—inside a rock wall?" Salimen gasped.

"Not as you term the word, 'alive,'" Sasheer assured him after a long moment's consideration. "Magics are unpredictable. Especially when used in far from ideal situations."

Ryland looked at Sasheer then moved his eyes over to encompass Salimen. "So, he is neither alive, nor is he dead," he said. "You have a twisted sense of humor, Mage."

Sasheer snorted humorlessly but didn't answer.

"Could we get him out of the wall?" Salimen asked.

"If we do, then the Ravener may emerge as well," Sasheer mused, really starting to think about the dilemma. The possibilities were endless. "Then we would be faced with the same problem. And Peleyia would still die. Only very painfully this time."

Salimen continued to glare at the Mage. "So is there a chance he could still be alive? Alive inside that wall?"

"In a manner of speaking. Yes." Sasheer nodded. He watched Salimen raise a brow in exasperation. Next to the Ihovian, Crizkerisomia's expression was unreadable, but Ryland's eyes showed a mix of puzzlement and growing horror.

"Okay, I'll ask the damn question," Salimen growled. "But just for the record, I want you to know that I think you are a twisted bastard, Sasheer. Even when ill."

Sasheer smiled in acknowledgment. "Your opinion is noted."

"So," Salimen asked, "in what manner of speaking could Peleyia still be alive?"

CHAPTER FIFTY-SEVEN

He was falling, spiraling down uncontrollably.

Panic engulfed him as he slapped into unseen, sticky threads of webs, roots, and vines. The filthy objects breached the darkness, scratching him, entangling him in formless horrors, and he clutched at everything in desperation. But each vine and sticky piece of netting gave way, plummeting him even further down into the endless blackness of the abyss.

He could see nothing. His body was numb from pain and cold, his face, hands, and legs bleeding from the numerous cuts and scratches from the unseen, whiplike protrusions he struck. They smacked into him repeatedly until he tasted both blood and bile in his mouth. He made another reckless grab for a stronghold, feeling himself tumble in wild confusion, crashing into a cold, slimy wall before sliding down its rough surface.

He gasped, hanging on with all his strength, dreading the slow slide that was worse than the original free fall. The vine between his fingers gave way, and he slithered unrestrained down the damp, muddy-textured surface. He grunted in pain, hitting obstacles both soft and hard.

Then, abruptly, he was jerked to a halt, every inch of his body vibrating in agony, and he sucked in a pain-filled breath. With his fingers, he felt for the slimy wall and found his precarious perch to be nothing more than two vines sticking out of the mud above a small indented ledge. The ledge would not hold him long, but he sagged in exhaustion, feeling the mud already oozing away under his knees. Releasing one vine, he searched around for something else to hold on to. But there was nothing, and the more he wiggled, the quicker his ledge disintegrated.

A sob of despair bubbled up in the back of his throat, and he battled to suppress it, not sure if he was alone in this alien environment, not sure what vile creatures lived in this abyss. He squinted up into the darkness but could see absolutely nothing—no light, not even a speck of illumination to show the abyss' mouth. So how far had he fallen? And was there a bottom to this nightmare?

He cautiously stretched out a hand and searched with his fingers for another root or vine that would hold his weight. But his bruised hands only encountered more slippery rock edges and oozing mud. Moving a little more, he cried out in a mixture of fright and anguish when the ledge under him disappeared completely. He slipped further, grimly hanging on to the remaining vines, and knowing his efforts were in vain.

He dug his fingers into the soft ooze, gritting his teeth against the cramp in his hands. Nothing seemed real anymore, and he cursed Kalern, then cursed Sasheer, deciding both men were as bad as each other. *And brothers!* Though that tidbit of information had not been a total shock. *It makes a crazy sort of sense*, he mused, wiggling his toes and trying to relieve the cramp in his calf muscles. The vine supporting his weight sagged further, and he forced himself to relax. Then another, not so pleasant, thought hit him. If he was a descendant of Kalern's line then that would mean he was also related to Sasheer.

"Cursed stars and to the ten levels of hell with them all!" he half-yelled. The verbalized anger relieved his tension, and he pressed his face into the cold, wet wall, wishing with all his heart that just for once the secretive Mage could have been honest with him. *Not that it is going to matter now*, he acknowledged. For very soon he was going to find out the hard way if an abyss actually had a bottom. "Damn you, Sasheer!"

"Don't tell me you are still thinking of those you have left behind."

The quiet words startled Kellen, and he jumped, almost losing his purchase on the two sagging vines. Looking around anxiously, it took him a long moment to feel the presence of another and then to see a pair of shining silver eyes.

"Shard?"

"Who else did you expect? Your mentor, Sasheer?" The little snow dragon half-sneered the name. "As I recall, mud offends his fine sensibilities."

Sensing the controlled anger behind the whispered words, Kellen wondered what nasty little game the dragon was playing now. "Are you here to make sure I fall all the way to the bottom? Well don't worry, I won't disappoint your perverted master," he cut back, deciding that at least he could vent his frustration and anger on this creature before he died.

"No," Shard said.

Waiting for more, Kellen just blinked in the direction of the hovering form. "So why are you here?" he demanded, hating the manipulations. Then abruptly he fell another few feet, his fingers slicing a trail through the mud.

"Don't ask," Shard growled, his wings creating a cool breeze.

"Oh, this is just great!" Kellen snapped as one vine broke completely free, and he was left clutching the second vine in desperation. "I get to play guessing games while I fall," he snapped as his own anger resurfaced acutely. "Do you have a musical instrument stashed somewhere? Maybe you could play the death march or something while I slide down this wall!"

"Sarcasm," Shard gave him a reproachful look. "A trait you obviously picked up from Sasheer."

Glaring at the hovering little dragon, Kellen fervently wished he had a hand free, so he could throw some mud at the annoyance.

"Kellen . . ."

"Get lost!" he shouted, peeved, just as his second root snapped, and he slid down the wet, cold rock face again. Only this time, he did not go far, managing to snag another root to hang on to. It pulled him up short, and he gasped for breath.

"Kellen?"

"You still here?" It was more a wheeze, and he turned his head to cough out muddy water and dirt.

"I am here, and I will always be here."

"Cute, but pointless."

"Listen!" Shard hissed, some of his annoyance returning.

"Get away from me!" Kellen slapped at the small dragon as it flew in closer. But his actions overbalanced him, and he fell, slamming into the slimy wall before he managed to grab a support. He came to an undignified halt and groaned. "This . . . is going to be a . . . a . . . painful experience," he gasped to no one in particular. "I think I almost preferred the . . . quick free fall to this s—slow torture."

"Kellen, listen to me."

Opening his eyes, Kellen wiped mud from his face and saw the vague outline of the little creature hovering just above him. "Shard, what do you want?" he asked. "If Lichien has sent you down here to finish me off, then just get on with it. I have no energy left to fight."

"No." The snow dragon was sounding more and more exasperated. One of its soft wings batted gently at Kellen's shoulder. "I am free of Lichien."

"What?" Confused, Kellen squinted, trying to see the dragon better in the darkness, only making out bright eyes as Shard flew in closer. Shining silver.

"I am free of his control. Sasheer has won a small victory, but the main battle is yet to be fought."

"What main battle?" Kellen asked curious, despite himself. He had seen Sasheer send the spell that would destroy Lichien. Had seen the stone start to fragment. "What happened up in the cavern?"

"The prophecy was fulfilled," Shard almost lisped, his tone altering and becoming very serious. "You challenged and won. You restored my soul and made me whole. And the price—was Kessendra's innocence."

Kellen stared at Shard, not sure if he wanted to believe. "Lichien is gone?"

"The stone was destroyed. But Lichien lives on," Shard said. "It lives on inside Kessendra."

"Kessendra," Kellen whispered the name, remembering her beauty, her tears of despair, her softness and warmth. He shivered, also remembering how Kalern had wanted her to conceive his child. He blinked, refocusing on Shard's face. "Lichien survived?"

"It now lives in the body of beauty and innocence."

"Bright stars..."

"Its power is unlimited. Unrestrained. Its wants and desires uncharted. Its hate unequaled," Shard said. "Unless you stop it."

"Stop it?" Kellen asked incredulously. He could feel water dripping on his head, running down his neck. *Just another annoyance.* "In case you haven't noticed—I am stuck down an abyss!" he hissed.

"You are stating the obvious. Again."

"So tell me—what do you possibly think I can do?" Kellen snarled with deliberate sarcasm. "Spit at Lichien from down here, perhaps?"

"Fight Lichien," Shard said ignoring the jest. "Fight for supremacy."

"Supremacy? Of what?" Kellen demanded. "Mud Island? And what of Sasheer? Surely, His Royal Cleverness can come up with a better plan than this?"

"I do not presume to guess Sasheer's mind. Nor do I know if Sasheer survived the backlash of his spell," Shard said.

Kellen closed his mouth, feeling suddenly ill, like all the wind had been knocked out of him with those simple words. Was Sasheer dead? He closed his eyes, feeling suddenly defeated. "So everything we attempted to do was all for nothing? I distracted Lichien, yet Sasheer still died? The stone is destroyed yet Lichien still lives? Kessendra was rescued only to be consumed by a worse evil?" he let out an explosive breath. "In that case, the four lands are lost."

"Maybe not," Shard offered.

Lifting his head, Kellen wished he could see Shard better, so that he could discern the dragon's true meanings. "Shard?" he asked suspiciously.

"You have the ability, Kellen, to balance the odds. Kessendra carries your unborn child. But any child born from her womb will be totally evil, totally corrupted by Lichien. Only you will be able to stop it."

Appalled, shocked, and disgusted, Kellen snorted. "So you want me to kill Kessendra? Kill my unborn child?" He shook his head in disbelief. "I'm not exactly in a winning position."

"But you will be," the little creature assured him.

"How?" Despite himself, Kellen had to ask. He could sense the dragon's confidence, and that intrigued him.

"I will show you, but we must hurry before she gains full power and detects your life force. For Lichien will search for you and kill you."

Feeling a prickling of apprehension, Kellen sucked in a startled breath as the small snow dragon flew closer and gently touched his chest before leaning forward until they were nose to nose. It was intimate and bewitching.

"I will teach you," Shard whispered.

"What will you teach?" Kellen found he was whispering, and he peered harder at the dragon settling against his chest.

"All that you need to know about Magery. All about my creator's life and loves. All that you will need in order to make you an equal to Lichien's challenge."

His unease increased, and Kellen dragged in a breath, spellbound by Shard's passionate words. Slowly he reached forward and ran a dirty finger over the dragon's nose. "Shard—how is this possible? Serine is dead."

"But not forgotten," Shard said. "You have his focus stone; you have me, and you will have all the old knowledge of Mitthsombaine."

Swallowing, Kellen eyed the object Shard uncovered from beneath its soft wings. It was a round crystal. It shone dully in the darkness, and he gazed at the palm-sized gem in awe. "I still don't see how," he stopped again as he felt the formation of a magical spell start to weave around him. "Shard?" he whispered, urgent.

"I will entomb us," the dragon explained in a soft whisper. "It is necessary, as it will hide us from all prying eyes and senses. You will sleep and heal. Sleep and learn. Sleep and understand."

"But . . ."

The cold nose touched his again in gentle petition. "I will guard your sleep. Fear nothing, my young trainee, for you and I will be forever bound."

At a loss to fully comprehend what was happening to him,

Kellen found his eyelids treacherously closing as his limbs relaxed. Around him the icy mud and water vanished. He felt cushioned, warmed, and oddly secure as the layered spell feathered over him in repeated strength.

"F—For . . . for how . . . long . . ." He tried to say the words, not sure if they were verbal or mental. Then it didn't matter as he drifted down into a deeper trance. Nothing could touch him here, his mind free of stress and filled with images of long, long ago, of a world so different to the one he had seen. In this new magical world, he held a focus stone, the pendant of invisibility, and a magnificent Shade.

Shard continued to weave the spell around him, locking them together. Hiding them from prying senses. "Sleep, relax, and learn, my young master," Shard whispered.

The magical spell sent them both into a state of slumber, until the two existed only in the world of memory.

:*Sleep, my young lord . . . for this could take us years. Decades. Even an eternity until one of your blood comes to unlock the enchantment.*:

* * *

Here ends book 1. In book 2—The Soul of Lichien—Kellen wakens in a world gone mad, learning the fate of his friends. Disorientated, he must decide what to do about the woman he has fallen in love with, and what to tell Tich, the woman he is betrothed to. He also must decide if he wants to use the old knowledge Shard has gifted him with or leave the curse of Mitthsombaine buried for all time.